MAPMAKERS

AND THE Flickering FORTRESS

Also by Cameron Chittock and Amanda Castillo

Mapmakers and the Lost Magic

Mapmakers and the Enchanted Mountain

MAPMAKERS

AND THE Flickering Fortress

Written by
CAMERON CHITTOCK

Illustrated by
AMANDA CASTILLO

Colored by
Sara Calhoun

RH GRAPHIC

New York

Mapmakers and the Flickering Fortress was written with pencil and paper before being transferred to a Word document. It was drawn and colored digitally in Photoshop and lettered with the artist's own handwritten font.

Text copyright © 2024 by Cameron Chittock
Cover art and interior illustrations copyright © 2024 by Amanda Castillo
Colors by Sara Calhoun and title design by Walter Parenton

All rights reserved. Published in the United States by RH Graphic, an imprint of Random House Children's Books, a division of Penguin Random House LLC, New York.

RH Graphic with the book design is a trademark of Penguin Random House LLC.

Visit us on the web! RHKidsGraphic.com • @RHKidsGraphic

Educators and librarians, for a variety of teaching tools, visit us at RHTeachersLibrarians.com

Library of Congress Cataloging-in-Publication Data is available upon request.
ISBN 978-0-593-17295-7 (trade) — ISBN 978-0-593-17294-0 (pbk.)
ISBN 978-0-593-17297-1 (ebook)

Editor: Whitney Leopard
Designers: Patrick Crotty and Bob Bianchini
Production Editor: Melinda Ackell
Managing Editor: Katy Miller
Production Manager: Jen Jie Li

MANUFACTURED IN CHINA
10 9 8 7 6 5 4 3 2 1
First Edition

RH GRAPHIC

A comic on every bookshelf.

For Taren

—C.C.

For everyone who made this adventure possible

—A.C.

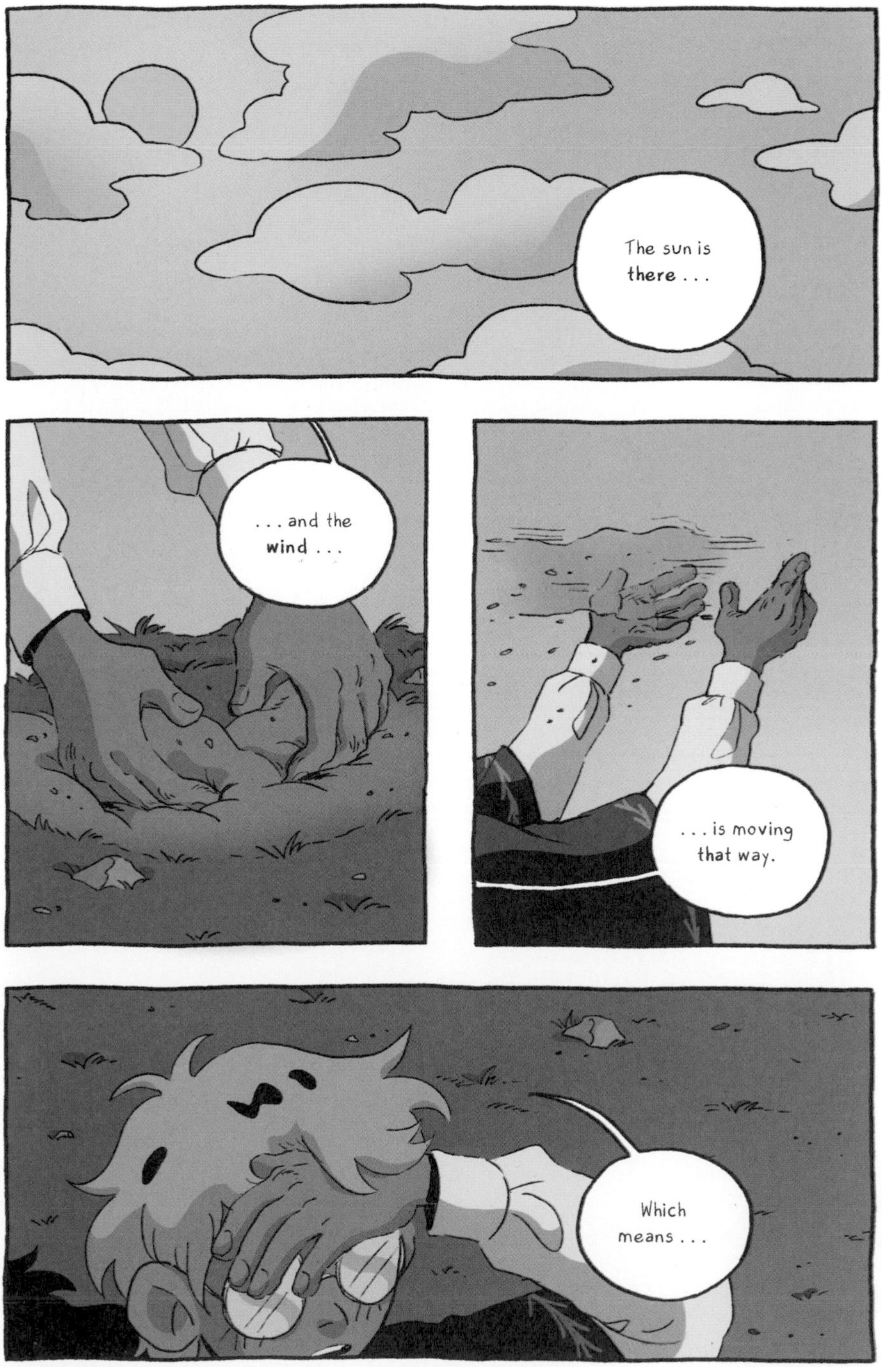
The sun is there . . .
. . . and the wind . . .
. . . is moving that way.
Which means . . .

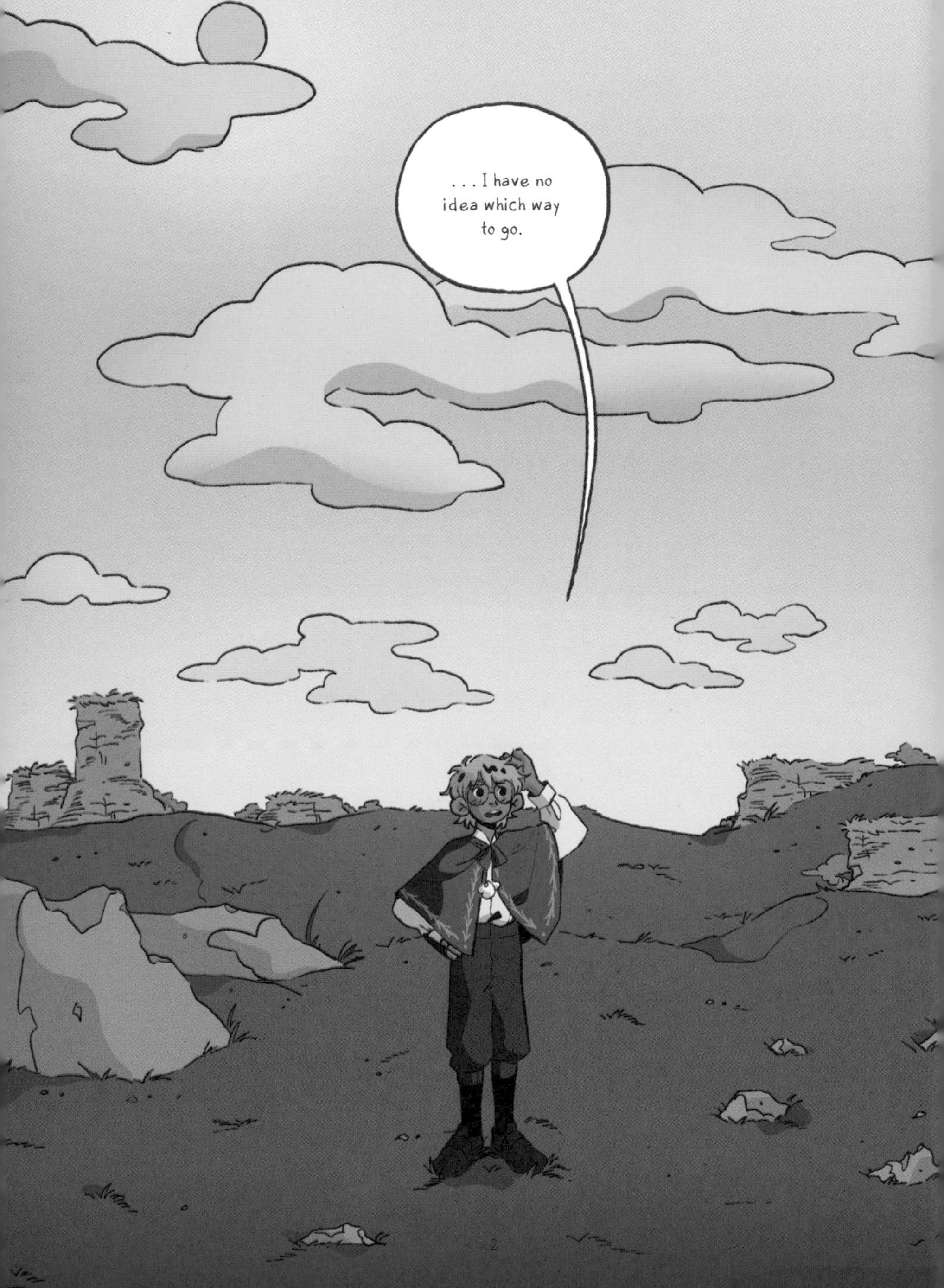
. . . I have no idea which way to go.

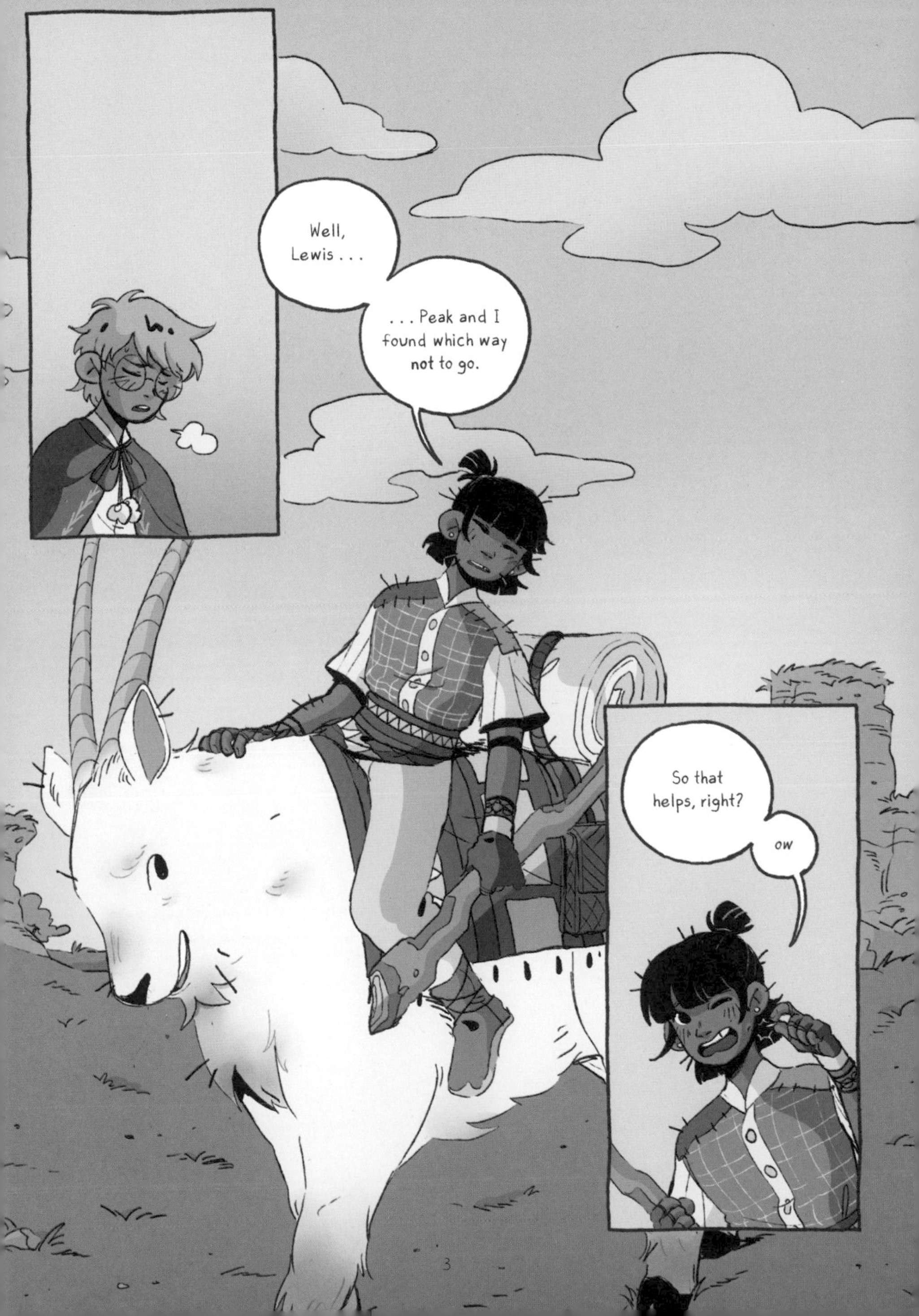

Well, Lewis . . .
. . . Peak and I found which way not to go.
So that helps, right?
ow

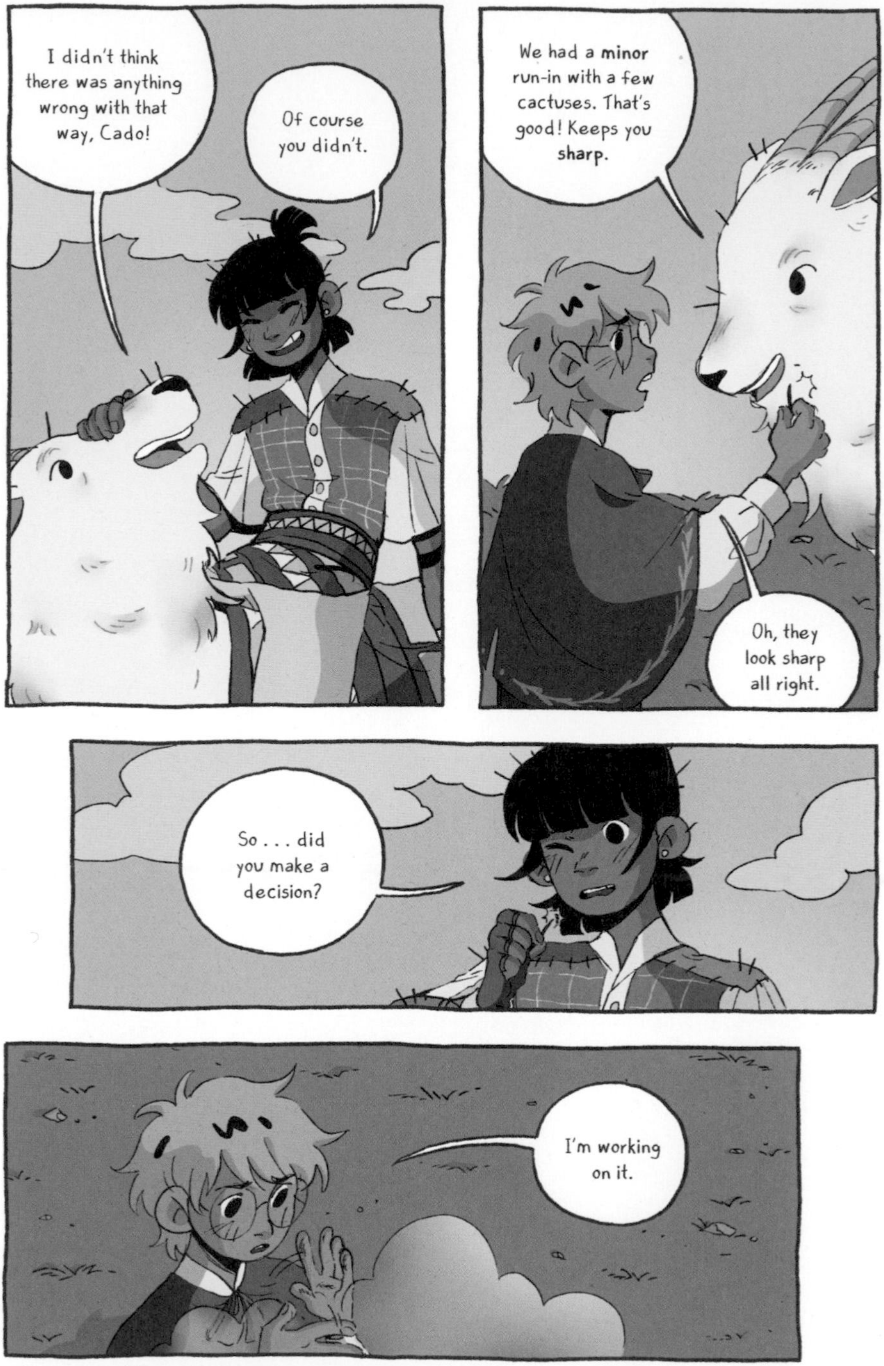
I didn't think there was anything wrong with that way, Cado!
Of course you didn't.
We had a **minor** run-in with a few cactuses. That's good! Keeps you **sharp**.
Oh, they look sharp all right.
So . . . did you make a decision?
I'm working on it.

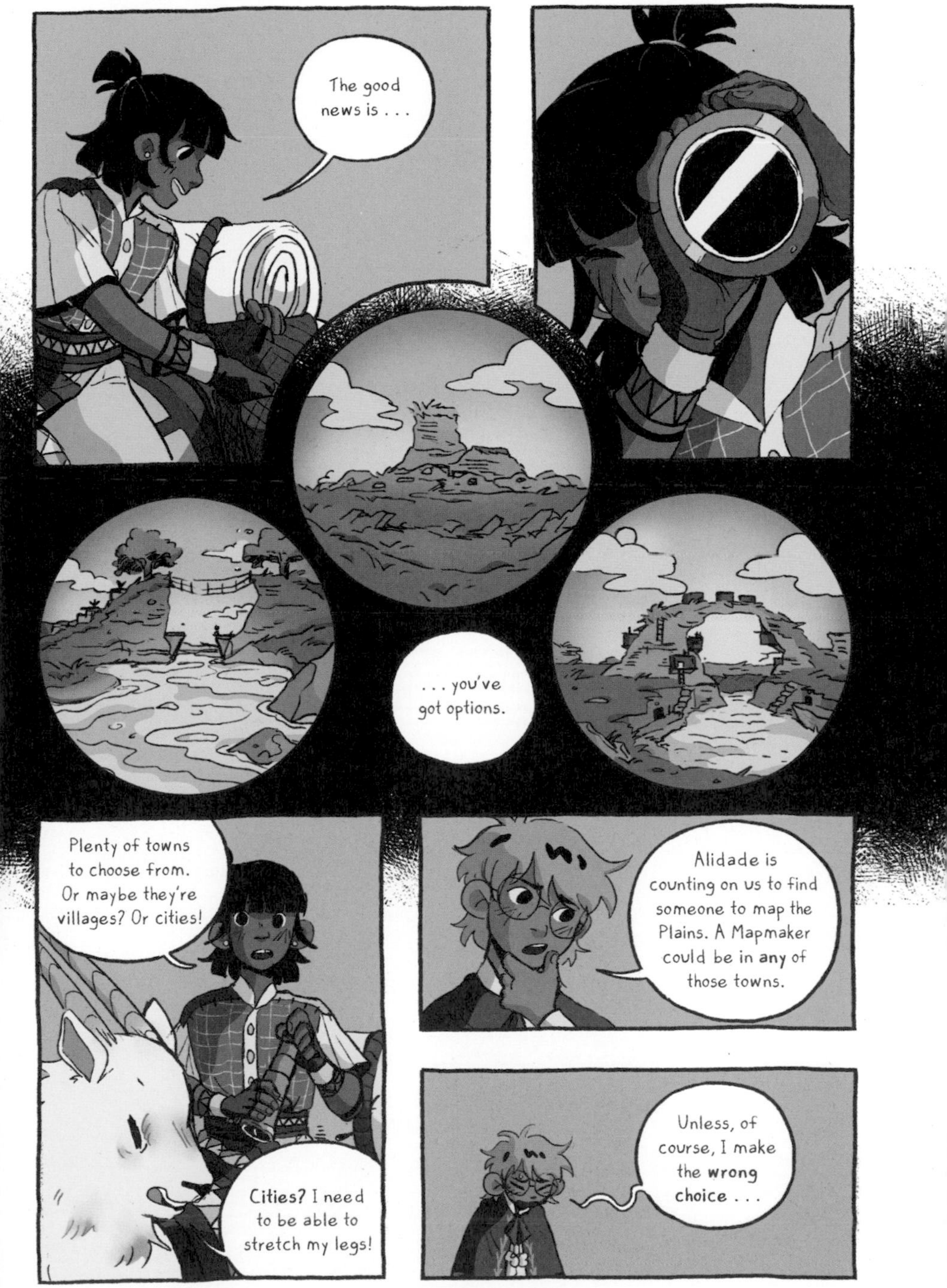
The good news is . . .
. . . you've got options.
Plenty of towns to choose from. Or maybe they're villages? Or cities!
Cities? I need to be able to stretch my legs!
Alidade is counting on us to find someone to map the Plains. A Mapmaker could be in **any** of those towns.
Unless, of course, I make the **wrong choice** . . .

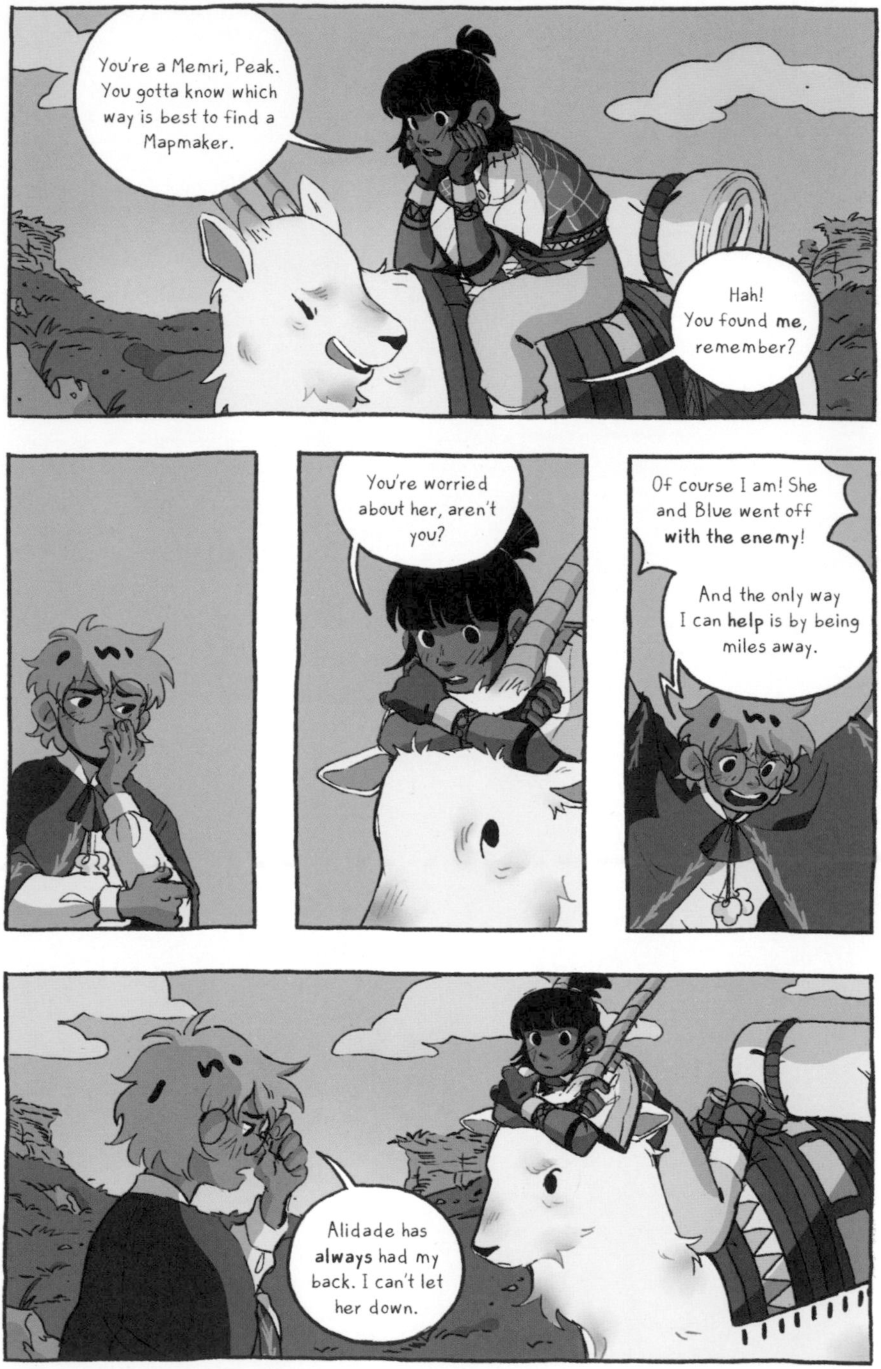
You're a Memri, Peak. You gotta know which way is best to find a Mapmaker.
Hah! You found **me**, remember?
You're worried about her, aren't you?
Of course I am! She and Blue went off **with the enemy**!
And the only way I can **help** is by being miles away.
Alidade has **always** had my back. I can't let her down.

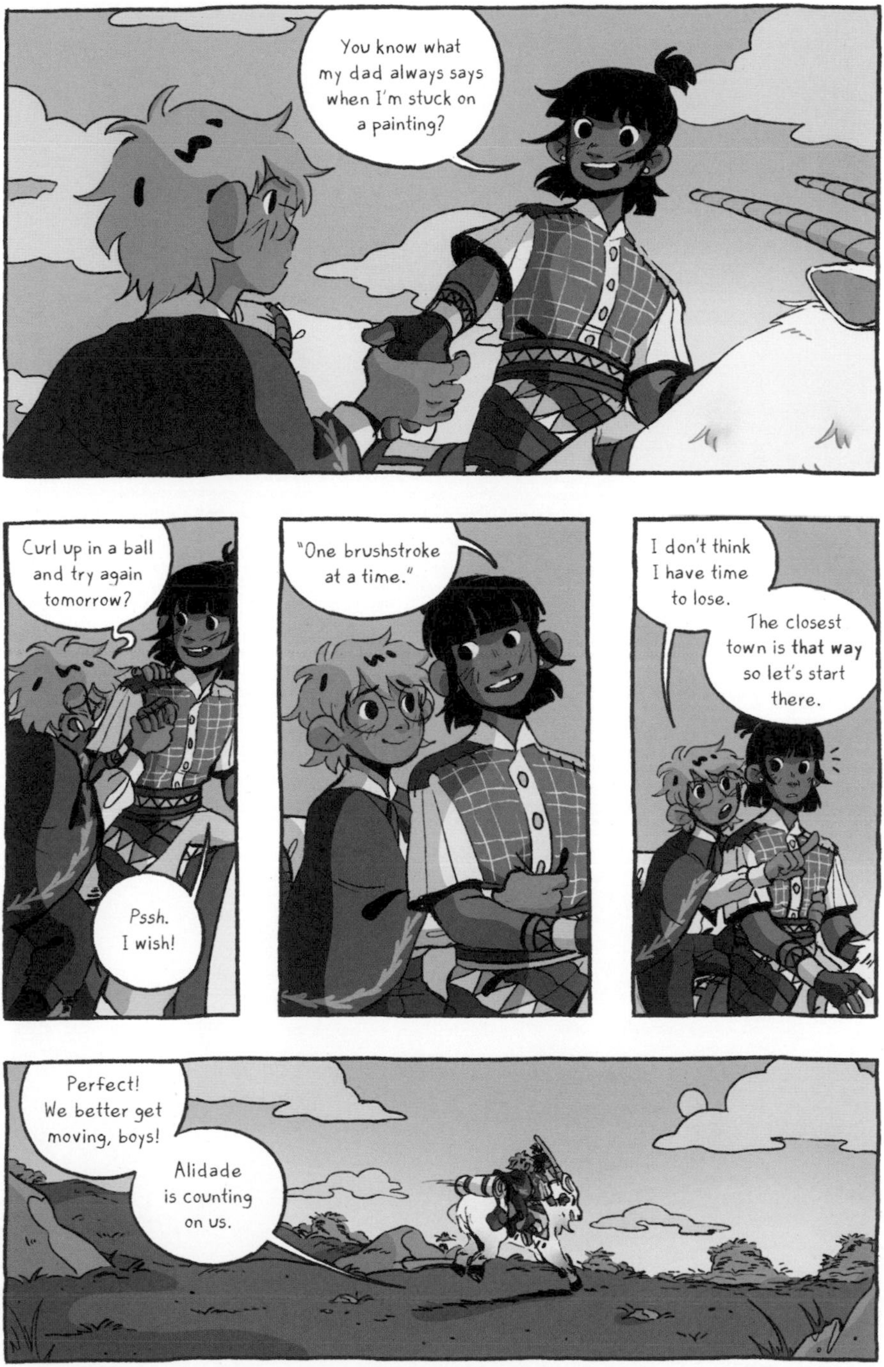
You know what my dad always says when I'm stuck on a painting?
Curl up in a ball and try again tomorrow?
Pssh. I wish!
"One brushstroke at a time."
I don't think I have time to lose.
The closest town is **that way** so let's start there.
Perfect! We better get moving, boys!
Alidade is counting on us.

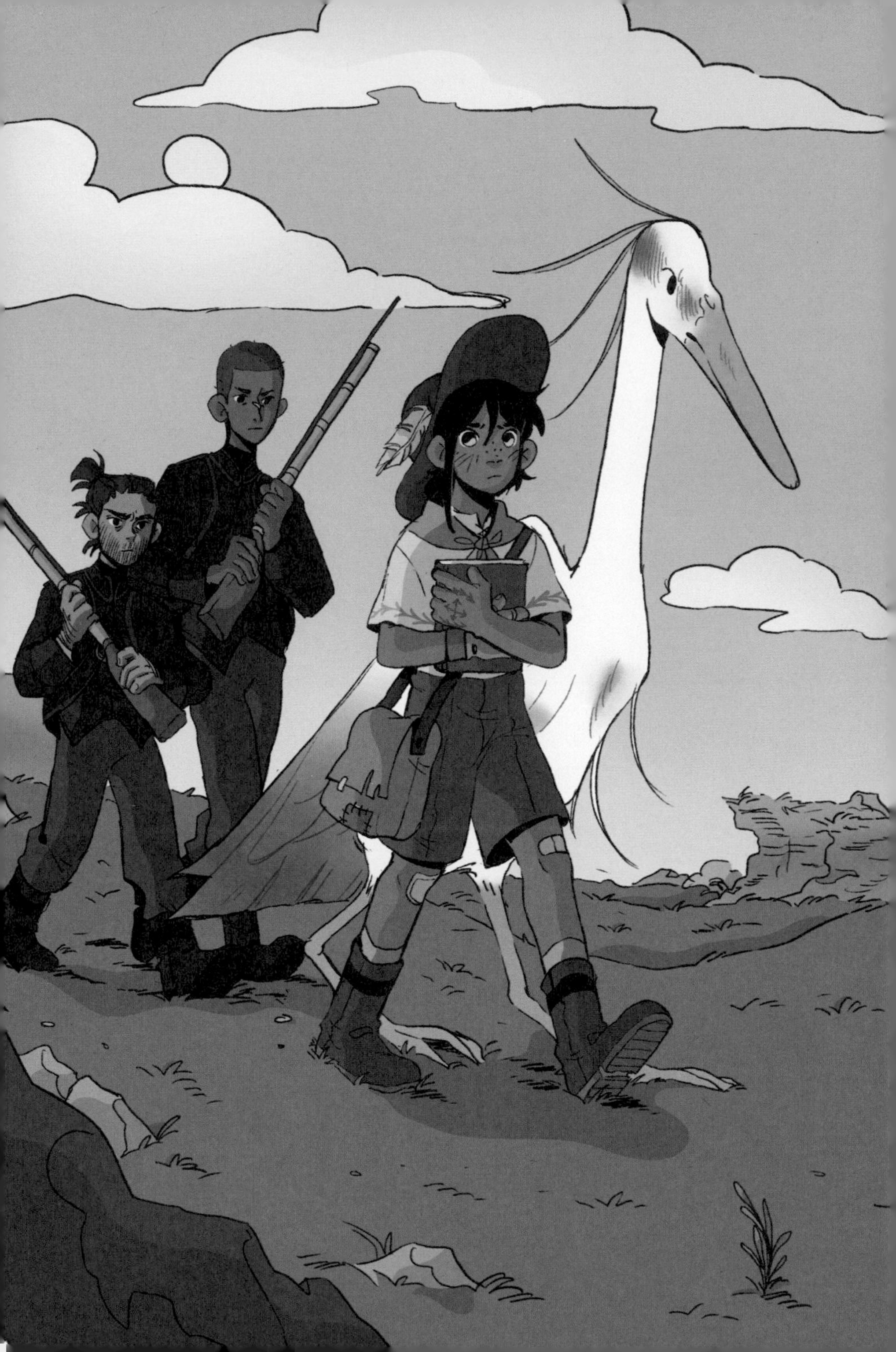

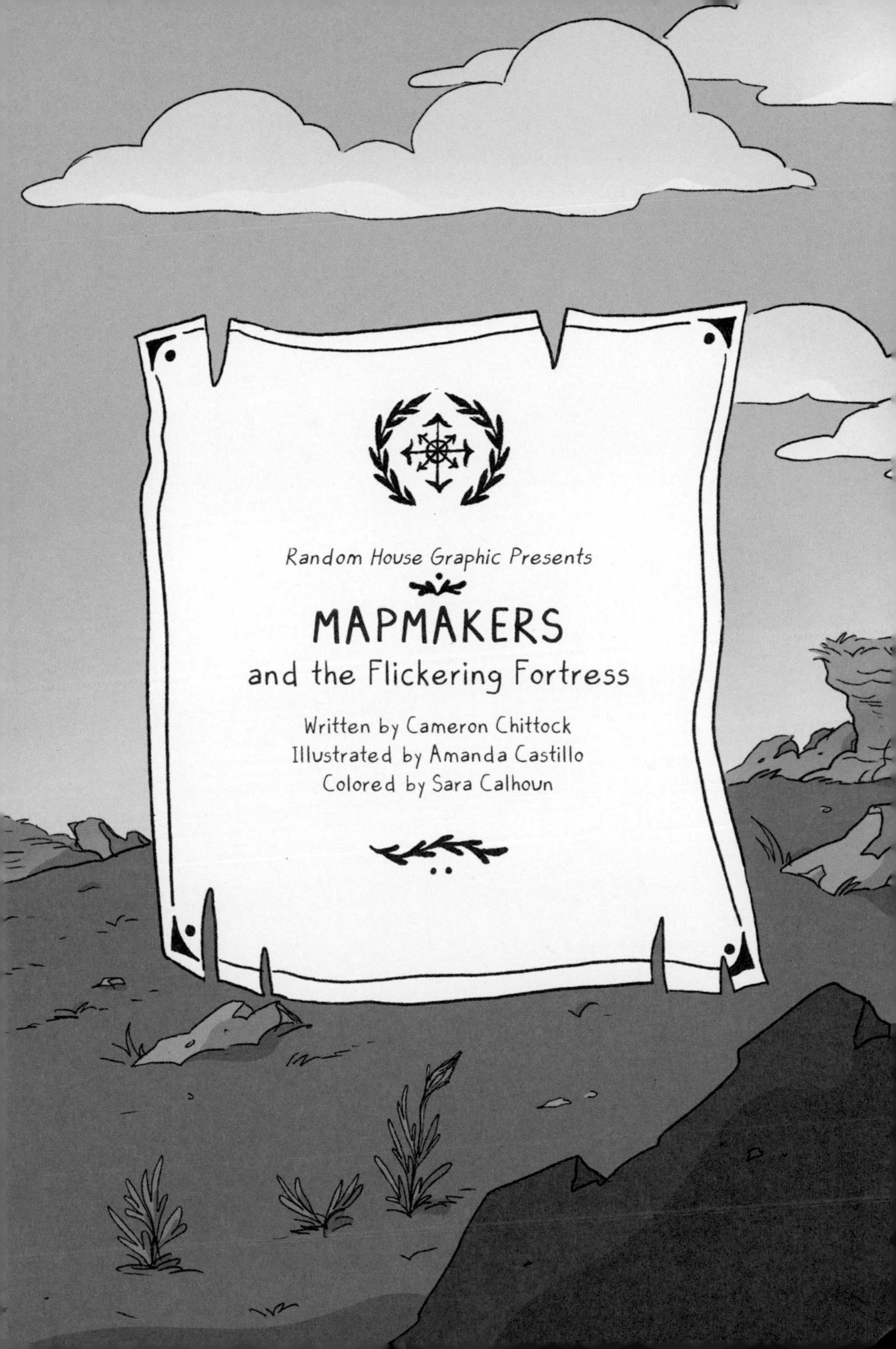
Random House Graphic Presents
MAPMAKERS
and the Flickering Fortress
Written by Cameron Chittock
Illustrated by Amanda Castillo
Colored by Sara Calhoun

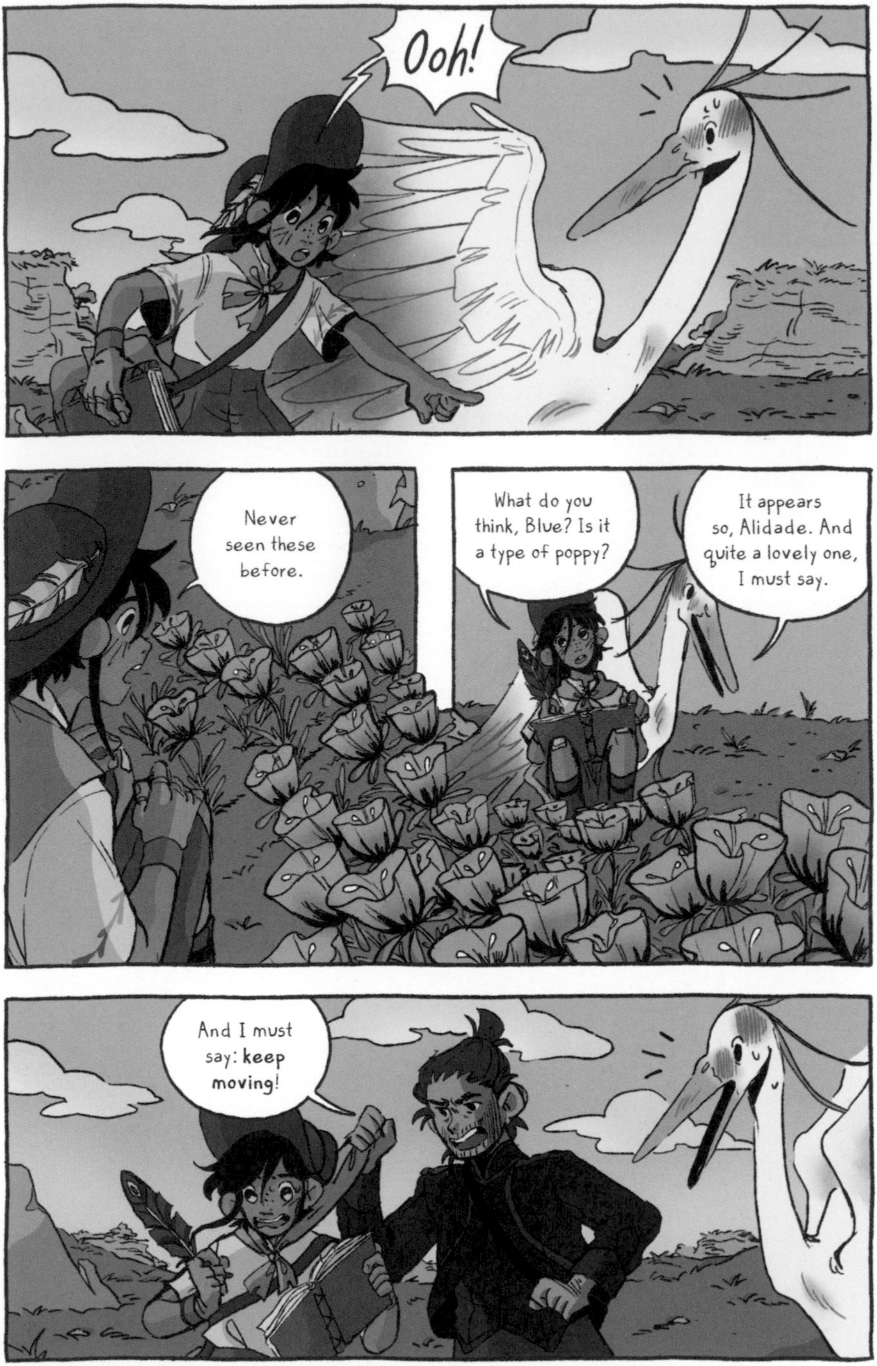

Ooh!
Never seen these before.
What do you think, Blue? Is it a type of poppy?
It appears so, Alidade. And quite a lovely one, I must say.
And I must say: **keep moving**!

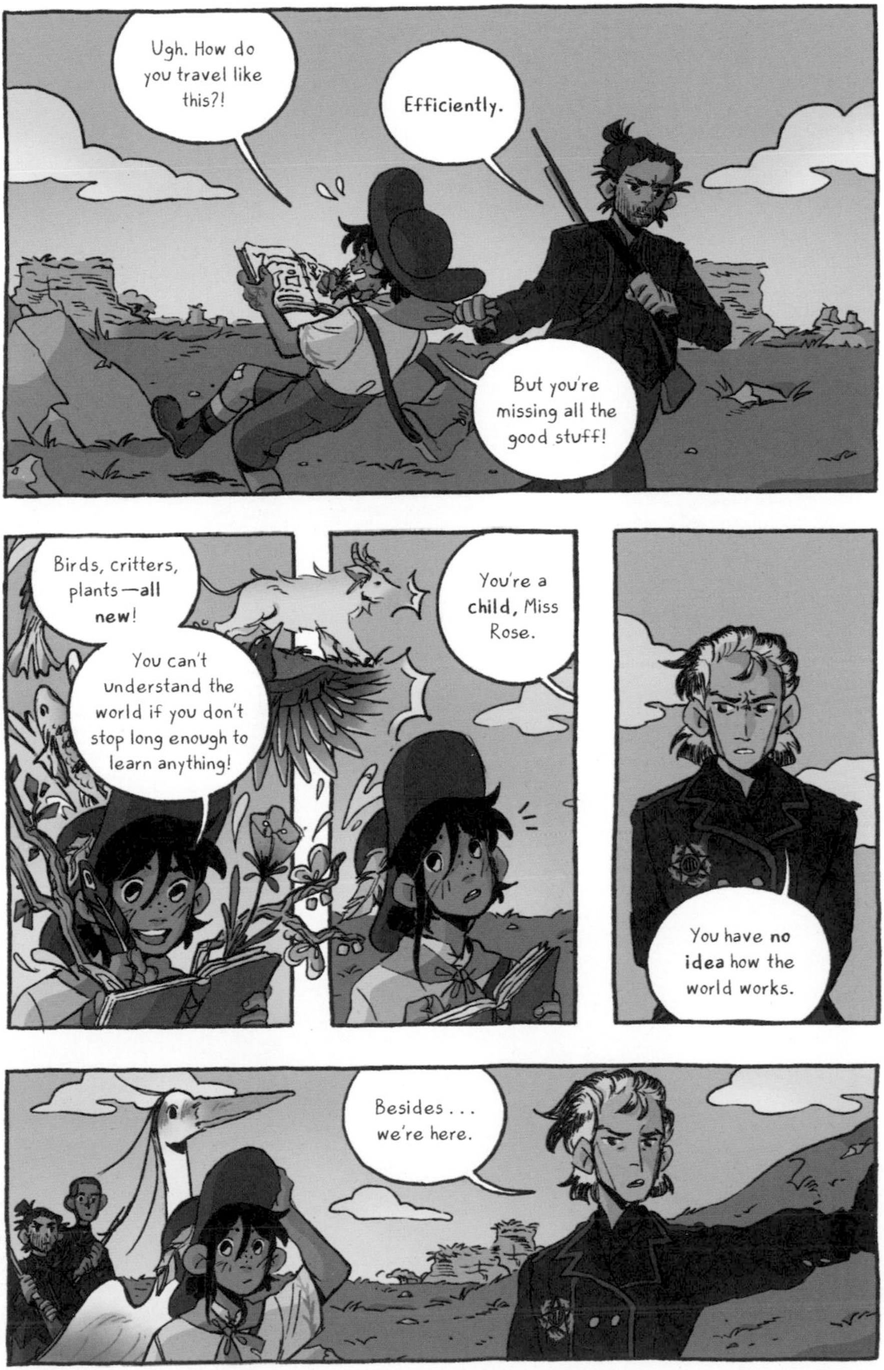
Ugh. How do you travel like this?!
Efficiently.
But you're missing all the good stuff!
Birds, critters, plants—all new!
You can't understand the world if you don't stop long enough to learn anything!
You're a child, Miss Rose.
You have no idea how the world works.
Besides . . . we're here.

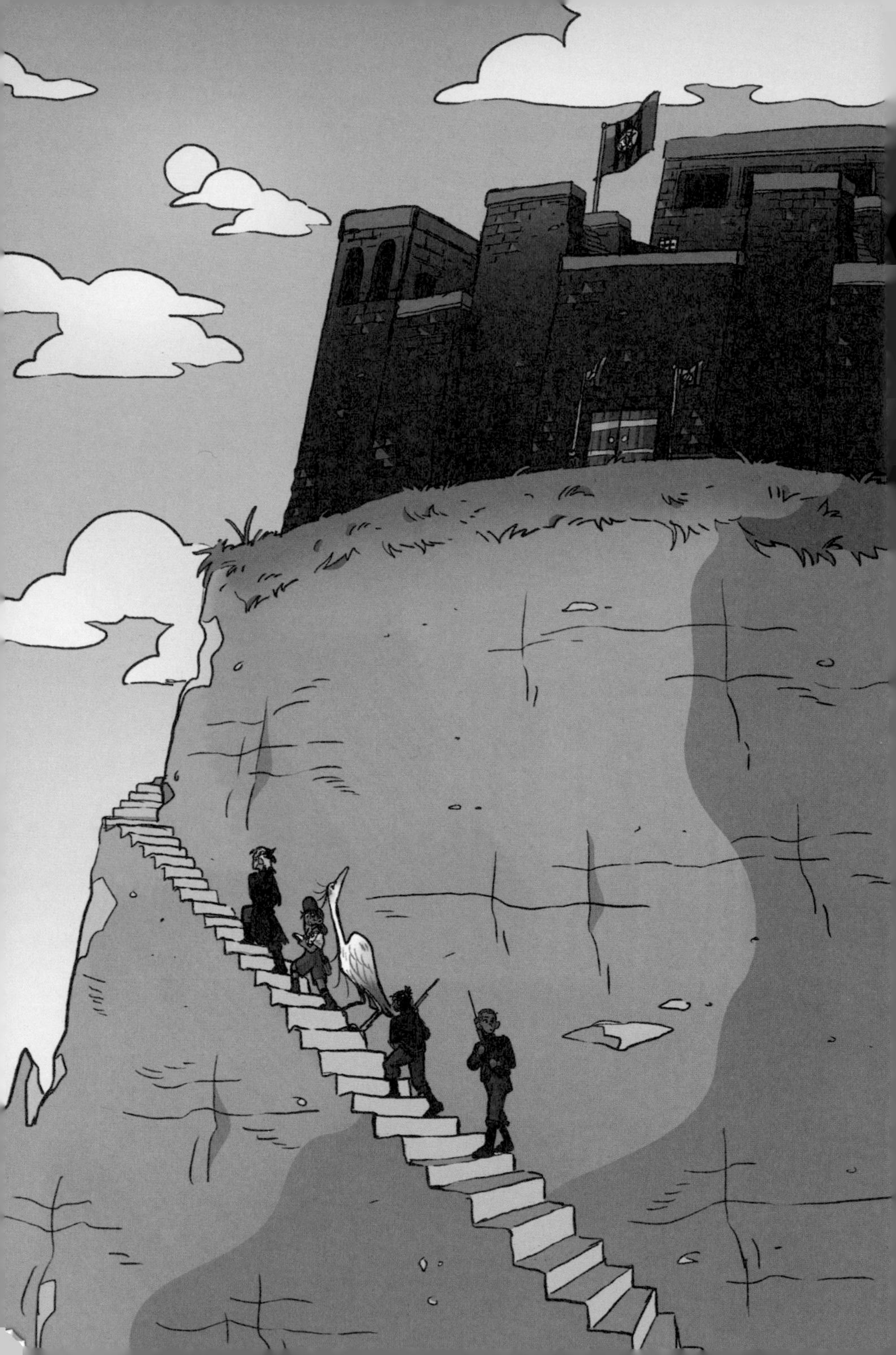

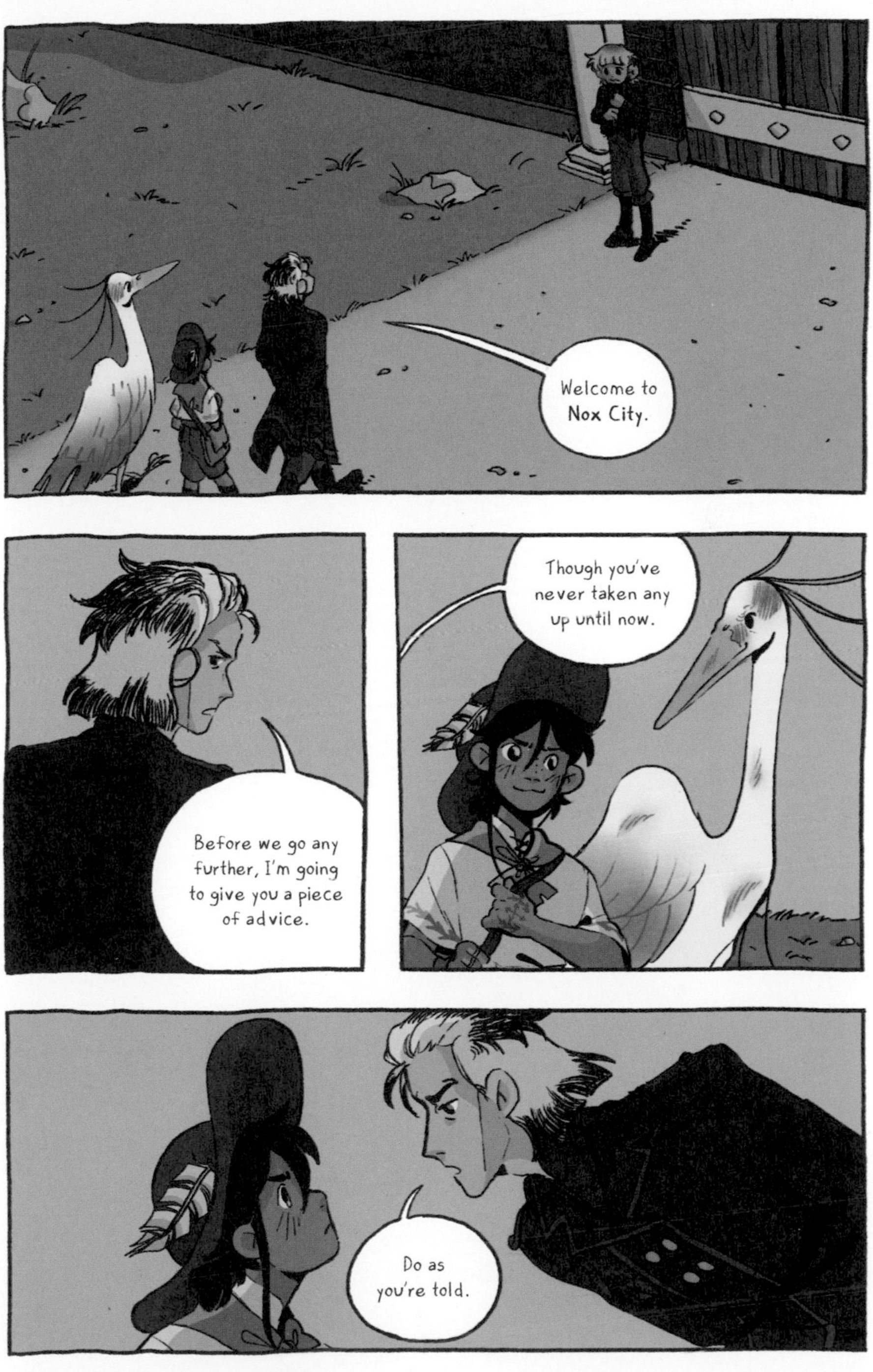

Welcome to Nox City.
Before we go any further, I'm going to give you a piece of advice.
Though you've never taken any up until now.
Do as you're told.

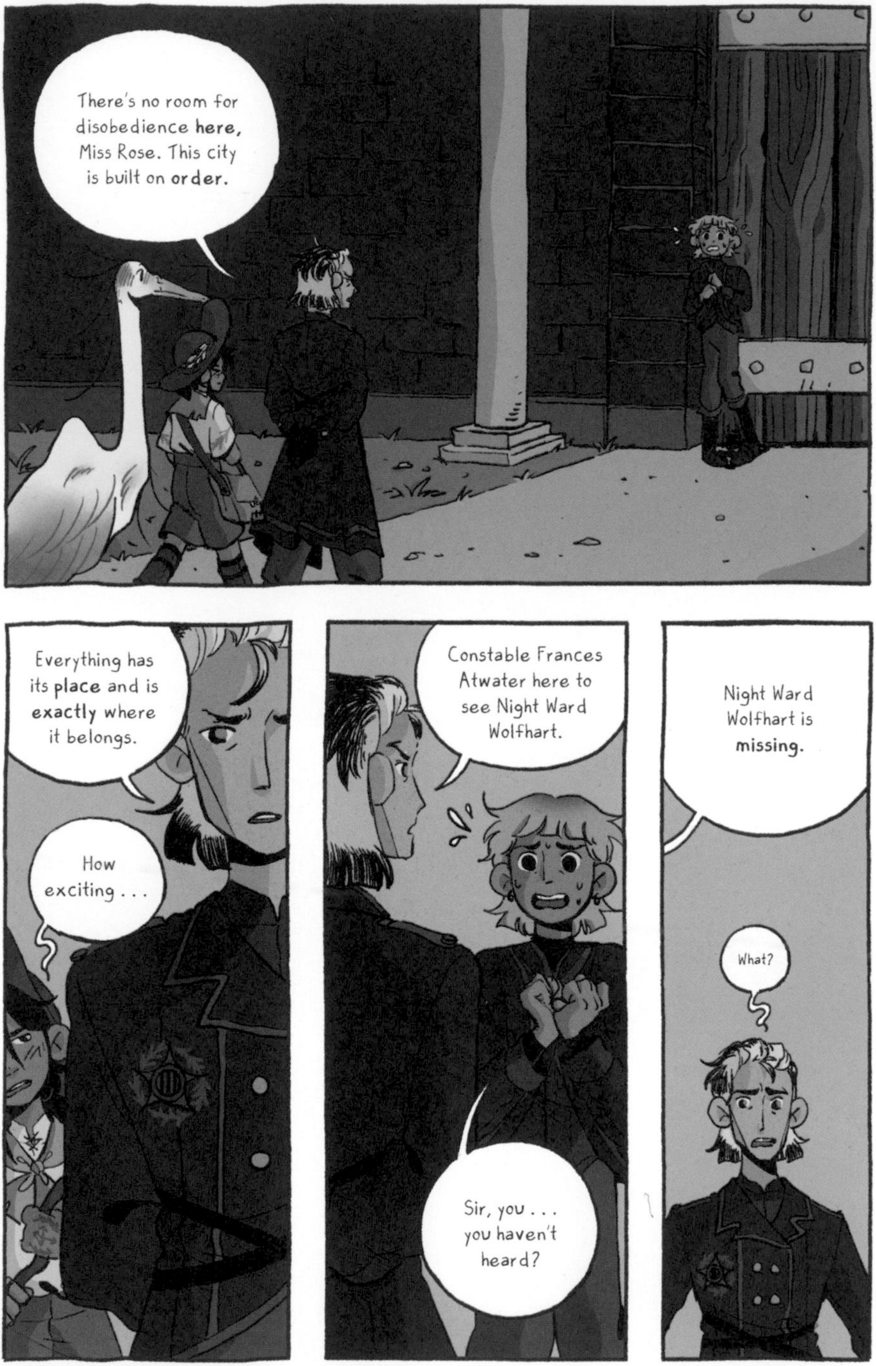
There's no room for disobedience here, Miss Rose. This city is built on order.
Everything has its place and is exactly where it belongs.
How exciting . . .
Constable Frances Atwater here to see Night Ward Wolfhart.
Sir, you . . . you haven't heard?
Night Ward Wolfhart is missing.
What?

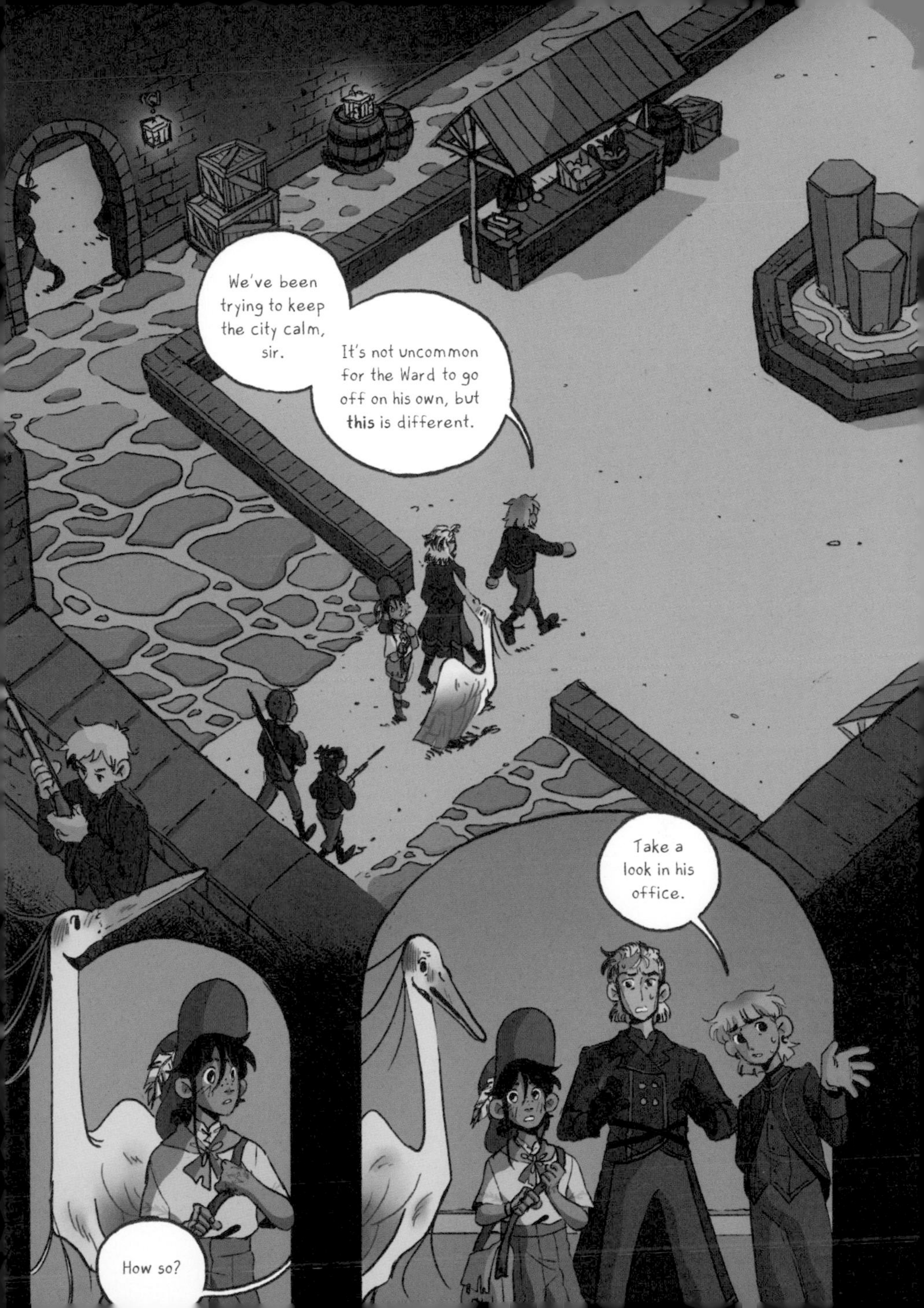
We've been trying to keep the city calm, sir.
It's not uncommon for the Ward to go off on his own, but **this** is different.
How so?
Take a look in his office.

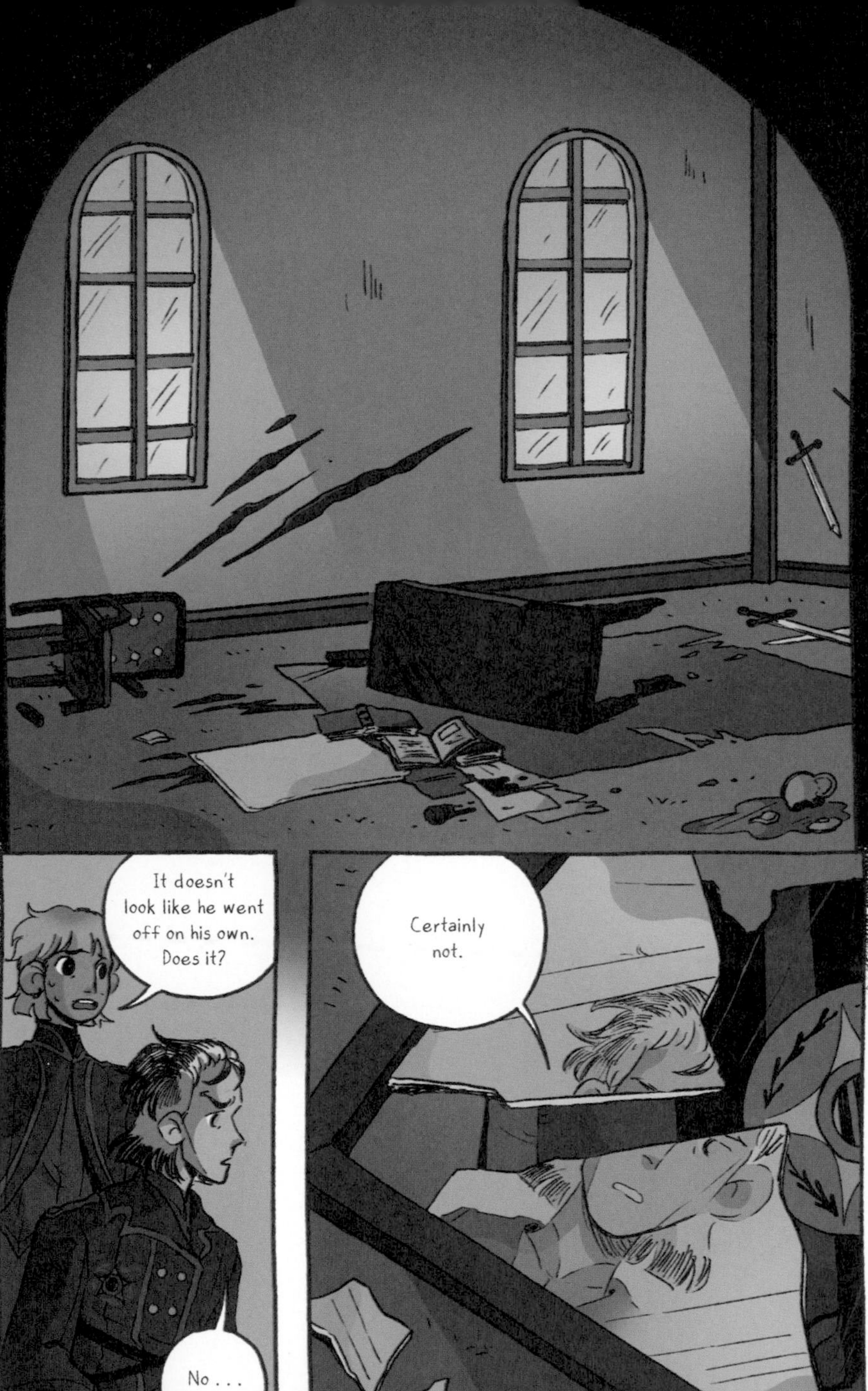
It doesn't look like he went off on his own. Does it?
No . . .
Certainly not.

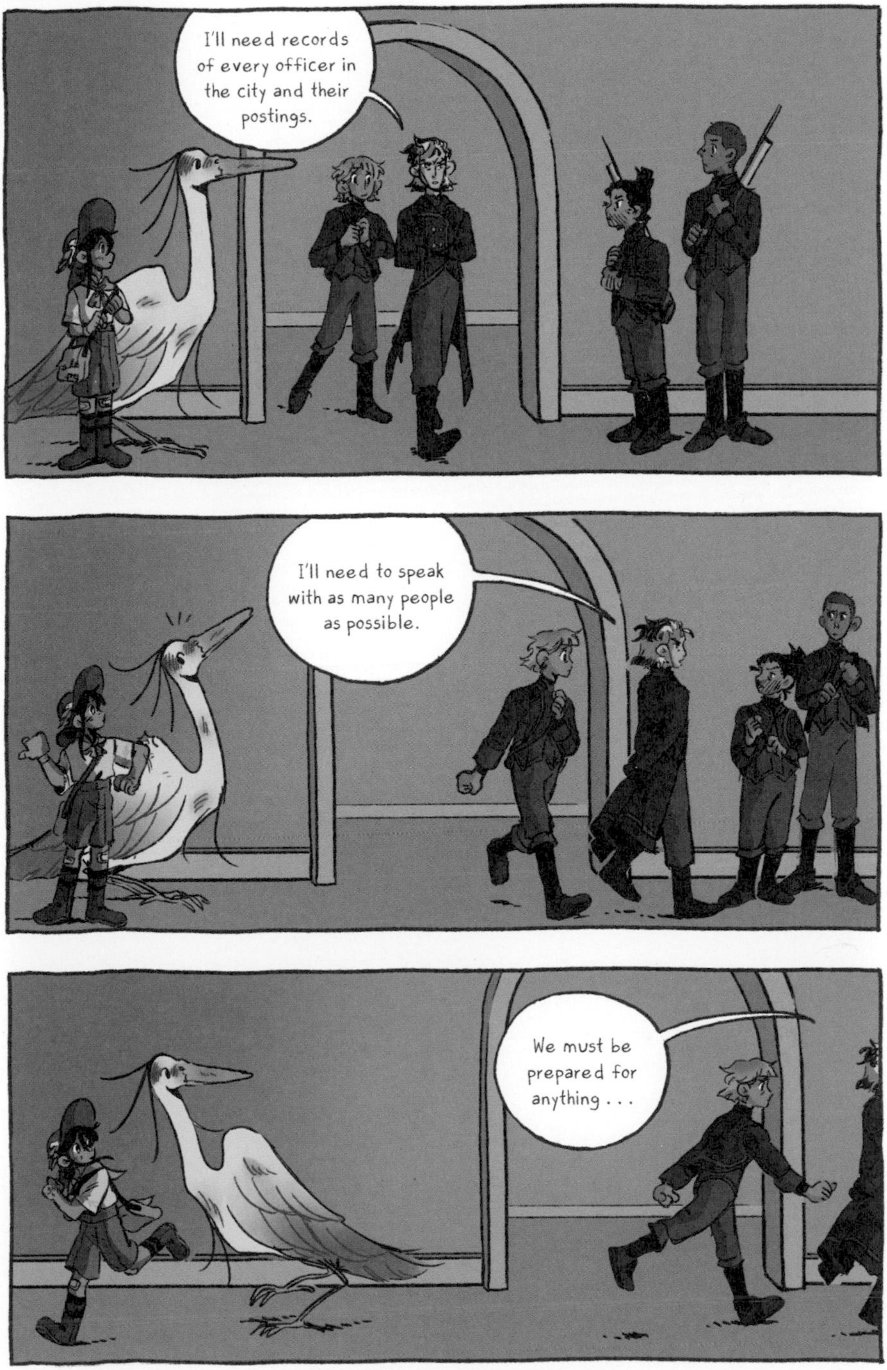
I'll need records of every officer in the city and their postings.
I'll need to speak with as many people as possible.
We must be prepared for anything . . .

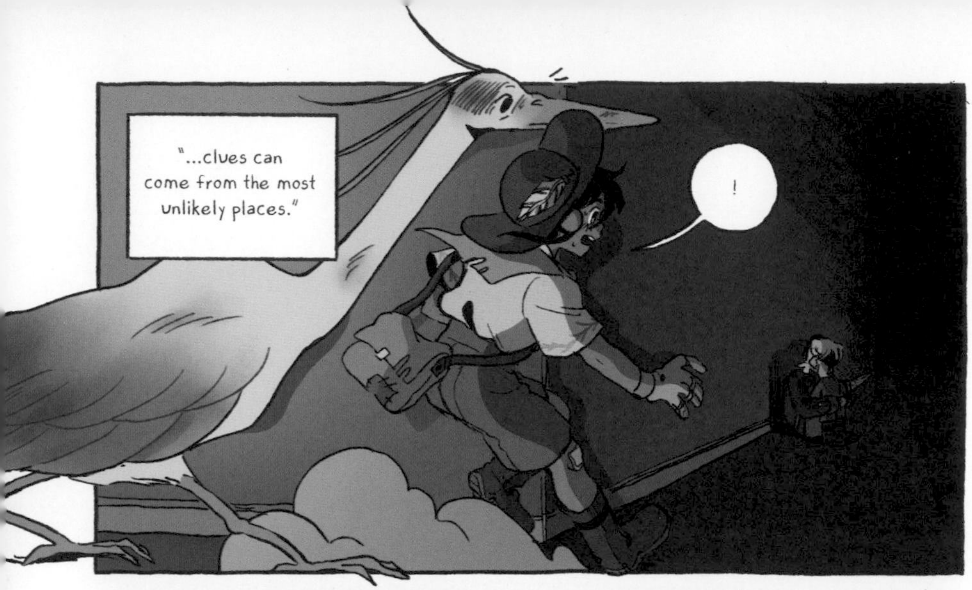
"...clues can come from the most unlikely places."
!

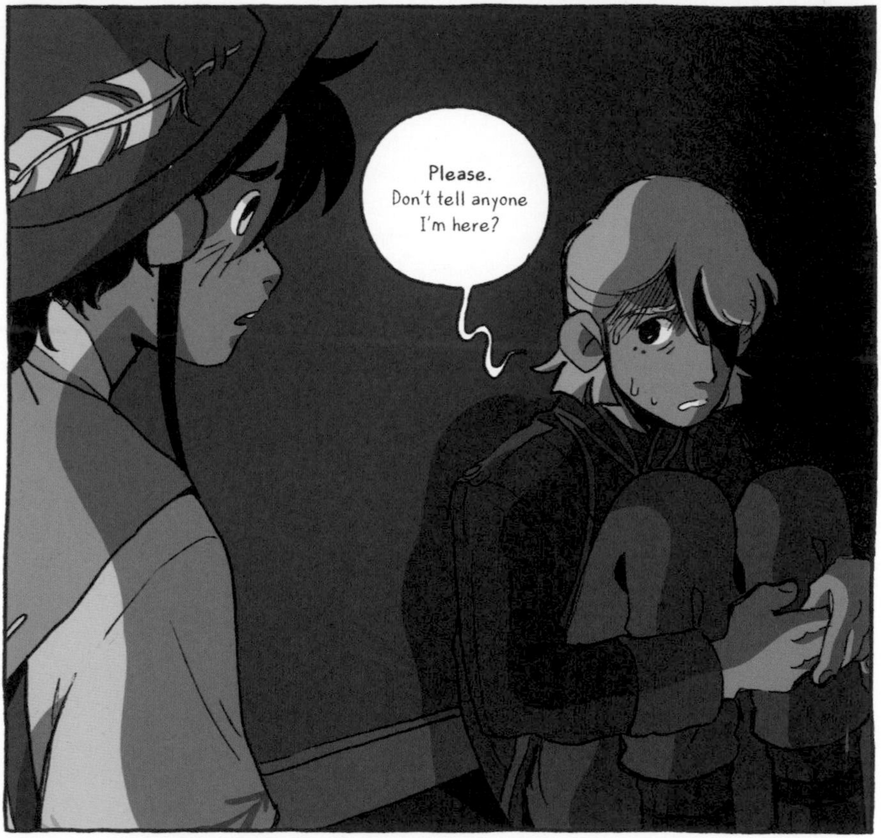
Please.
Don't tell anyone I'm here?

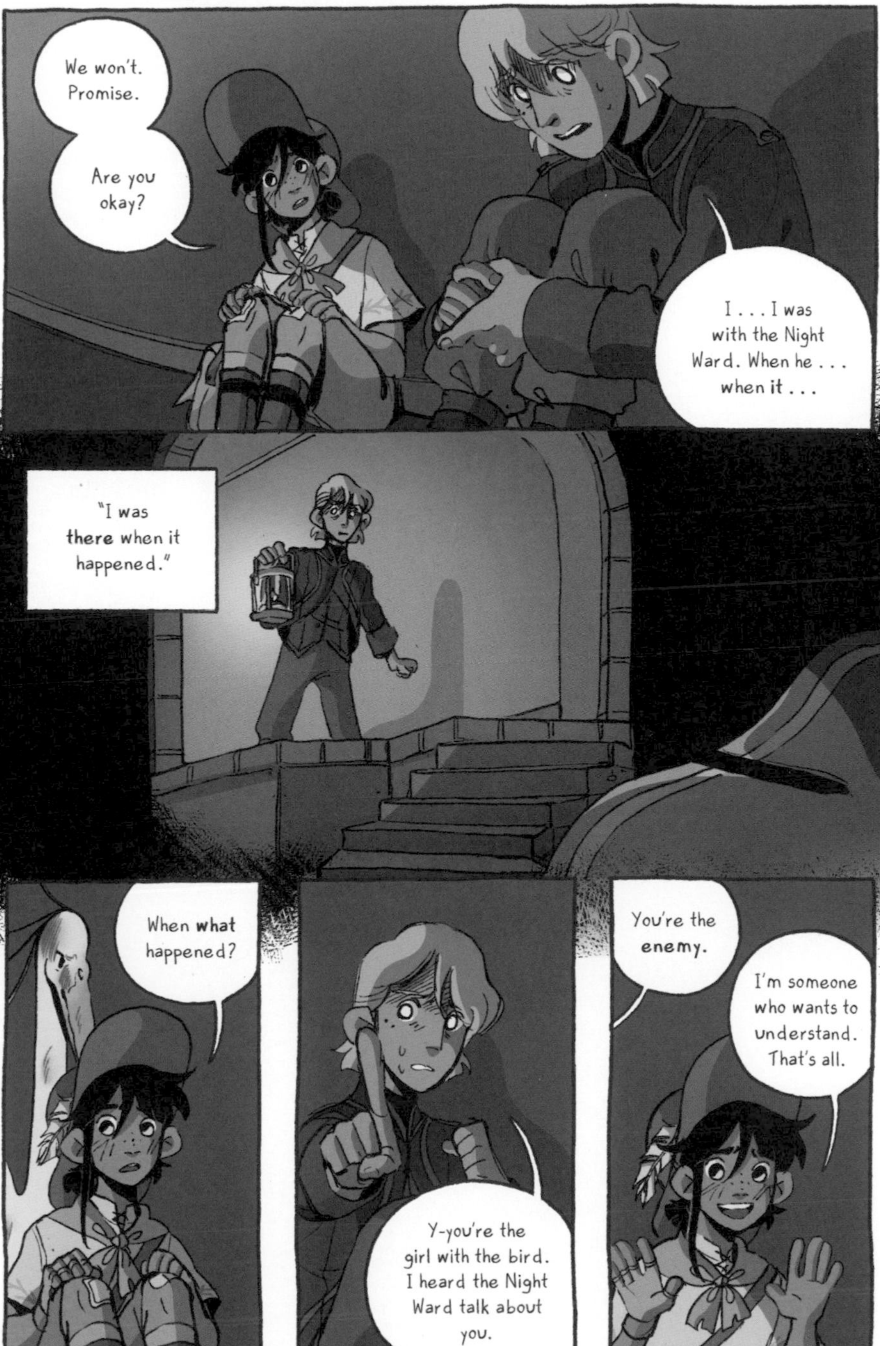
We won't.
Promise.
Are you okay?
I . . . I was with the Night Ward. When he . . . when **it** . . .
"I was **there** when it happened."
When **what** happened?
Y-you're the girl with the bird. I heard the Night Ward talk about you.
You're the **enemy.**
I'm someone who wants to understand. That's all.

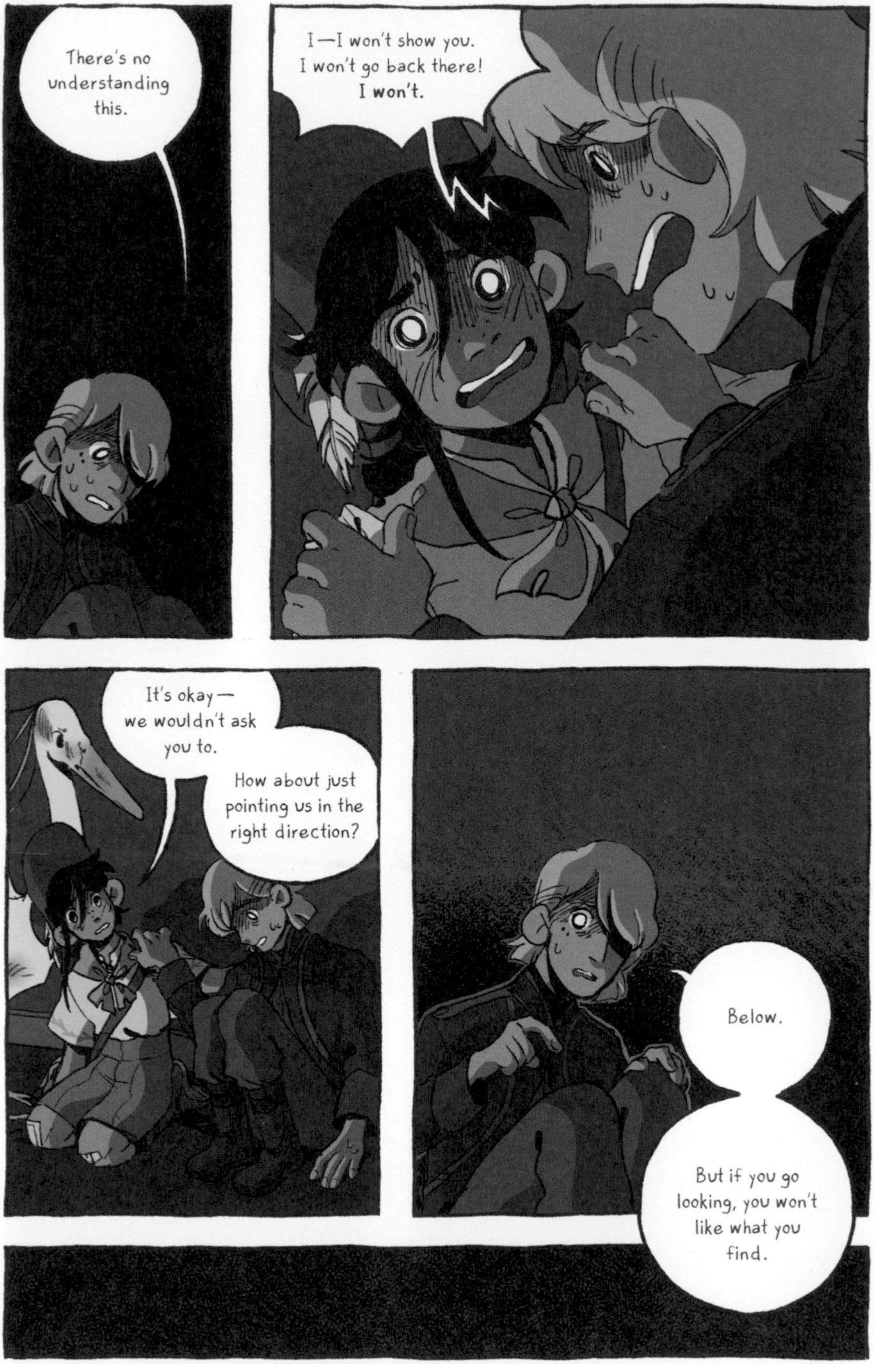
There's no understanding this.
I—I won't show you. I won't go back there! **I won't.**
It's okay—we wouldn't ask you to.
How about just pointing us in the right direction?
Below.
But if you go looking, you won't like what you find.

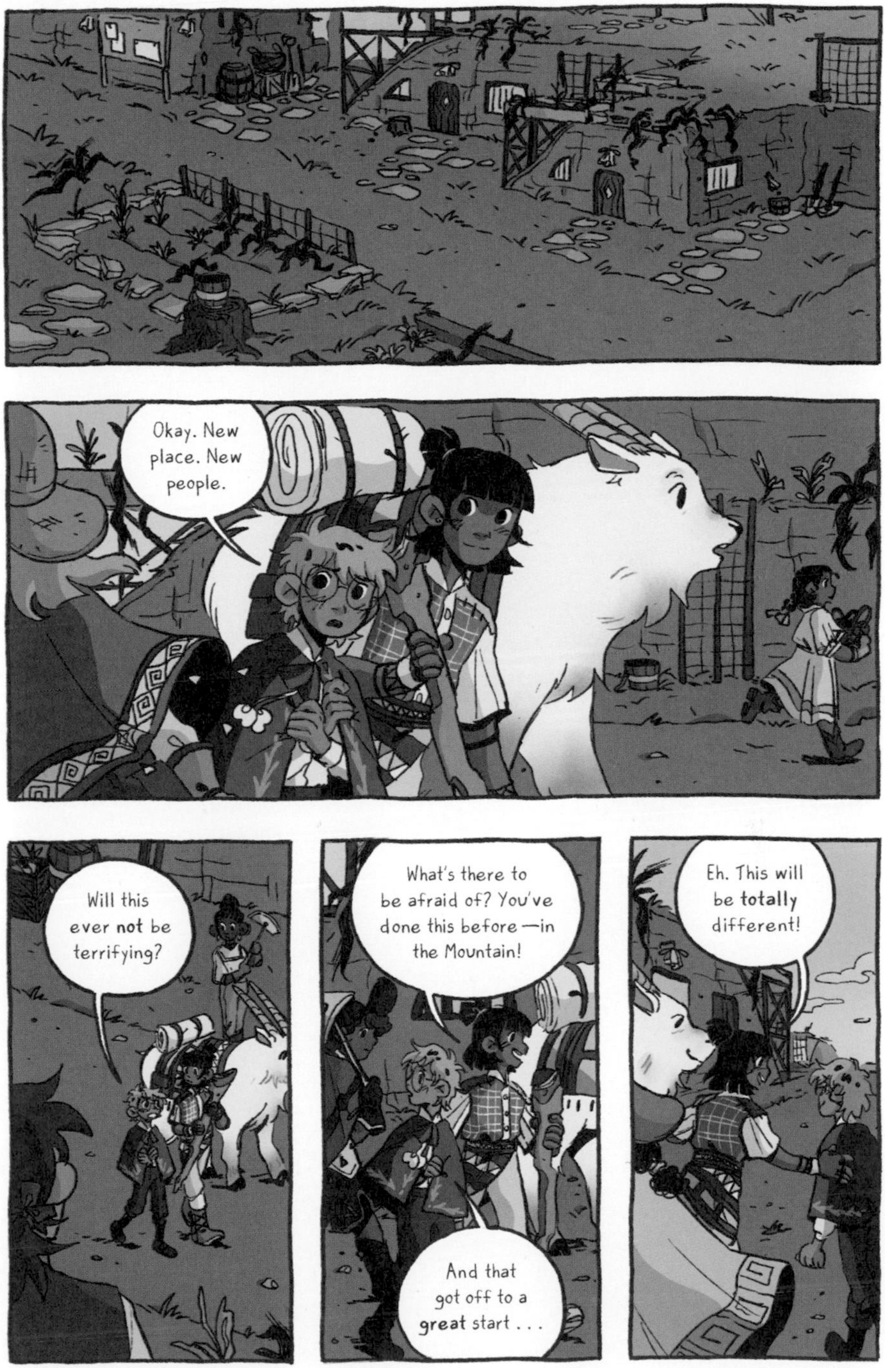
Okay. New place. New people.
Will this ever **not** be terrifying?
What's there to be afraid of? You've done this before—in the Mountain!
And that got off to a **great** start . . .
Eh. This will be **totally** different!

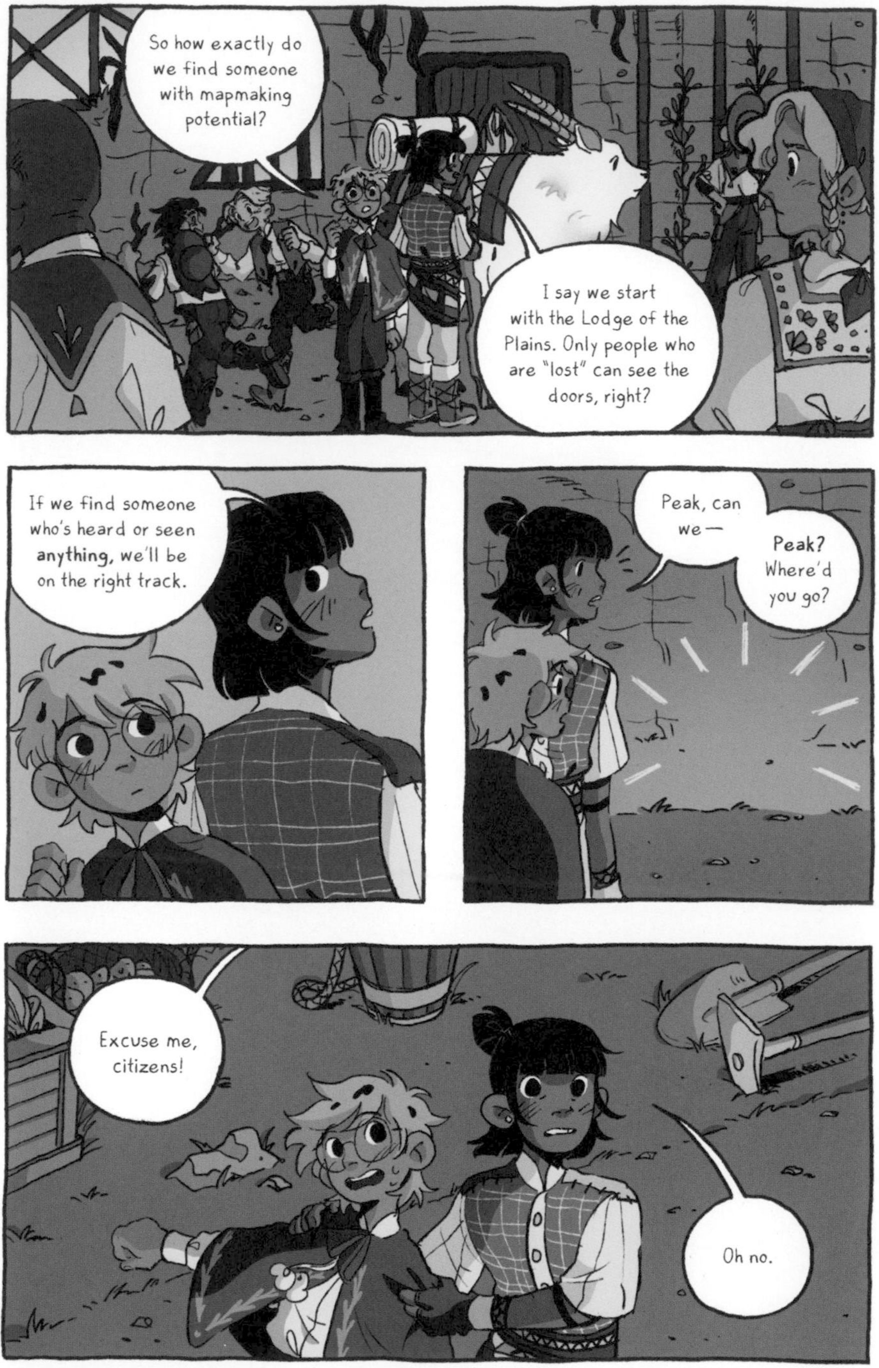
So how exactly do we find someone with mapmaking potential?
I say we start with the Lodge of the Plains. Only people who are "lost" can see the doors, right?
If we find someone who's heard or seen **anything**, we'll be on the right track.
Peak, can we—
Peak? Where'd you go?
Excuse me, citizens!
Oh no.

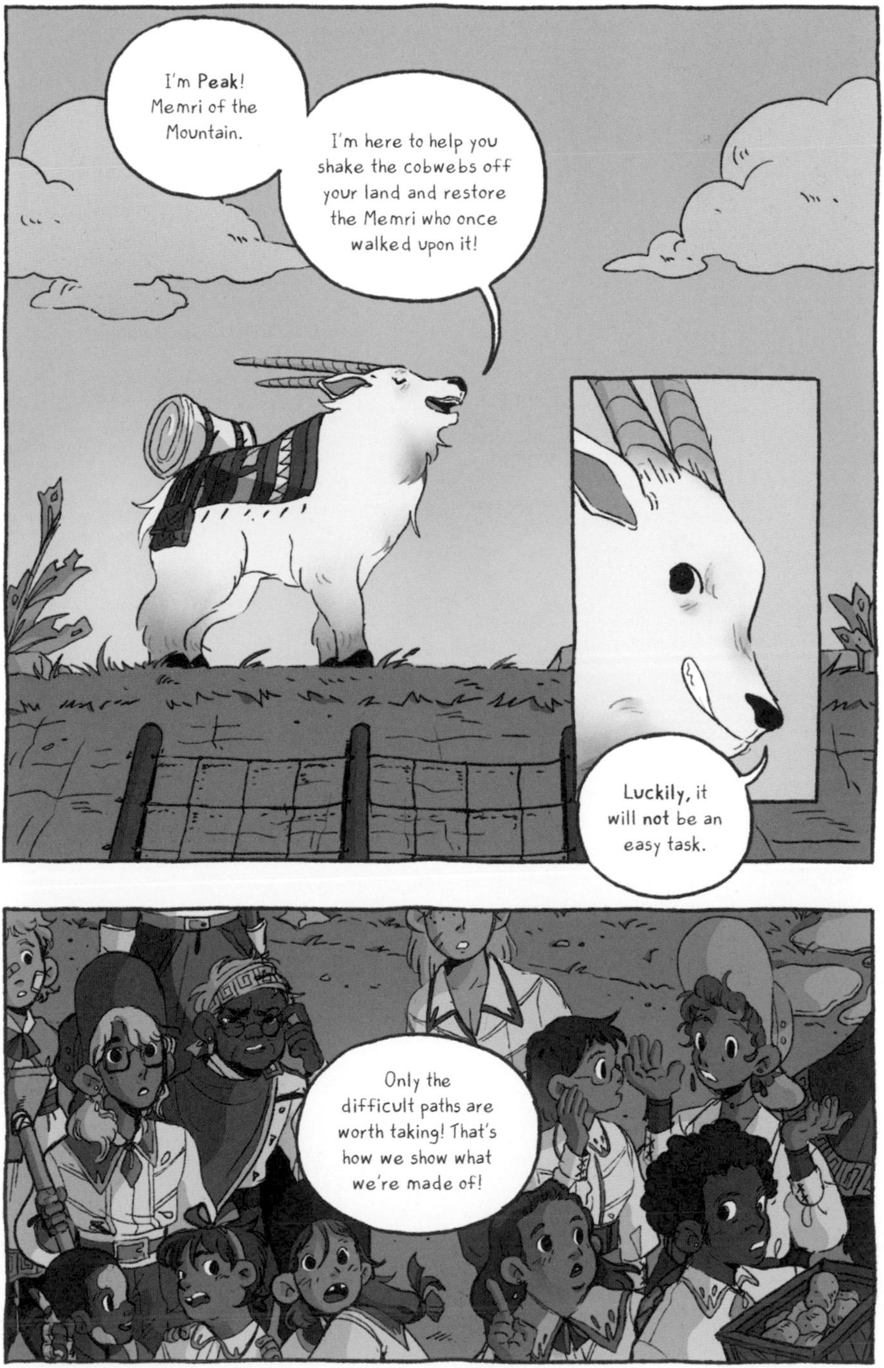
I'm **Peak**! Memri of the Mountain.
I'm here to help you shake the cobwebs off your land and restore the Memri who once walked upon it!
Luckily, it will **not** be an easy task.
Only the difficult paths are worth taking! That's how we show what we're made of!

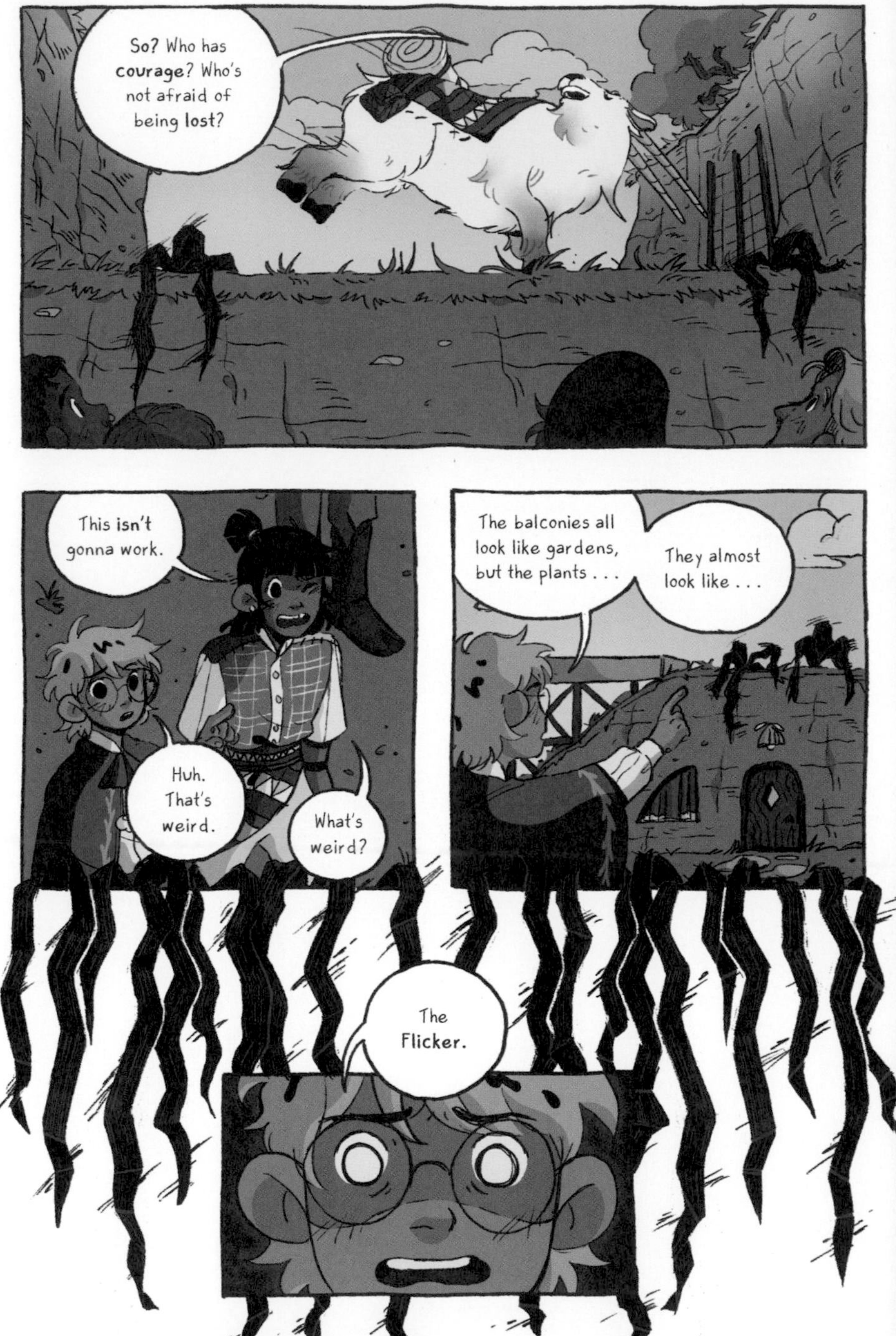
So? Who has courage? Who's not afraid of being lost?
This isn't gonna work.
Huh. That's weird.
What's weird?
The balconies all look like gardens, but the plants . . .
They almost look like . . .
The Flicker.

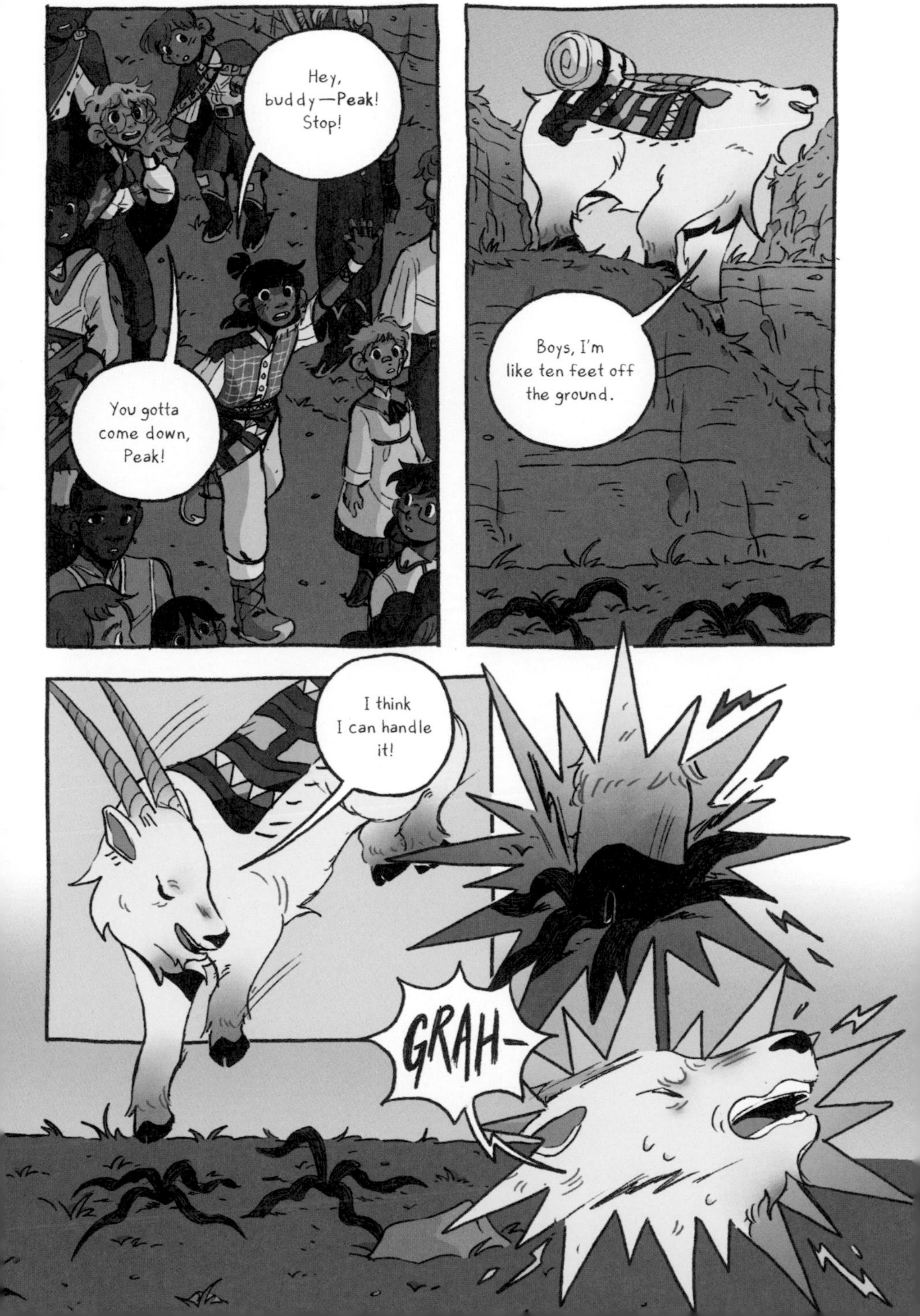

Hey, buddy—Peak! Stop!
You gotta come down, Peak!
Boys, I'm like ten feet off the ground.
I think I can handle it!
GRAH-

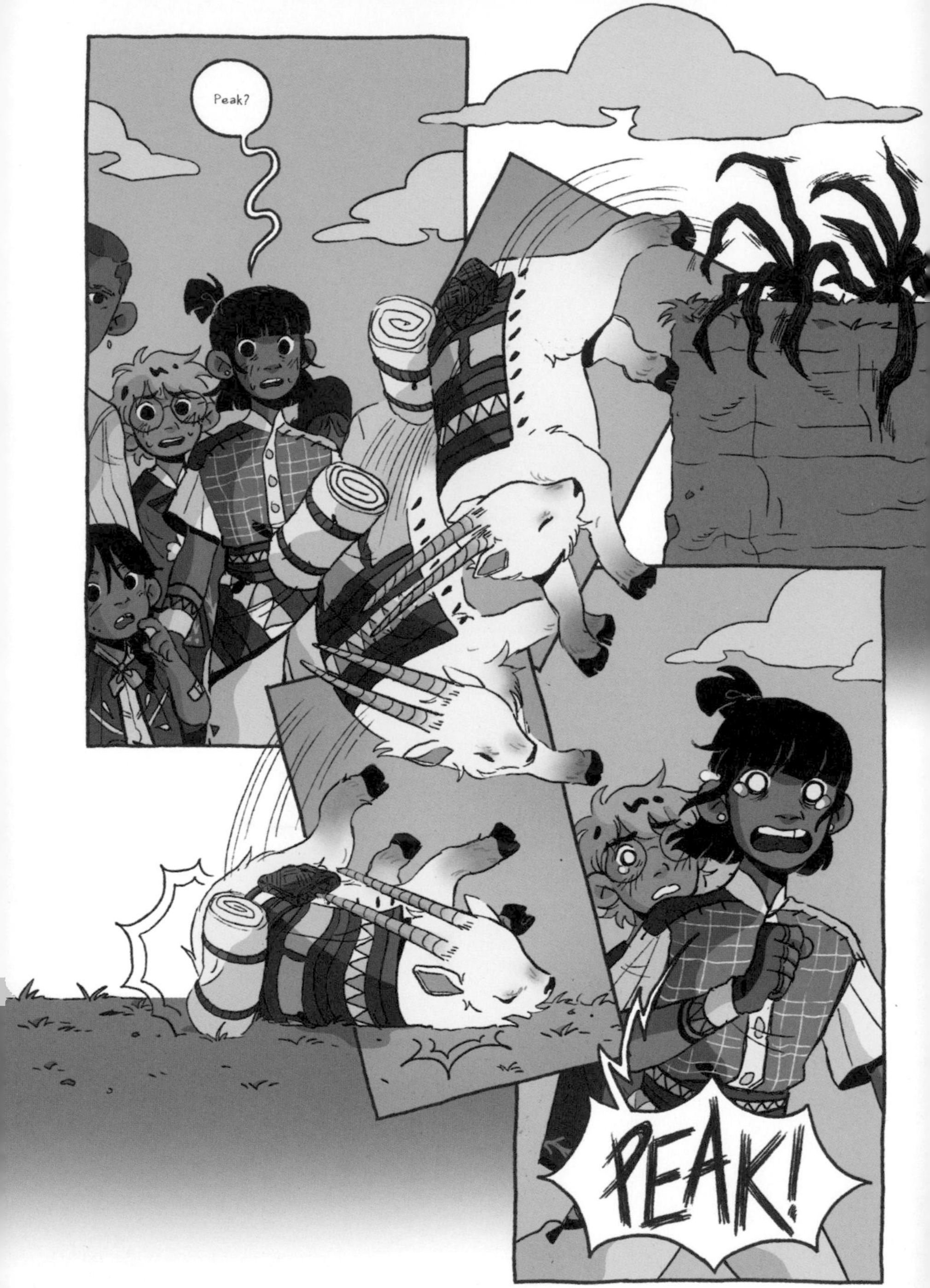
Peak?
PEAK!

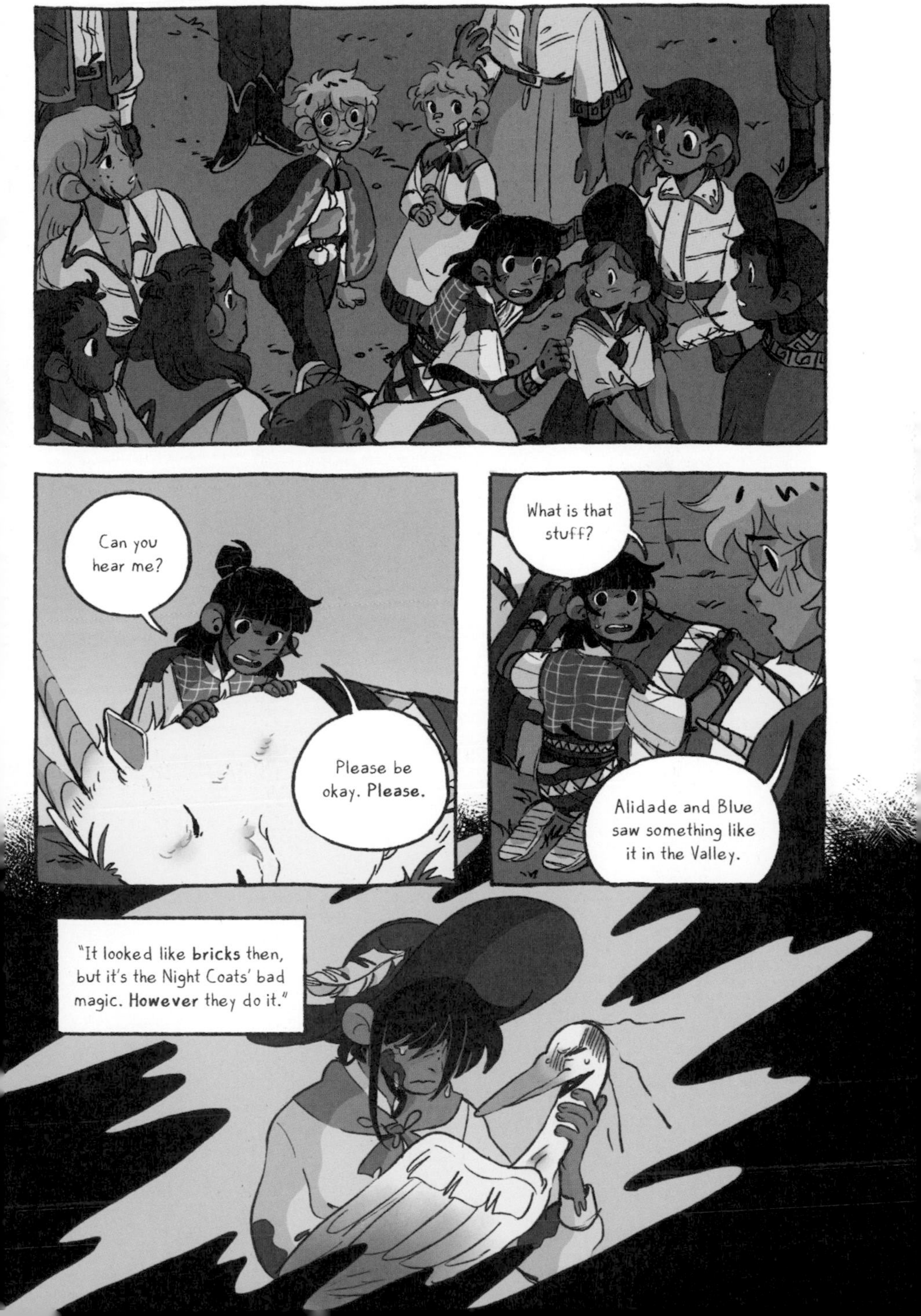
Can you hear me?
Please be okay. **Please.**
What is that stuff?
Alidade and Blue saw something like it in the Valley.
"It looked like **bricks** then, but it's the Night Coats' bad magic. **However** they do it."

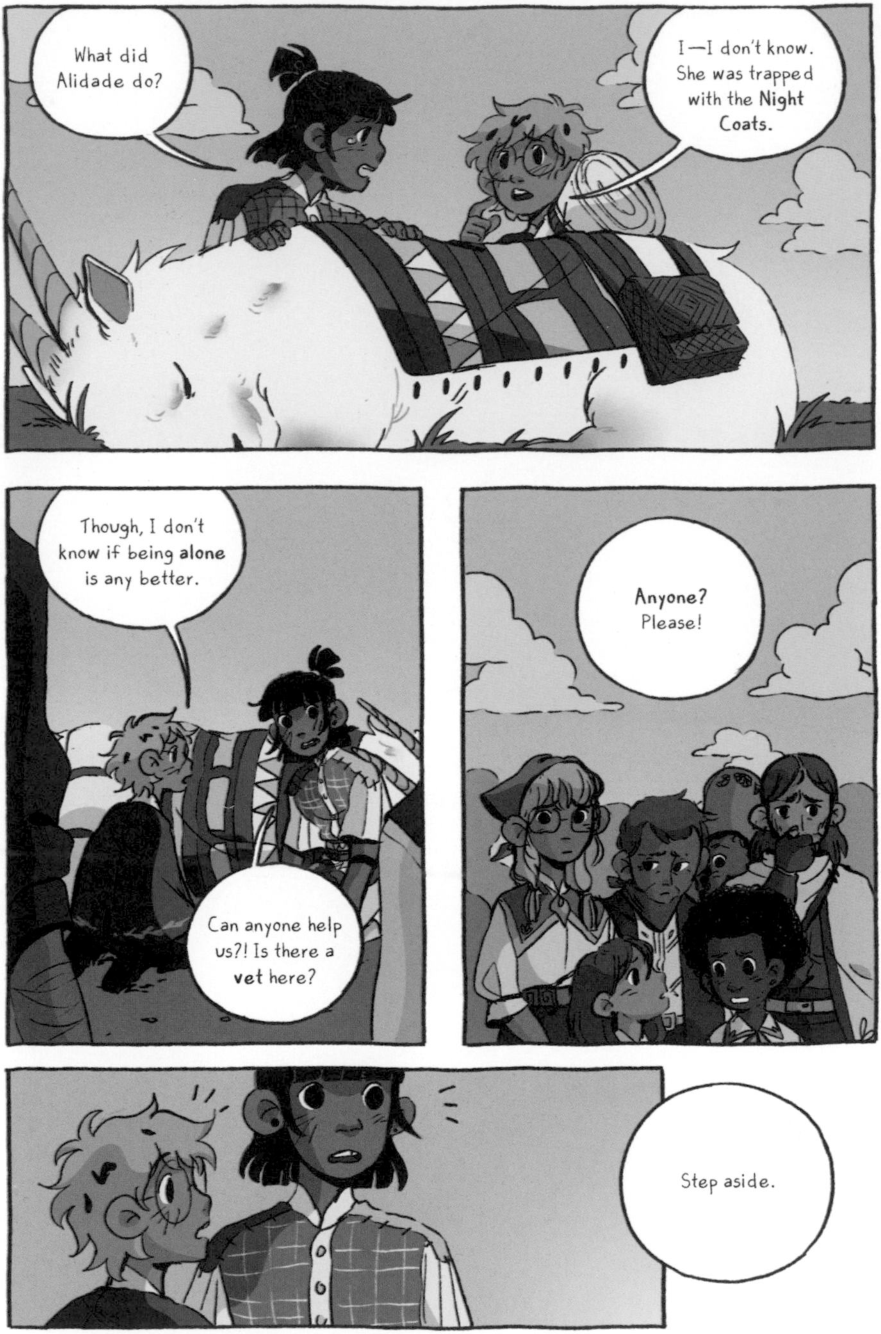

What did Alidade do?
I—I don't know. She was trapped with the **Night Coats.**
Though, I don't know if being **alone** is any better.
Can anyone help us?! Is there a **vet** here?
Anyone? Please!
Step aside.

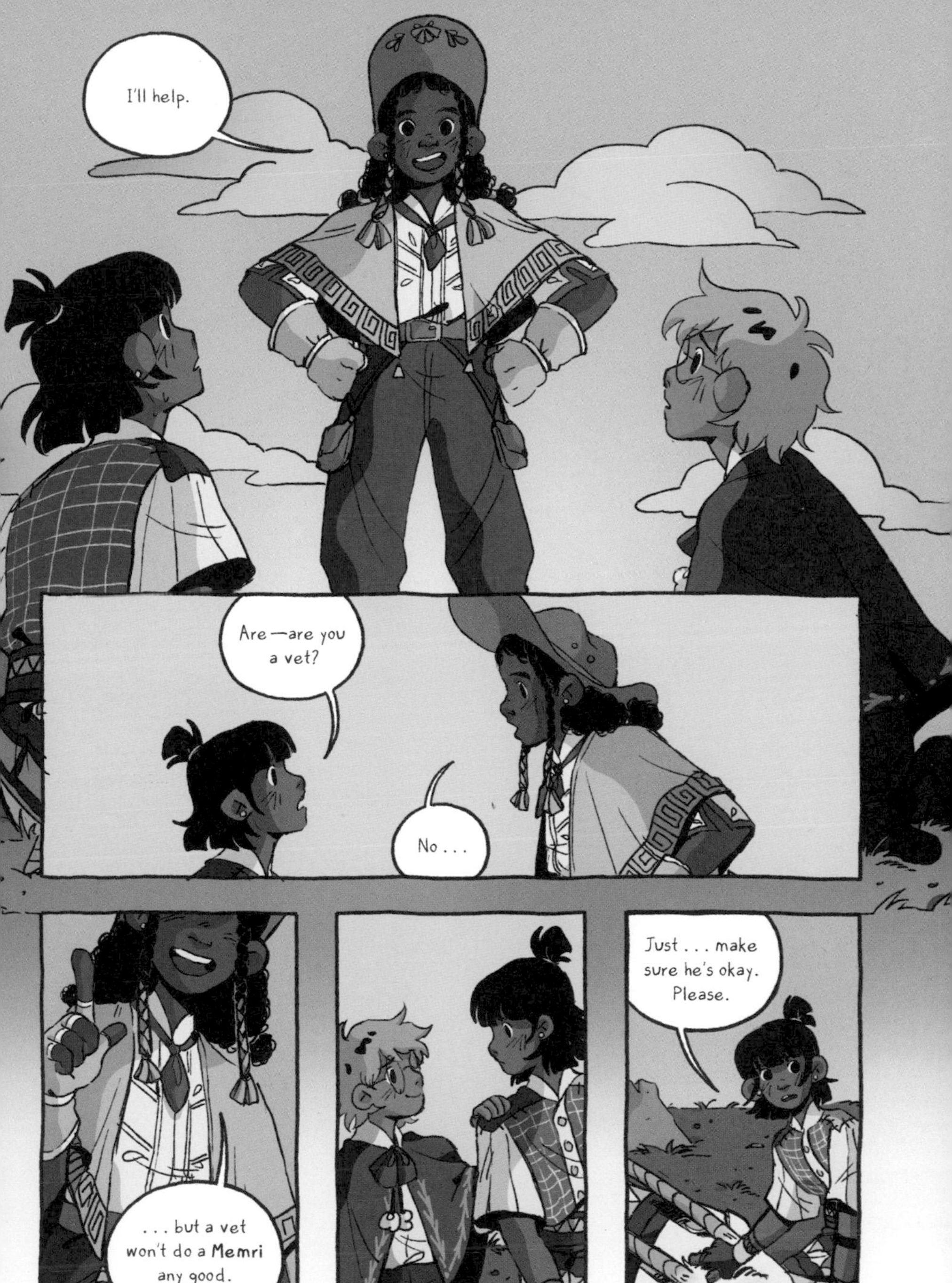
I'll help.
Are—are you a vet?
No . . .
. . . but a vet won't do a **Memri** any good.
Just . . . make sure he's okay. Please.

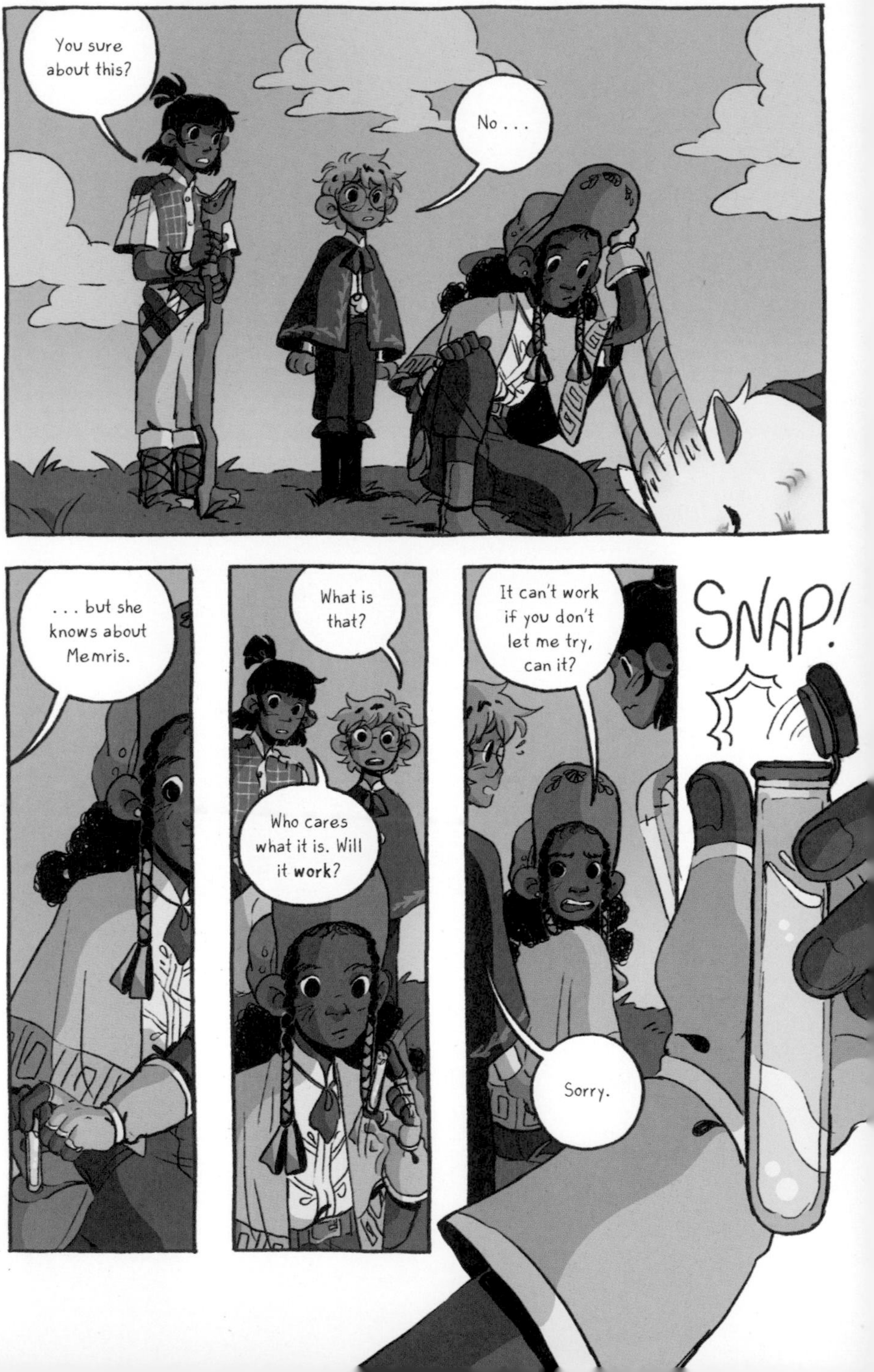
You sure about this?
No . . .
. . . but she knows about Memris.
What is that?
Who cares what it is. Will it **work**?
It can't work if you don't let me try, can it?
Sorry.
SNAP!

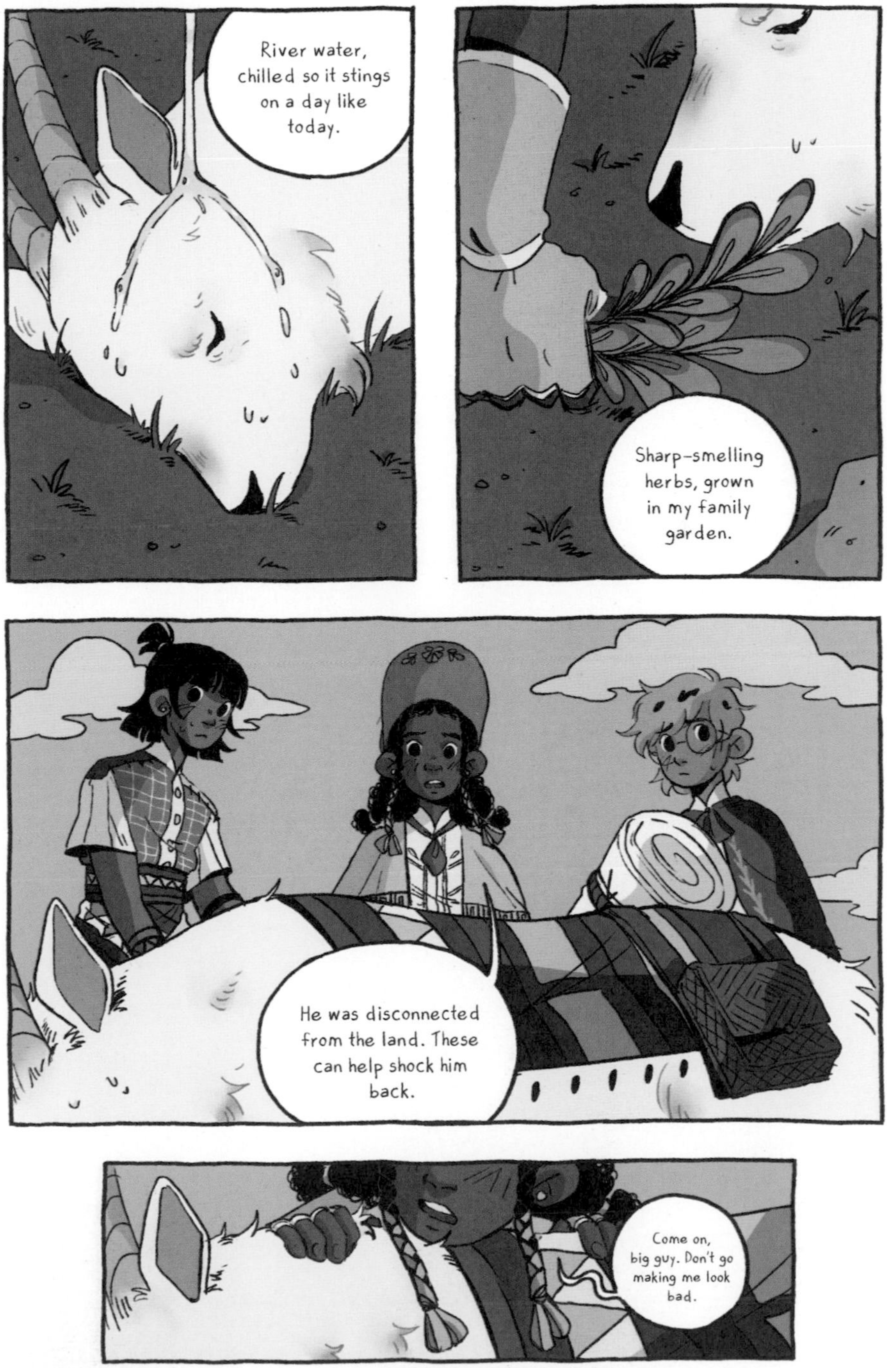
River water, chilled so it stings on a day like today.
Sharp-smelling herbs, grown in my family garden.
He was disconnected from the land. These can help shock him back.
Come on, big guy. Don't go making me look bad.

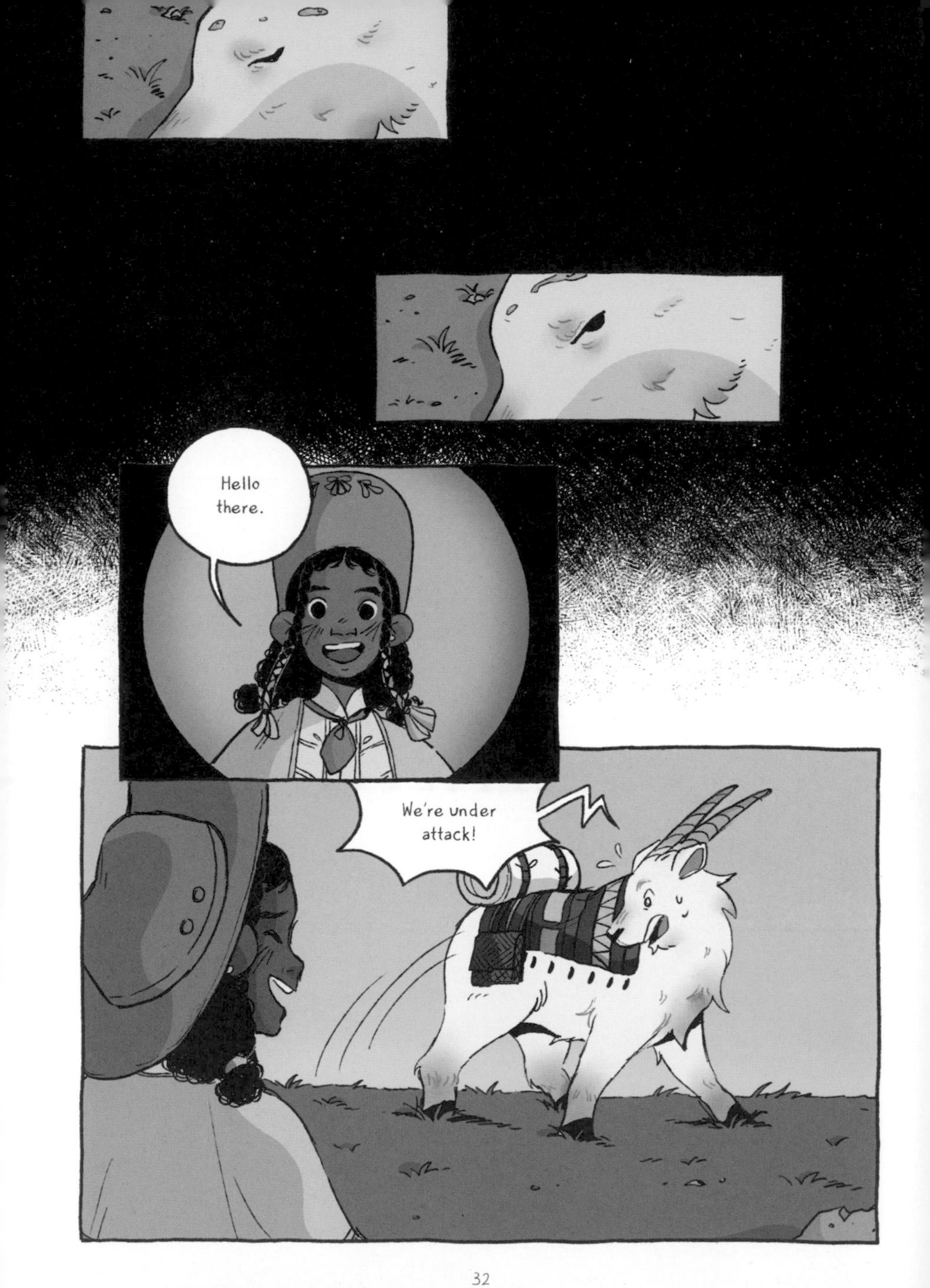
Hello there.
We're under attack!

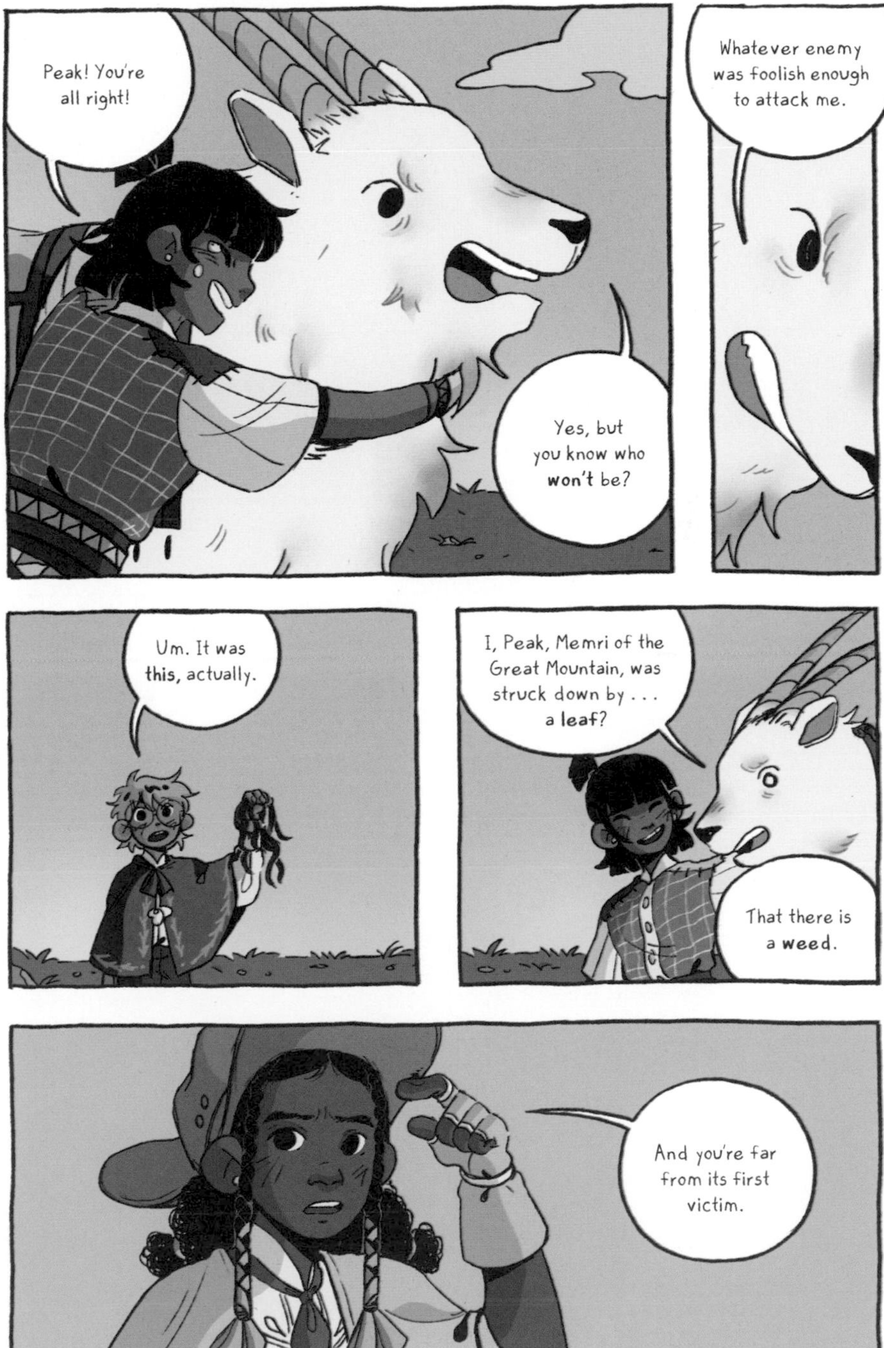
Peak! You're all right!
Whatever enemy was foolish enough to attack me.
Yes, but you know who **won't** be?
Um. It was **this**, actually.
I, Peak, Memri of the Great Mountain, was struck down by . . . a **leaf**?
That there is a **weed**.
And you're far from its first victim.

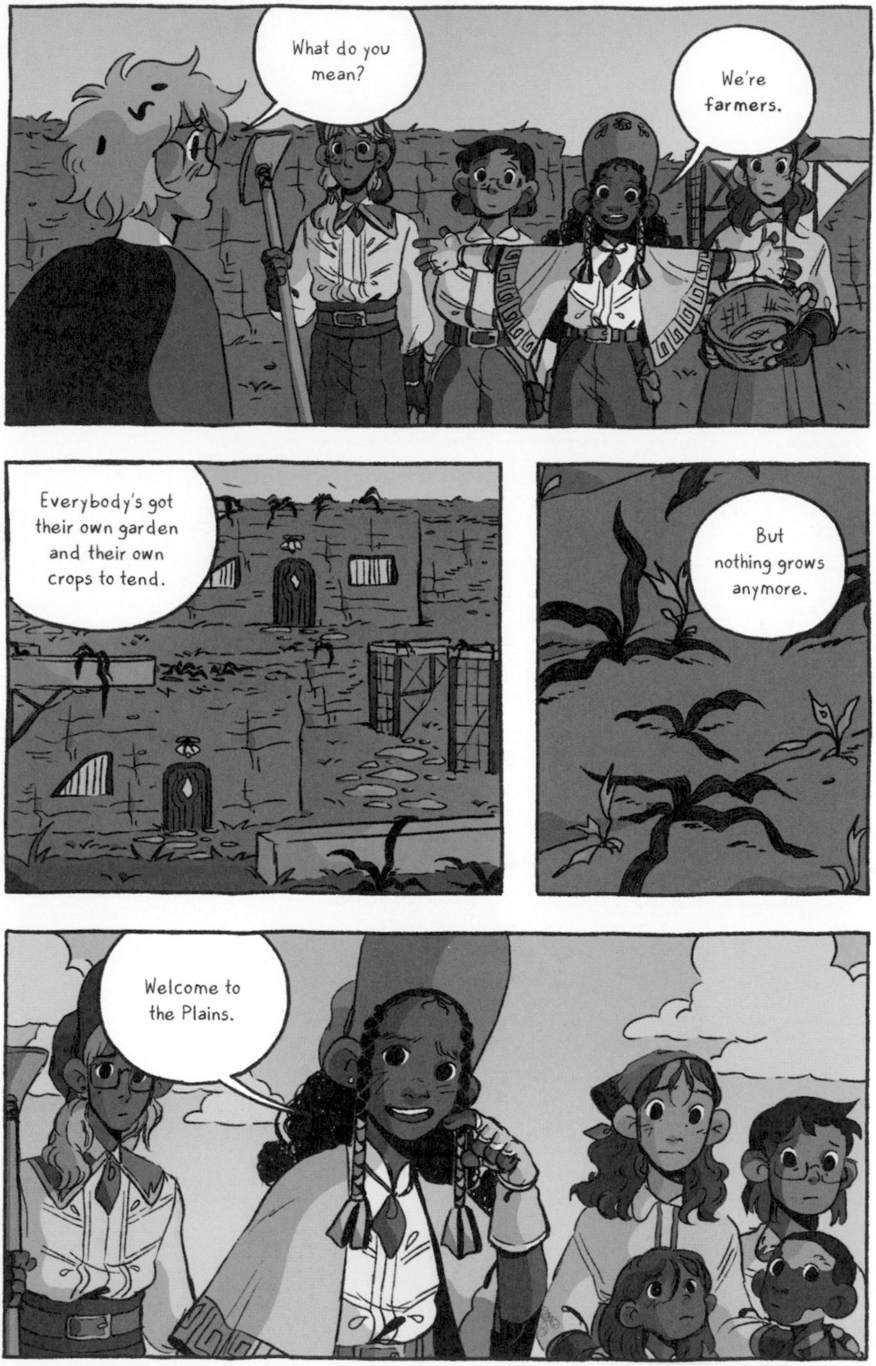
What do you mean?
We're farmers.
Everybody's got their own garden and their own crops to tend.
But nothing grows anymore.
Welcome to the Plains.

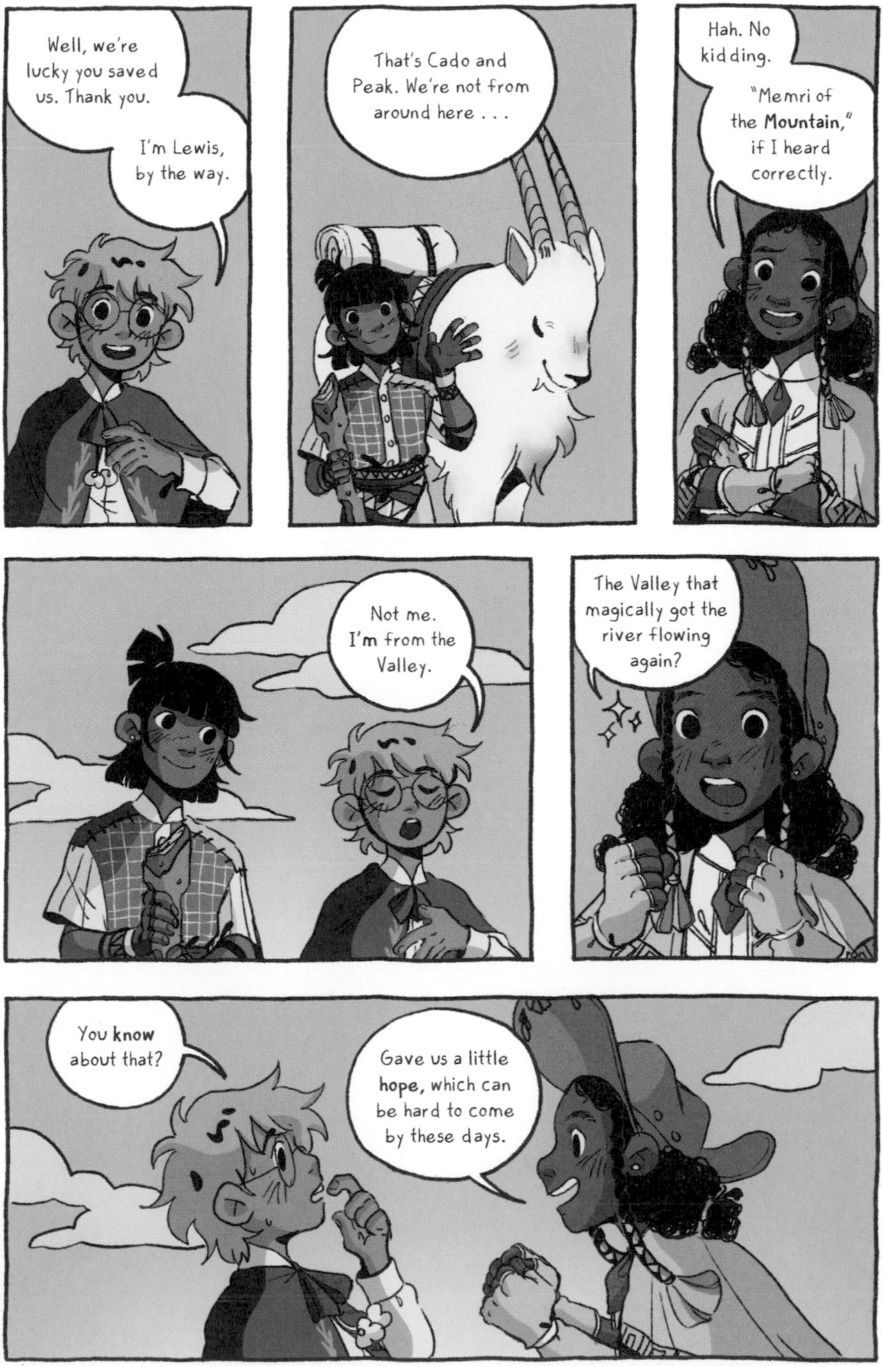
Well, we're lucky you saved us. Thank you.
I'm Lewis, by the way.
That's Cado and Peak. We're not from around here . . .
Hah. No kidding.
"Memri of the **Mountain**," if I heard correctly.
Not me. I'm from the Valley.
The Valley that magically got the river flowing again?
You **know** about that?
Gave us a little **hope**, which can be hard to come by these days.

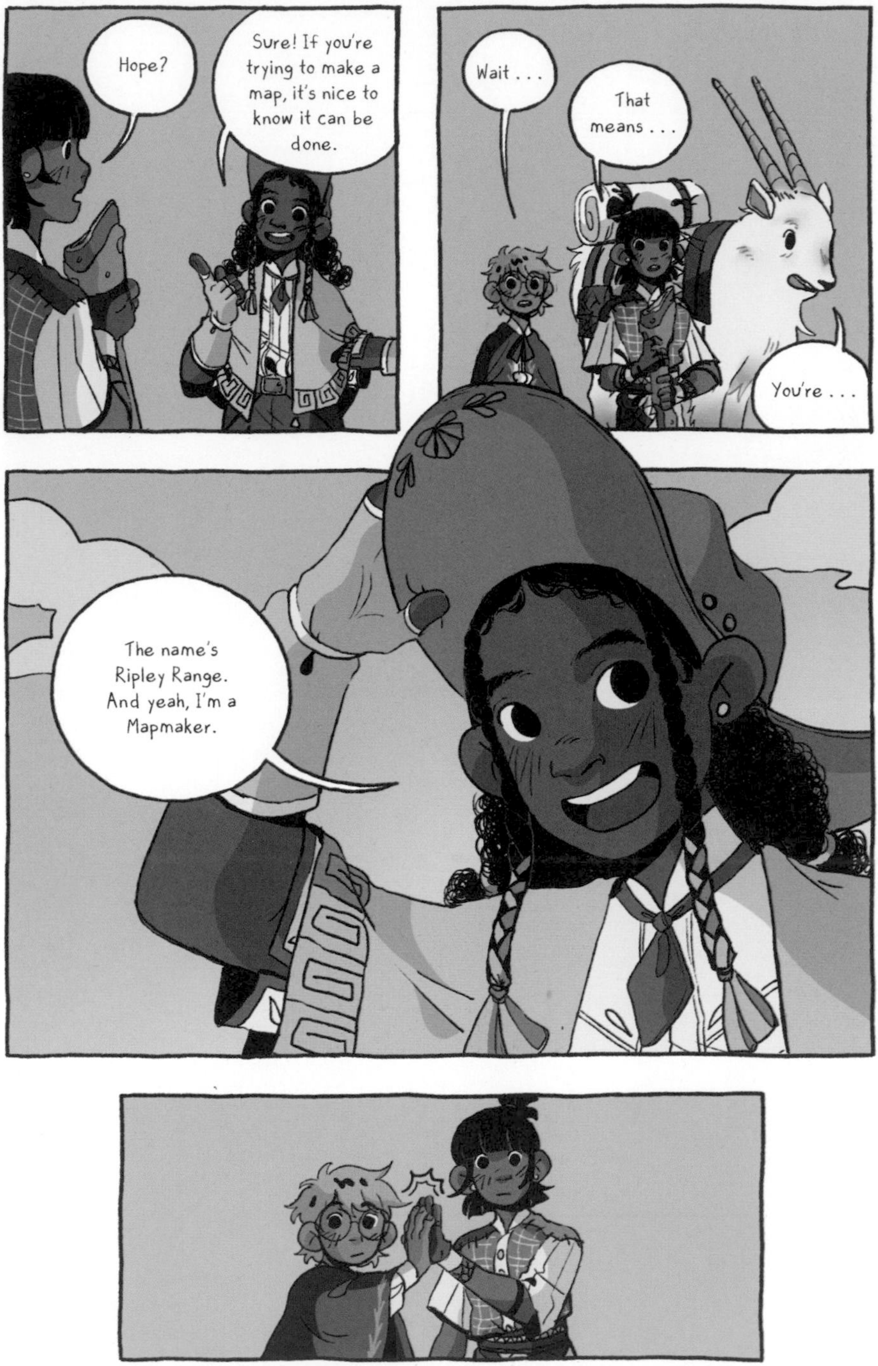
Hope?
Sure! If you're trying to make a map, it's nice to know it can be done.
Wait . . .
That means . . .
You're . . .
The name's Ripley Range. And yeah, I'm a Mapmaker.

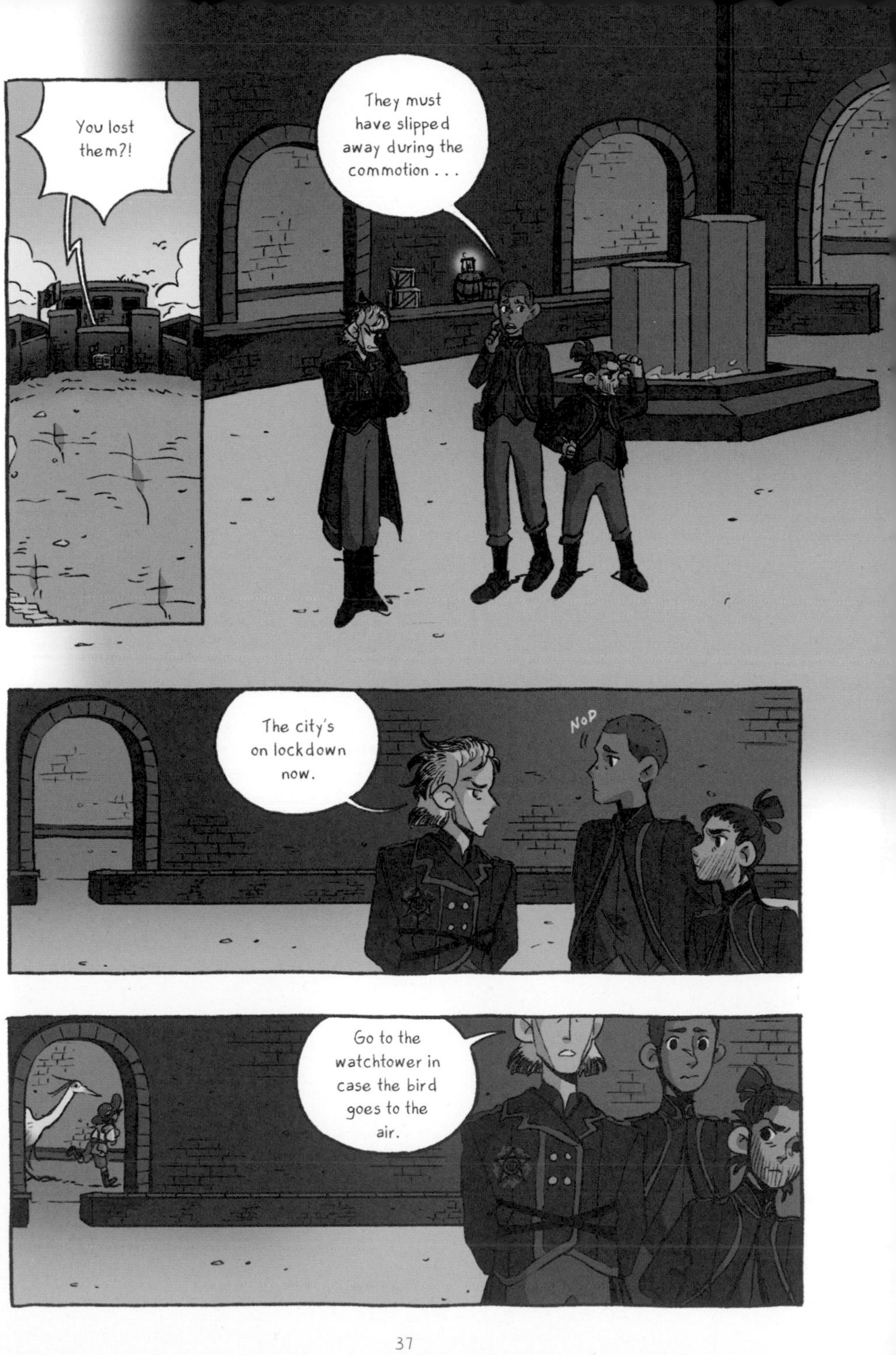
You lost them?!
They must have slipped away during the commotion . . .
The city's on lockdown now.
NOD
Go to the watchtower in case the bird goes to the air.

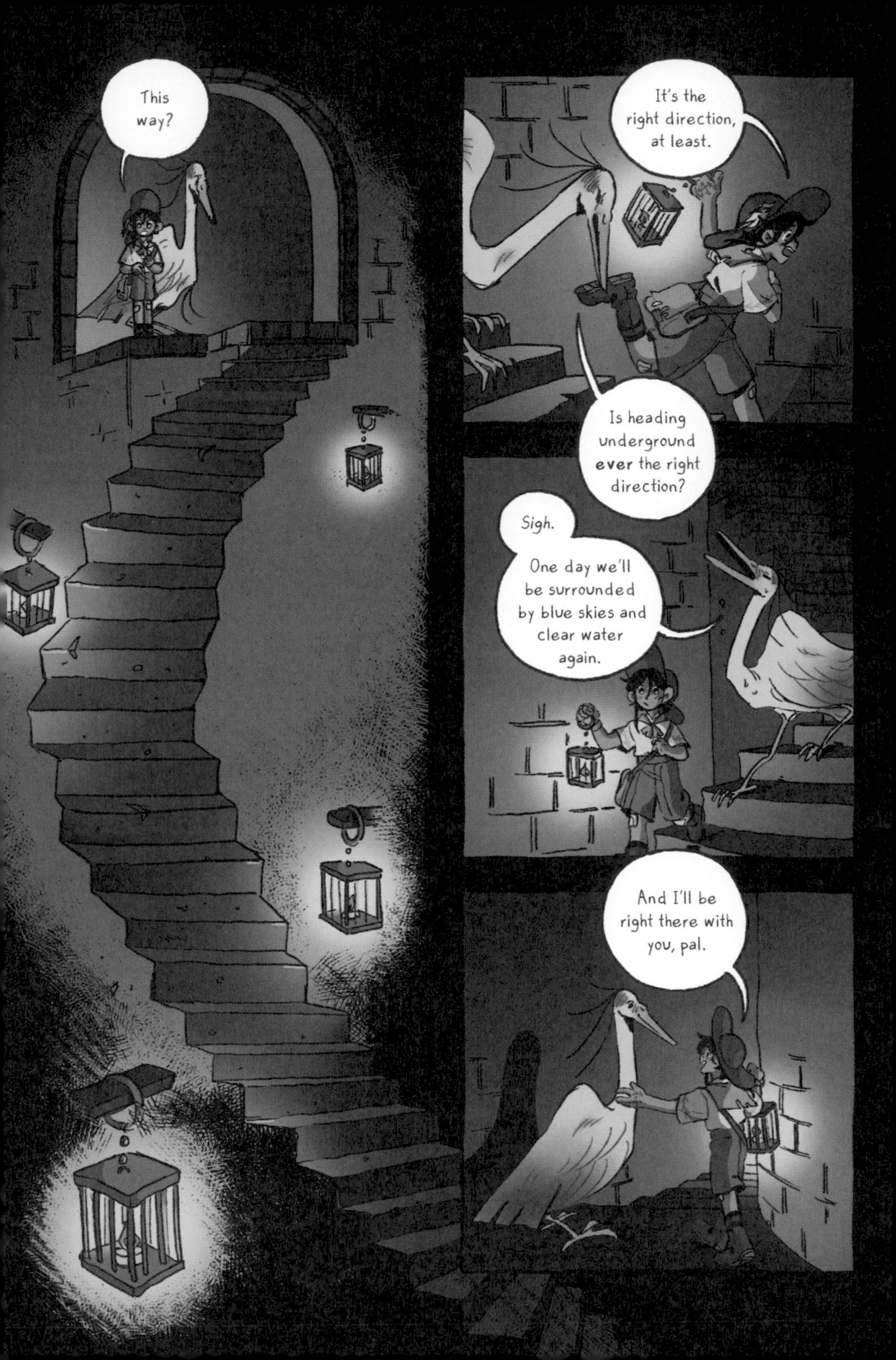
This way?
It's the right direction, at least.
Is heading underground **ever** the right direction?
Sigh.
One day we'll be surrounded by blue skies and clear water again.
And I'll be right there with you, pal.

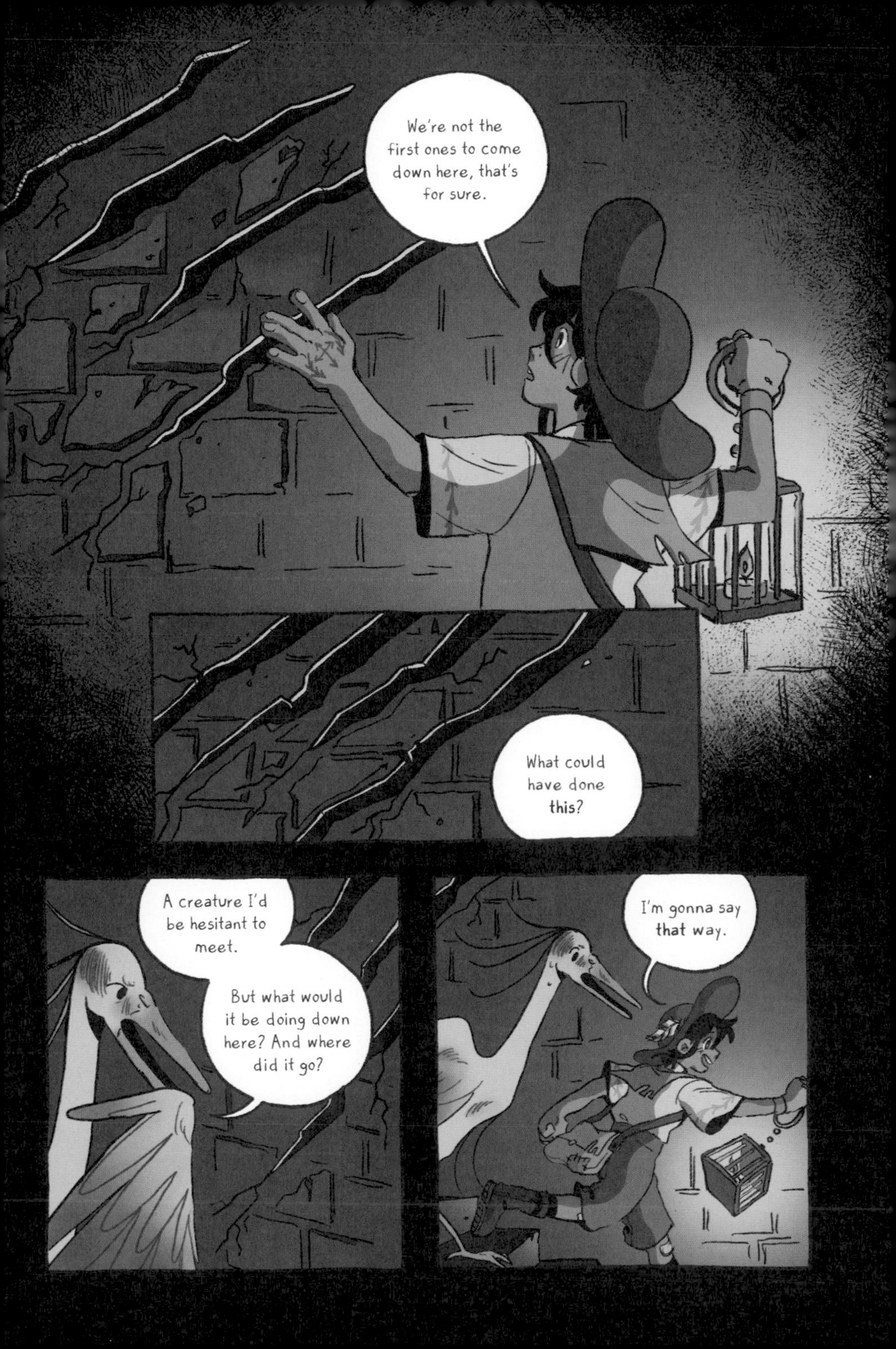
We're not the first ones to come down here, that's for sure.
What could have done **this**?
A creature I'd be hesitant to meet.
But what would it be doing down here? And where did it go?
I'm gonna say **that way**.

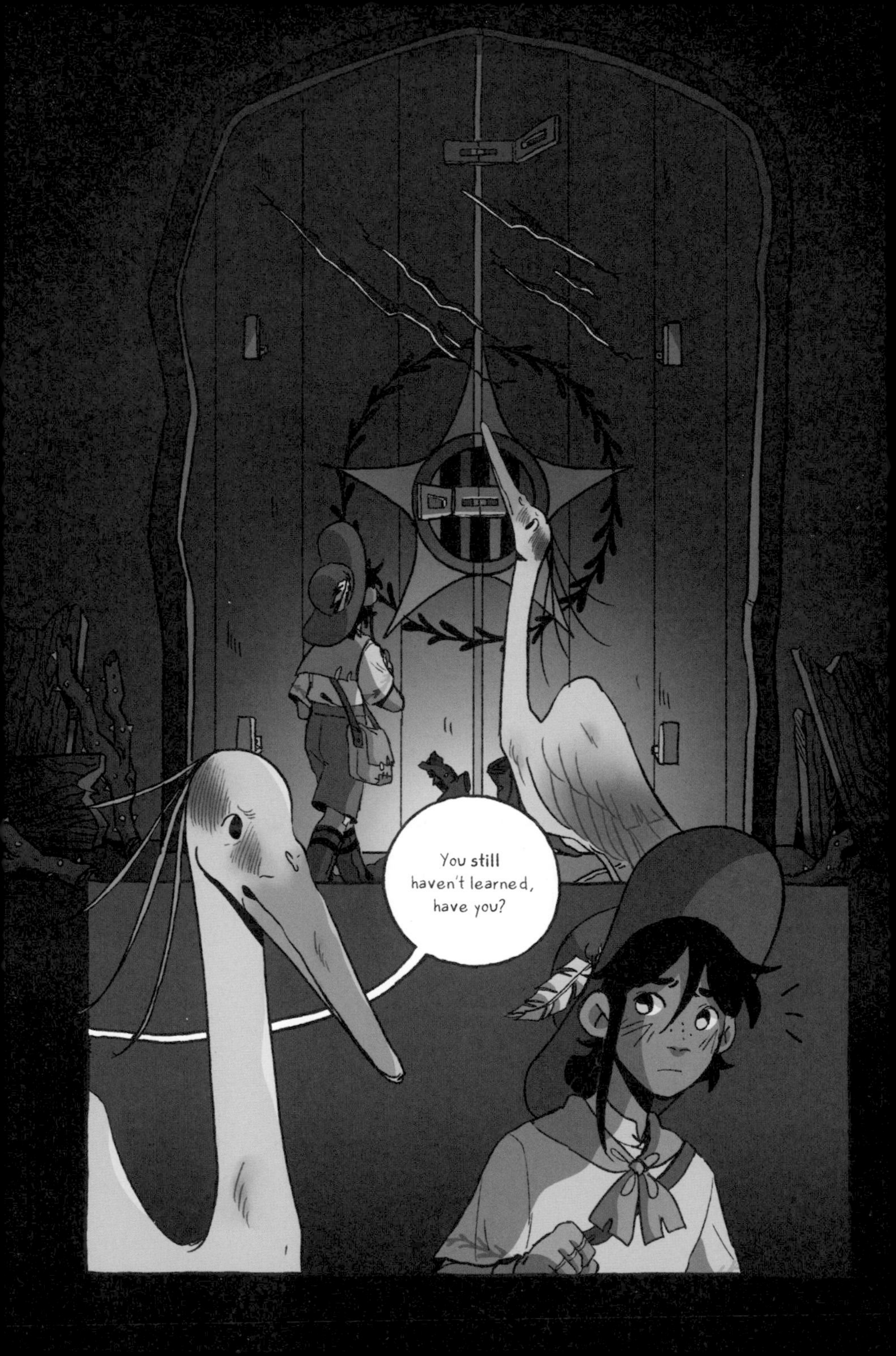
You still haven't learned, have you?

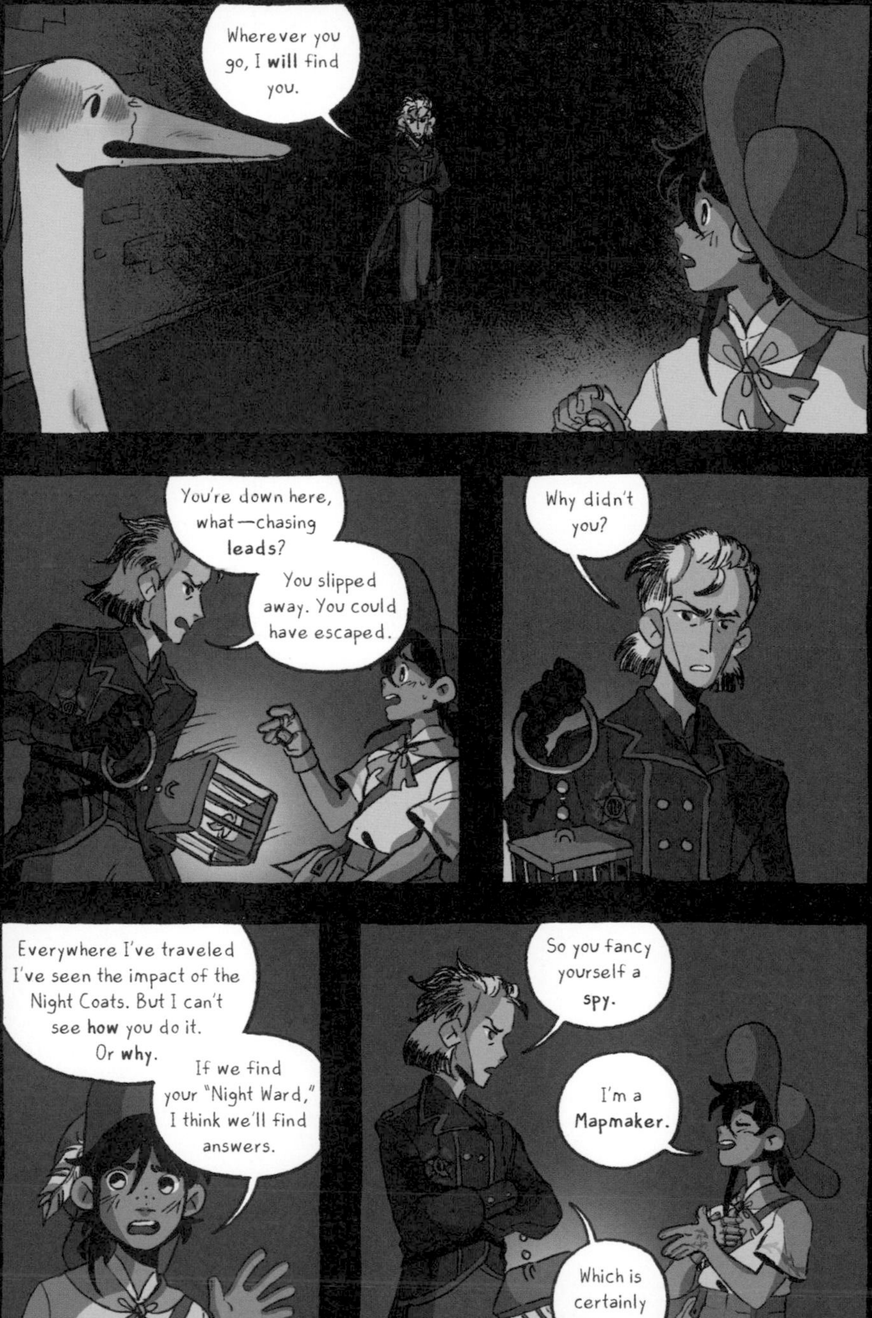
Wherever you go, I **will** find you.
You're down here, what—chasing **leads**?
You slipped away. You could have escaped.
Why didn't you?
Everywhere I've traveled I've seen the impact of the Night Coats. But I can't see **how** you do it. Or **why**.
If we find your "Night Ward," I think we'll find answers.
So you fancy yourself a **spy**.
I'm a **Mapmaker**.
Which is certainly worse.

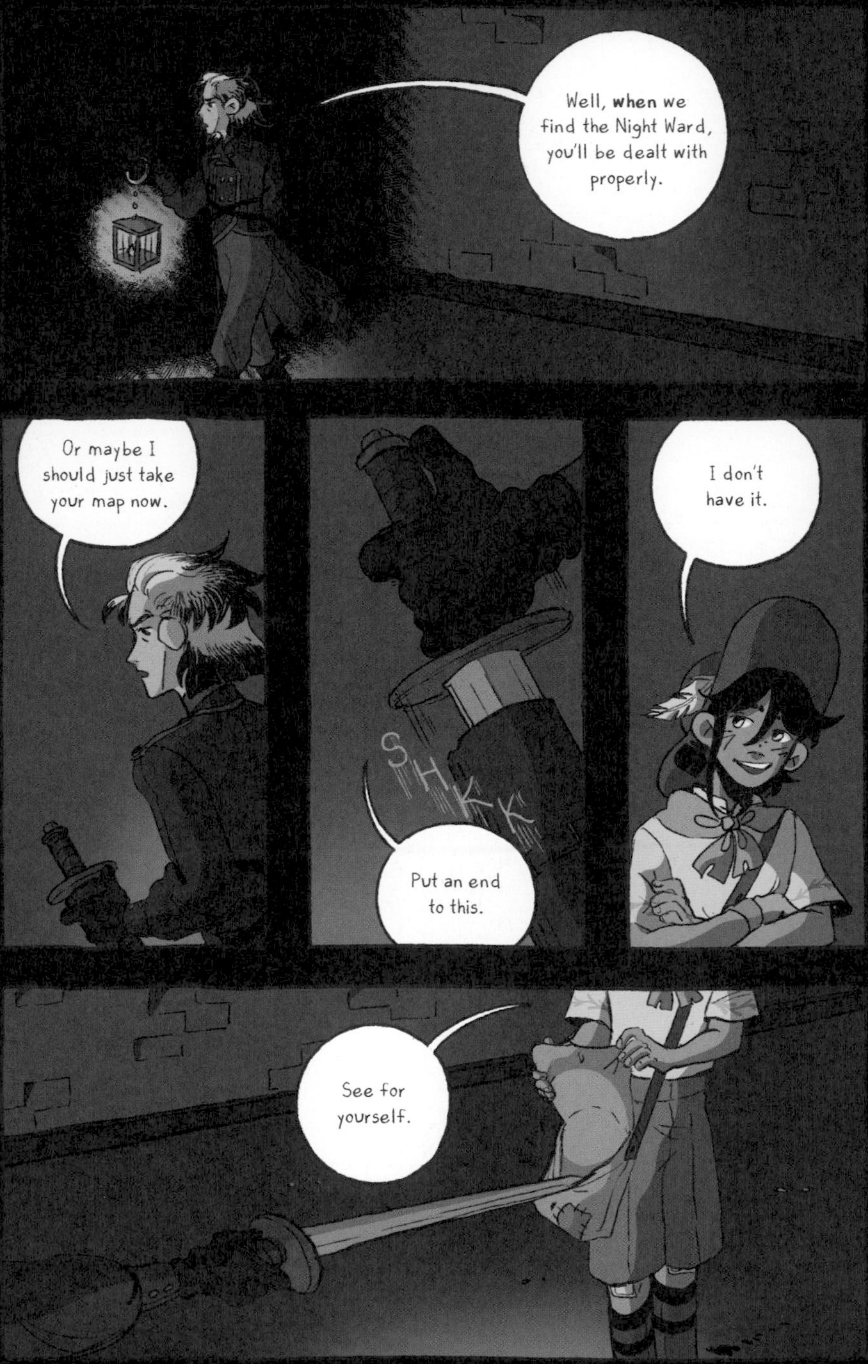
Well, **when** we find the Night Ward, you'll be dealt with properly.
Or maybe I should just take your map now.
SHKK
Put an end to this.
I don't have it.
See for yourself.

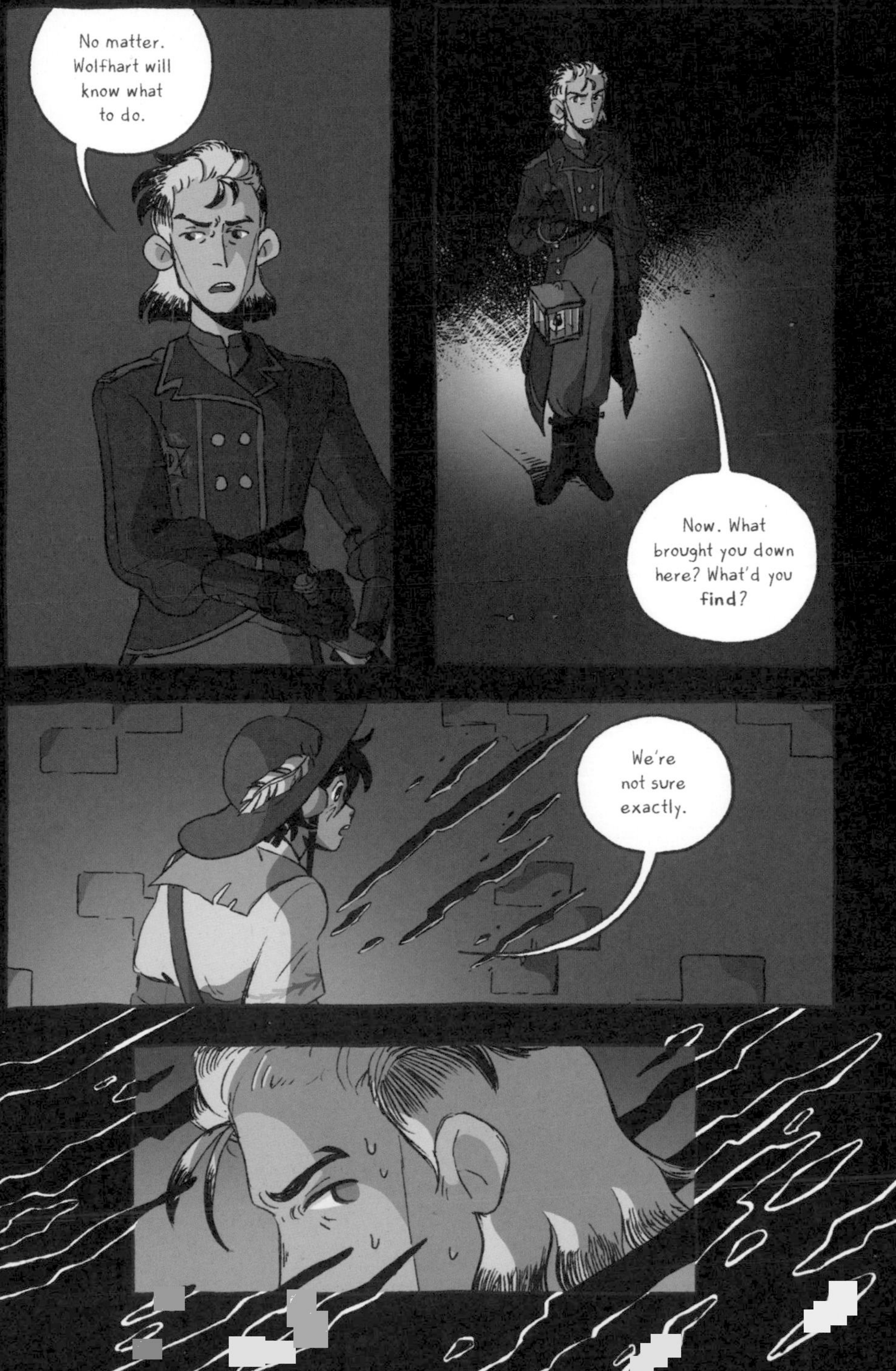
No matter. Wolfhart will know what to do.
Now. What brought you down here? What'd you find?
We're not sure exactly.

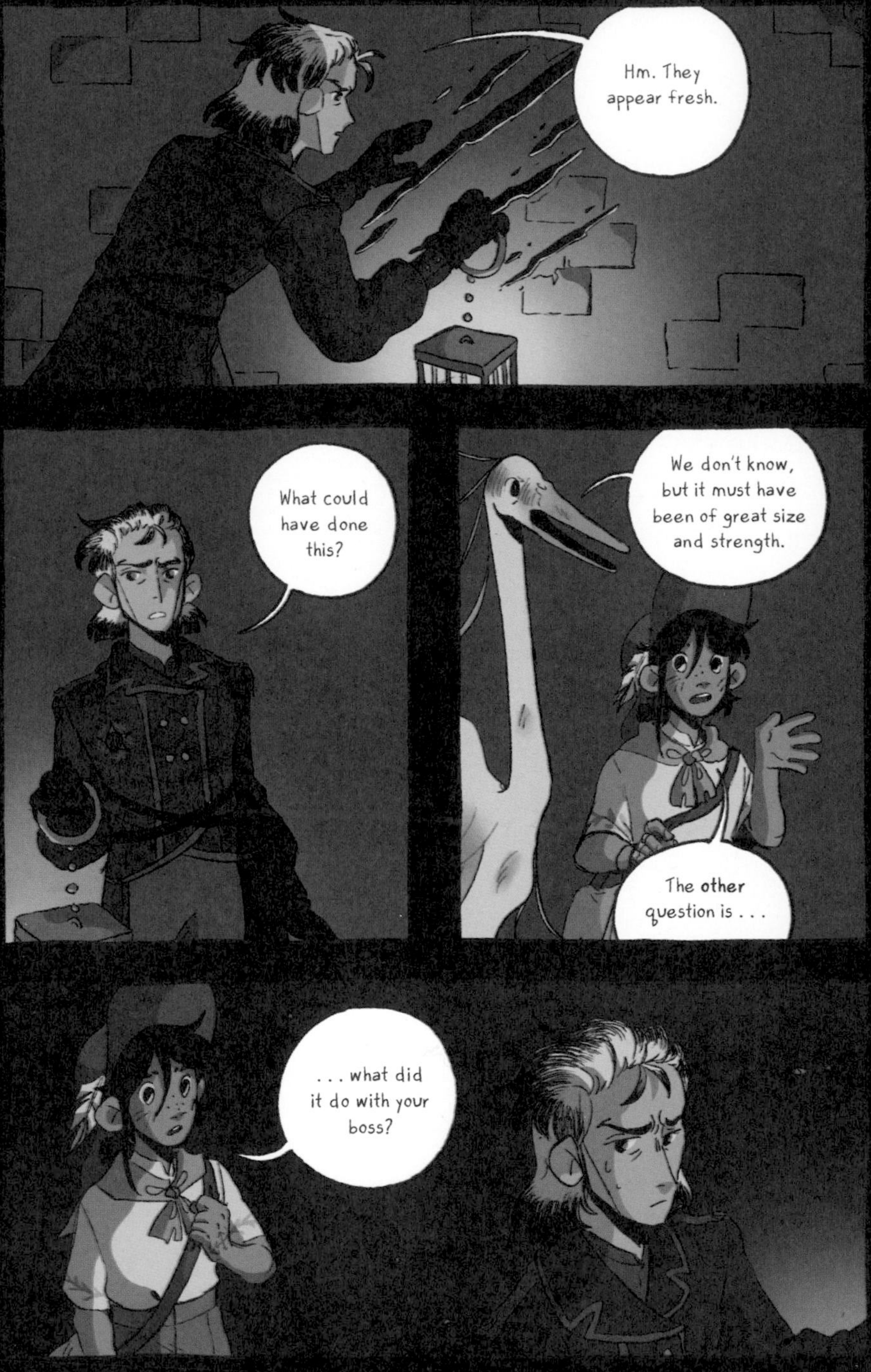
Hm. They appear fresh.
What could have done this?
We don't know, but it must have been of great size and strength.
The **other** question is . . .
. . . what did it do with your boss?

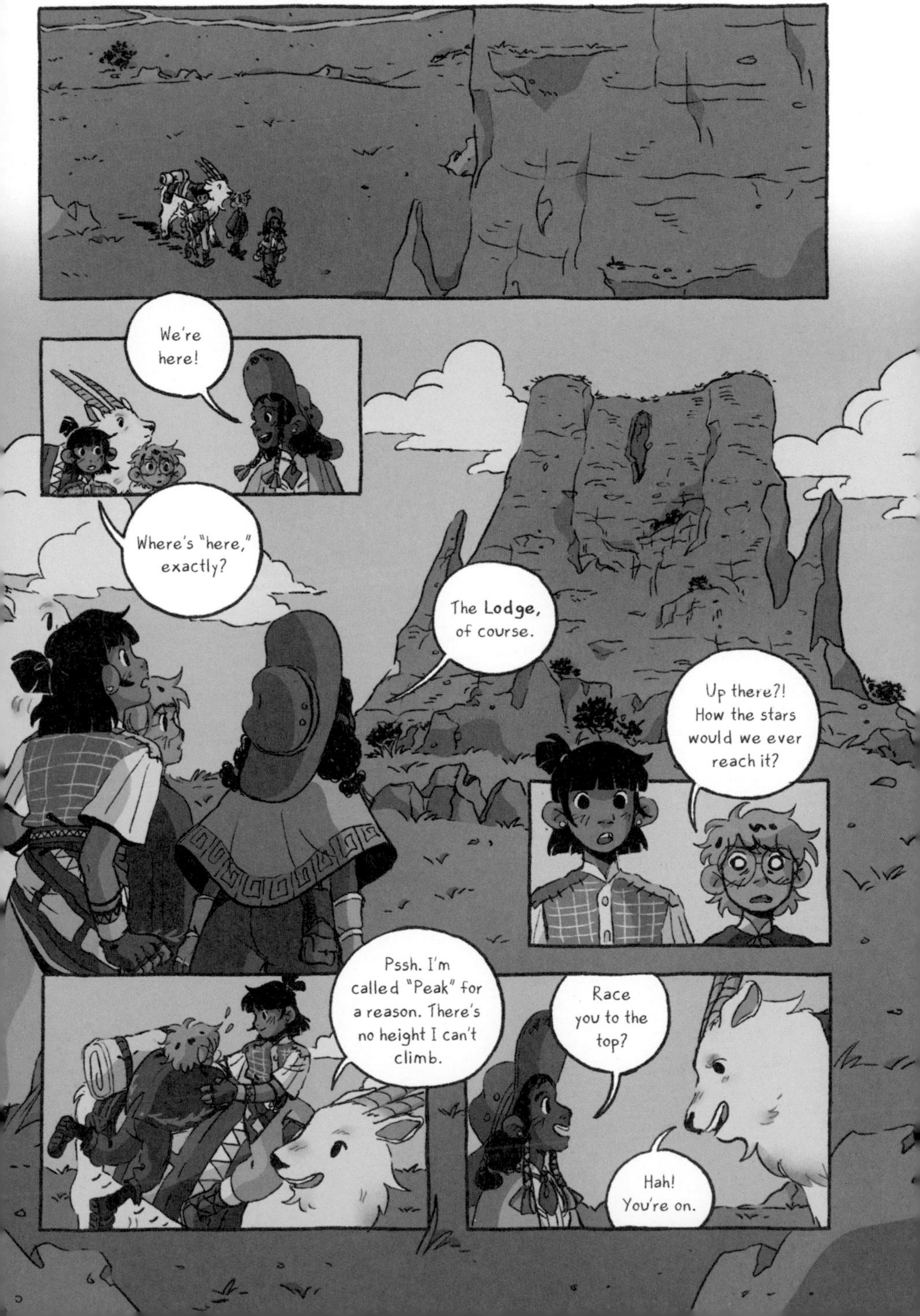
We're here!
Where's "here," exactly?
The **Lodge,** of course.
Up there?! How the stars would we ever reach it?
Pssh. I'm called "Peak" for a reason. There's no height I can't climb.
Race you to the top?
Hah! You're on.

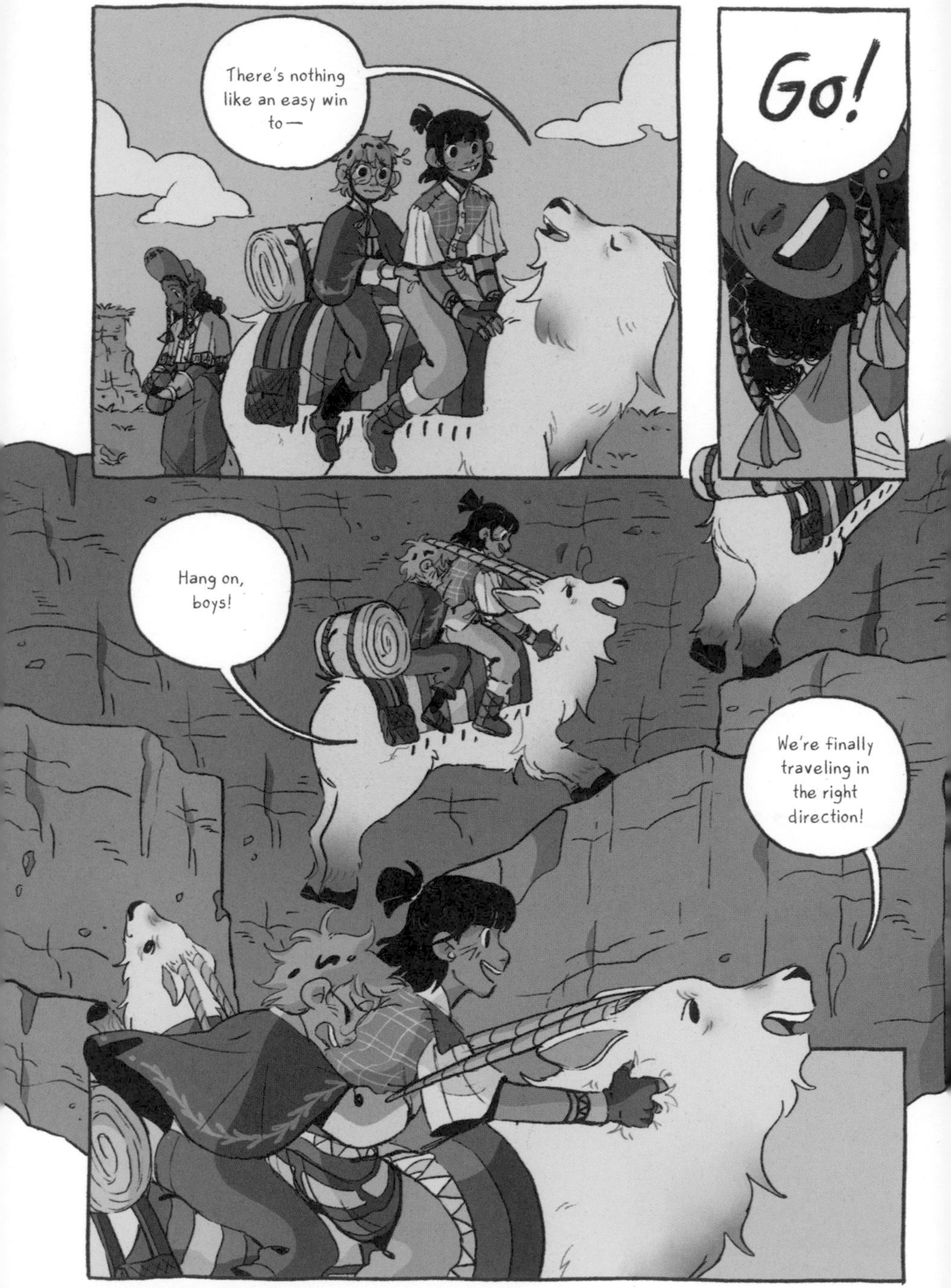

There's nothing like an easy win to—
Go!
Hang on, boys!
We're finally traveling in the right direction!

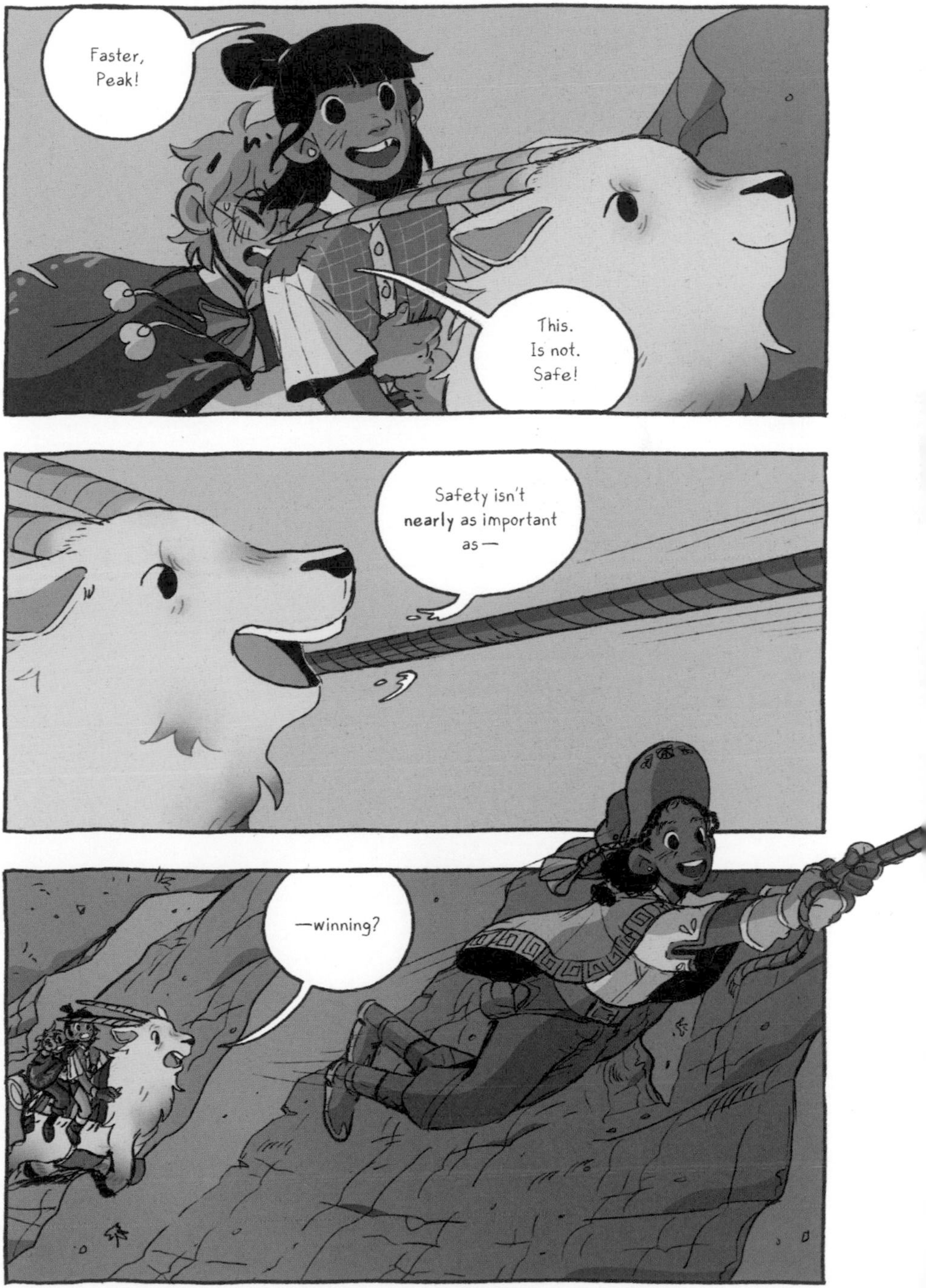
Faster, Peak!
This. Is not. Safe!
Safety isn't **nearly** as important as—
—winning?

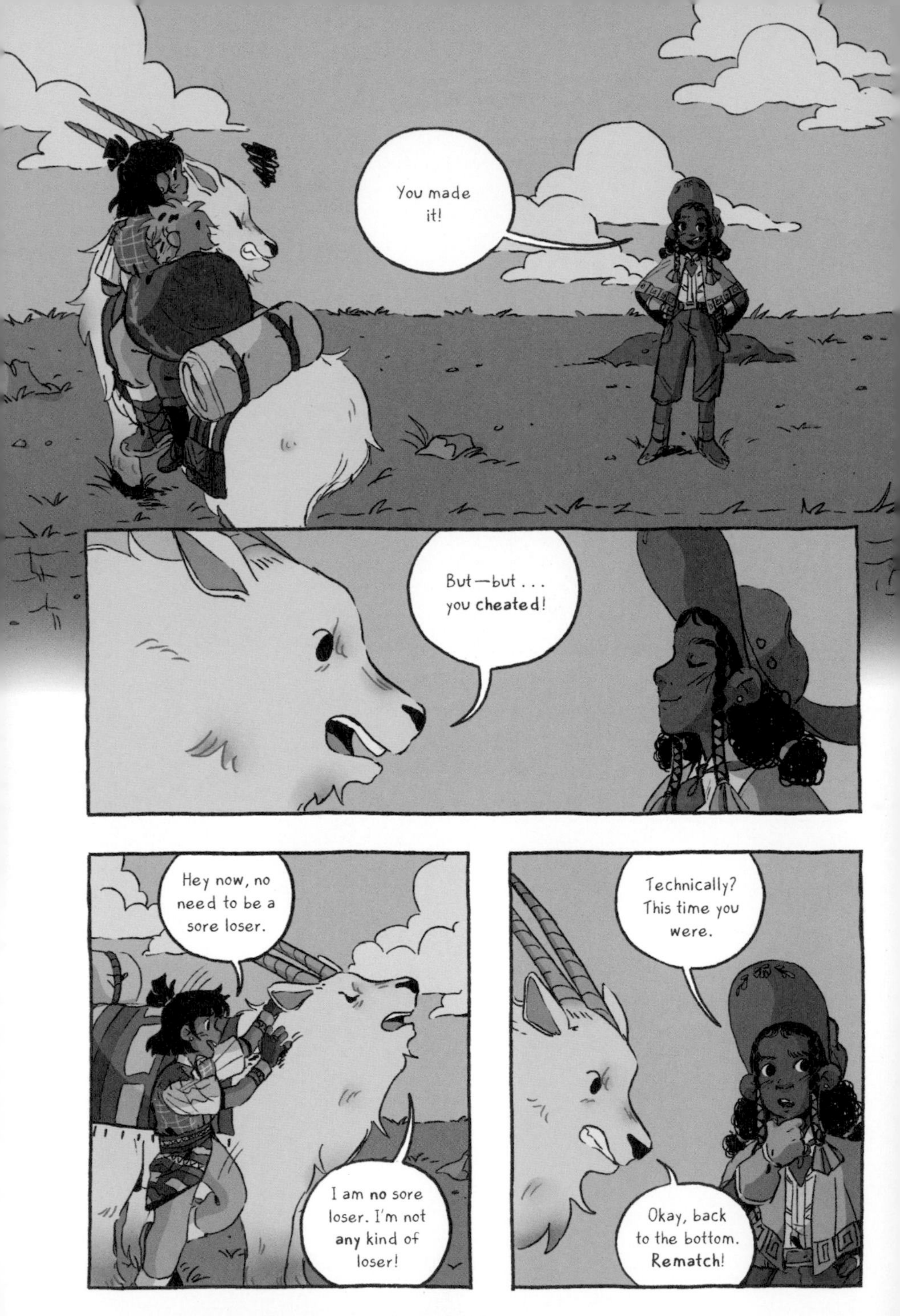
You made it!
But—but . . . you **cheated**!
Hey now, no need to be a sore loser.
I am **no** sore loser. I'm not **any** kind of loser!
Technically? This time you were.
Okay, back to the bottom. **Rematch**!

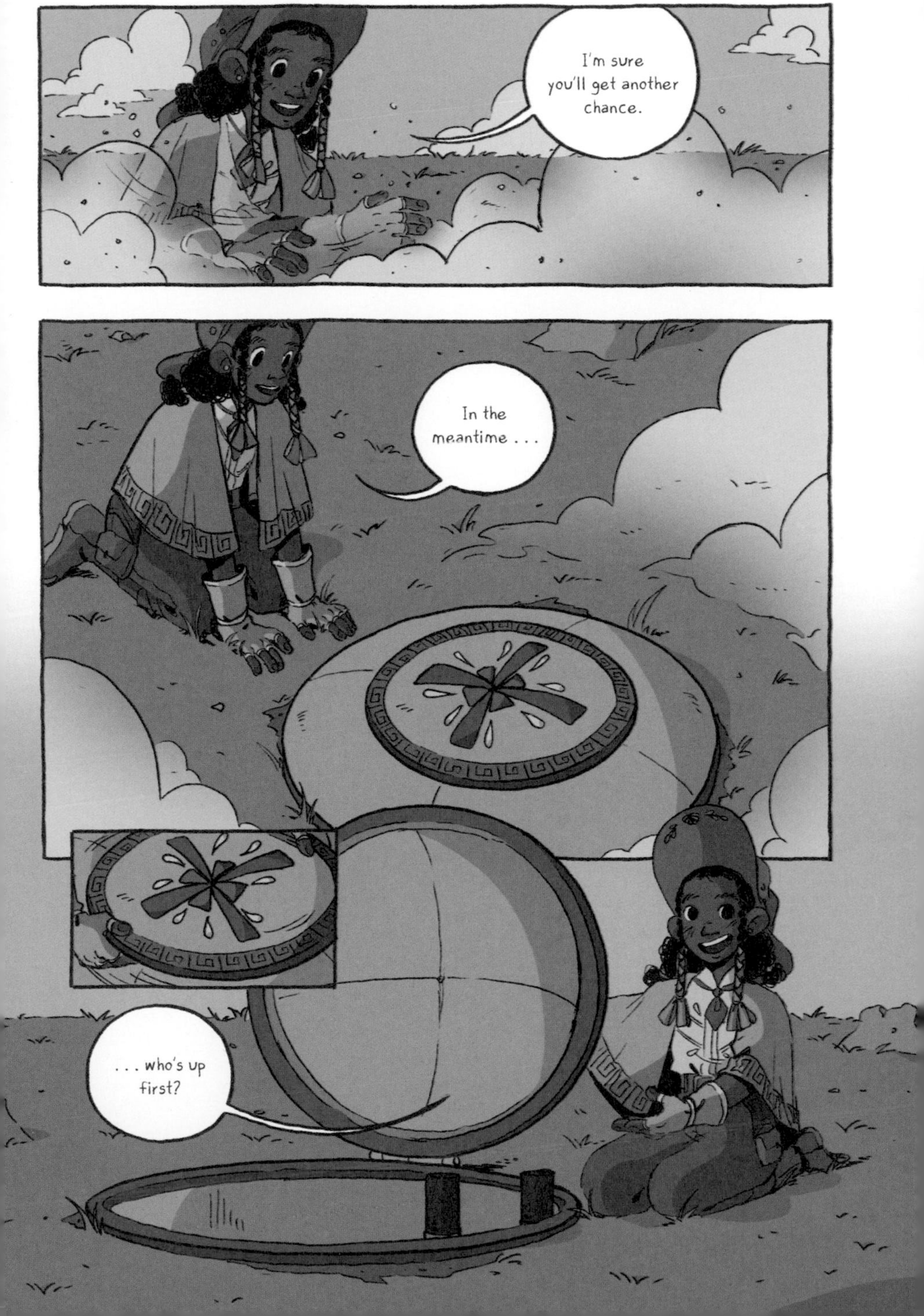
I'm sure you'll get another chance.
In the meantime . . .
. . . who's up first?

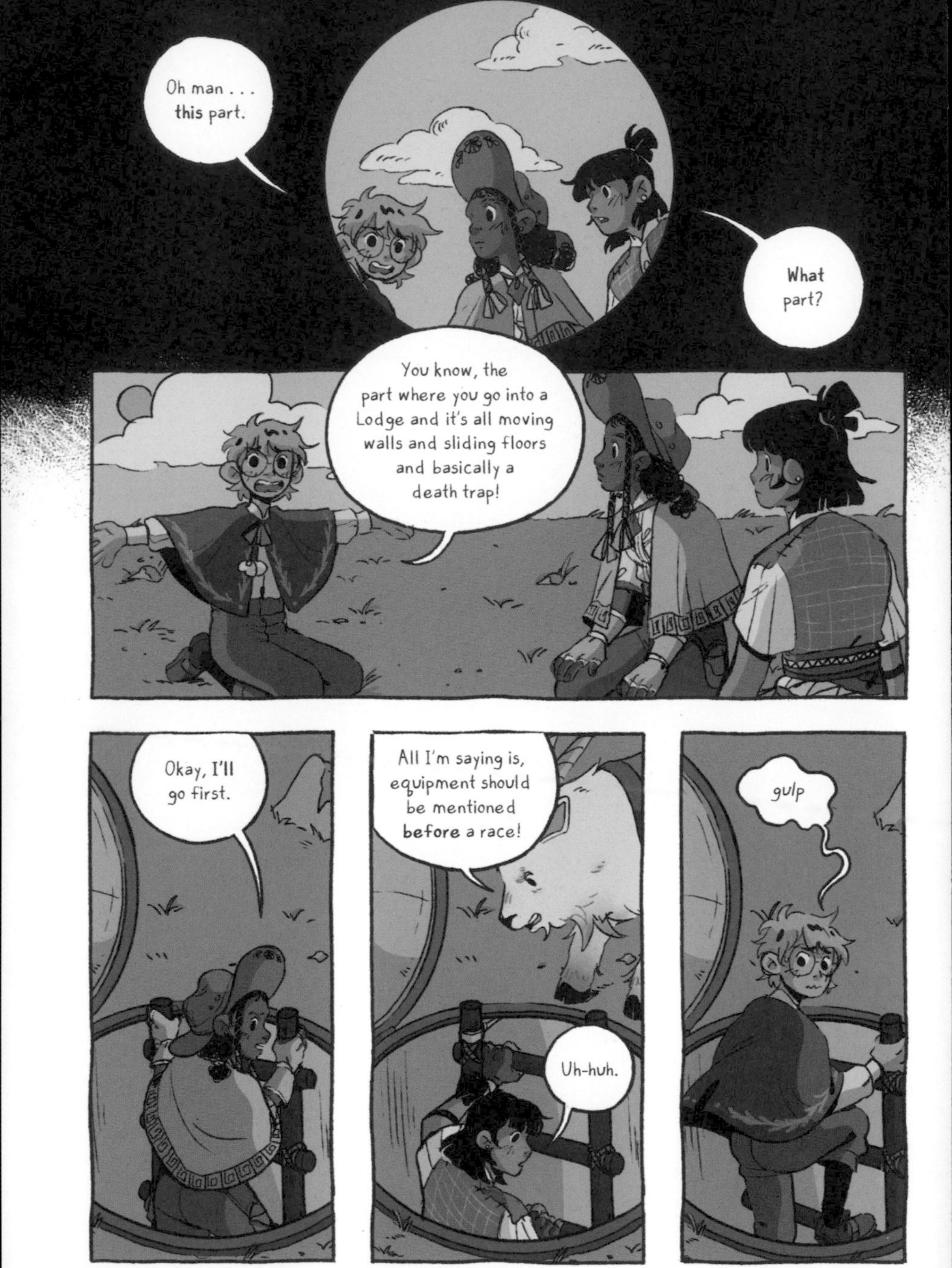
Oh man . . . this part.
What part?
You know, the part where you go into a Lodge and it's all moving walls and sliding floors and basically a death trap!
Okay, I'll go first.
All I'm saying is, equipment should be mentioned before a race!
Uh-huh.
gulp

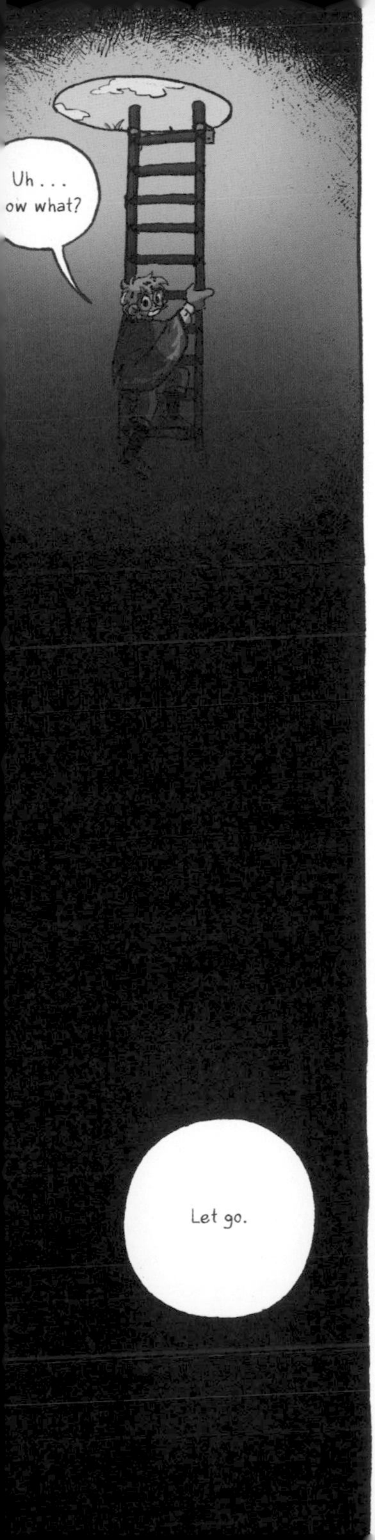
Uh . . .
ow what?
Let go.

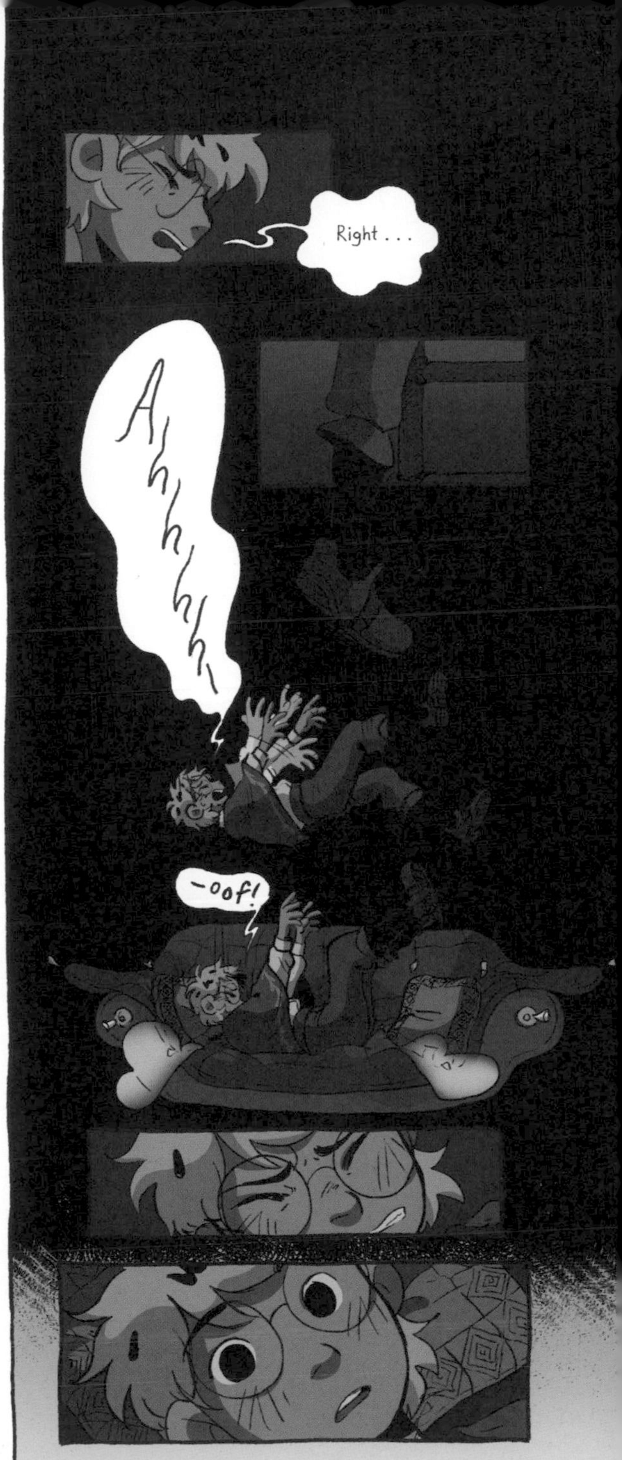
Right . . .
Ahhhhh
-oof!

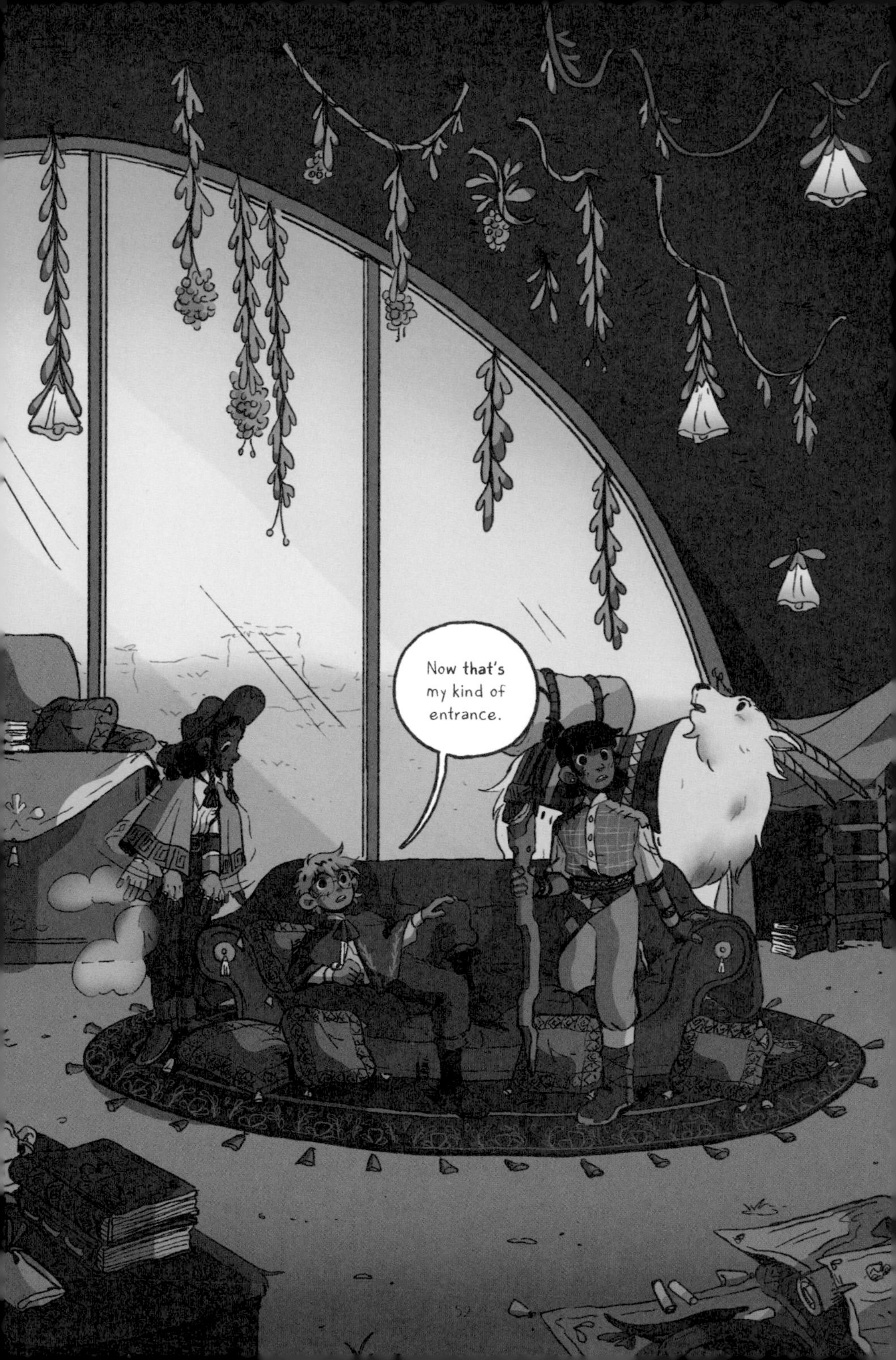
Now that's my kind of entrance.

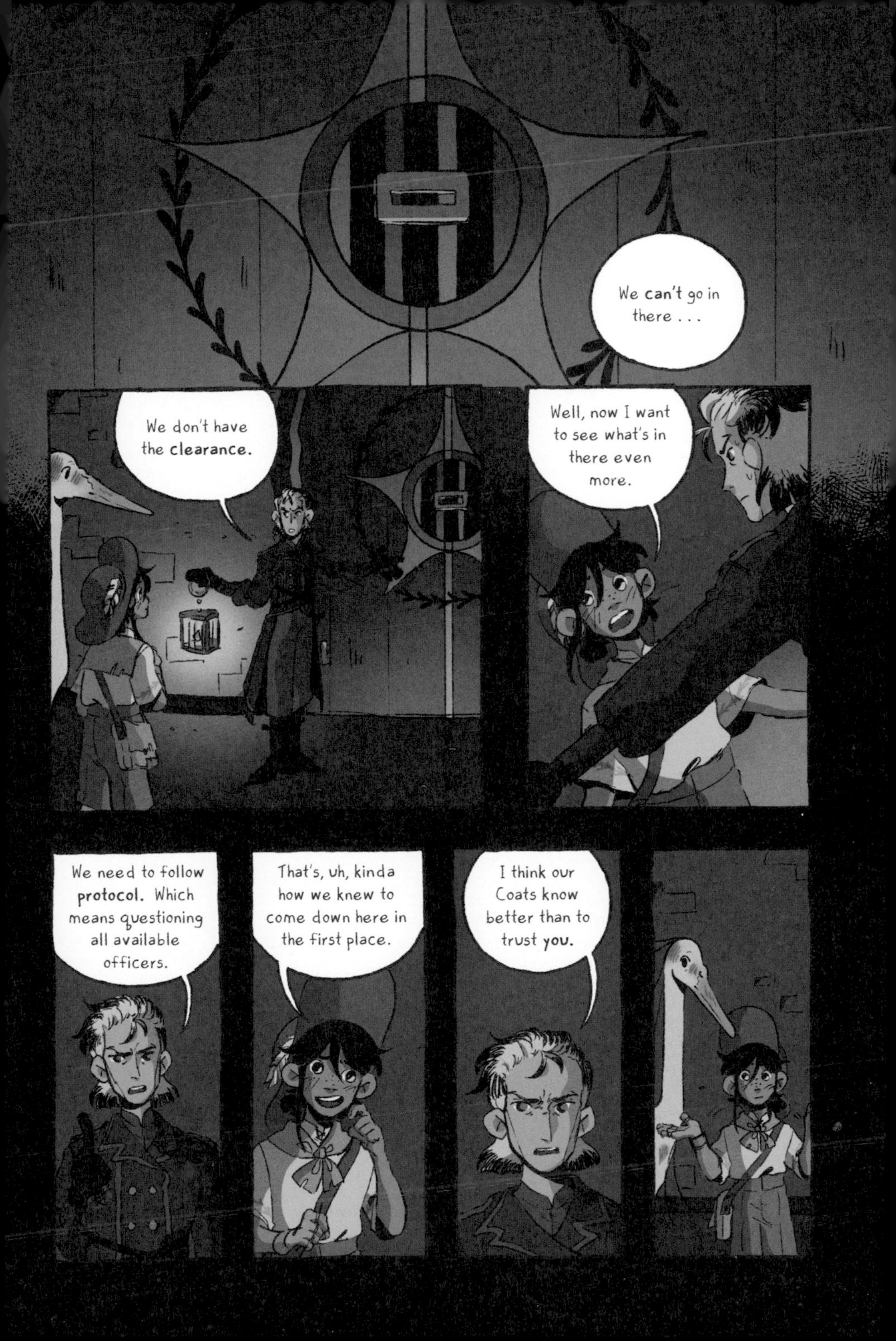
We can't go in there . . .
We don't have the clearance.
Well, now I want to see what's in there even more.
We need to follow protocol. Which means questioning all available officers.
That's, uh, kinda how we knew to come down here in the first place.
I think our Coats know better than to trust you.

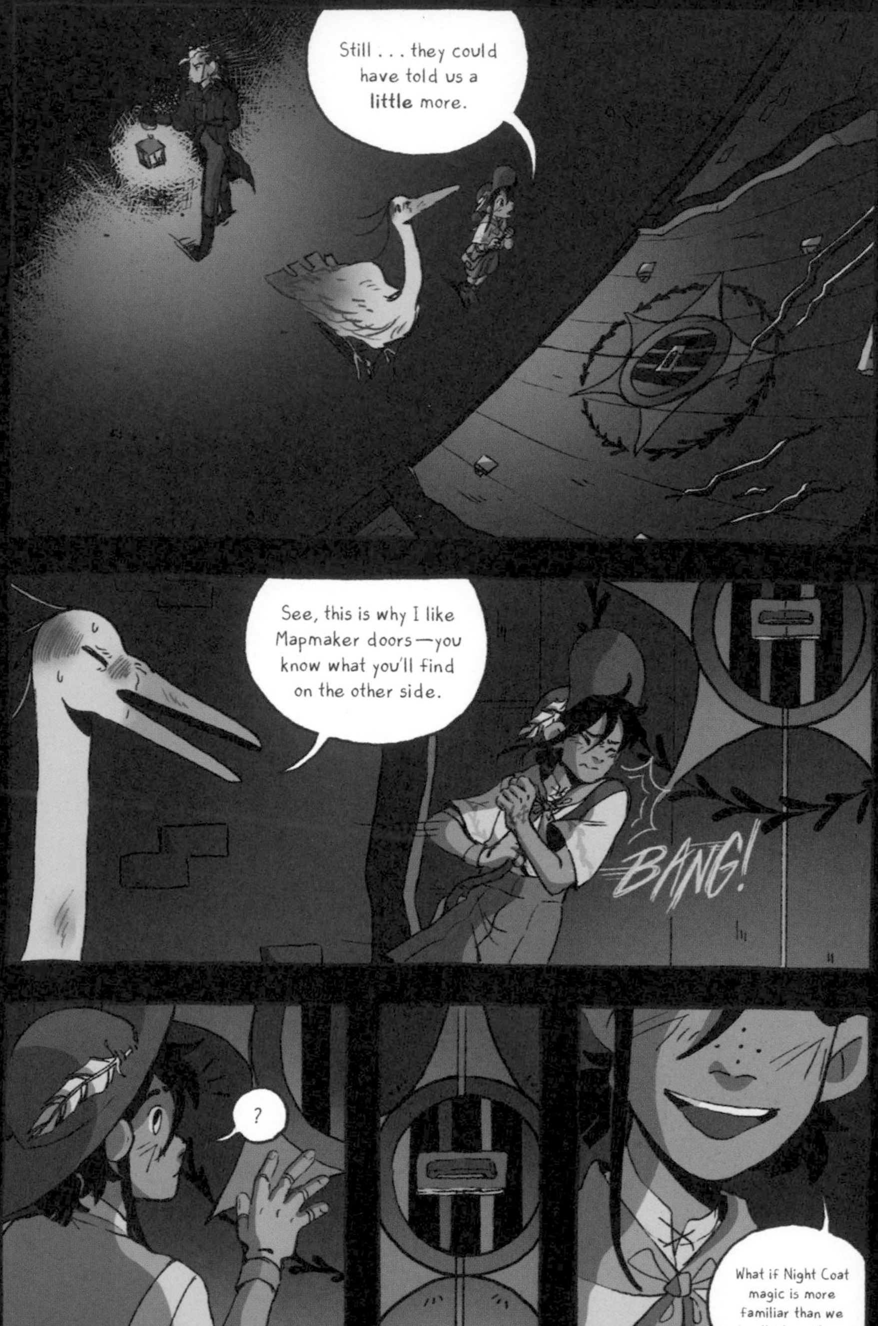
Still . . . they could have told us a little more.
See, this is why I like Mapmaker doors—you know what you'll find on the other side.
BANG!
?
What if Night Coat magic is more familiar than we think . . . ?

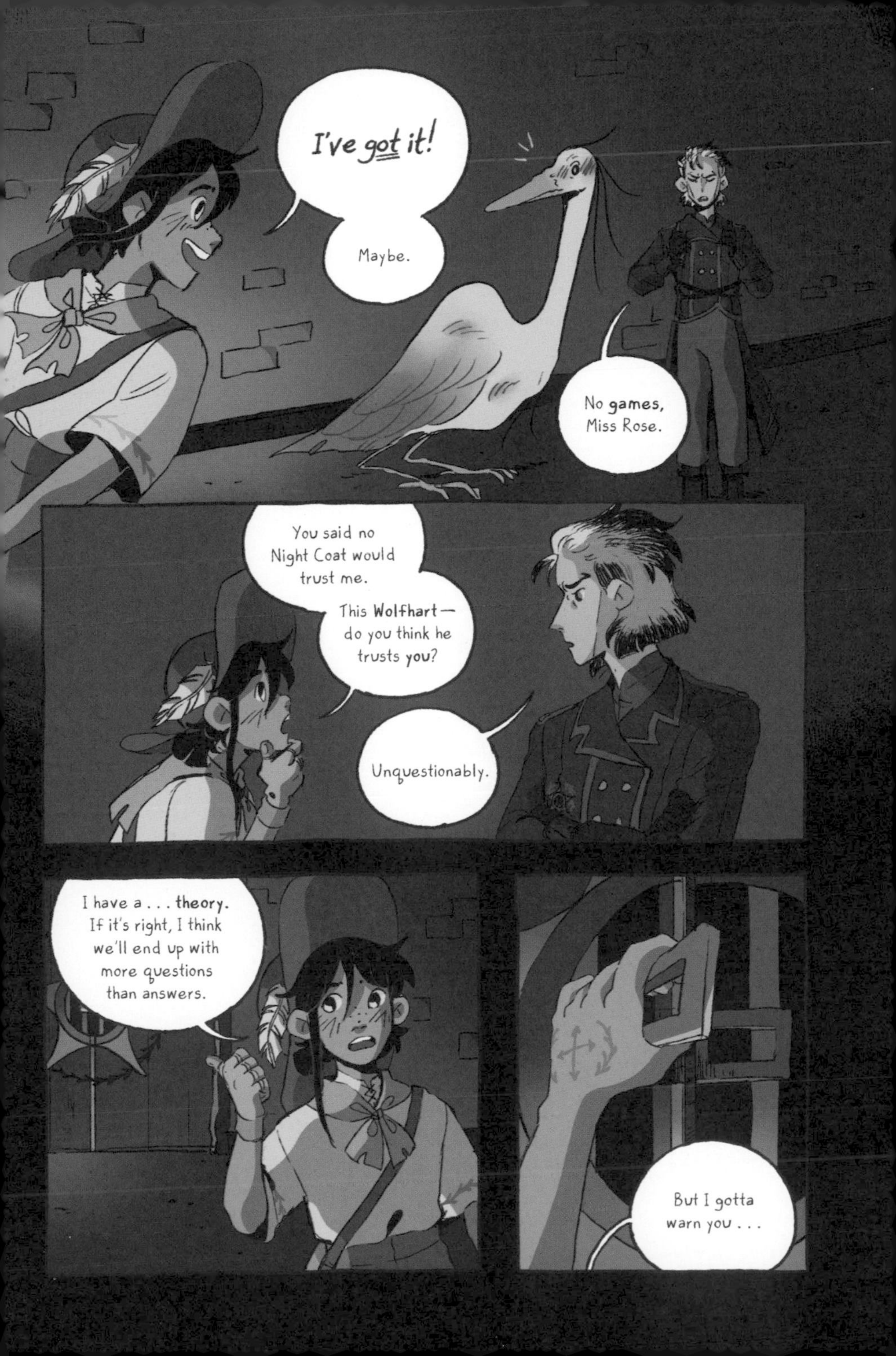
I've got it!
Maybe.
No games, Miss Rose.
You said no Night Coat would trust me.
This Wolfhart— do you think he trusts you?
Unquestionably.
I have a . . . theory. If it's right, I think we'll end up with more questions than answers.
But I gotta warn you . . .

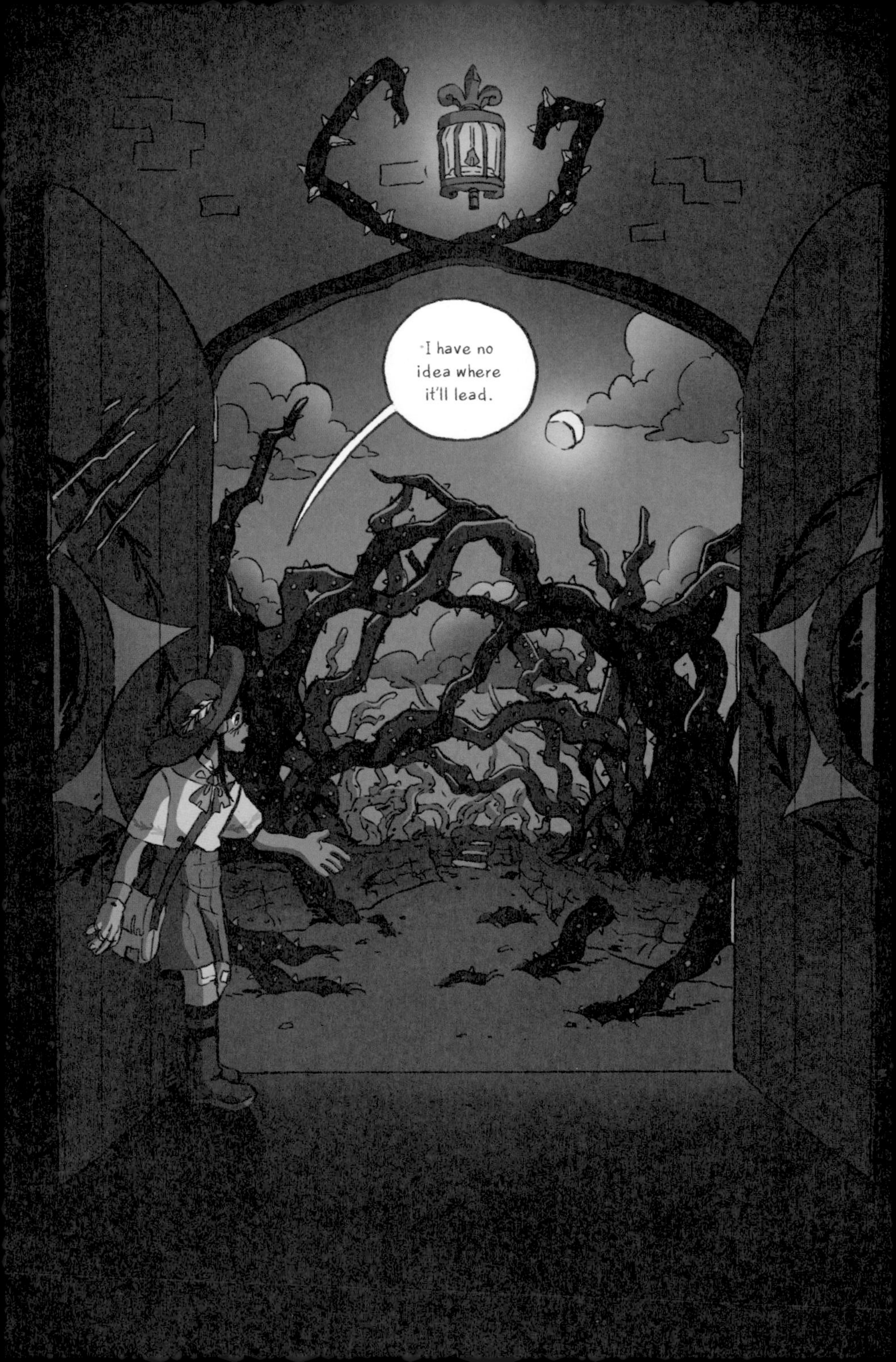
I have no idea where it'll lead.

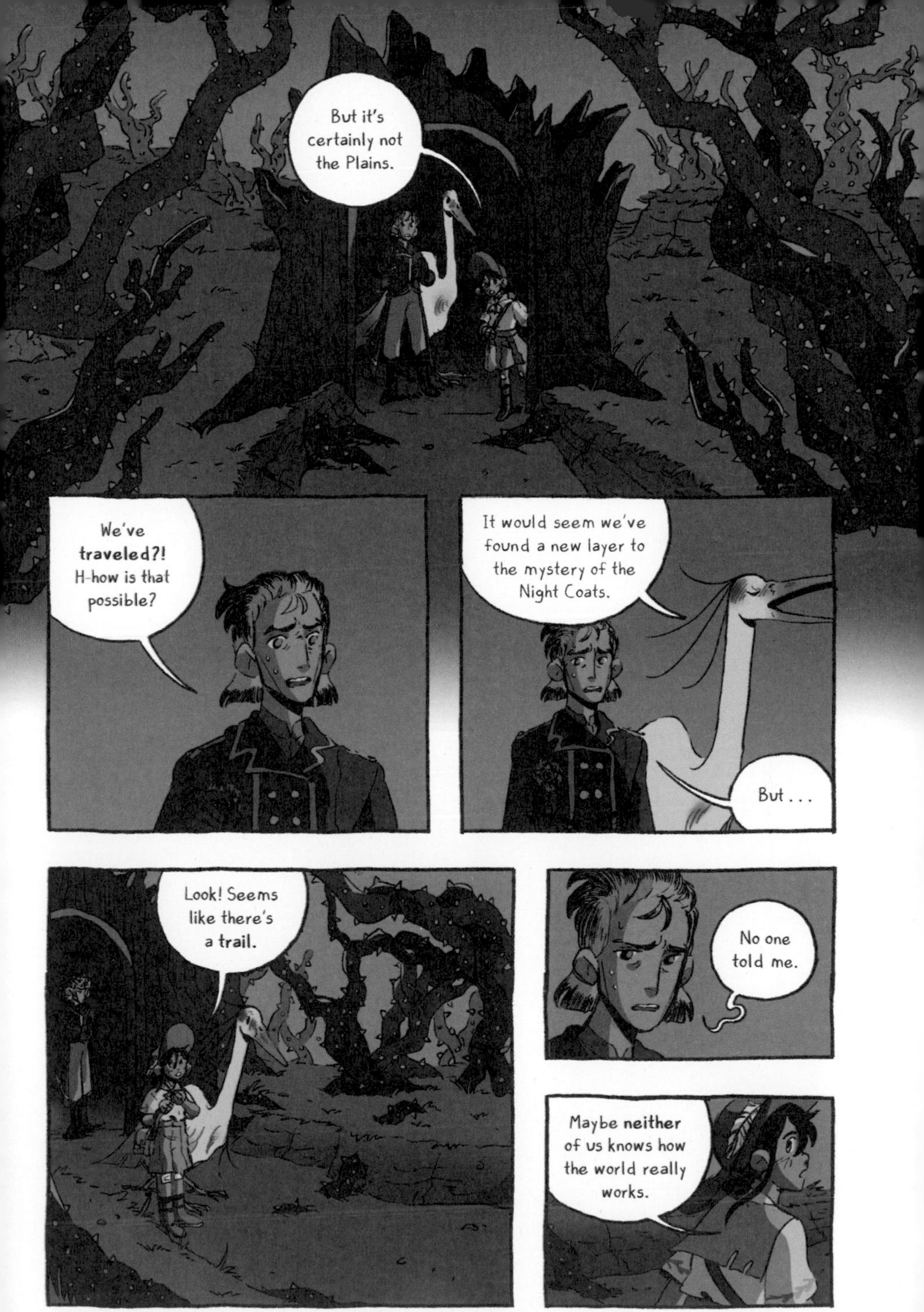
But it's certainly not the Plains.
We've **traveled?!** H-how is that possible?
It would seem we've found a new layer to the mystery of the Night Coats.
But . . .
Look! Seems like there's a **trail.**
No one told me.
Maybe **neither** of us knows how the world really works.

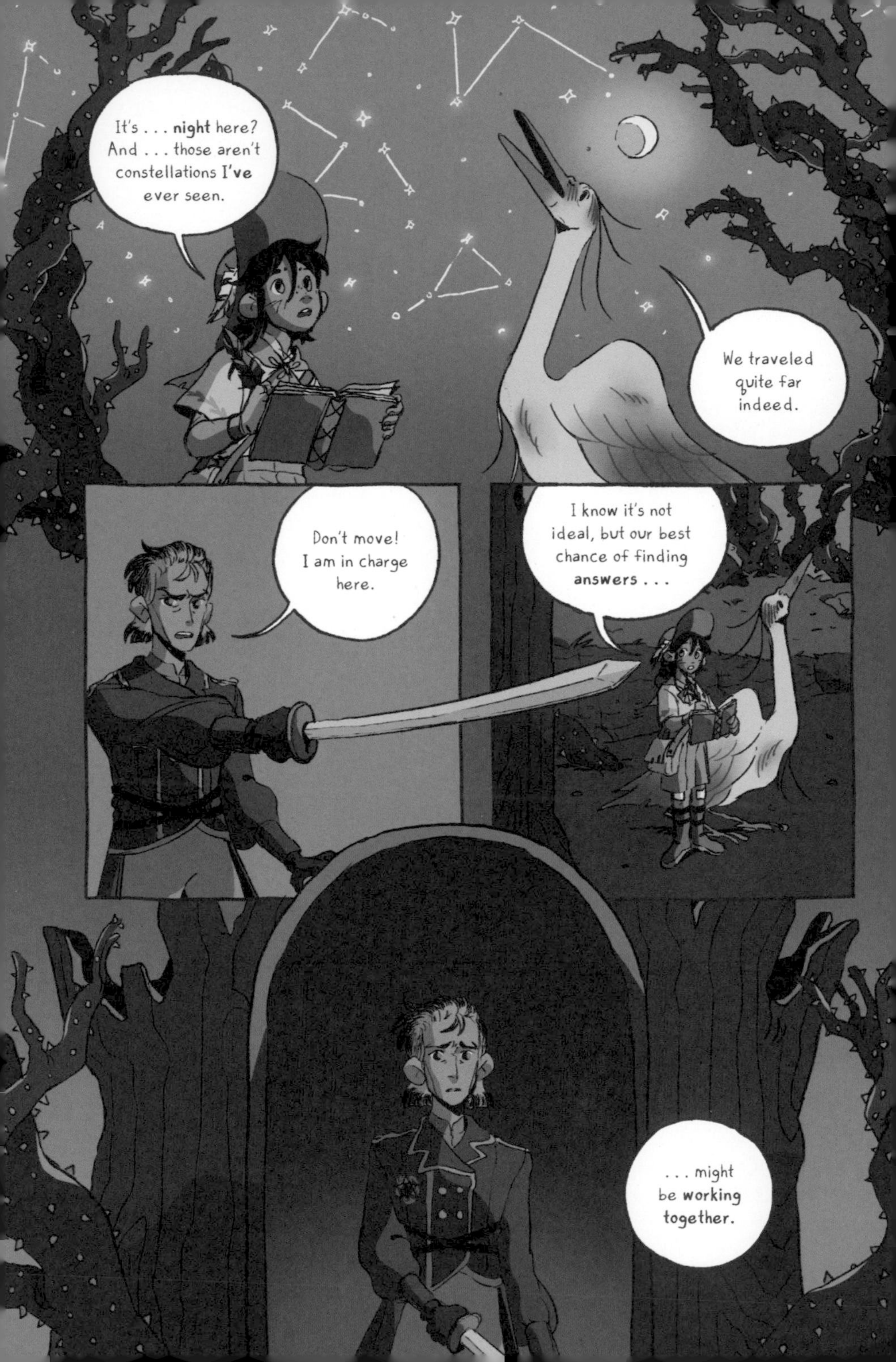
It's . . . **night** here? And . . . those aren't constellations **I've** ever seen.
We traveled quite far indeed.
Don't move! I am in charge here.
I know it's not ideal, but our best chance of finding **answers . . .**
. . . might be **working together.**

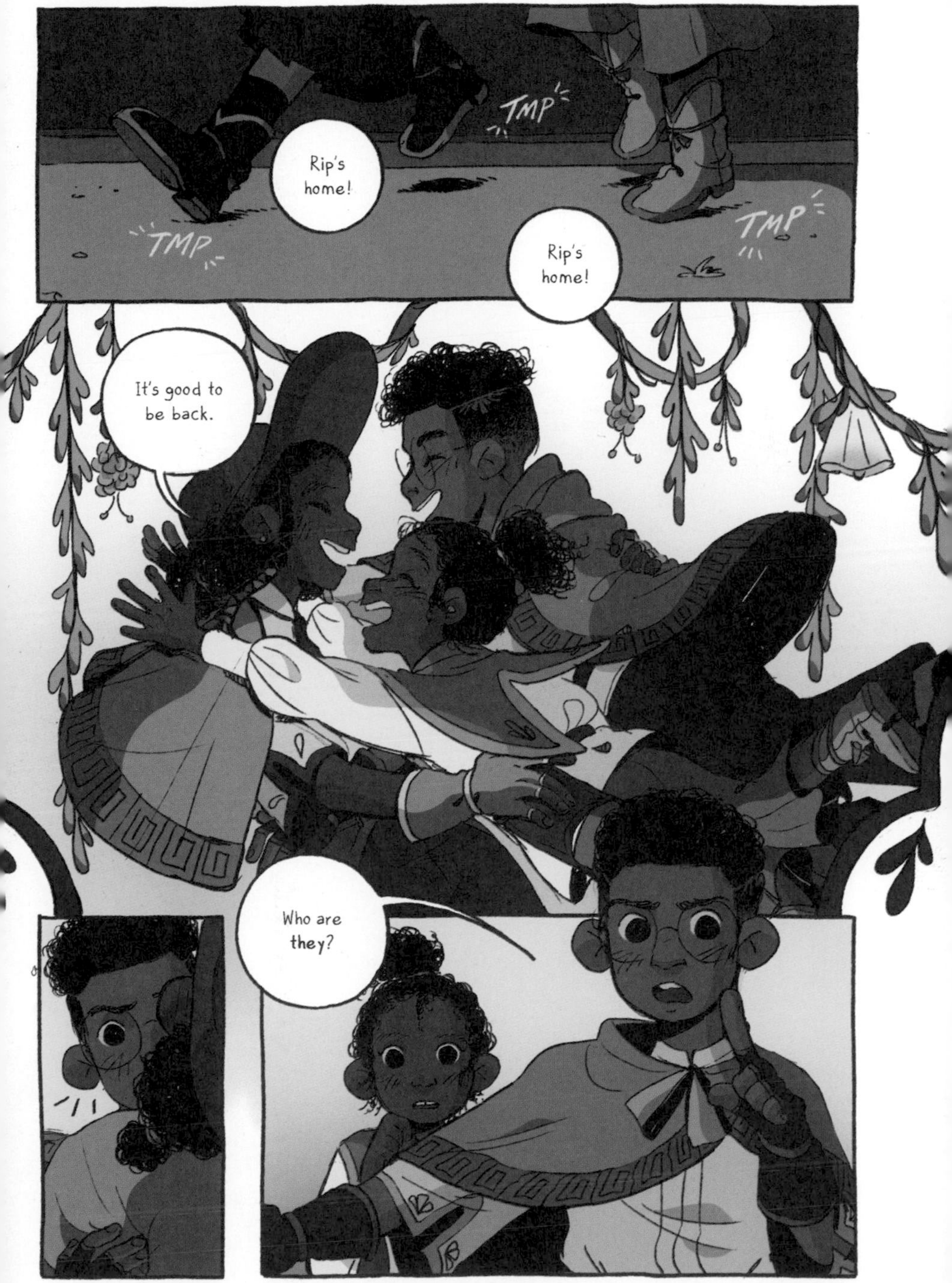
TMP
Rip's home!
TMP
TMP
Rip's home!
It's good to be back.
Who are they?

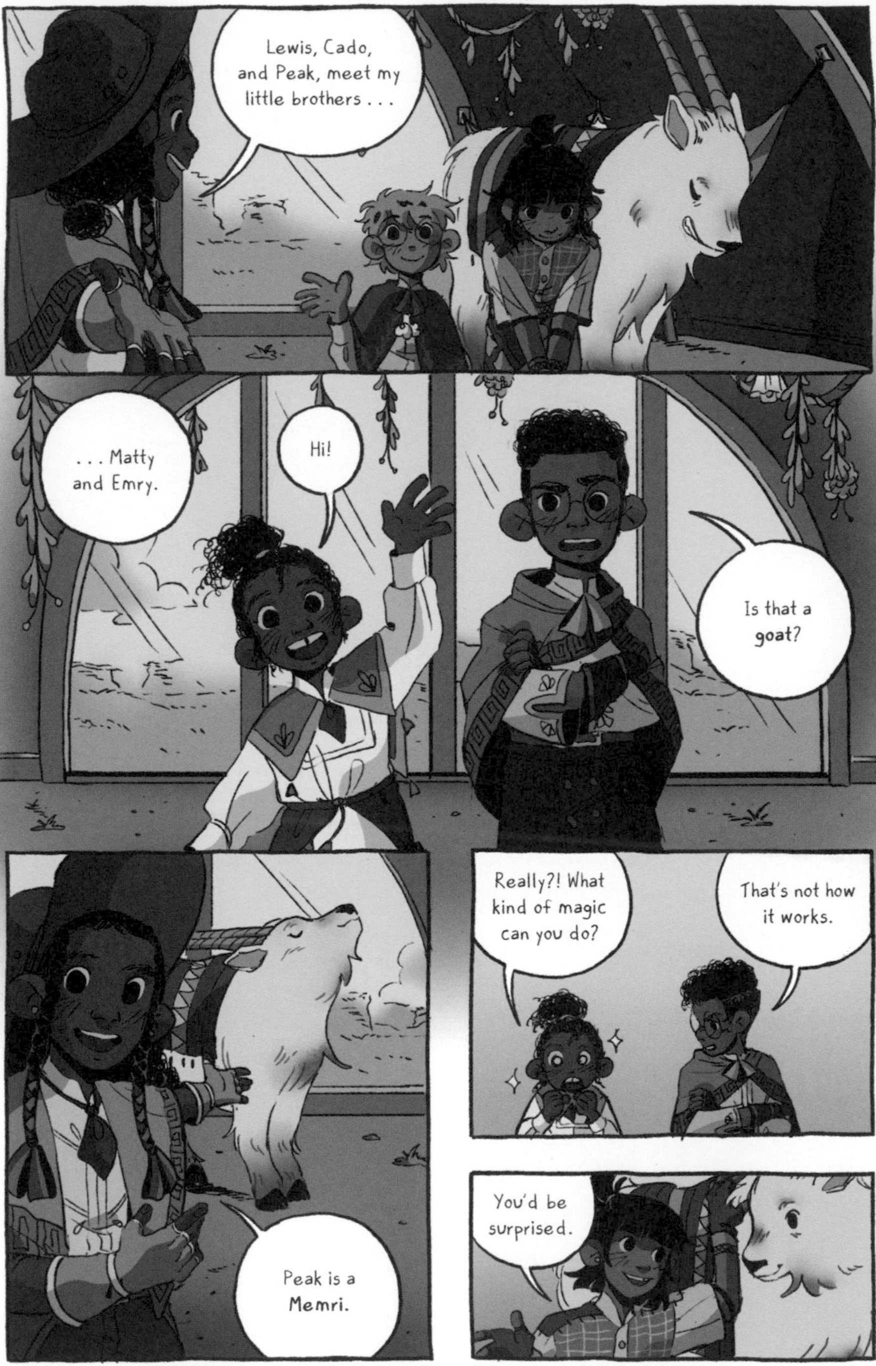
Lewis, Cado, and Peak, meet my little brothers . . .
. . . Matty and Emry.
Hi!
Is that a goat?
Peak is a Memri.
Really?! What kind of magic can you do?
That's not how it works.
You'd be surprised.

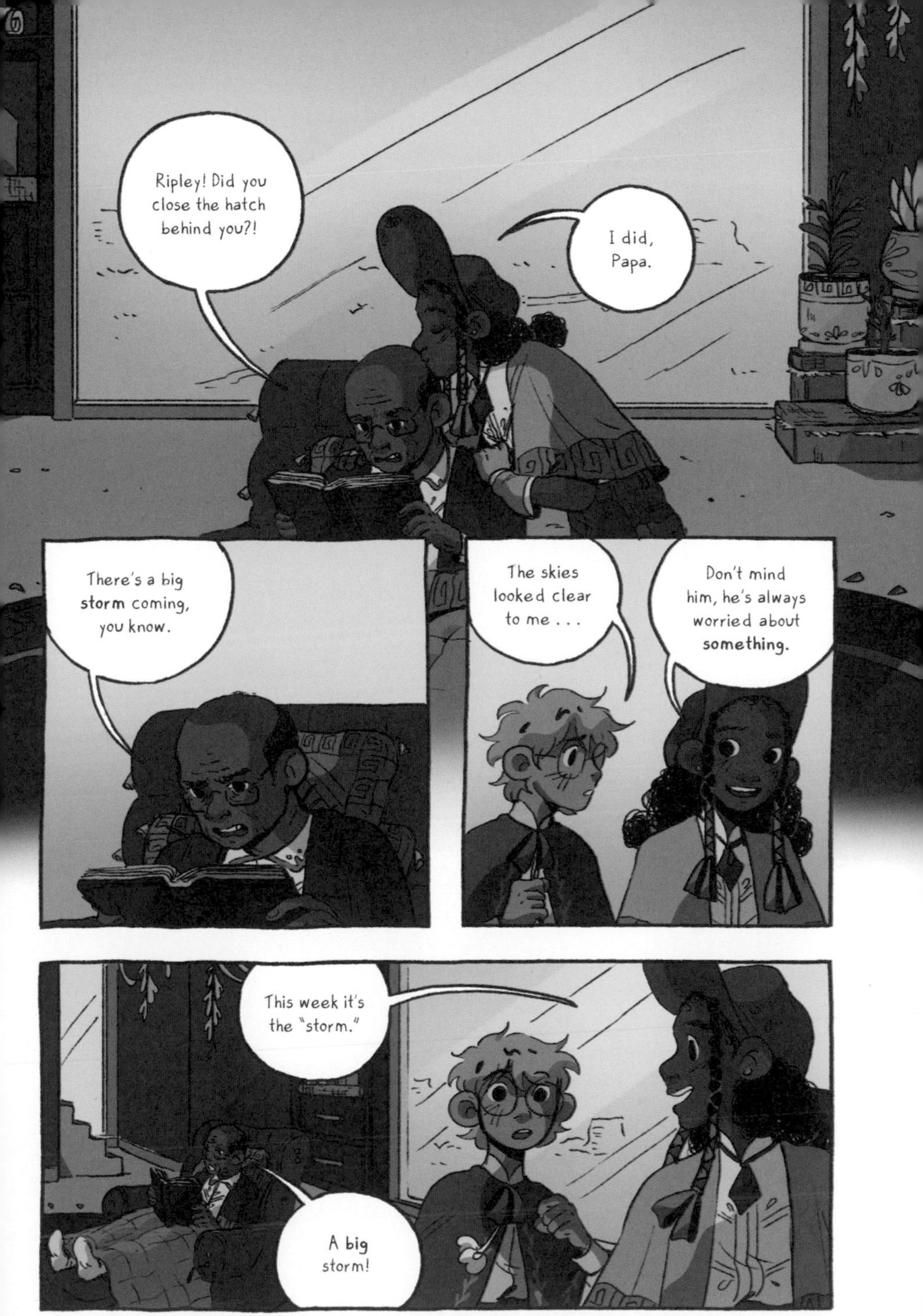
Ripley! Did you close the hatch behind you?!
I did, Papa.
There's a big **storm** coming, you know.
The skies looked clear to me . . .
Don't mind him, he's always worried about **something.**
This week it's the "storm."
A **big** storm!

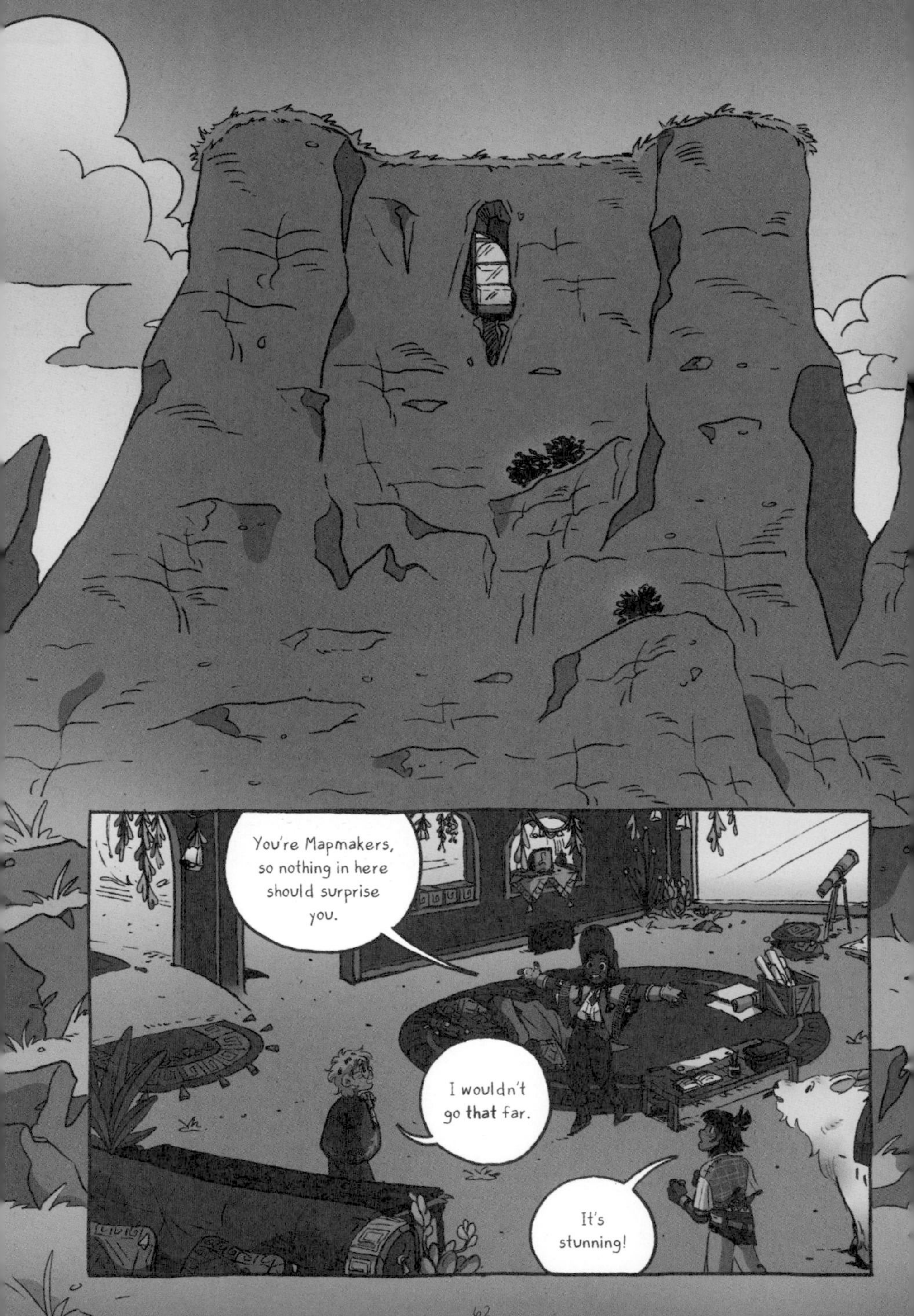
You're Mapmakers, so nothing in here should surprise you.
I wouldn't go that far.
It's stunning!

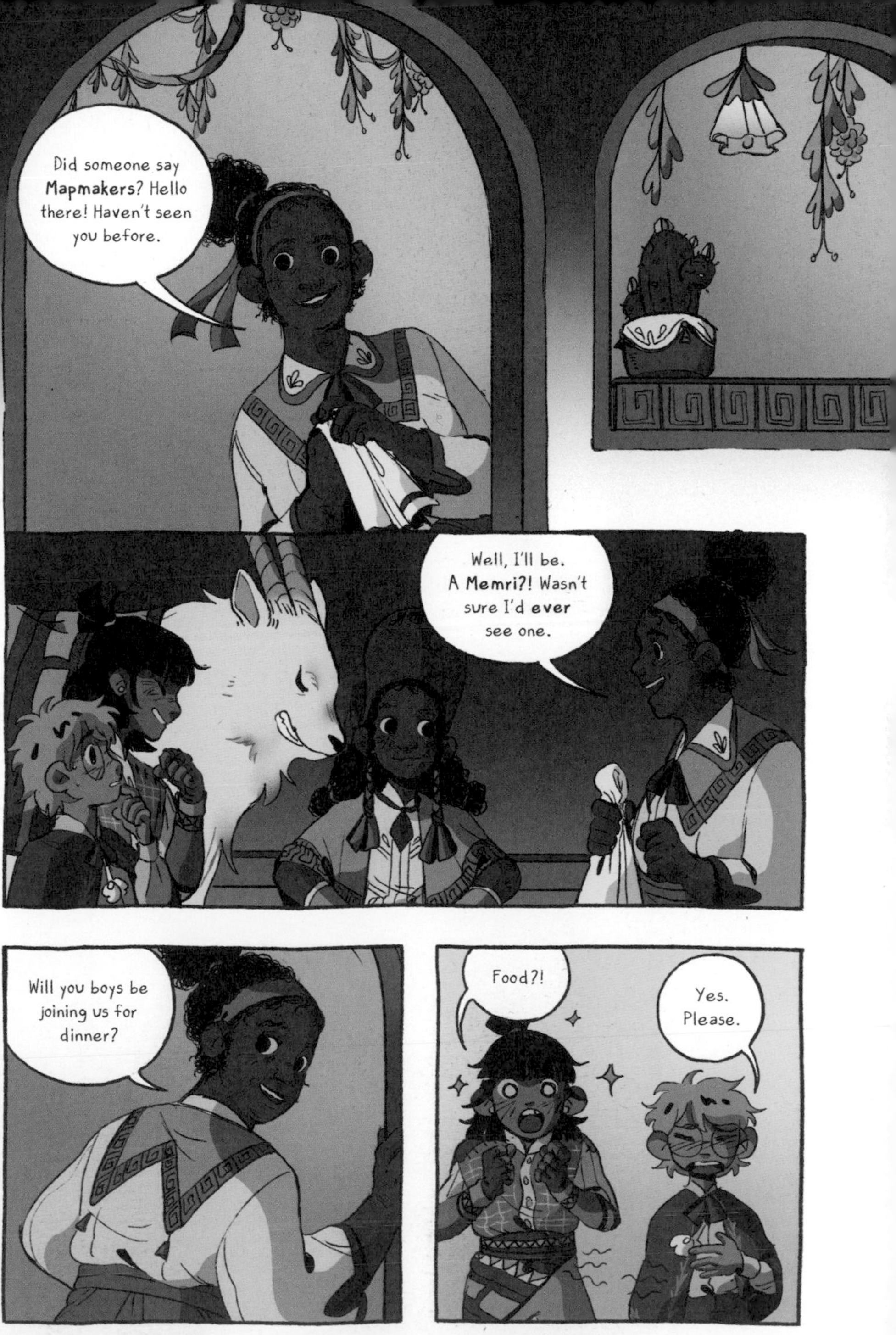
Did someone say **Mapmakers**? Hello there! Haven't seen you before.
Well, I'll be. A **Memri?!** Wasn't sure I'd **ever** see one.
Will you boys be joining us for dinner?
Food?!
Yes. Please.

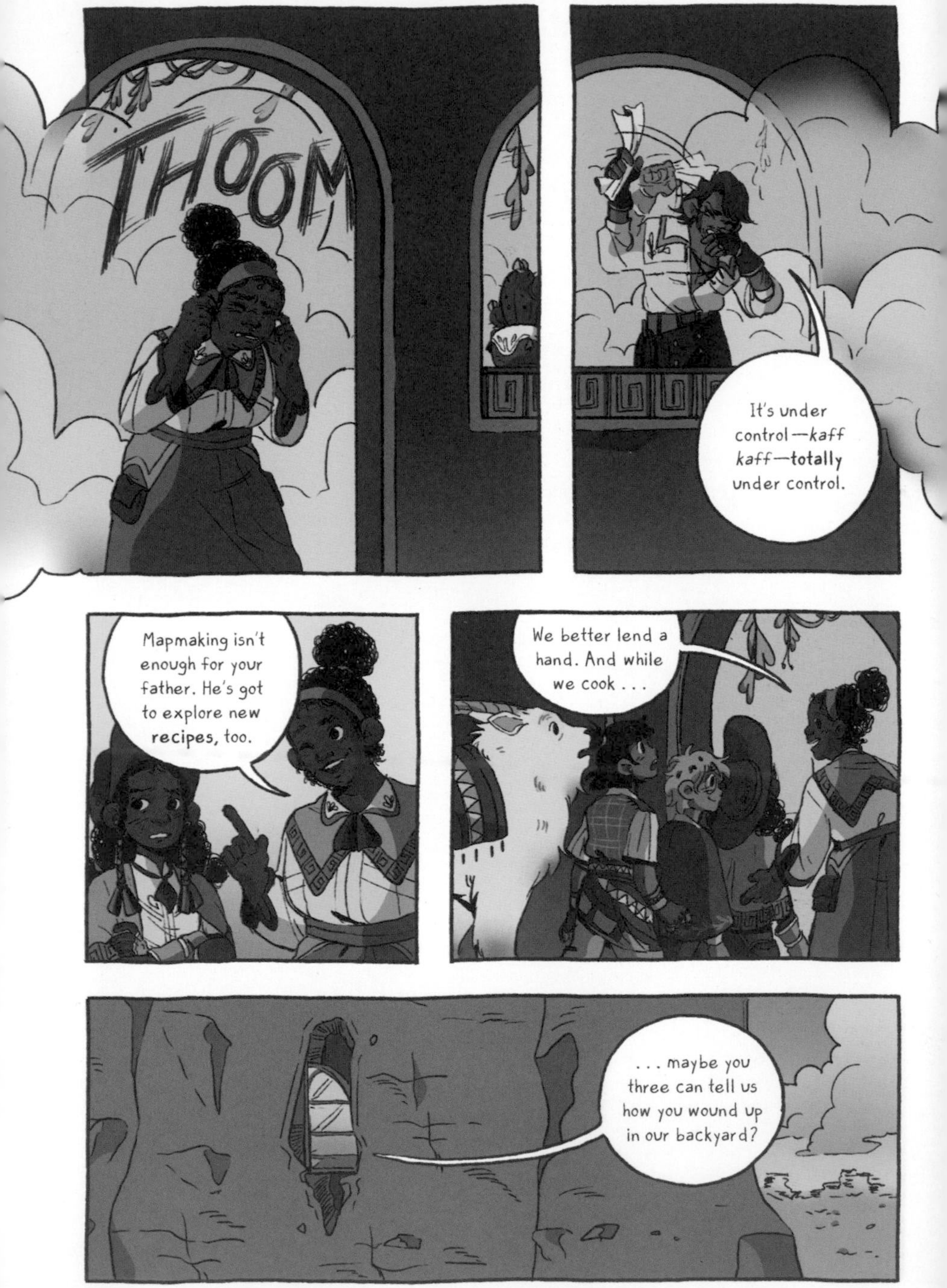
THOOM
It's under control—*kaff kaff*—**totally** under control.
Mapmaking isn't enough for your father. He's got to explore new **recipes**, too.
We better lend a hand. And while we cook . . .
. . . maybe you three can tell us how you wound up in our backyard?

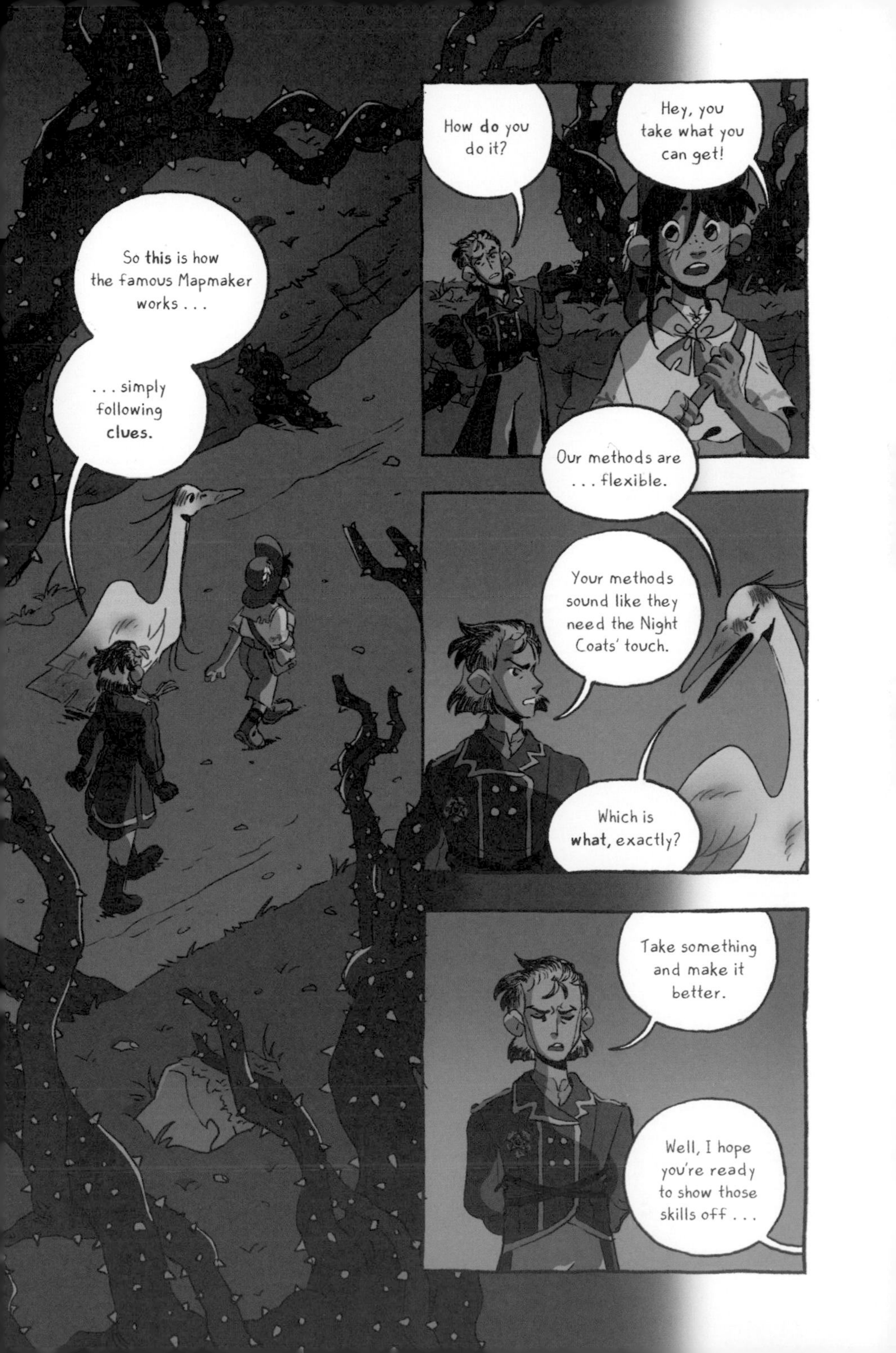

So this is how the famous Mapmaker works . . .
. . . simply following clues.
How do you do it?
Hey, you take what you can get!
Our methods are . . . flexible.
Your methods sound like they need the Night Coats' touch.
Which is what, exactly?
Take something and make it better.
Well, I hope you're ready to show those skills off . . .

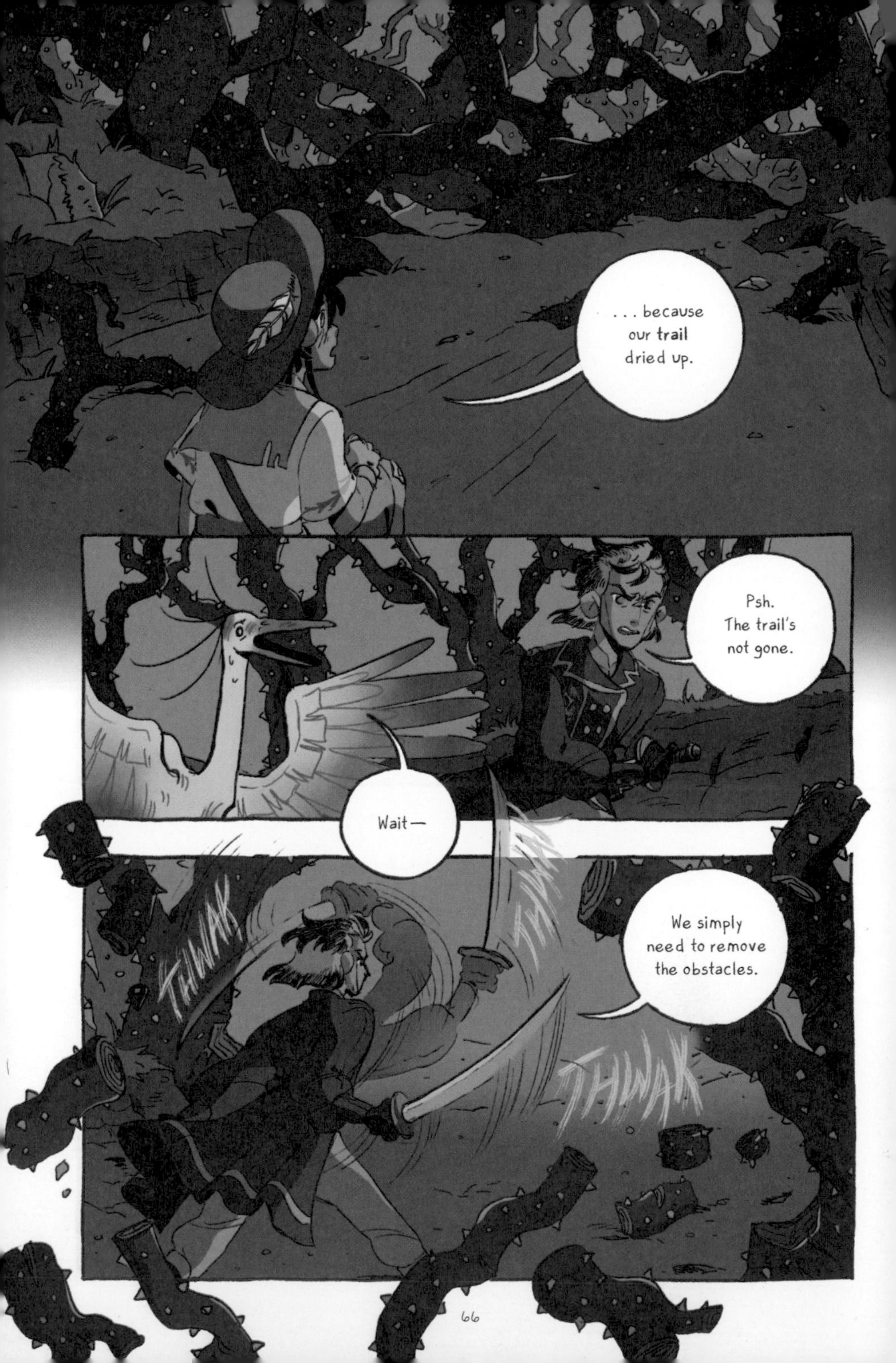

. . . because our trail dried up.
Psh. The trail's not gone.
Wait—
THWAK
We simply need to remove the obstacles.
THWAK

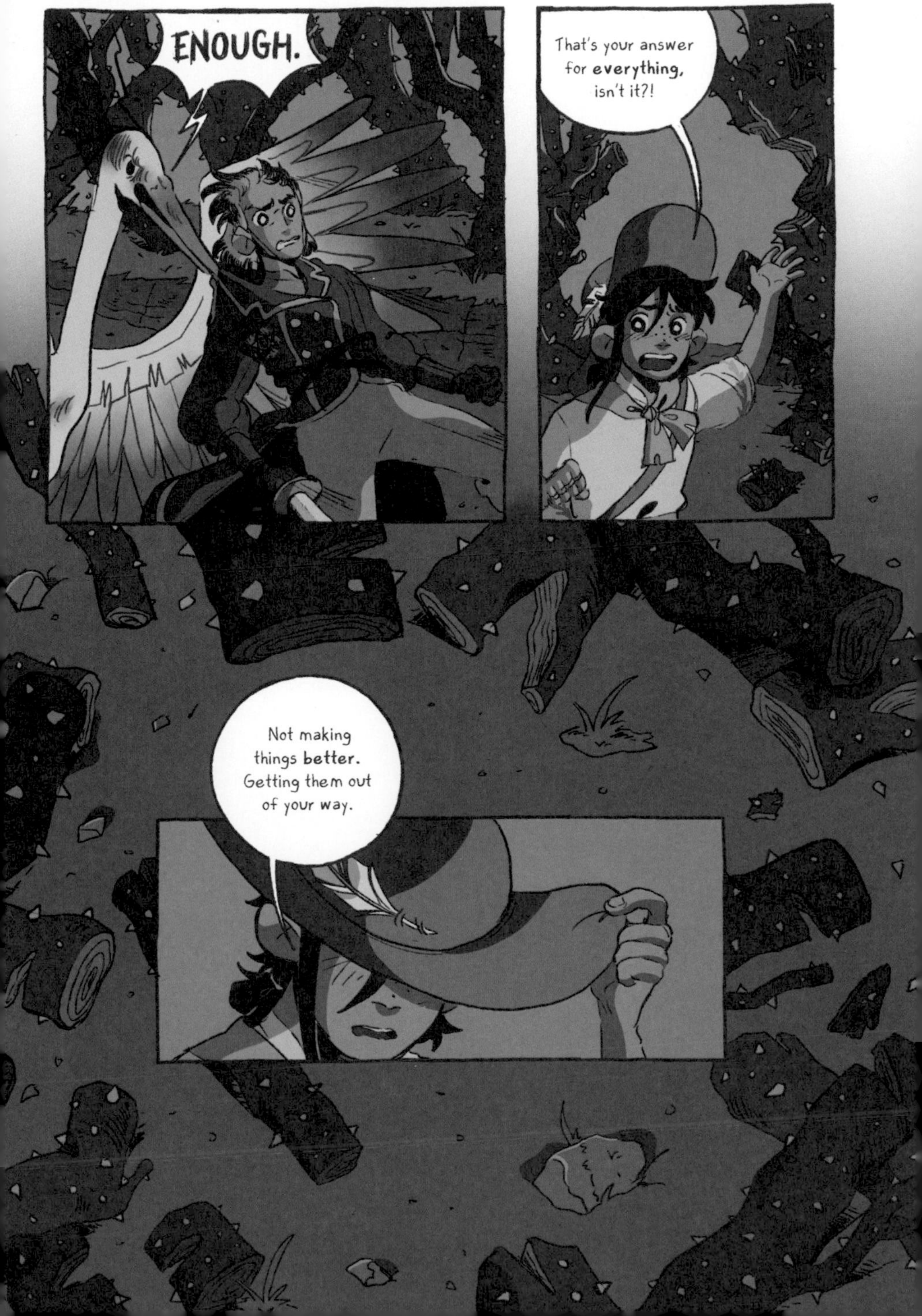
ENOUGH.
That's your answer for everything, isn't it?!
Not making things better. Getting them out of your way.

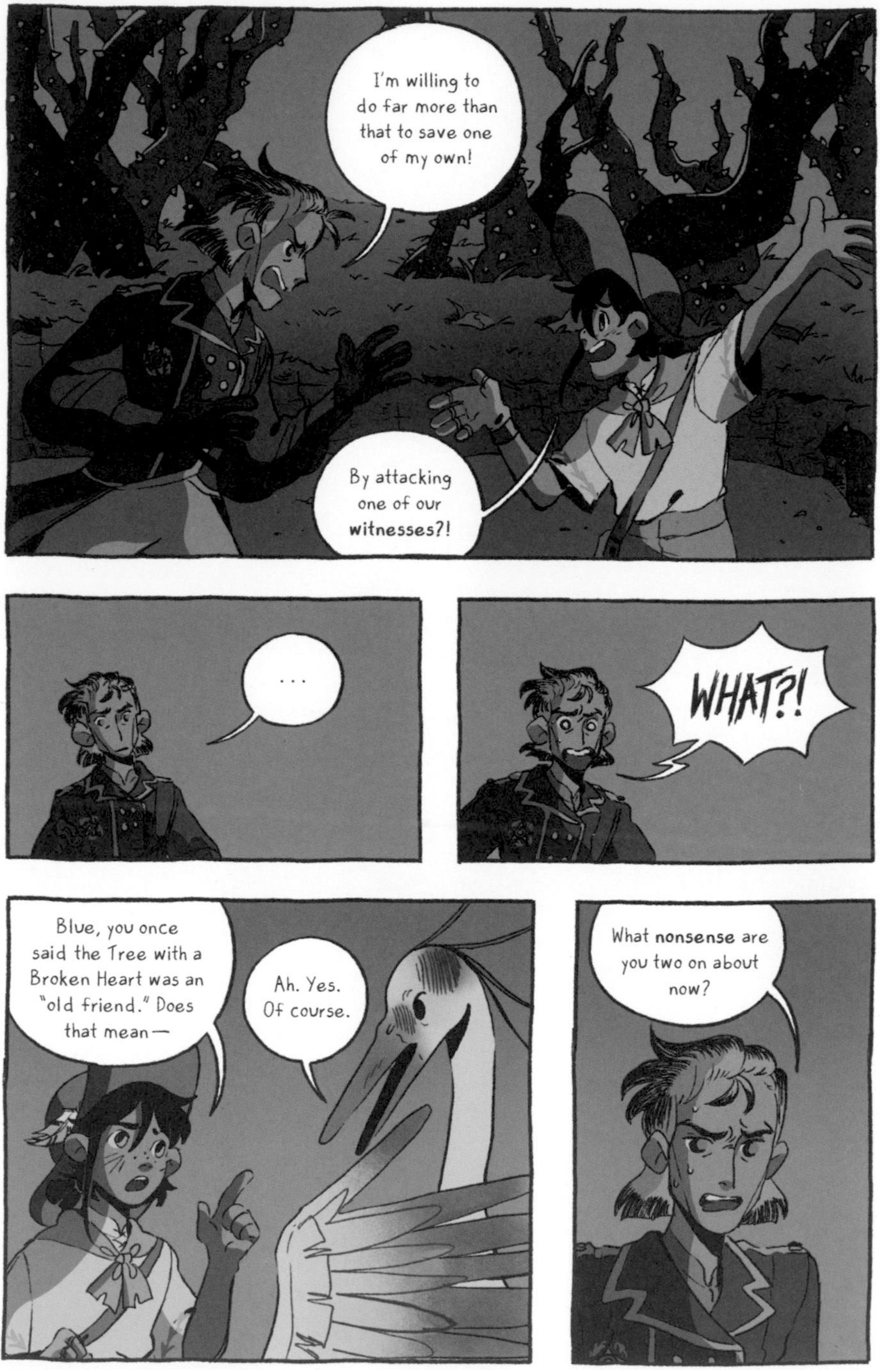
I'm willing to do far more than that to save one of my own!
By attacking one of our witnesses?!
. . .
WHAT?!
Blue, you once said the Tree with a Broken Heart was an "old friend." Does that mean—
Ah. Yes. Of course.
What nonsense are you two on about now?

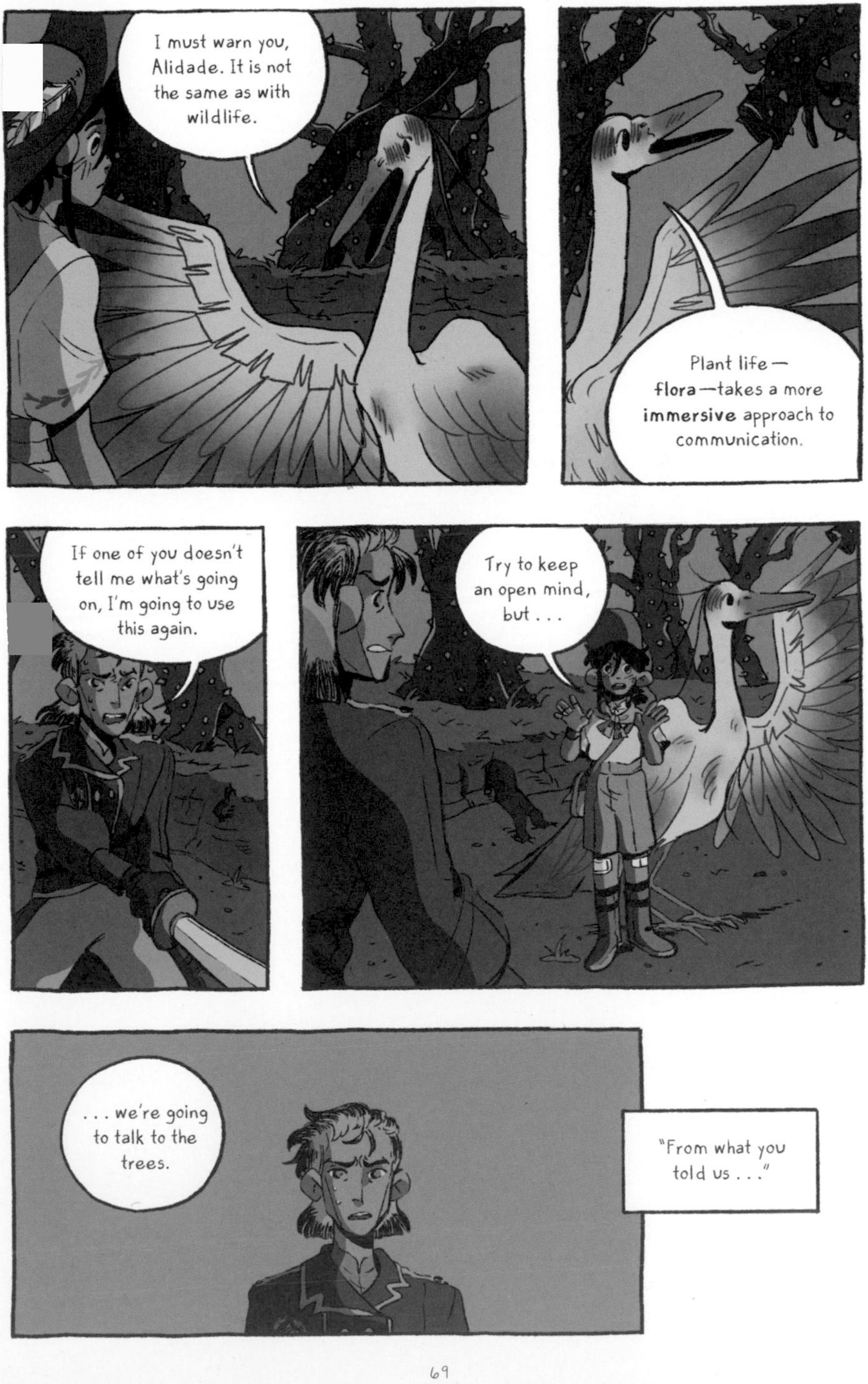
I must warn you, Alidade. It is not the same as with wildlife.
Plant life— flora—takes a more immersive approach to communication.
If one of you doesn't tell me what's going on, I'm going to use this again.
Try to keep an open mind, but . . .
. . . we're going to talk to the trees.
"From what you told us . . ."

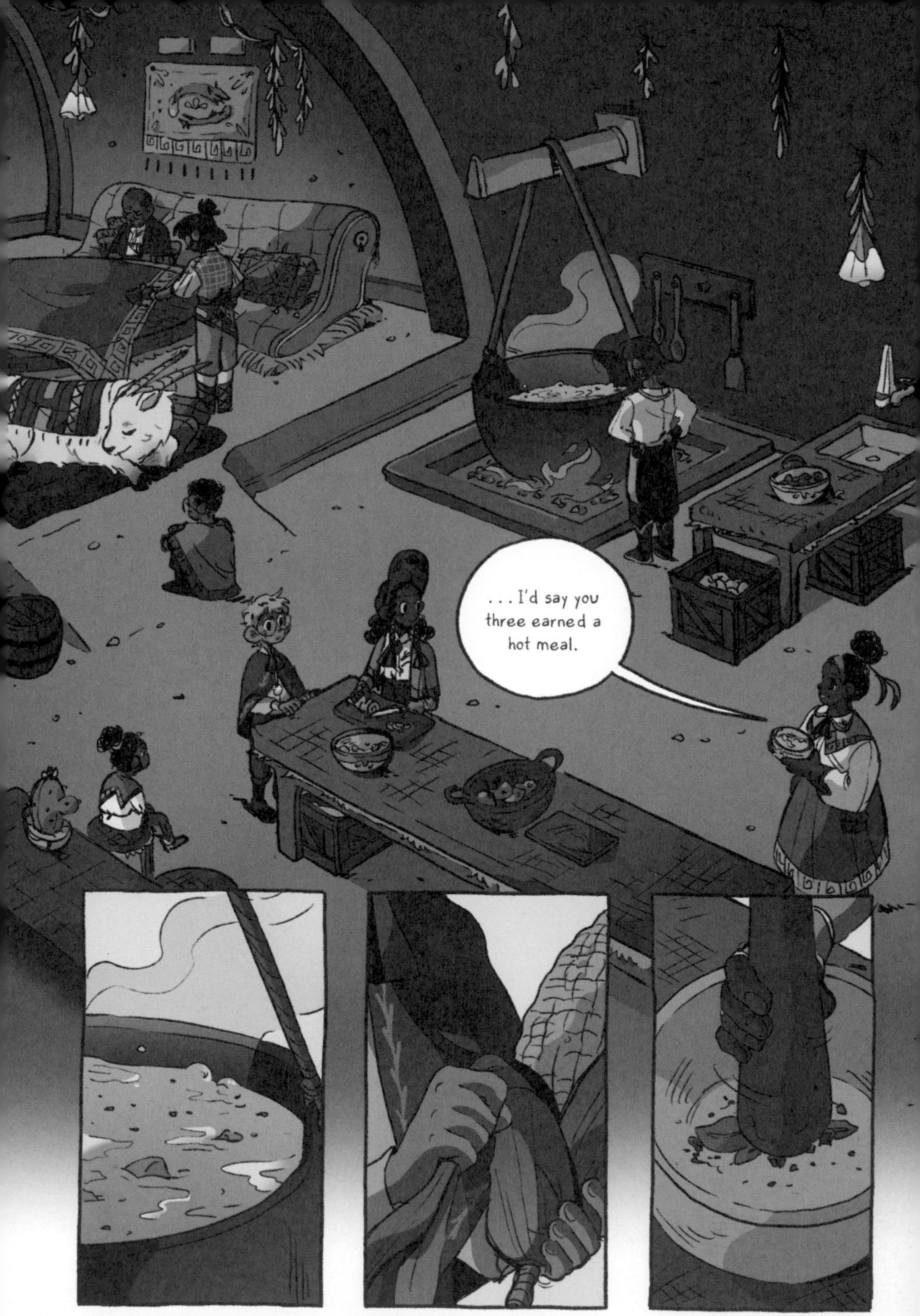
. . . I'd say you three earned a hot meal.

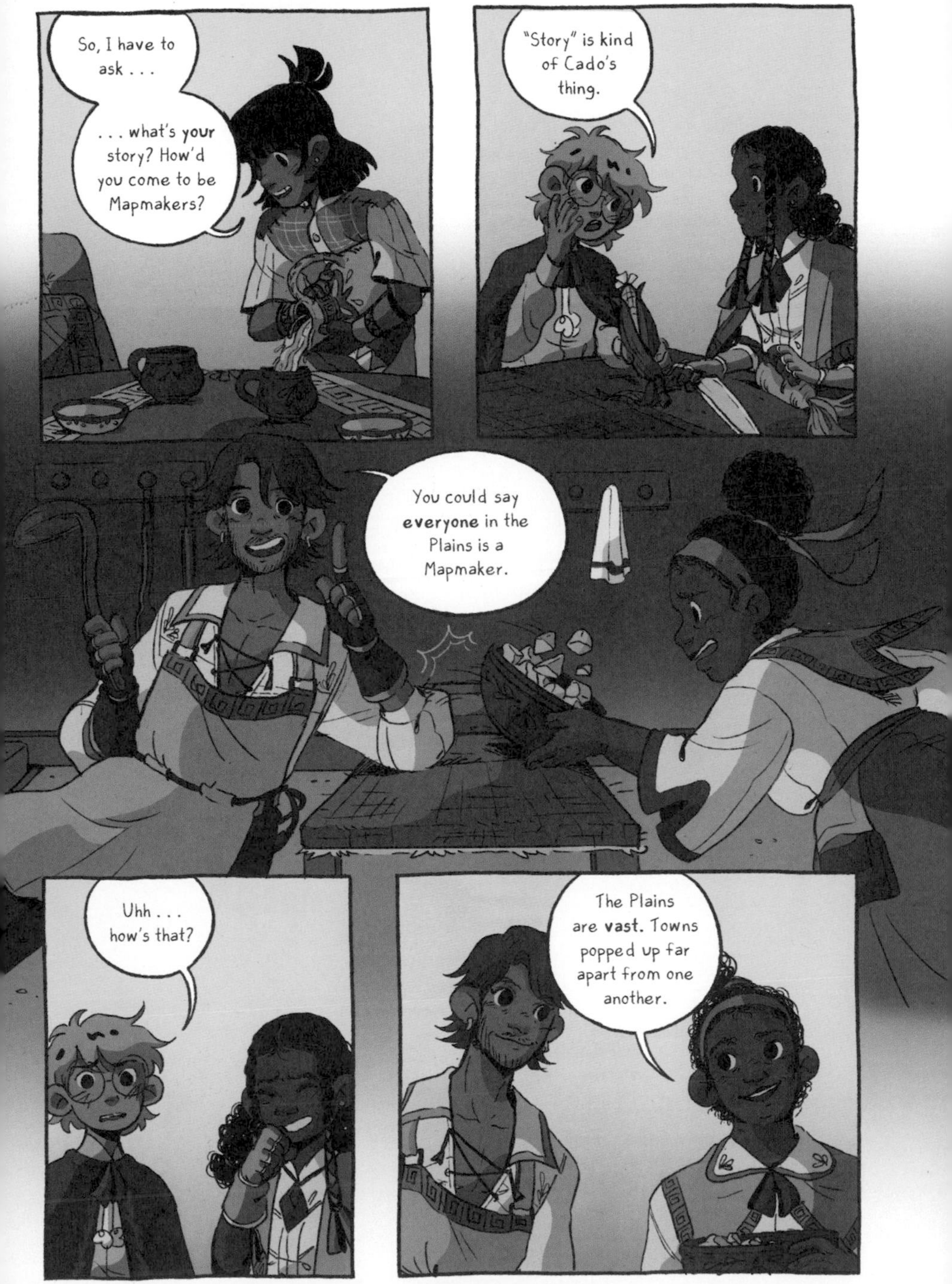
So, I have to ask . . .
. . . what's **your** story? How'd you come to be Mapmakers?
"Story" is kind of Cado's thing.
You could say **everyone** in the Plains is a Mapmaker.
Uhh . . . how's that?
The Plains are **vast.** Towns popped up far apart from one another.

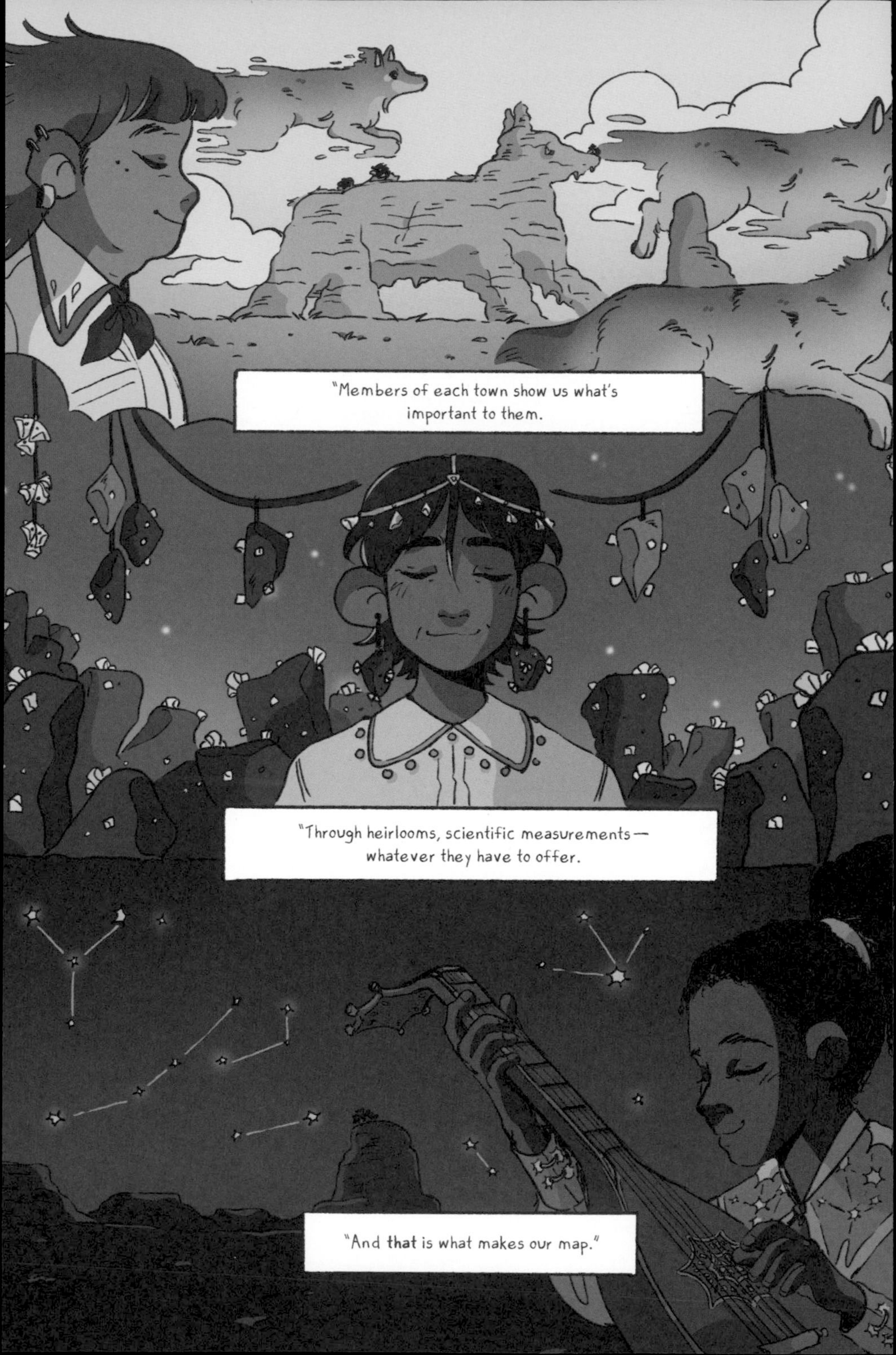
"Members of each town show us what's important to them.
"Through heirlooms, scientific measurements—whatever they have to offer.
"And **that** is what makes our map."

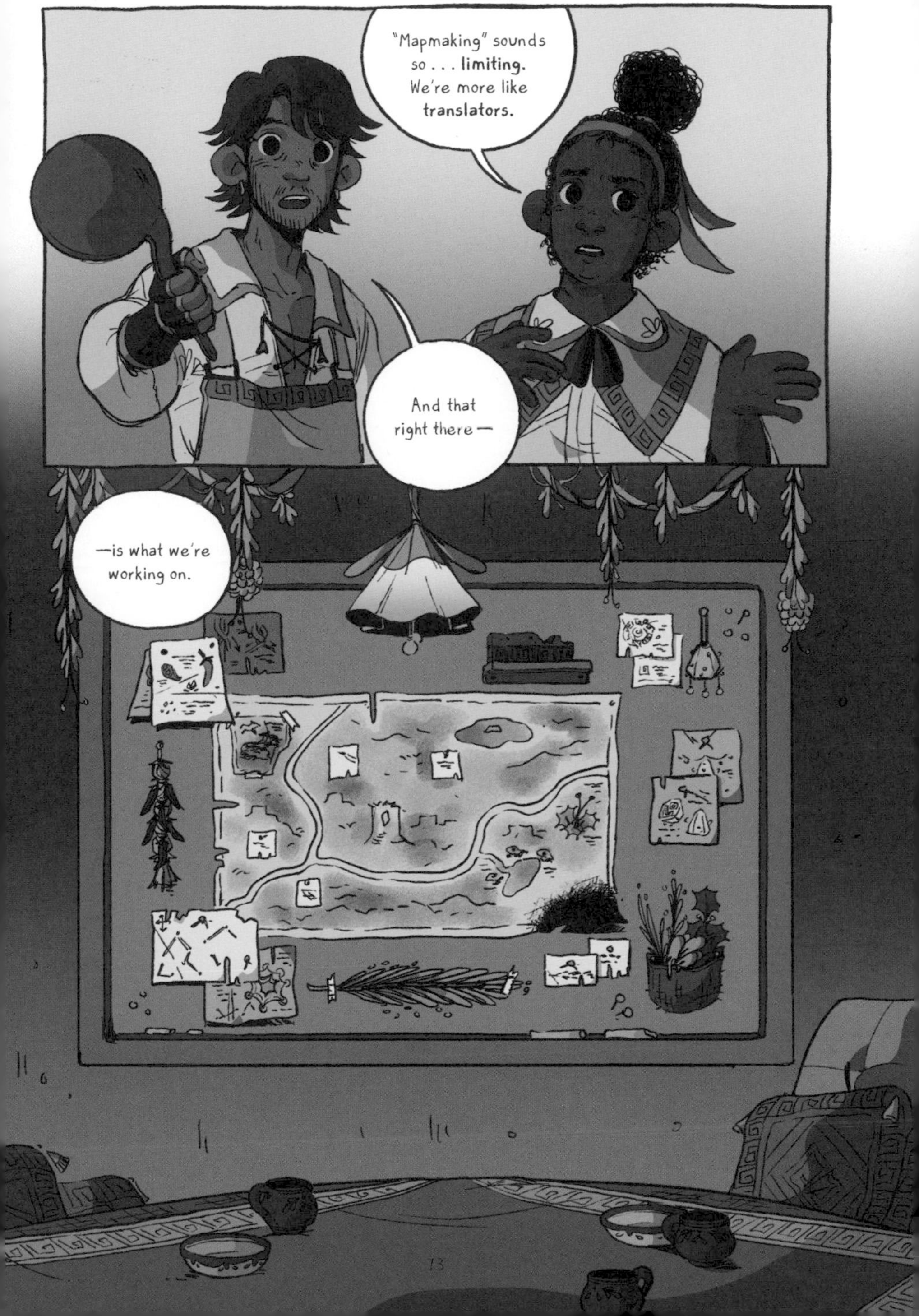
"Mapmaking" sounds so . . . **limiting.** We're more like **translators.**
And that right there—
—is what we're working on.

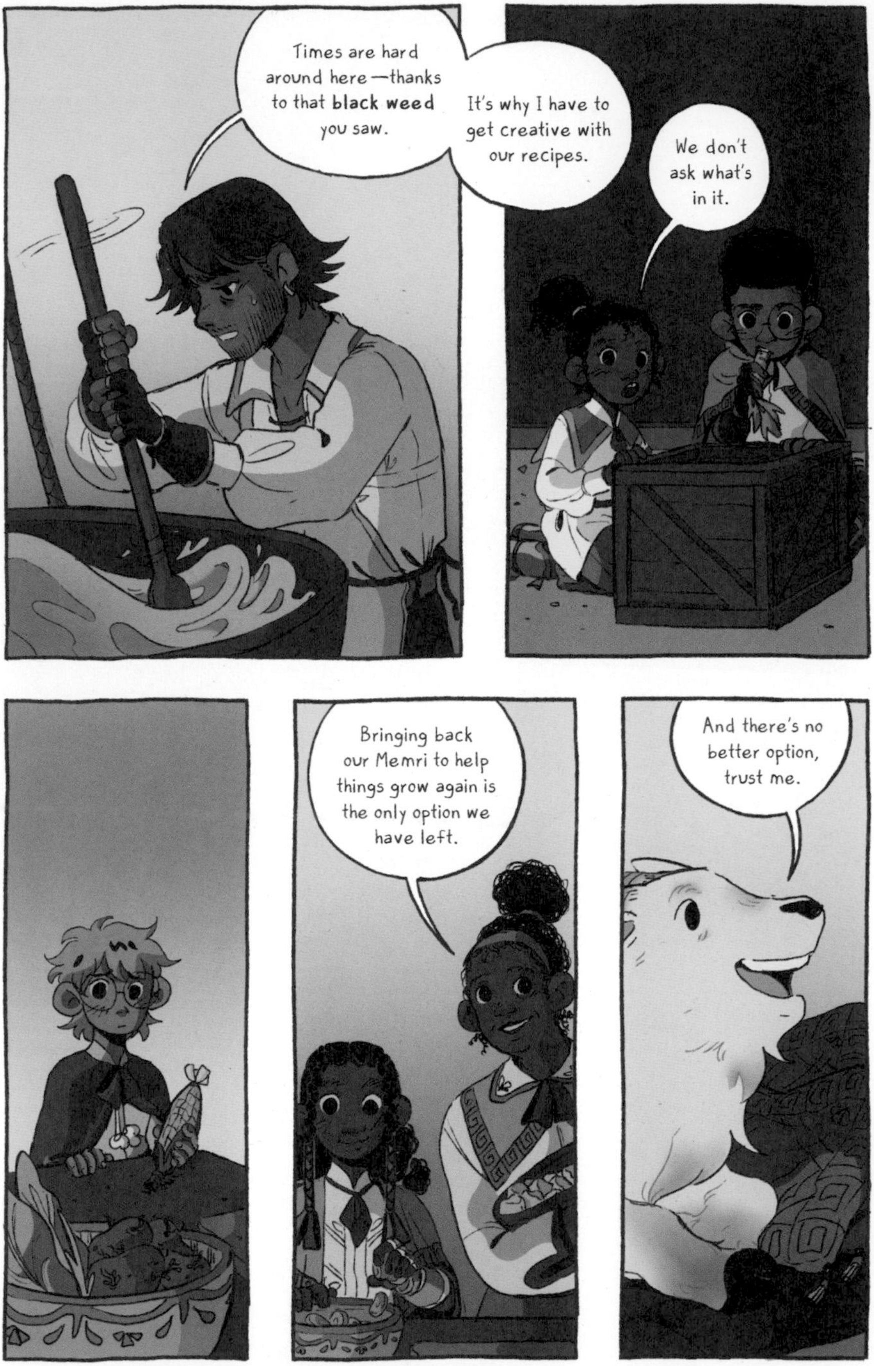
Times are hard around here—thanks to that **black weed** you saw.
It's why I have to get creative with our recipes.
We don't ask what's in it.
Bringing back our Memri to help things grow again is the only option we have left.
And there's no better option, trust me.

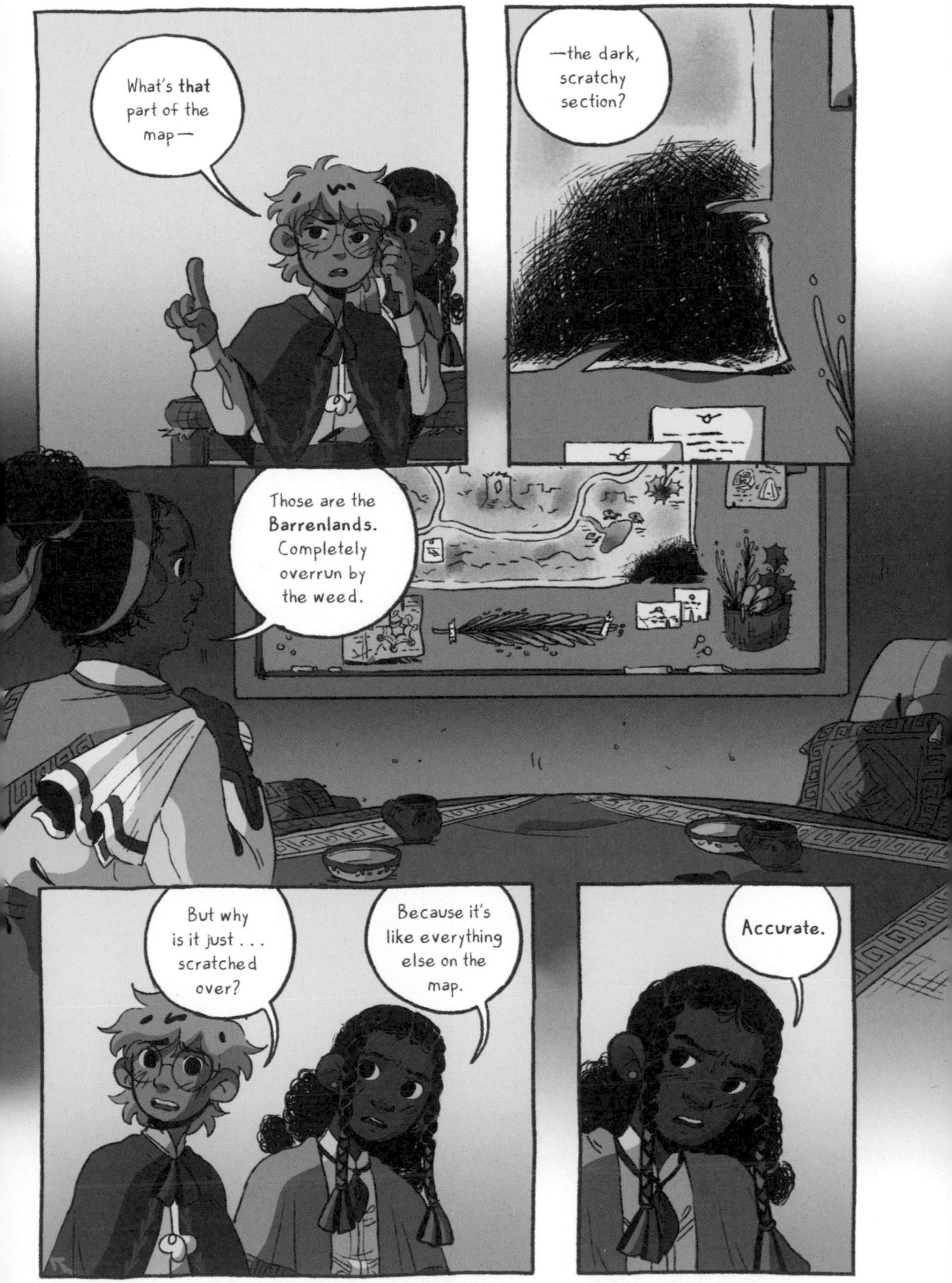

What's **that** part of the map—
—the dark, scratchy section?
Those are the **Barrenlands.** Completely overrun by the weed.
But why is it just . . . scratched over?
Because it's like everything else on the map.
Accurate.

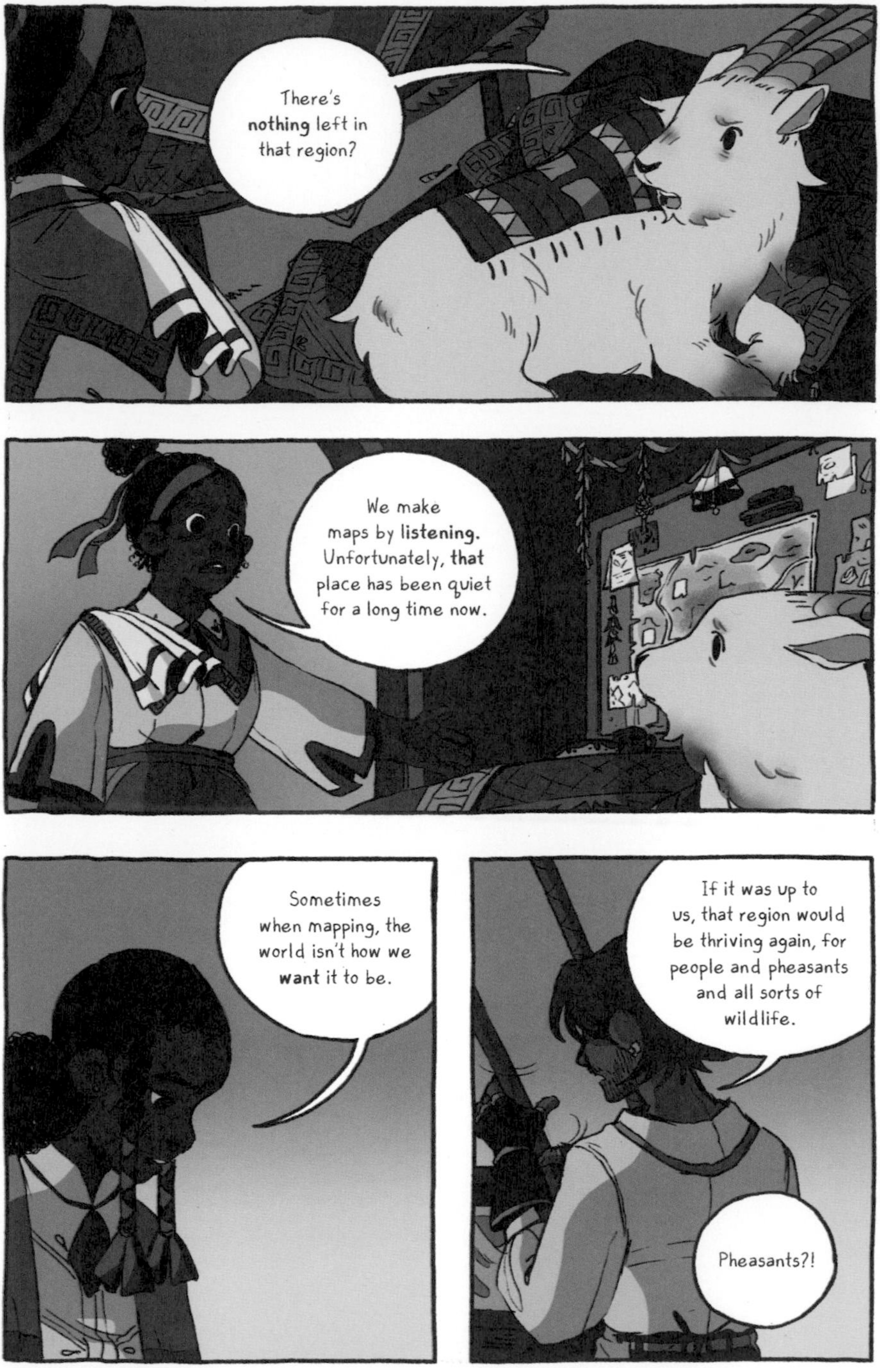

There's **nothing** left in that region?
We make maps by **listening.** Unfortunately, **that** place has been quiet for a long time now.
Sometimes when mapping, the world isn't how we **want** it to be.
If it was up to us, that region would be thriving again, for people and pheasants and all sorts of wildlife.
Pheasants?!

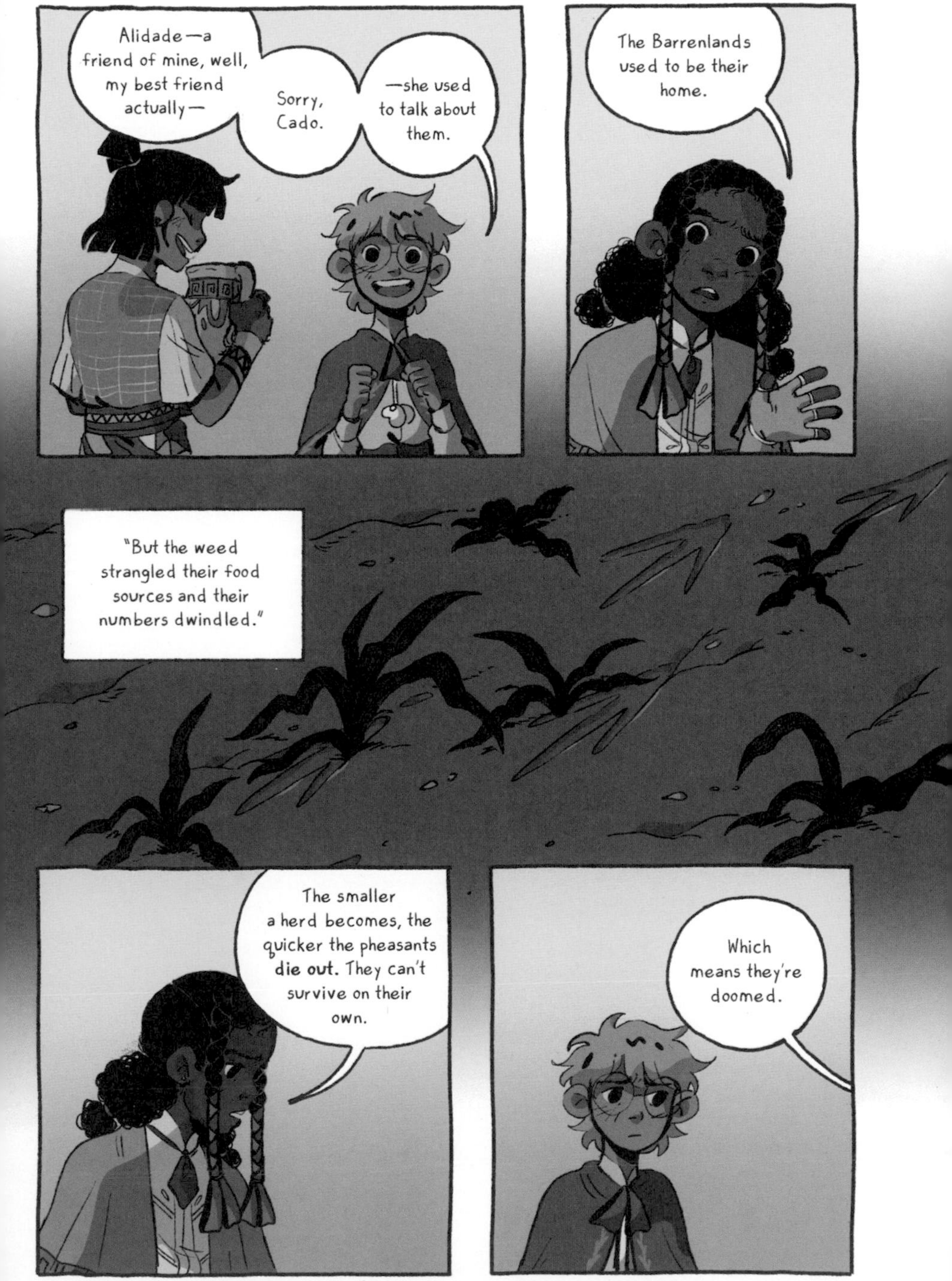
Alidade—a friend of mine, well, my best friend actually—
Sorry, Cado.
—she used to talk about them.
The Barrenlands used to be their home.
"But the weed strangled their food sources and their numbers dwindled."
The smaller a herd becomes, the quicker the pheasants **die out.** They can't survive on their own.
Which means they're doomed.

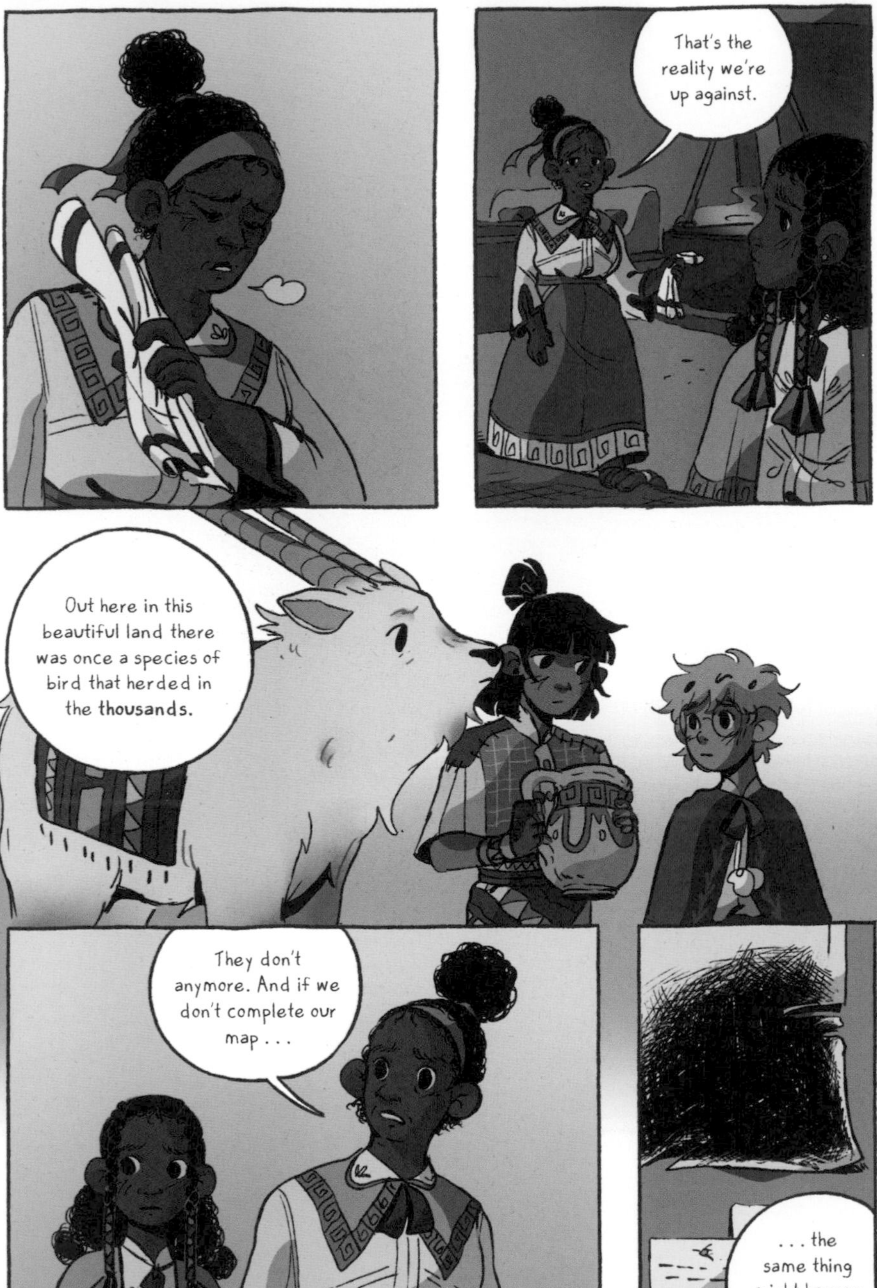
That's the reality we're up against.
Out here in this beautiful land there was once a species of bird that herded in the **thousands.**
They don't anymore. And if we don't complete our map . . .
. . . the same thing might happen to us.

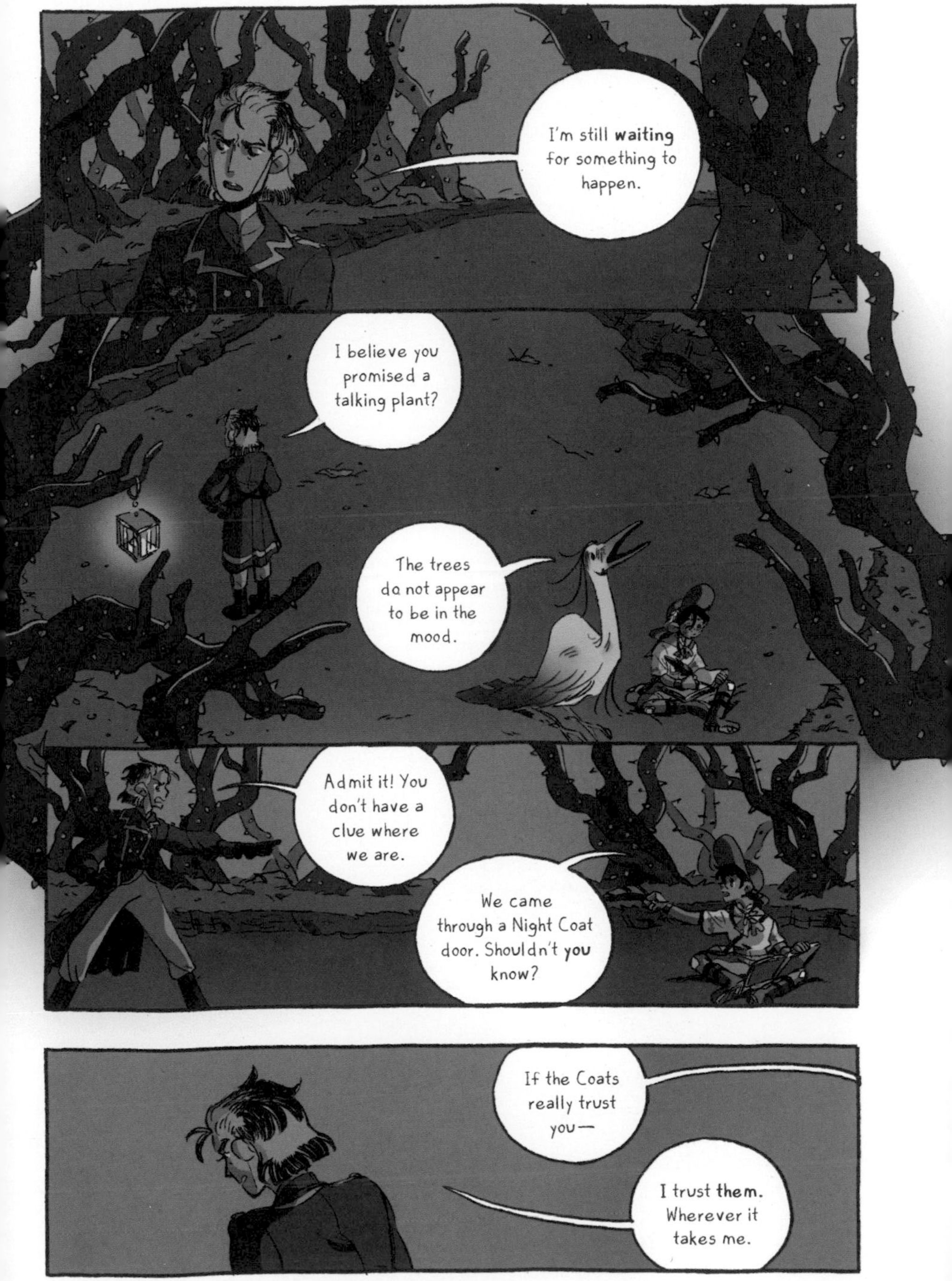
I'm still **waiting** for something to happen.
I believe you promised a talking plant?
The trees do not appear to be in the mood.
Admit it! You don't have a clue where we are.
We came through a Night Coat door. Shouldn't **you** know?
If the Coats really trust you—
I trust **them.** Wherever it takes me.

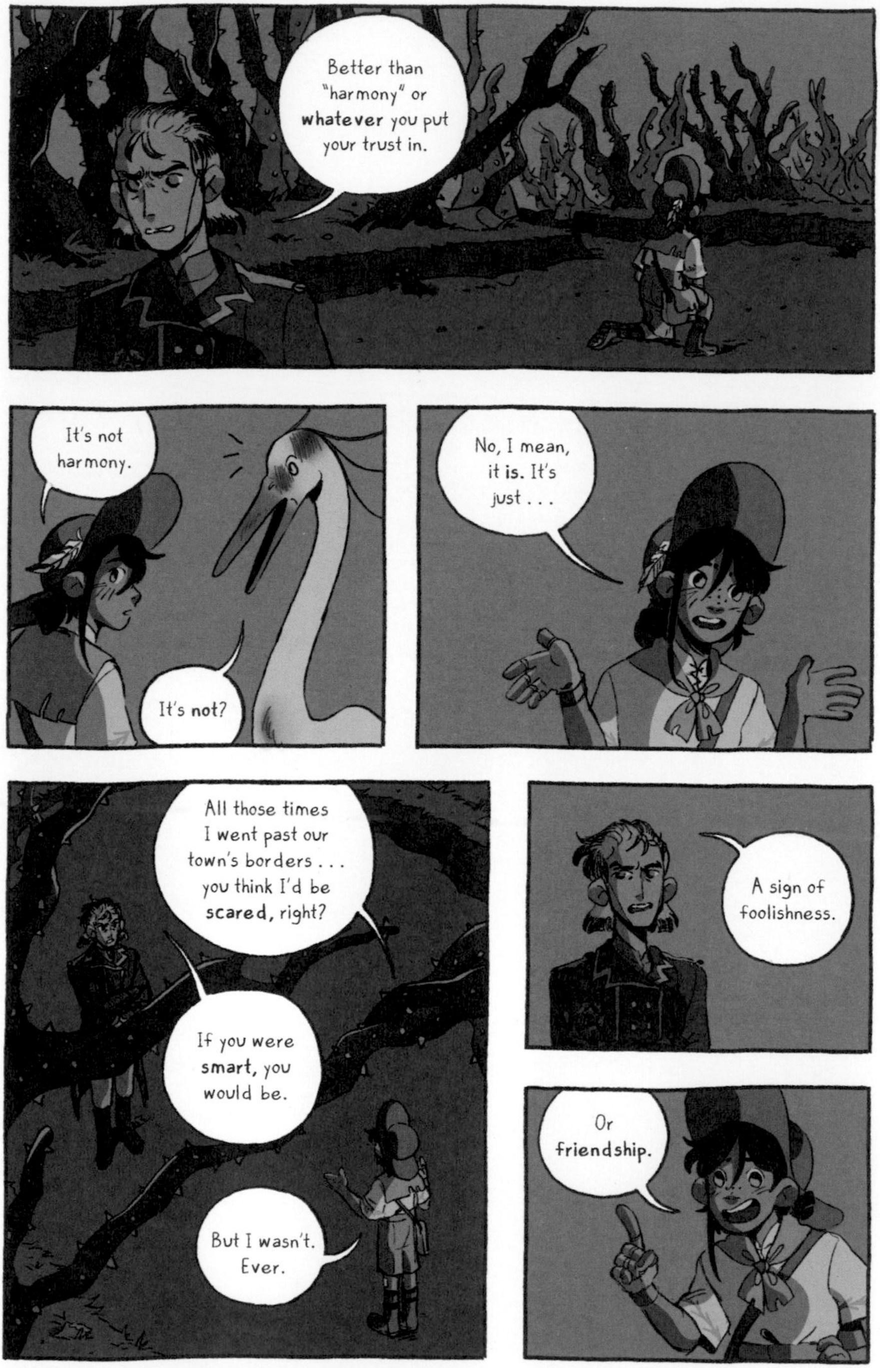
Better than "harmony" or **whatever** you put your trust in.
It's not harmony.
It's **not**?
No, I mean, it **is**. It's just . . .
All those times I went past our town's borders . . . you think I'd be **scared**, right?
If you were **smart**, you would be.
But I wasn't. Ever.
A sign of foolishness.
Or **friendship**.

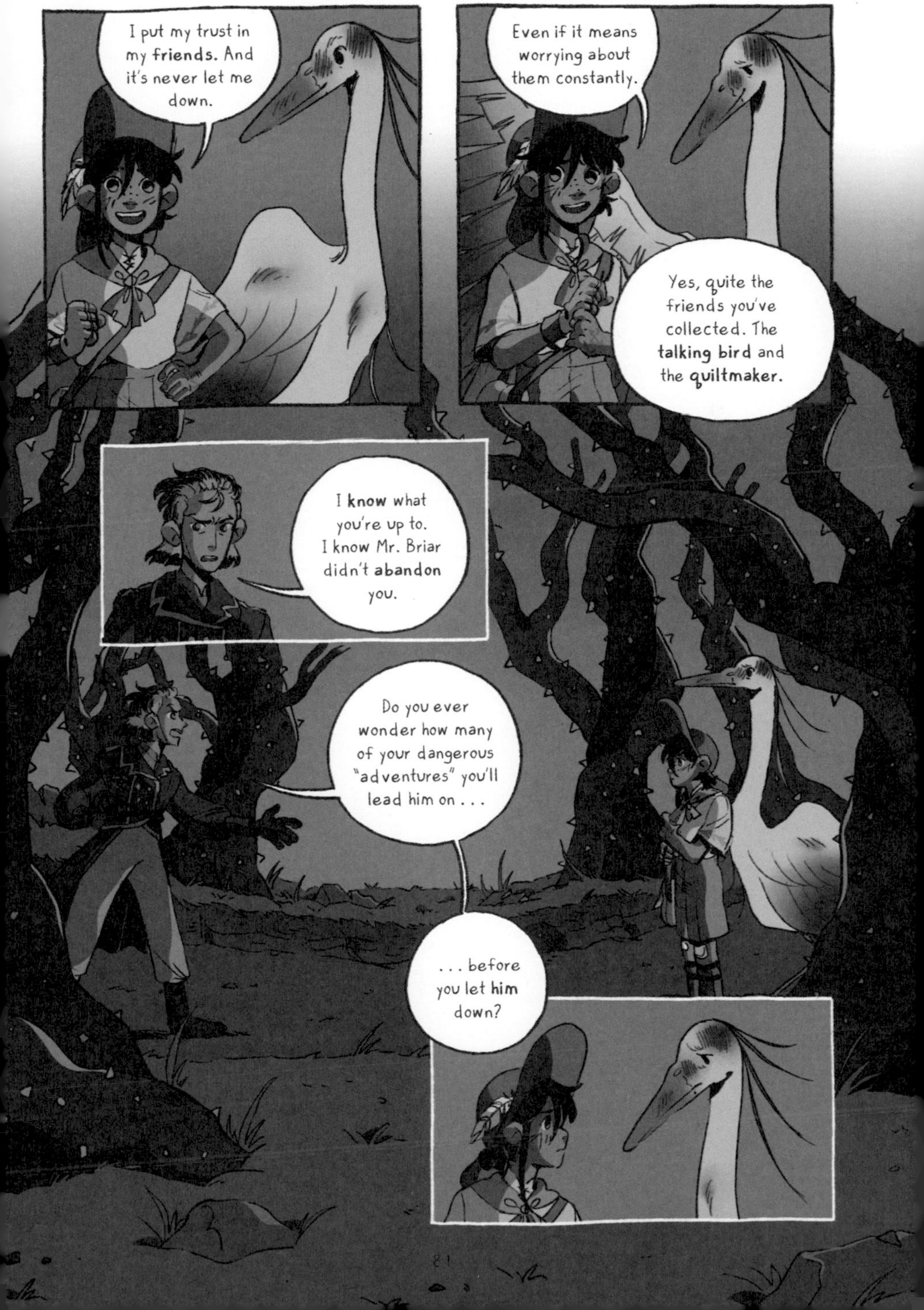
I put my trust in my **friends.** And it's never let me down.
Even if it means worrying about them constantly.
Yes, quite the friends you've collected. The **talking bird** and the **quiltmaker.**
I **know** what you're up to. I know Mr. Briar didn't **abandon** you.
Do you ever wonder how many of your dangerous "adventures" you'll lead him on . . .
. . . before you let **him** down?

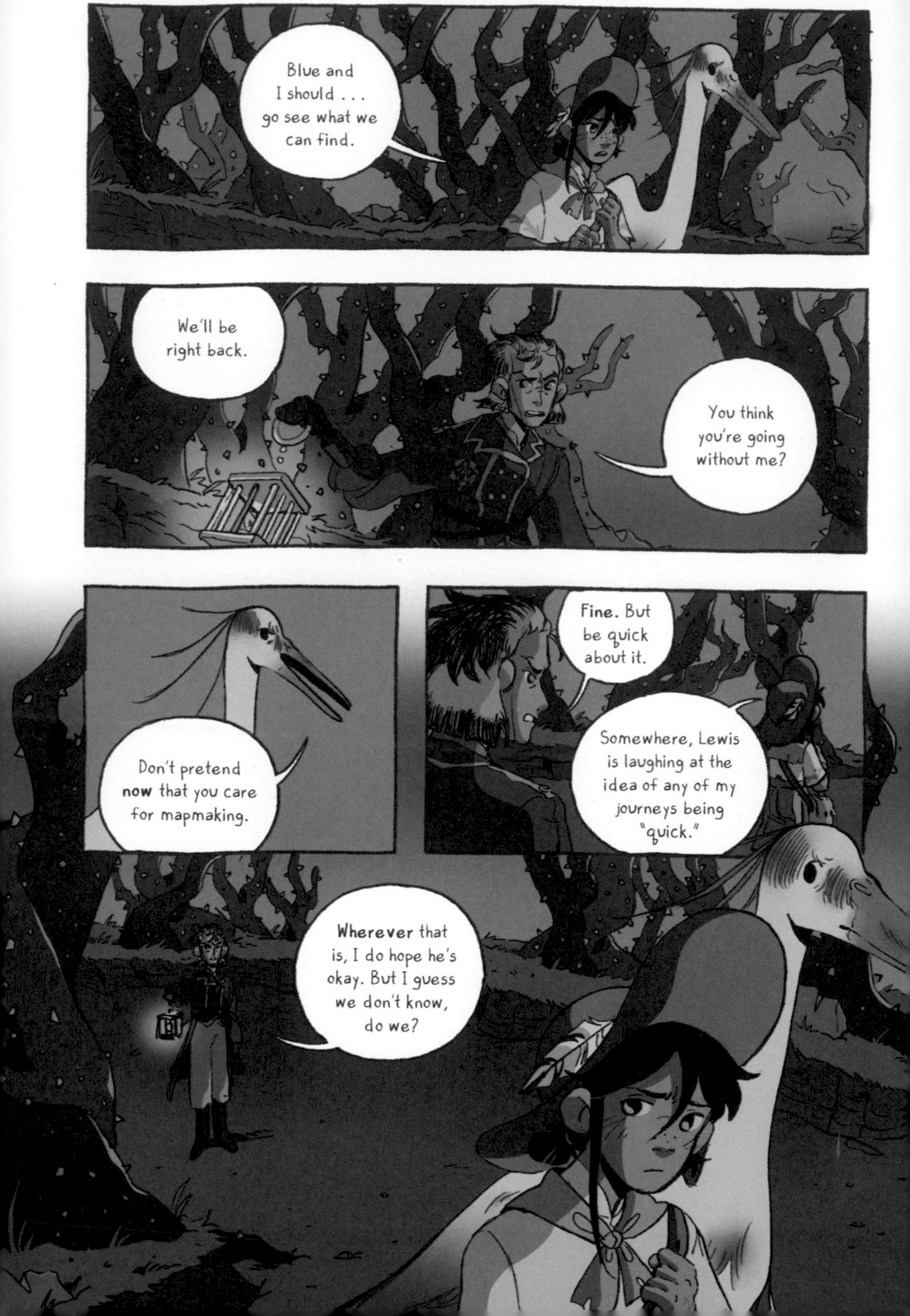
Blue and I should . . . go see what we can find.
We'll be right back.
You think you're going without me?
Don't pretend **now** that you care for mapmaking.
Fine. But be quick about it.
Somewhere, Lewis is laughing at the idea of any of my journeys being "quick."
Wherever that is, I do hope he's okay. But I guess we don't know, do we?

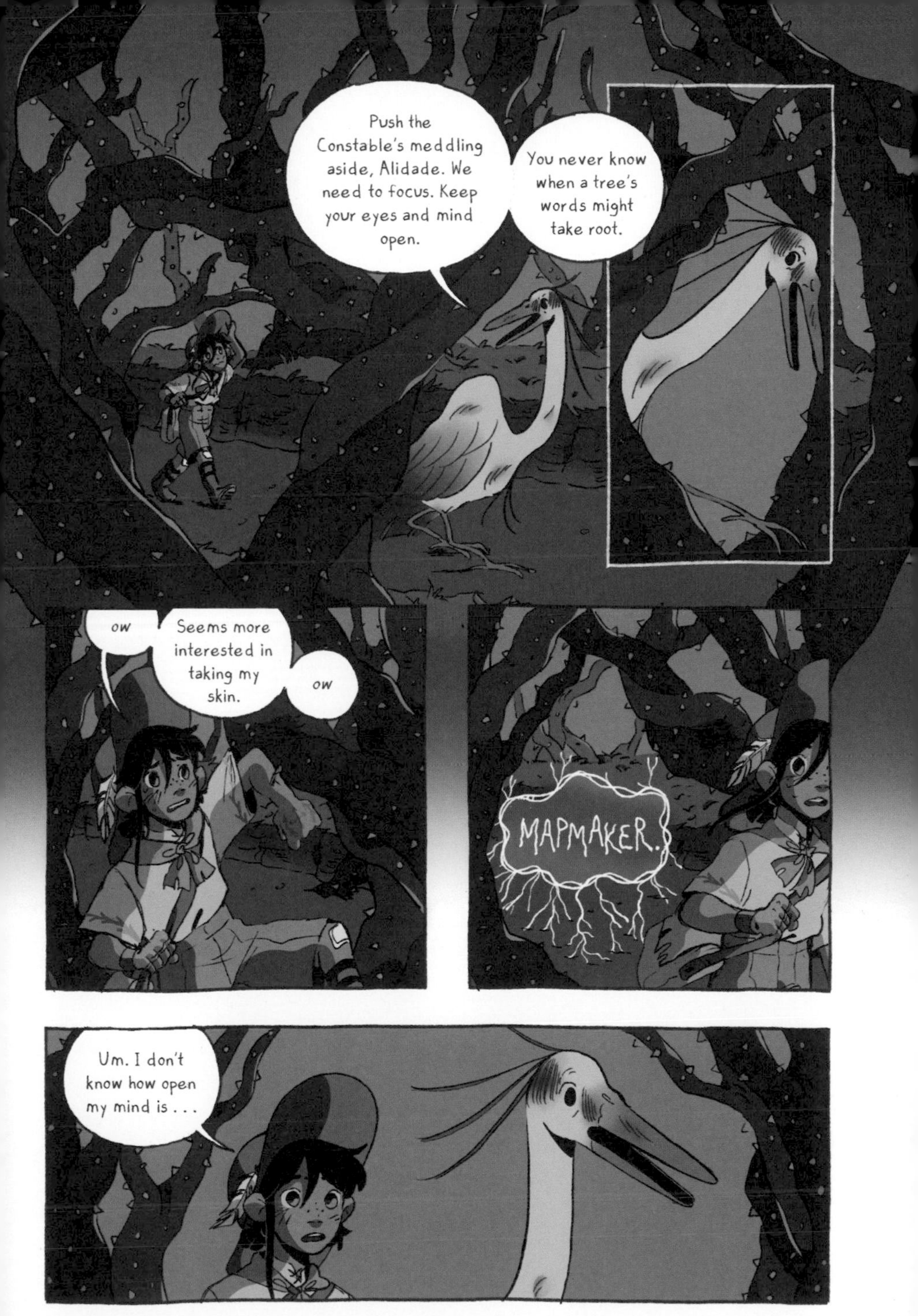
Push the Constable's meddling aside, Alidade. We need to focus. Keep your eyes and mind open.
You never know when a tree's words might take root.
ow
Seems more interested in taking my skin.
ow
MAPMAKER.
Um. I don't know how open my mind is . . .

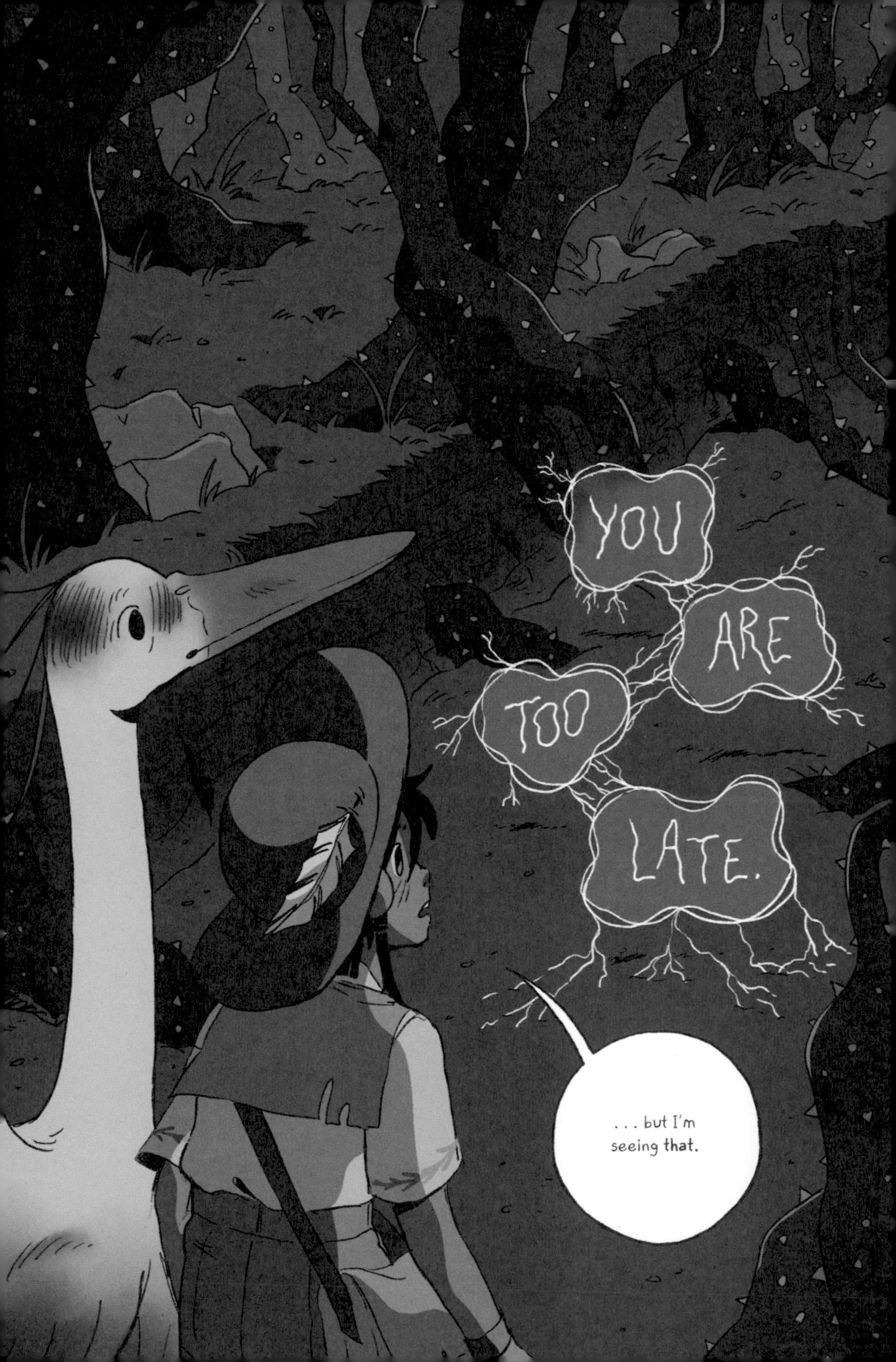
YOU
ARE
TOO
LATE.
. . . but I'm seeing that.

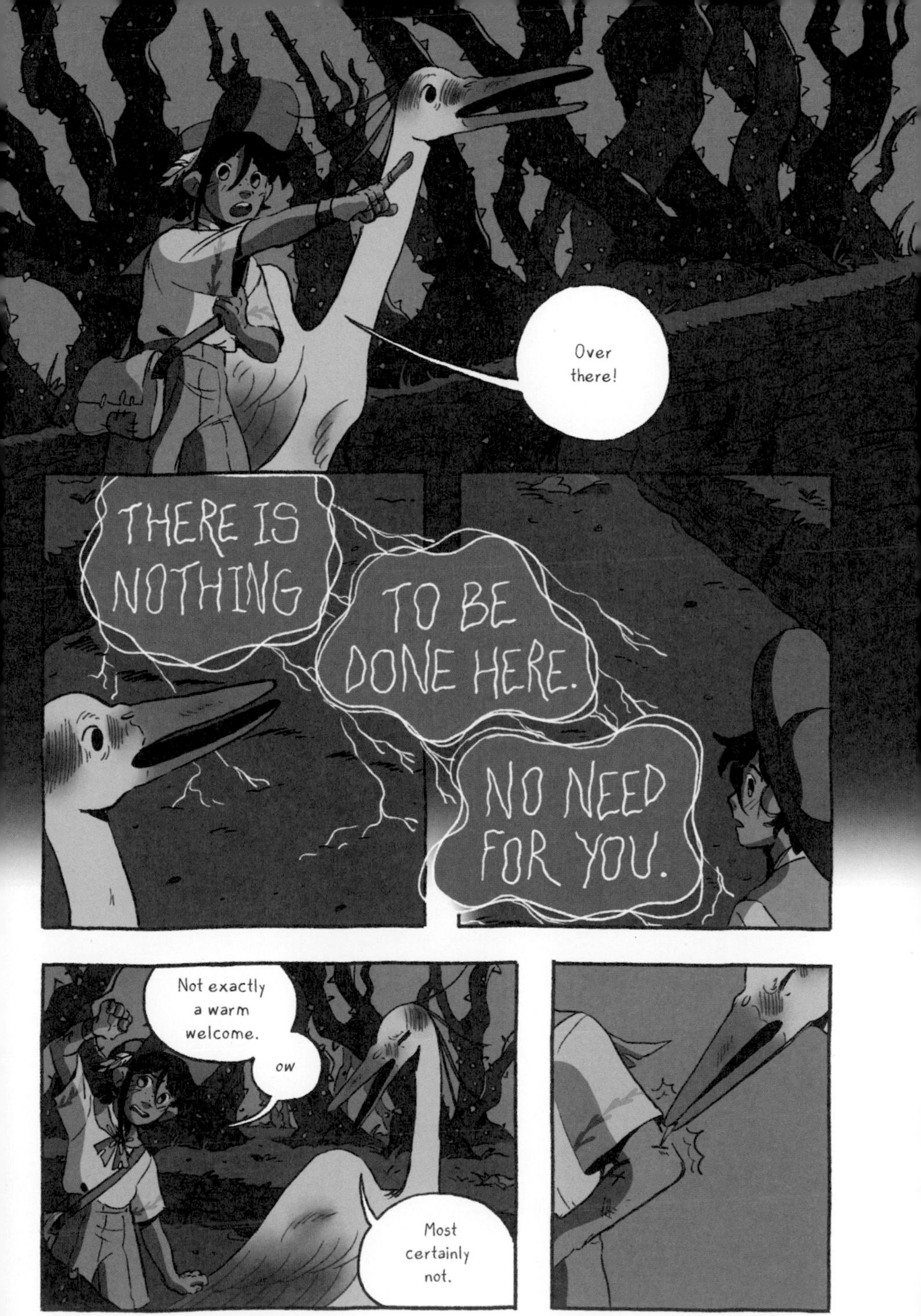
Over there!
THERE IS NOTHING
TO BE DONE HERE.
NO NEED FOR YOU.
Not exactly a warm welcome.
ow
Most certainly not.

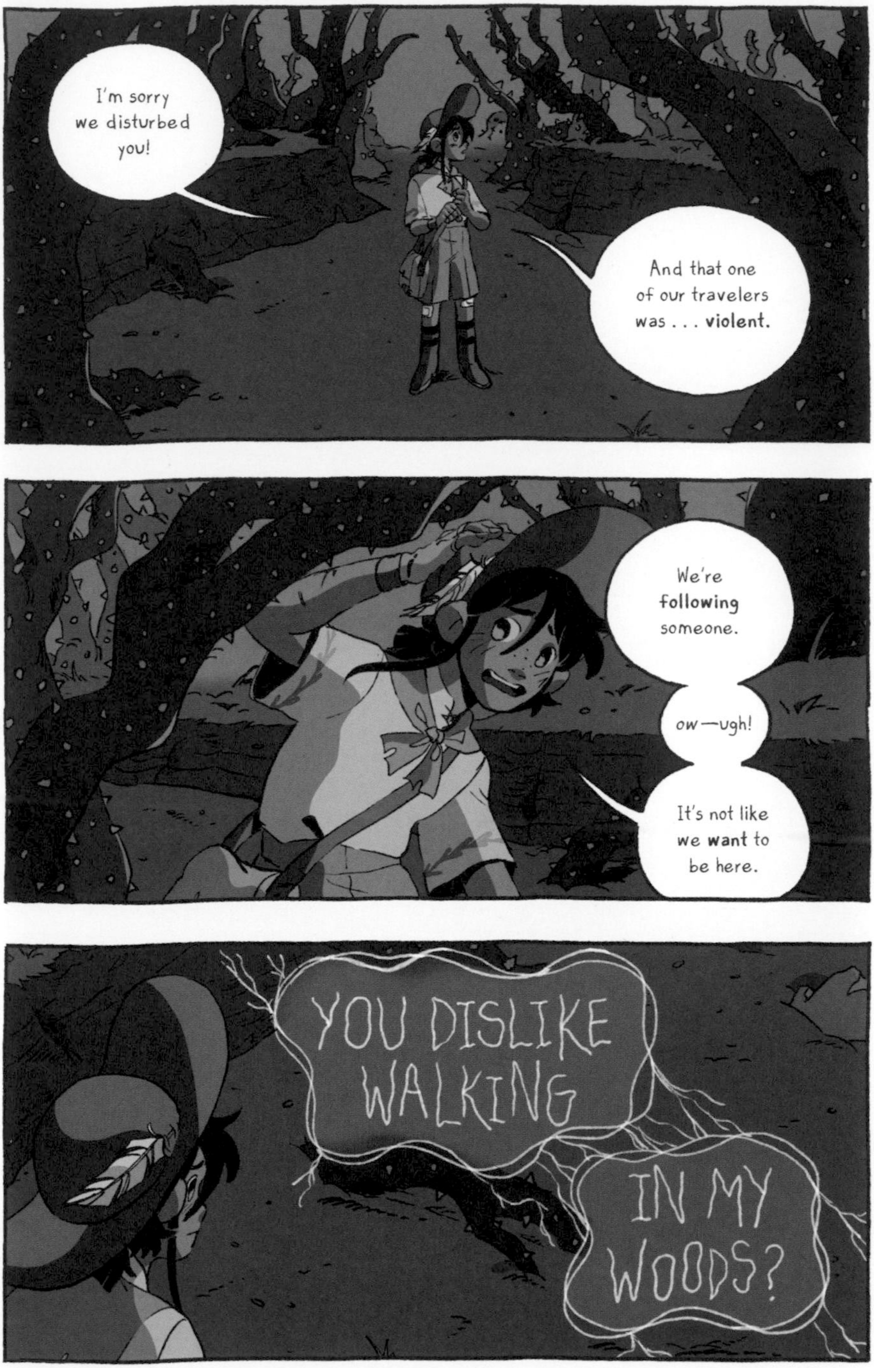

I'm sorry we disturbed you!
And that one of our travelers was . . . **violent.**
We're **following** someone.
ow—ugh!
It's not like we **want** to be here.
YOU DISLIKE WALKING
IN MY WOODS?

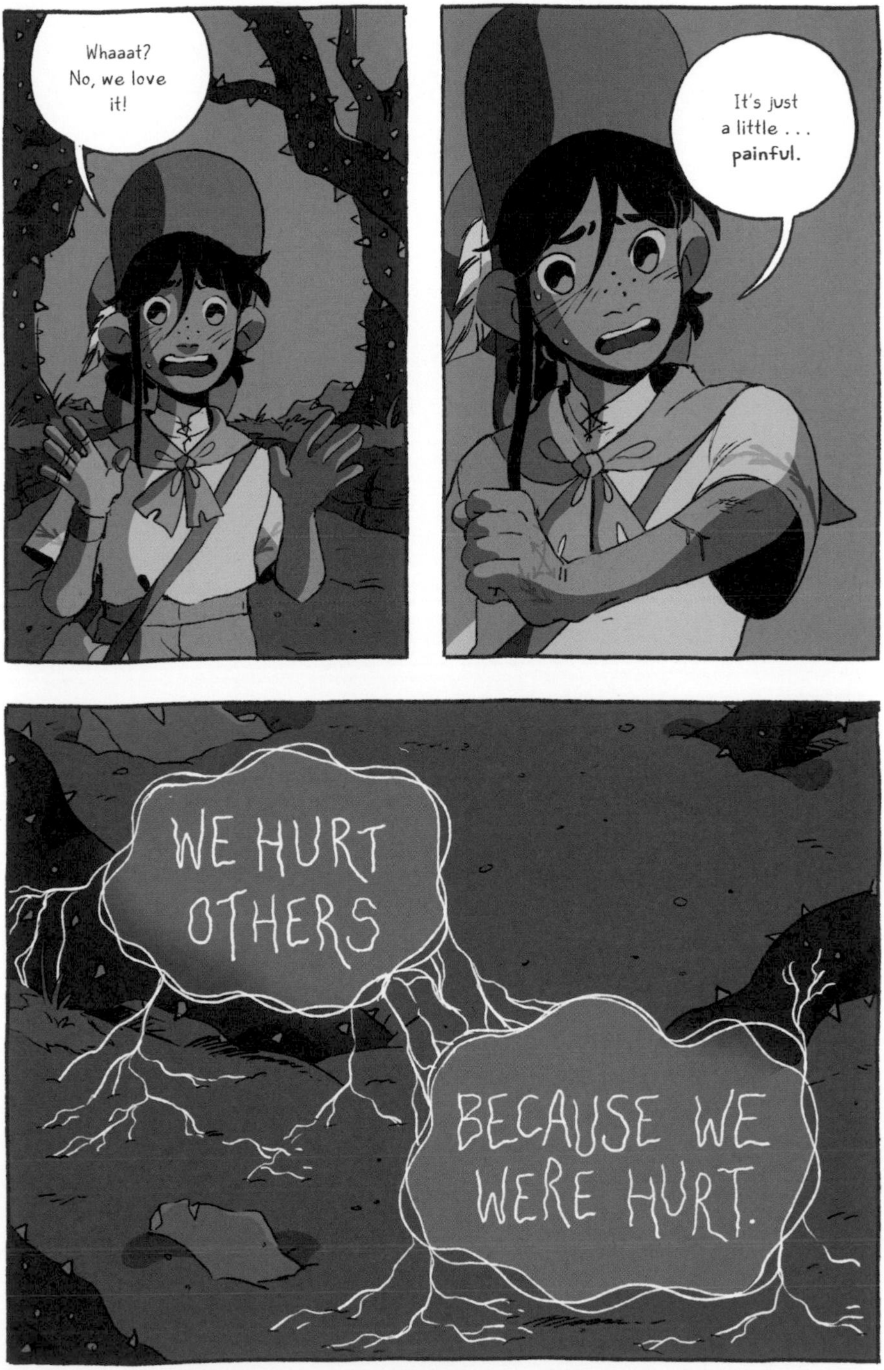
Whaaat?
No, we love it!
It's just a little . . . painful.
WE HURT OTHERS
BECAUSE WE WERE HURT.

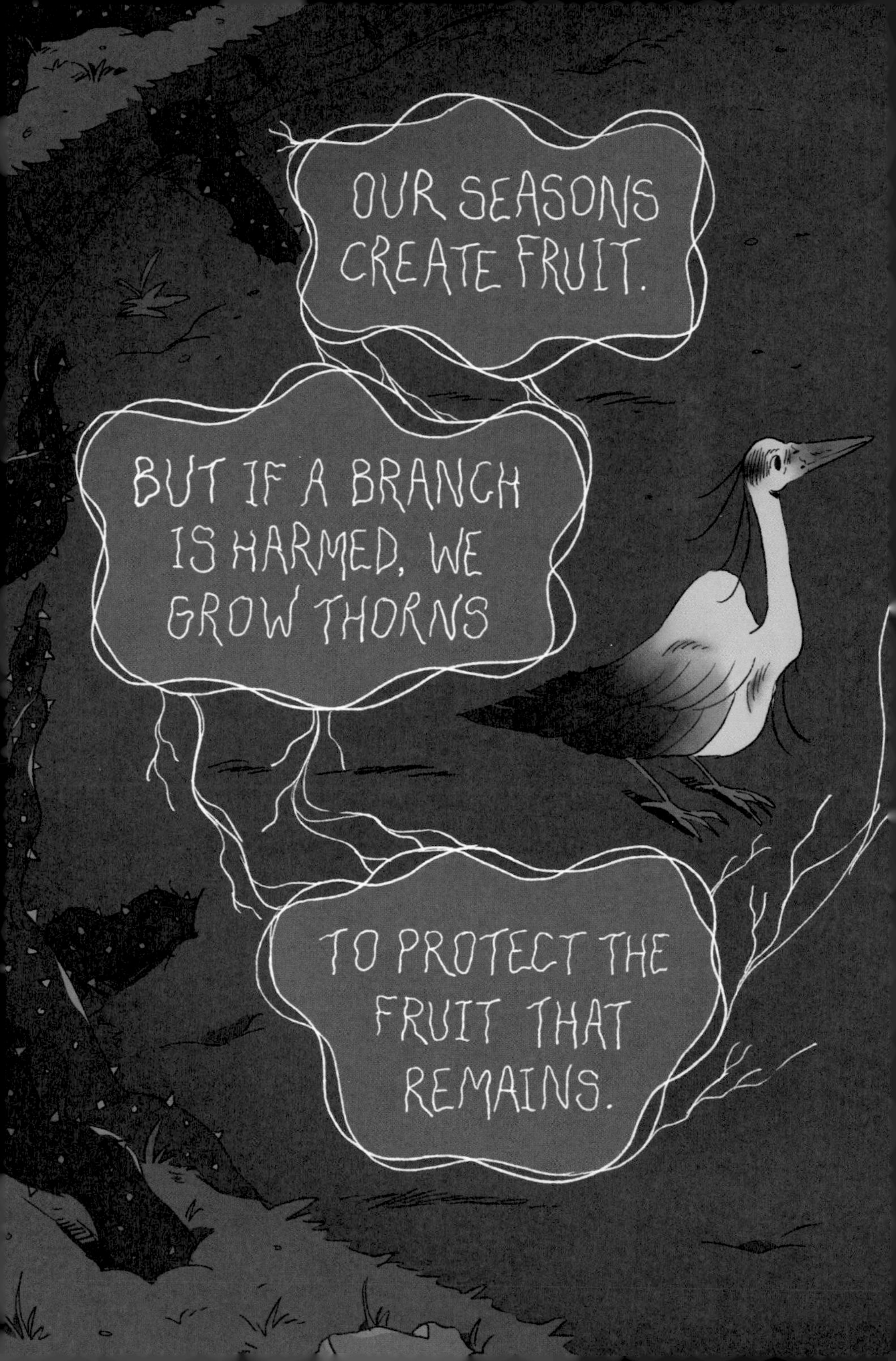
OUR SEASONS CREATE FRUIT.
BUT IF A BRANCH IS HARMED, WE GROW THORNS
TO PROTECT THE FRUIT THAT REMAINS.

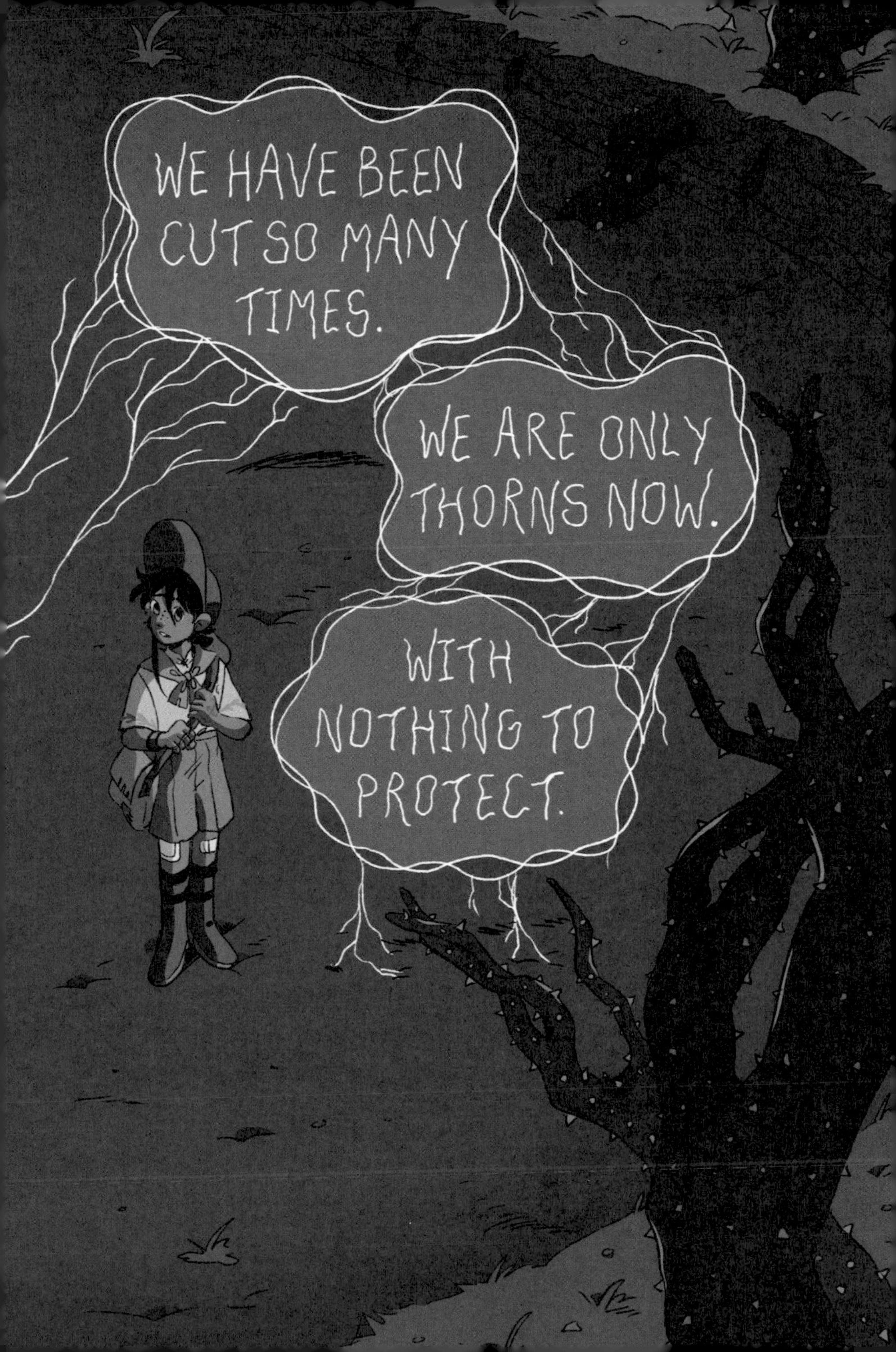
WE HAVE BEEN CUT SO MANY TIMES.
WE ARE ONLY THORNS NOW.
WITH NOTHING TO PROTECT.

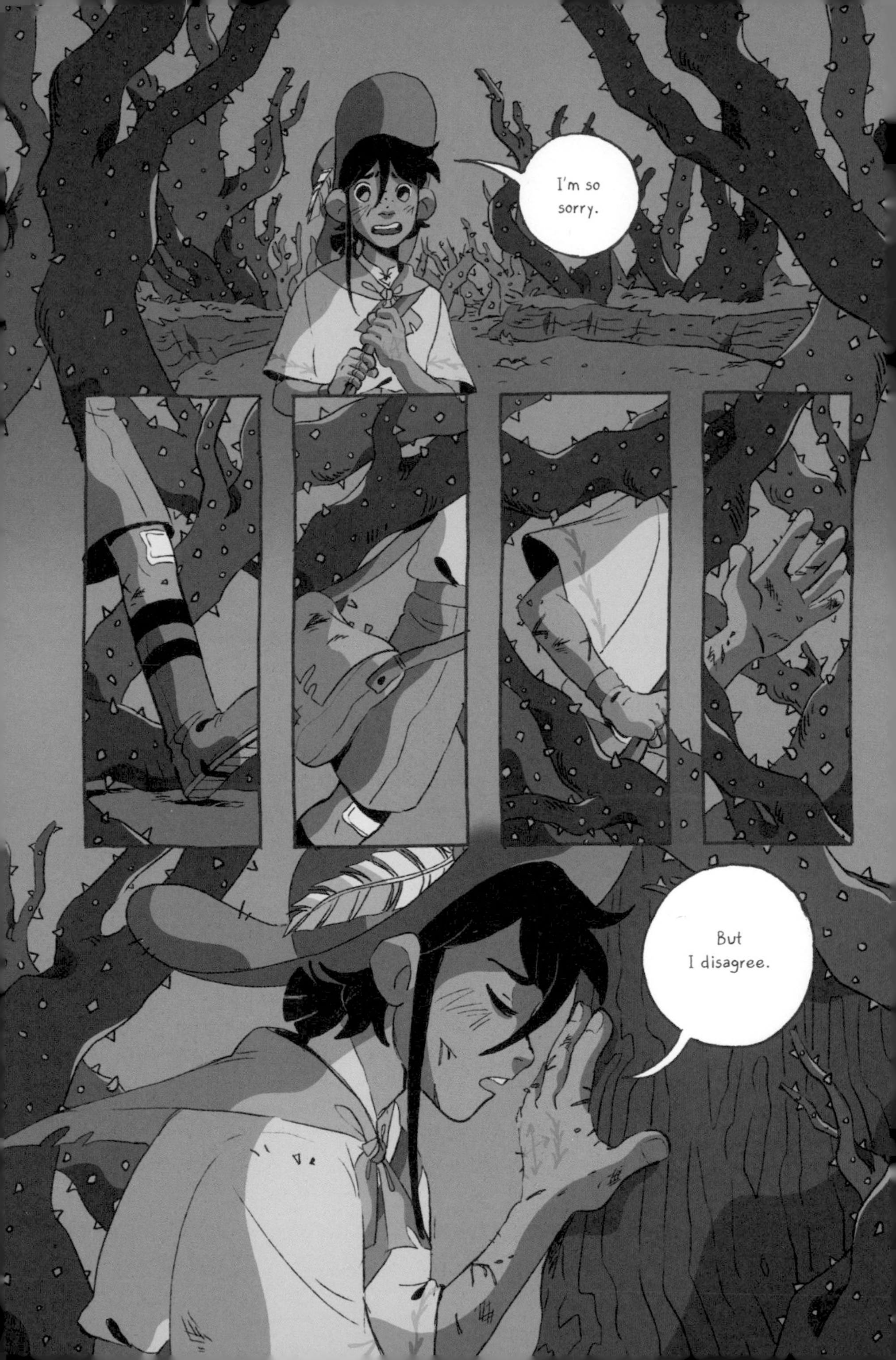
I'm so sorry.
But I disagree.

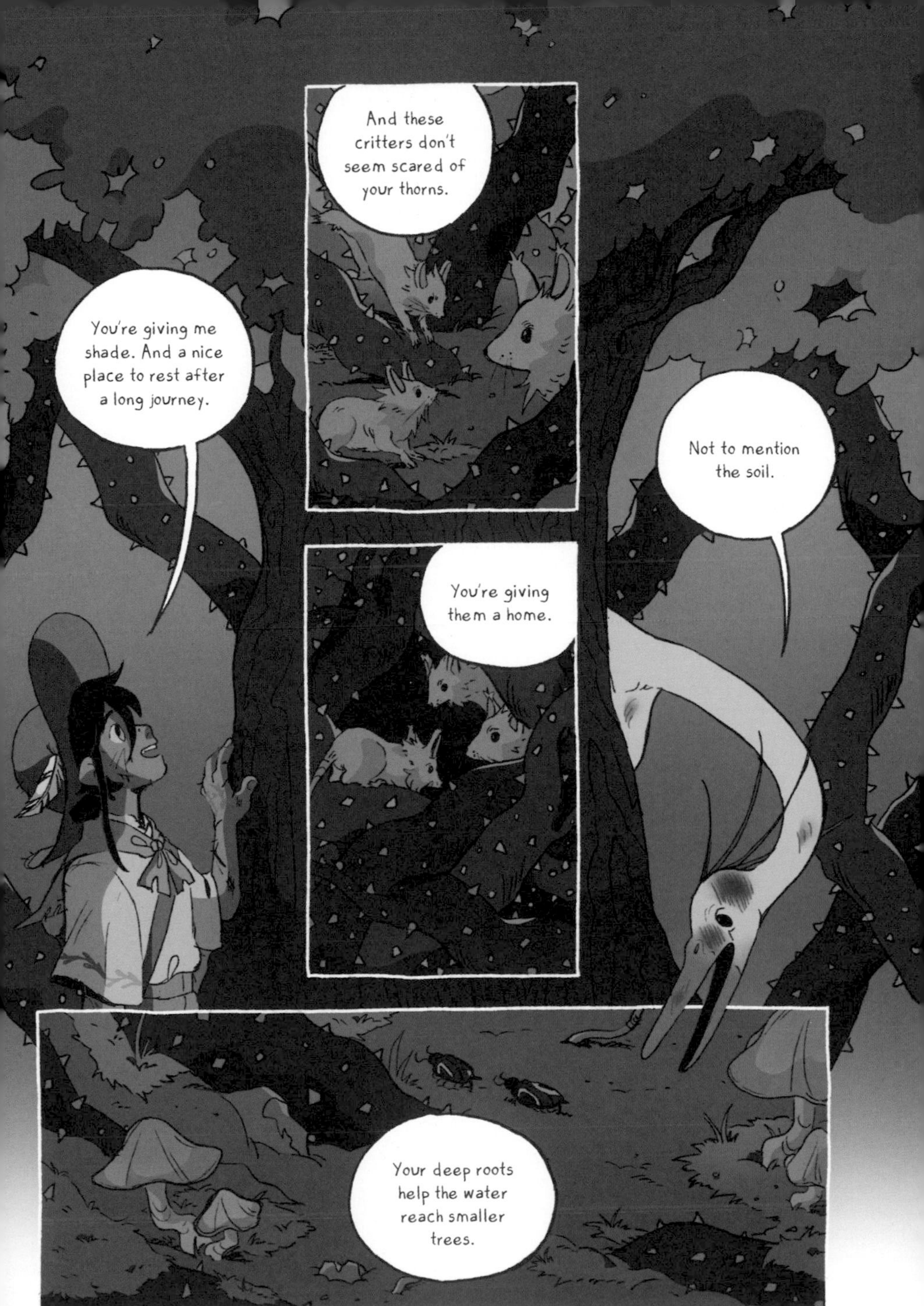

And these critters don't seem scared of your thorns.
You're giving me shade. And a nice place to rest after a long journey.
Not to mention the soil.
You're giving them a home.
Your deep roots help the water reach smaller trees.

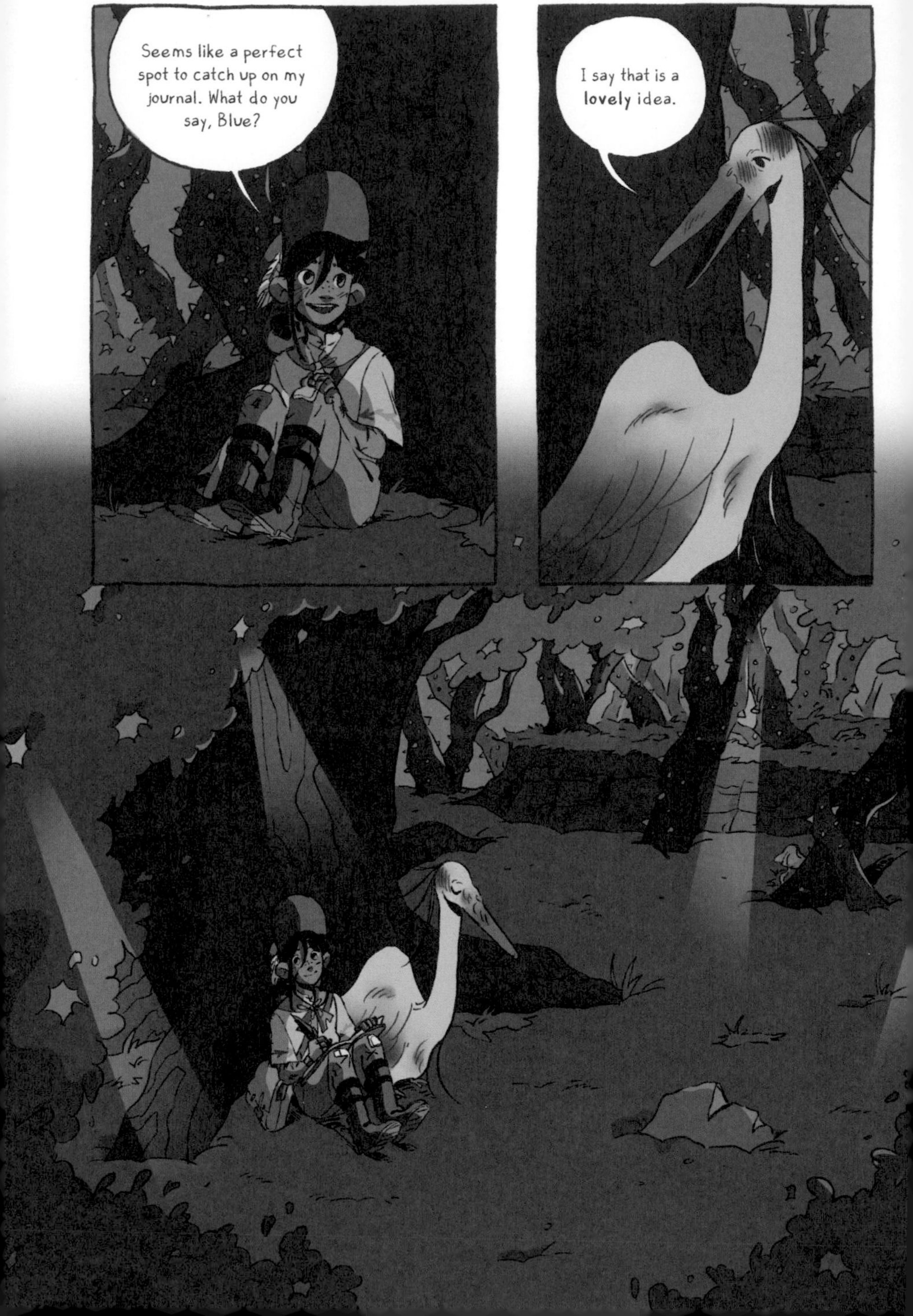
Seems like a perfect spot to catch up on my journal. What do you say, Blue?
I say that is a **lovely** idea.

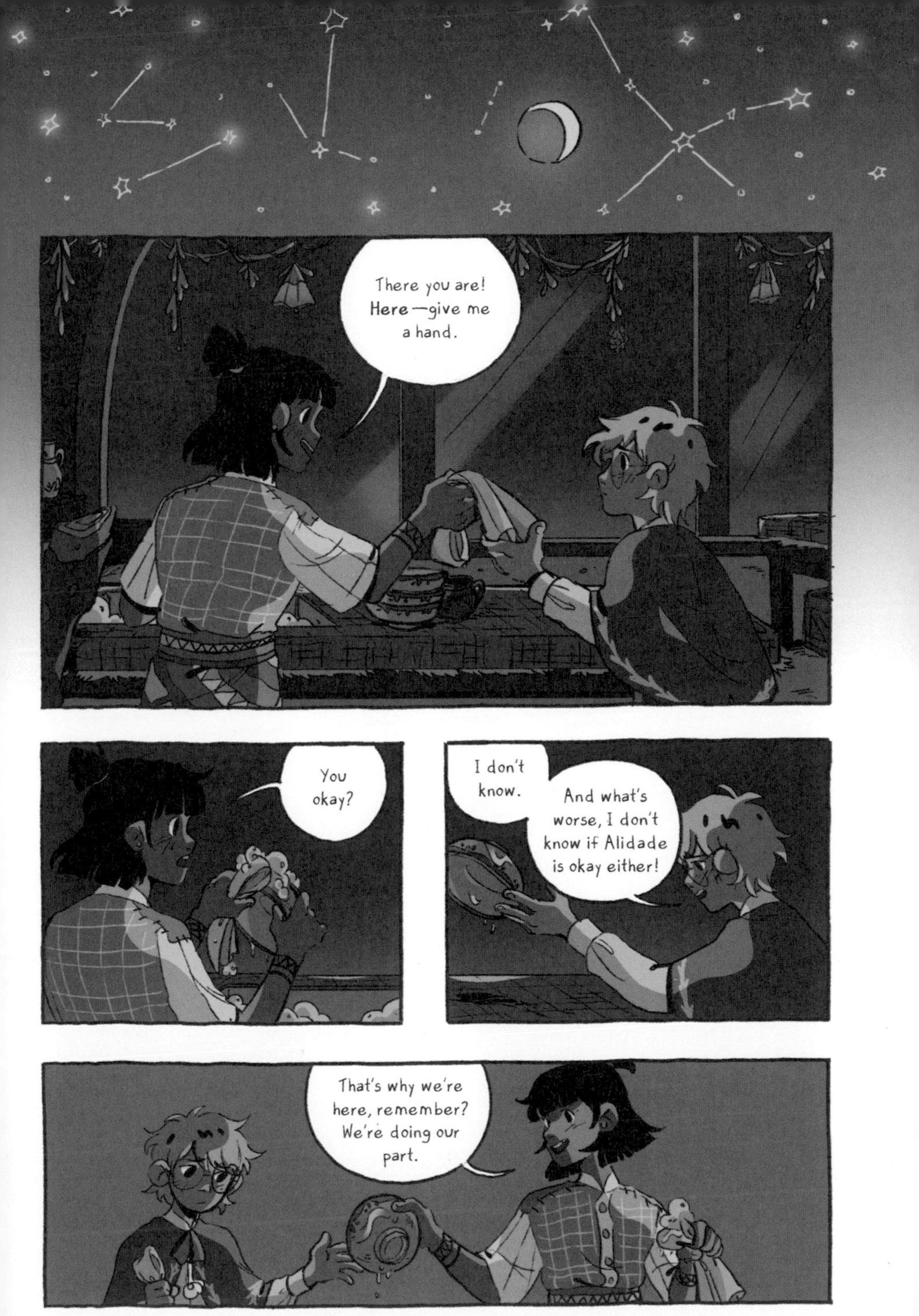
There you are! Here—give me a hand.
You okay?
I don't know.
And what's worse, I don't know if Alidade is okay either!
That's why we're here, remember? We're doing our part.

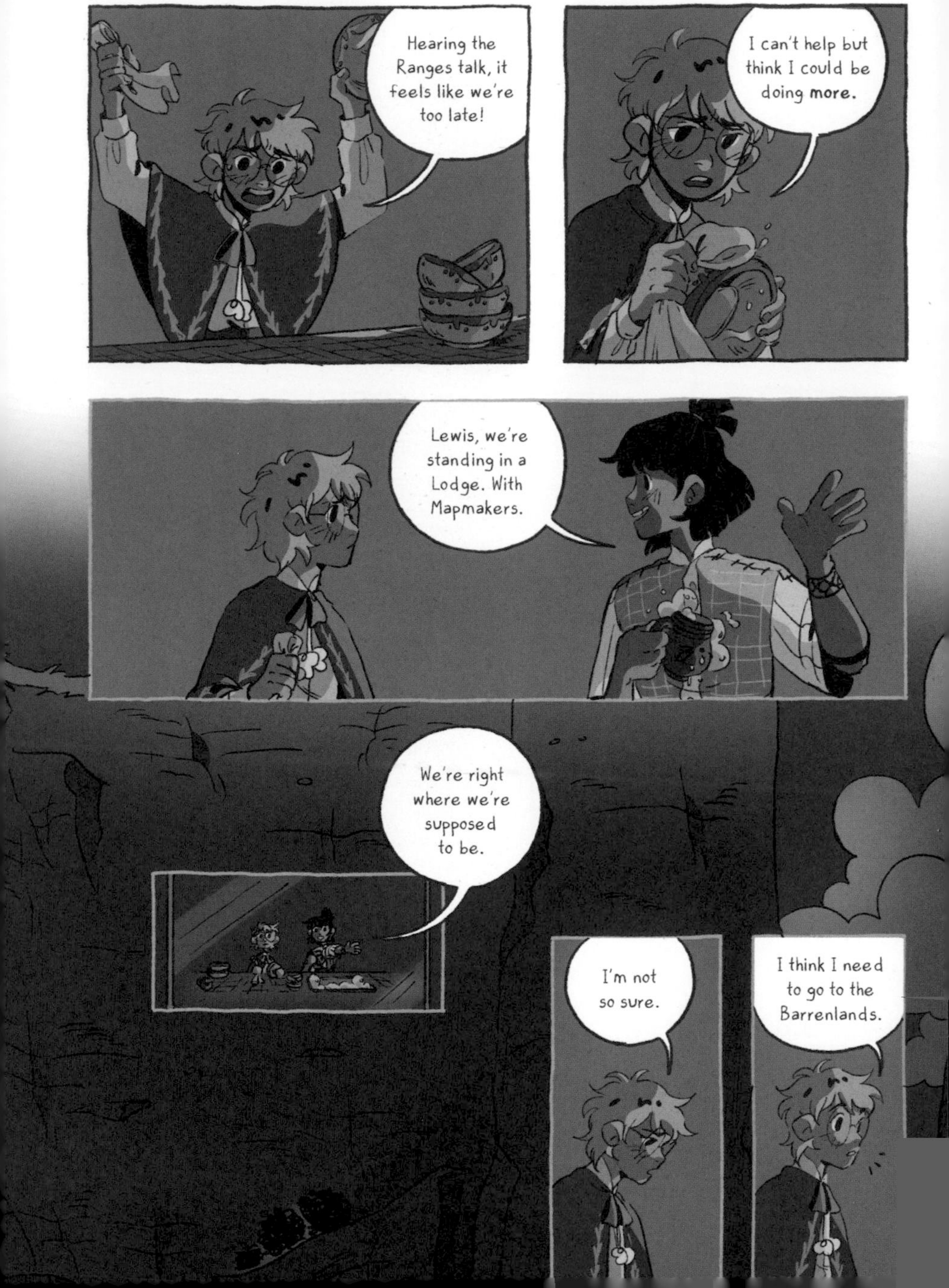
Hearing the Ranges talk, it feels like we're too late!
I can't help but think I could be doing **more.**
Lewis, we're standing in a Lodge. With Mapmakers.
We're right where we're supposed to be.
I'm not so sure.
I think I need to go to the Barrenlands.

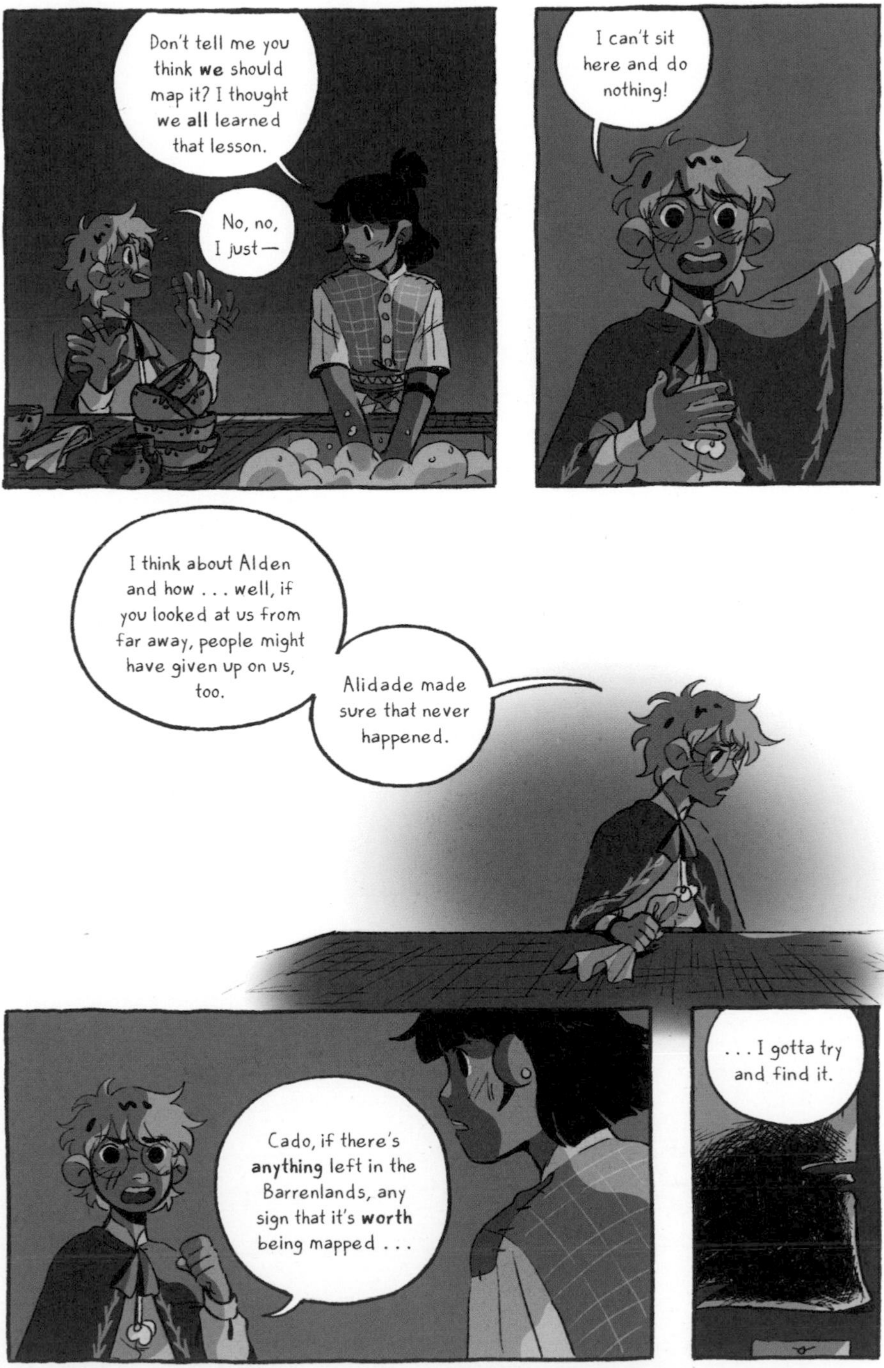
Don't tell me you think **we** should map it? I thought we **all** learned that lesson.
No, no, I just—
I can't sit here and do nothing!
I think about Alden and how . . . well, if you looked at us from far away, people might have given up on us, too.
Alidade made sure that never happened.
Cado, if there's **anything** left in the Barrenlands, any sign that it's **worth** being mapped . . .
. . . I gotta try and find it.

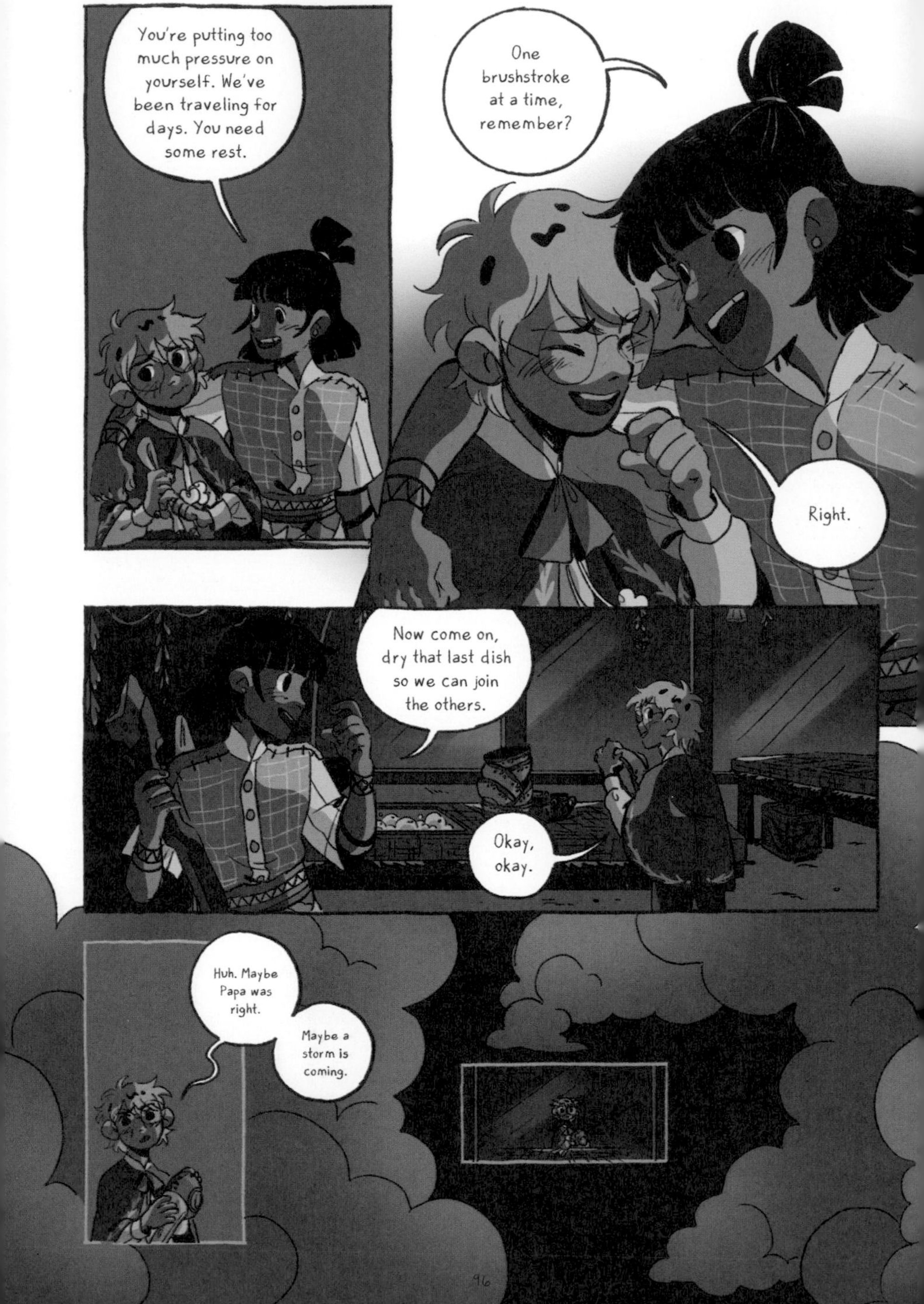
You're putting too much pressure on yourself. We've been traveling for days. You need some rest.
One brushstroke at a time, remember?
Right.
Now come on, dry that last dish so we can join the others.
Okay, okay.
Huh. Maybe Papa was right.
Maybe a storm is coming.

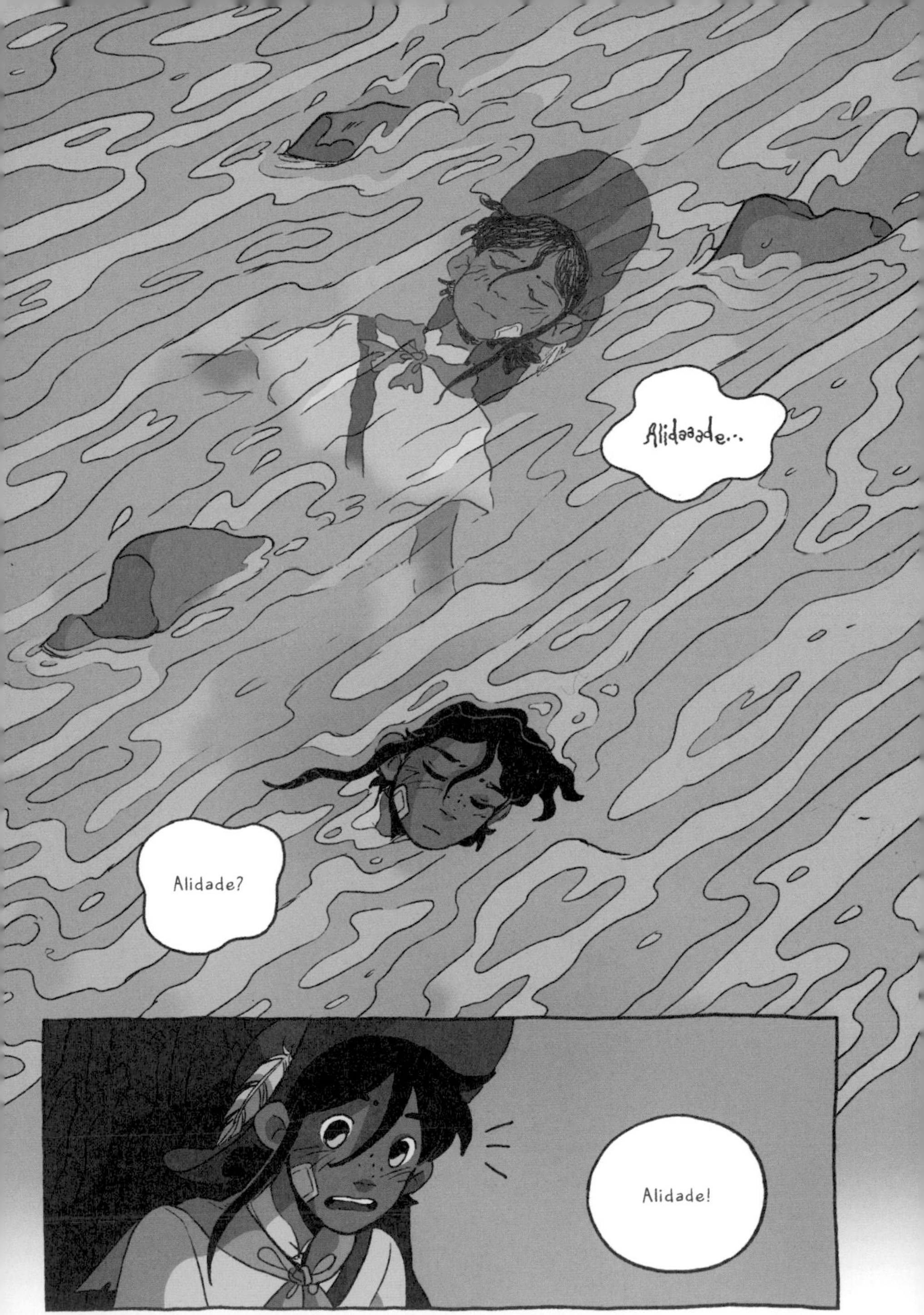
Alidaaade...
Alidade?
Alidade!

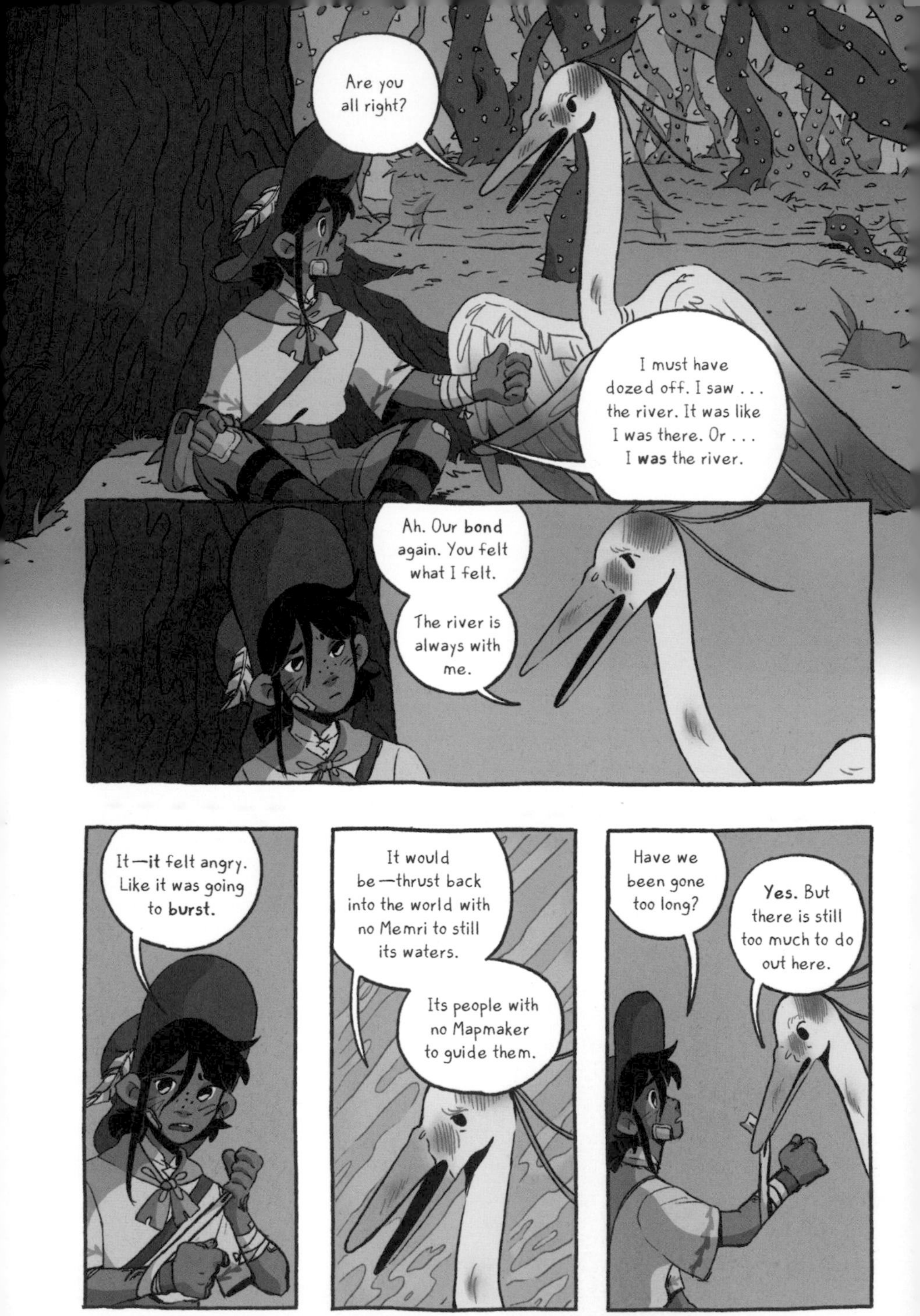
Are you all right?
I must have dozed off. I saw . . . the river. It was like I was there. Or . . . I **was** the river.
Ah. Our **bond** again. You felt what I felt.
The river is always with me.
It—**it** felt angry. Like it was going to **burst**.
It would be—thrust back into the world with no Memri to still its waters.
Its people with no Mapmaker to guide them.
Have we been gone too long?
Yes. But there is still too much to do out here.

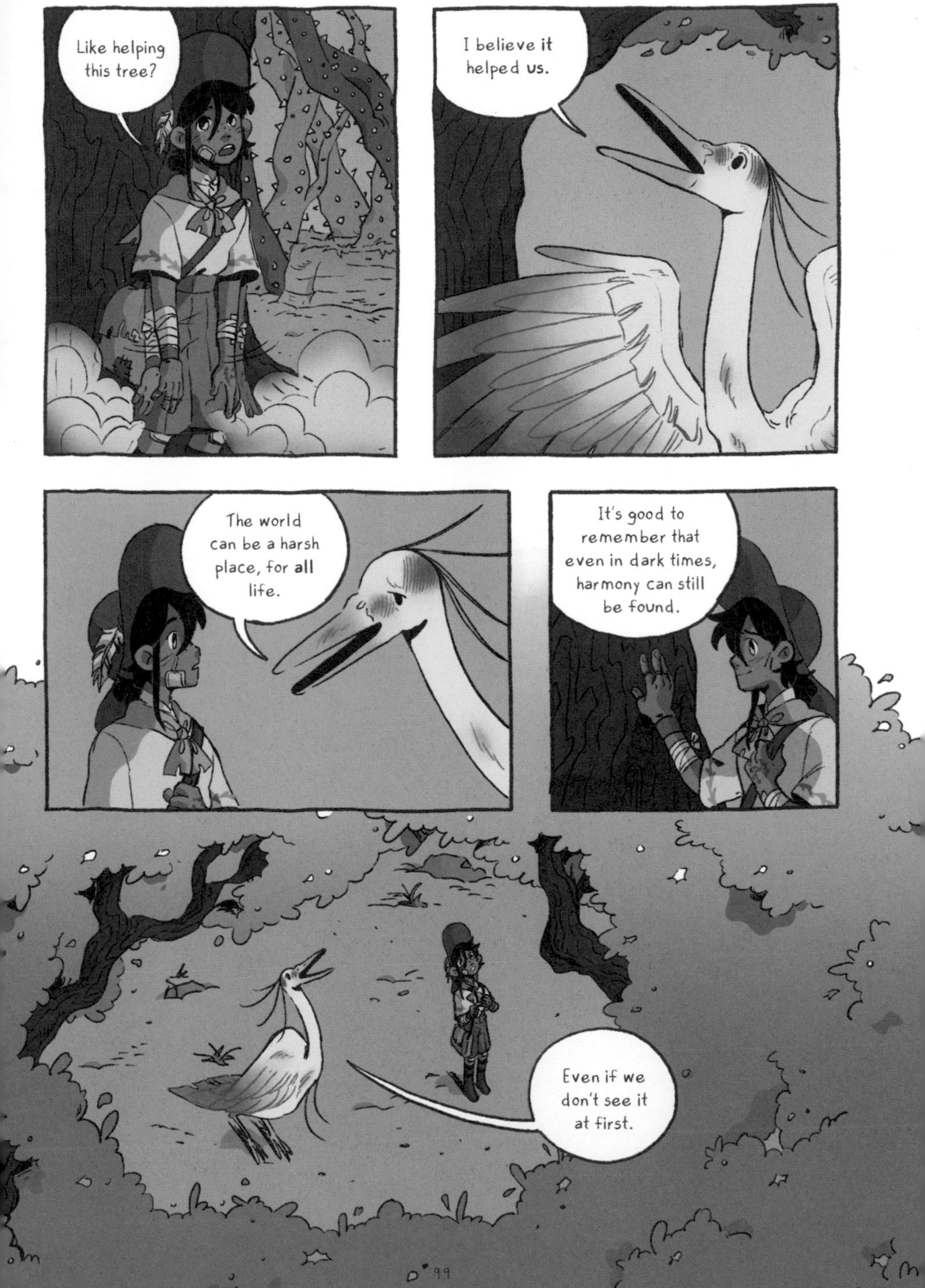
Like helping this tree?
I believe it helped us.
The world can be a harsh place, for all life.
It's good to remember that even in dark times, harmony can still be found.
Even if we don't see it at first.

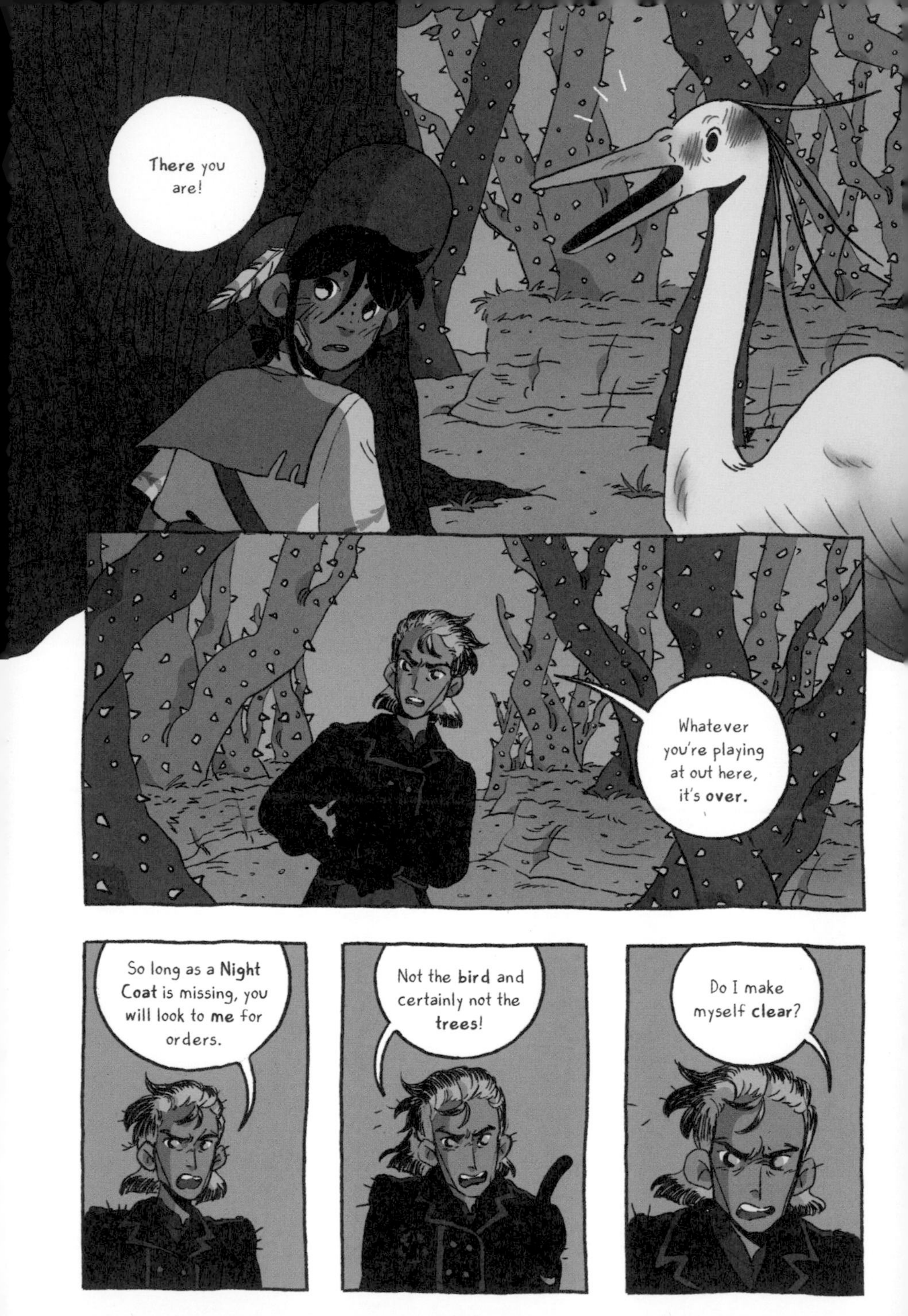
There you are!
Whatever you're playing at out here, it's over.
So long as a Night Coat is missing, you will look to me for orders.
Not the bird and certainly not the trees!
Do I make myself clear?

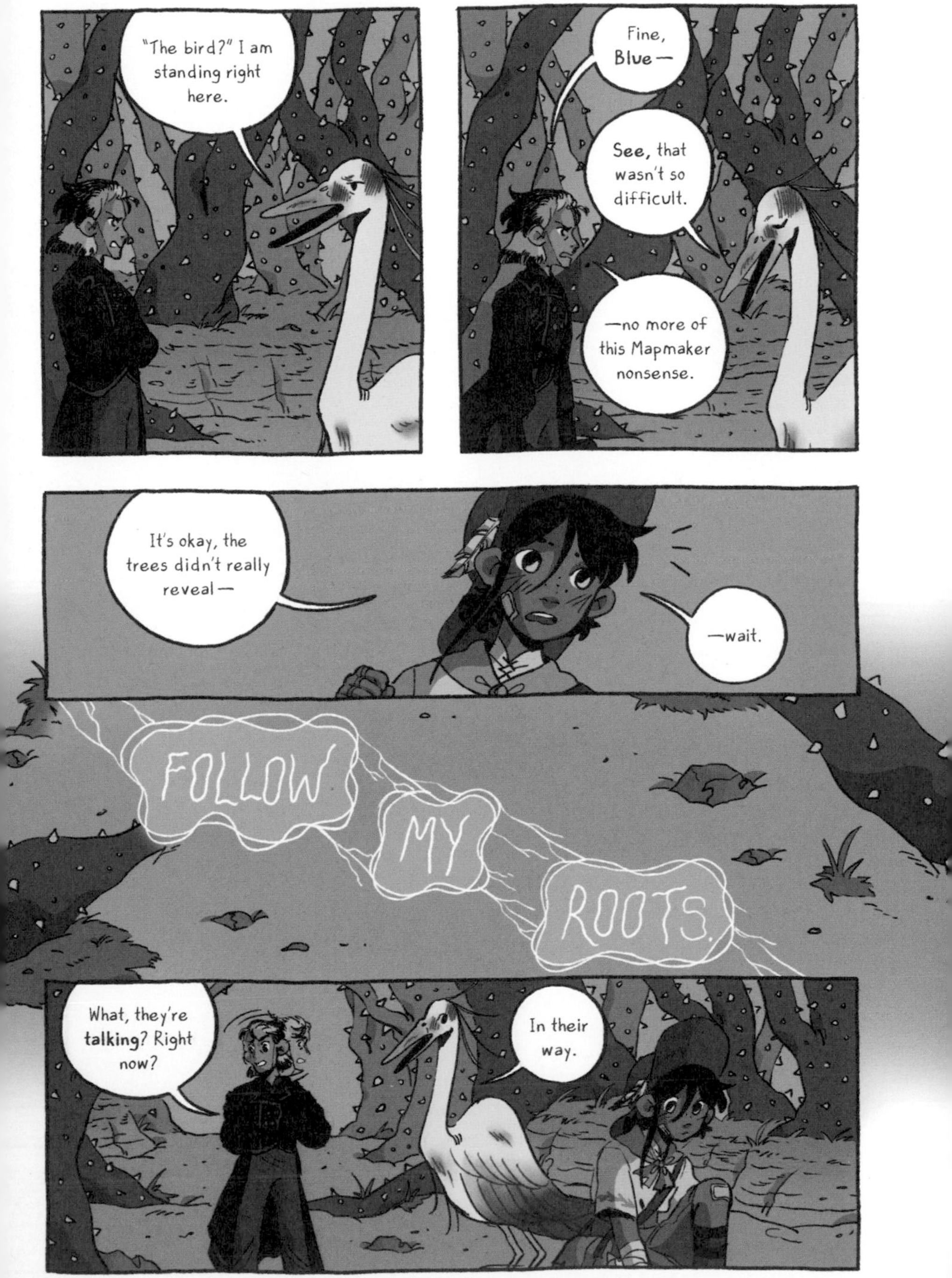
"The bird?" I am standing right here.
Fine, Blue—
See, that wasn't so difficult.
—no more of this Mapmaker nonsense.
It's okay, the trees didn't really reveal—
—wait.
FOLLOW
MY
ROOTS.
What, they're talking? Right now?
In their way.

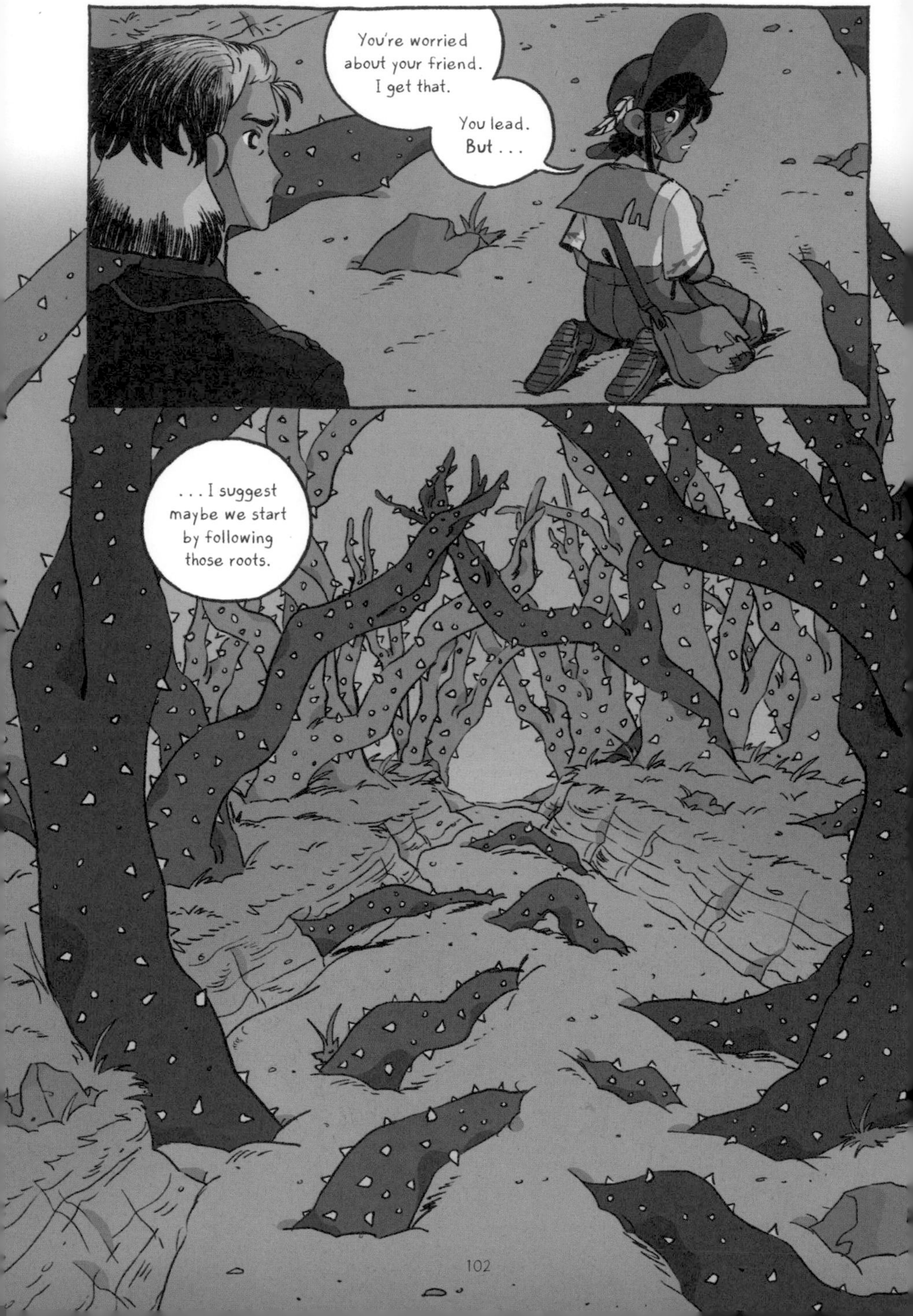
You're worried about your friend. I get that.
You lead. But . . .
. . . I suggest maybe we start by following those roots.

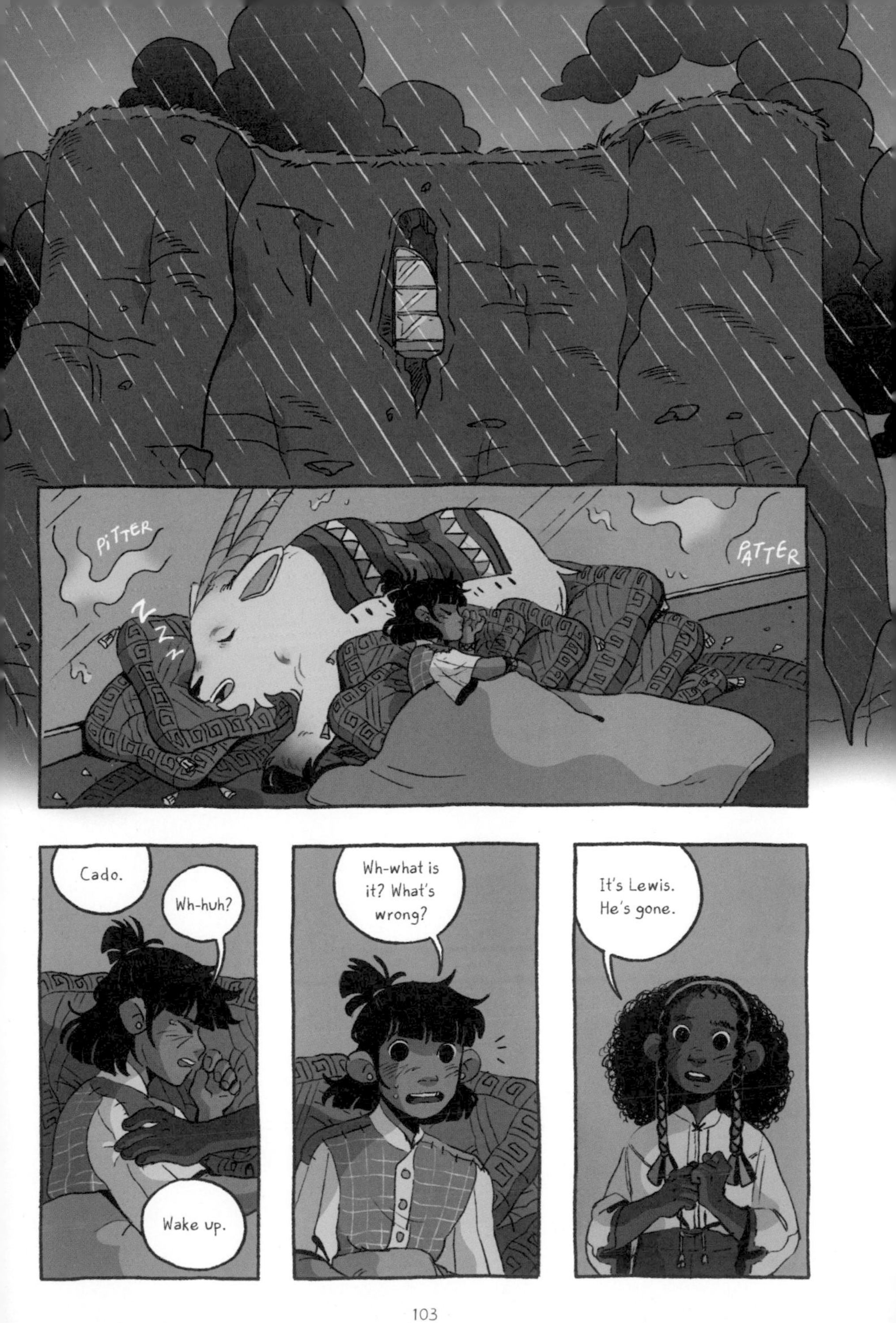
PITTER
PATTER
Z Z Z
Cado.
Wh-huh?
Wake up.
Wh-what is it? What's wrong?
It's Lewis. He's gone.

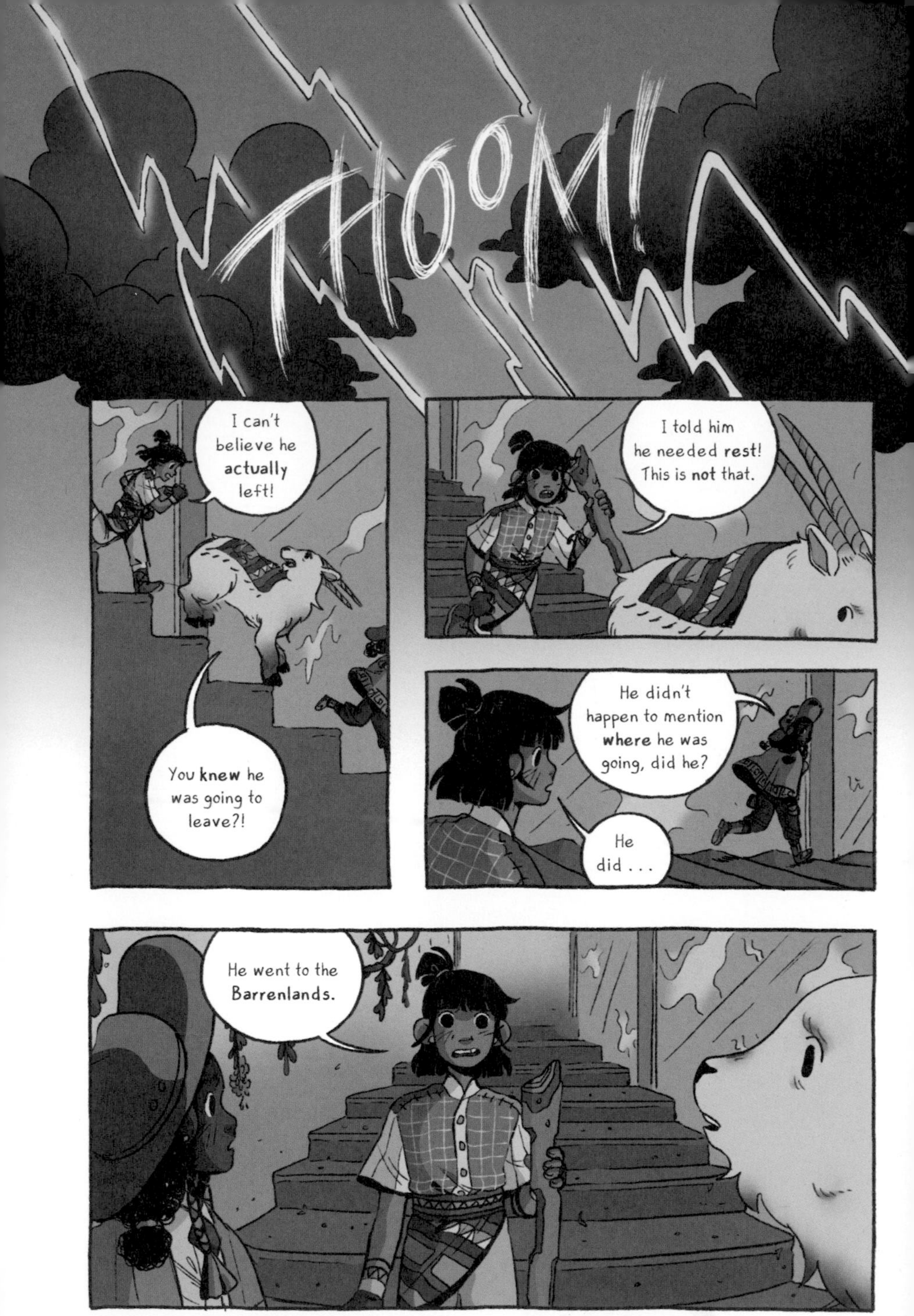
THOOM!
I can't believe he actually left!
You knew he was going to leave?!
I told him he needed rest! This is not that.
He didn't happen to mention where he was going, did he?
He did . . .
He went to the Barrenlands.

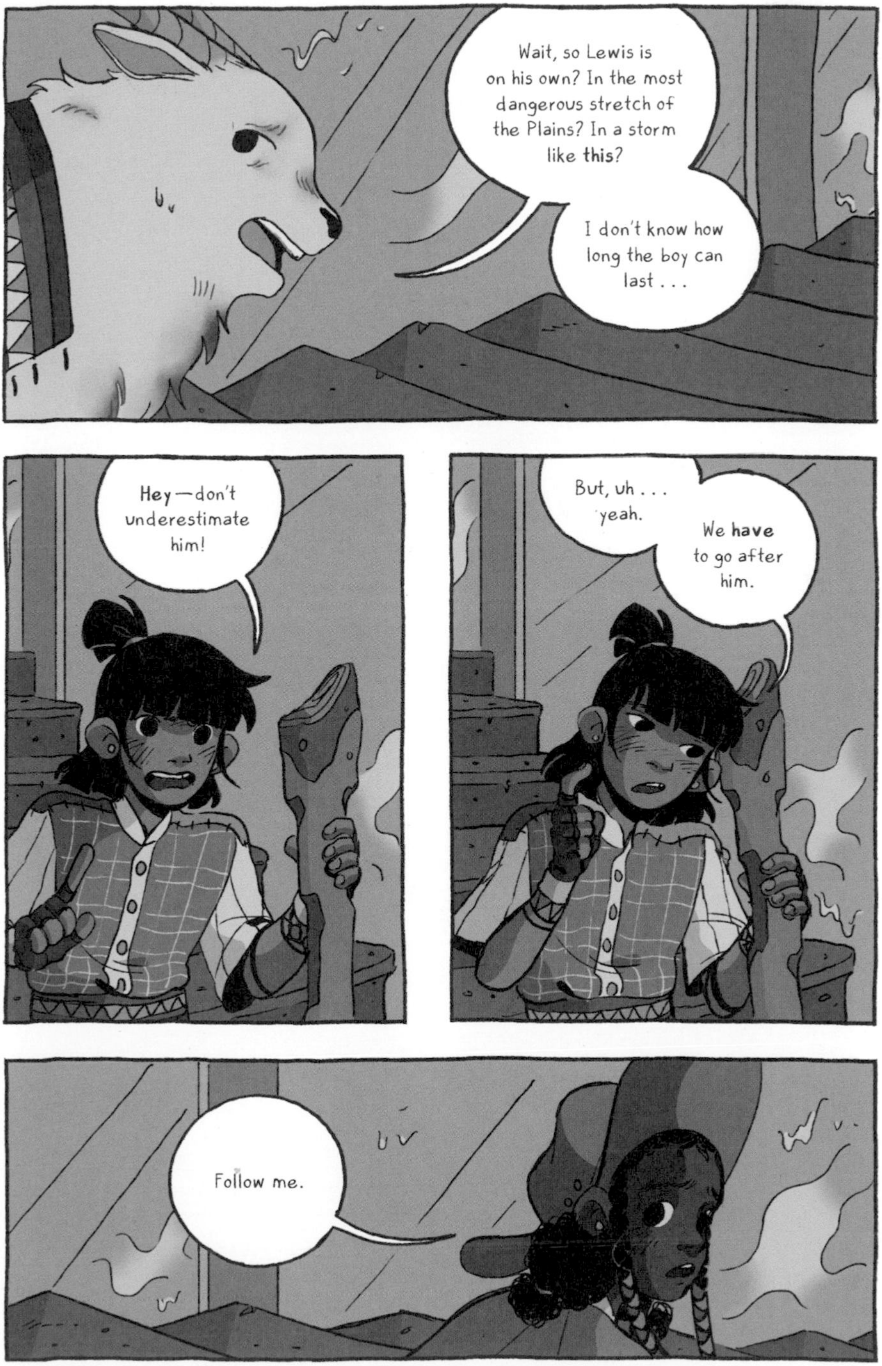
Wait, so Lewis is on his own? In the most dangerous stretch of the Plains? In a storm like **this**?
I don't know how long the boy can last . . .
Hey—don't underestimate him!
But, uh . . . yeah.
We **have** to go after him.
Follow me.

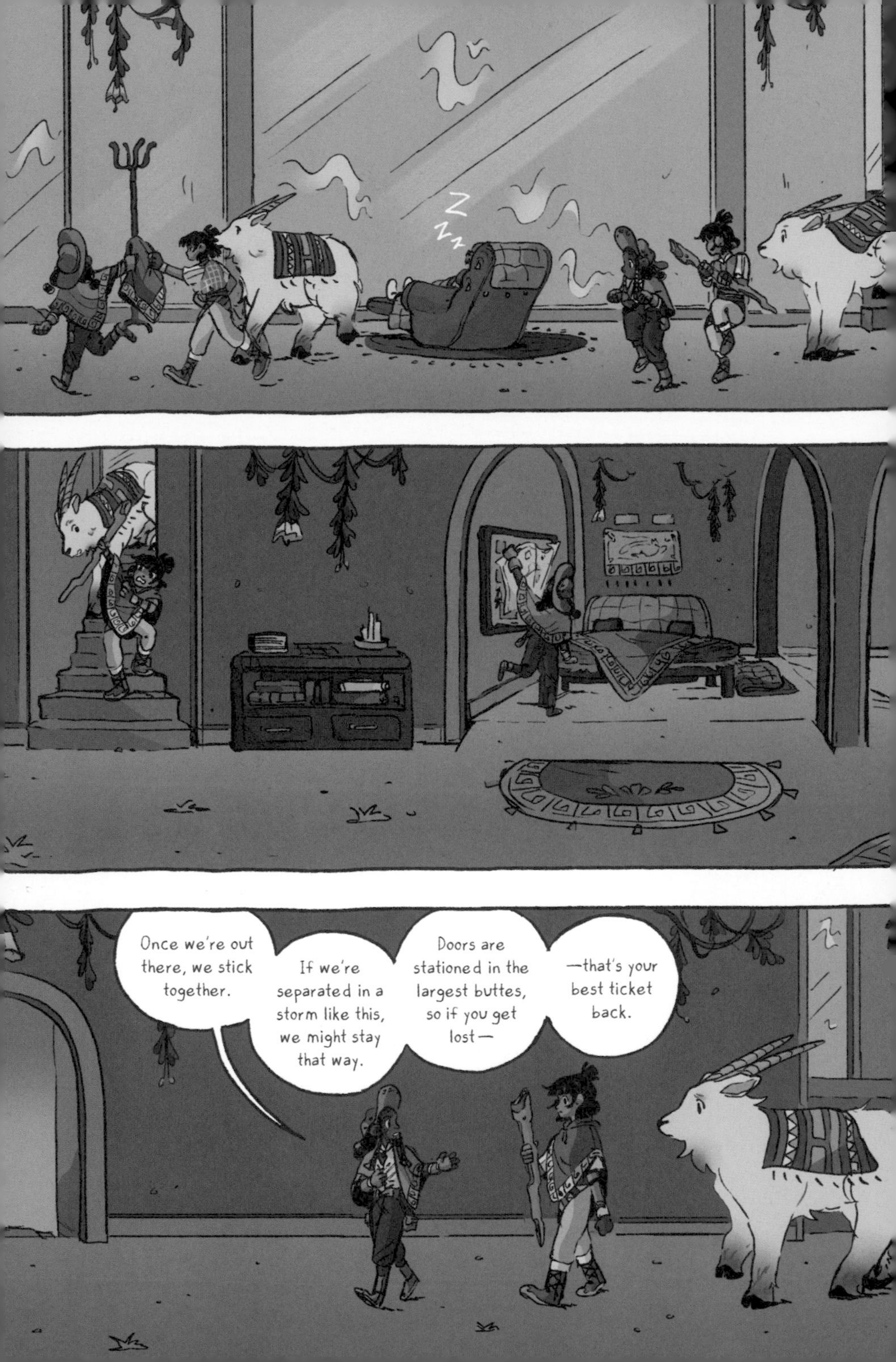
Z Z Z
Once we're out there, we stick together.
If we're separated in a storm like this, we might stay that way.
Doors are stationed in the largest buttes, so if you get lost—
—that's your best ticket back.

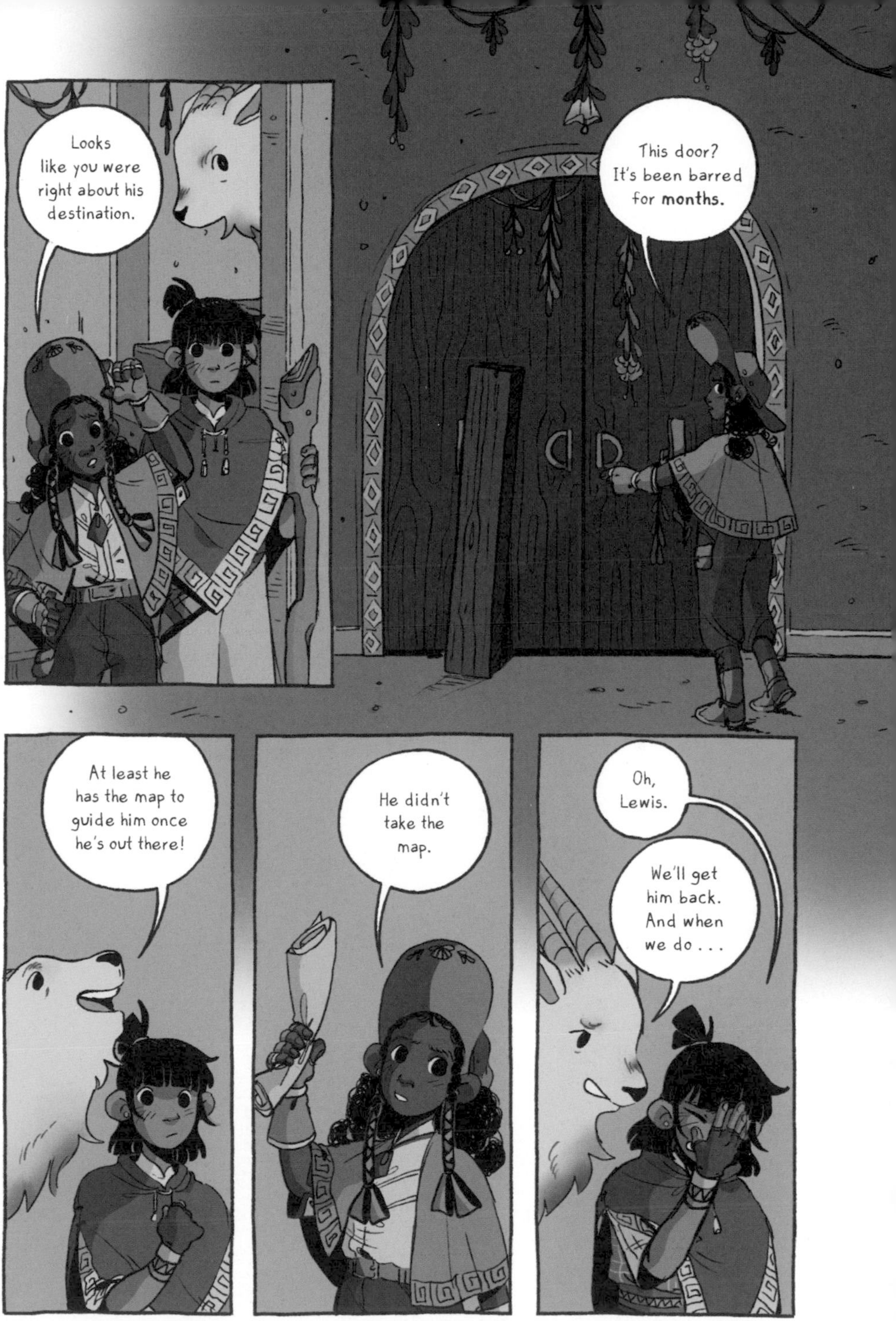
Looks like you were right about his destination.
This door? It's been barred for **months.**
At least he has the map to guide him once he's out there!
He didn't take the map.
Oh, Lewis.
We'll get him back. And when we do . . .

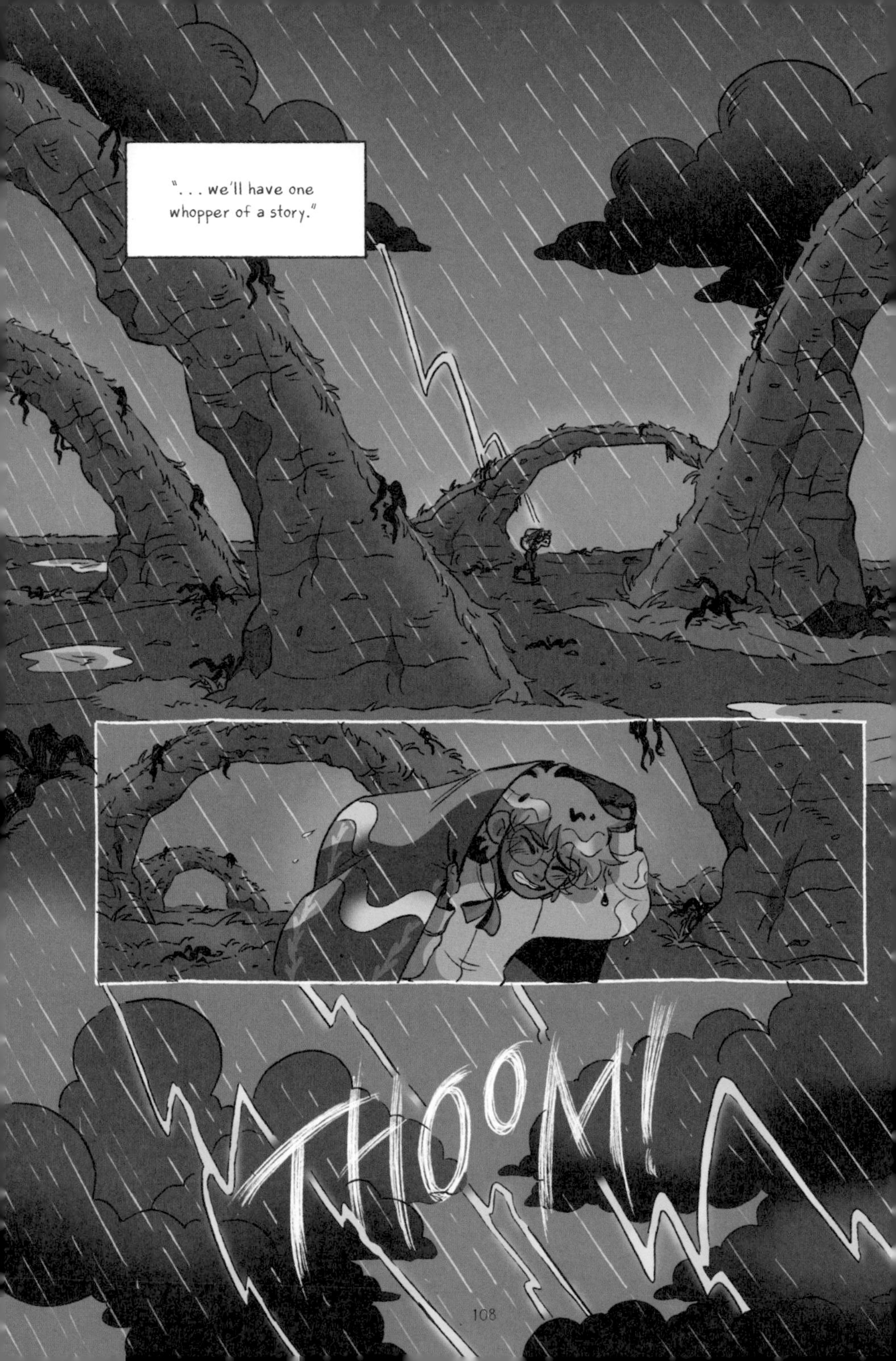
". . . we'll have one whopper of a story."
THOOM!

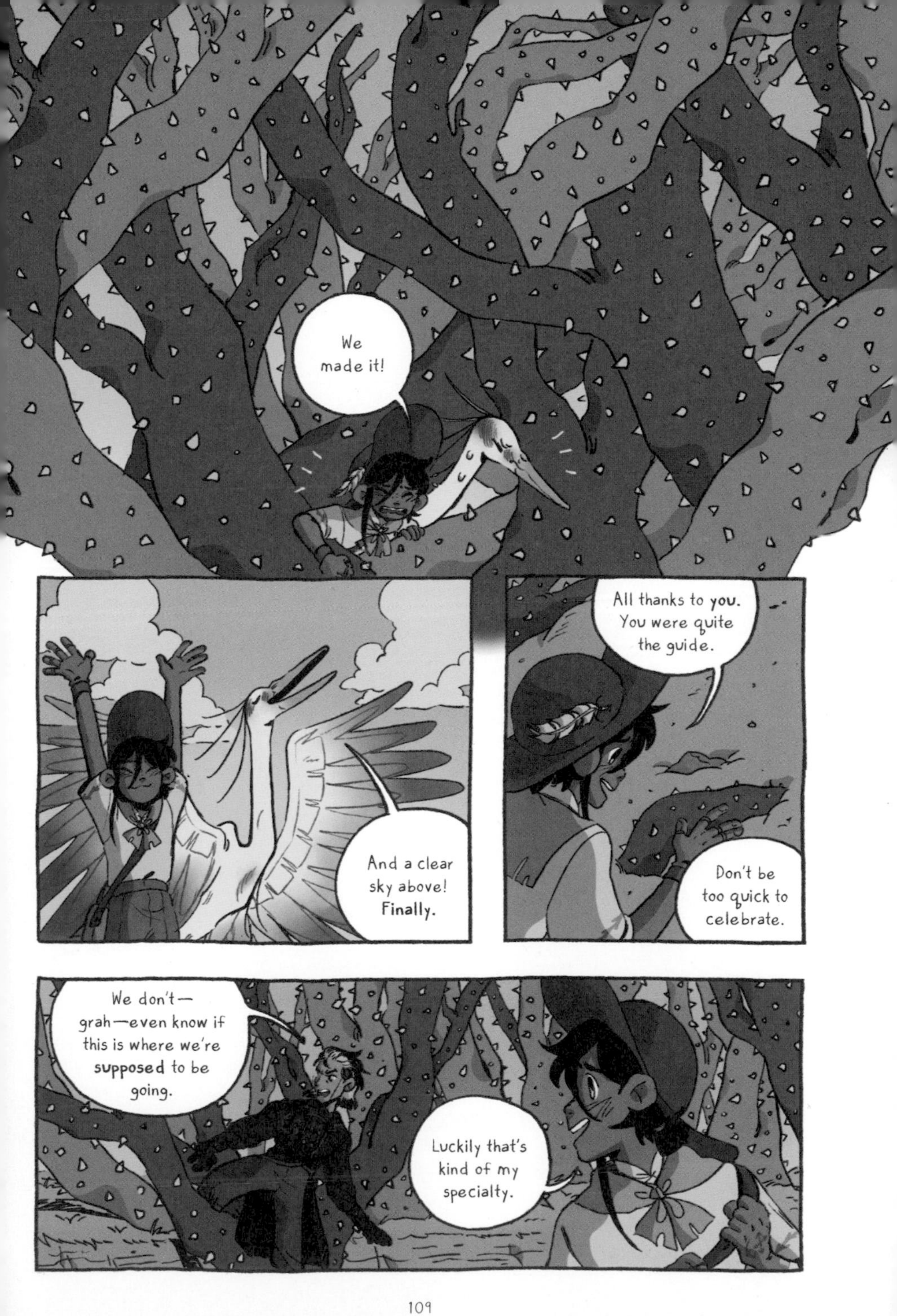
We made it!
And a clear sky above! **Finally.**
All thanks to **you.** You were quite the guide.
Don't be too quick to celebrate.
We don't—grah—even know if this is where we're **supposed** to be going.
Luckily that's kind of my specialty.

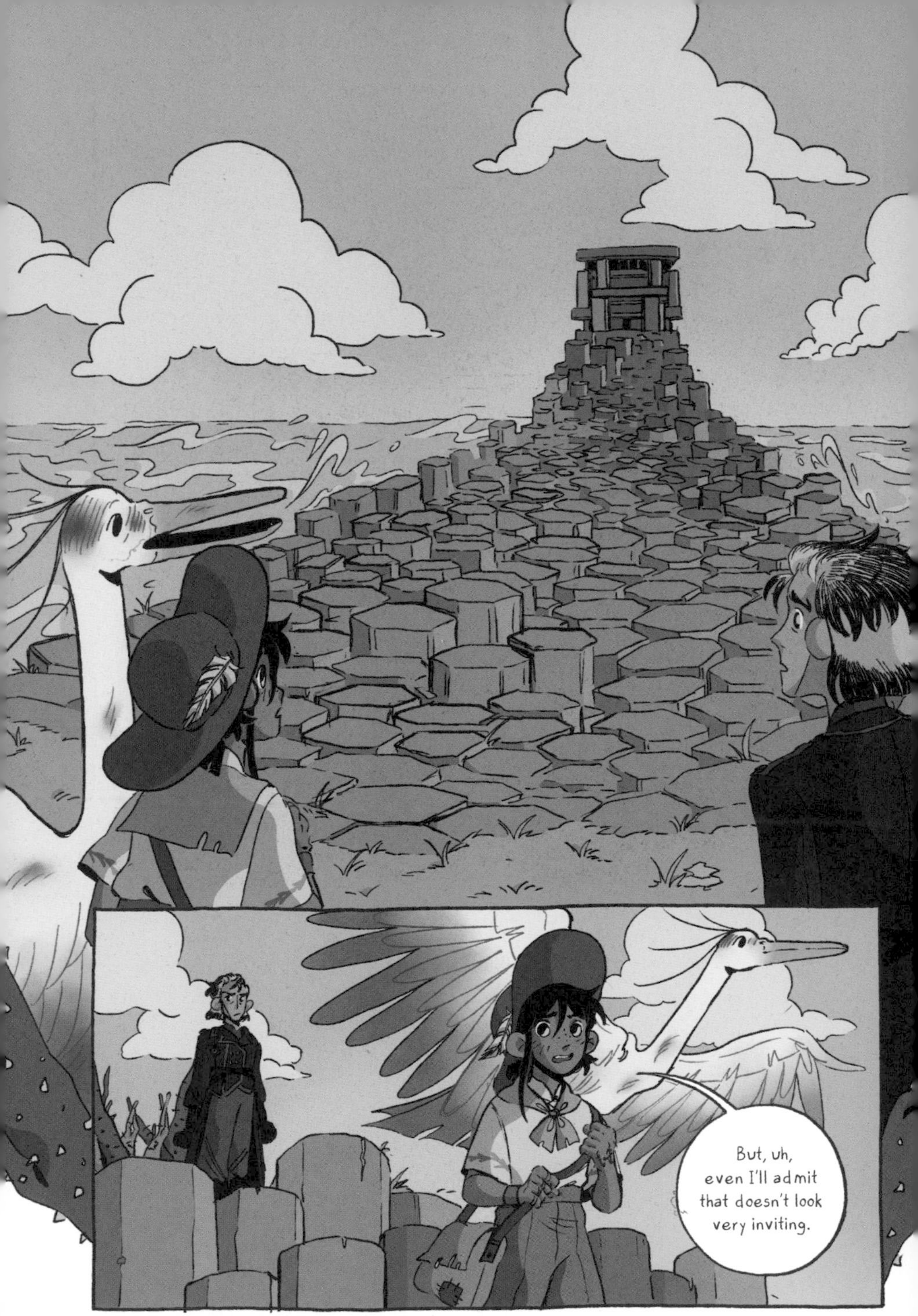
But, uh, even I'll admit that doesn't look very inviting.

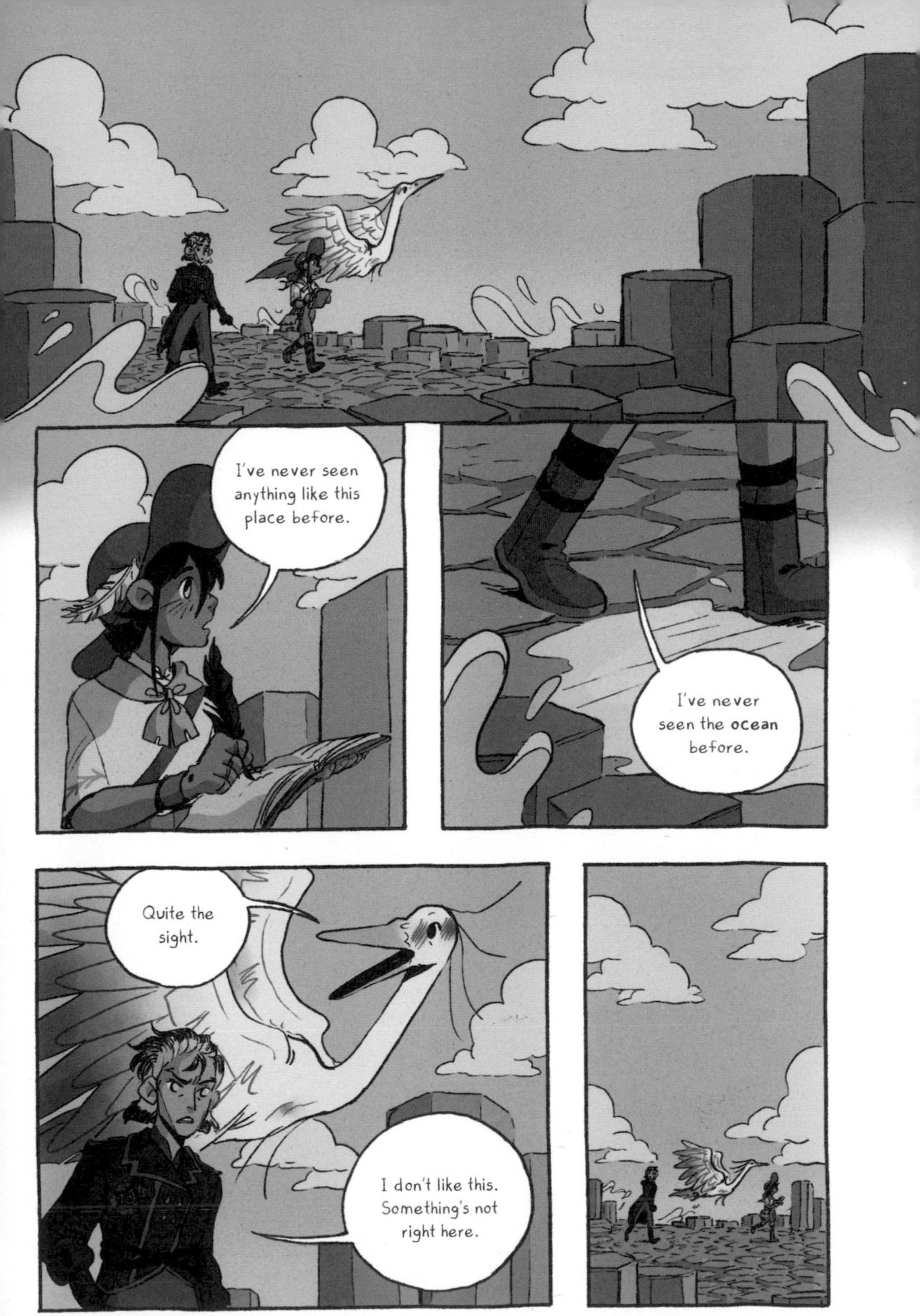
I've never seen anything like this place before.
I've never seen the **ocean** before.
Quite the sight.
I don't like this. Something's not right here.

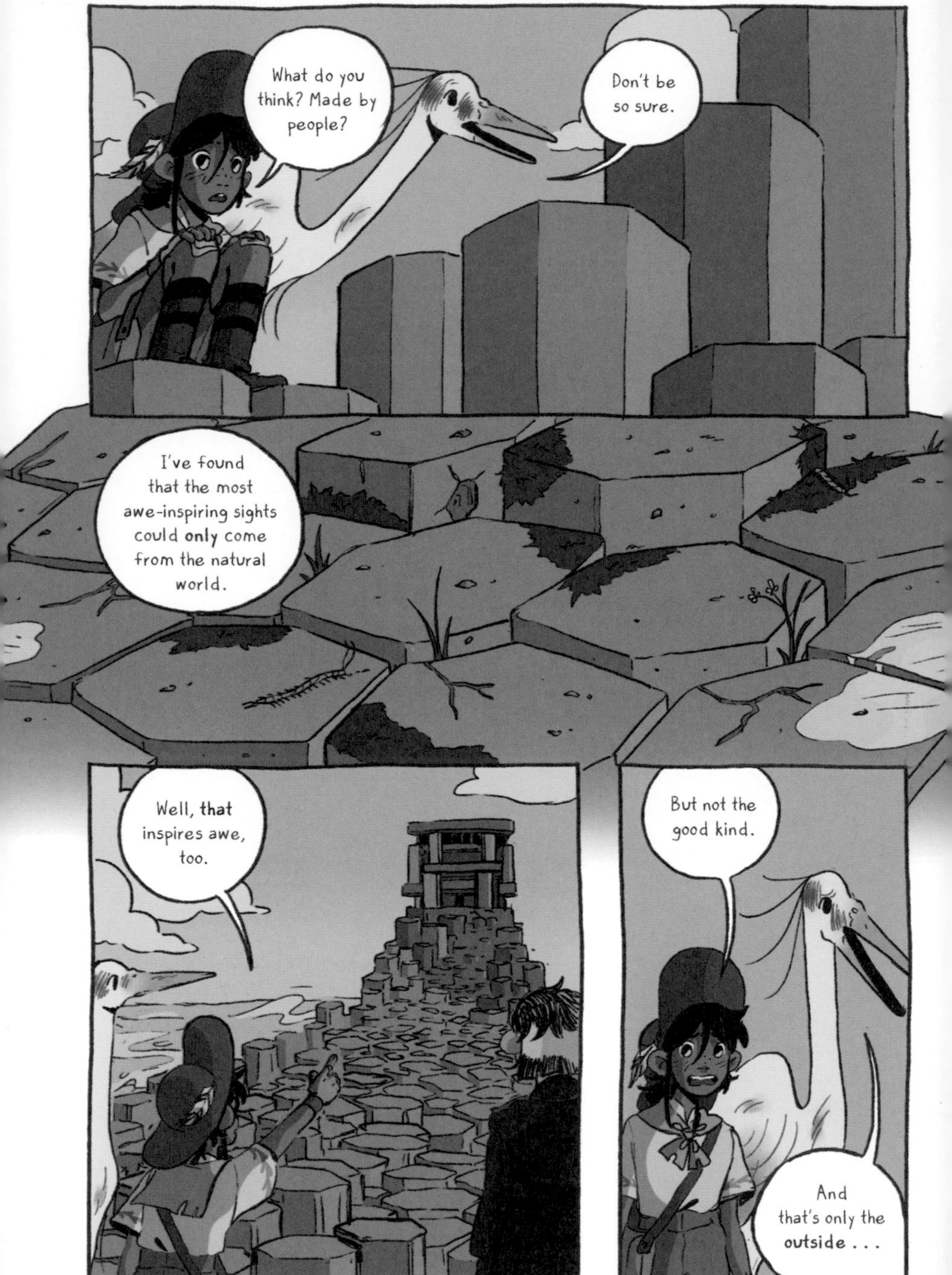

What do you think? Made by people?
Don't be so sure.
I've found that the most awe-inspiring sights could **only** come from the natural world.
Well, **that** inspires awe, too.
But not the good kind.
And that's only the **outside** . . .

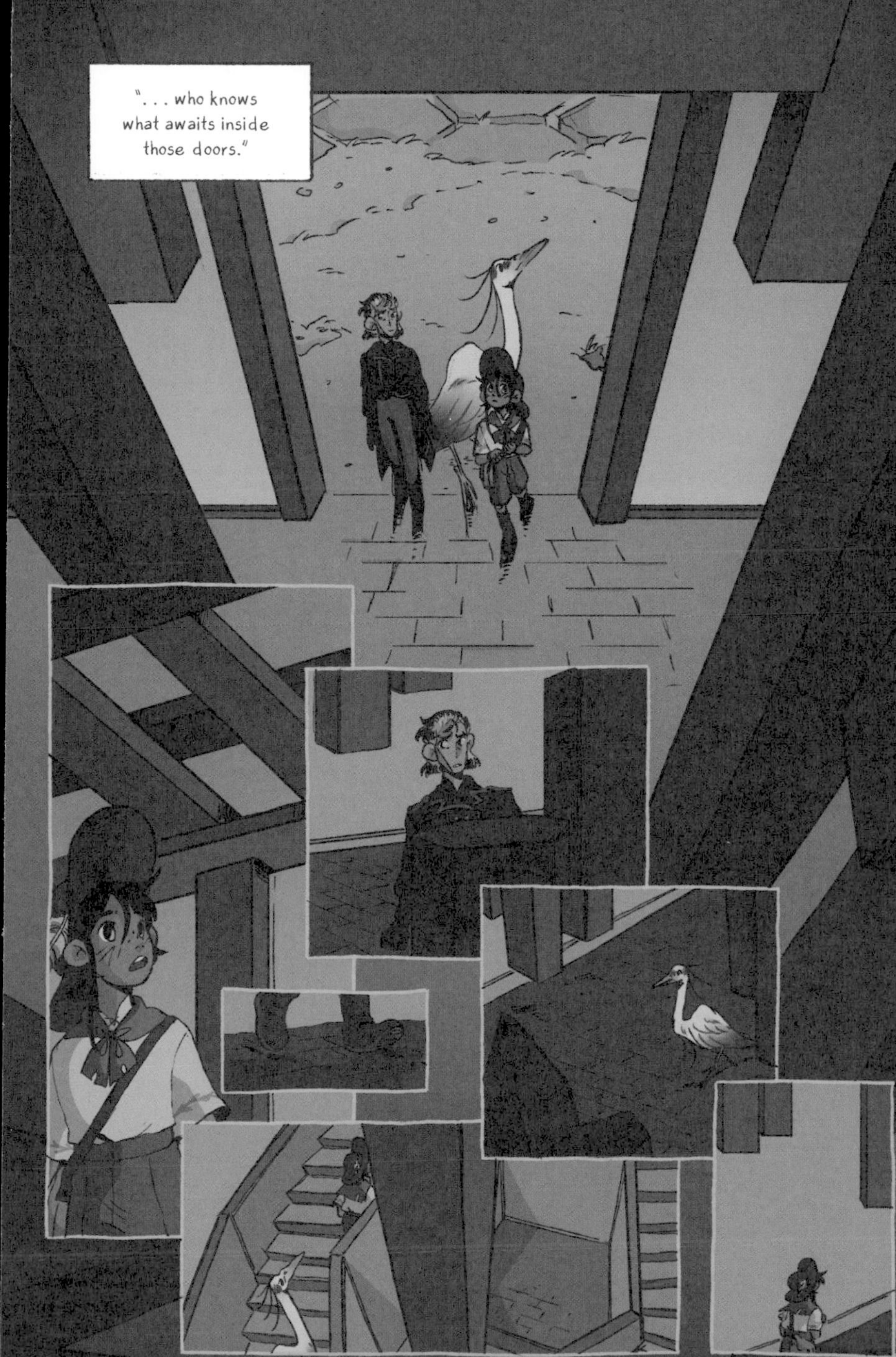
". . . who knows what awaits inside those doors."

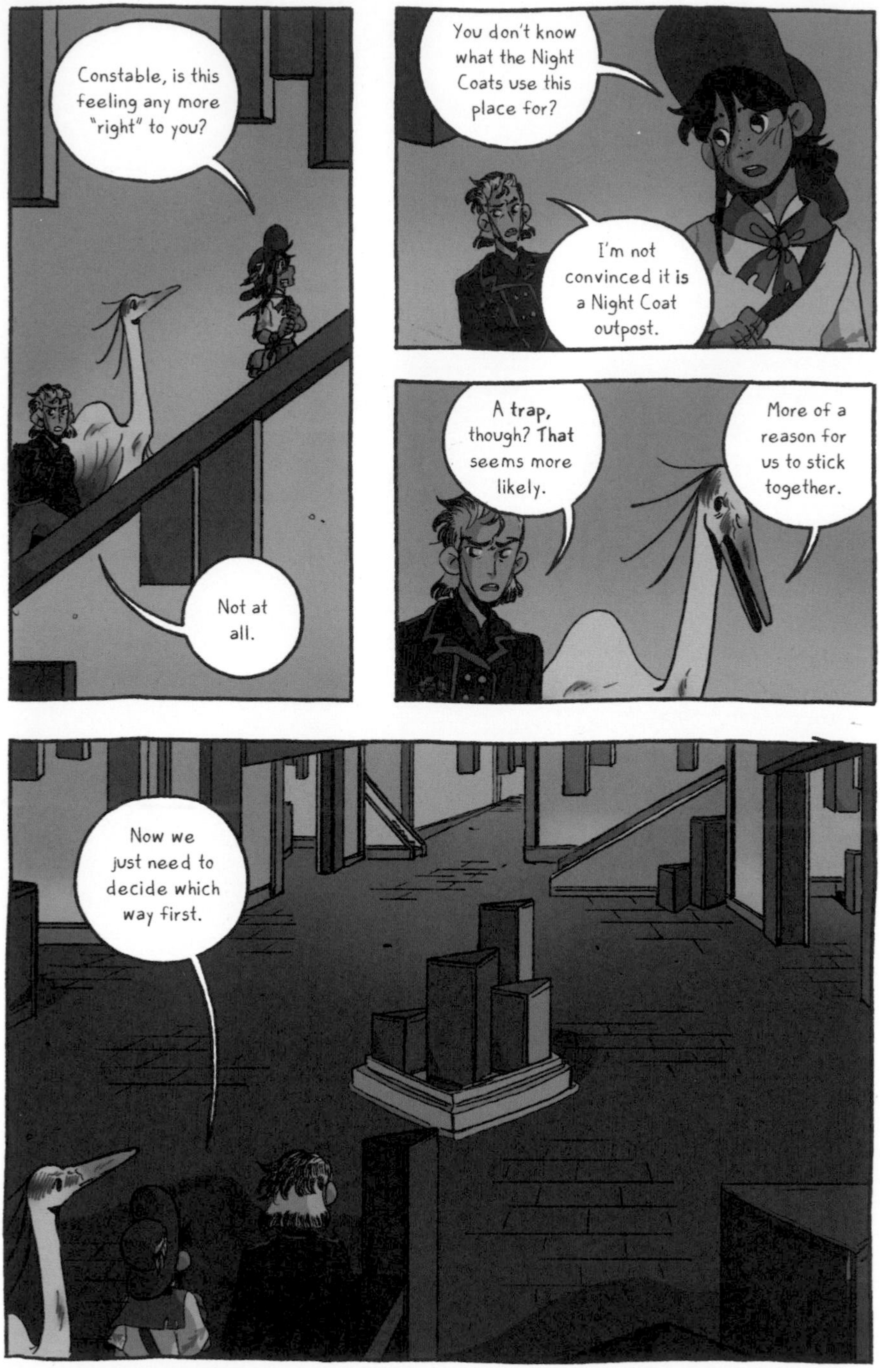
Constable, is this feeling any more "right" to you?
Not at all.
You don't know what the Night Coats use this place for?
I'm not convinced it **is** a Night Coat outpost.
A **trap**, though? **That** seems more likely.
More of a reason for us to stick together.
Now we just need to decide which way first.

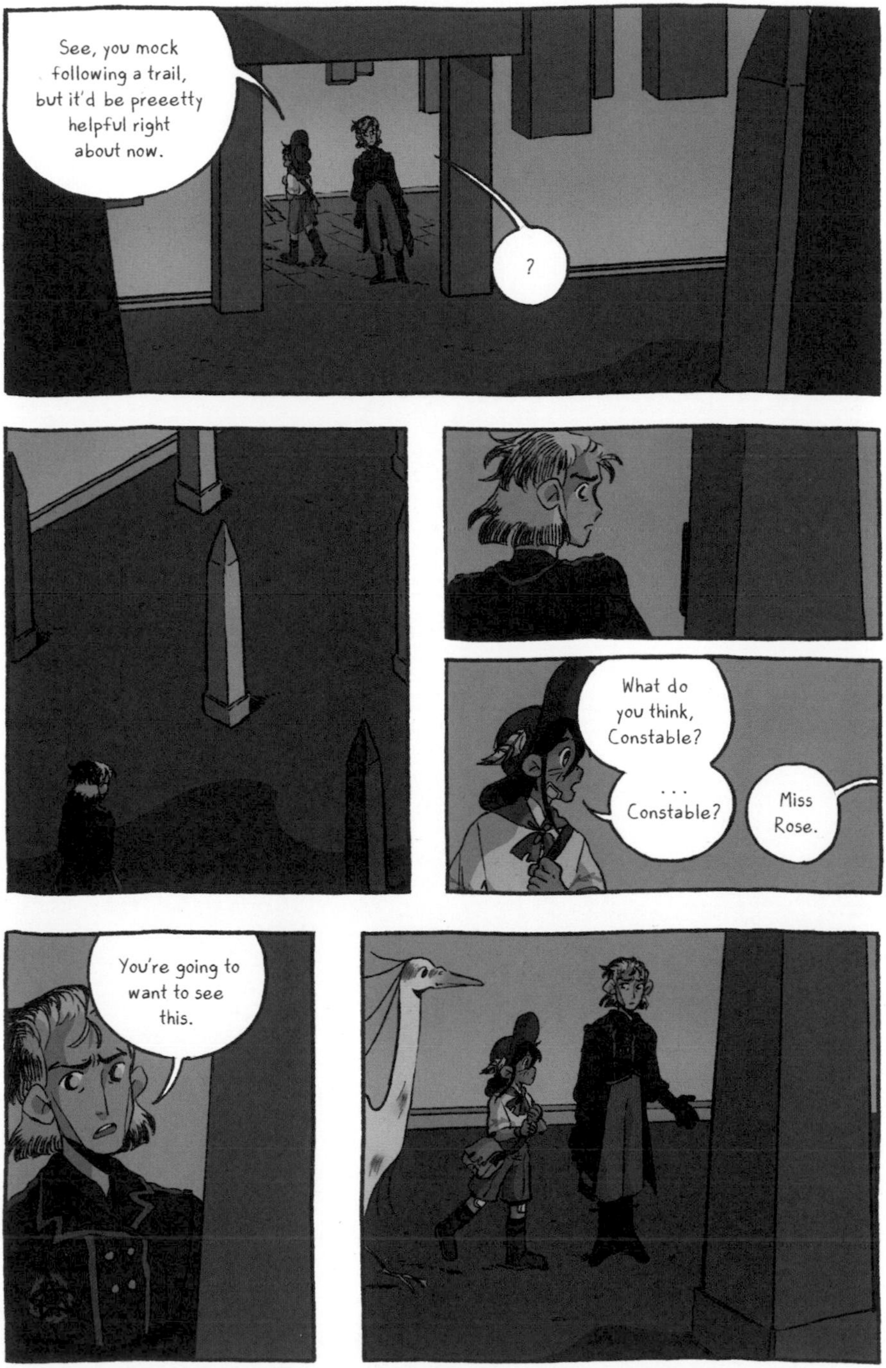
See, you mock following a trail, but it'd be preeetty helpful right about now.
?
What do you think, Constable?
... Constable?
Miss Rose.
You're going to want to see this.

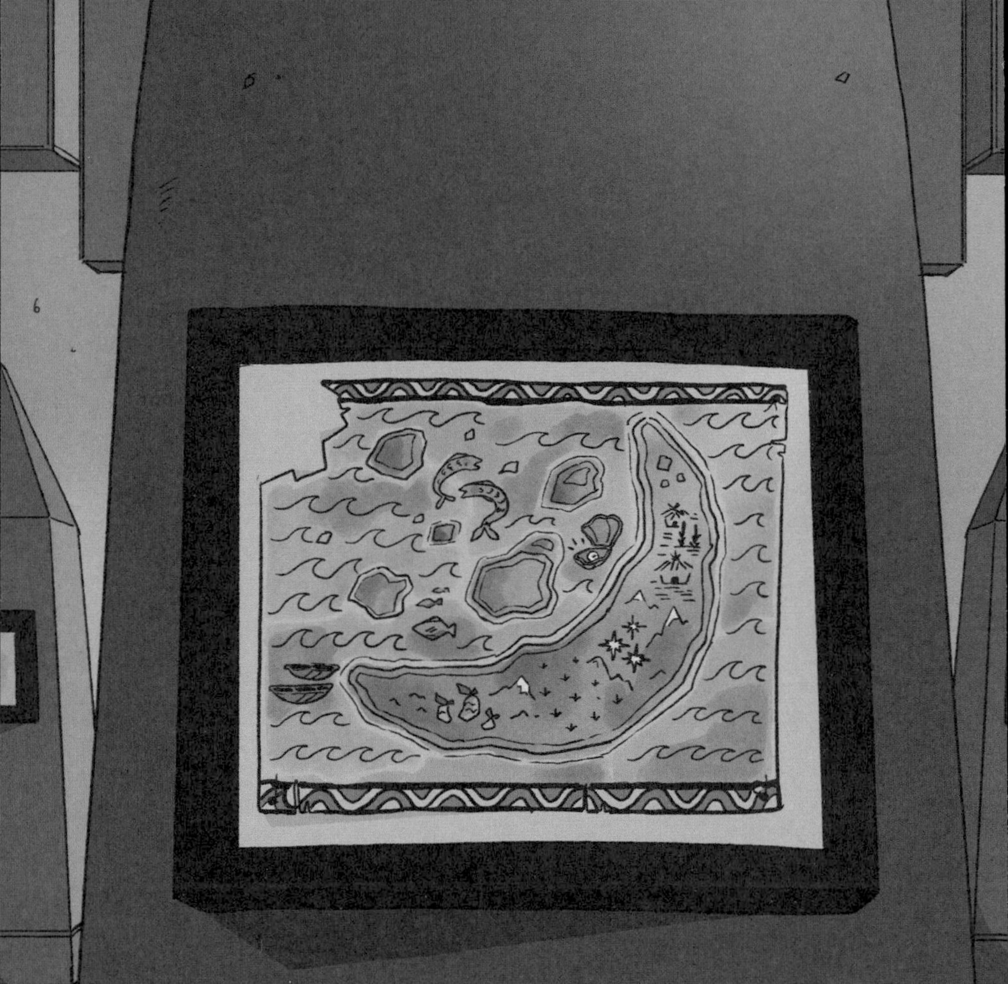

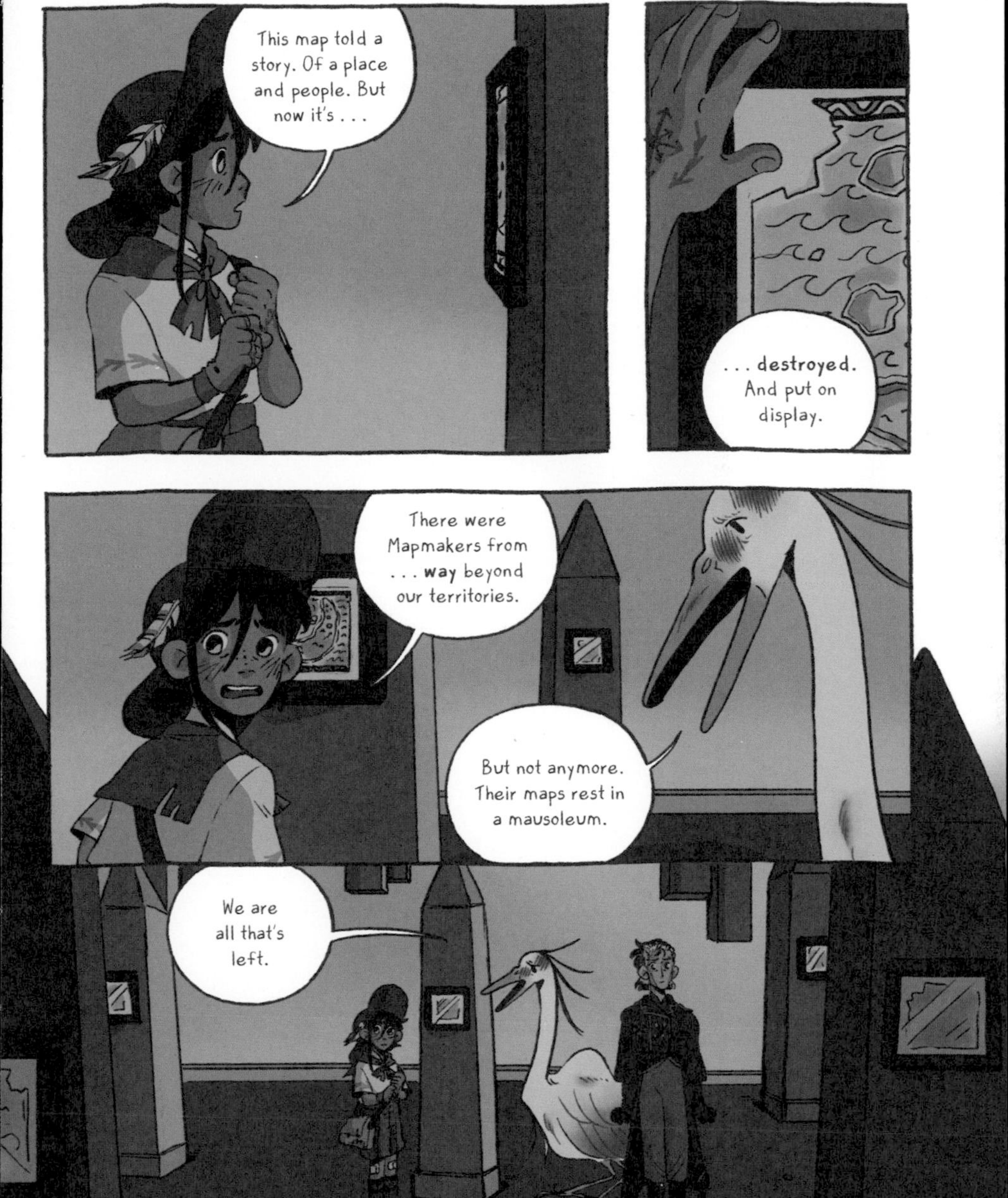
This map told a story. Of a place and people. But now it's . . .
. . . **destroyed.** And put on display.
There were Mapmakers from . . . **way** beyond our territories.
But not anymore. Their maps rest in a mausoleum.
We are all that's left.

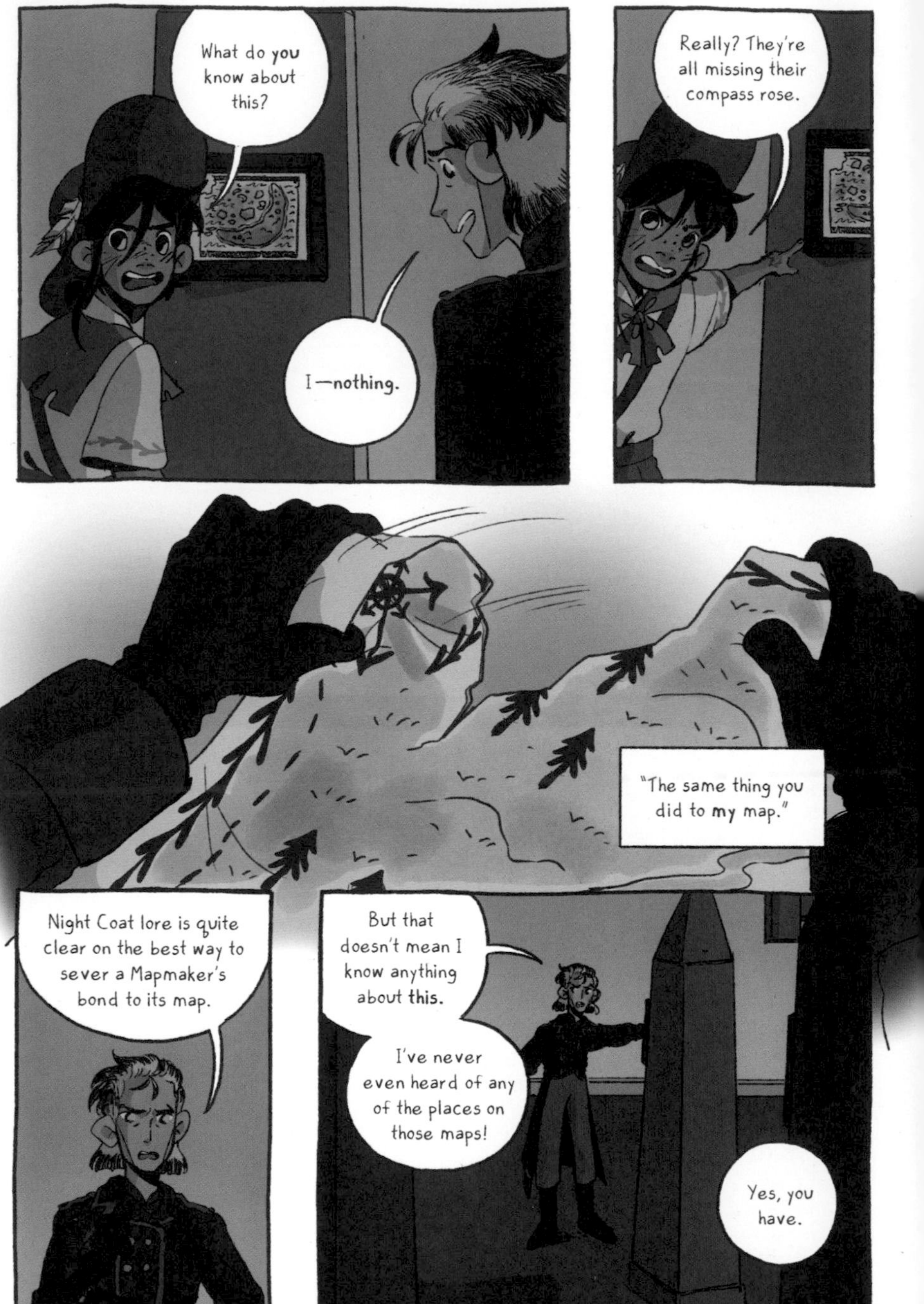

What do you know about this?
I—nothing.
Really? They're all missing their compass rose.
"The same thing you did to my map."
Night Coat lore is quite clear on the best way to sever a Mapmaker's bond to its map.
But that doesn't mean I know anything about this.
I've never even heard of any of the places on those maps!
Yes, you have.

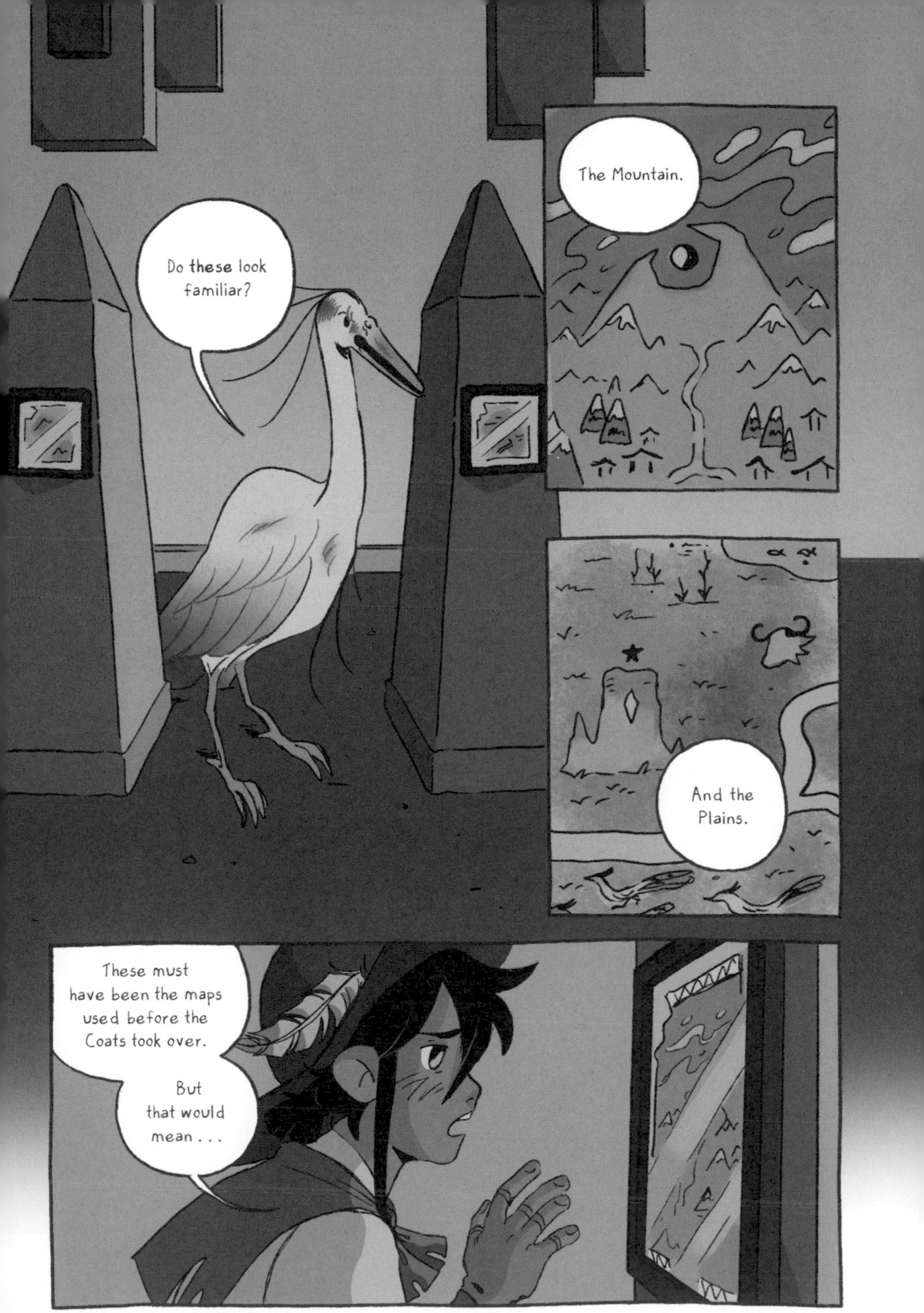
Do these look familiar?
The Mountain.
And the Plains.
These must have been the maps used before the Coats took over.
But that would mean . . .

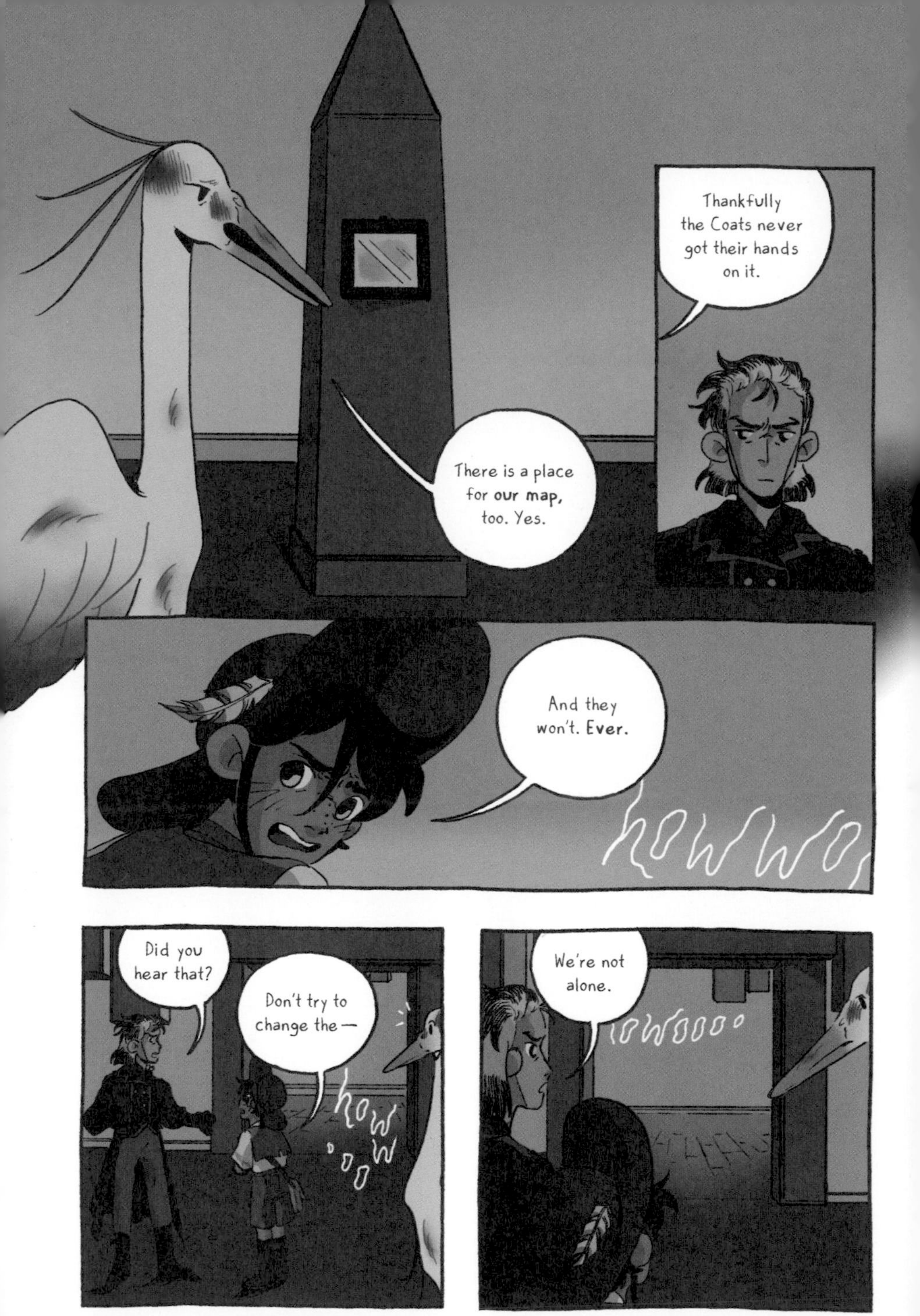

Thankfully the Coats never got their hands on it.
There is a place for **our map,** too. Yes.
And they won't. **Ever.**
HOWWOO
Did you hear that?
Don't try to change the—
HOWOOO
We're not alone.
OWOOOO

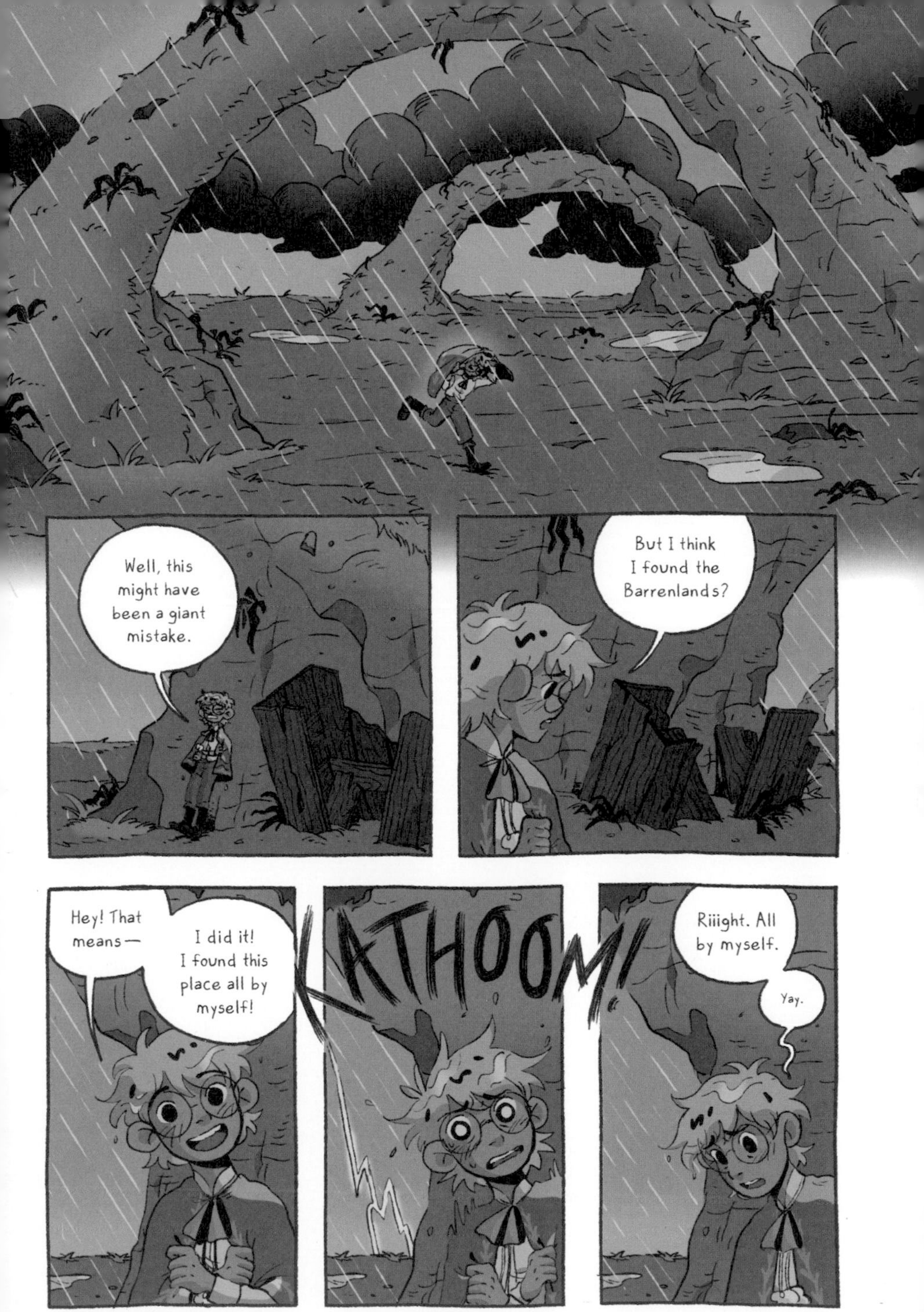

Well, this might have been a giant mistake.
But I think I found the Barrenlands?
Hey! That means—
I did it! I found this place all by myself!
KATHOOM!
Riiight. All by myself.
Yay.

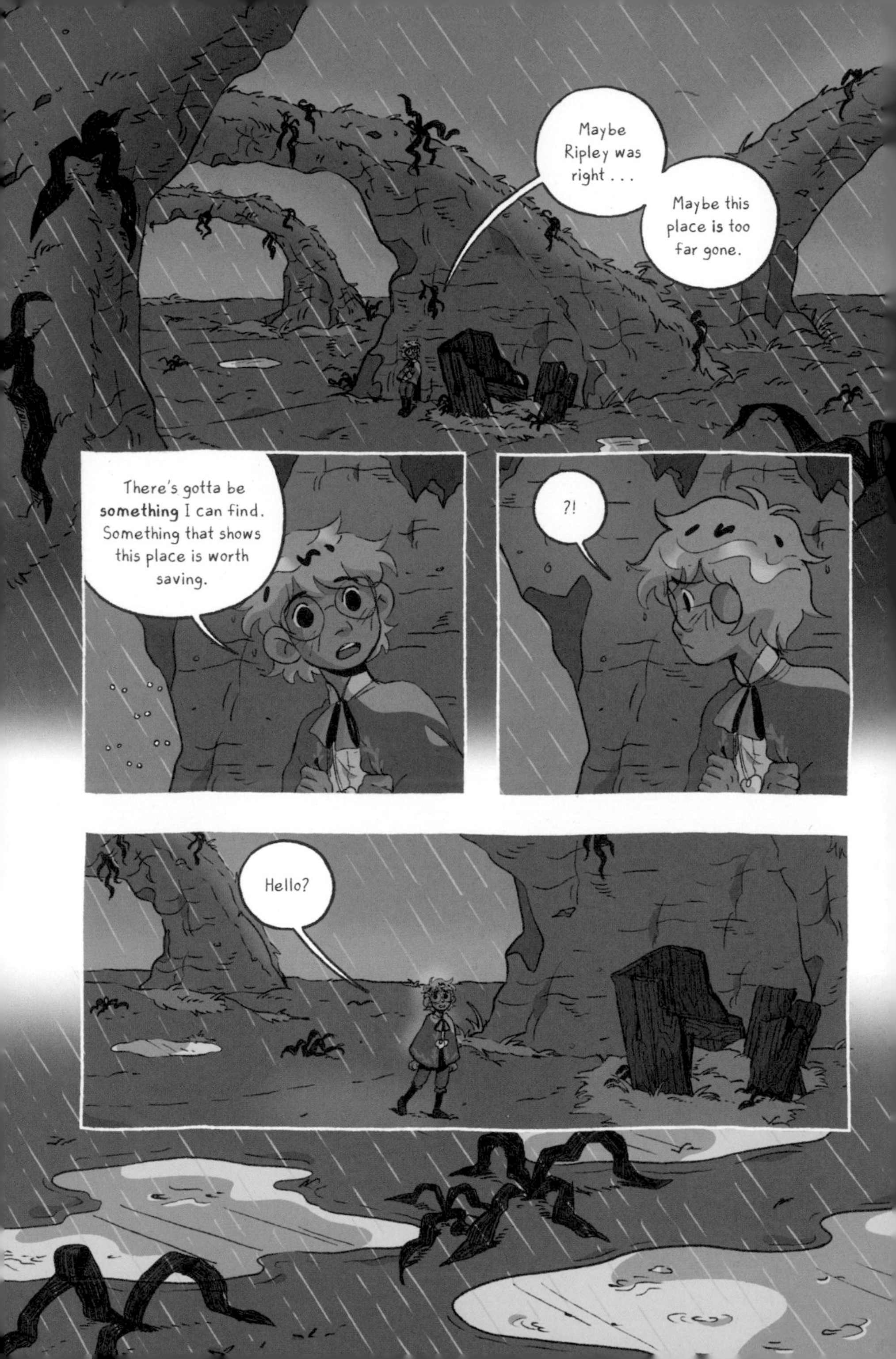
Maybe Ripley was right . . .
Maybe this place **is** too far gone.
There's gotta be **something** I can find. Something that shows this place is worth saving.
?!
Hello?

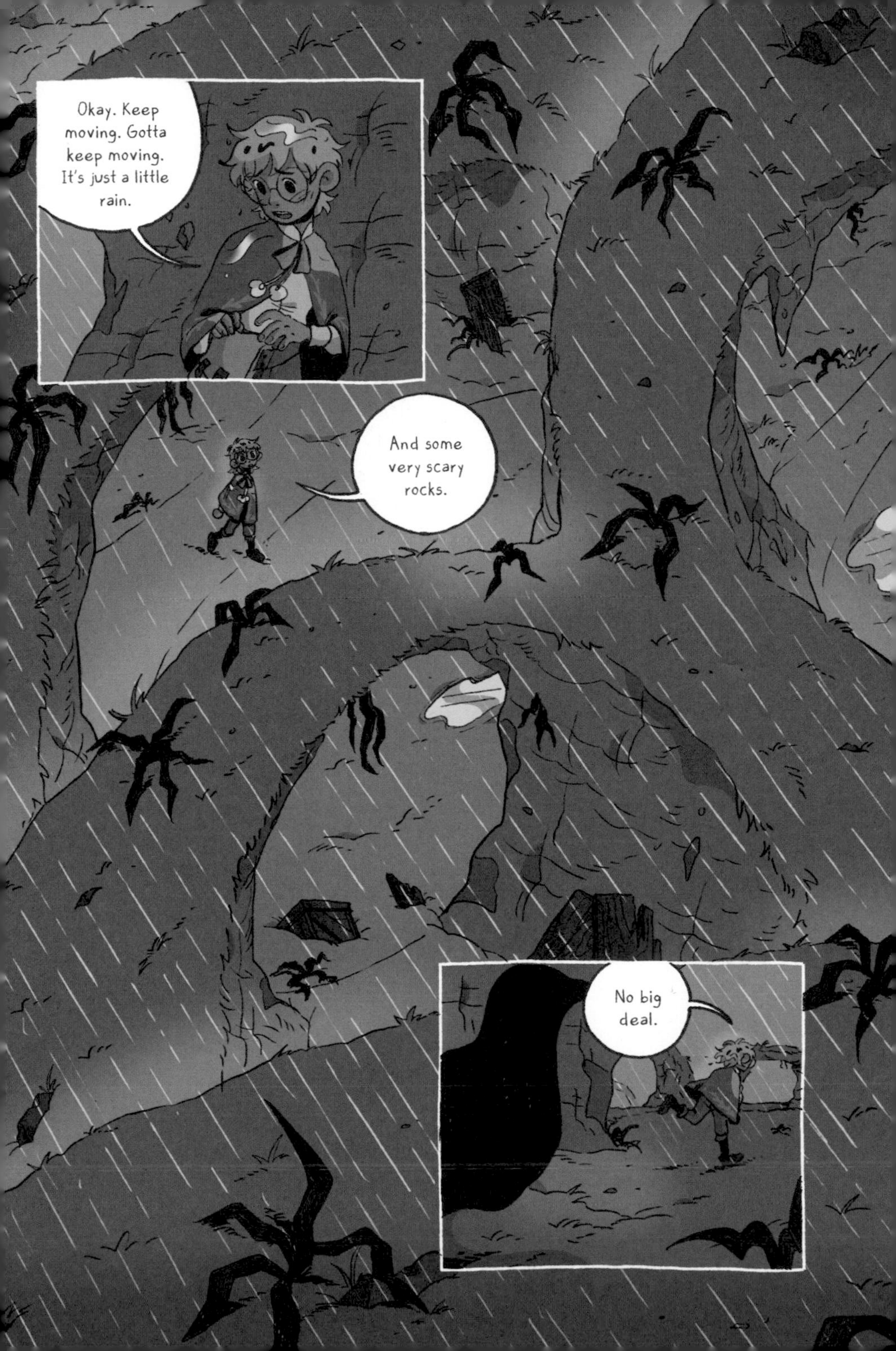
Okay. Keep moving. Gotta keep moving. It's just a little rain.
And some very scary rocks.
No big deal.

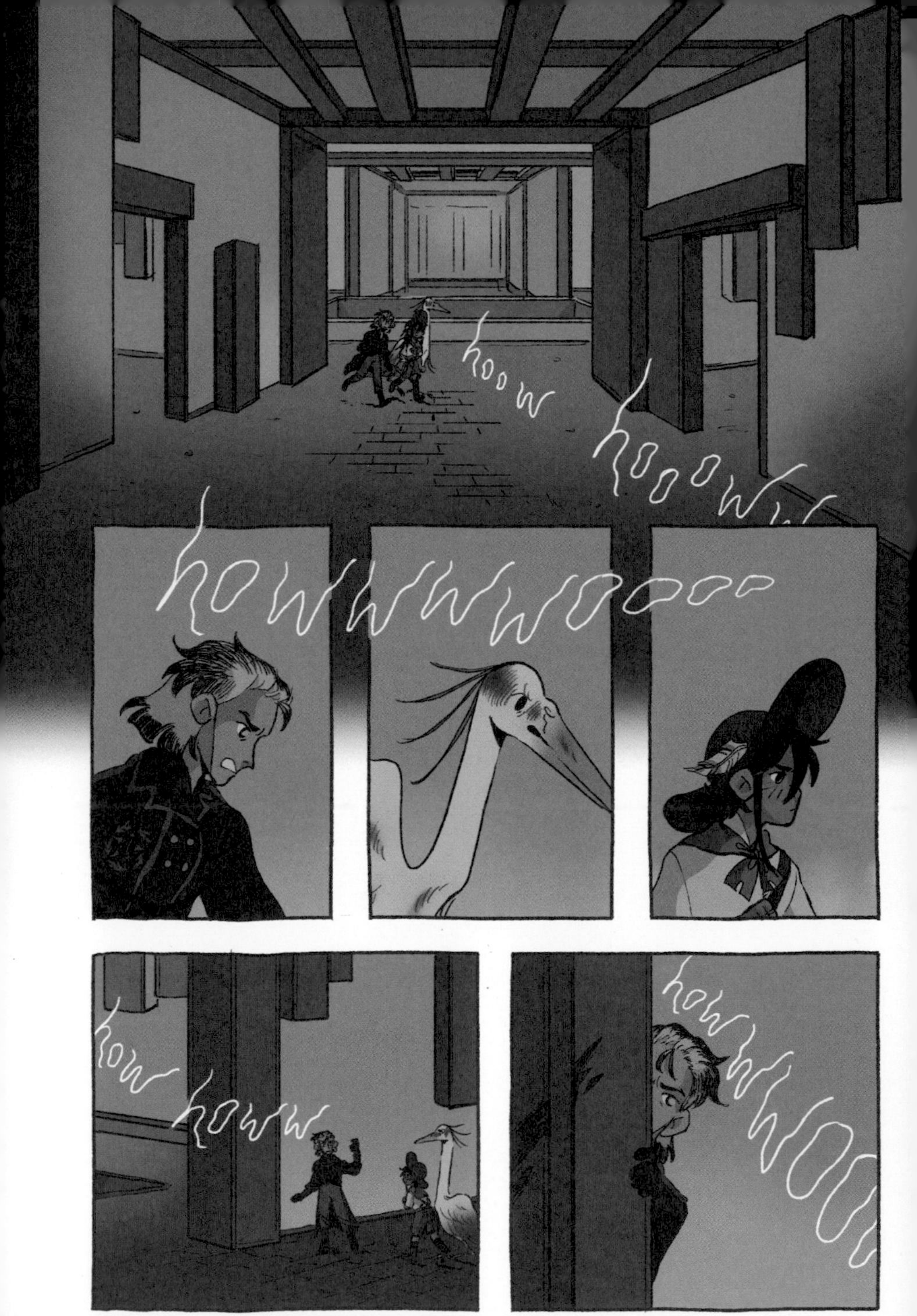
hoow
hooowww
howwwwoooooo
how howw
howwwooo

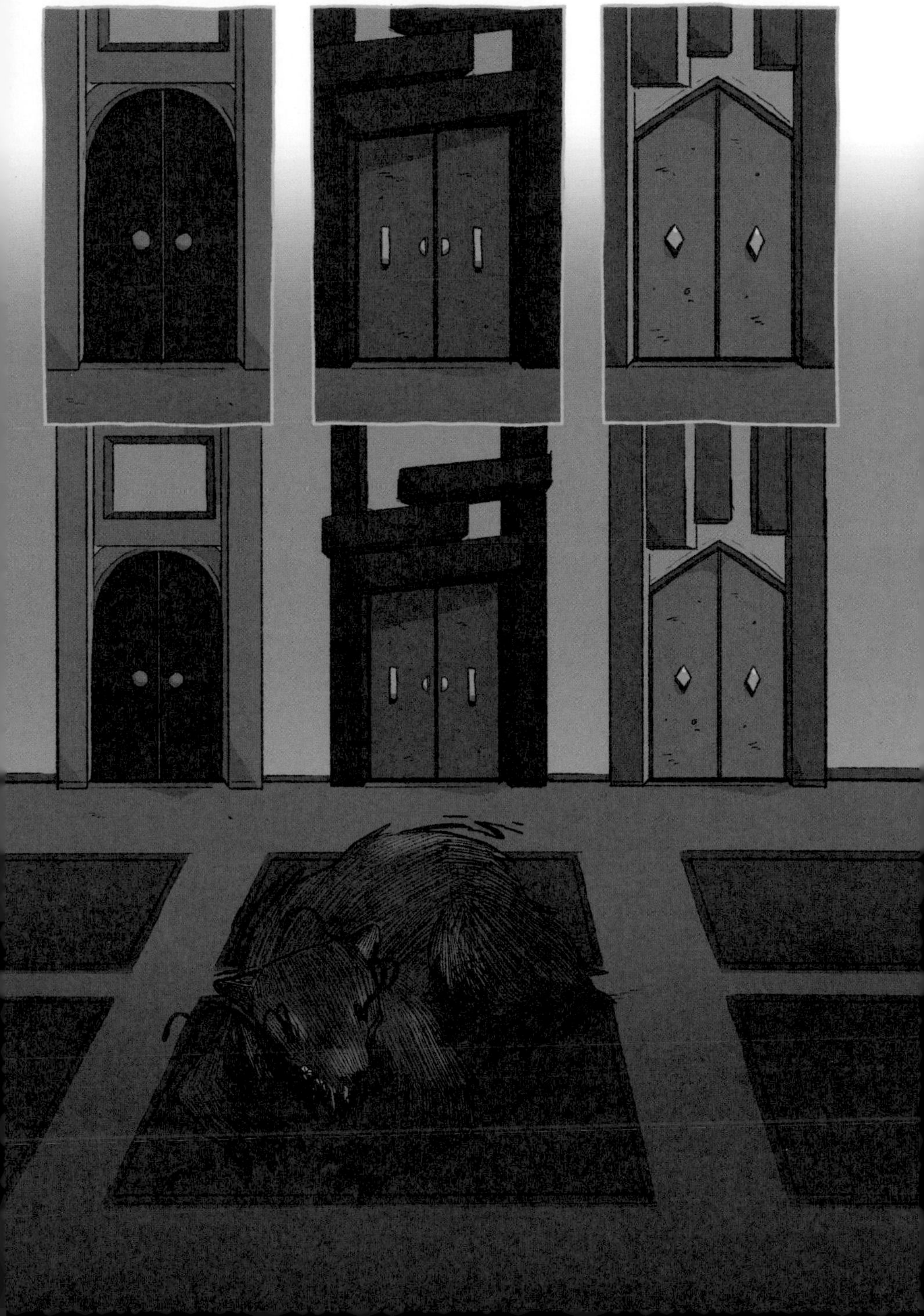

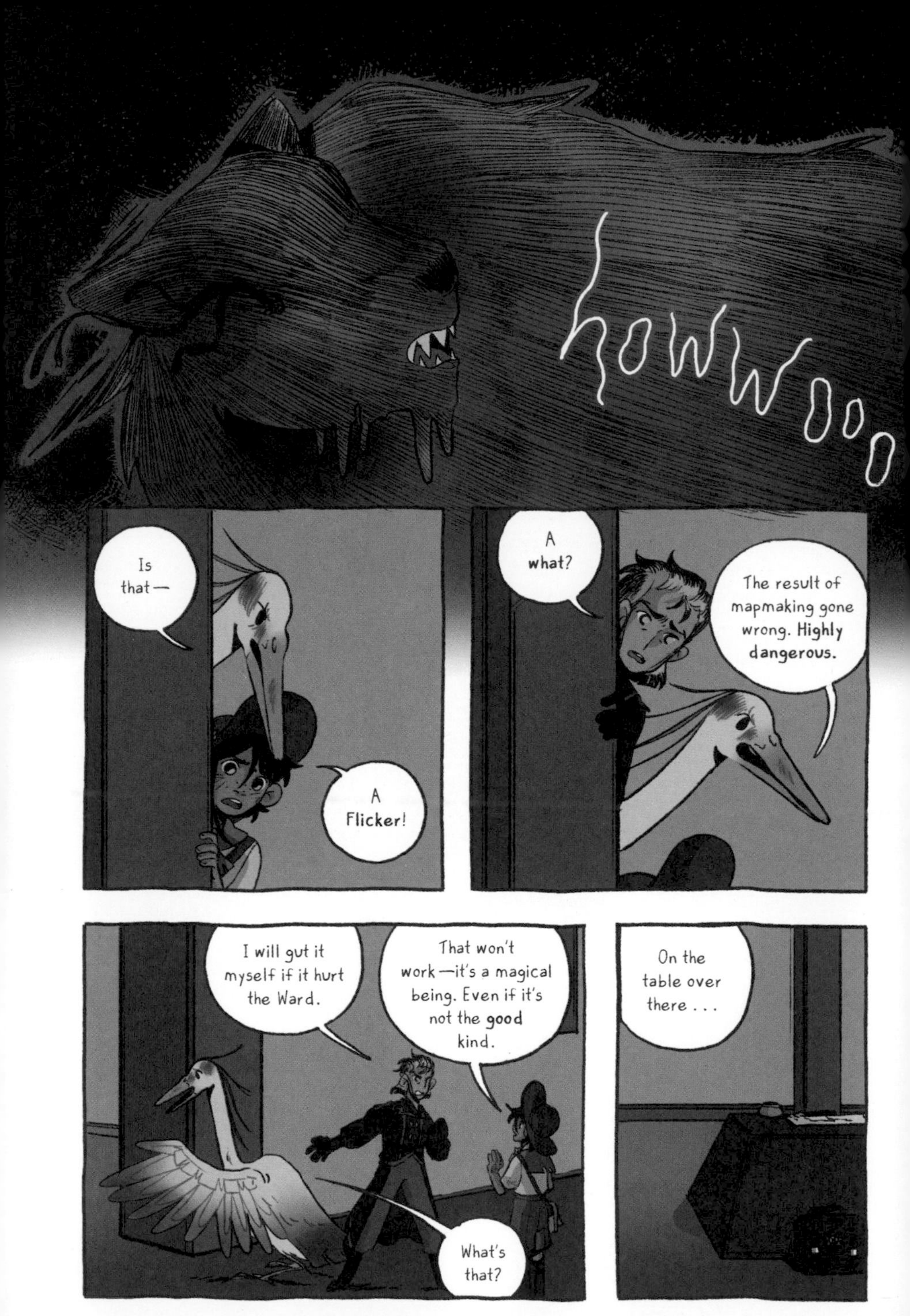
howwooo
Is that—
A Flicker!
A what?
The result of mapmaking gone wrong. **Highly dangerous.**
I will gut it myself if it hurt the Ward.
That won't work—it's a magical being. Even if it's not the **good** kind.
What's that?
On the table over there . . .

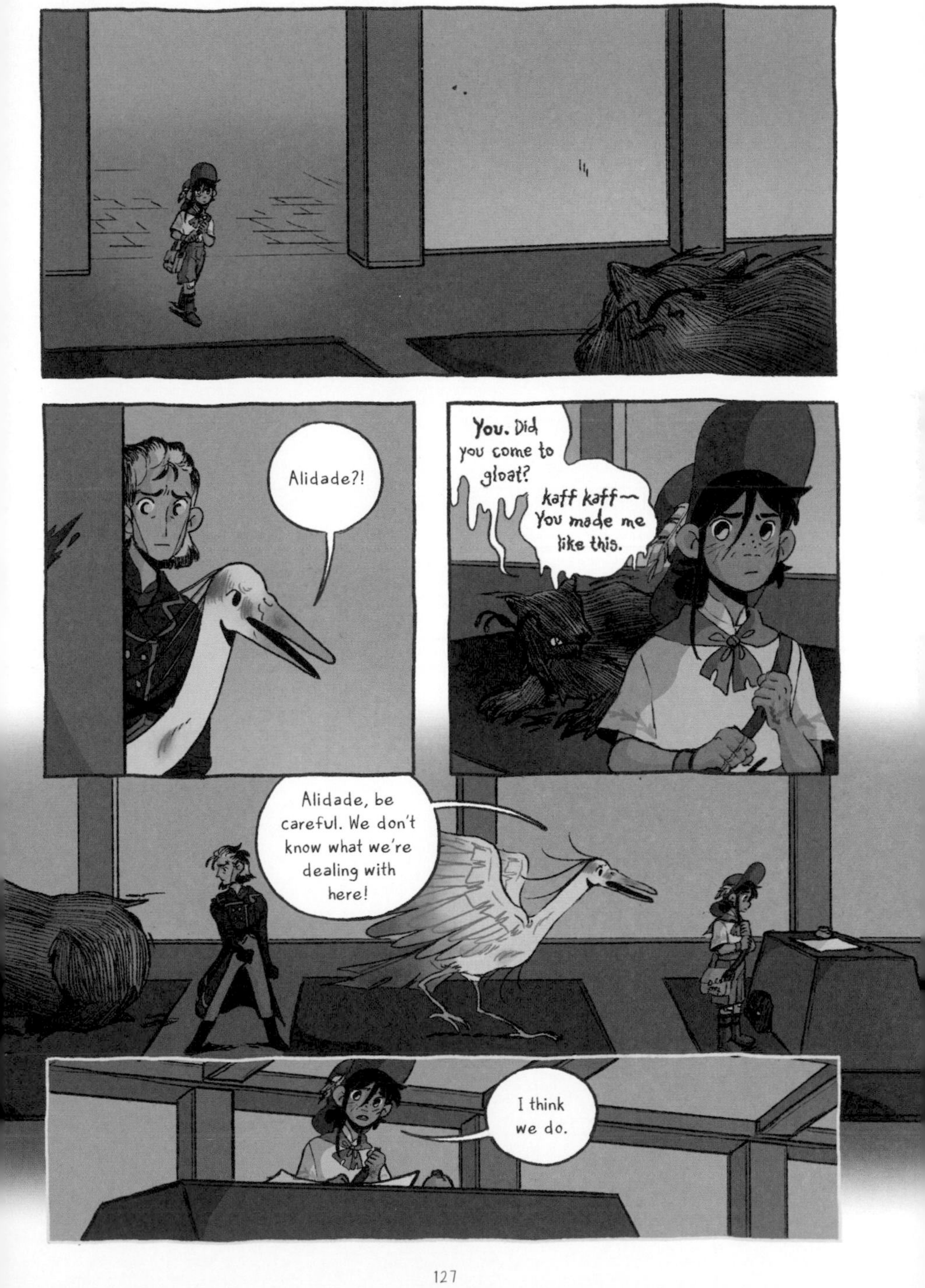

Alidade?!
You. Did you come to gloat?
kaff kaff~ You made me like this.
Alidade, be careful. We don't know what we're dealing with here!
I think we do.

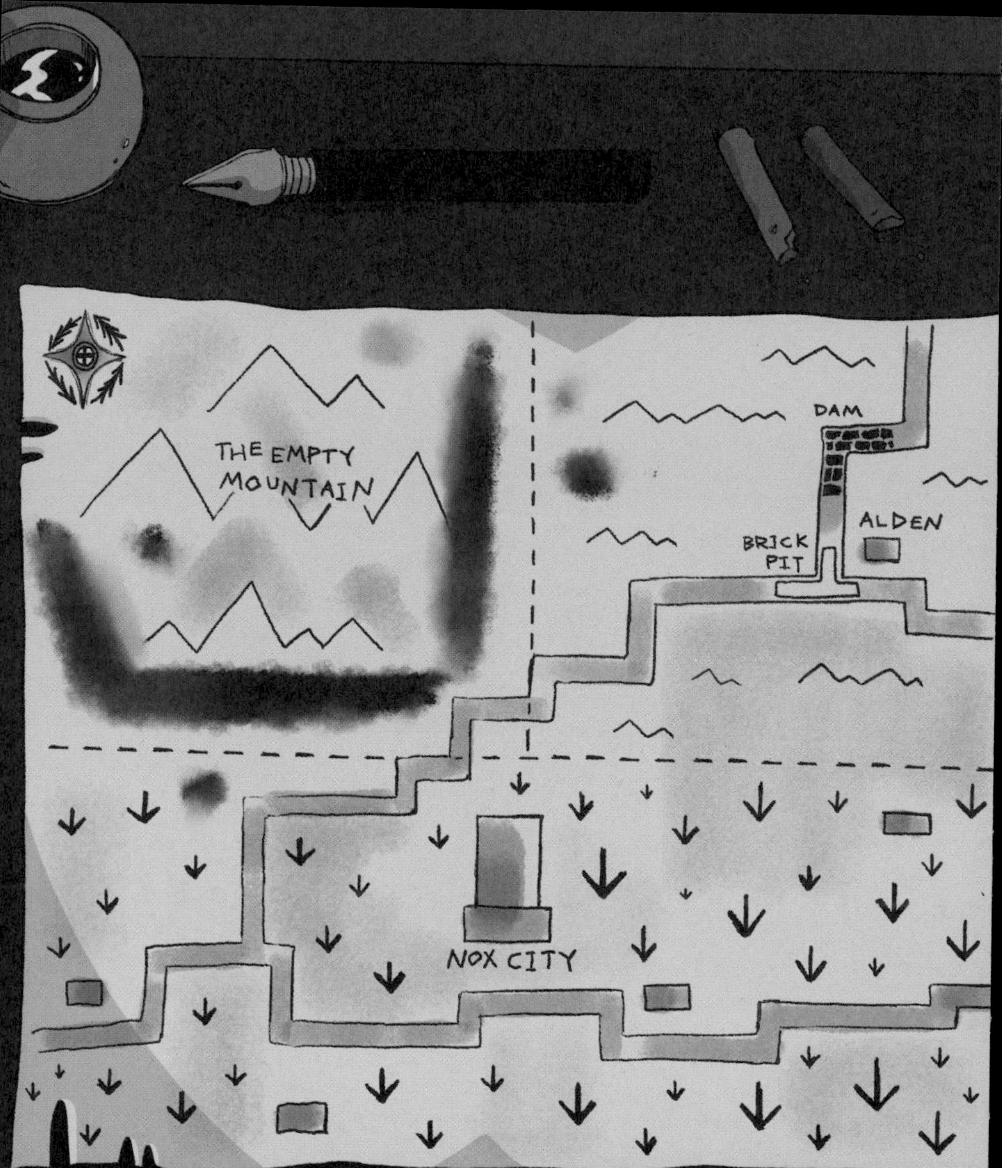
THE EMPTY MOUNTAIN
DAM
ALDEN
BRICK PIT
NOX CITY

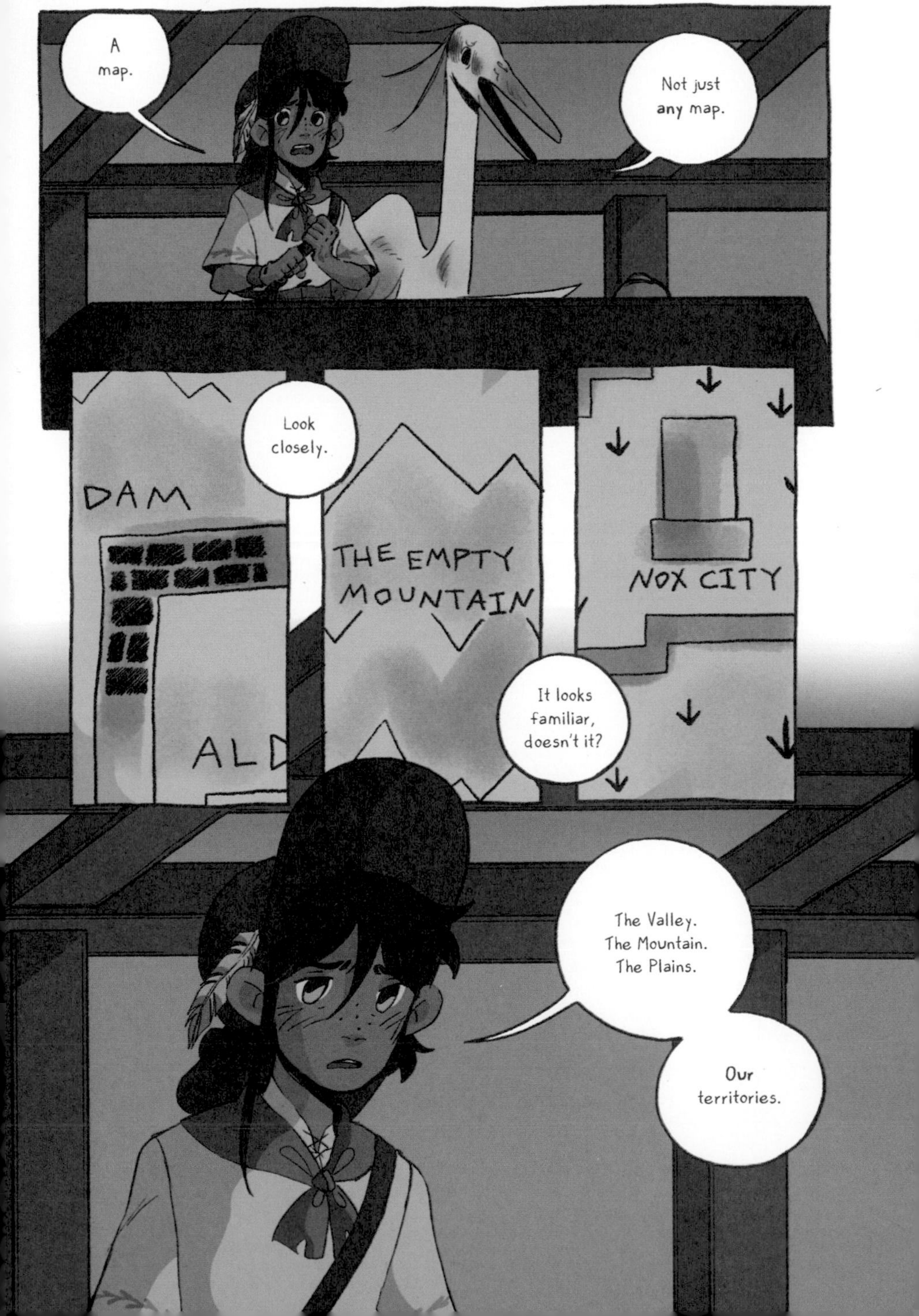
A map.
Not just any map.
Look closely.
DAM
ALD
THE EMPTY MOUNTAIN
NOX CITY
It looks familiar, doesn't it?
The Valley. The Mountain. The Plains.
Our territories.

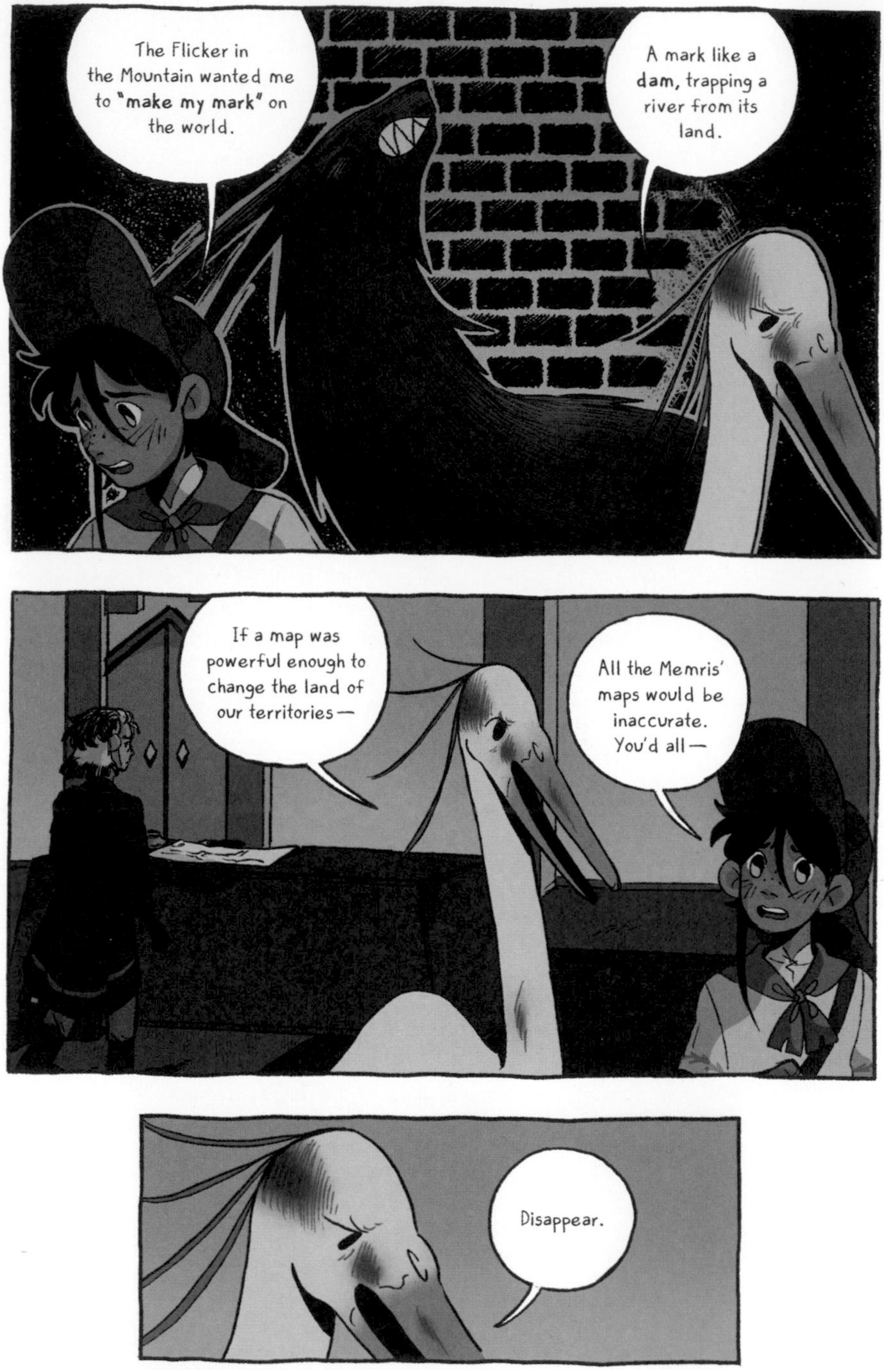
The Flicker in the Mountain wanted me to "make my mark" on the world.
A mark like a dam, trapping a river from its land.
If a map was powerful enough to change the land of our territories—
All the Memris' maps would be inaccurate. You'd all—
Disappear.

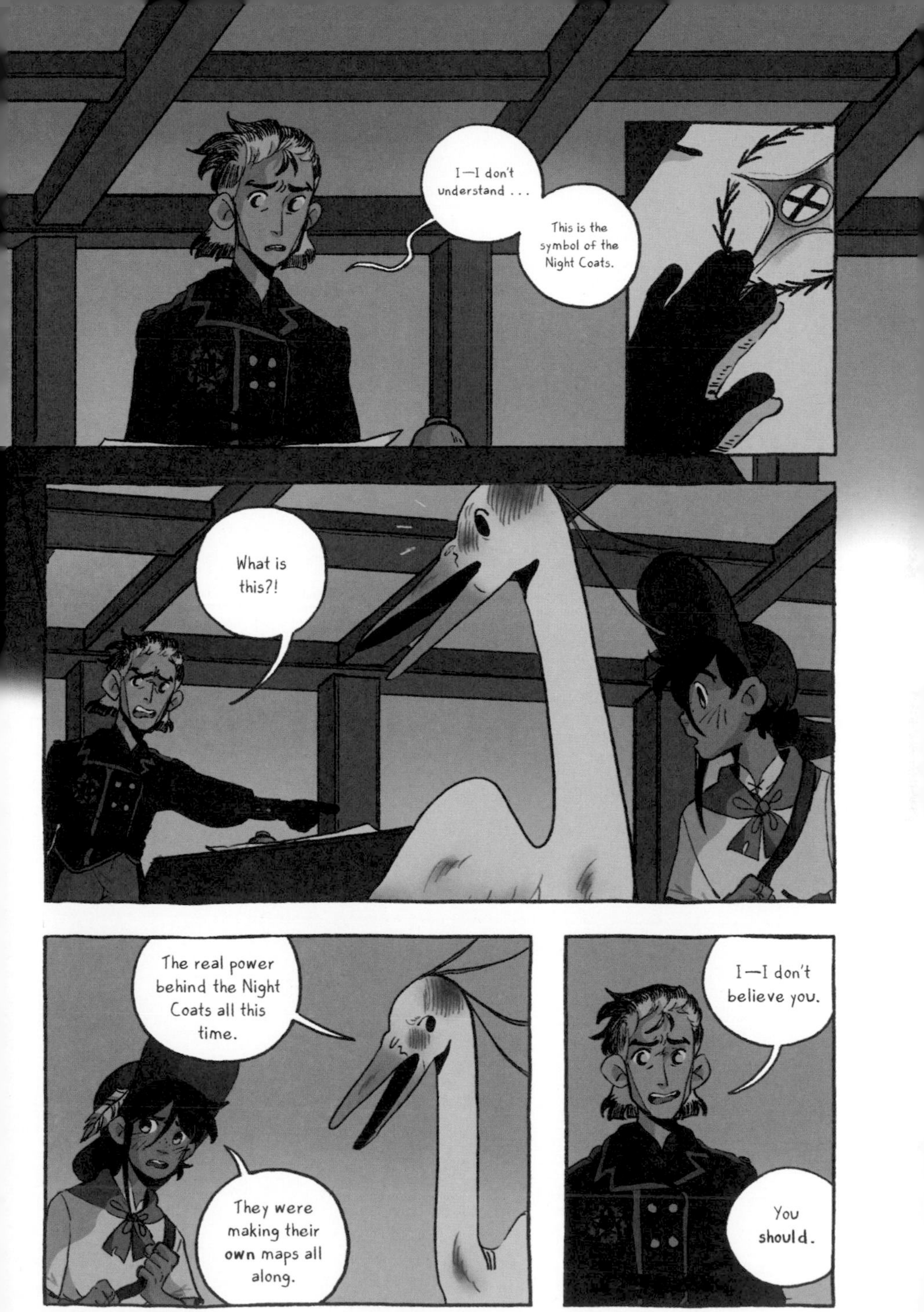
I—I don't understand . . .
This is the symbol of the Night Coats.
What is this?!
The real power behind the Night Coats all this time.
They were making their **own** maps all along.
I—I don't believe you.
You **should**.

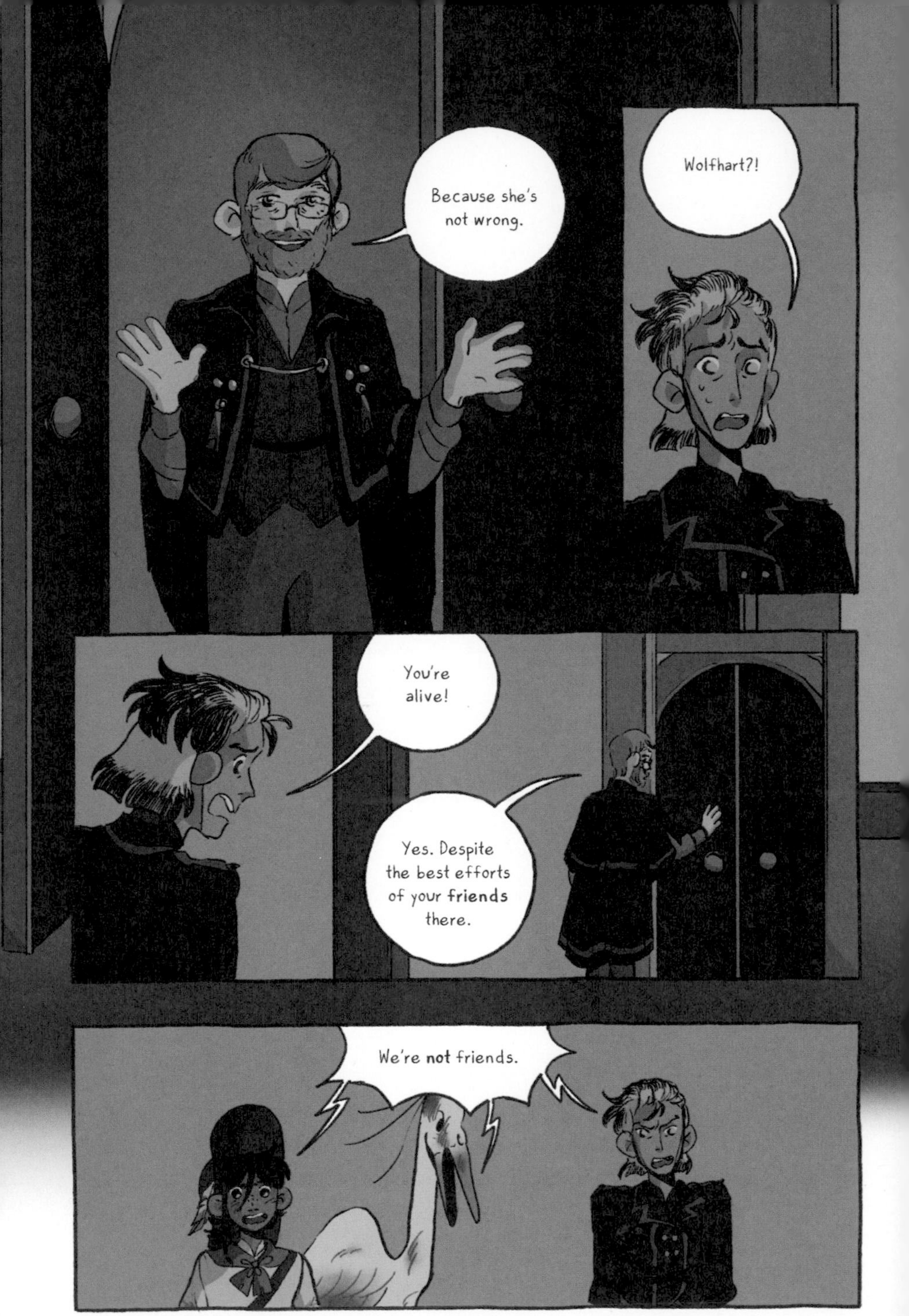
Because she's not wrong.
Wolfhart?!
You're alive!
Yes. Despite the best efforts of your **friends** there.
We're **not** friends.

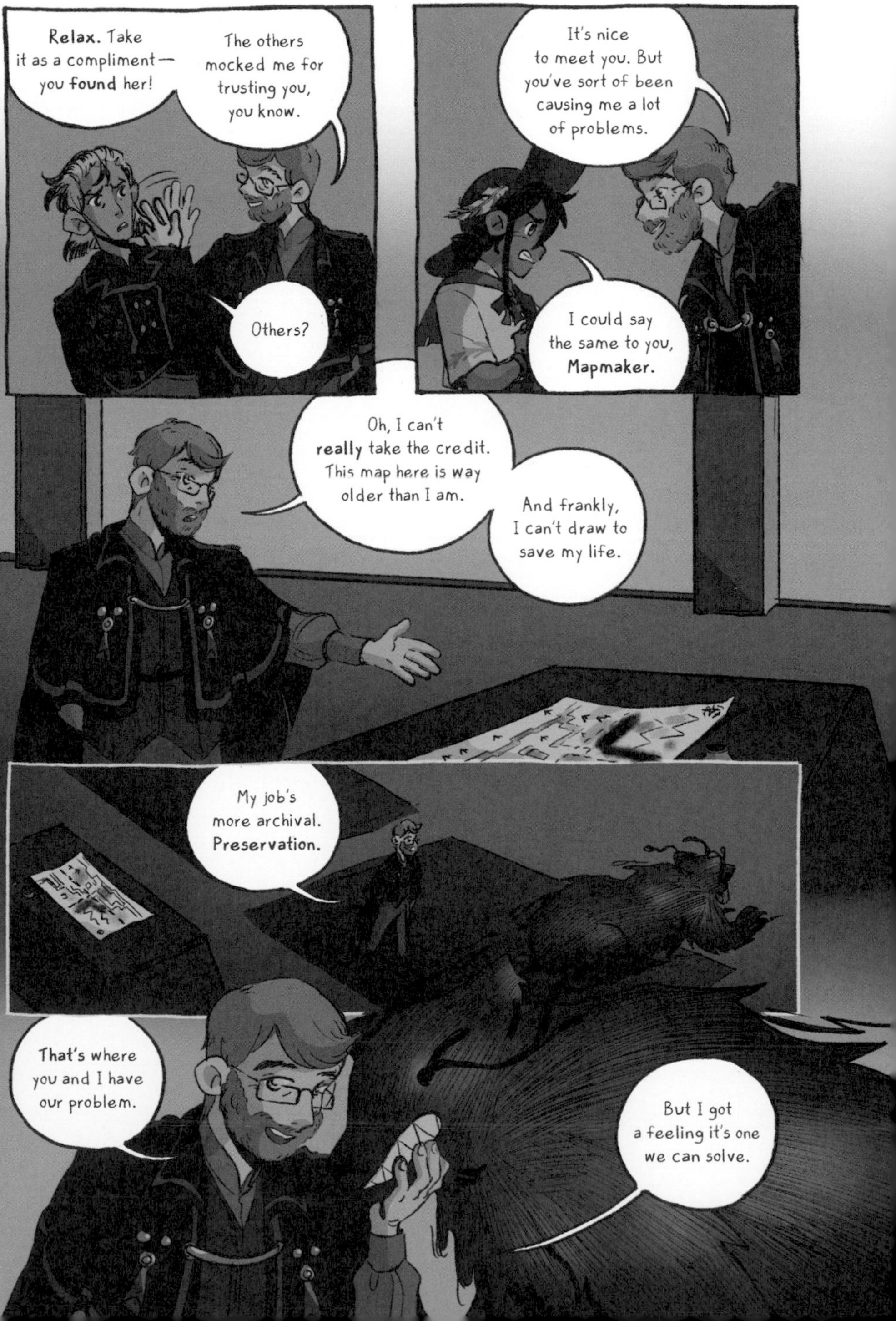
Relax. Take it as a compliment— you found her!
The others mocked me for trusting you, you know.
Others?
It's nice to meet you. But you've sort of been causing me a lot of problems.
I could say the same to you, Mapmaker.
Oh, I can't really take the credit. This map here is way older than I am.
And frankly, I can't draw to save my life.
My job's more archival. Preservation.
That's where you and I have our problem.
But I got a feeling it's one we can solve.

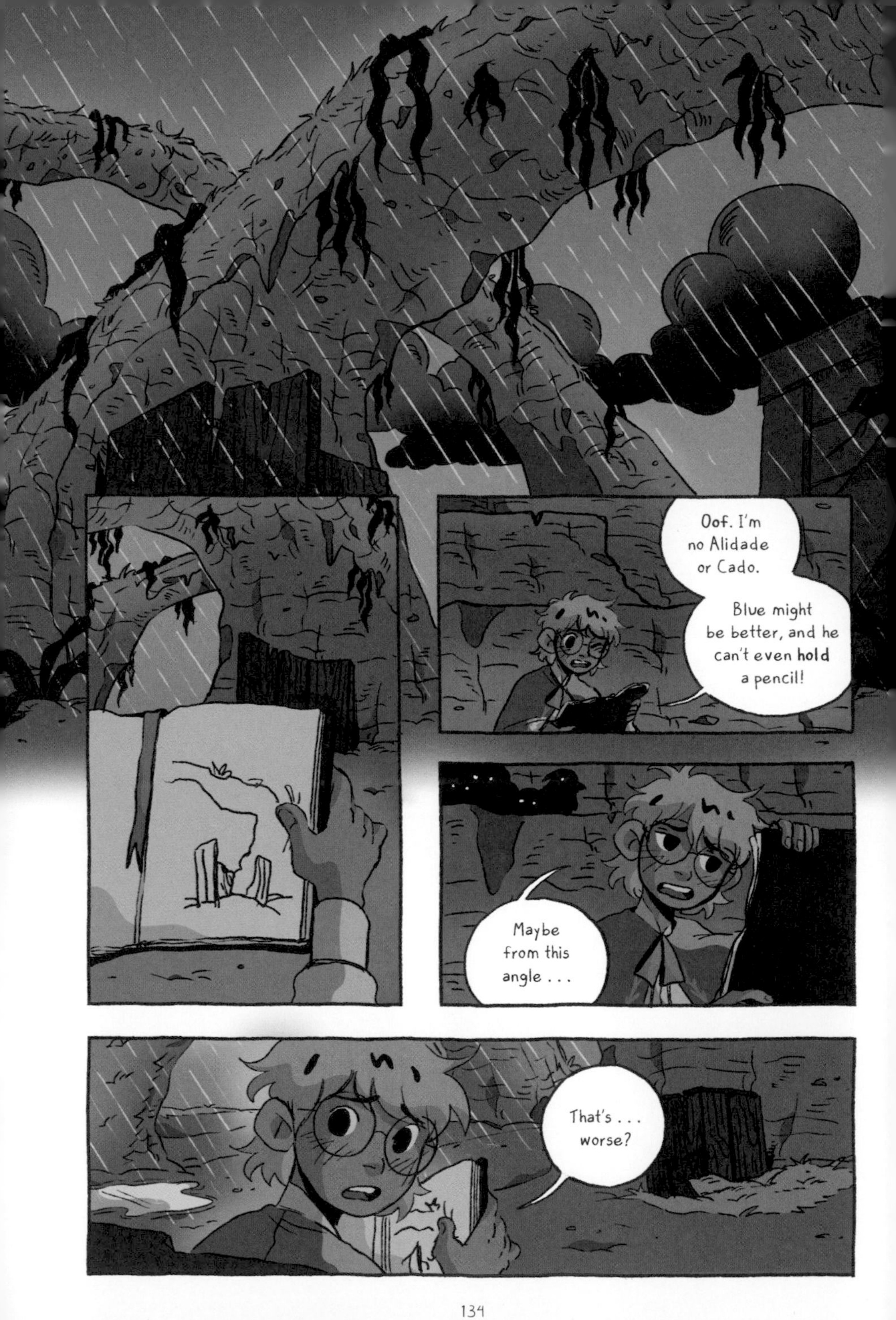
Oof. I'm no Alidade or Cado.
Blue might be better, and he can't even **hold** a pencil!
Maybe from this angle . . .
That's . . . worse?

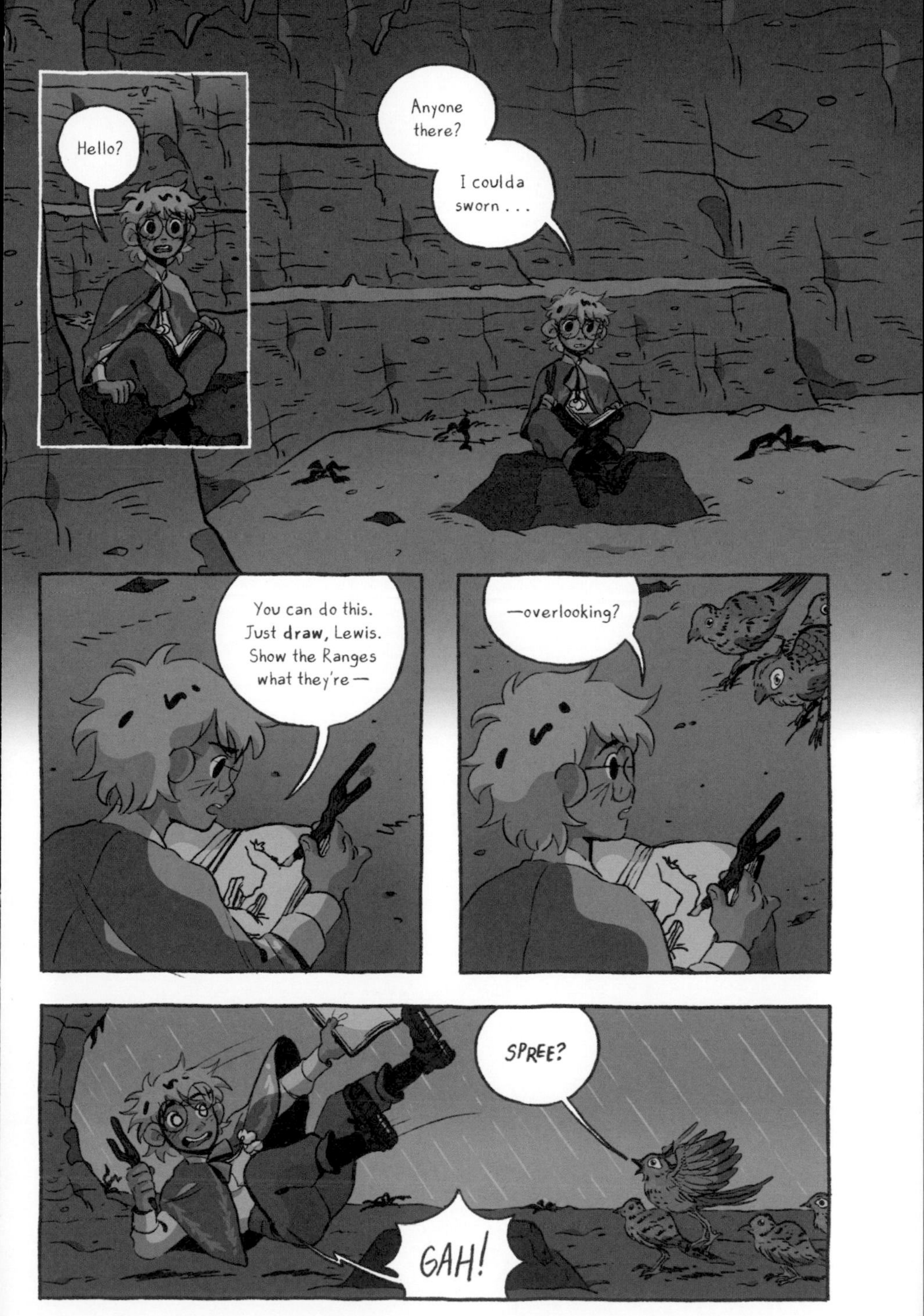
Hello?
Anyone there?
I coulda sworn . . .
You can do this. Just draw, Lewis. Show the Ranges what they're—
—overlooking?
SPREE?
GAH!

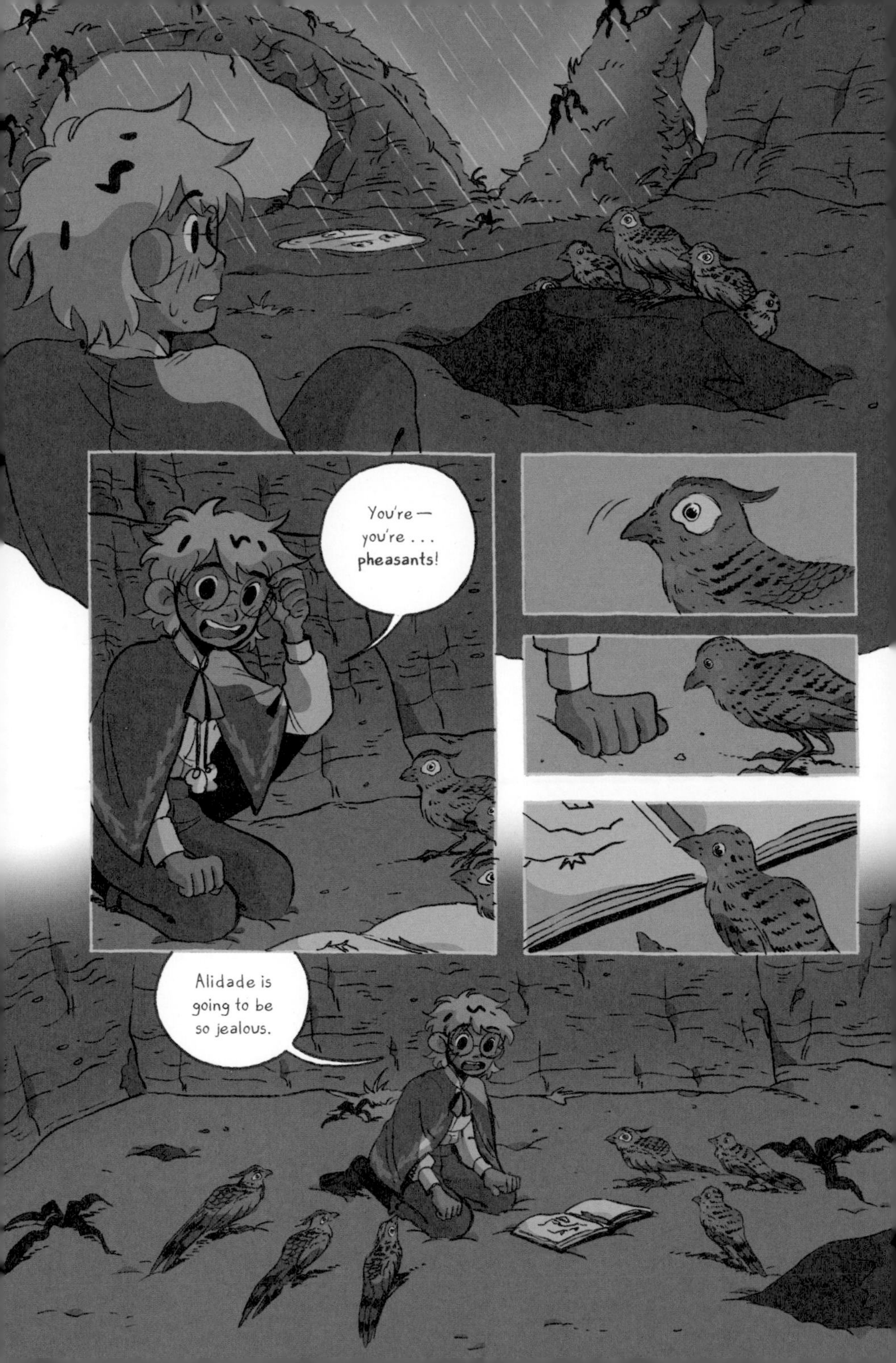
You're—
you're . . .
pheasants!
Alidade is going to be so jealous.

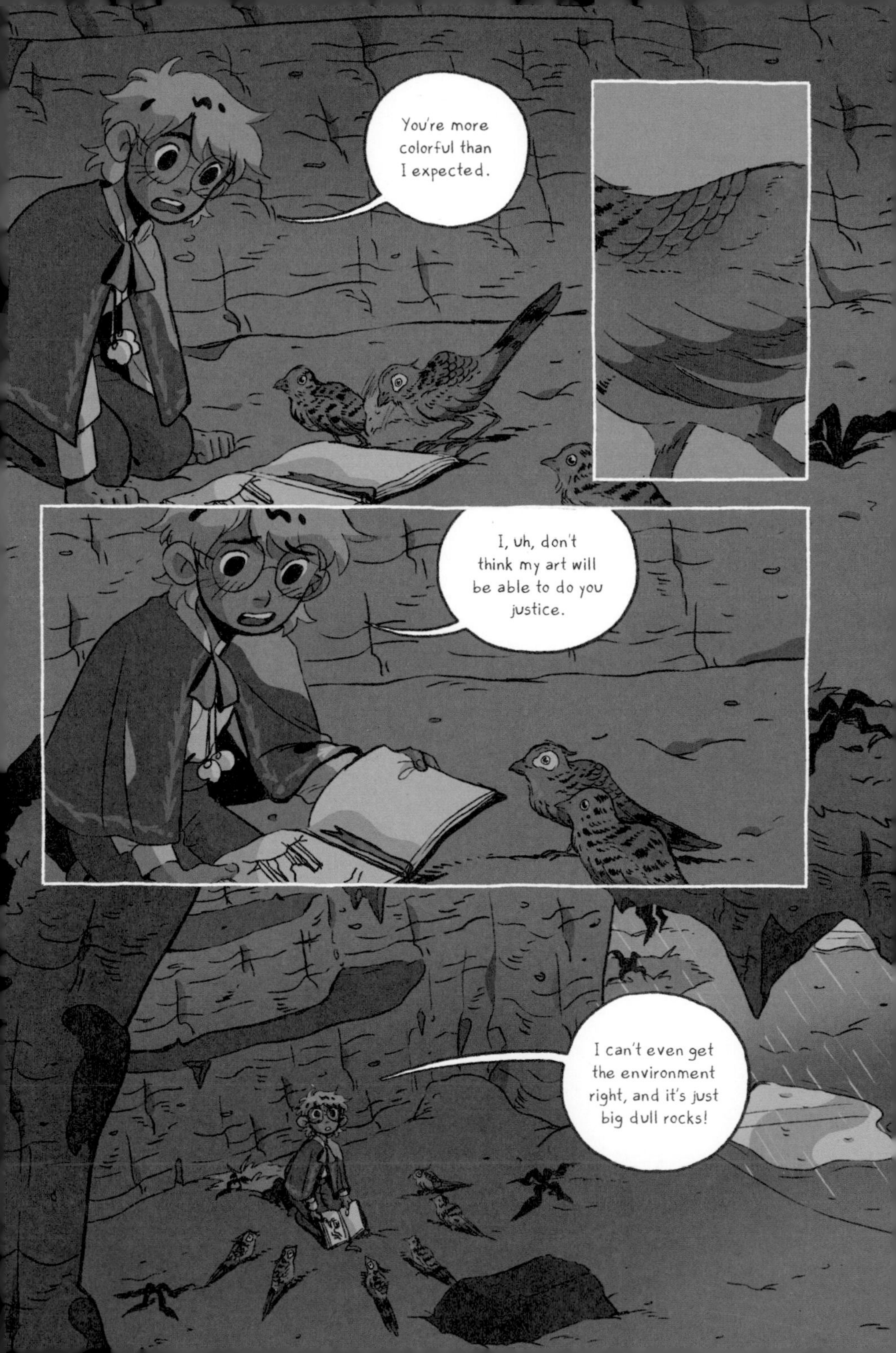
You're more colorful than I expected.
I, uh, don't think my art will be able to do you justice.
I can't even get the environment right, and it's just big dull rocks!

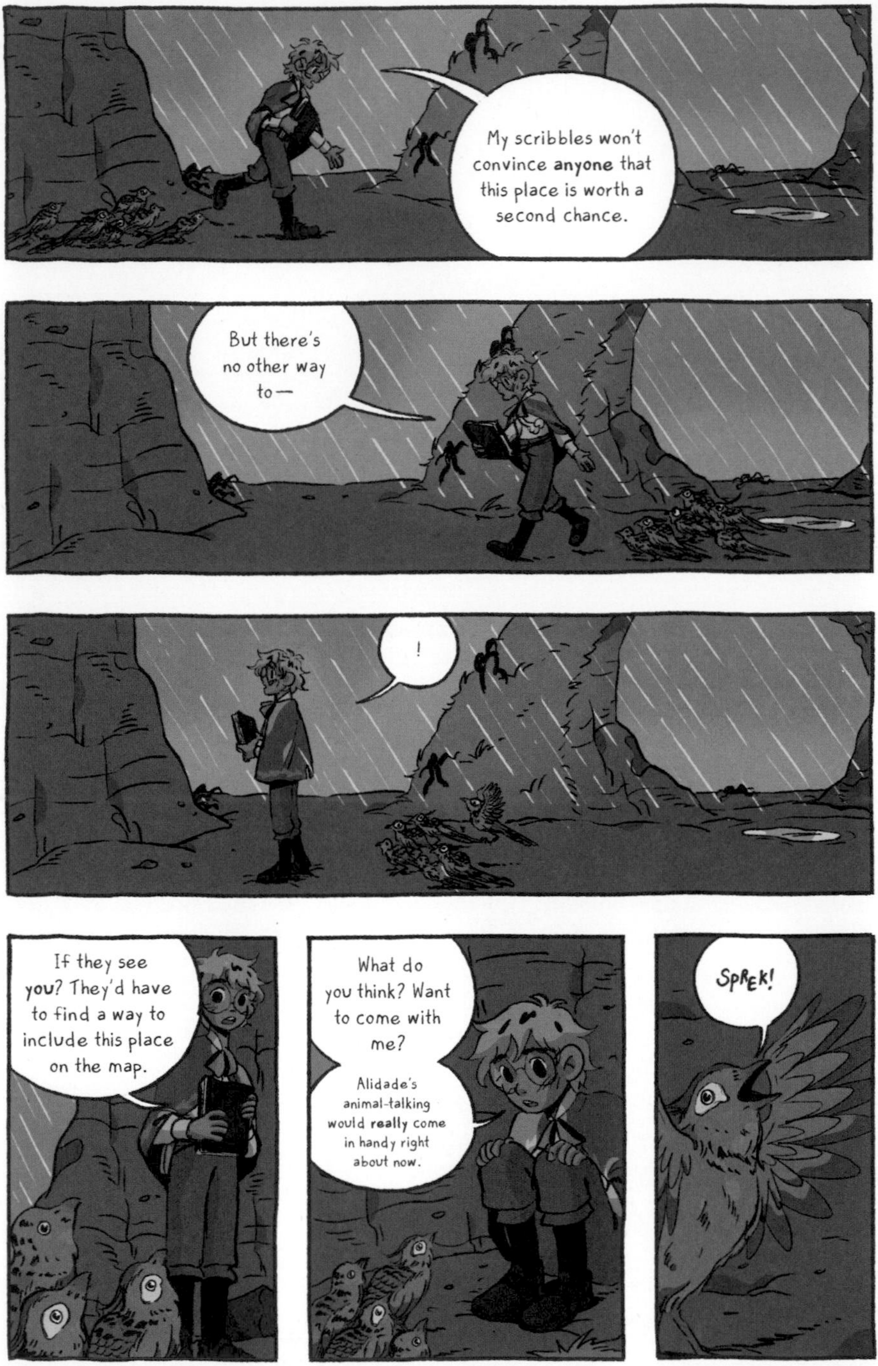
My scribbles won't convince **anyone** that this place is worth a second chance.
But there's no other way to—
!
If they see **you**? They'd have to find a way to include this place on the map.
What do you think? Want to come with me?
Alidade's animal-talking would **really** come in handy right about now.
SPREK!

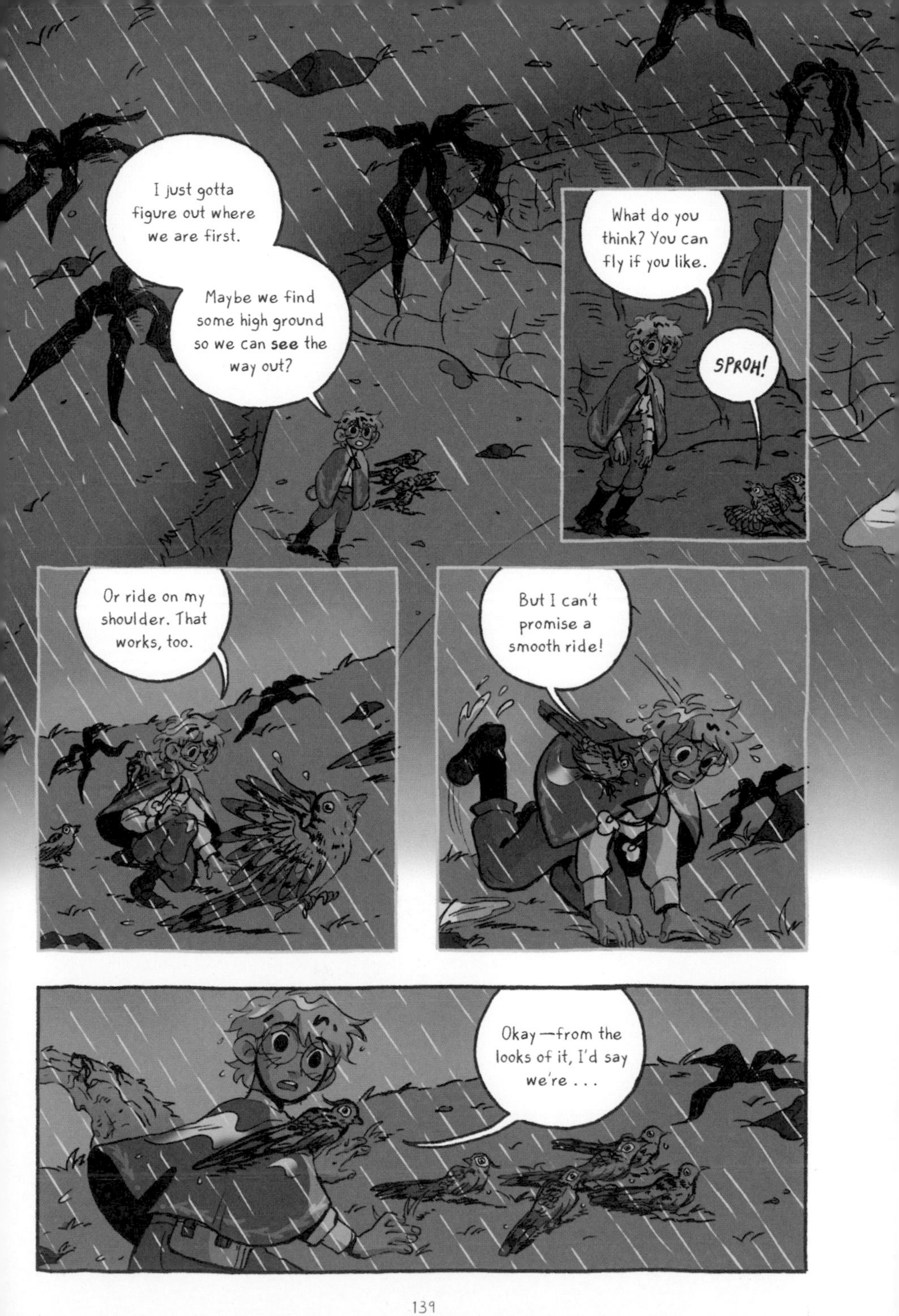
I just gotta figure out where we are first.
Maybe we find some high ground so we can **see** the way out?
What do you think? You can fly if you like.
SPROH!
Or ride on my shoulder. That works, too.
But I can't promise a smooth ride!
Okay—from the looks of it, I'd say we're . . .

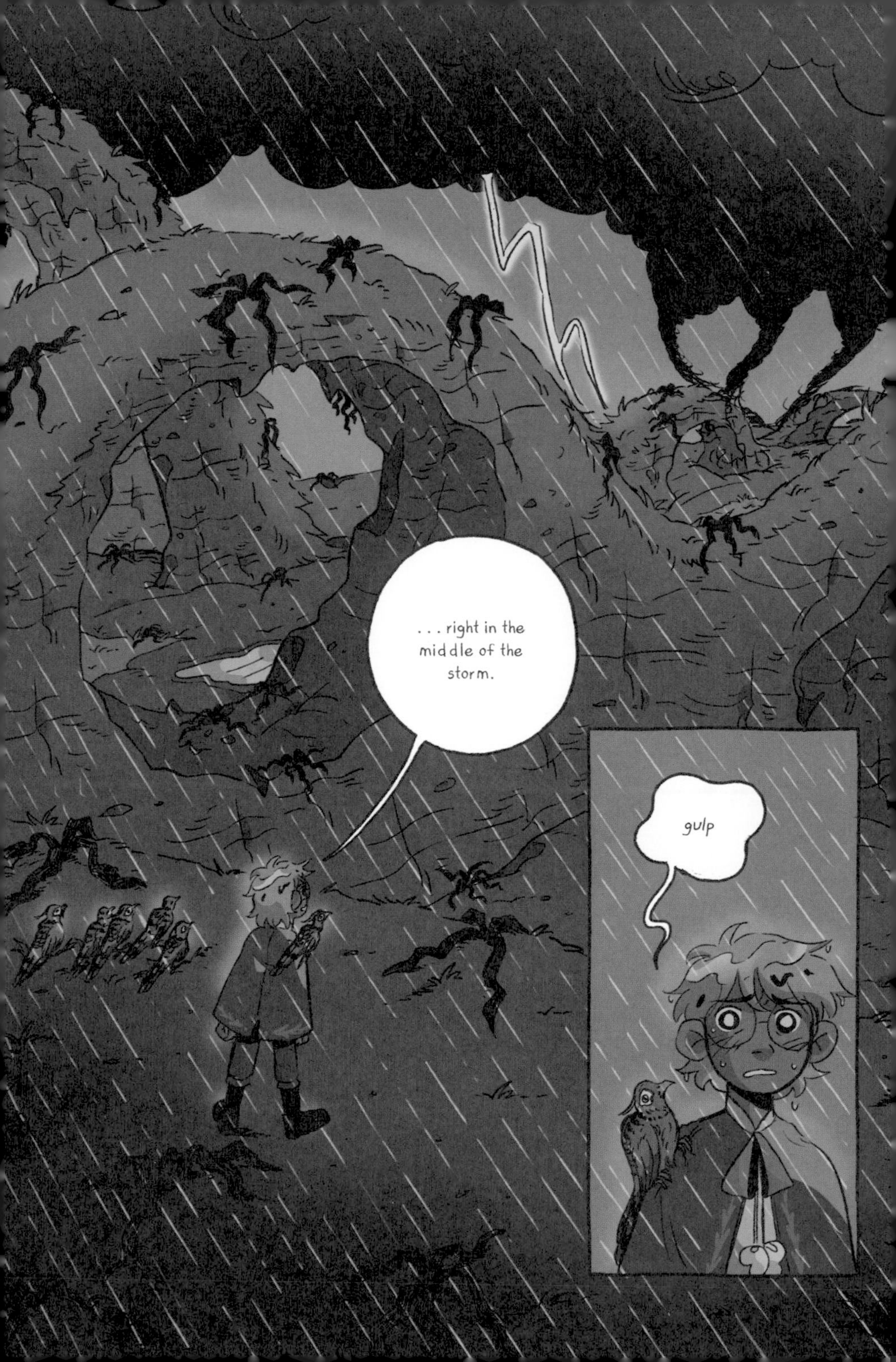
. . . right in the middle of the storm.
gulp

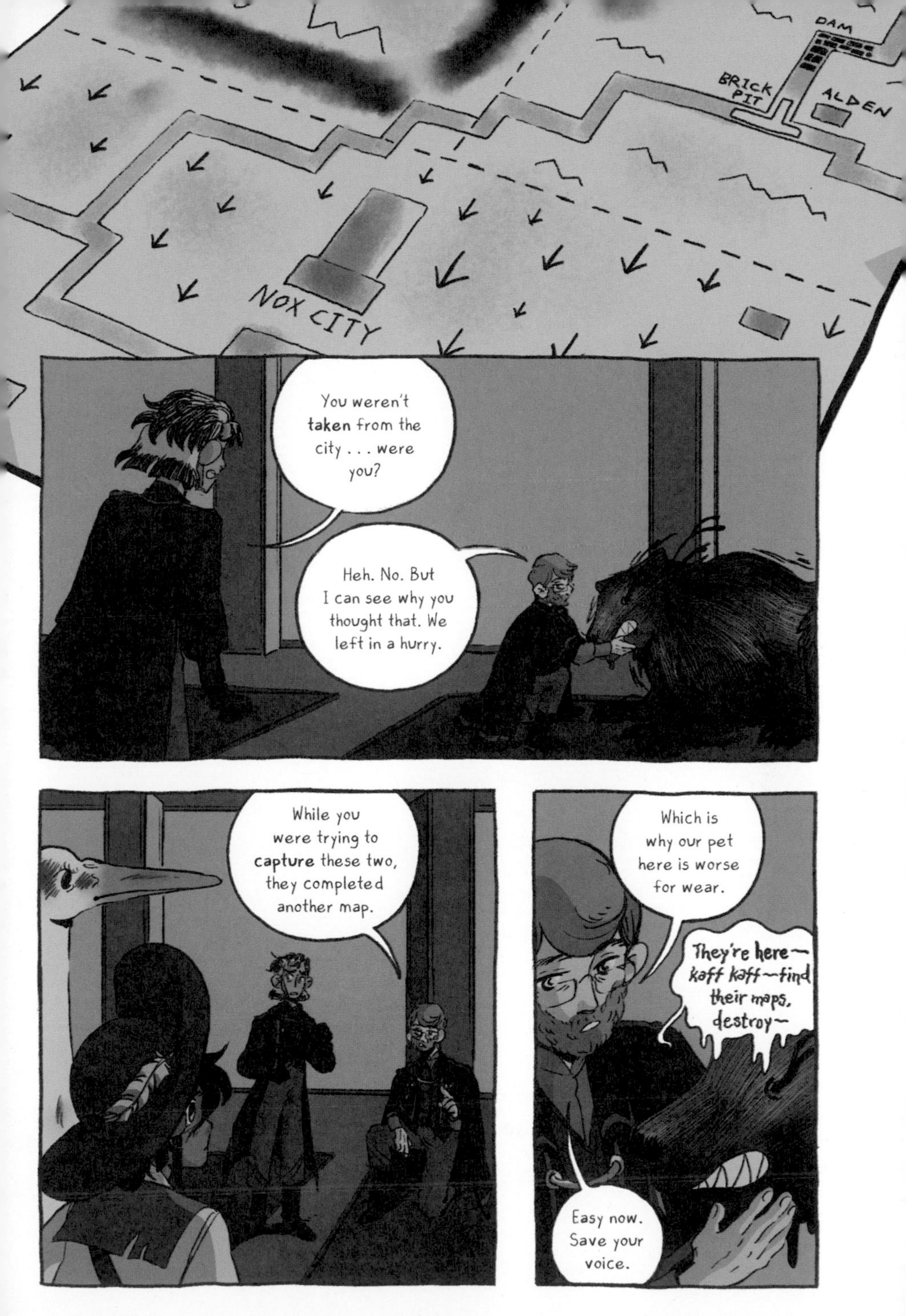
DAM
BRICK PIT
ALDEN
NOX CITY
You weren't **taken** from the city . . . were you?
Heh. No. But I can see why you thought that. We left in a hurry.
While you were trying to **capture** these two, they completed another map.
Which is why our pet here is worse for wear.
They're here—kaff kaff—find their maps, destroy—
Easy now. Save your voice.

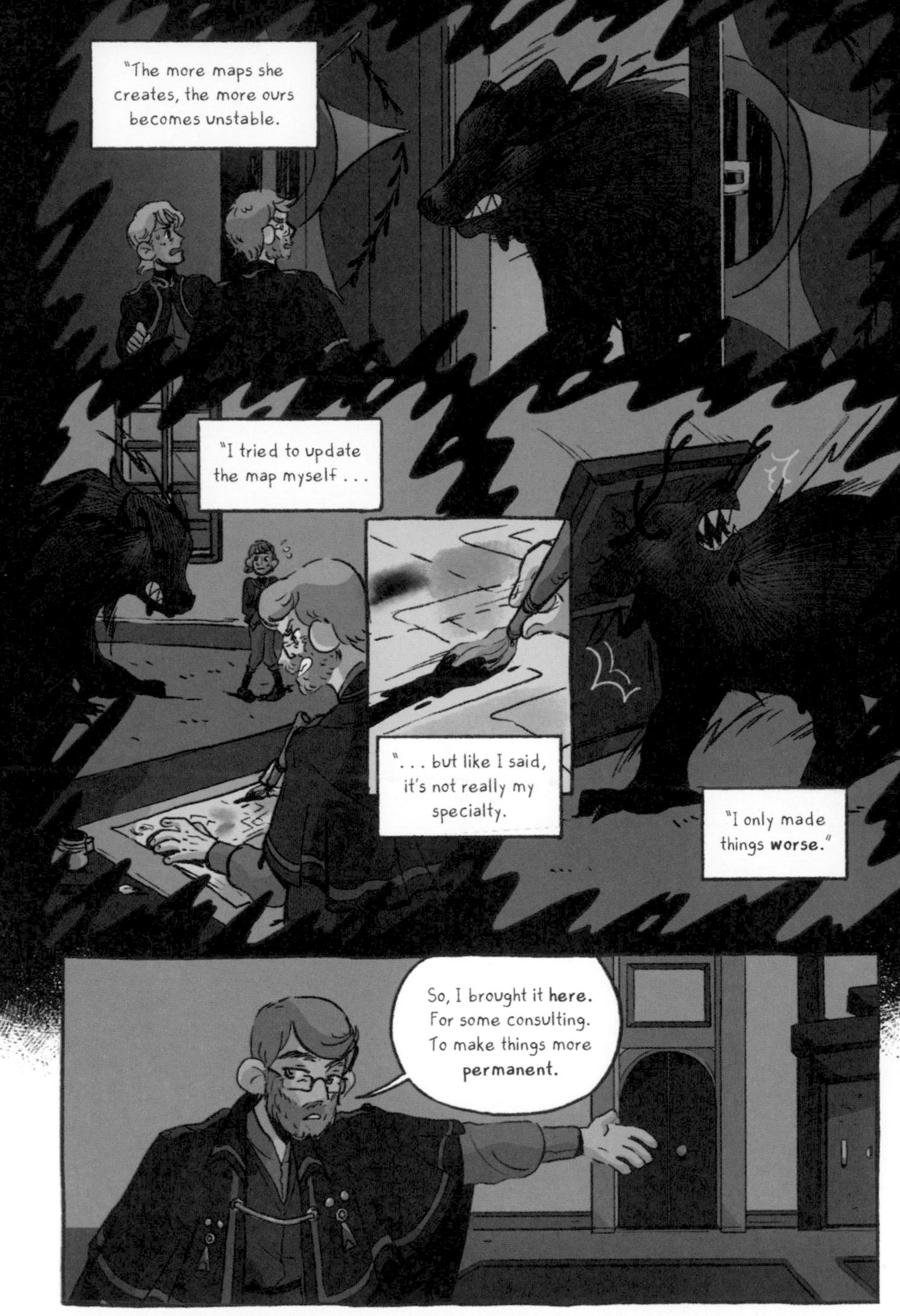
"The more maps she creates, the more ours becomes unstable.
"I tried to update the map myself . . .
". . . but like I said, it's not really my specialty.
"I only made things **worse**."
So, I brought it **here**. For some consulting. To make things more **permanent**.

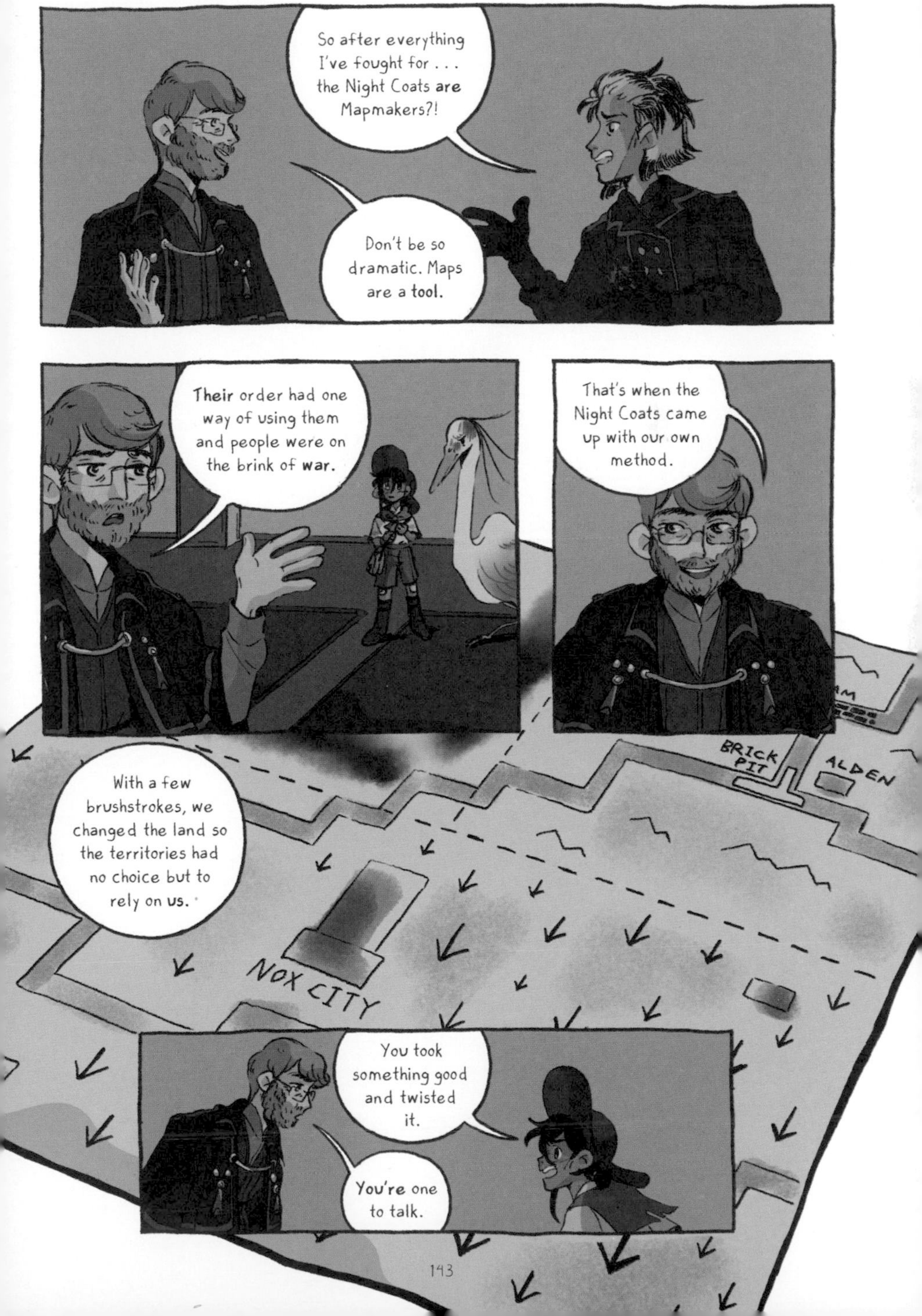
So after everything I've fought for . . . the Night Coats **are** Mapmakers?!
Don't be so dramatic. Maps are a **tool.**
Their order had one way of using them and people were on the brink of **war.**
That's when the Night Coats came up with our own method.
BRICK PIT
ALDEN
With a few brushstrokes, we changed the land so the territories had no choice but to rely on **us.**
NOX CITY
You took something good and twisted it.
You're one to talk.

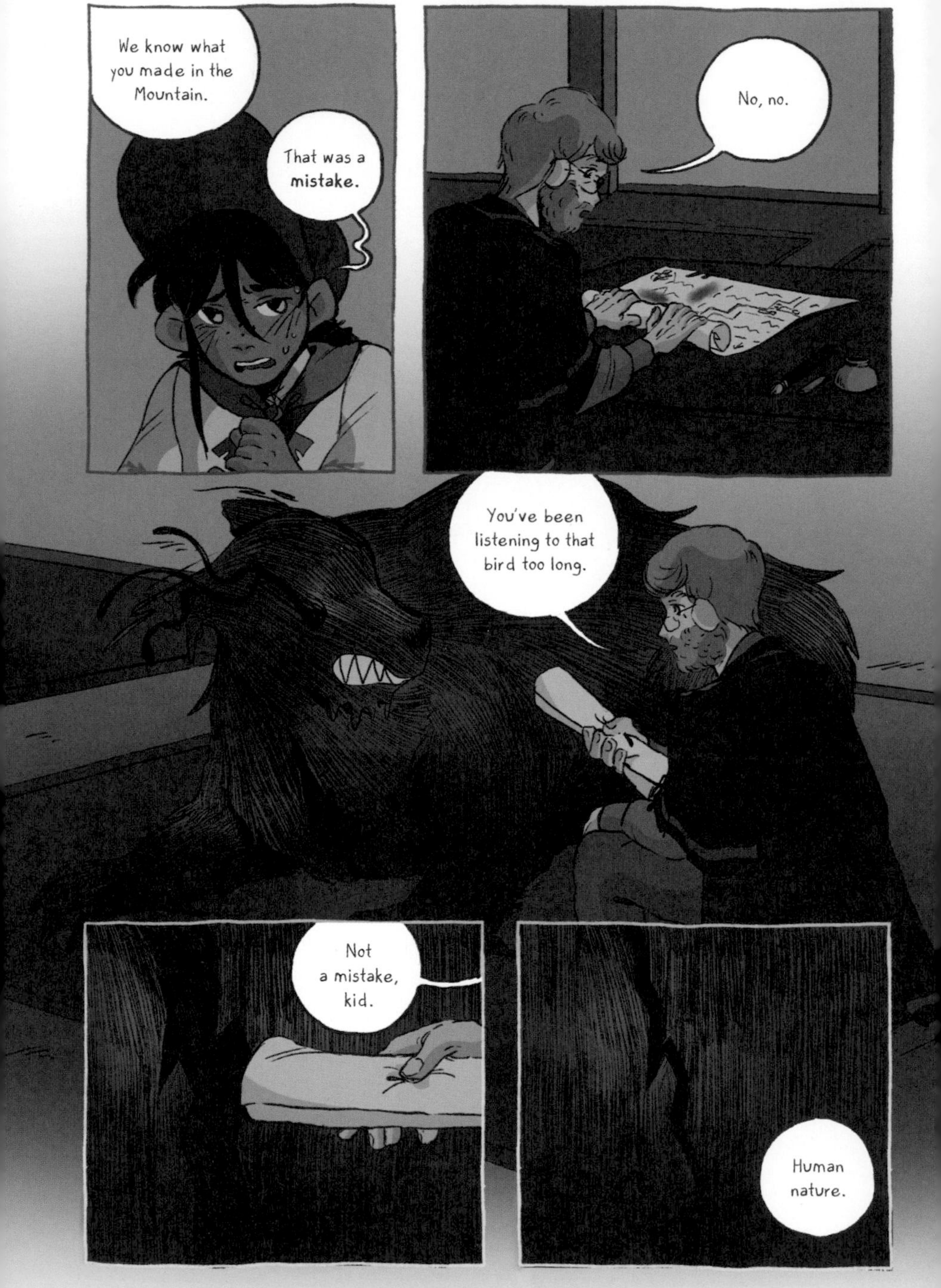
We know what you made in the Mountain.
That was a mistake.
No, no.
You've been listening to that bird too long.
Not a mistake, kid.
Human nature.

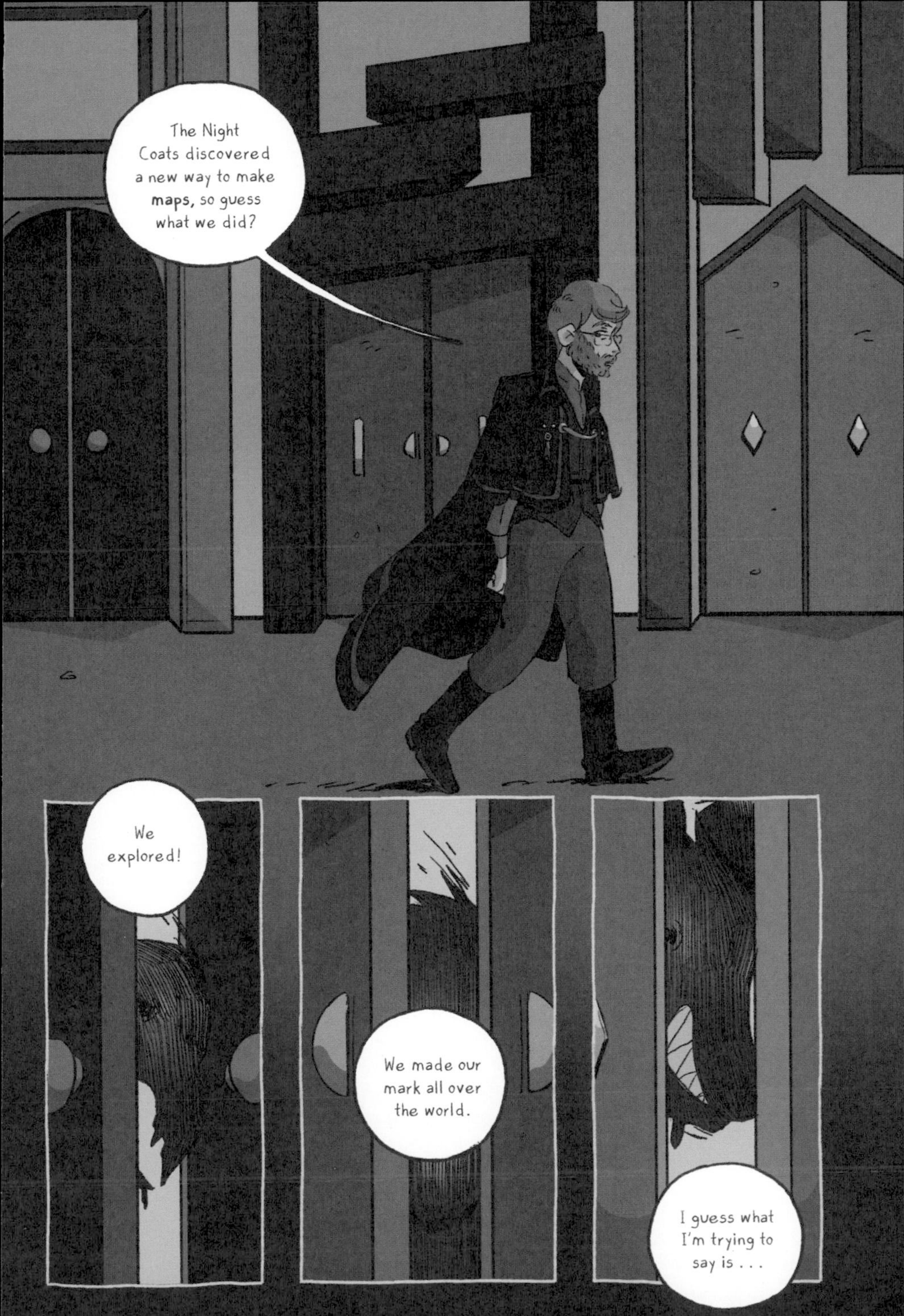
The Night Coats discovered a new way to make **maps**, so guess what we did?
We explored!
We made our mark all over the world.
I guess what I'm trying to say is . . .

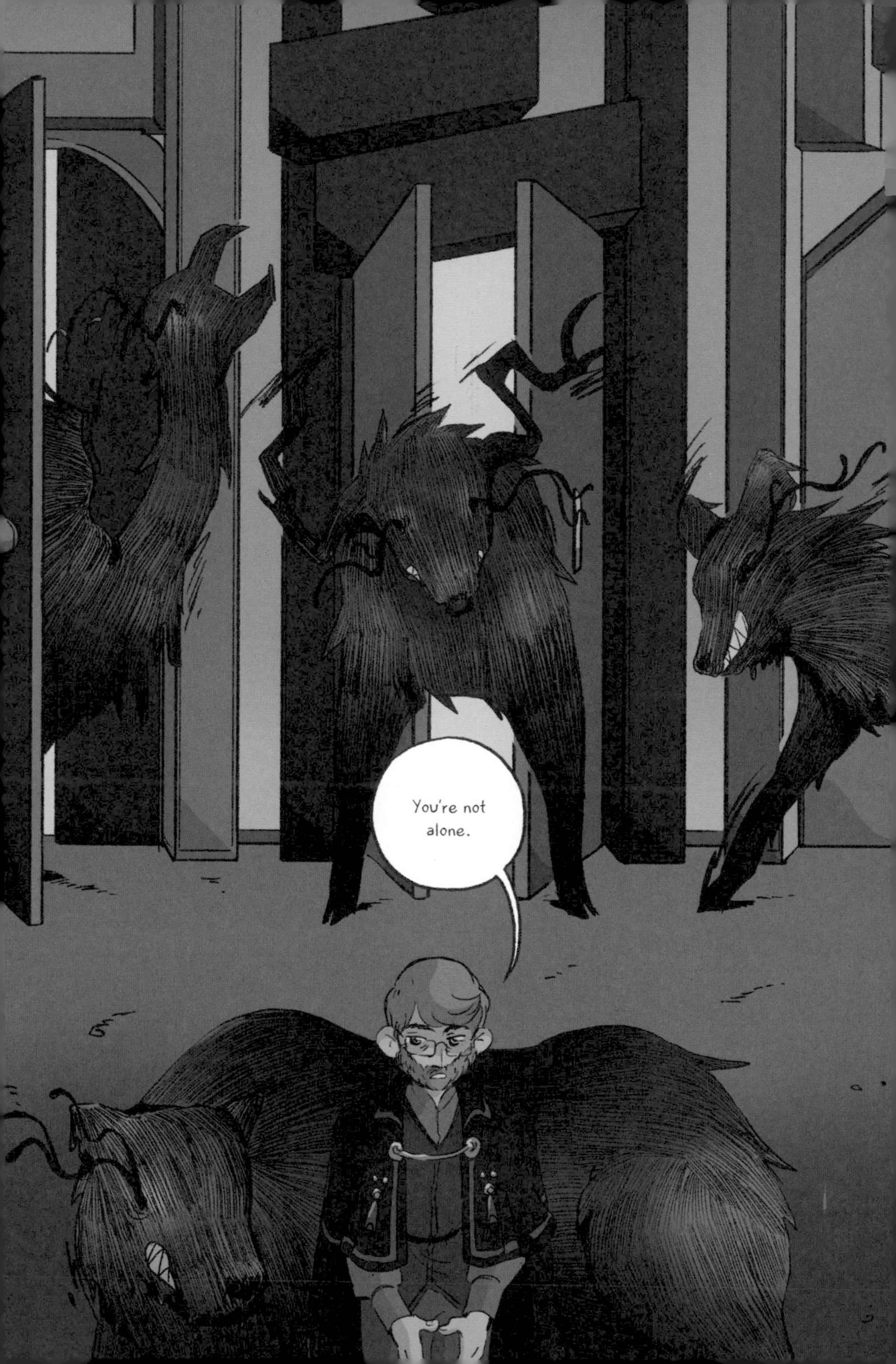
You're not alone.

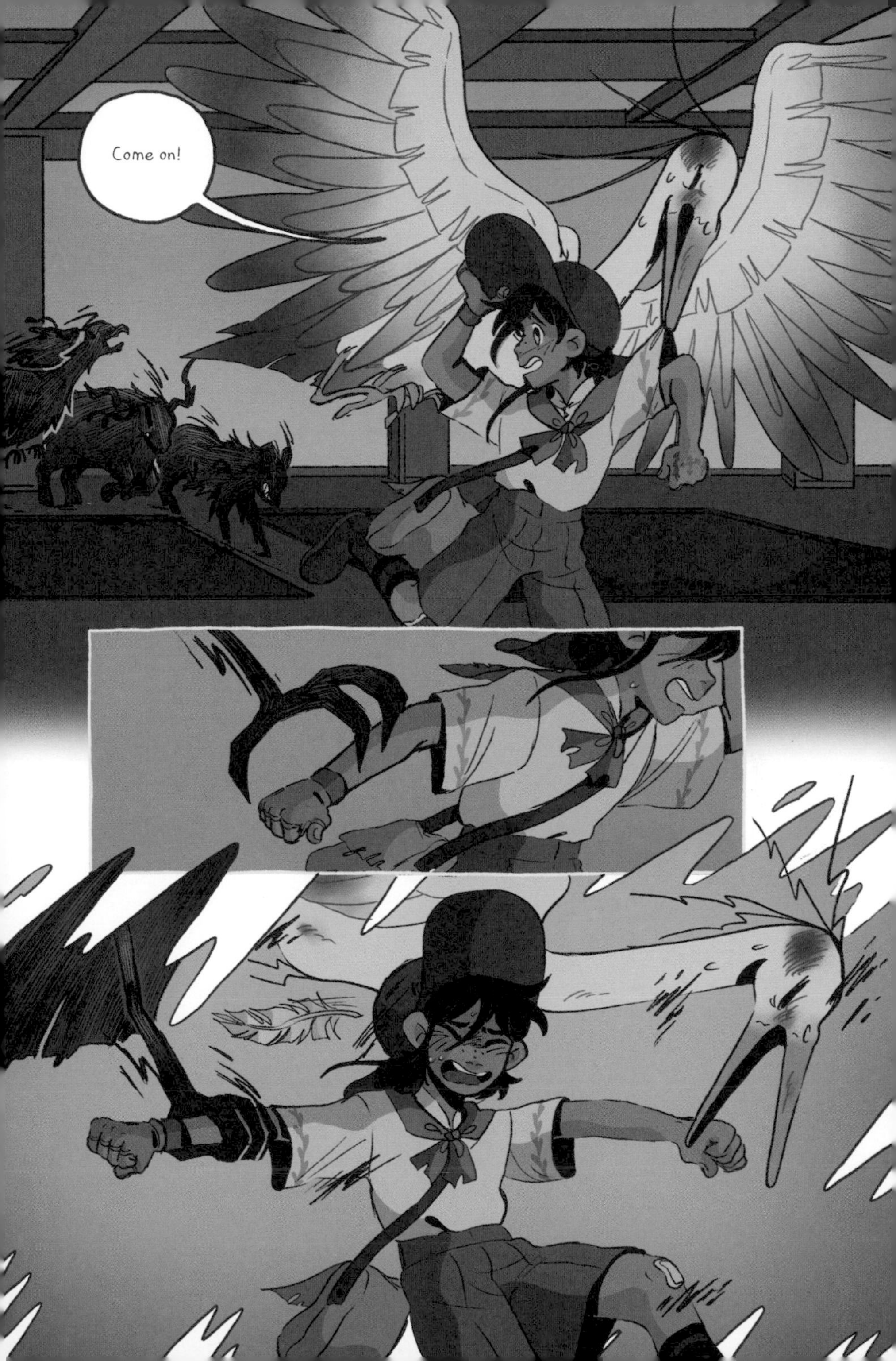
Come on!

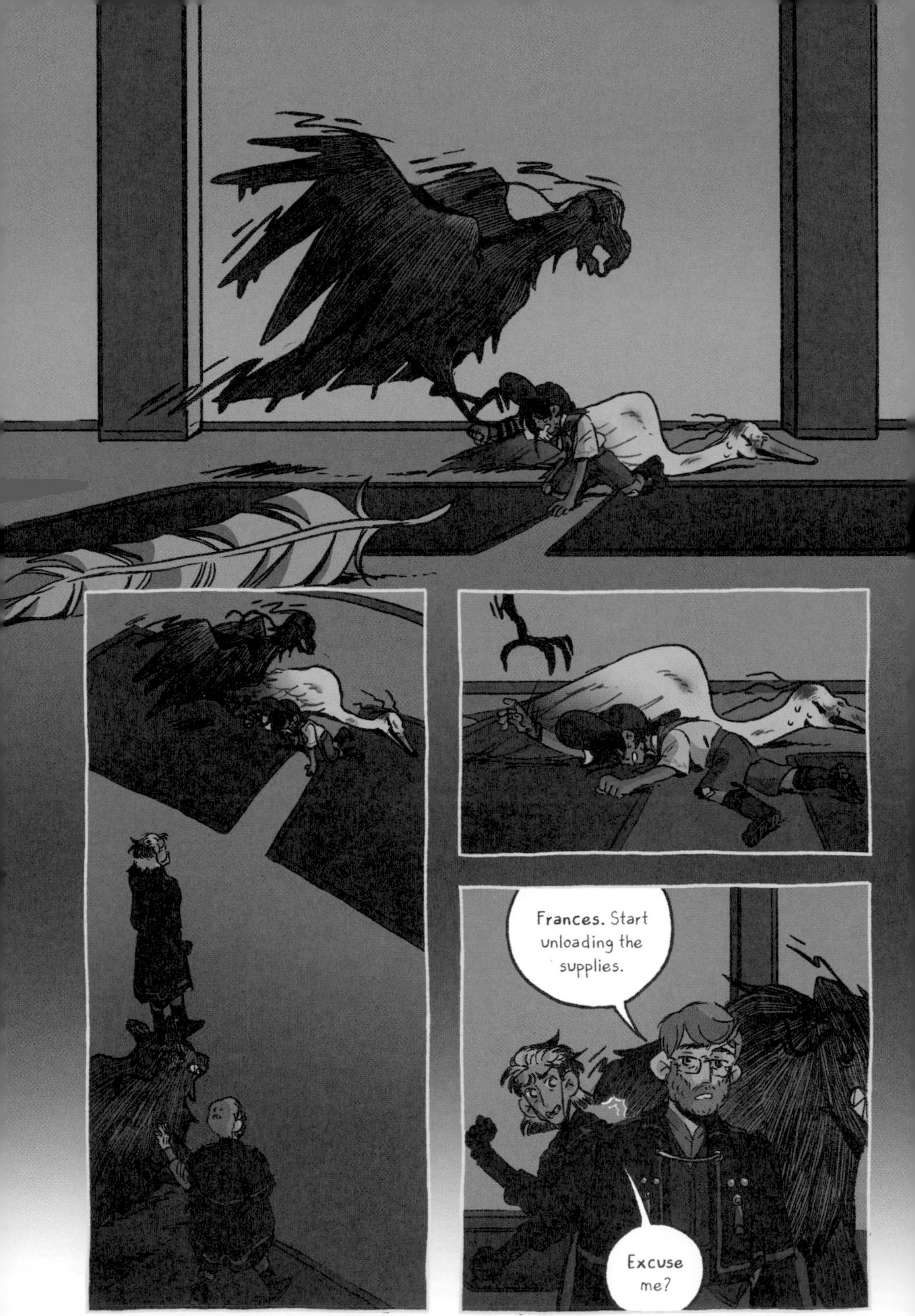
Frances. Start unloading the supplies.
Excuse me?

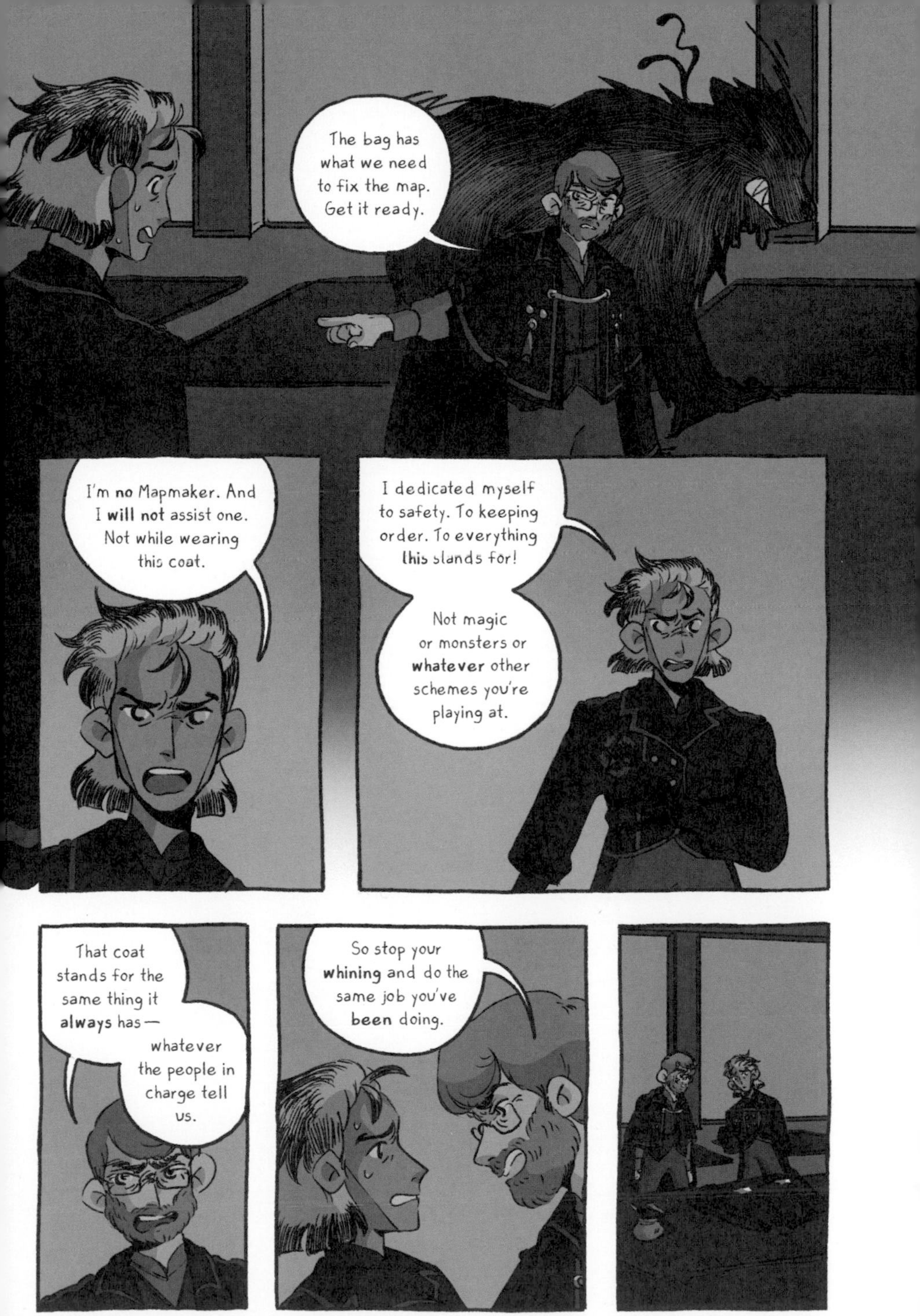
The bag has what we need to fix the map. Get it ready.
I'm **no** Mapmaker. And I **will not** assist one. Not while wearing this coat.
I dedicated myself to safety. To keeping order. To everything **this** stands for!
Not magic or monsters or **whatever** other schemes you're playing at.
That coat stands for the same thing it **always** has—
whatever the people in charge tell us.
So stop your **whining** and do the same job you've **been** doing.

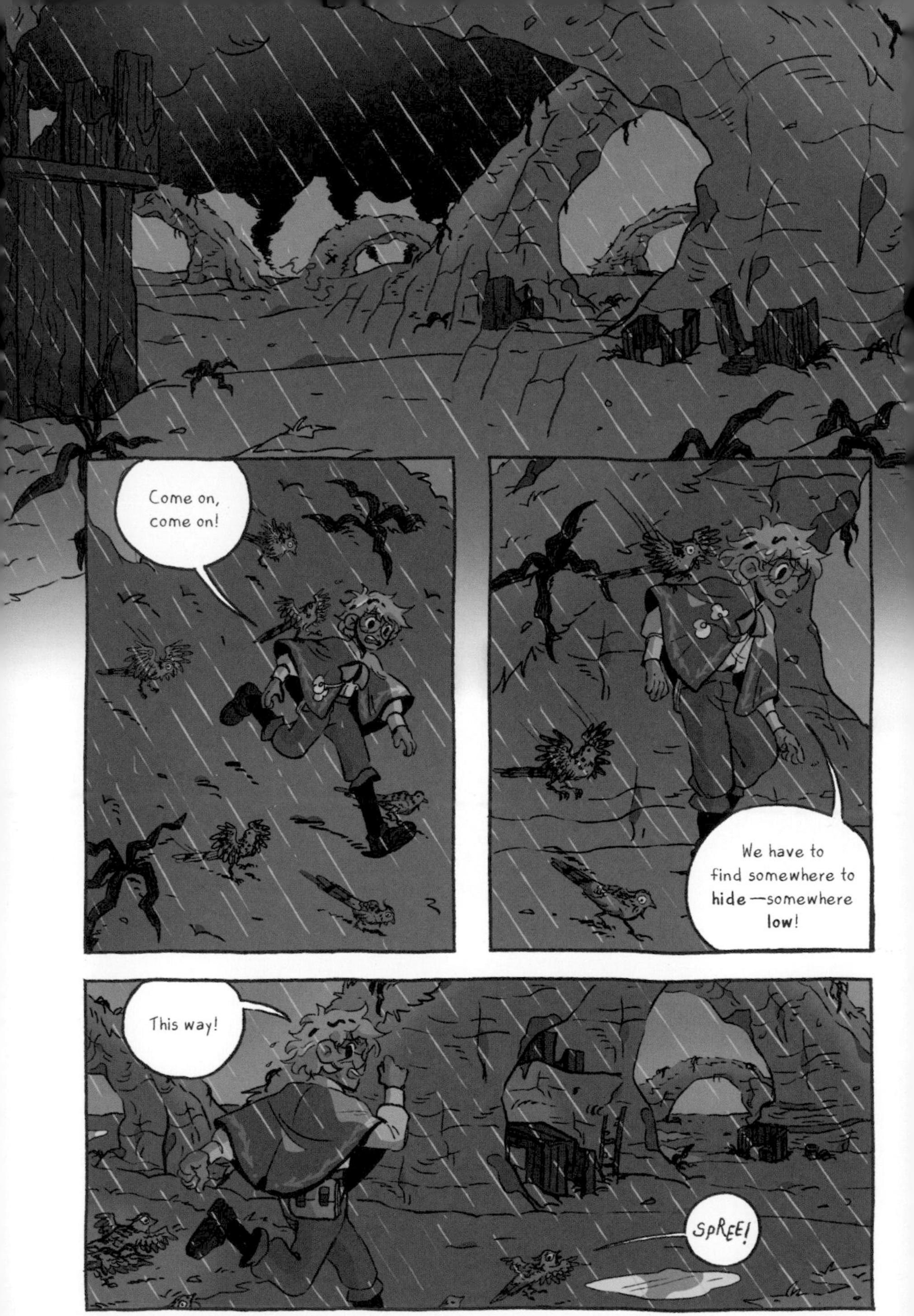
Come on, come on!
We have to find somewhere to **hide**—somewhere **low**!
This way!
SPREE!

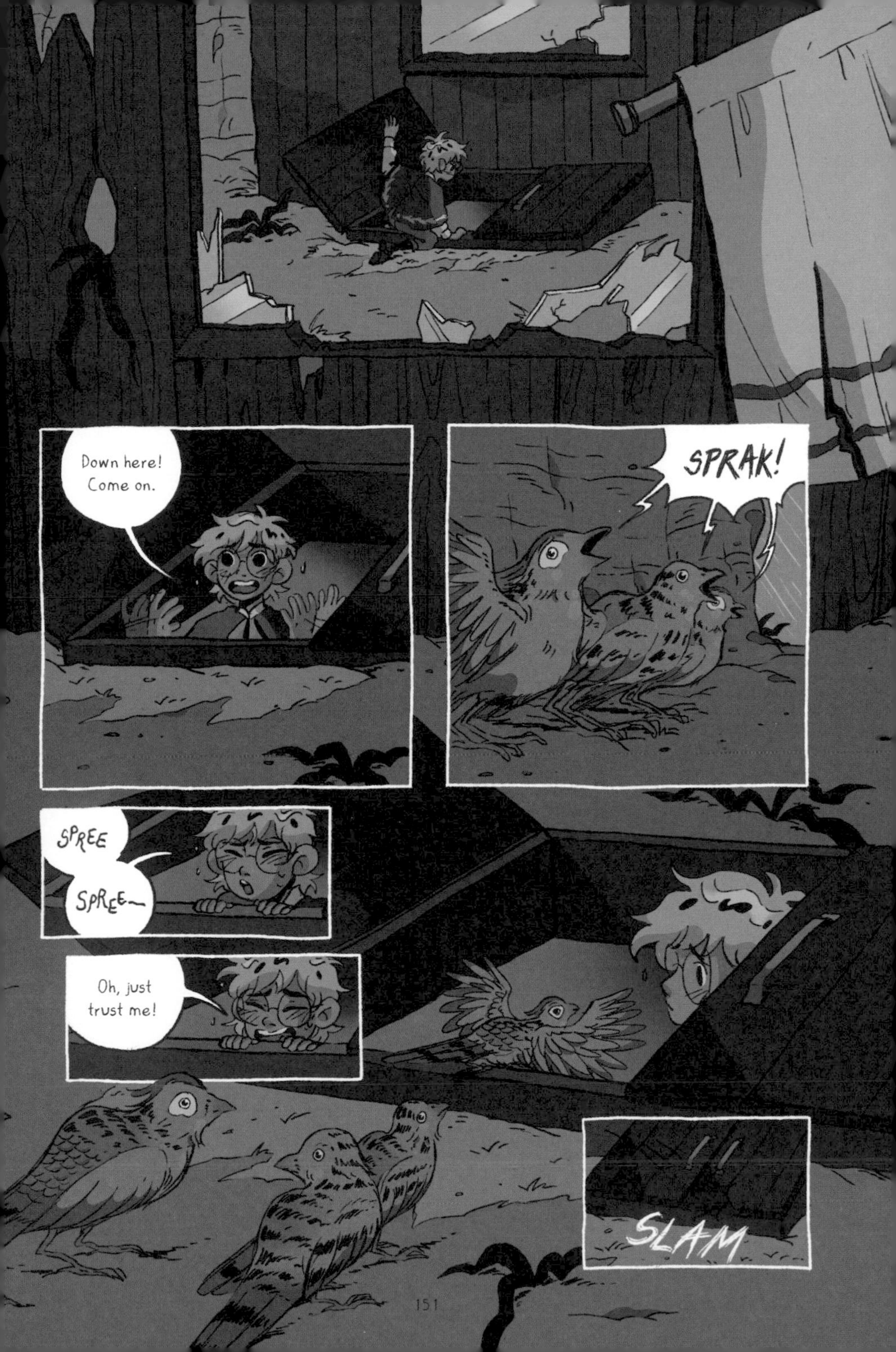
Down here! Come on.
SPRAK!
SPREE
SPREE~
Oh, just trust me!
SLAM

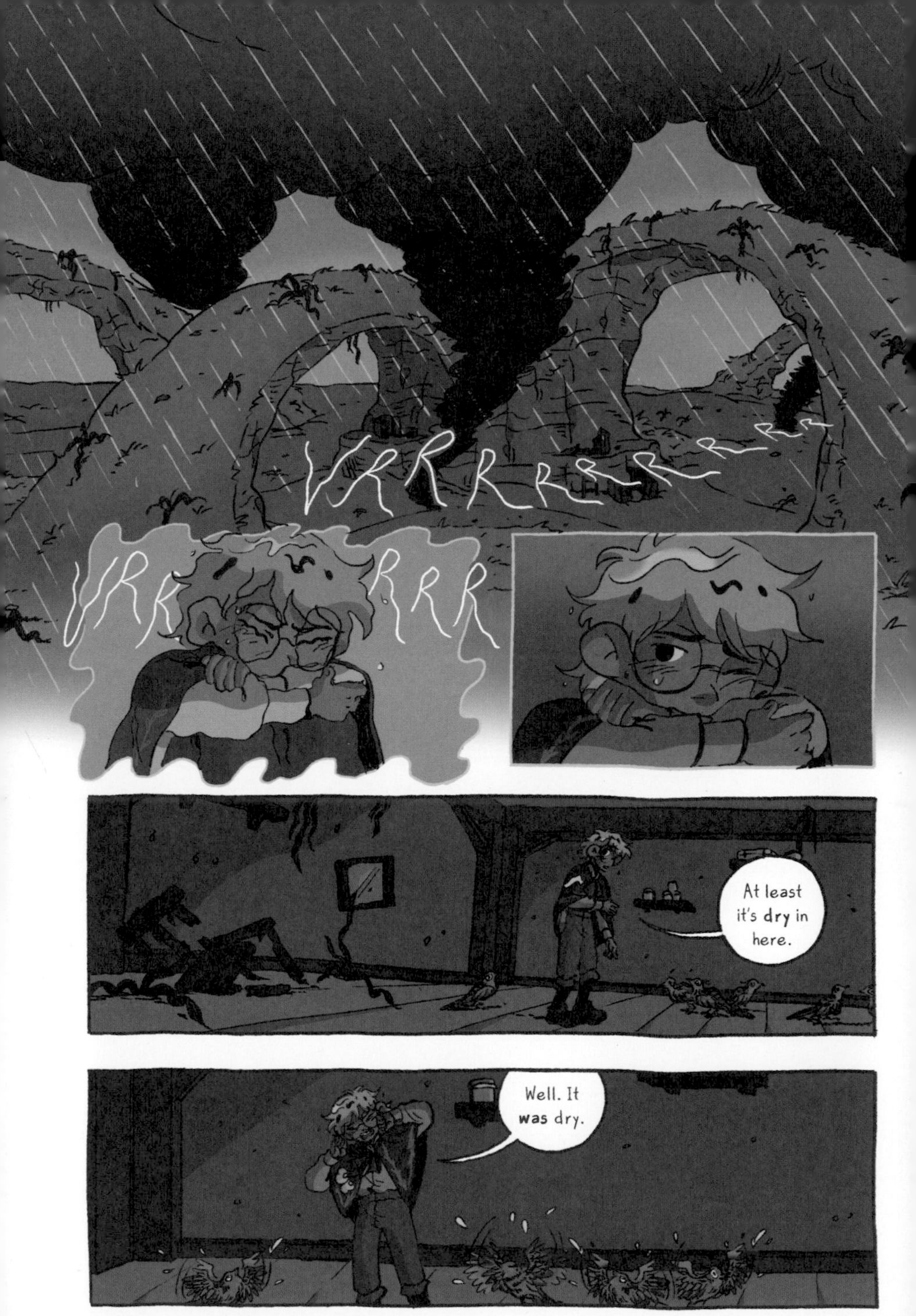
VRRRRRRRRRR
VRRRRR
At least it's dry in here.
Well. It was dry.

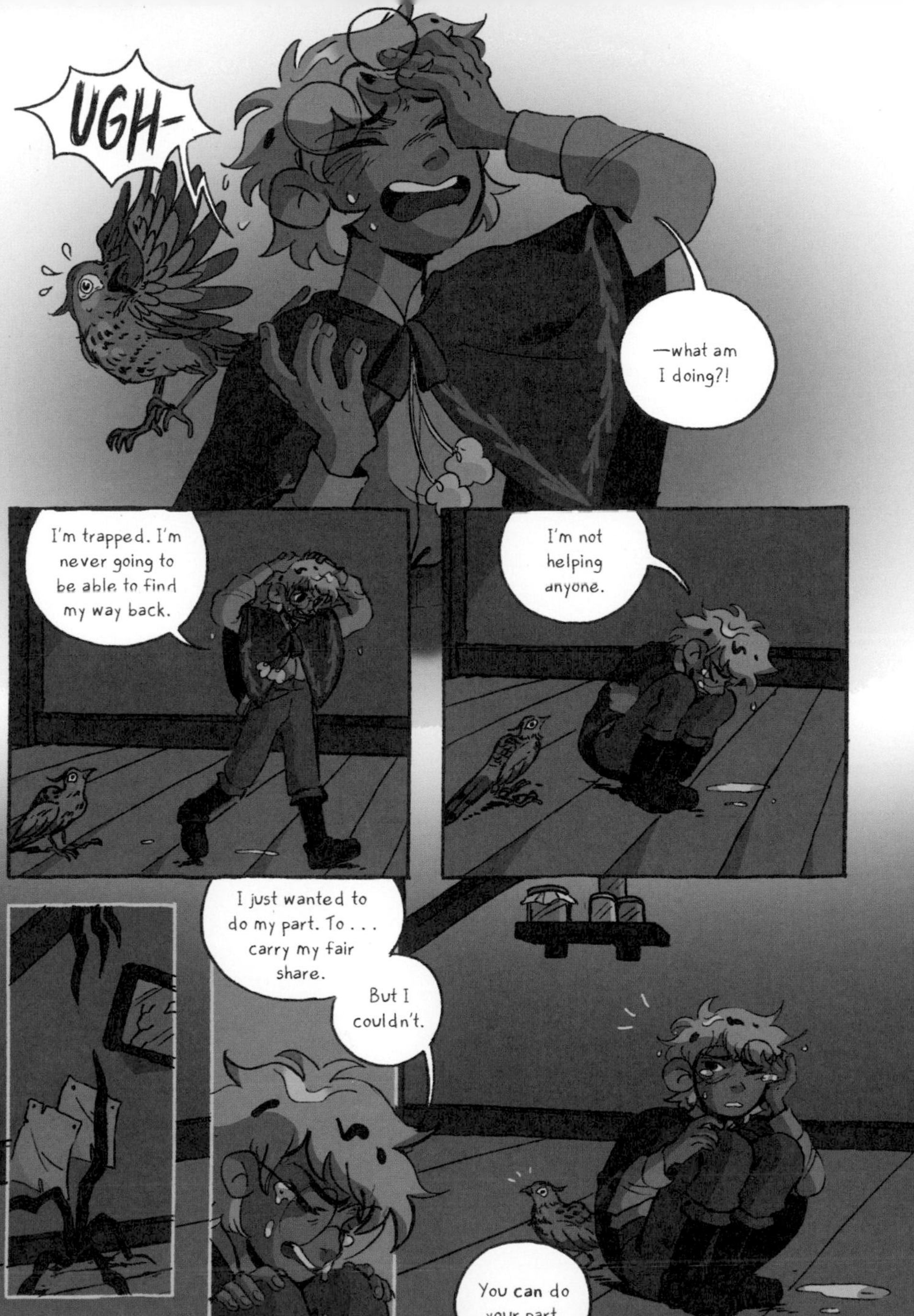
UGH-
—what am I doing?!
I'm trapped. I'm never going to be able to find my way back.
I'm not helping anyone.
I just wanted to do my part. To . . . carry my fair share.
But I couldn't.
You can do your part.

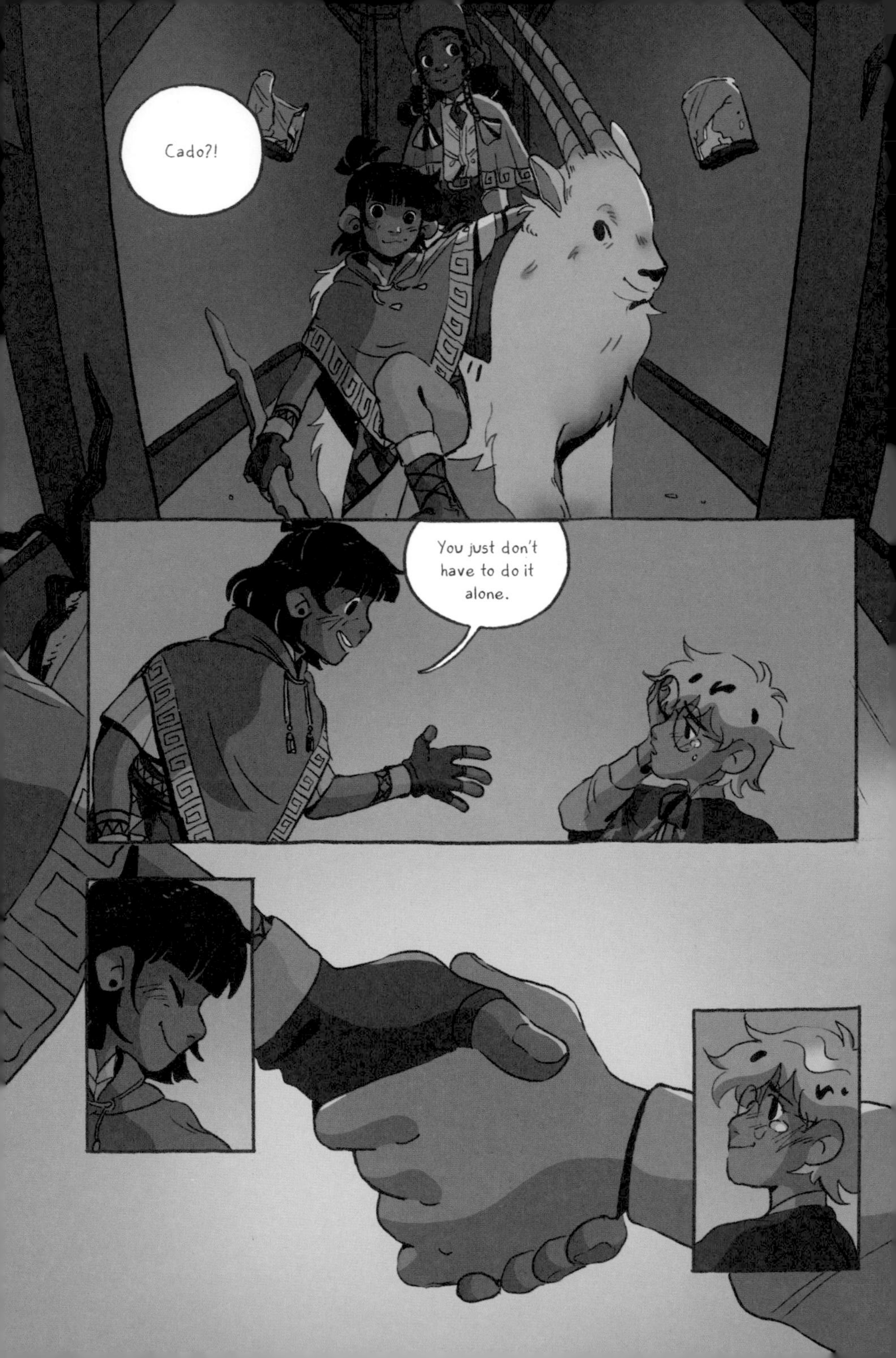
Cado?!
You just don't have to do it alone.

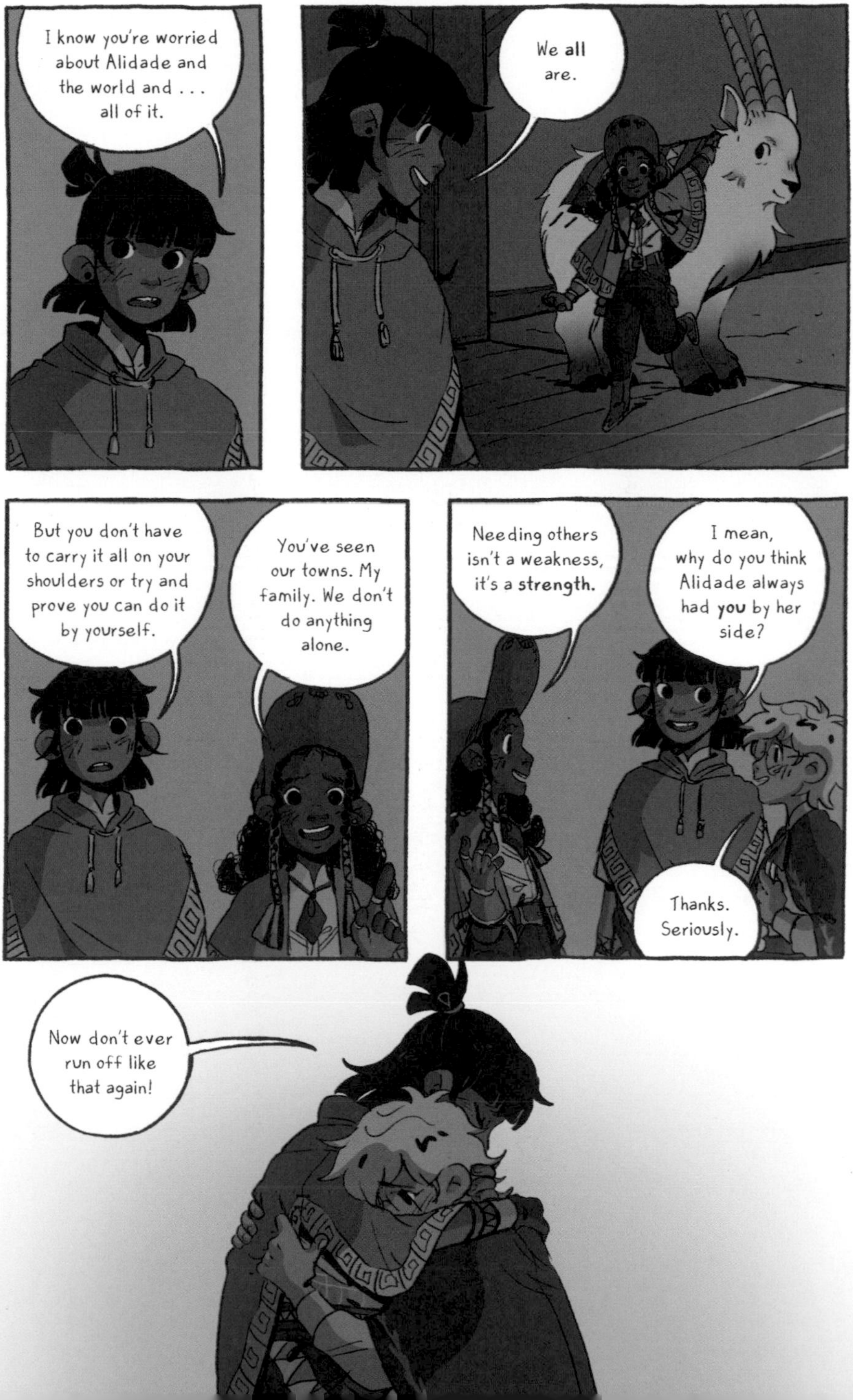
I know you're worried about Alidade and the world and . . . all of it.
We all are.
But you don't have to carry it all on your shoulders or try and prove you can do it by yourself.
You've seen our towns. My family. We don't do anything alone.
Needing others isn't a weakness, it's a strength.
I mean, why do you think Alidade always had you by her side?
Thanks. Seriously.
Now don't ever run off like that again!

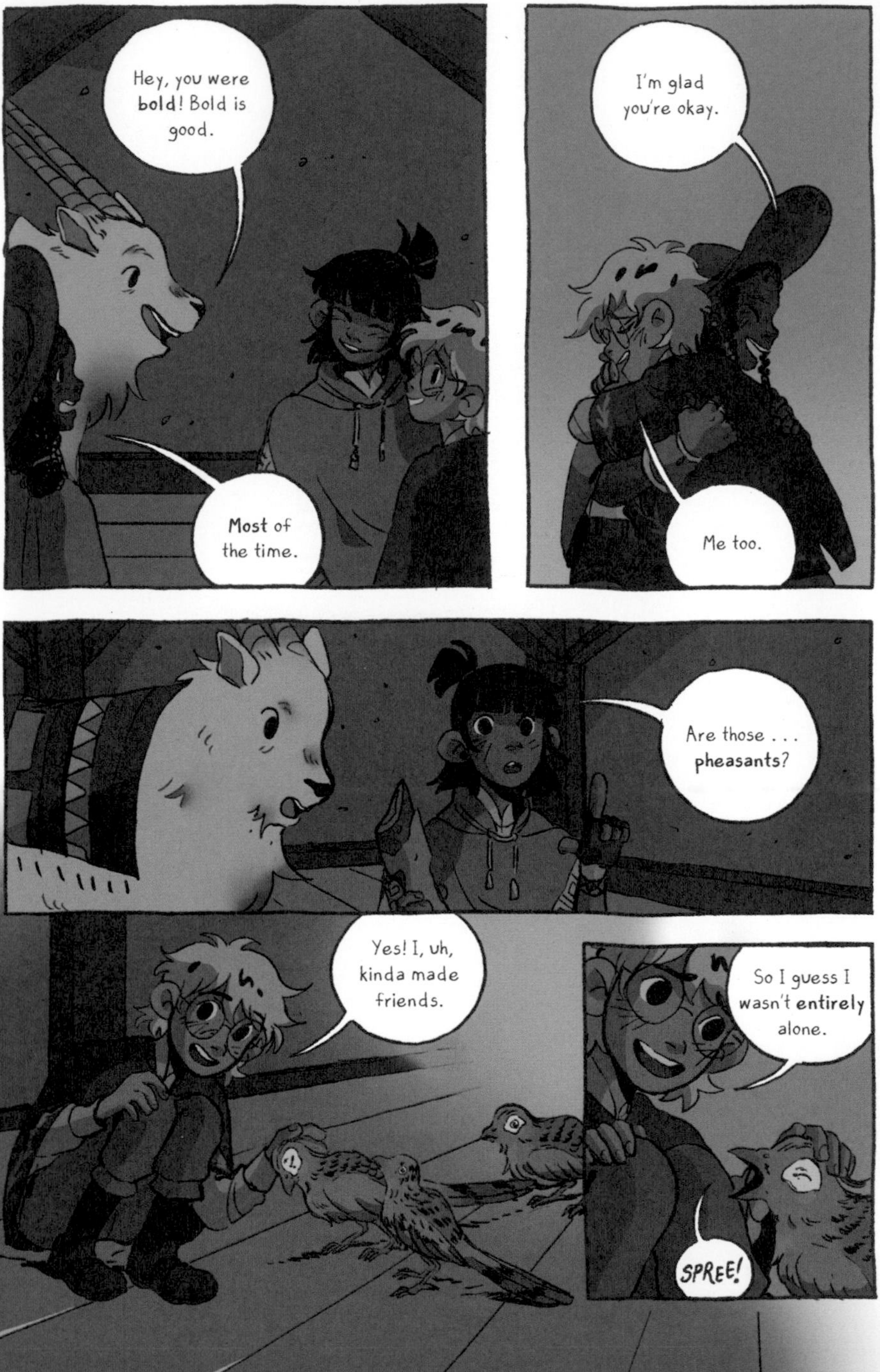

Hey, you were bold! Bold is good.
Most of the time.
I'm glad you're okay.
Me too.
Are those . . . pheasants?
Yes! I, uh, kinda made friends.
So I guess I wasn't entirely alone.
SPREE!

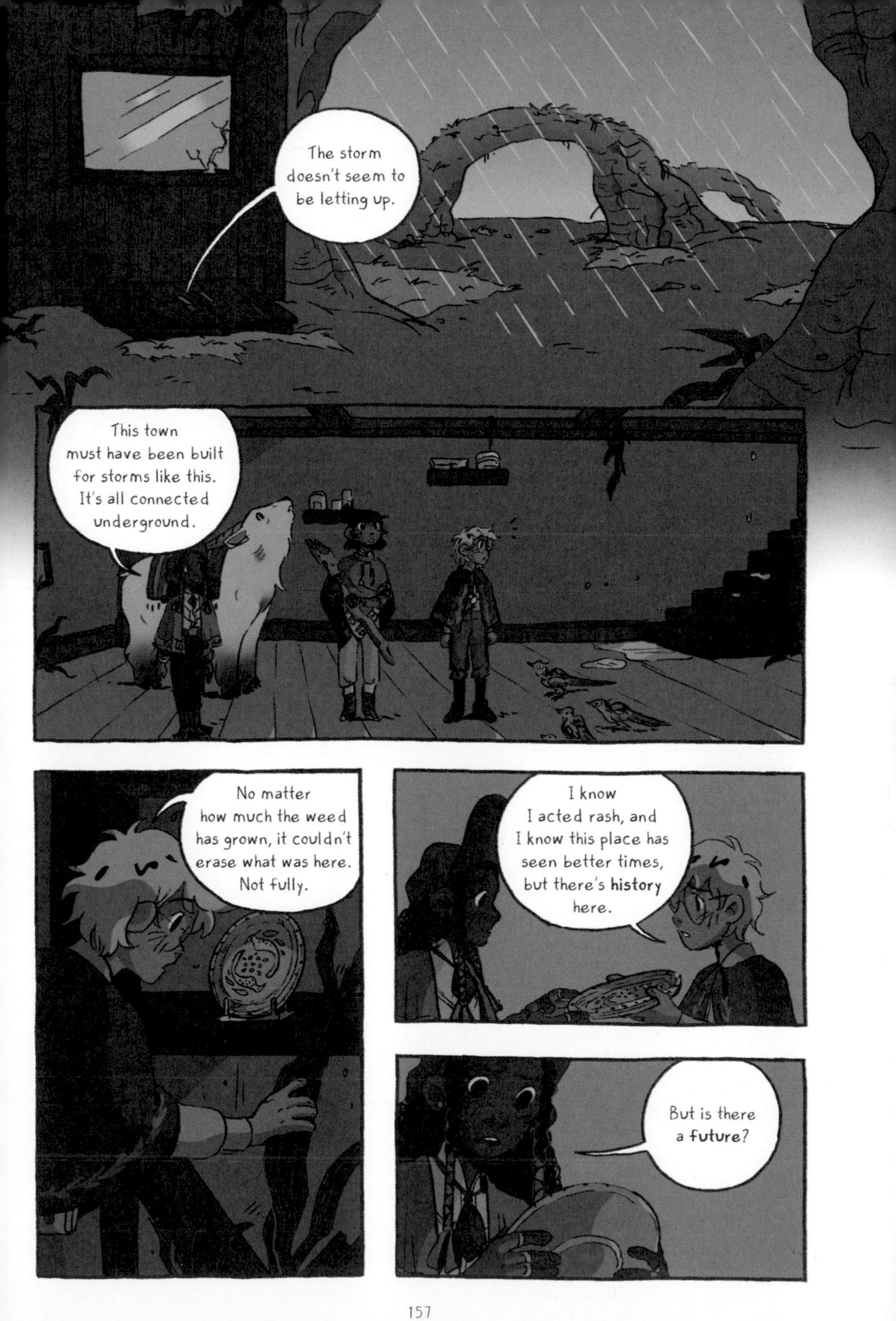
The storm doesn't seem to be letting up.
This town must have been built for storms like this. It's all connected underground.
No matter how much the weed has grown, it couldn't erase what was here. Not fully.
I know I acted rash, and I know this place has seen better times, but there's **history** here.
But is there a **future**?

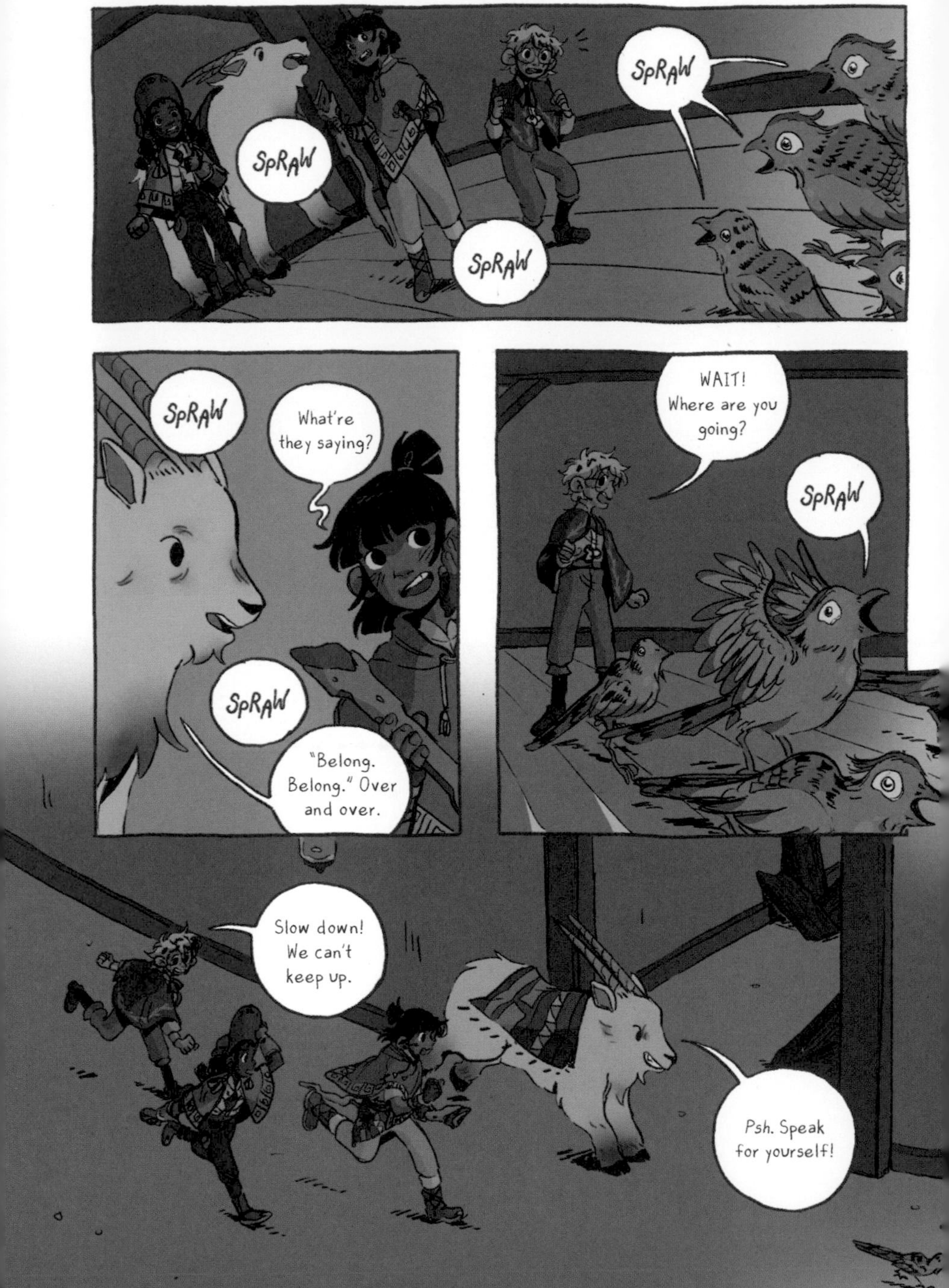
SpRAW
SpRAW
SpRAW
SpRAW
What're they saying?
SpRAW
"Belong. Belong." Over and over.
WAIT! Where are you going?
SpRAW
Slow down! We can't keep up.
Psh. Speak for yourself!

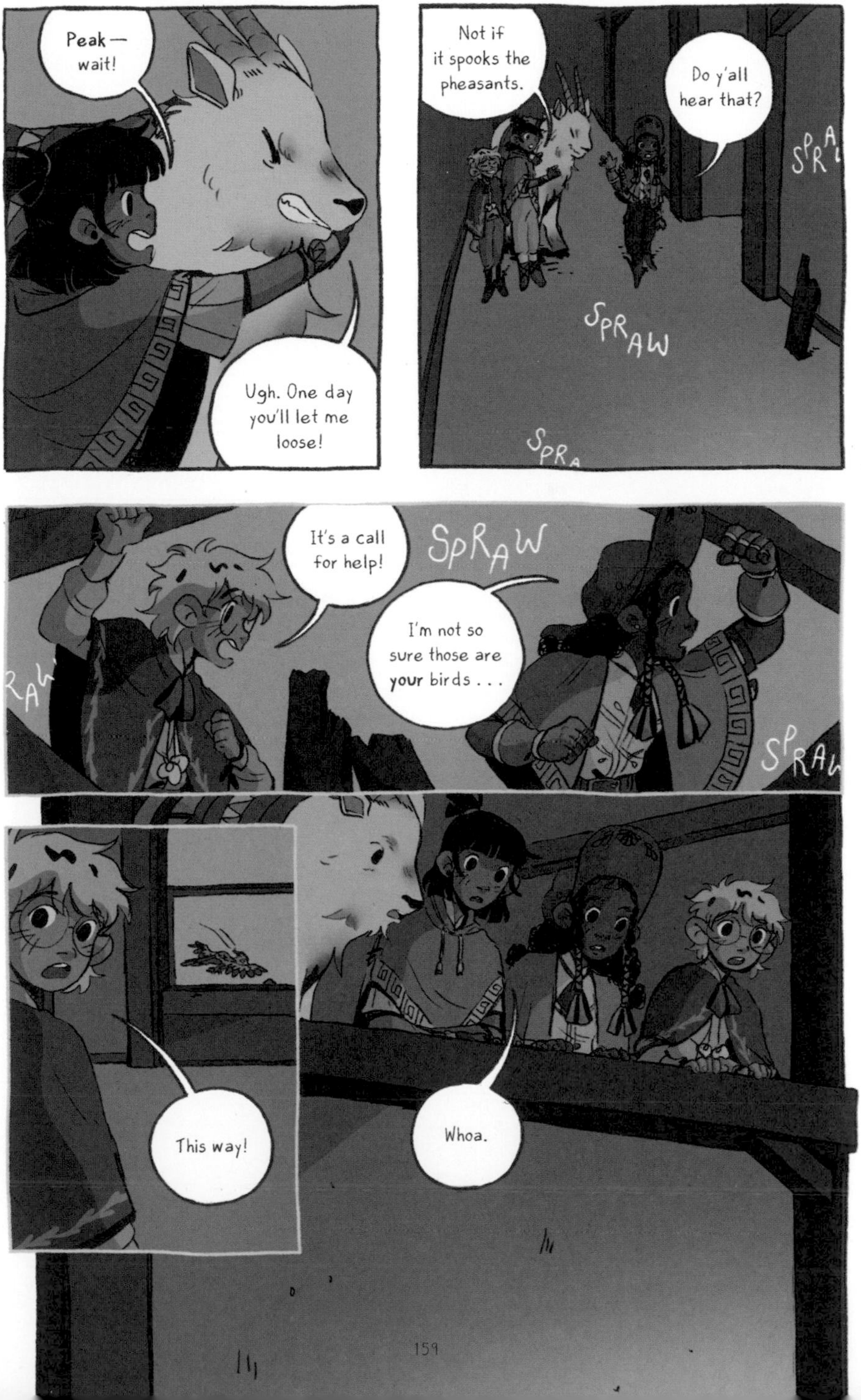
Peak—
wait!
Ugh. One day you'll let me loose!
Not if it spooks the pheasants.
Do y'all hear that?
SPRA
SPRAW
SPRA
It's a call for help!
SPRAW
I'm not so sure those are **your** birds . . .
RAW
SPRAW
This way!
Whoa.

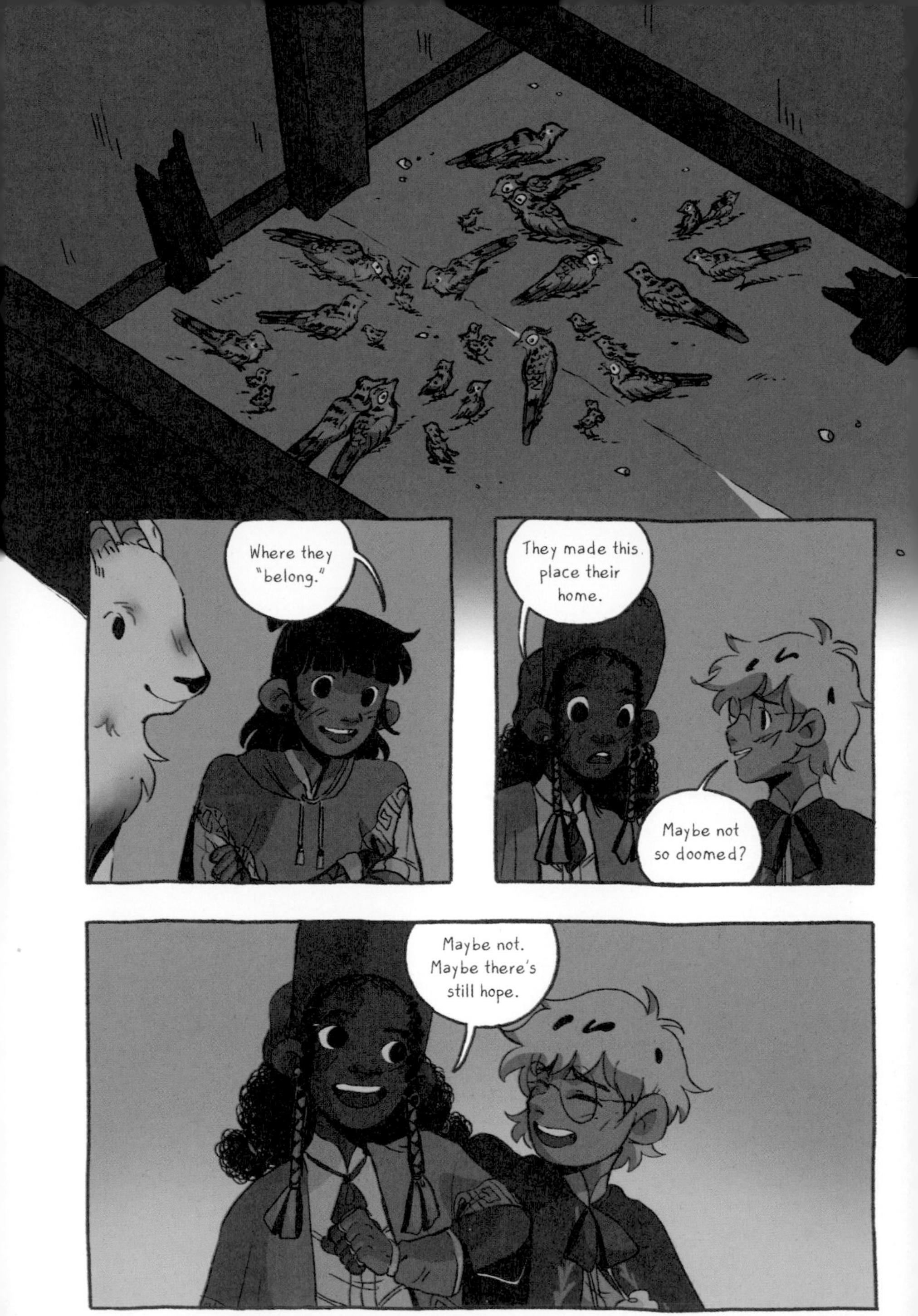
Where they "belong."
They made this place their home.
Maybe not so doomed?
Maybe not. Maybe there's still hope.

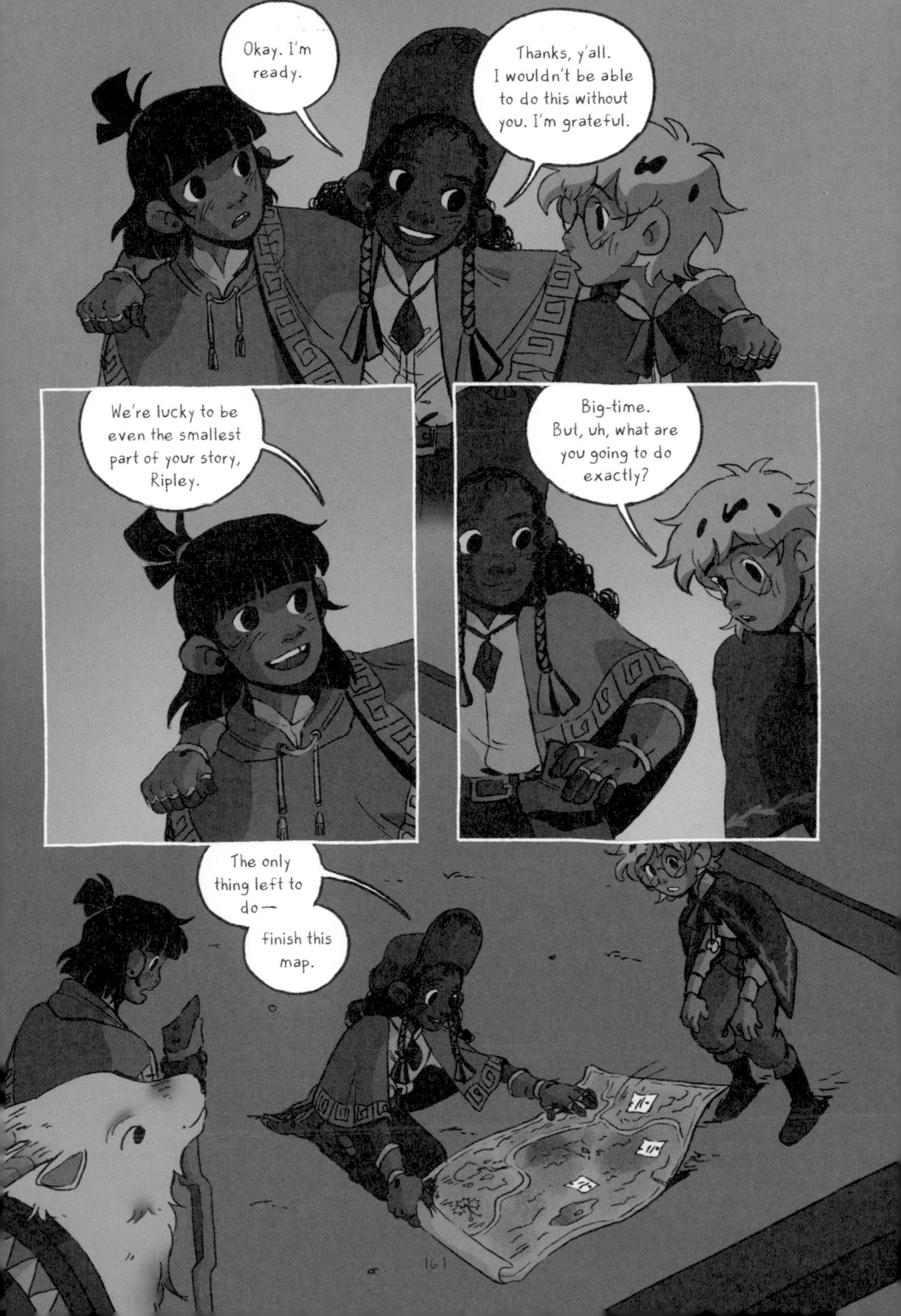
Okay. I'm ready.
Thanks, y'all. I wouldn't be able to do this without you. I'm grateful.
We're lucky to be even the smallest part of your story, Ripley.
Big-time. But, uh, what are you going to do exactly?
The only thing left to do—
finish this map.

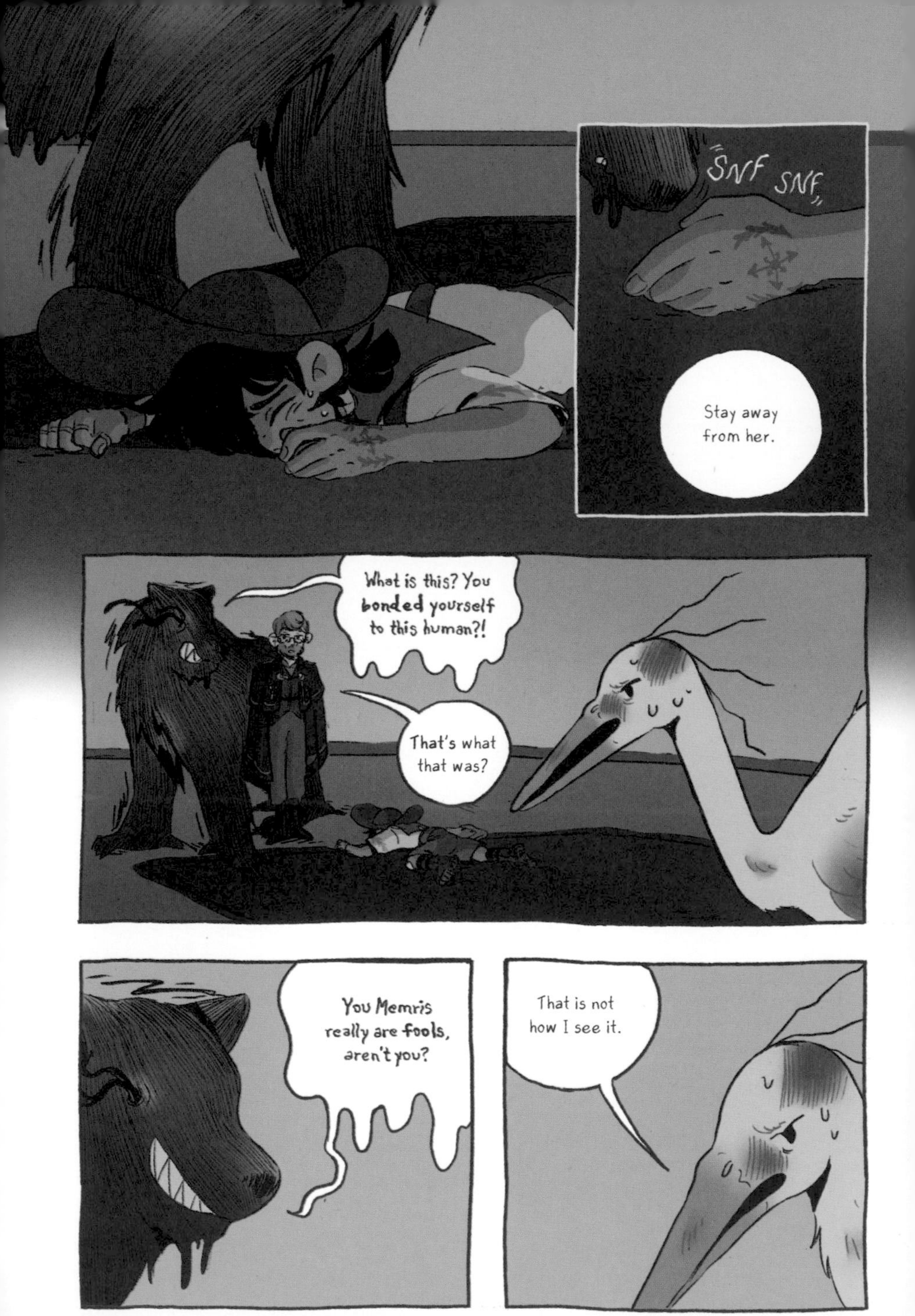
SNF SNF
Stay away from her.
What is this? You bonded yourself to this human?!
That's what that was?
You Memris really are fools, aren't you?
That is not how I see it.

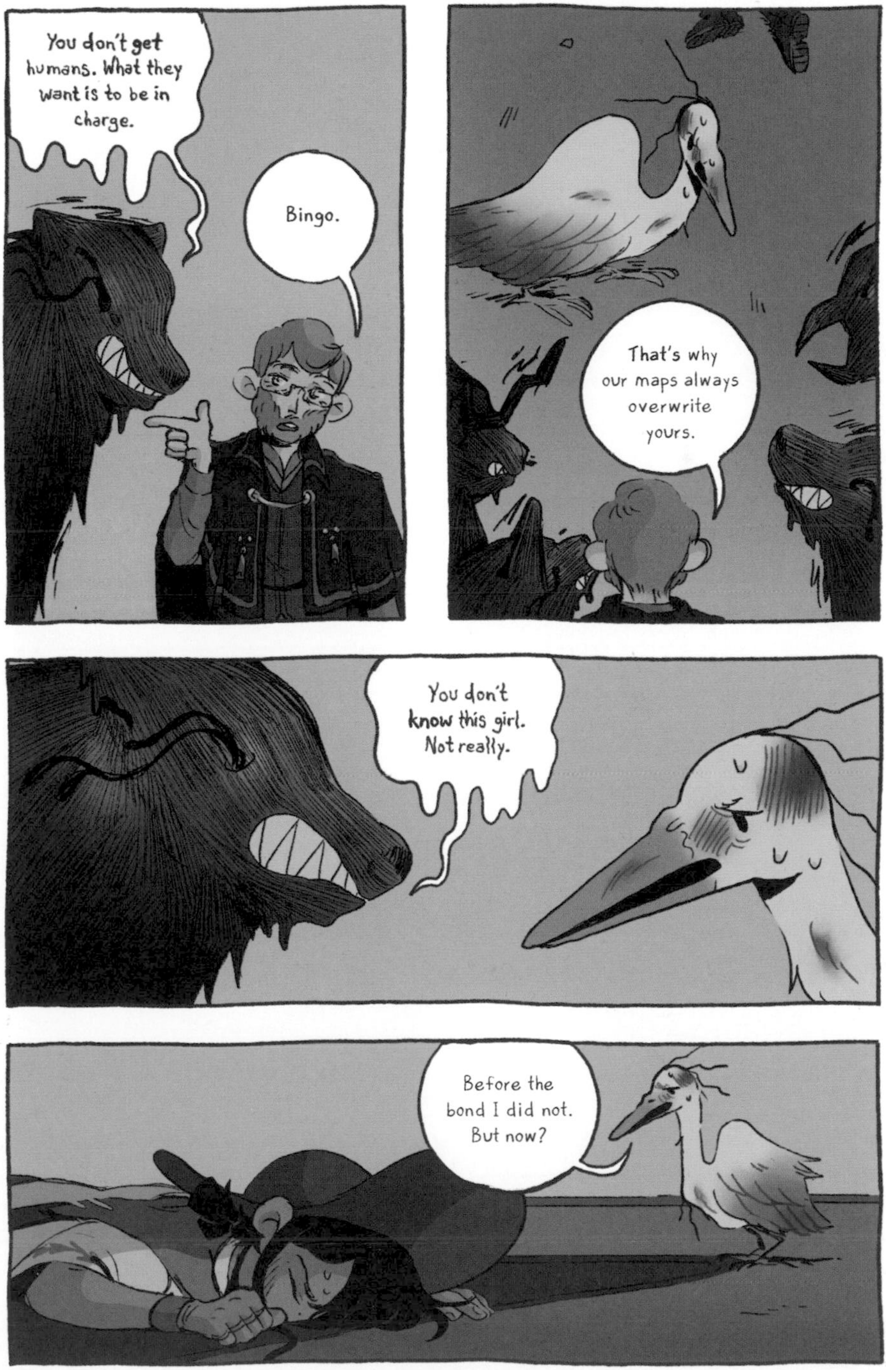
You don't get humans. What they want is to be in charge.
Bingo.
That's why our maps always overwrite yours.
You don't know this girl. Not really.
Before the bond I did not. But now?

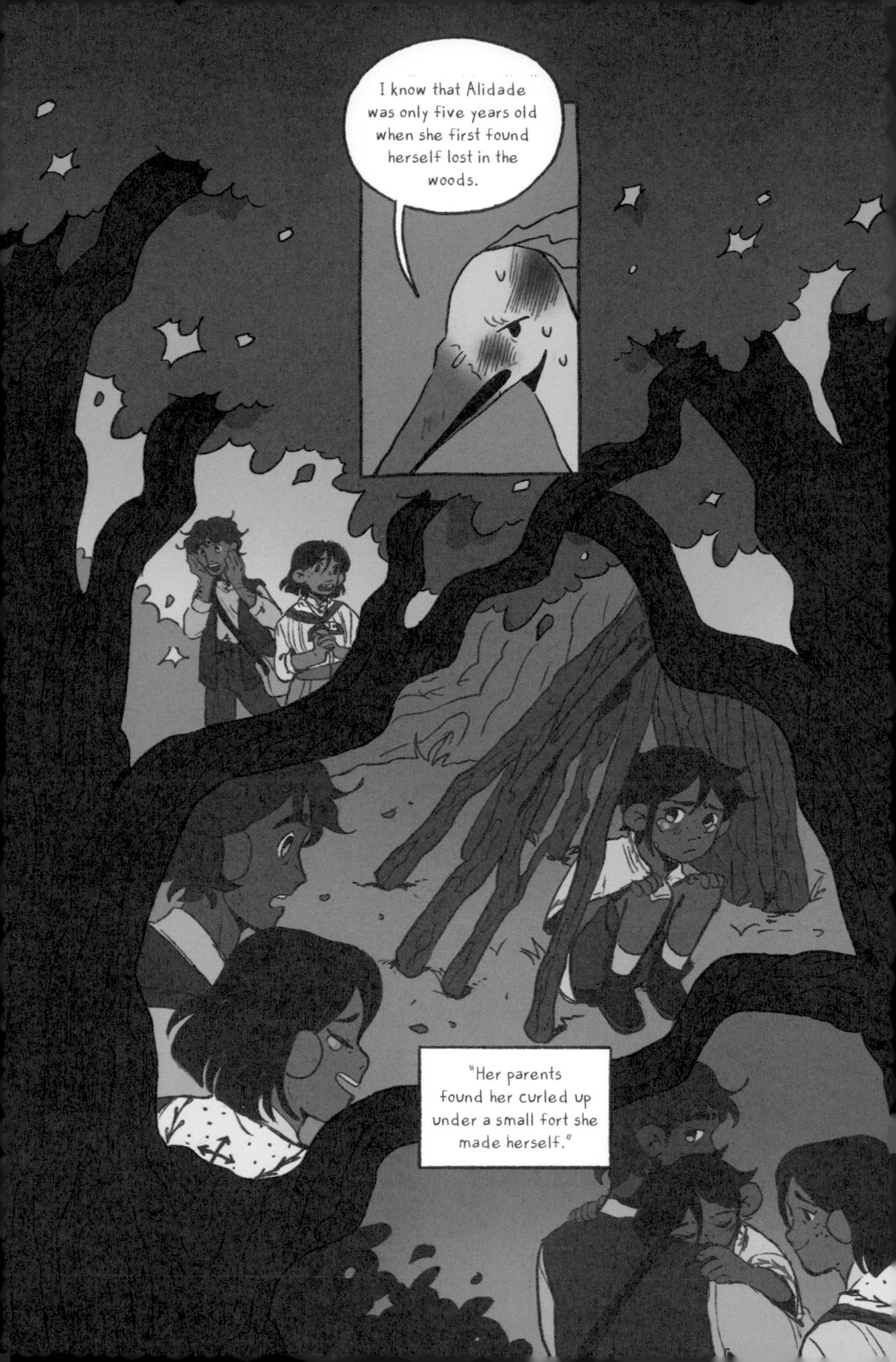
I know that Alidade was only five years old when she first found herself lost in the woods.
"Her parents found her curled up under a small fort she made herself."

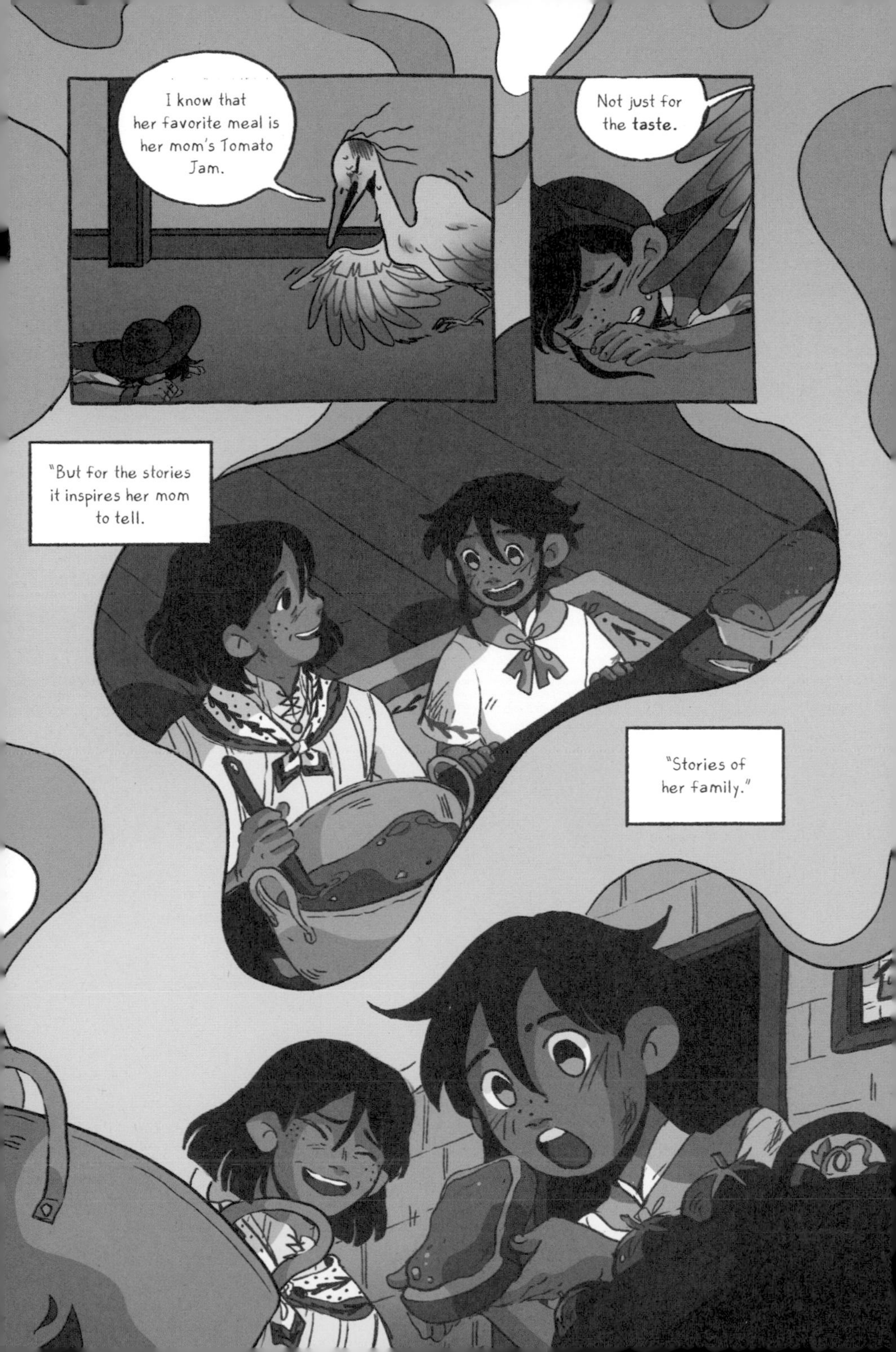
I know that her favorite meal is her mom's Tomato Jam.
Not just for the **taste.**
"But for the stories it inspires her mom to tell.
"Stories of her family."

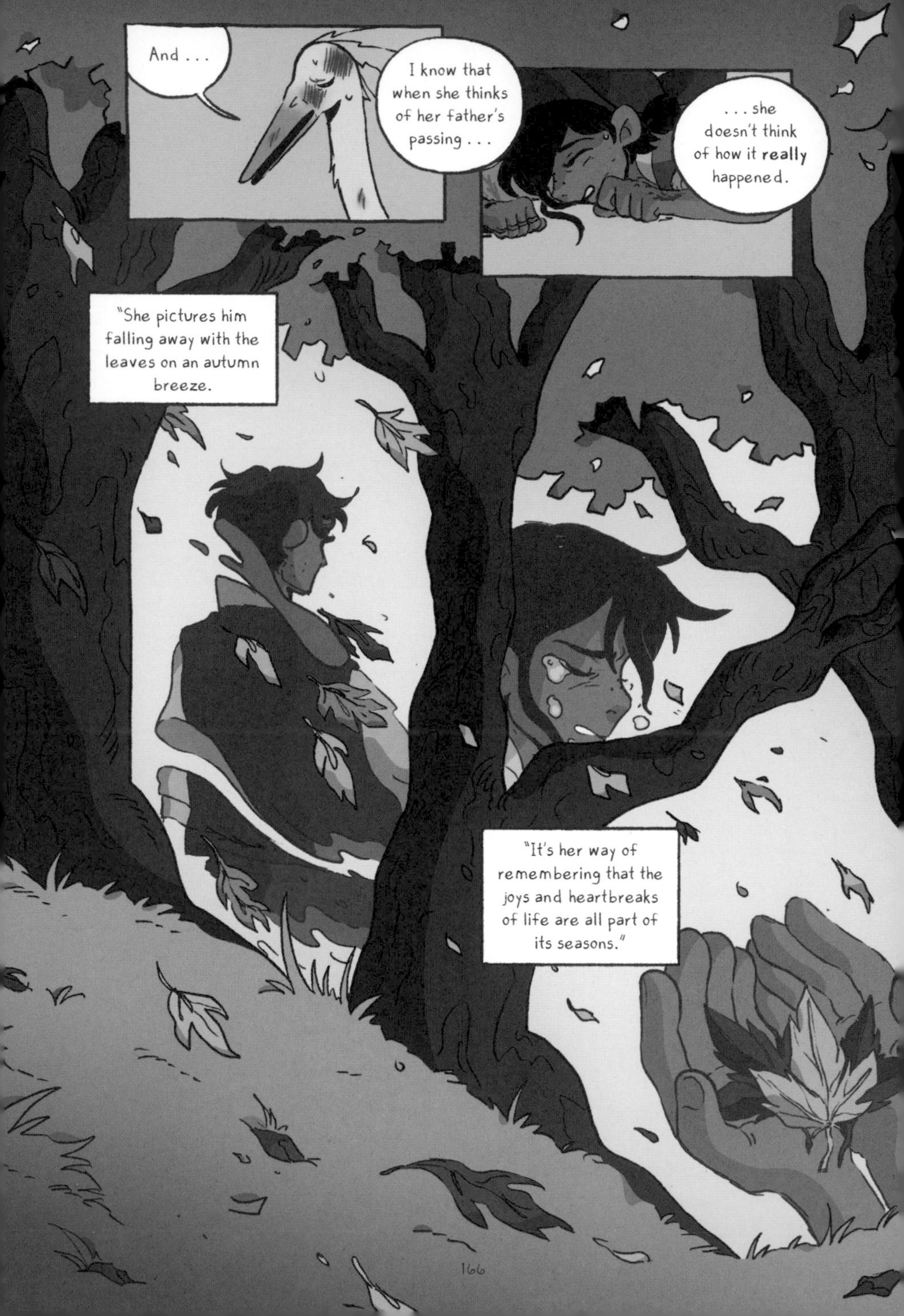
And . . .
I know that when she thinks of her father's passing . . .
. . . she doesn't think of how it **really** happened.
"She pictures him falling away with the leaves on an autumn breeze.
"It's her way of remembering that the joys and heartbreaks of life are all part of its seasons."

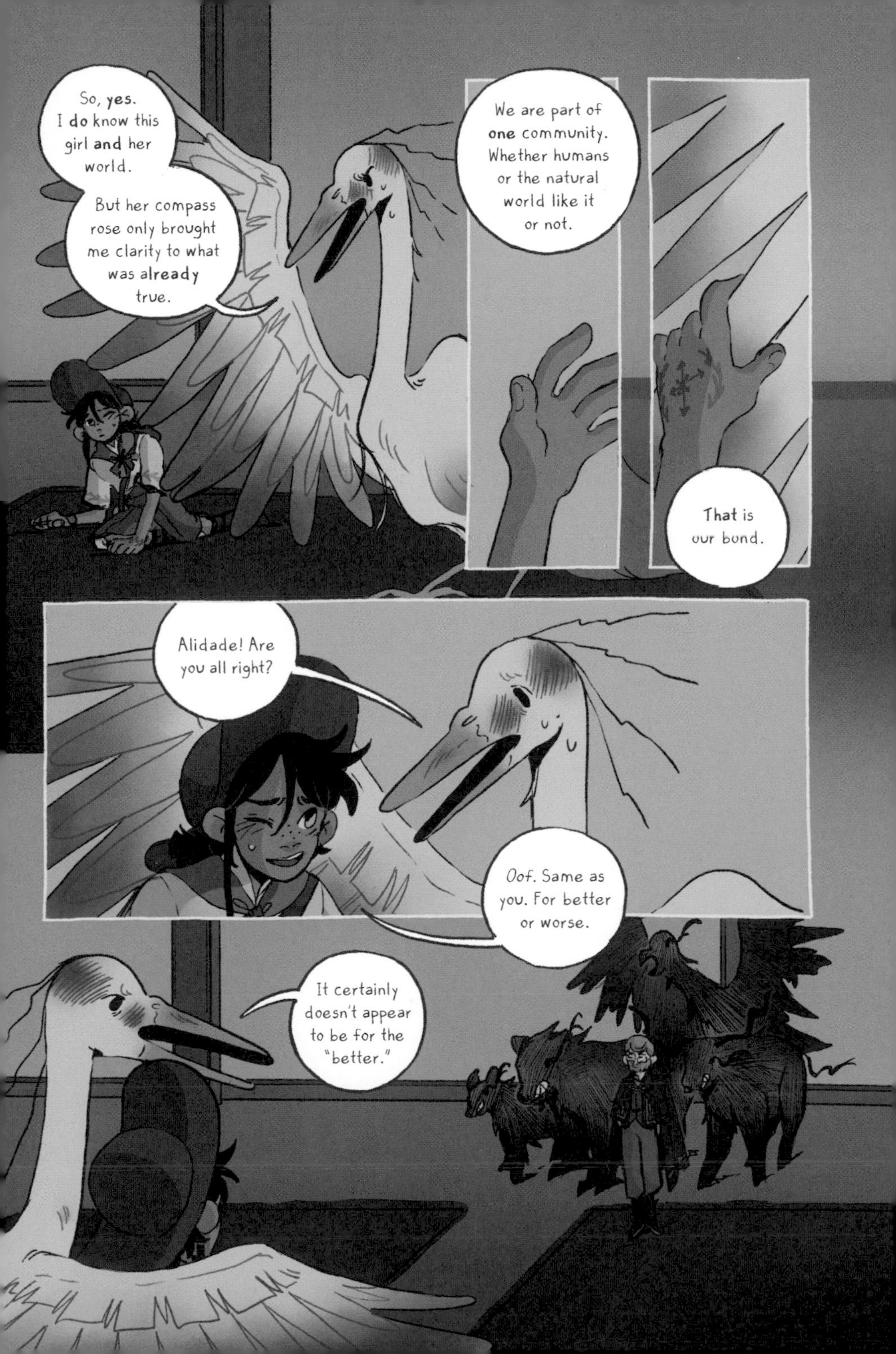
So, yes. I do know this girl and her world.
But her compass rose only brought me clarity to what was already true.
We are part of one community. Whether humans or the natural world like it or not.
That is our bond.
Alidade! Are you all right?
Oof. Same as you. For better or worse.
It certainly doesn't appear to be for the "better."

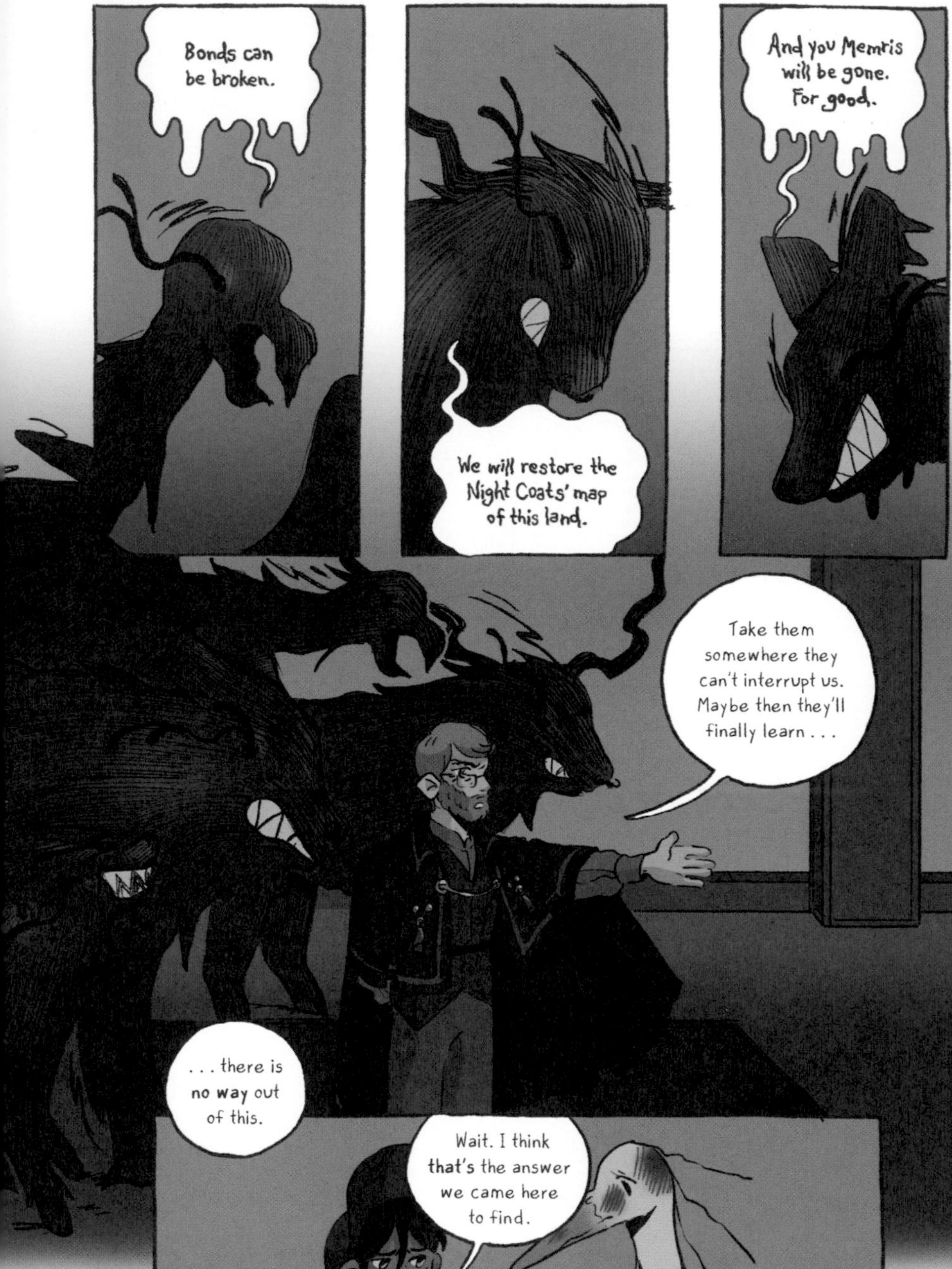

Bonds can be broken.
We will restore the Night Coats' map of this land.
And you Memris will be gone. For good.
Take them somewhere they can't interrupt us. Maybe then they'll finally learn . . .
. . . there is **no way** out of this.
Wait. I think **that's** the answer we came here to find.

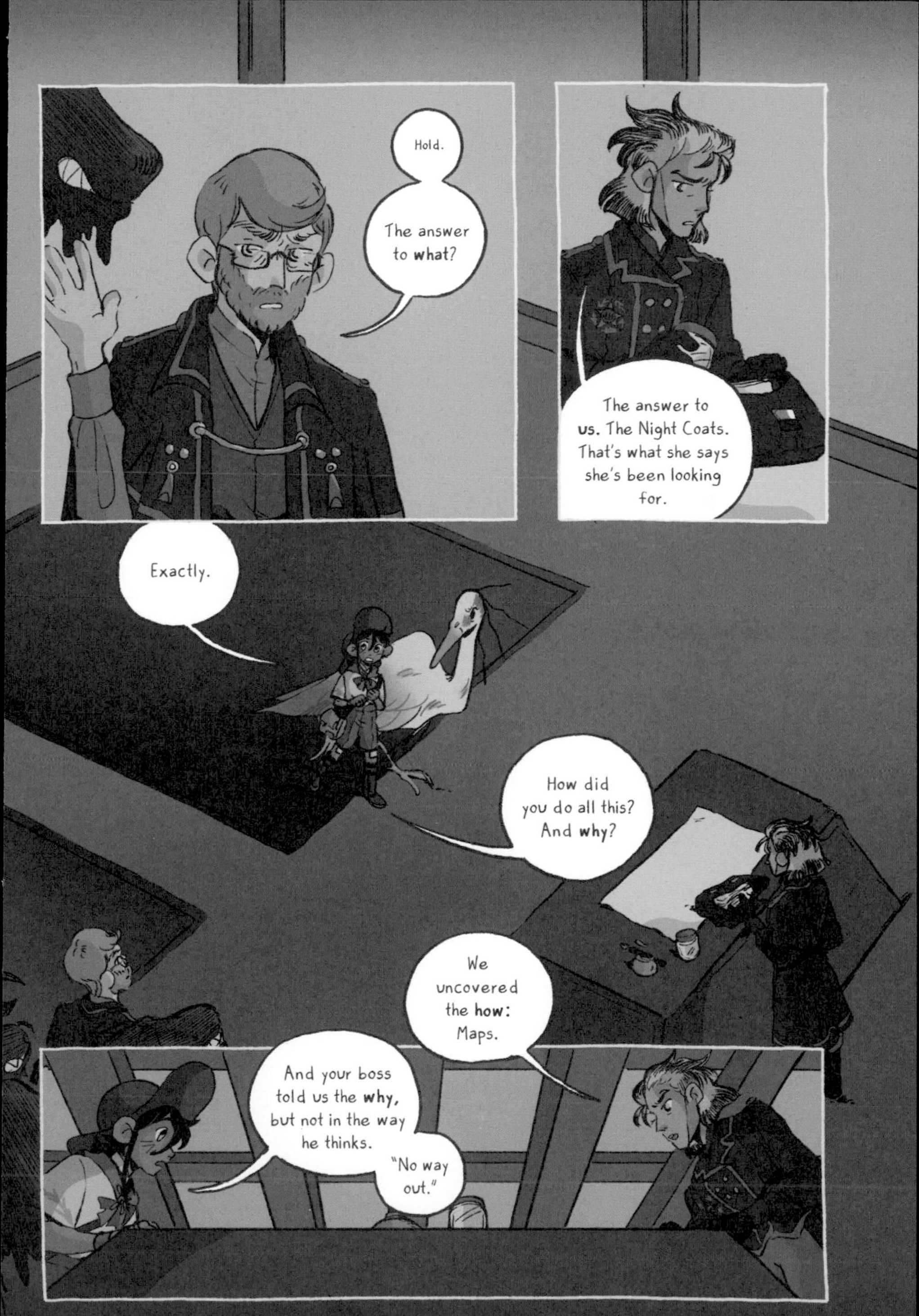
Hold.
The answer to what?
The answer to us. The Night Coats. That's what she says she's been looking for.
Exactly.
How did you do all this? And why?
We uncovered the how: Maps.
And your boss told us the why, but not in the way he thinks.
"No way out."

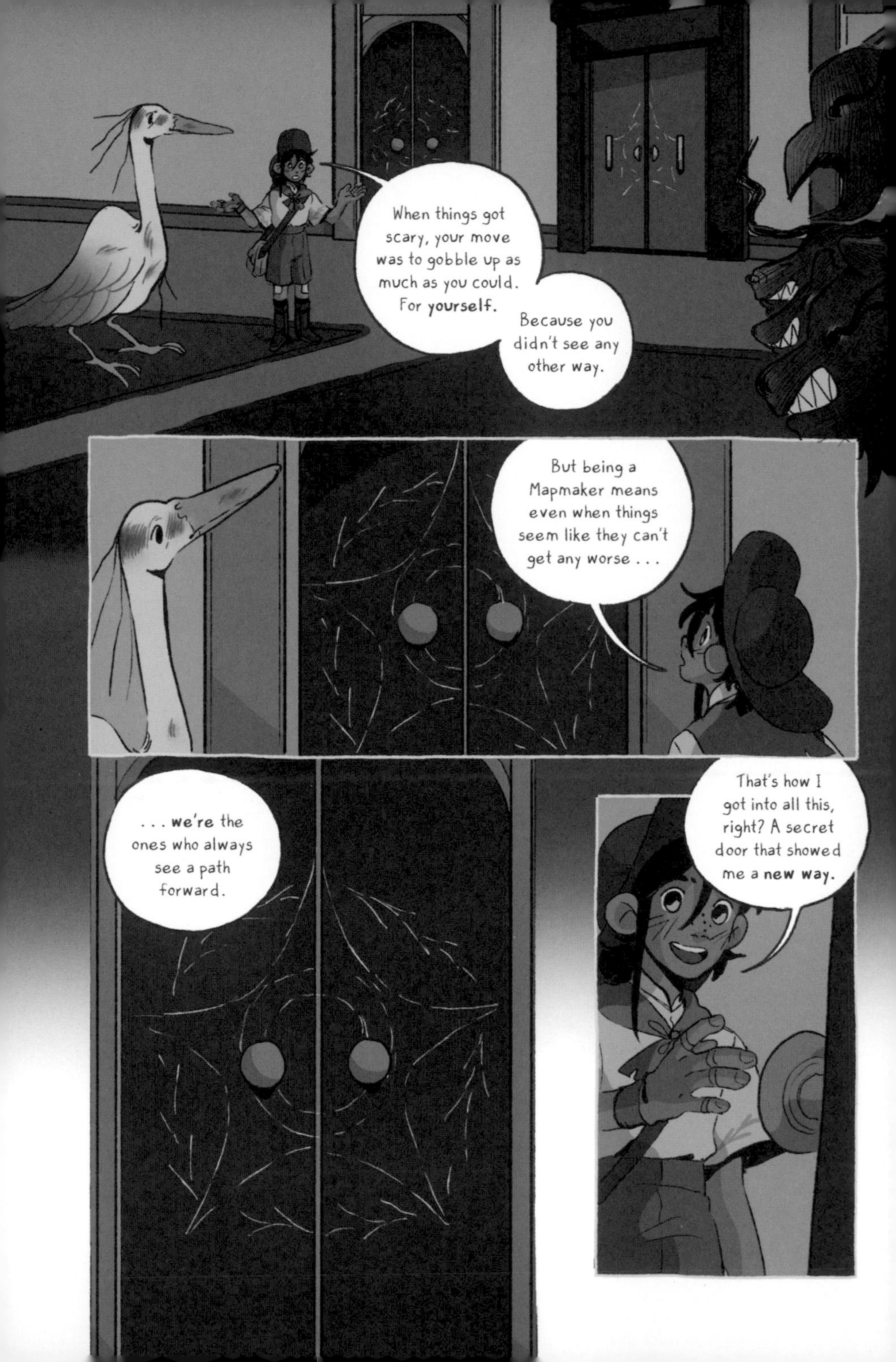
When things got scary, your move was to gobble up as much as you could. For **yourself**.
Because you didn't see any other way.
But being a Mapmaker means even when things seem like they can't get any worse . . .
. . . **we're** the ones who always see a path forward.
That's how I got into all this, right? A secret door that showed me a **new way.**

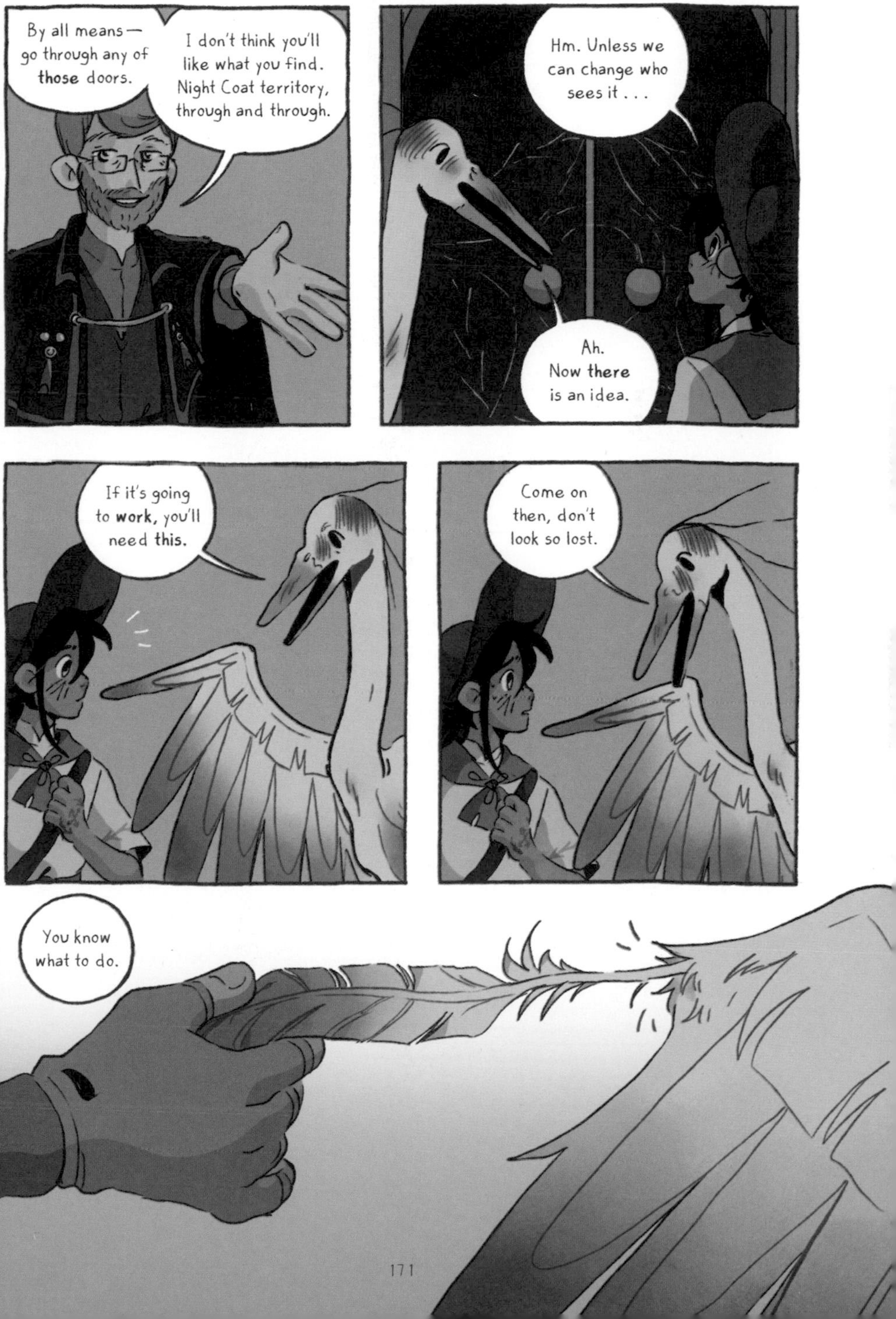
By all means — go through any of **those** doors.
I don't think you'll like what you find. Night Coat territory, through and through.
Hm. Unless we can change who sees it . . .
Ah. Now **there** is an idea.
If it's going to **work,** you'll need **this.**
Come on then, don't look so lost.
You know what to do.

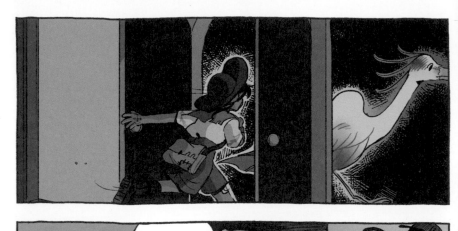

Enough of the stalling. Go on. Get them back.

Uh. Hiii. Don't mind us . . .

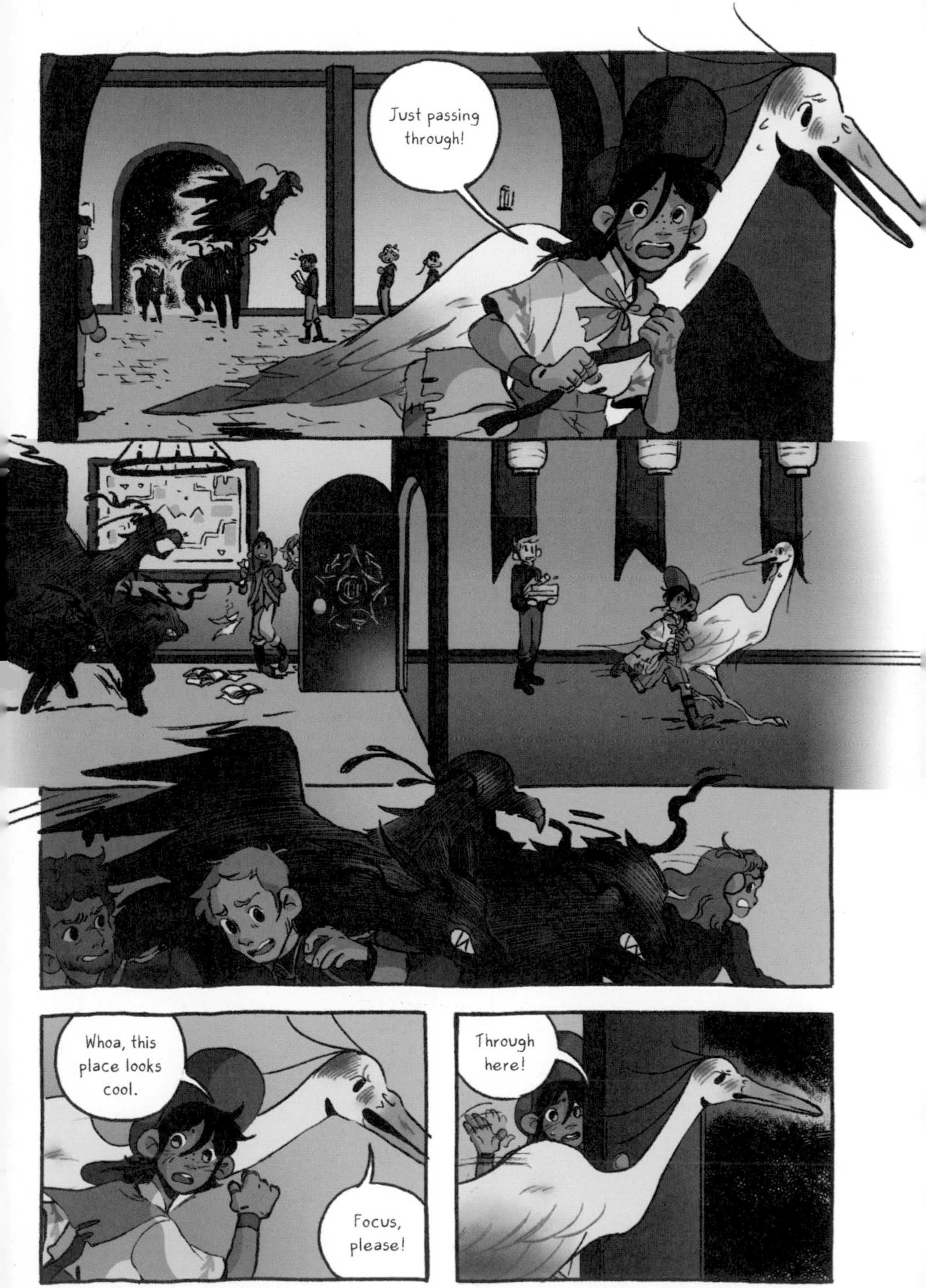
Just passing through!
Whoa, this place looks cool.
Focus, please!
Through here!

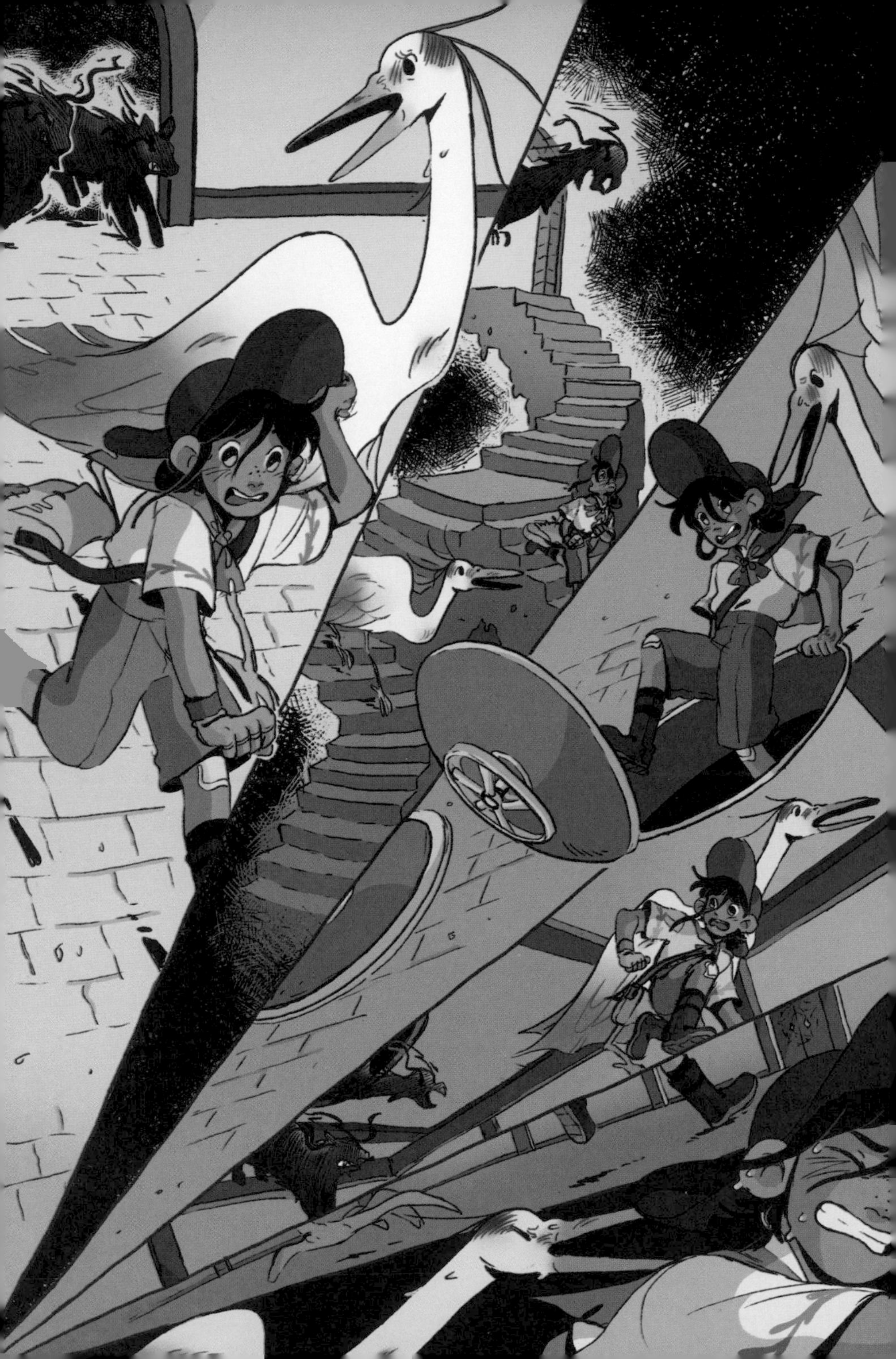

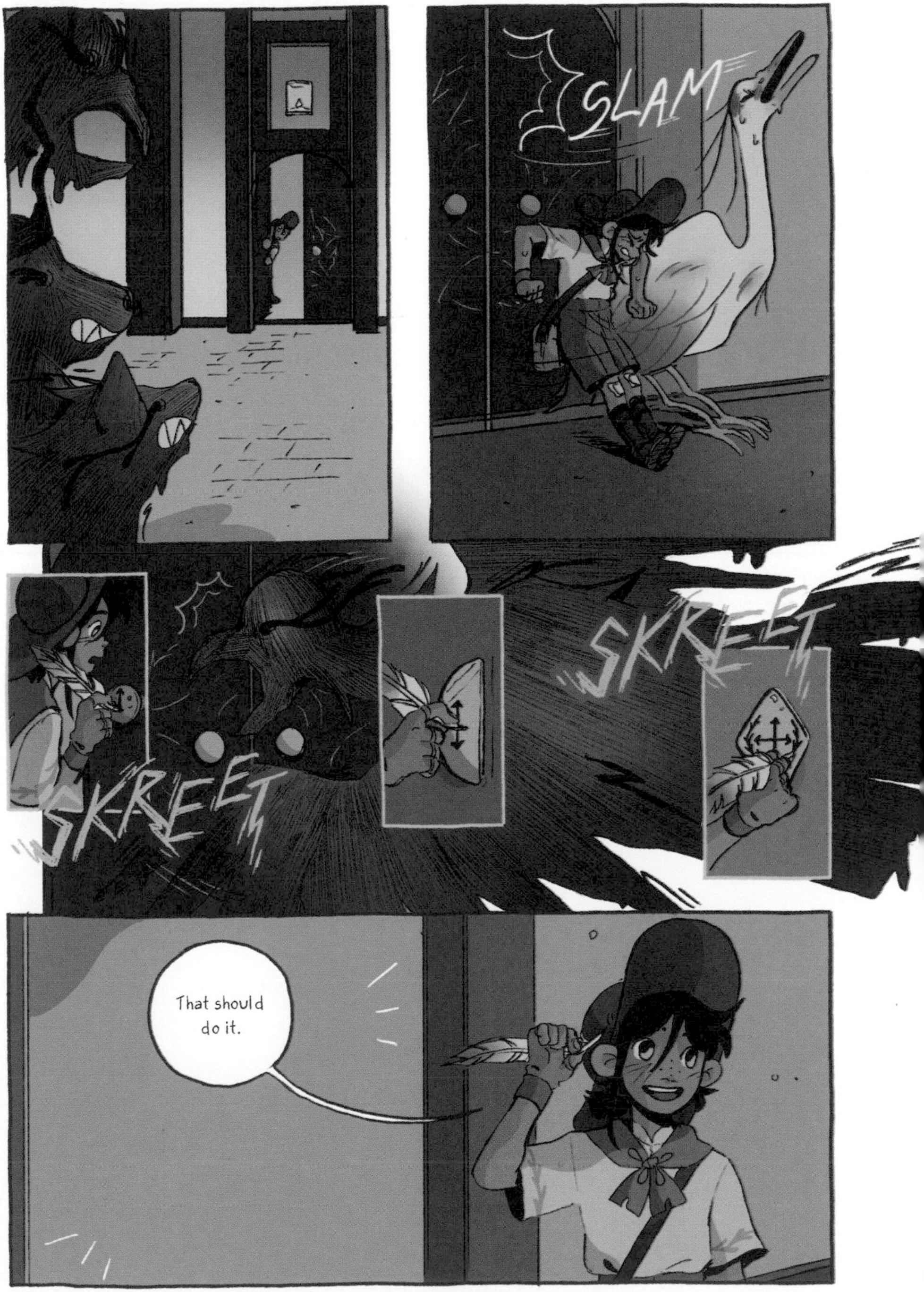
SLAM
SKREET
SKREET
That should do it.

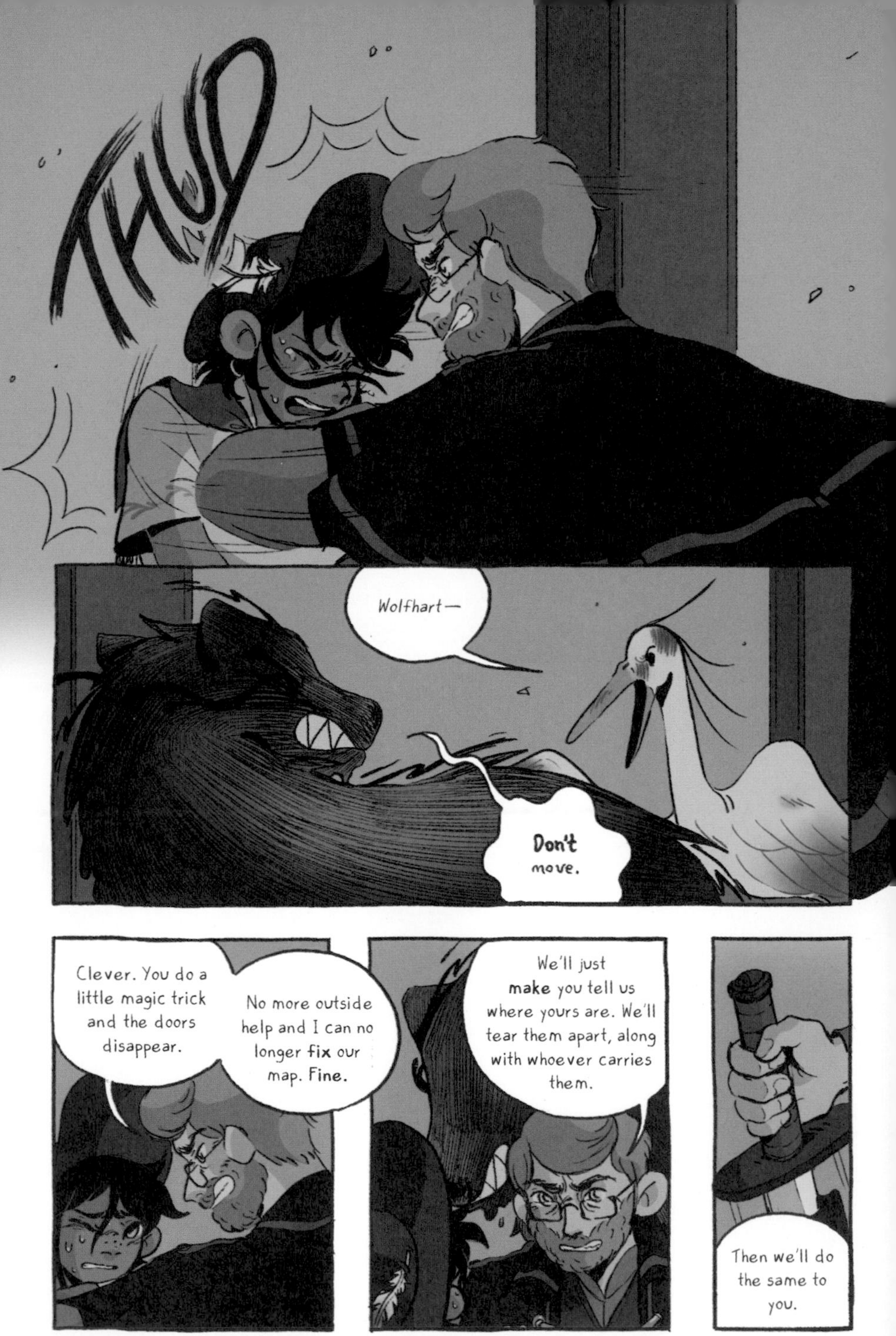
THUD
Wolfhart—
Don't move.
Clever. You do a little magic trick and the doors disappear.
No more outside help and I can no longer fix our map. Fine.
We'll just make you tell us where yours are. We'll tear them apart, along with whoever carries them.
Then we'll do the same to you.

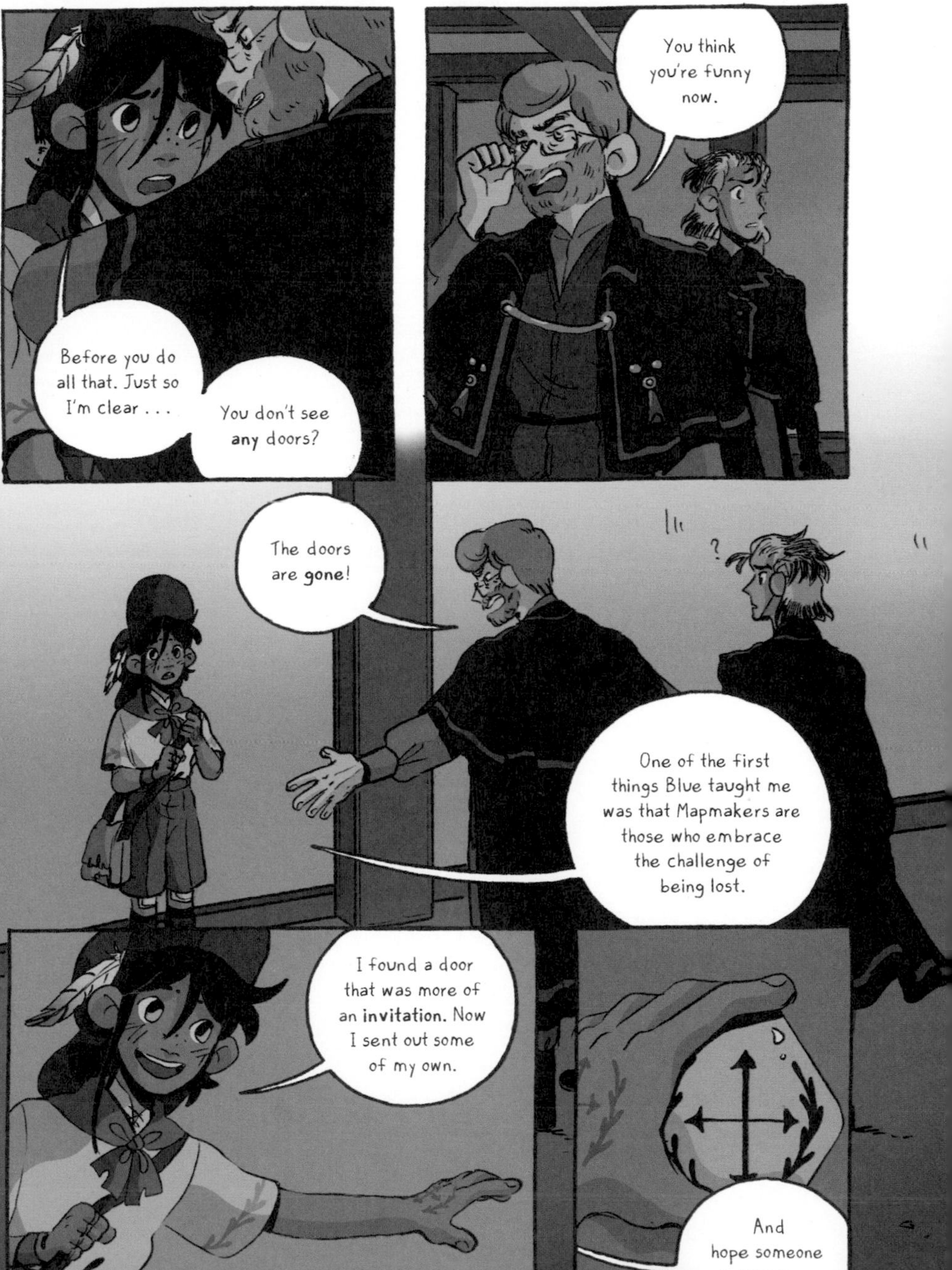
Before you do all that. Just so I'm clear . . .
You don't see **any** doors?
You think you're funny now.
The doors are **gone**!
One of the first things Blue taught me was that Mapmakers are those who embrace the challenge of being lost.
I found a door that was more of an **invitation.** Now I sent out some of my own.
And hope someone answers . . .

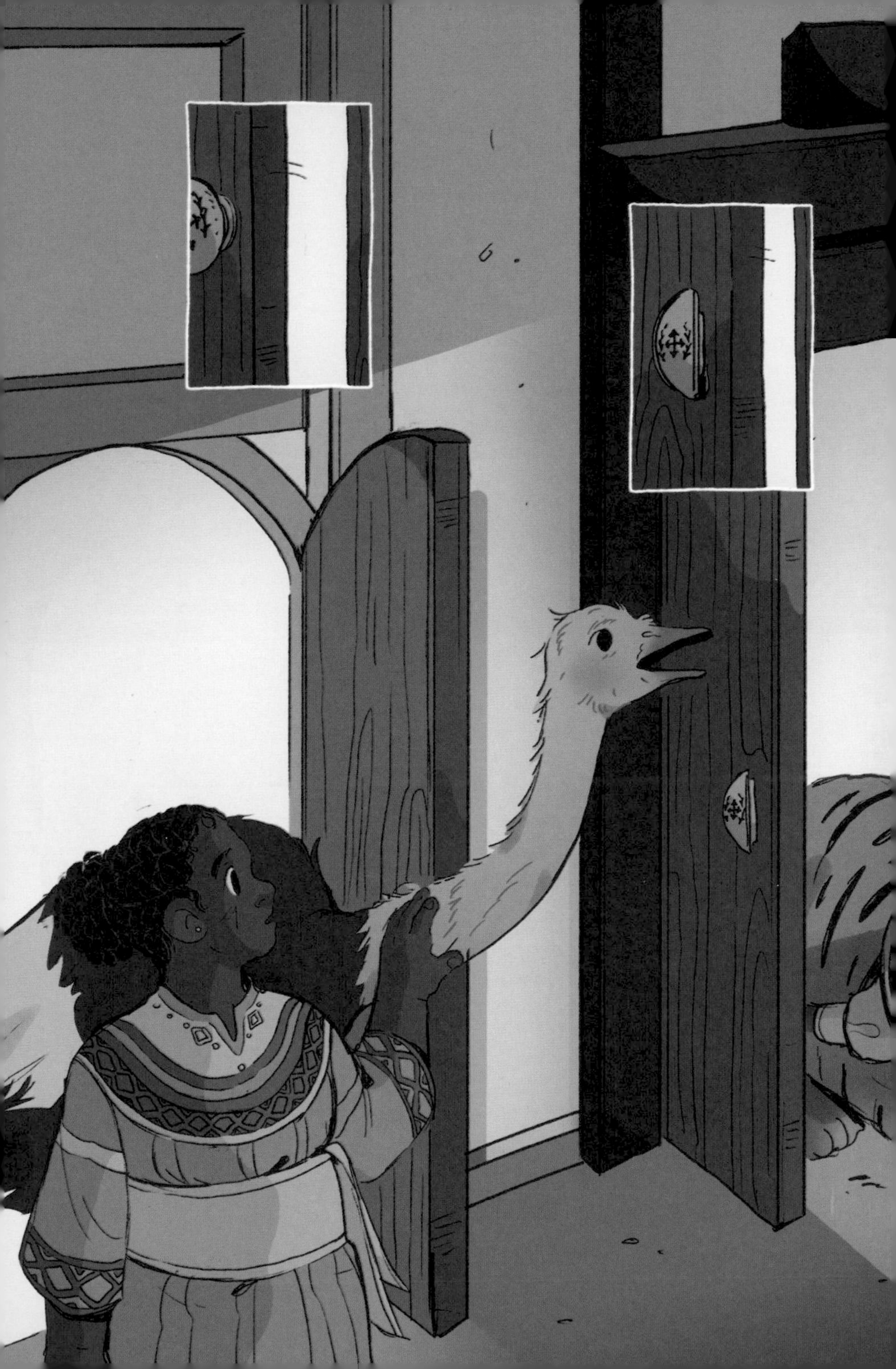

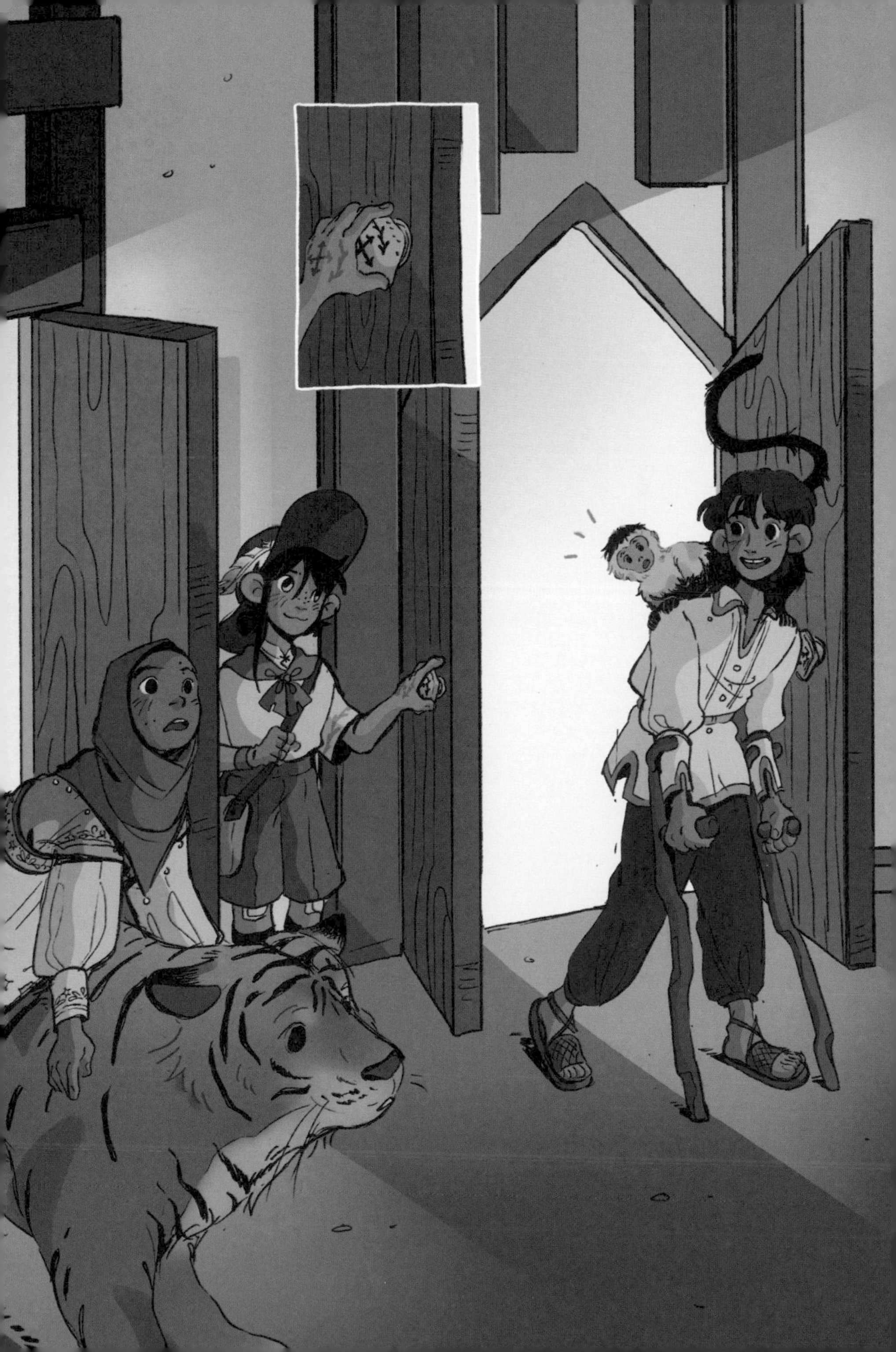

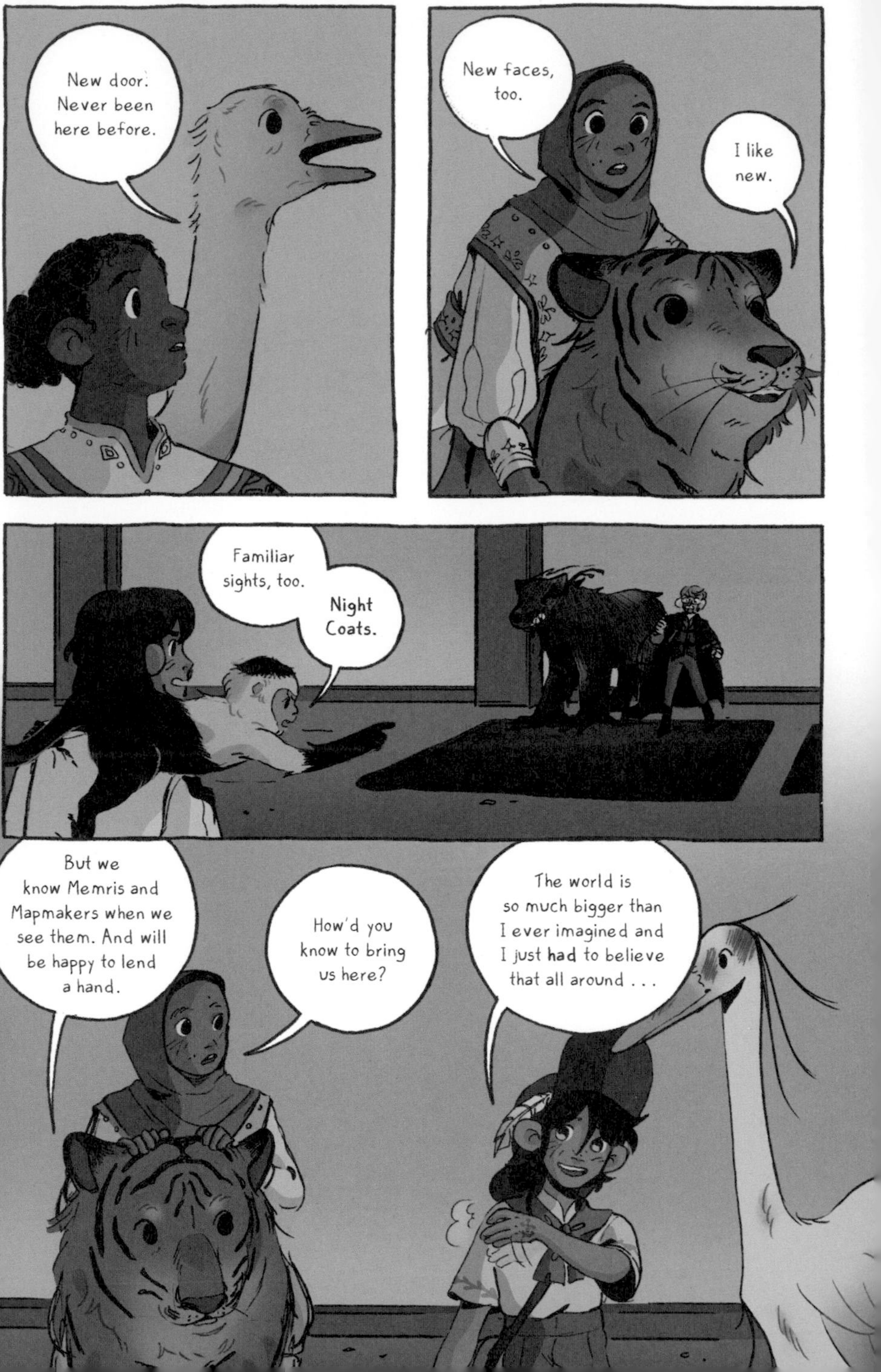
New door. Never been here before.
New faces, too.
I like new.
Familiar sights, too.
Night Coats.
But we know Memris and Mapmakers when we see them. And will be happy to lend a hand.
How'd you know to bring us here?
The world is so much bigger than I ever imagined and I just **had** to believe that all around . . .

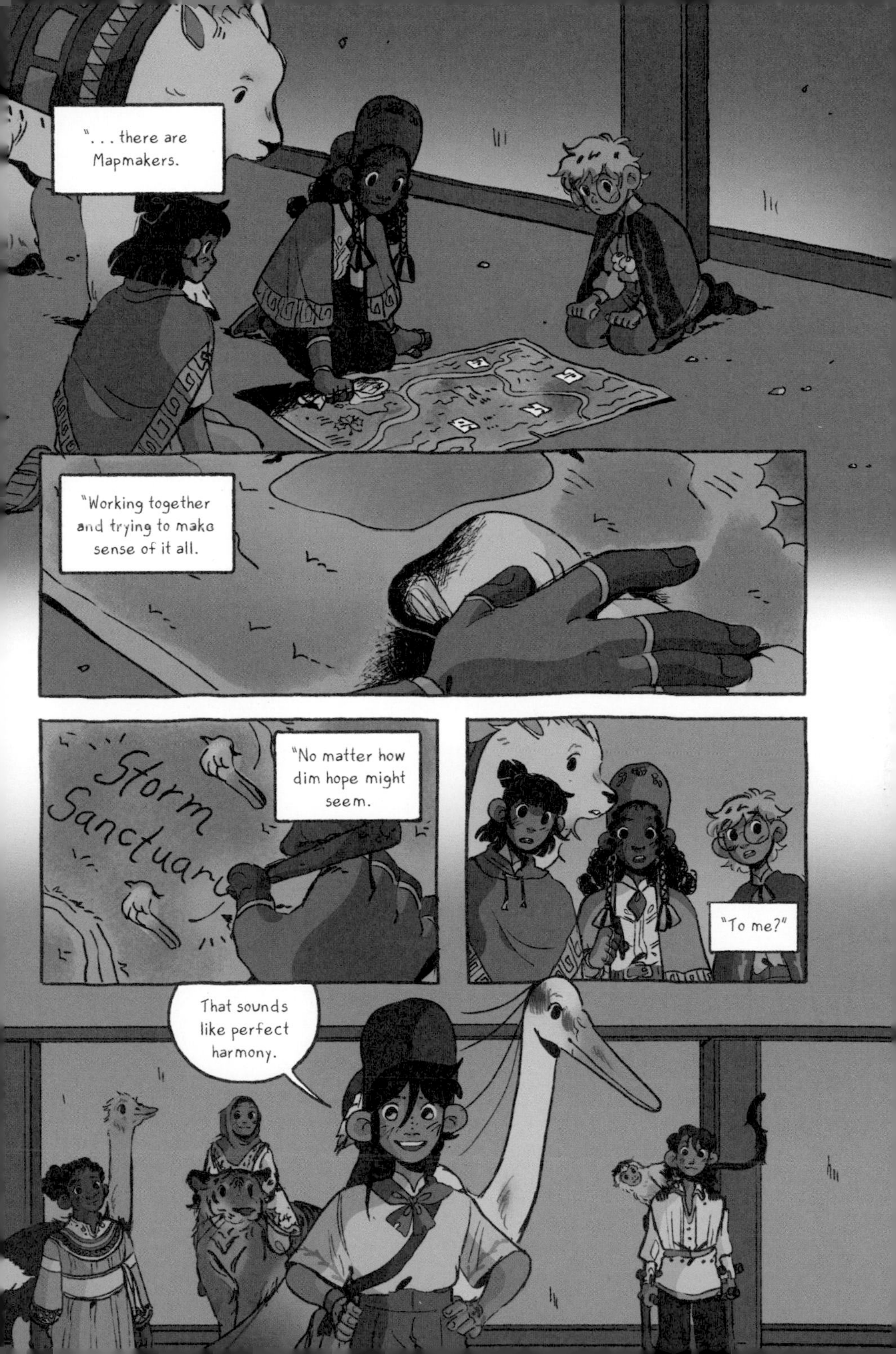
". . . there are Mapmakers.
"Working together and trying to make sense of it all.
"No matter how dim hope might seem.
Storm Sanctuary
"To me?"
That sounds like perfect harmony.

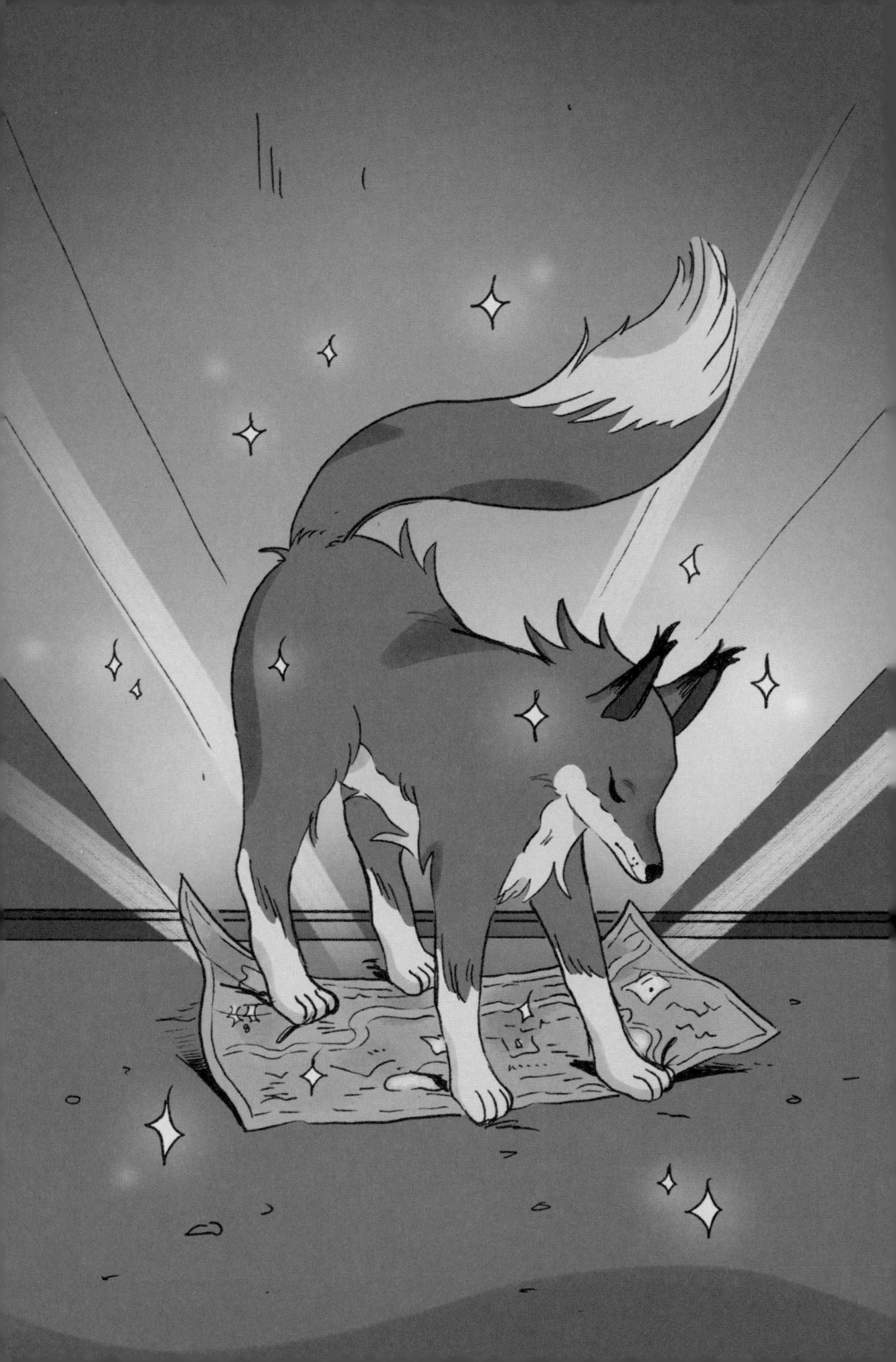

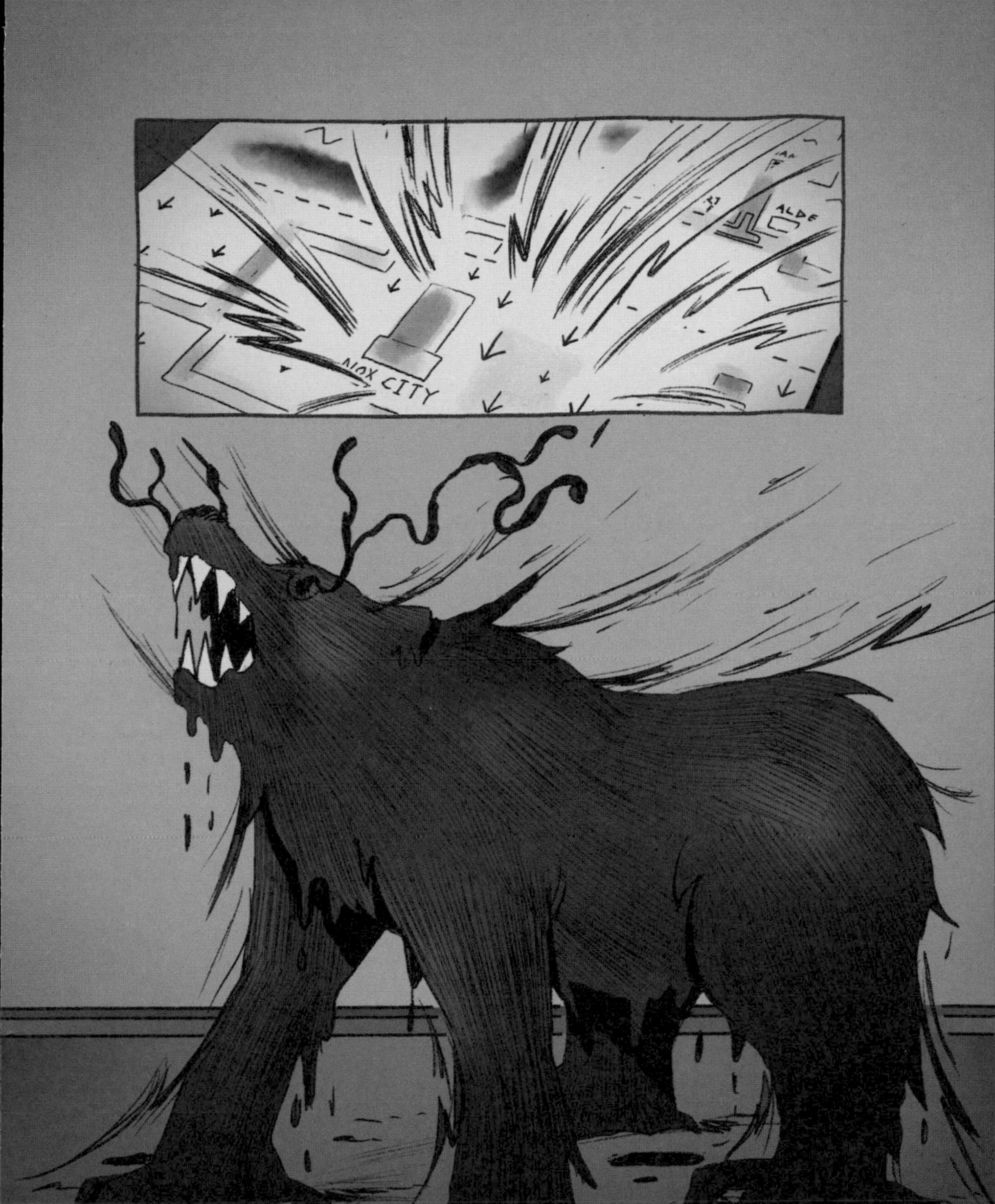
NOX CITY
ALDE

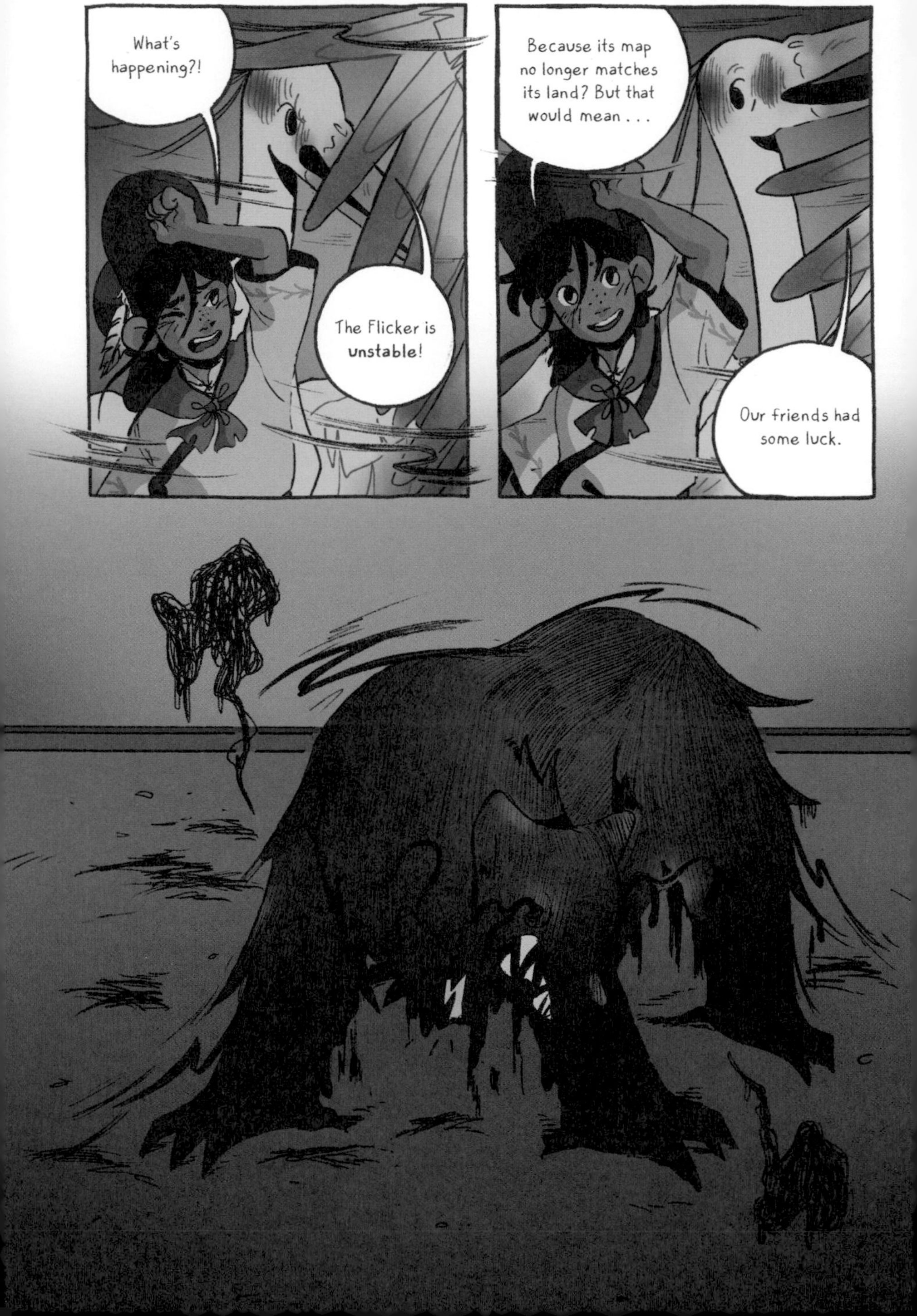
What's happening?!
The Flicker is **unstable**!
Because its map no longer matches its land? But that would mean . . .
Our friends had some luck.

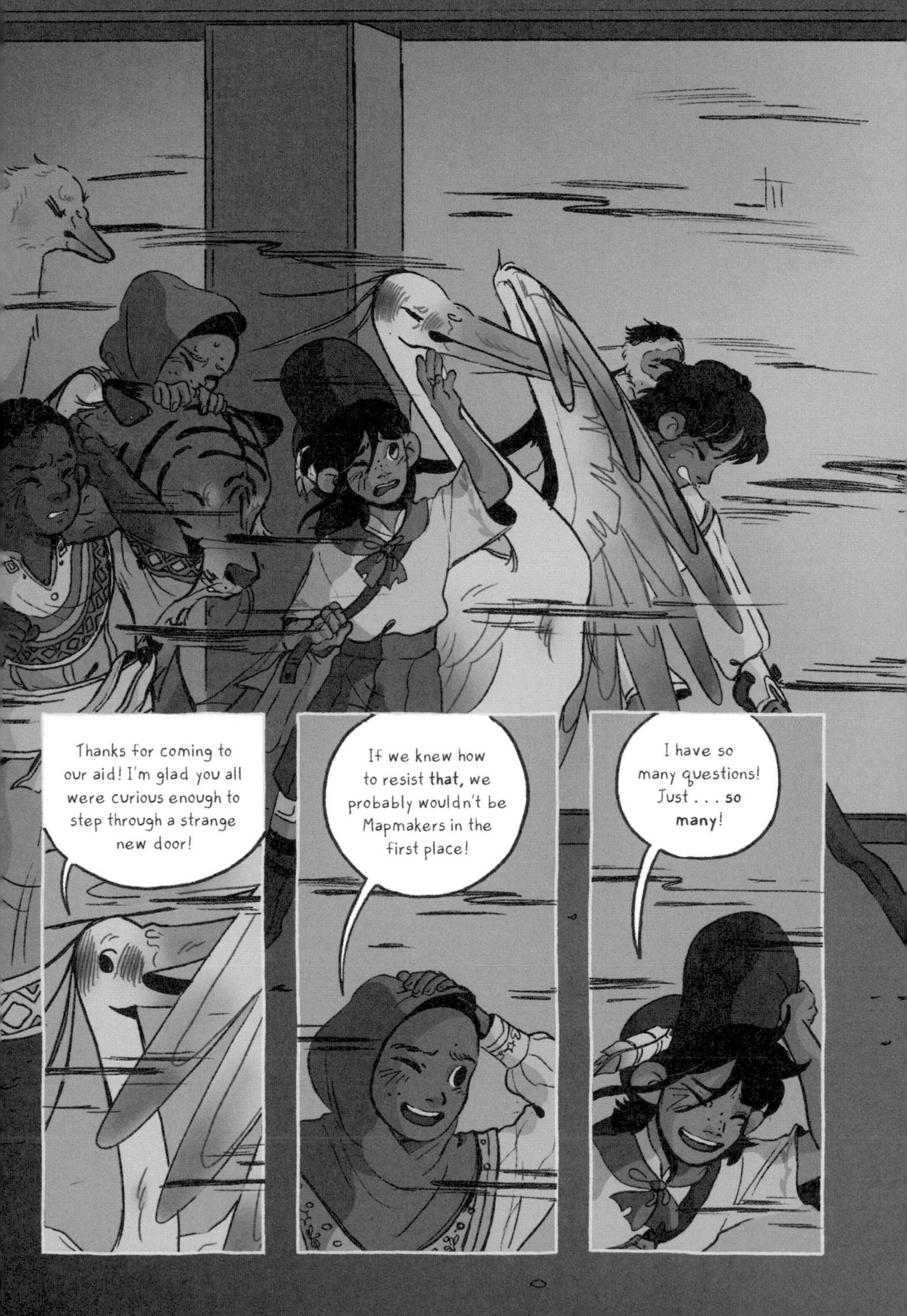
Thanks for coming to our aid! I'm glad you all were curious enough to step through a strange new door!
If we knew how to resist **that,** we probably wouldn't be Mapmakers in the first place!
I have so many questions! Just . . . **so many**!

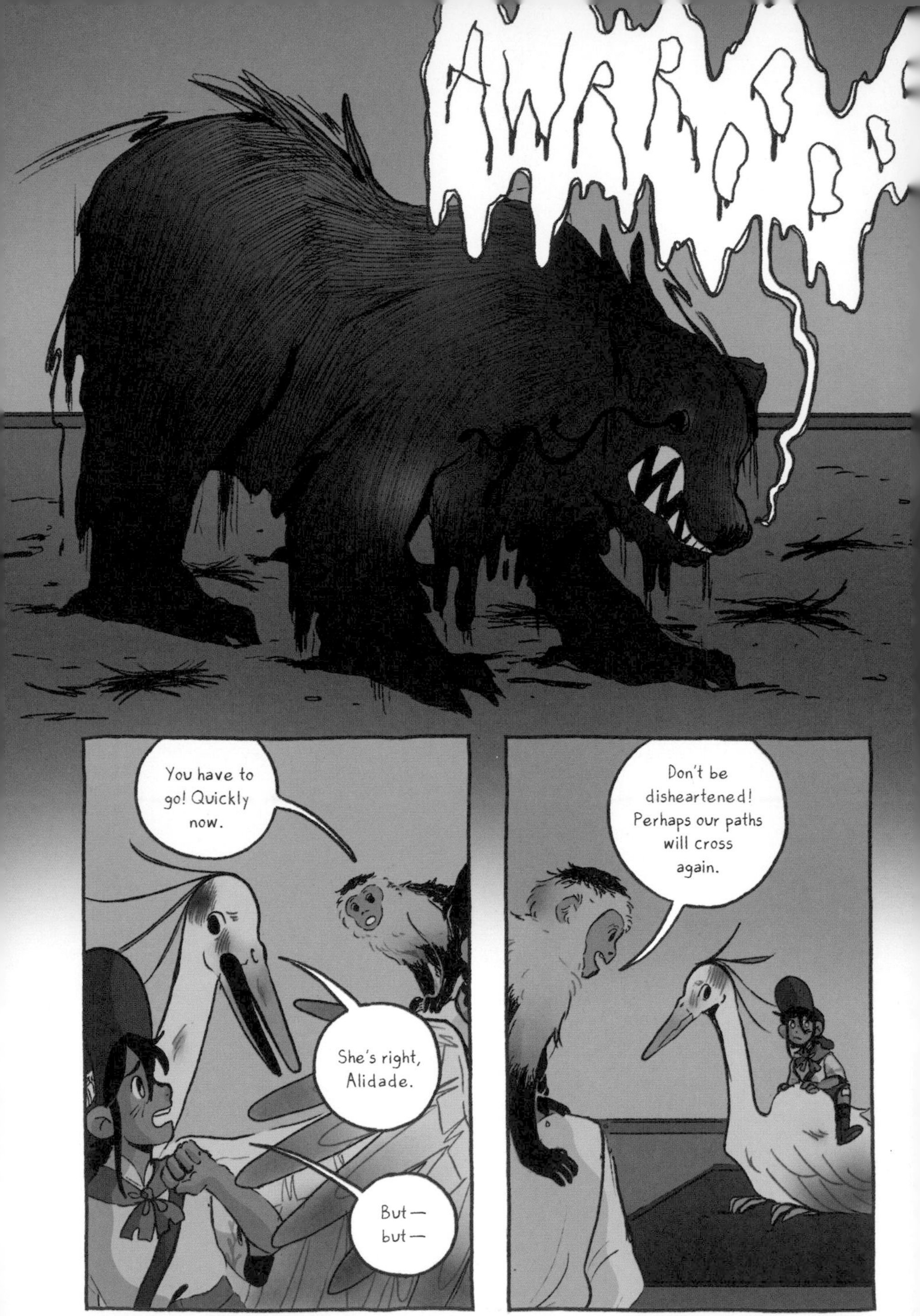
You have to go! Quickly now.
She's right, Alidade.
But— but—
Don't be disheartened! Perhaps our paths will cross again.

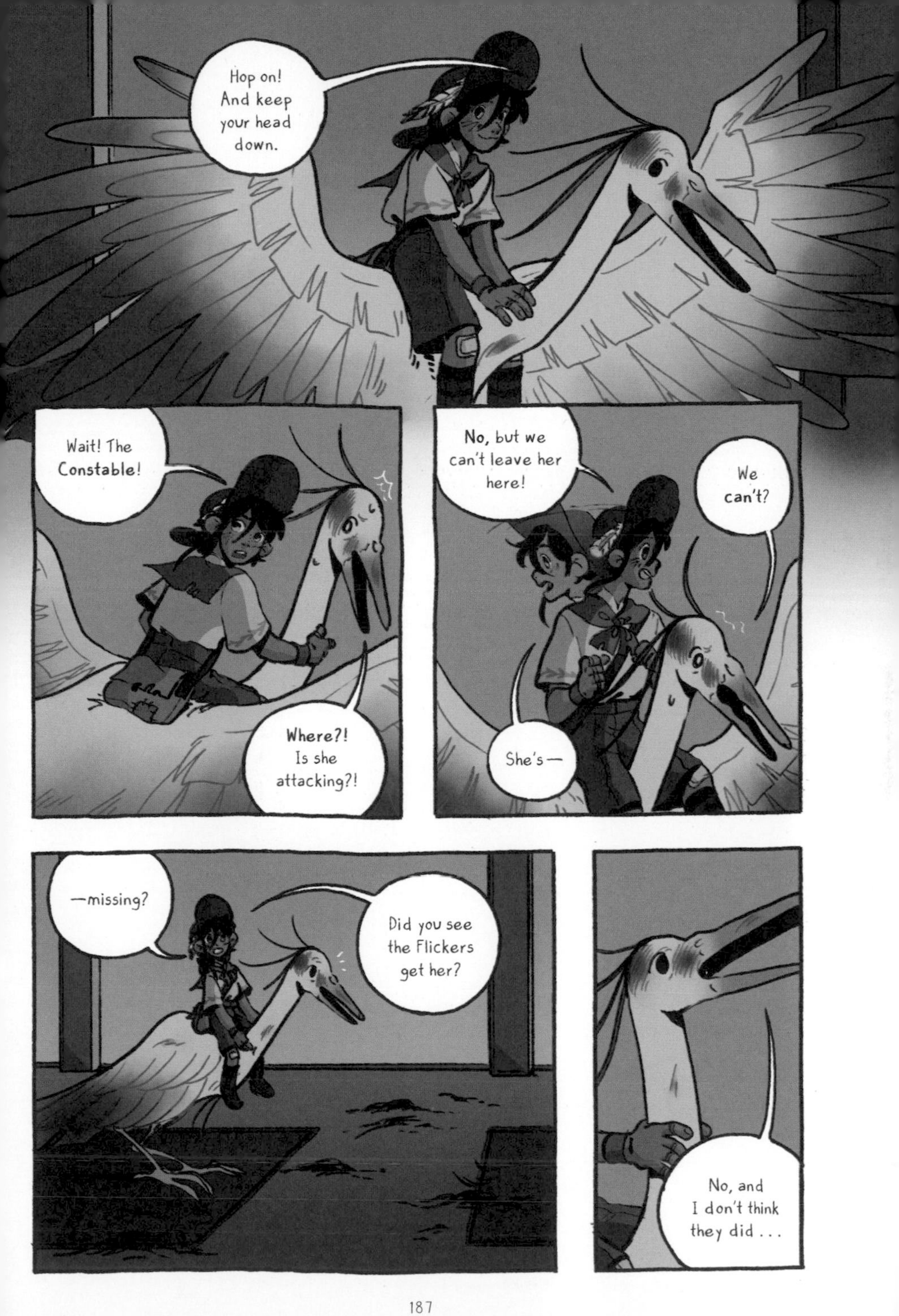
Hop on! And keep your head down.
Wait! The Constable!
Where?! Is she attacking?!
No, but we can't leave her here!
We can't?
She's—
—missing?
Did you see the Flickers get her?
No, and I don't think they did . . .

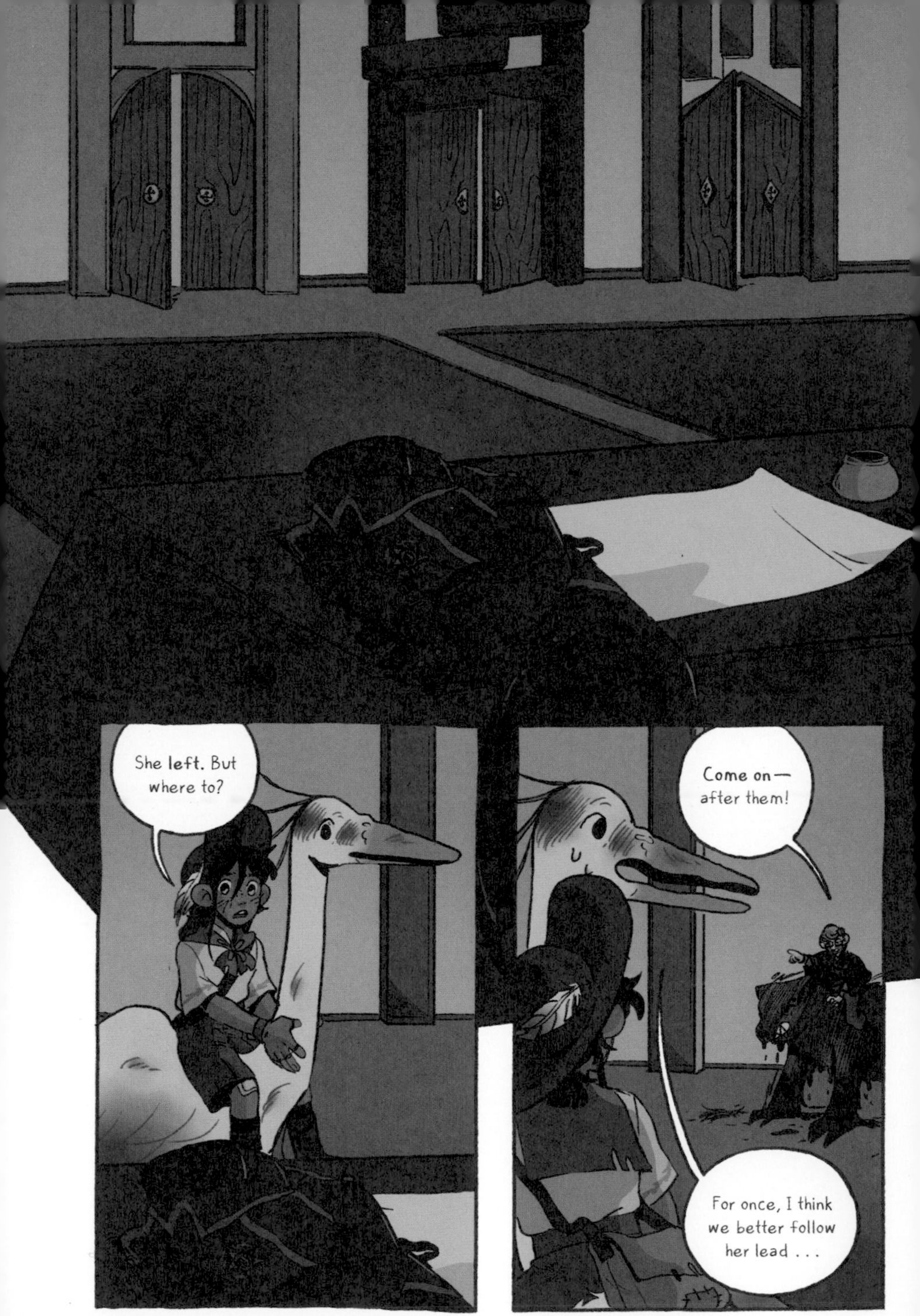
She left. But where to?
Come on— after them!
For once, I think we better follow her lead . . .

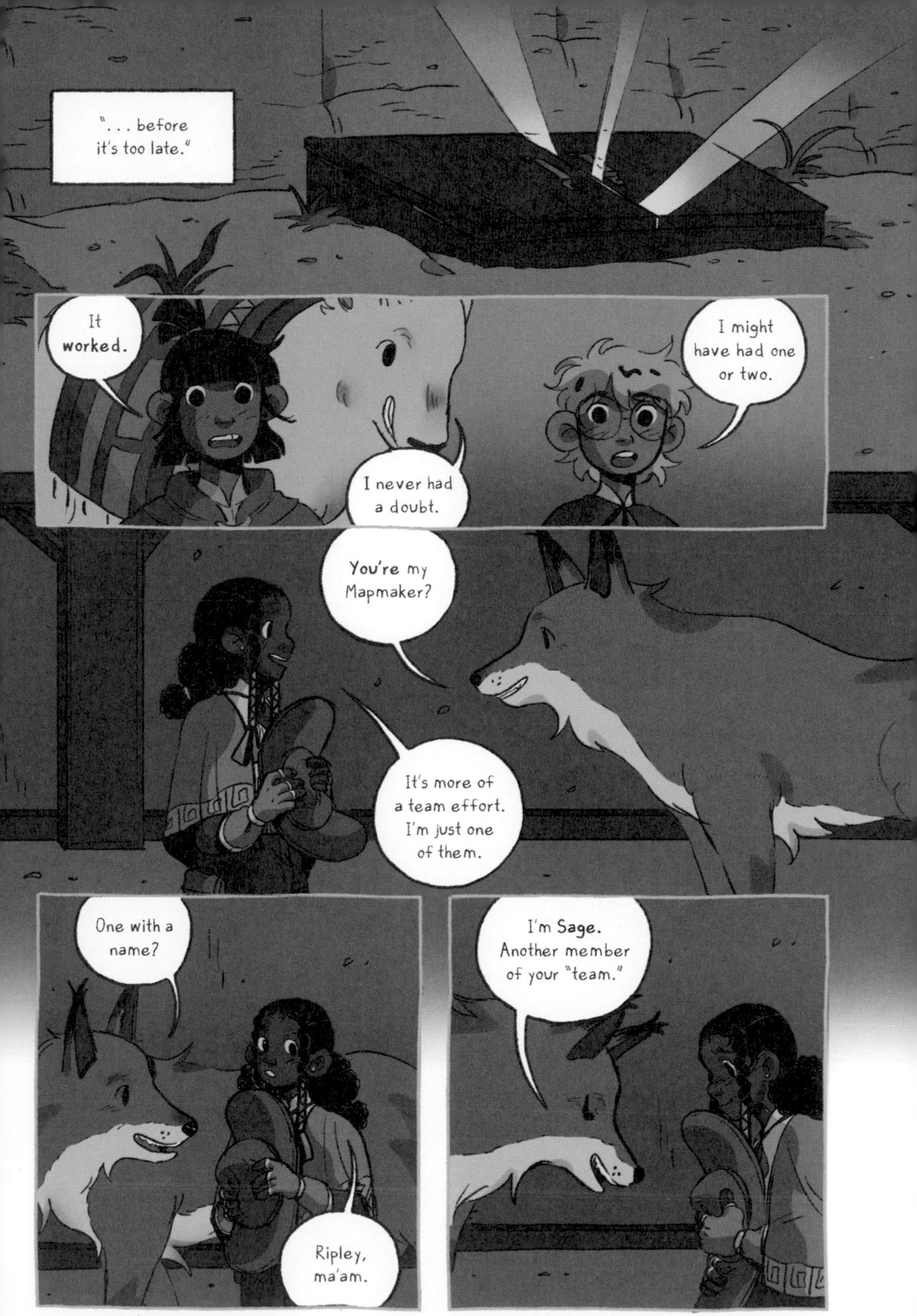
". . . before it's too late."
It worked.
I might have had one or two.
I never had a doubt.
You're my Mapmaker?
It's more of a team effort. I'm just one of them.
One with a name?
Ripley, ma'am.
I'm Sage. Another member of your "team."

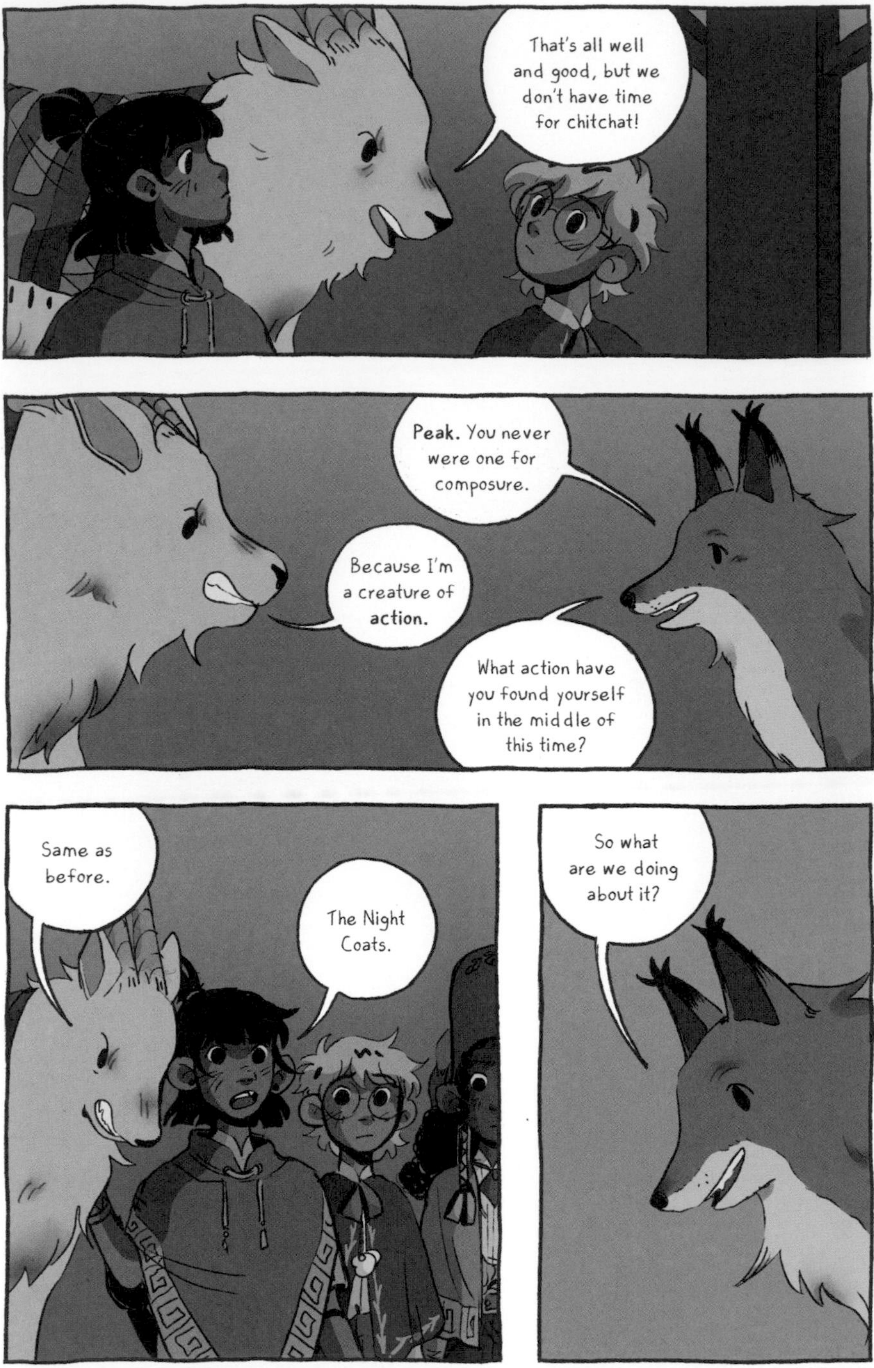
That's all well and good, but we don't have time for chitchat!
Peak. You never were one for composure.
Because I'm a creature of **action.**
What action have you found yourself in the middle of this time?
Same as before.
The Night Coats.
So what are we doing about it?

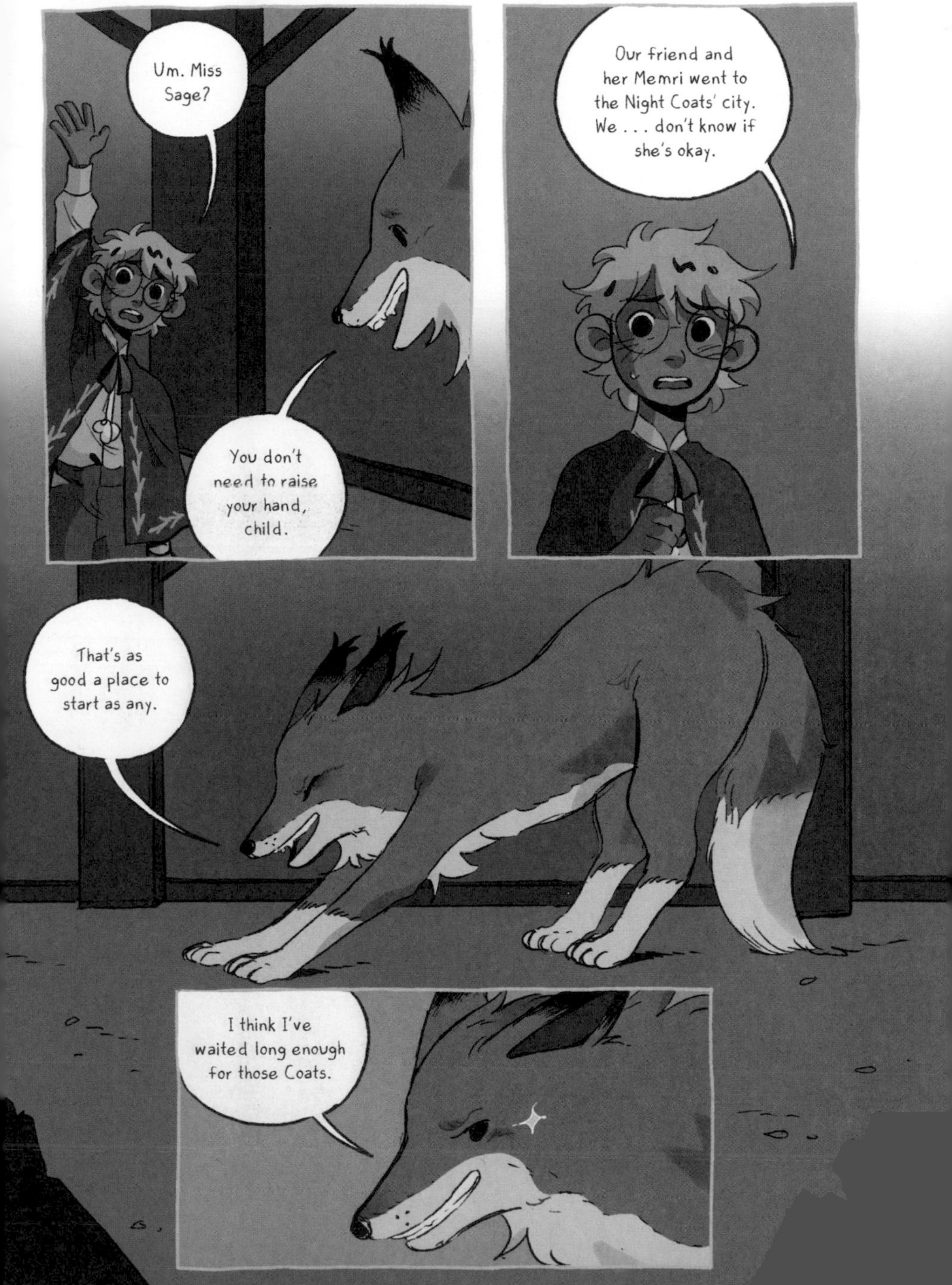
Um. Miss Sage?
You don't need to raise your hand, child.
Our friend and her Memri went to the Night Coats' city. We . . . don't know if she's okay.
That's as good a place to start as any.
I think I've waited long enough for those Coats.

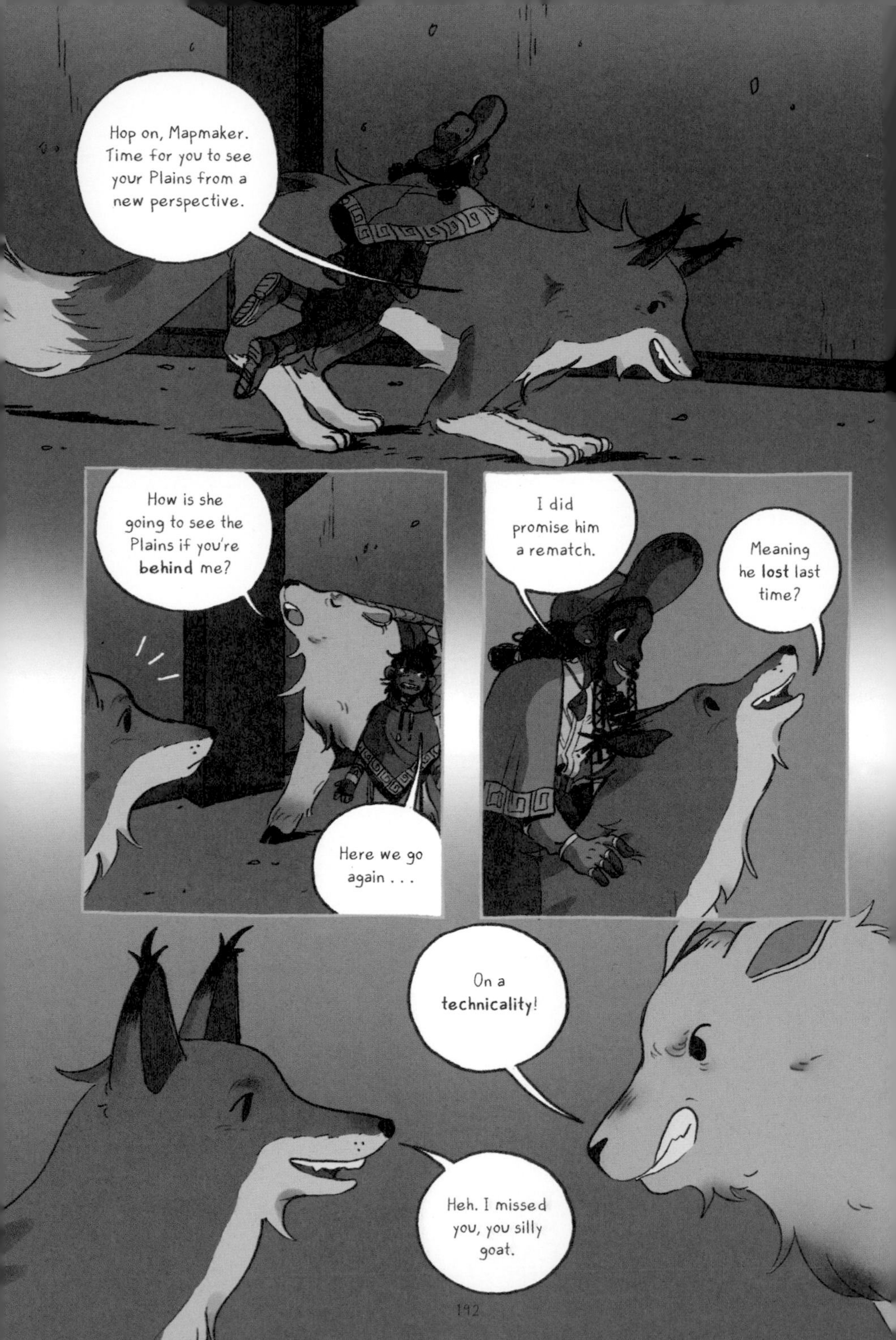
Hop on, Mapmaker. Time for you to see your Plains from a new perspective.
How is she going to see the Plains if you're **behind** me?
Here we go again . . .
I did promise him a rematch.
Meaning he **lost** last time?
On a **technicality**!
Heh. I missed you, you silly goat.

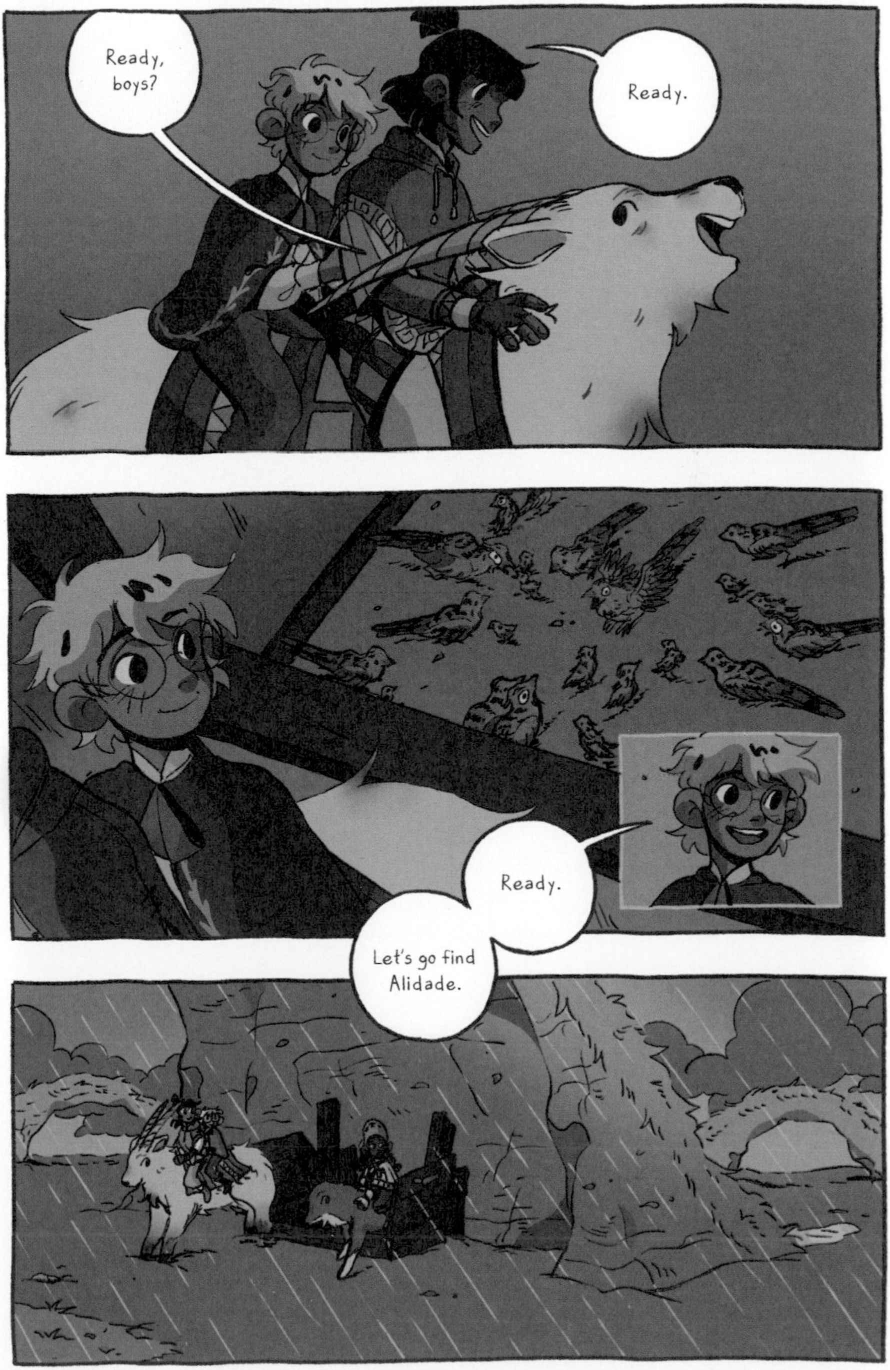
Ready, boys?
Ready.
Ready.
Let's go find Alidade.

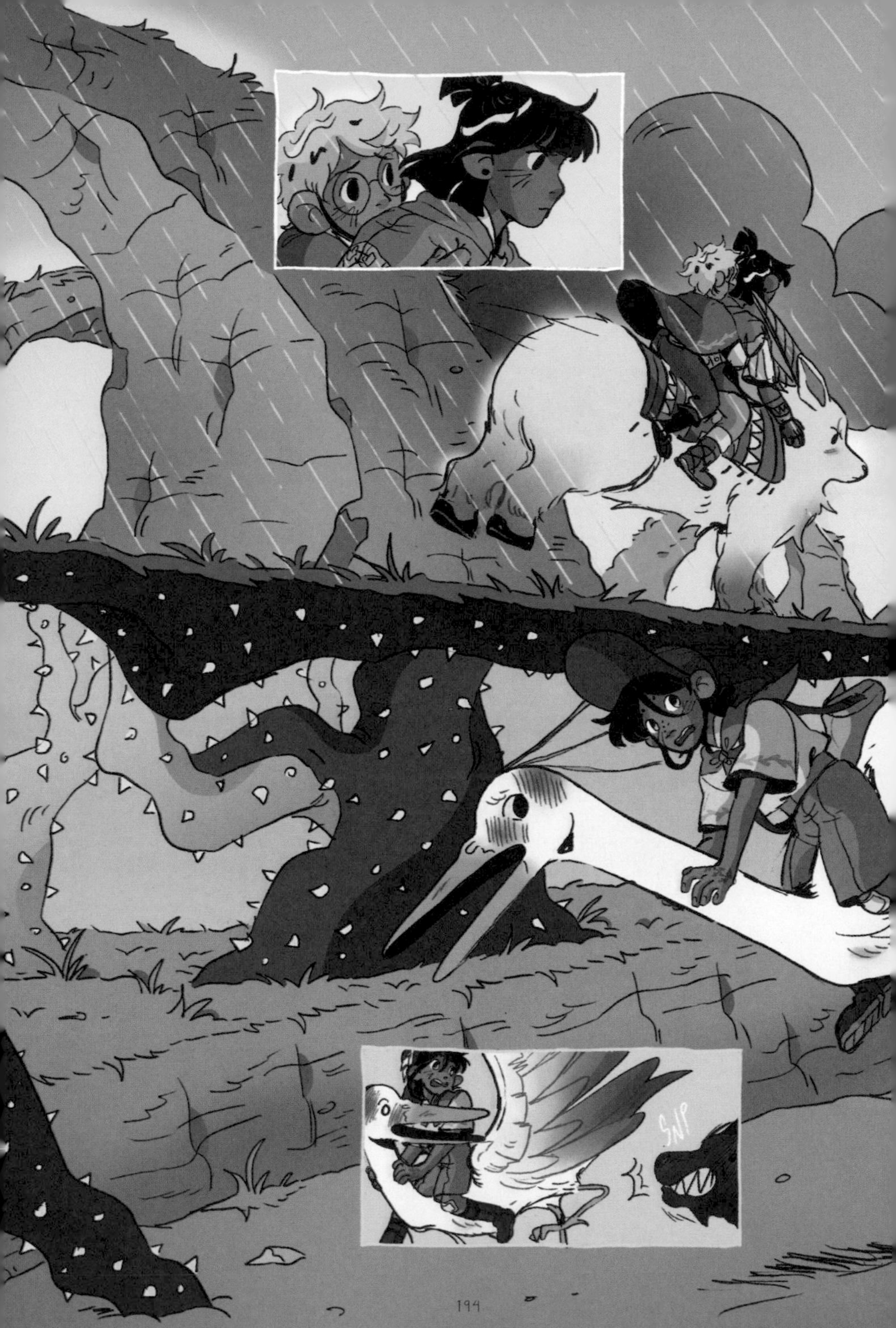
SNIP

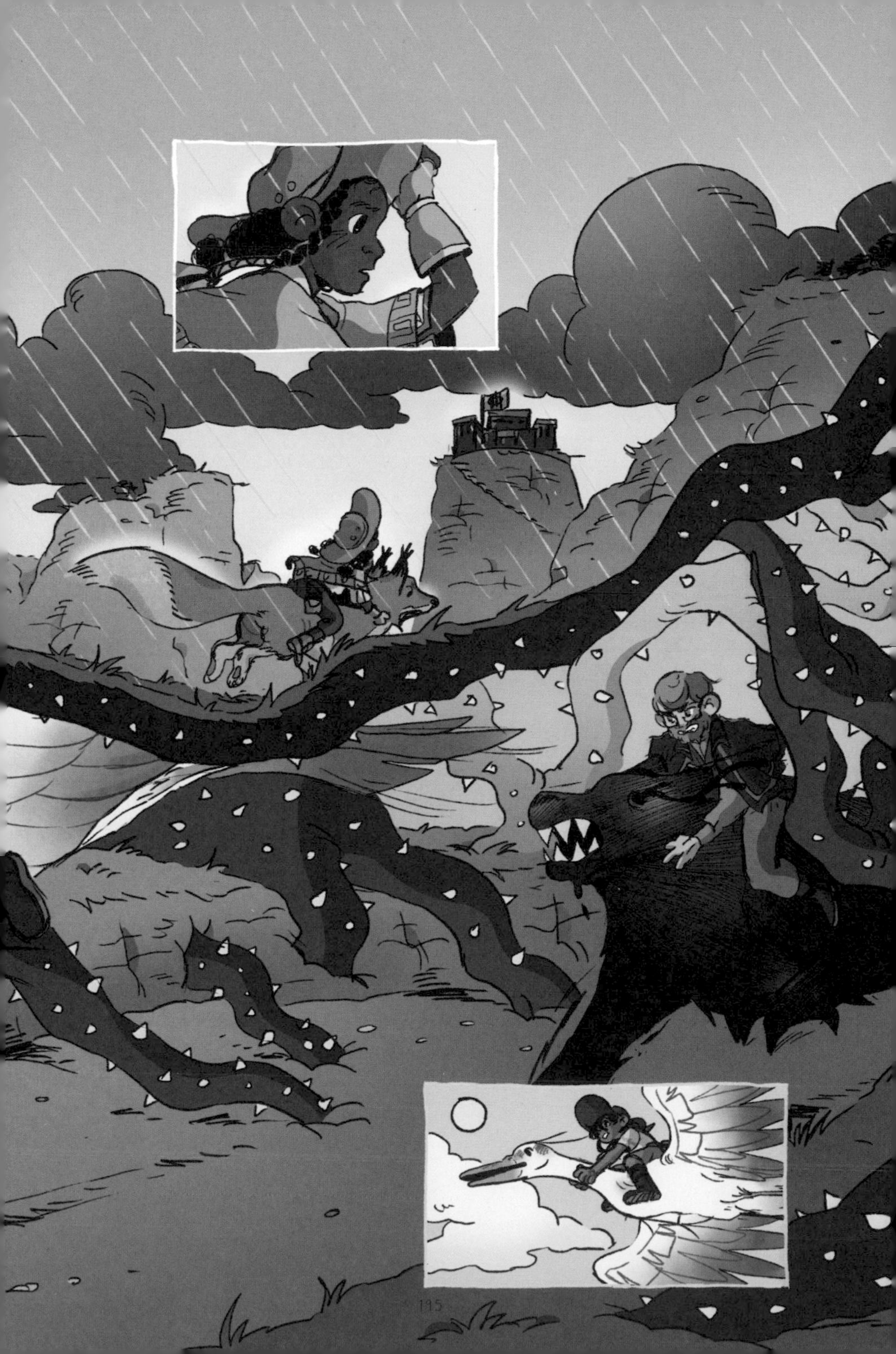

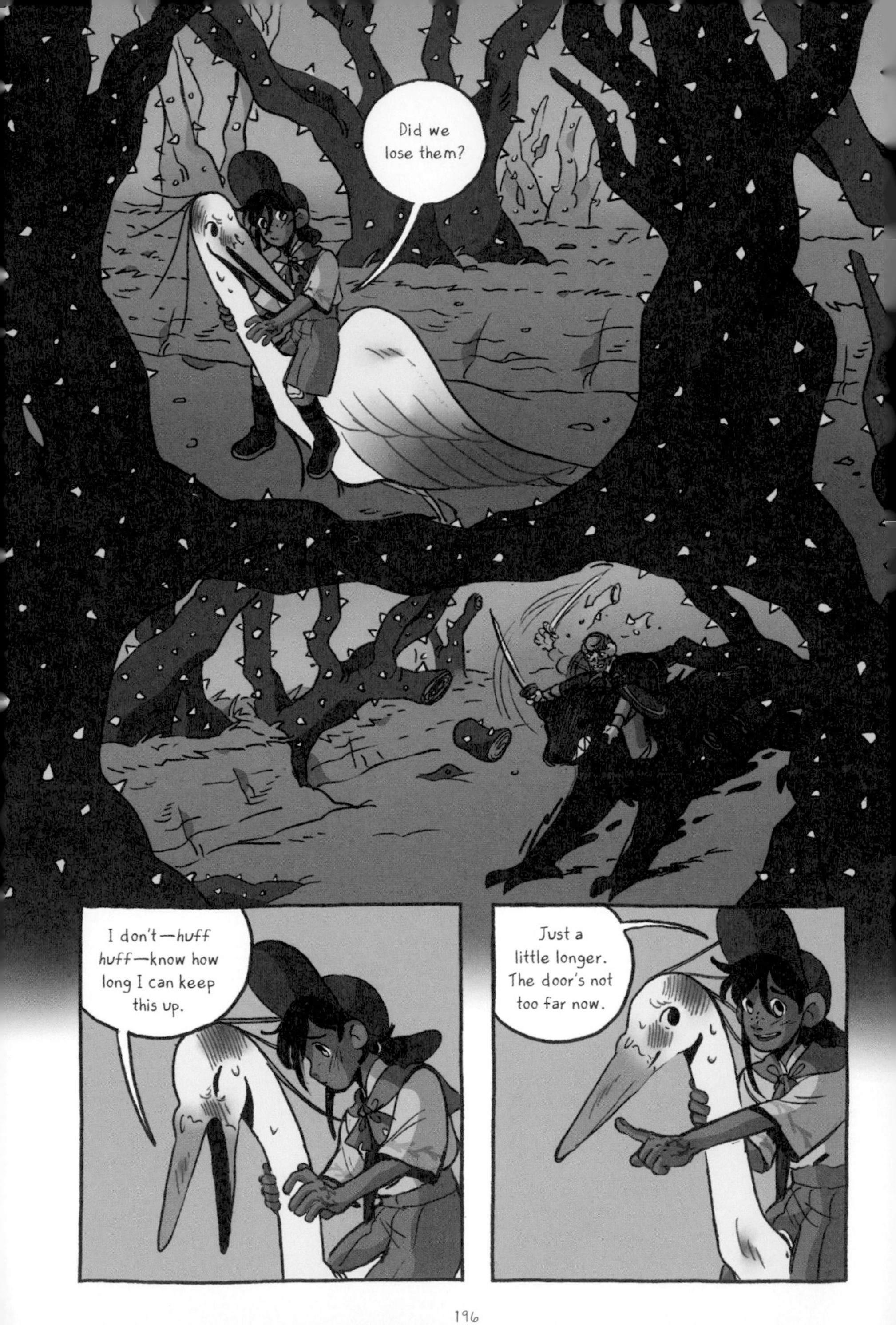
Did we lose them?
I don't—*huff huff*—know how long I can keep this up.
Just a little longer. The door's not too far now.

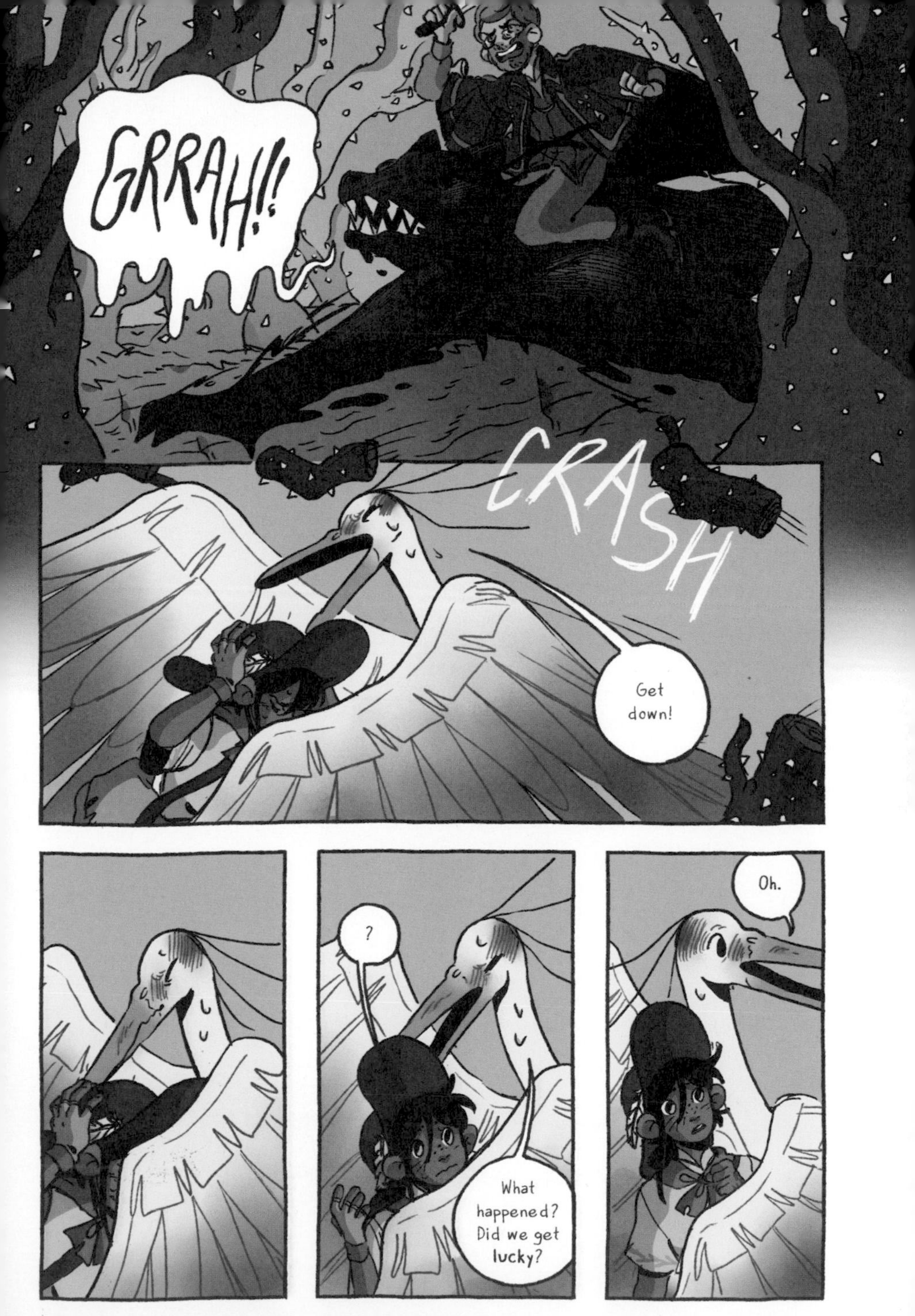
GRRAH!!
CRASH
Get down!
?
What happened? Did we get **lucky**?
Oh.

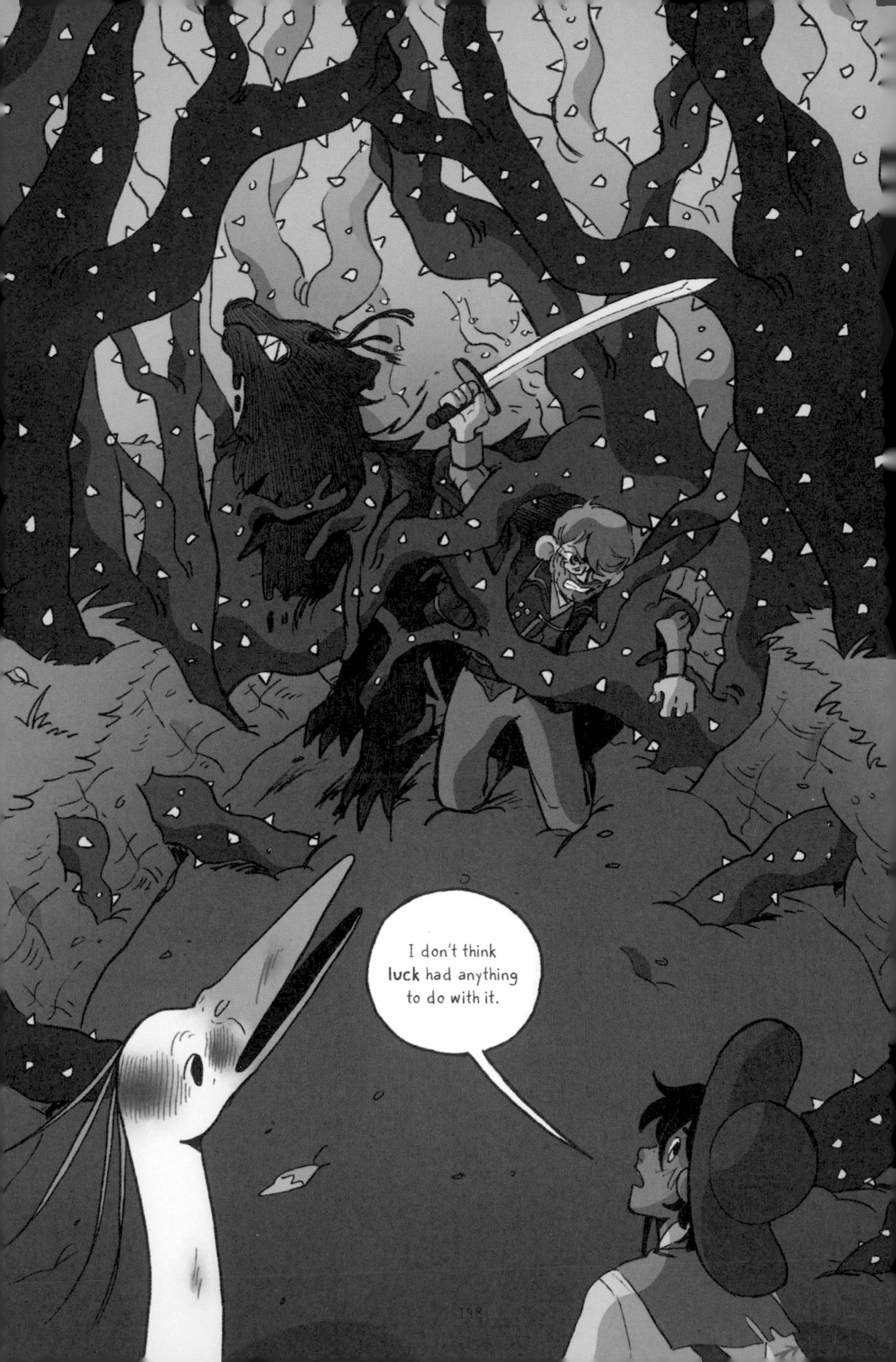
I don't think **luck** had anything to do with it.

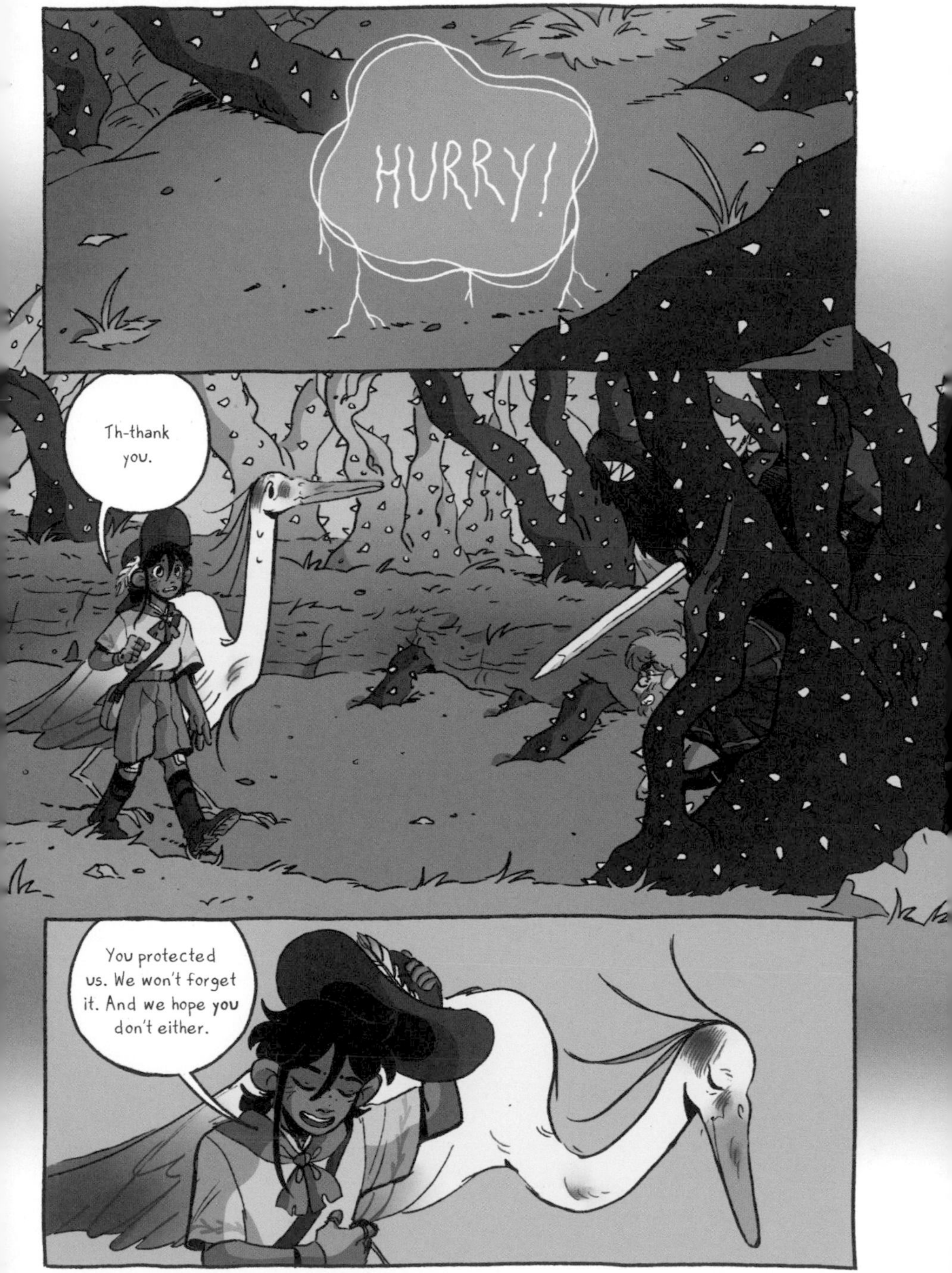
HURRY!
Th-thank you.
You protected us. We won't forget it. And we hope you don't either.

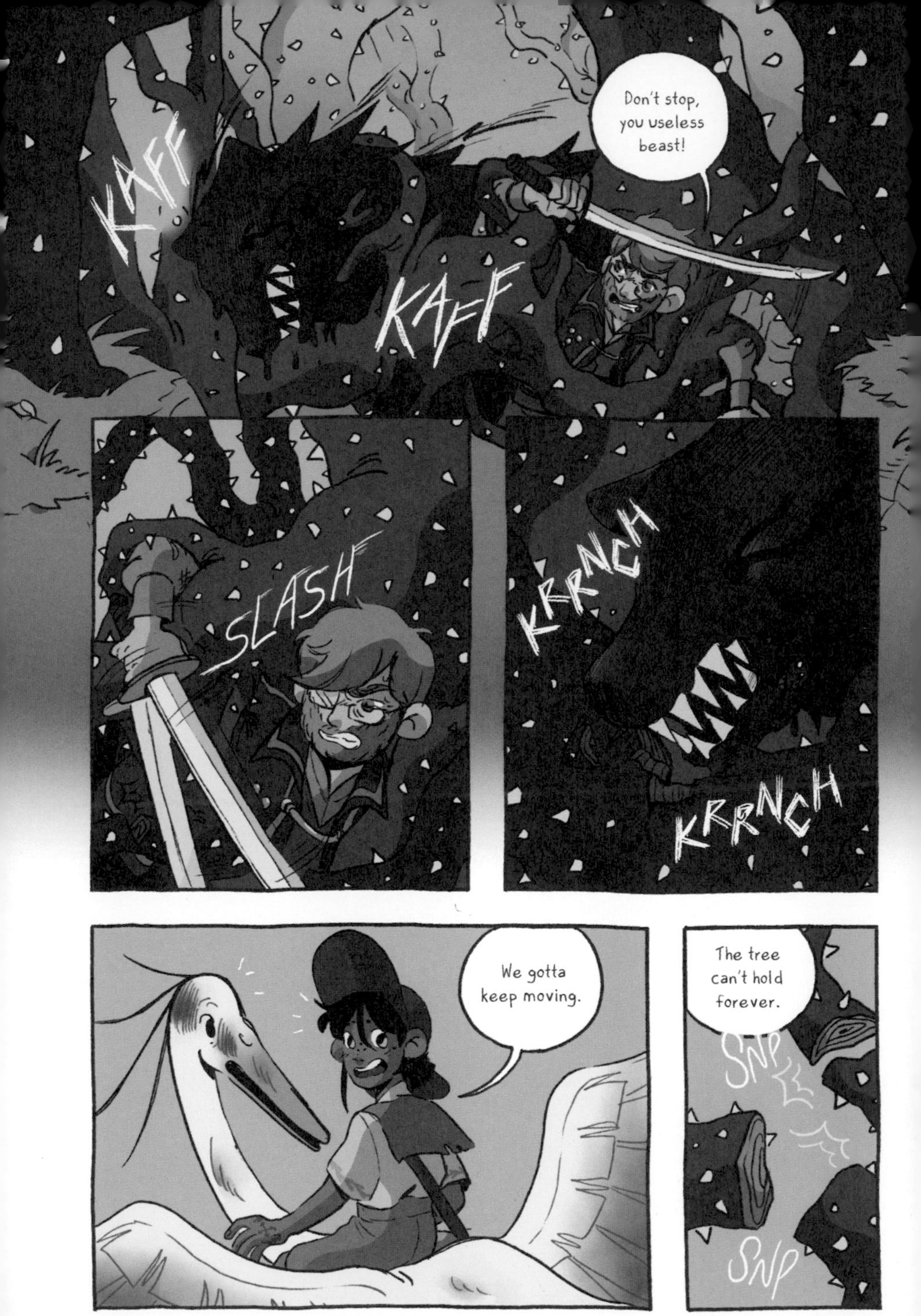
KAFF
KAFF
Don't stop, you useless beast!
SLASH
KRRNCH
KRRNCH
We gotta keep moving.
The tree can't hold forever.
SNP
SNP

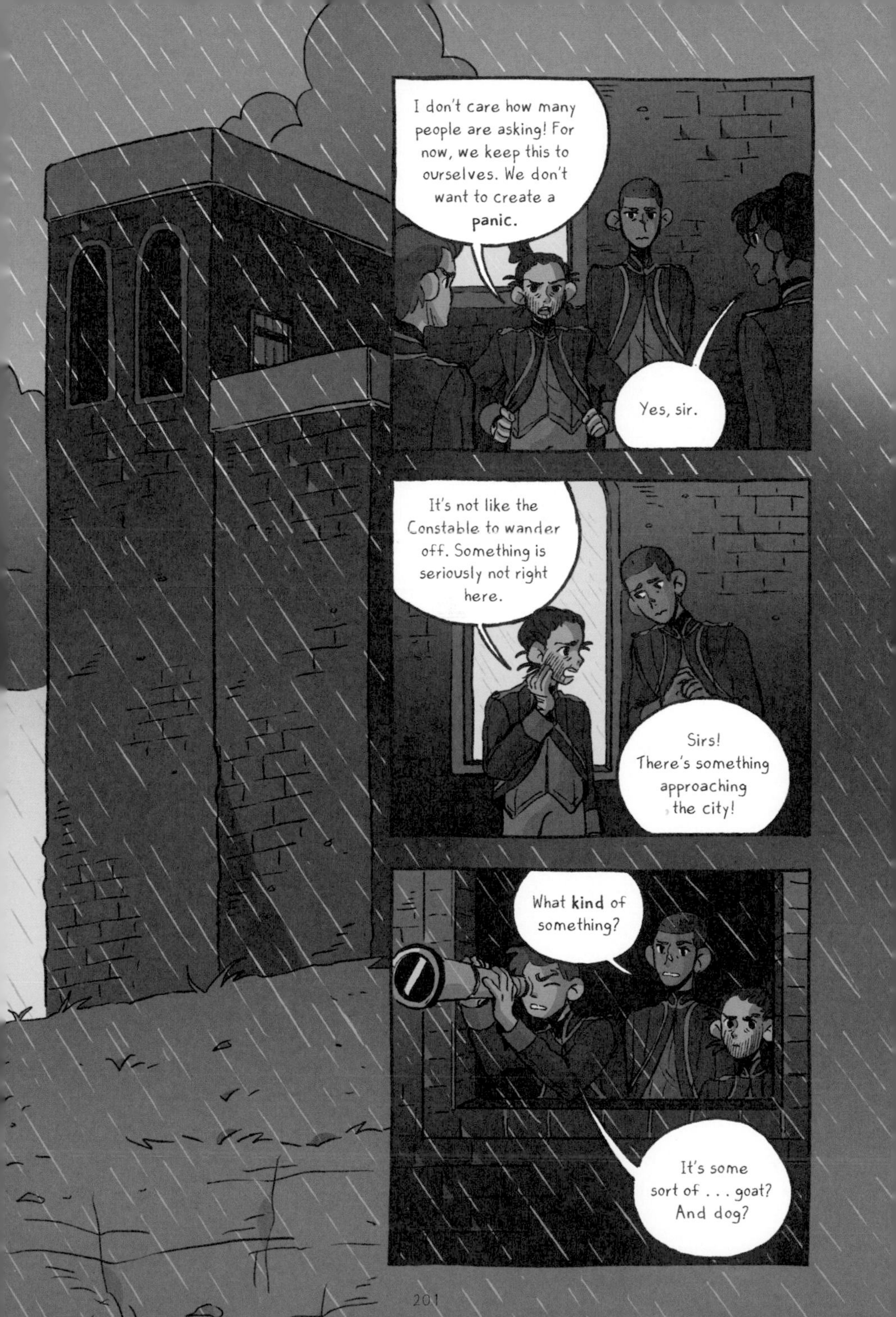
I don't care how many people are asking! For now, we keep this to ourselves. We don't want to create a **panic.**
Yes, sir.
It's not like the Constable to wander off. Something is seriously not right here.
Sirs! There's something approaching the city!
What **kind** of something?
It's some sort of . . . goat? And dog?

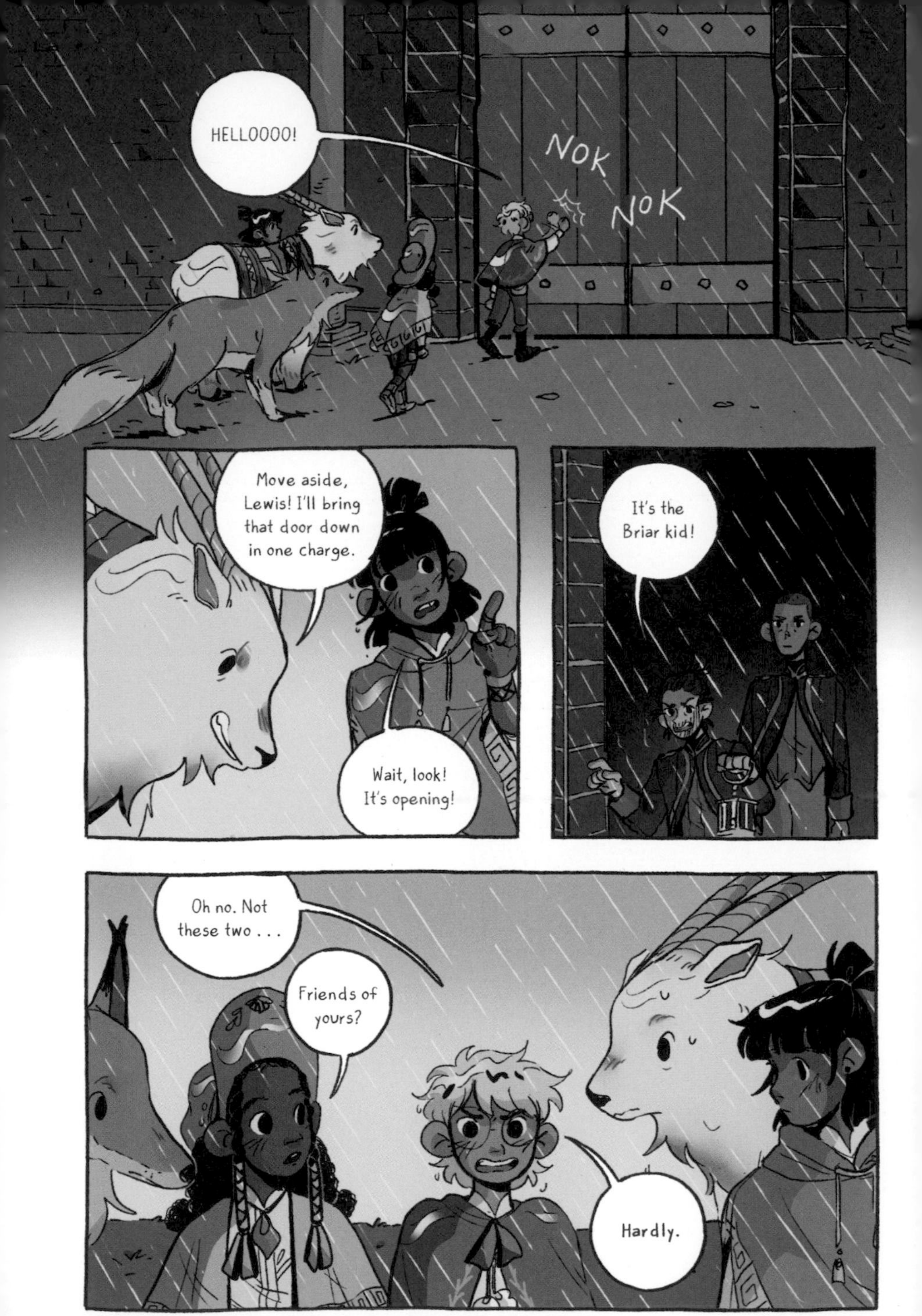
HELLOOOO!
NOK
NOK
Move aside, Lewis! I'll bring that door down in one charge.
Wait, look! It's opening!
It's the Briar kid!
Oh no. Not these two . . .
Friends of yours?
Hardly.

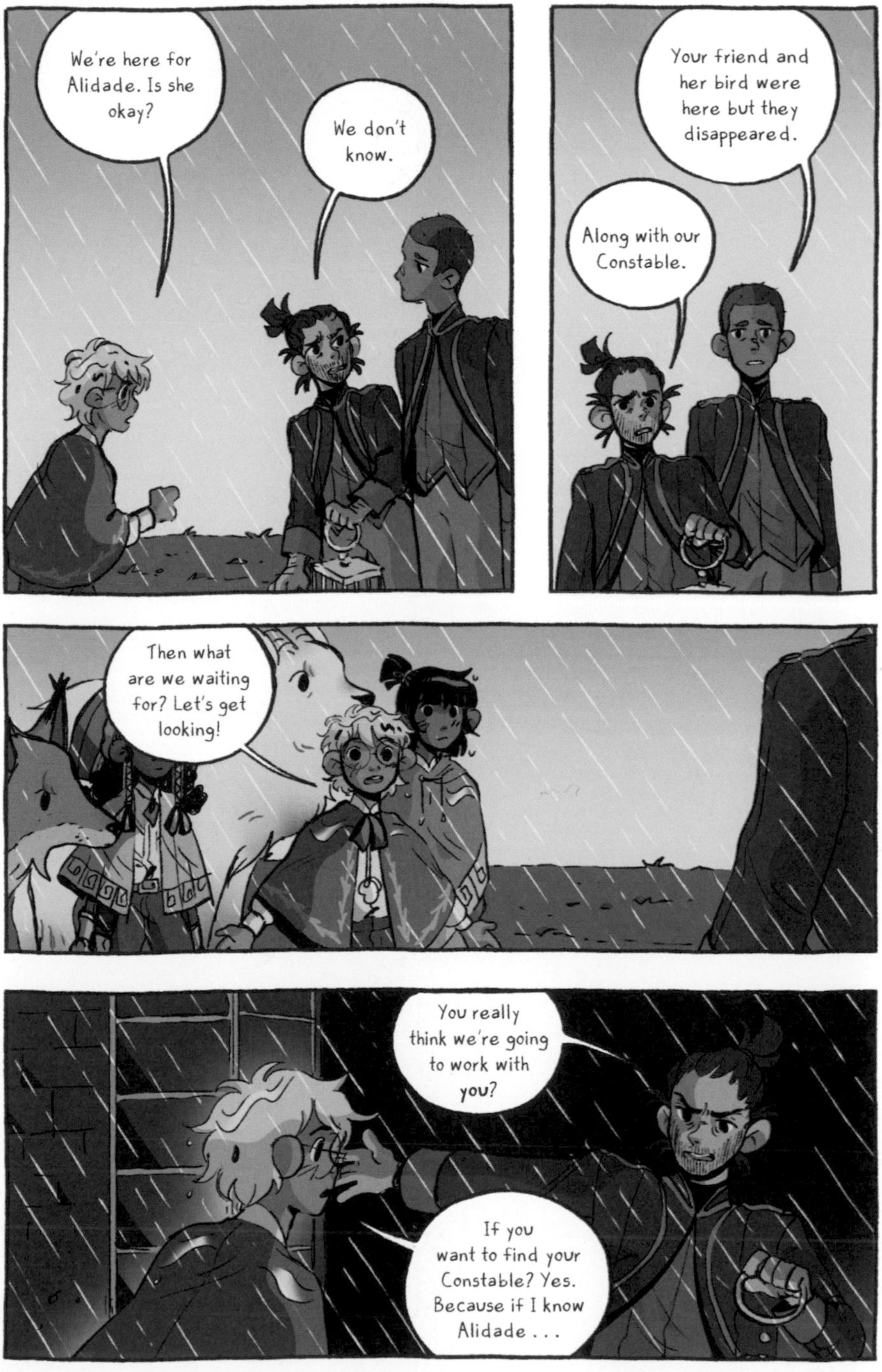
We're here for Alidade. Is she okay?
We don't know.
Your friend and her bird were here but they disappeared.
Along with our Constable.
Then what are we waiting for? Let's get looking!
You really think we're going to work with **you**?
If you want to find your Constable? Yes. Because if I know Alidade . . .

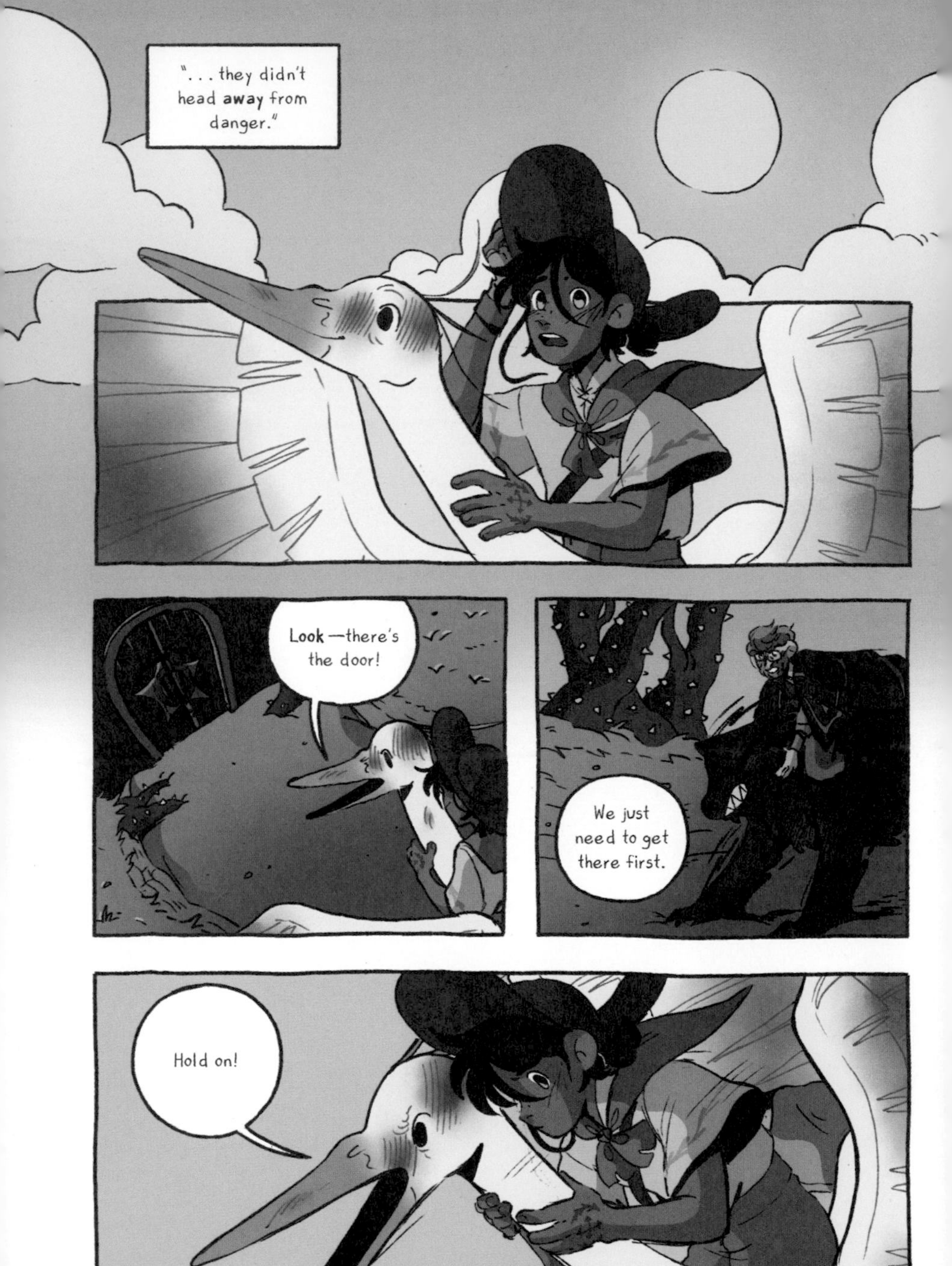
". . . they didn't head **away** from danger."
Look—there's the door!
We just need to get there first.
Hold on!

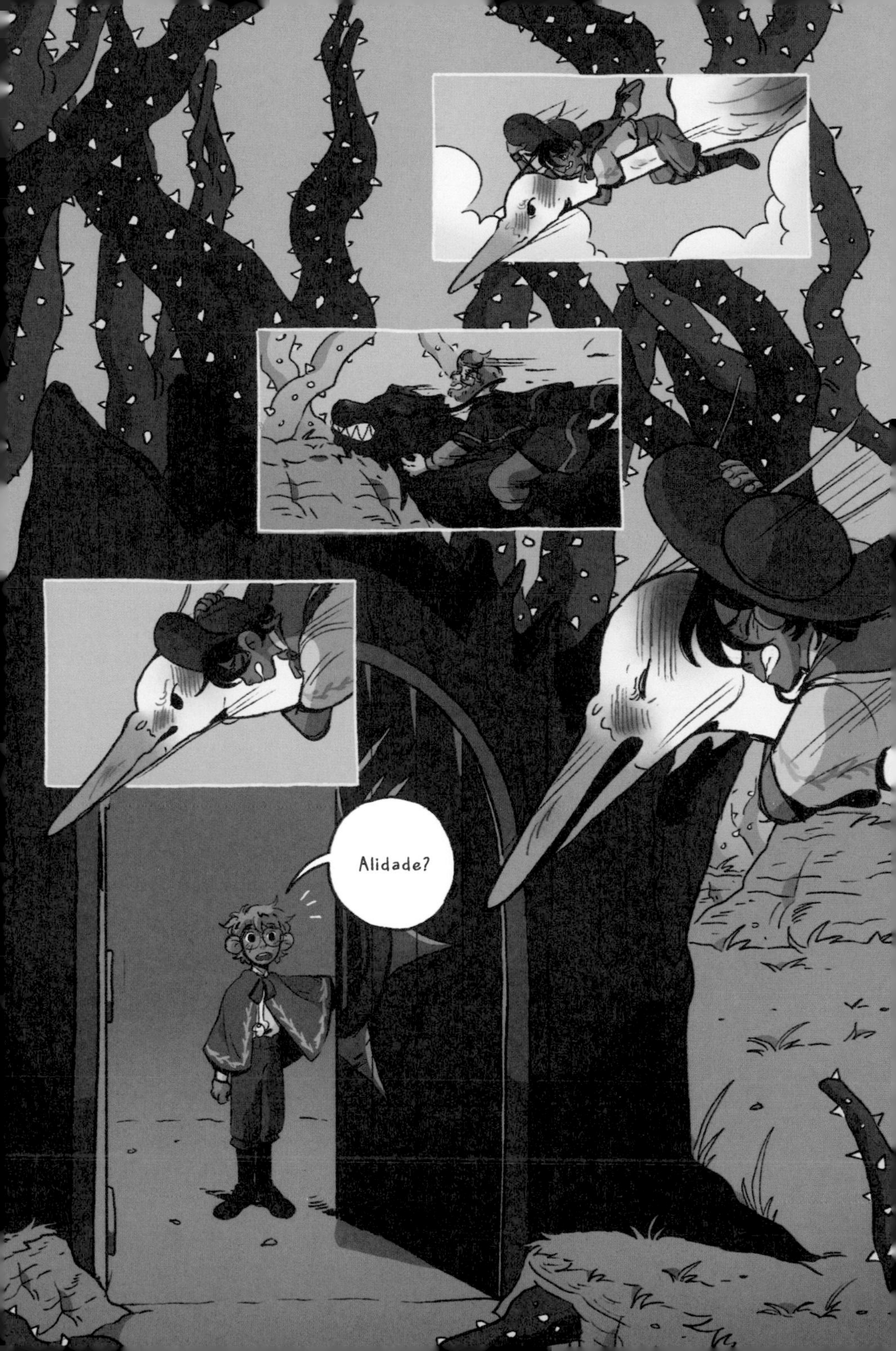
Alidade?

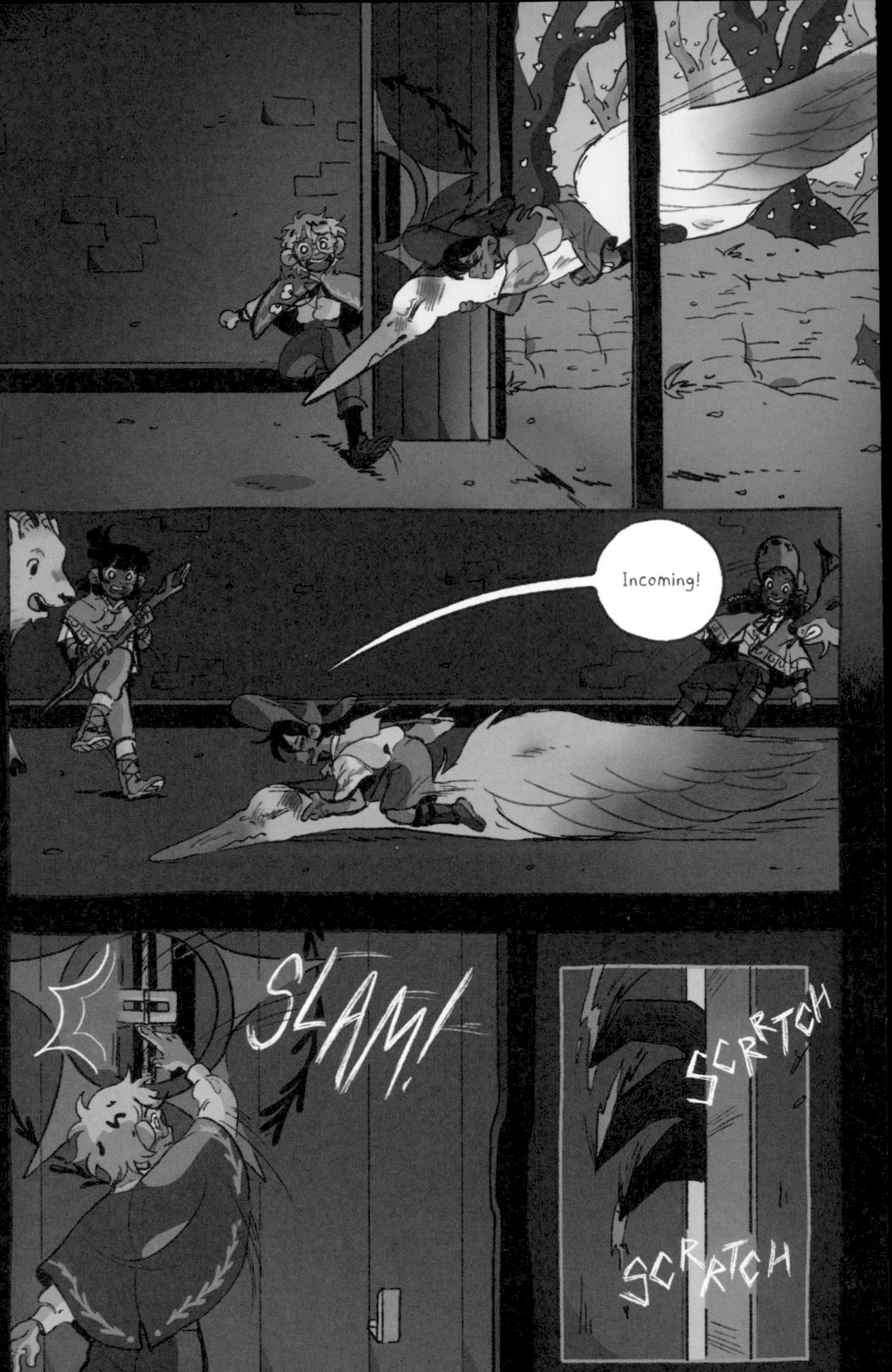

Incoming!
SLAM!
SCRRTCH
SCRRTCH

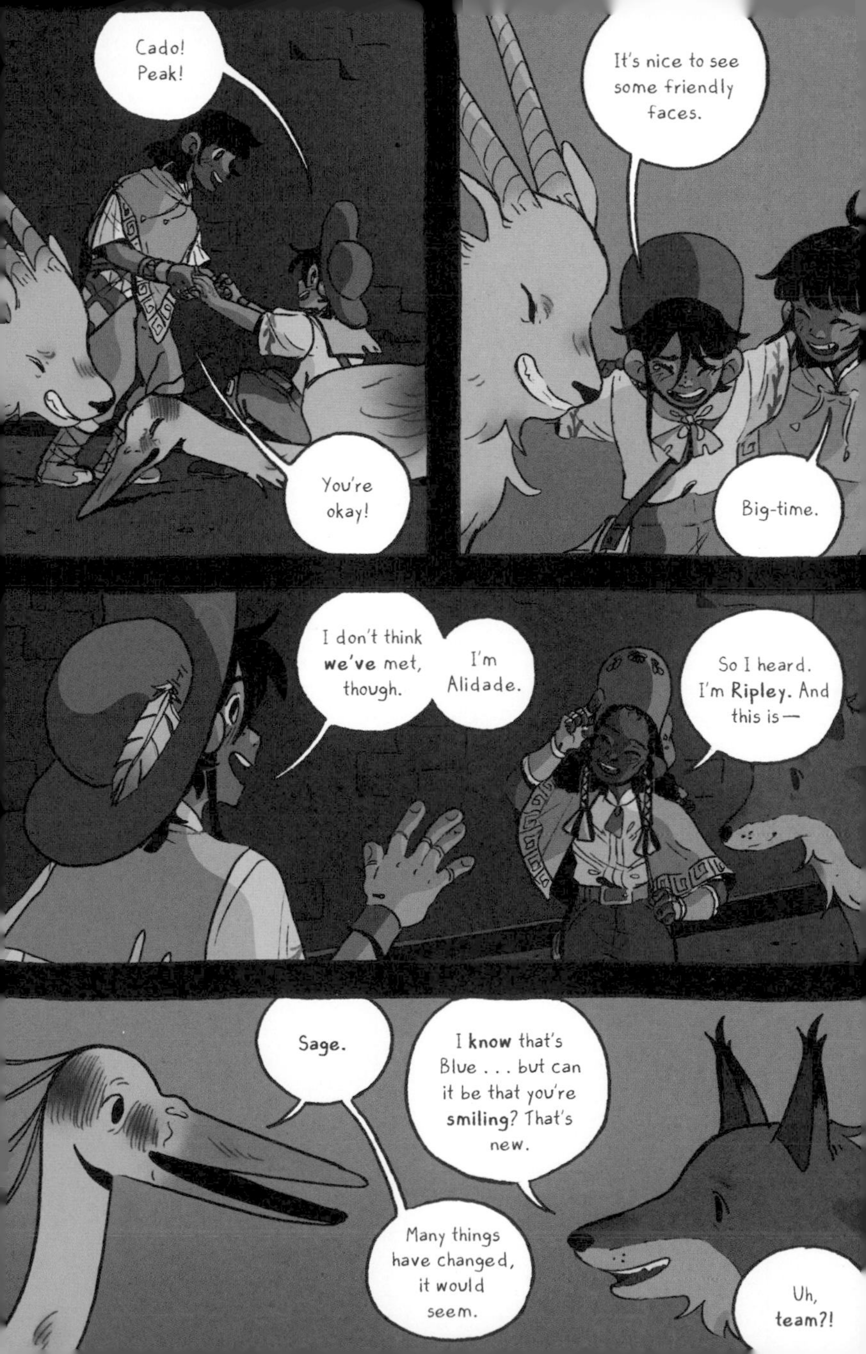
Cado! Peak!
You're okay!
It's nice to see some friendly faces.
Big-time.
I don't think **we've** met, though.
I'm Alidade.
So I heard. I'm **Ripley.** And this is—
Sage.
I **know** that's Blue . . . but can it be that you're **smiling**? That's new.
Many things have changed, it would seem.
Uh, **team?!**

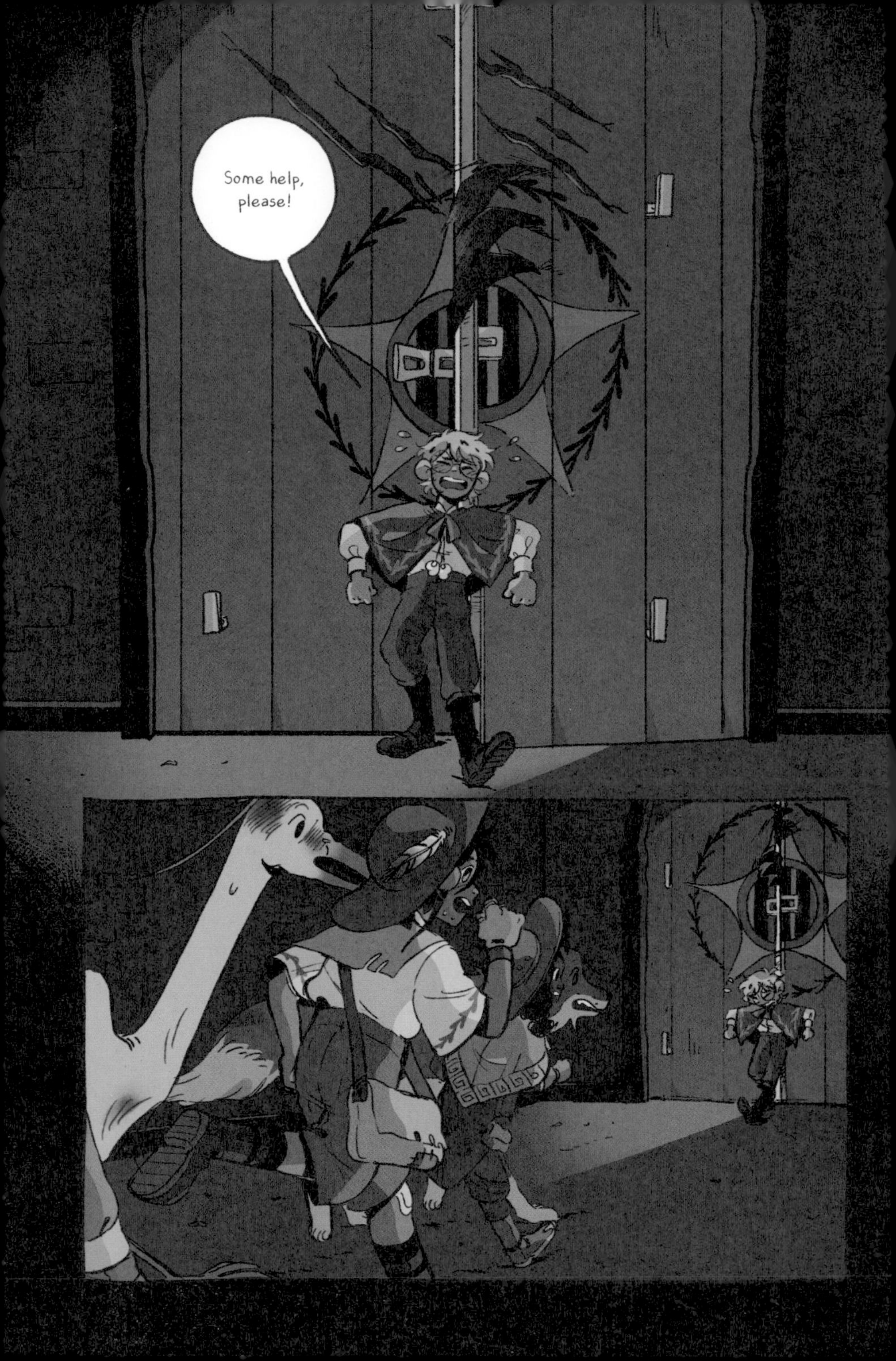
Some help, please!

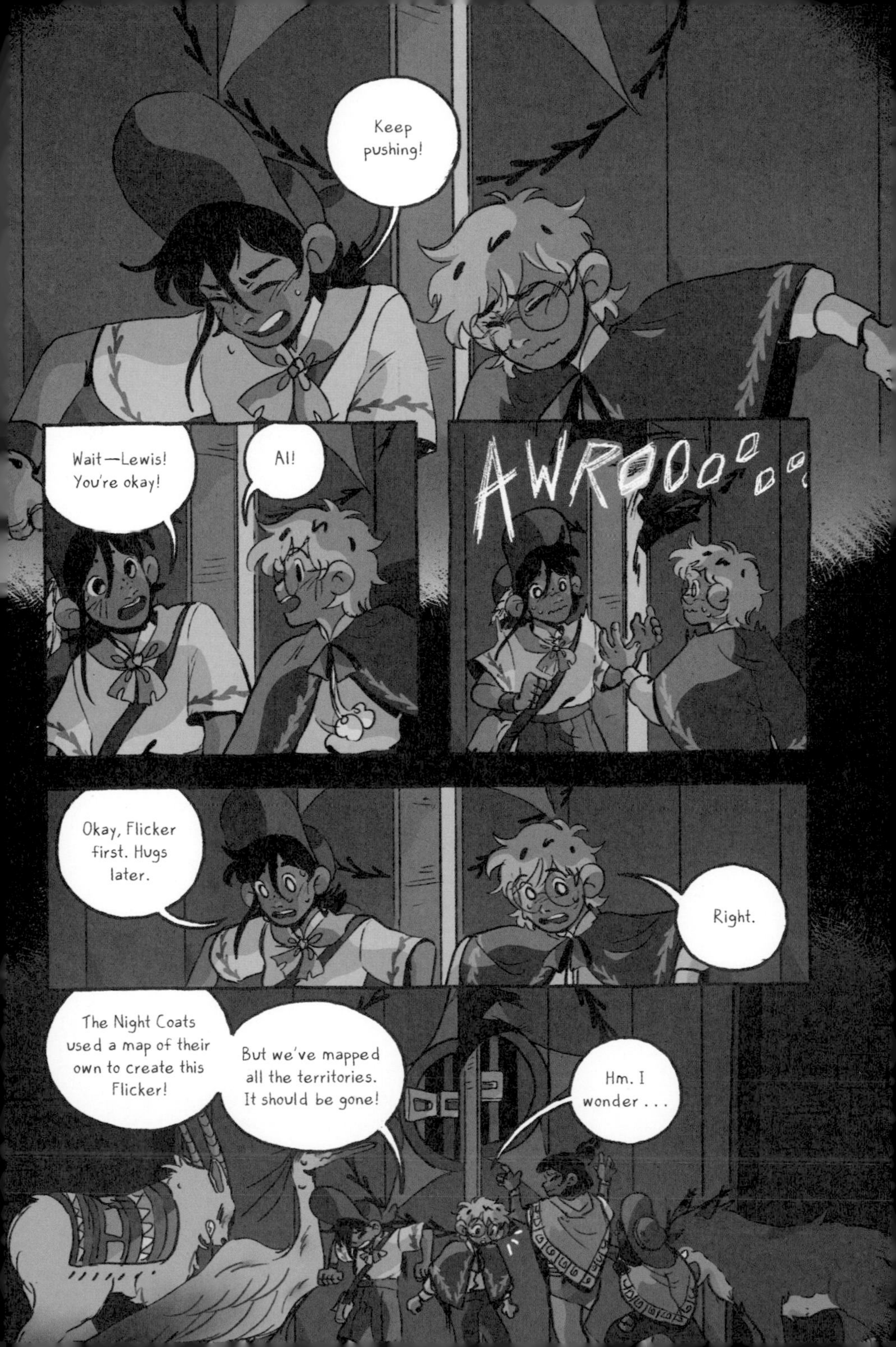
Keep pushing!
Wait—Lewis! You're okay!
Al!
AWROOOOooo
Okay, Flicker first. Hugs later.
Right.
The Night Coats used a map of their own to create this Flicker!
But we've mapped all the territories. It should be gone!
Hm. I wonder . . .

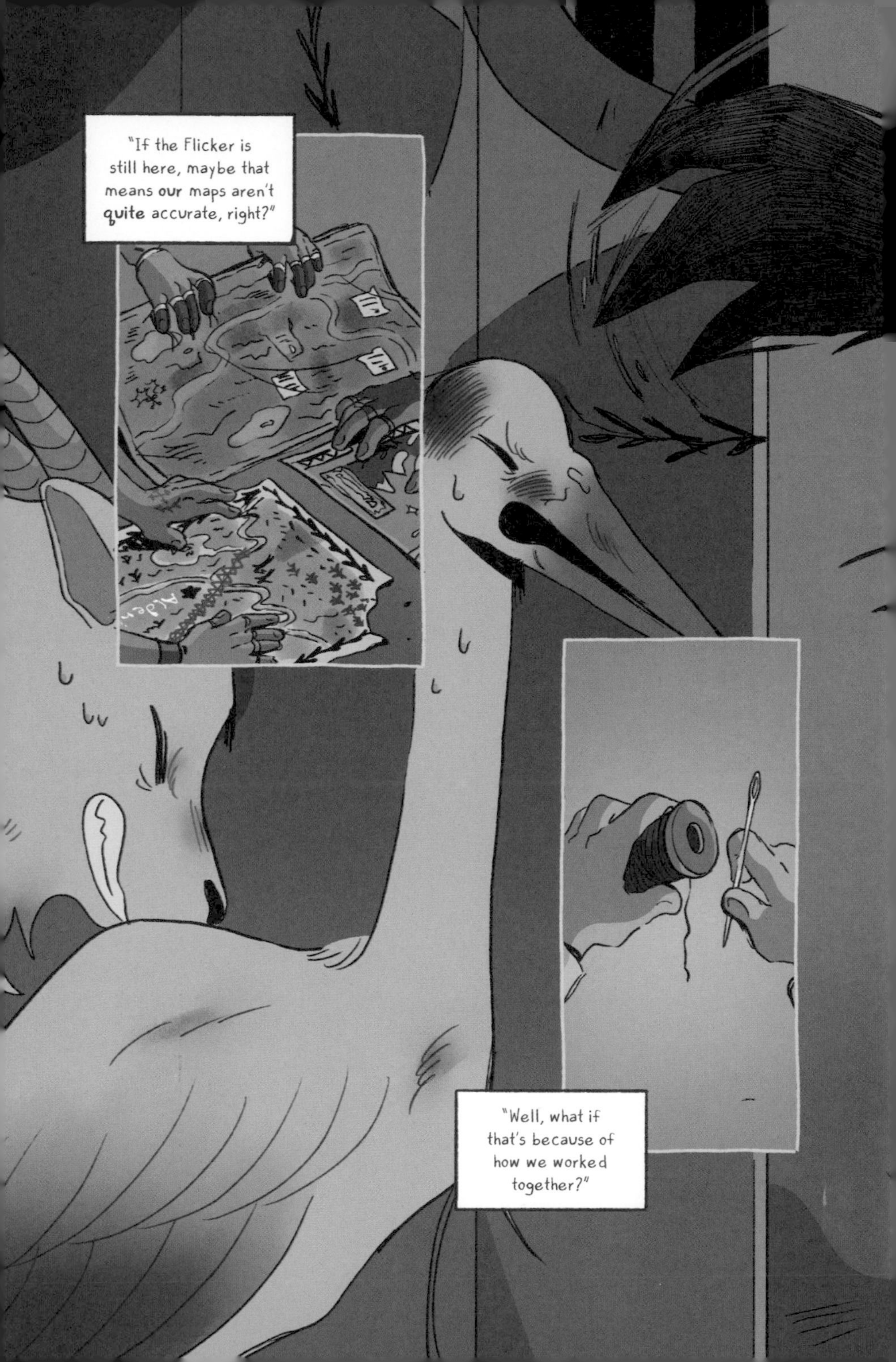
"If the Flicker is still here, maybe that means **our** maps aren't **quite** accurate, right?"
"Well, what if that's because of how we worked together?"

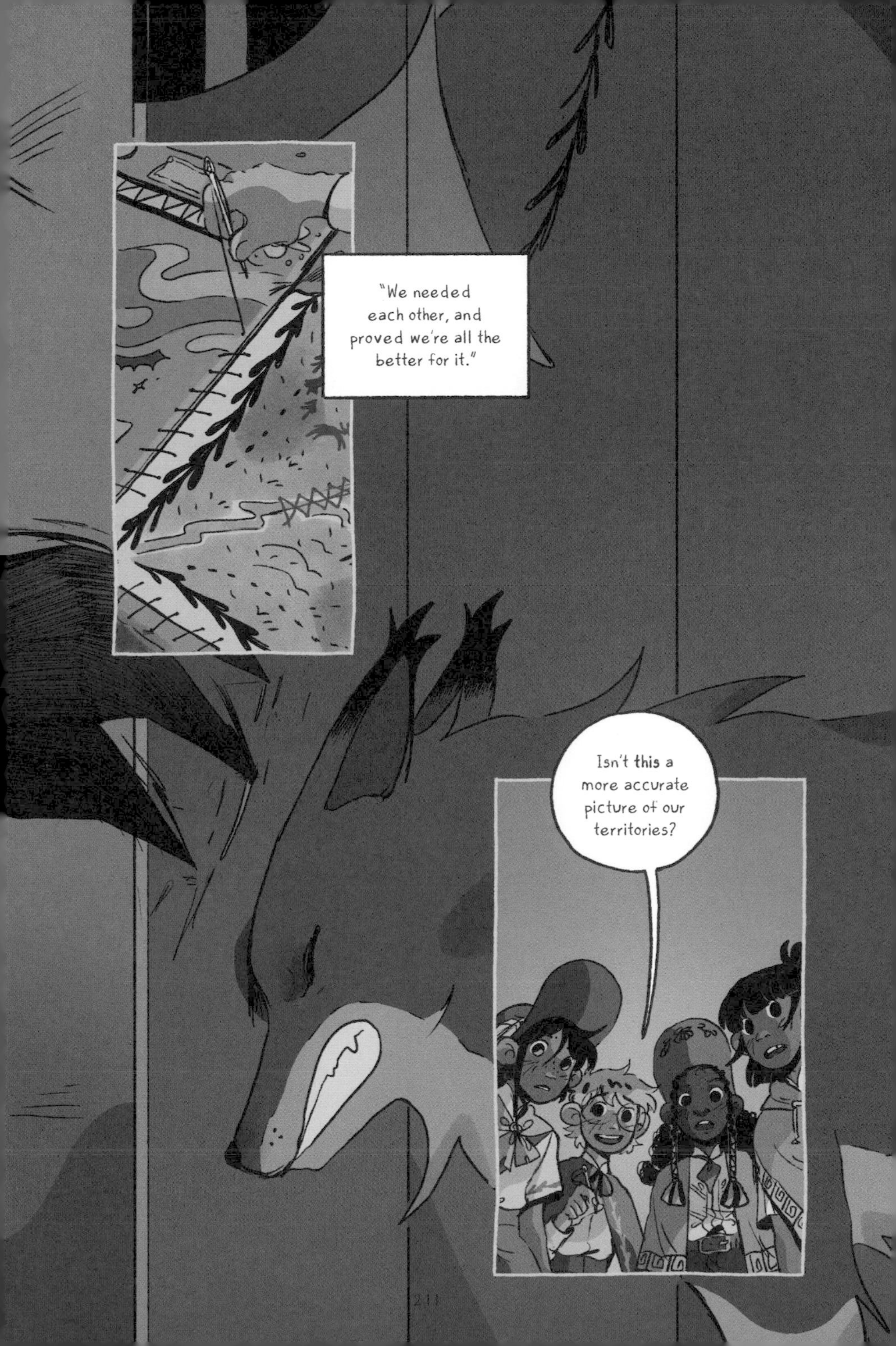
"We needed each other, and proved we're all the better for it."
Isn't this a more accurate picture of our territories?

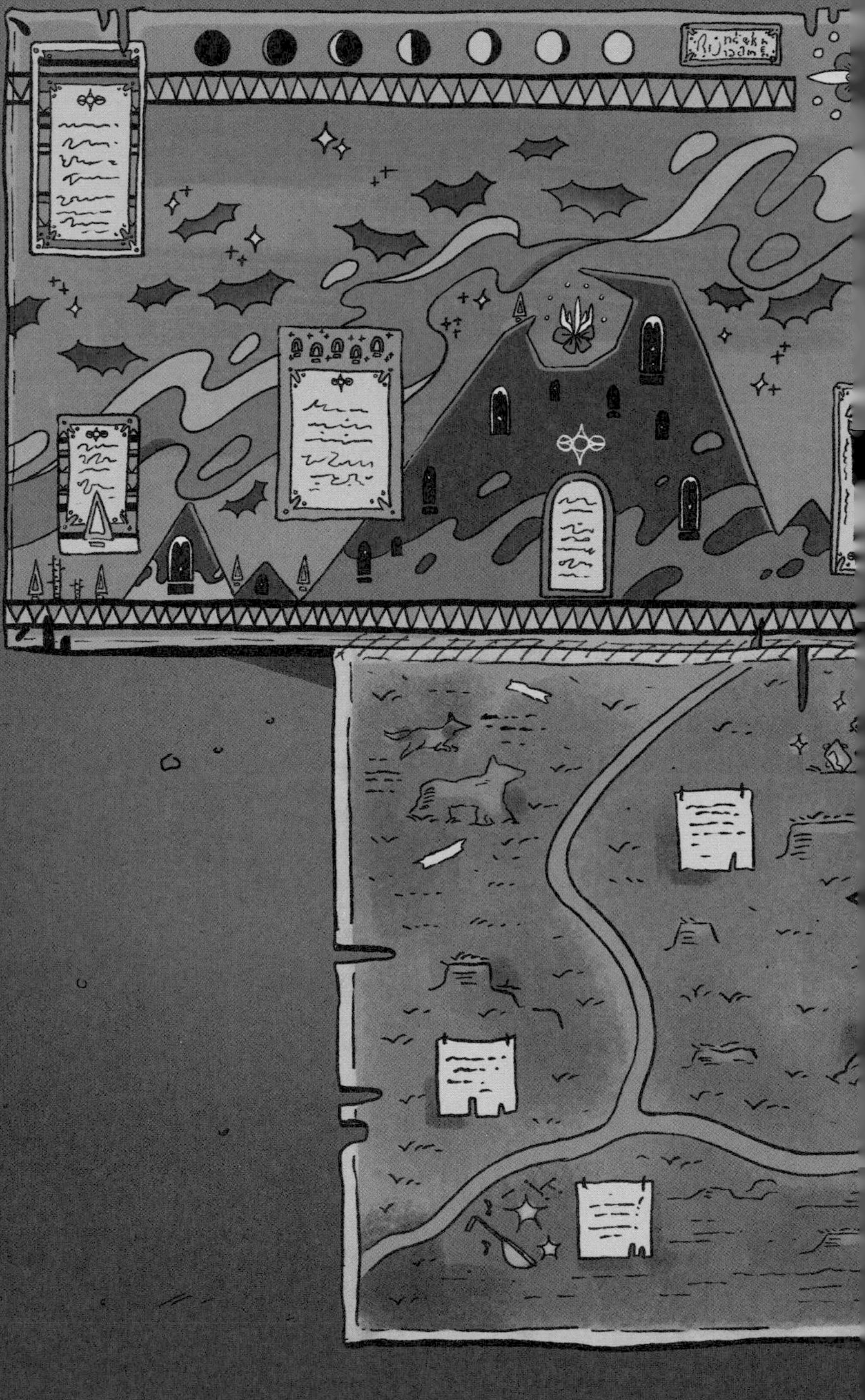

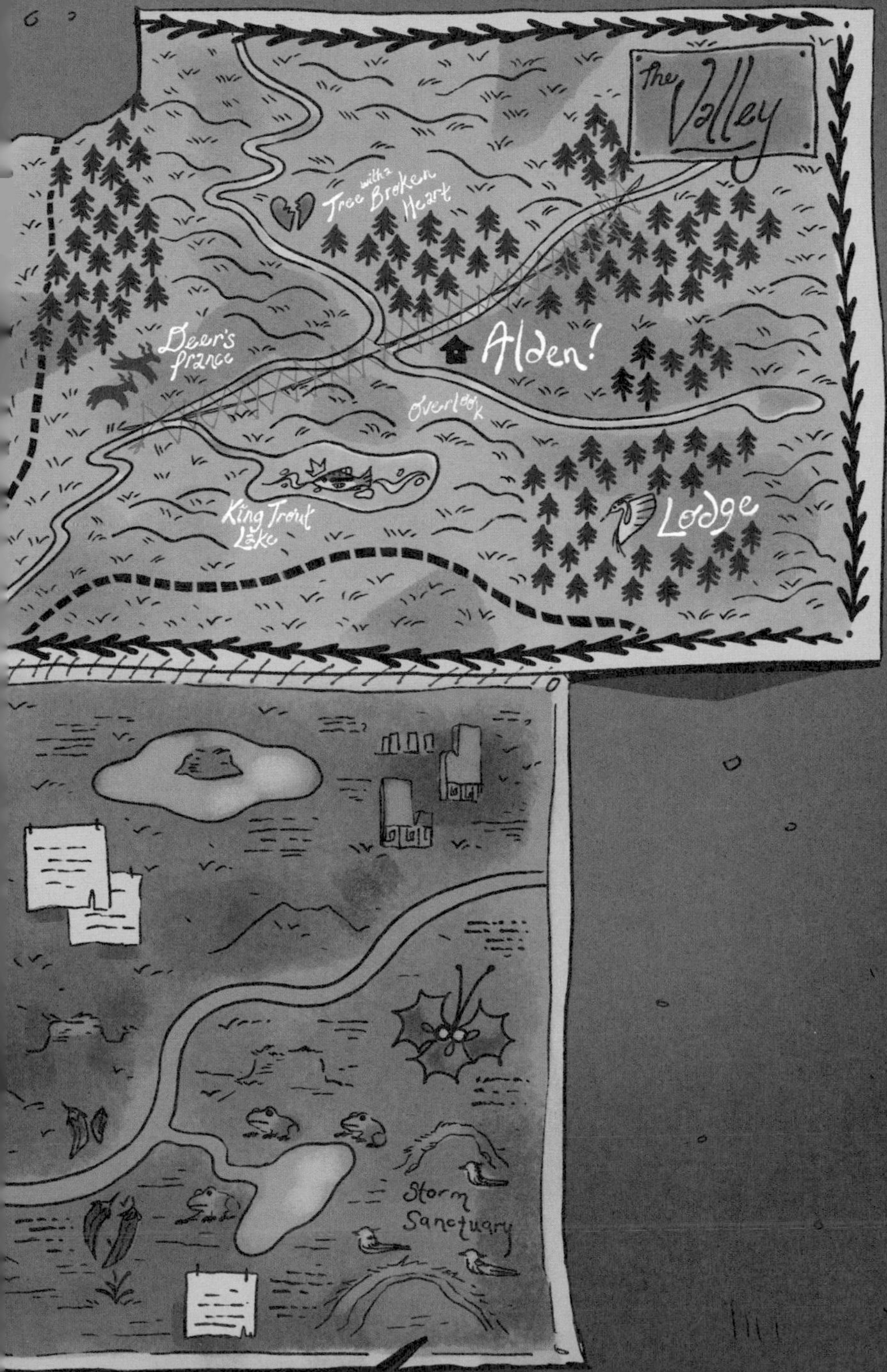
The Valley
Tree with a Broken Heart
Deer's prance
Alden!
Overlook
King Trout Lake
Lodge
Storm Sanctuary

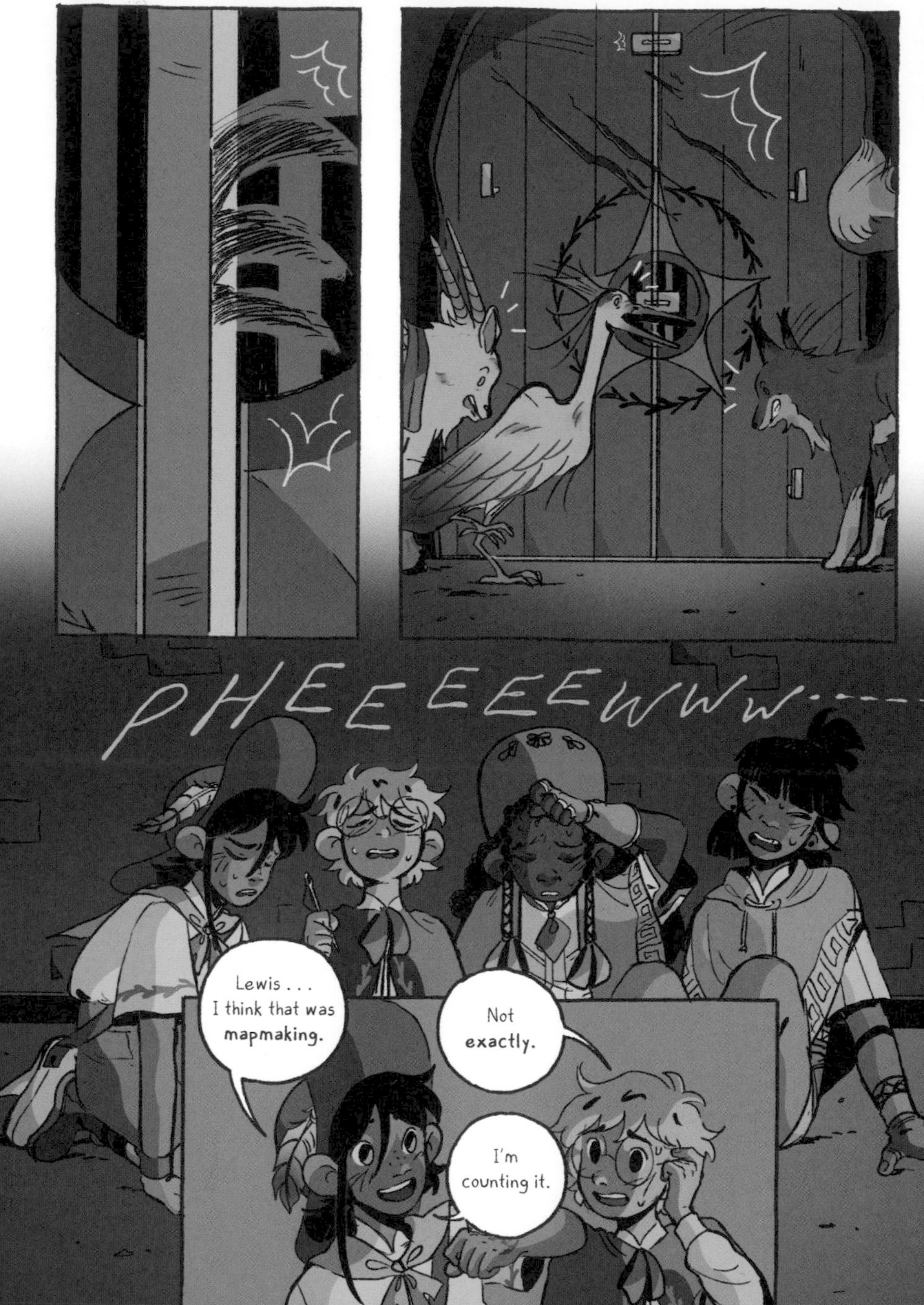
PHEEEEEWWW.....
Lewis . . . I think that was mapmaking.
Not exactly.
I'm counting it.

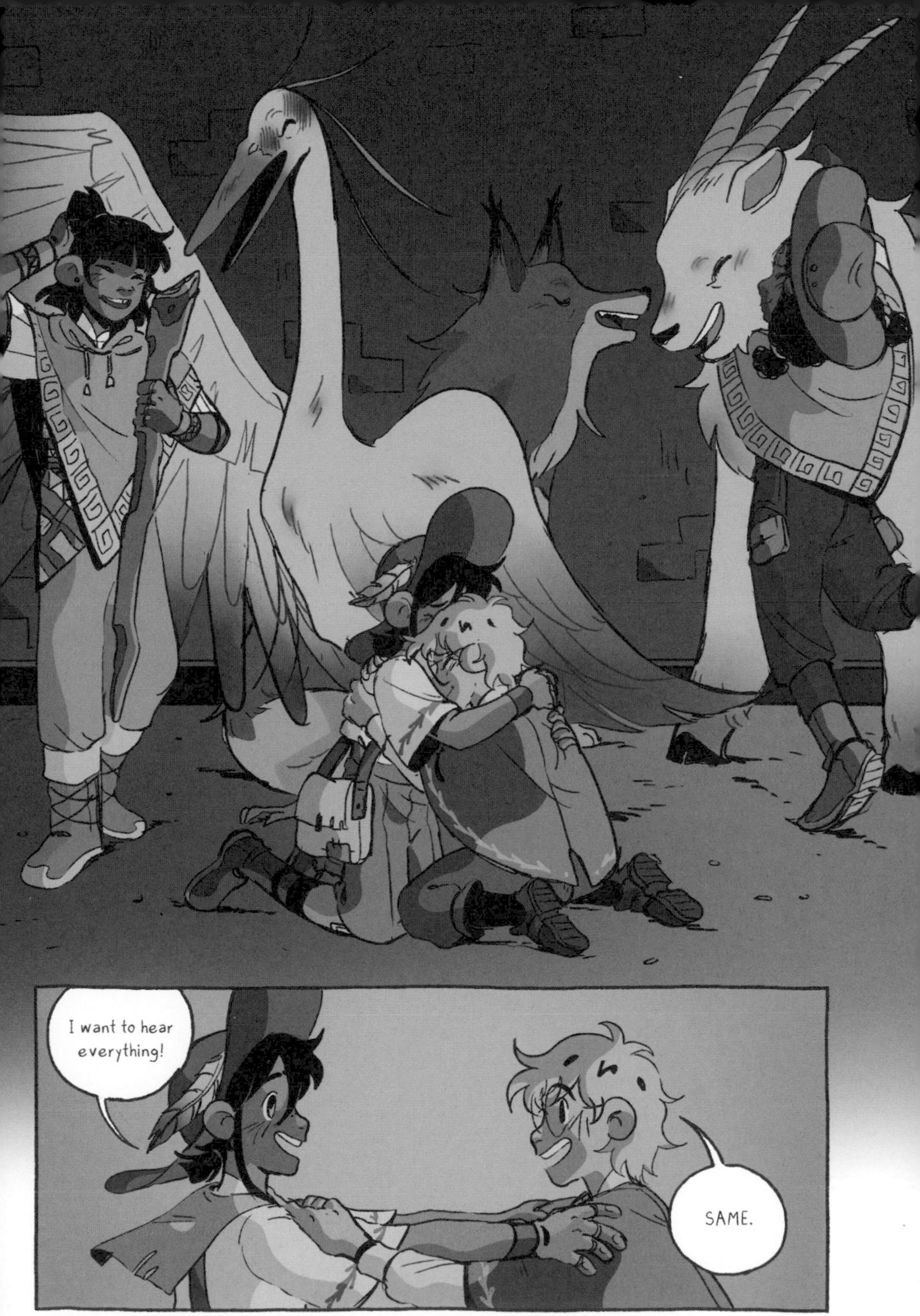
I want to hear everything!
SAME.

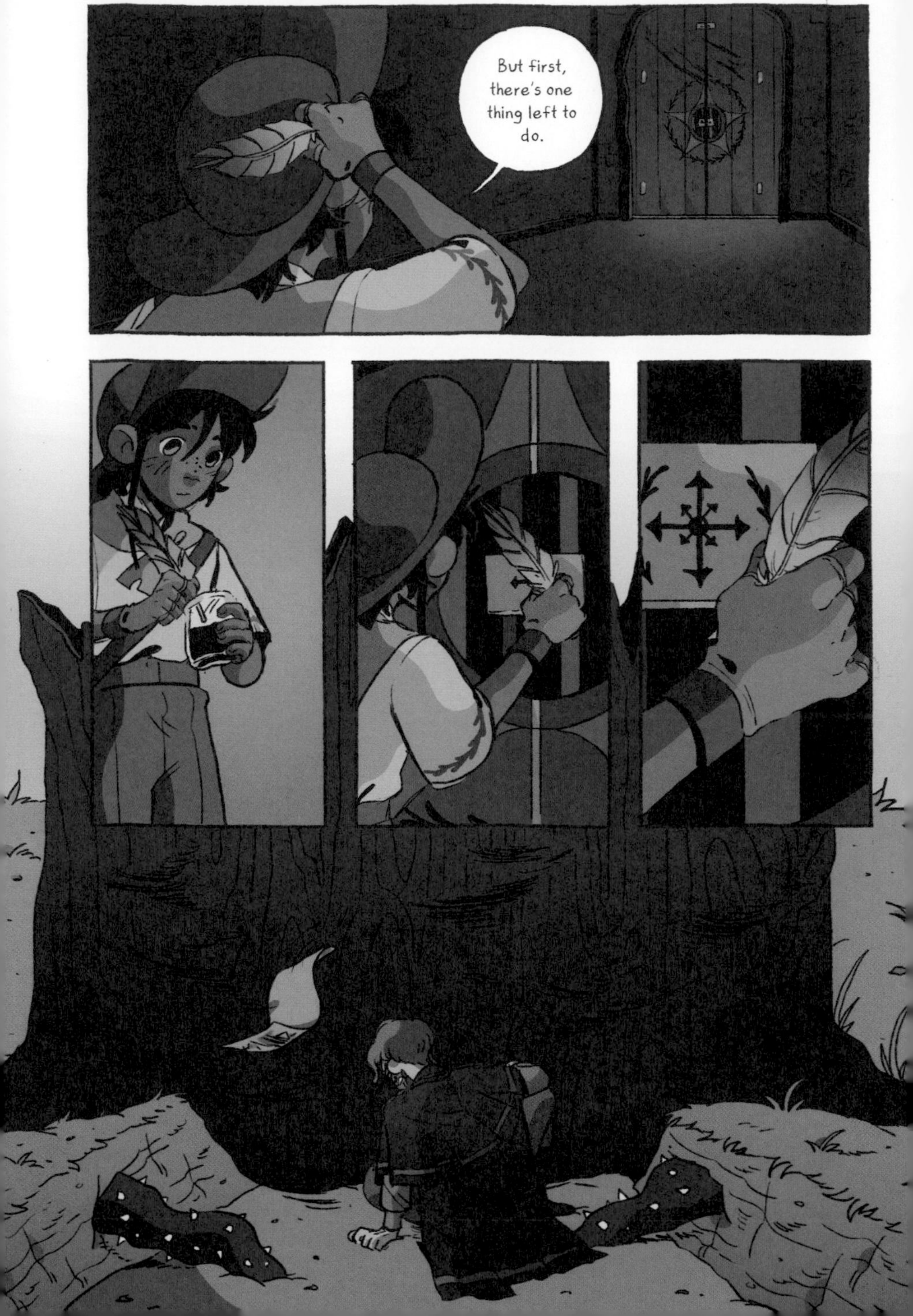

But first, there's one thing left to do.

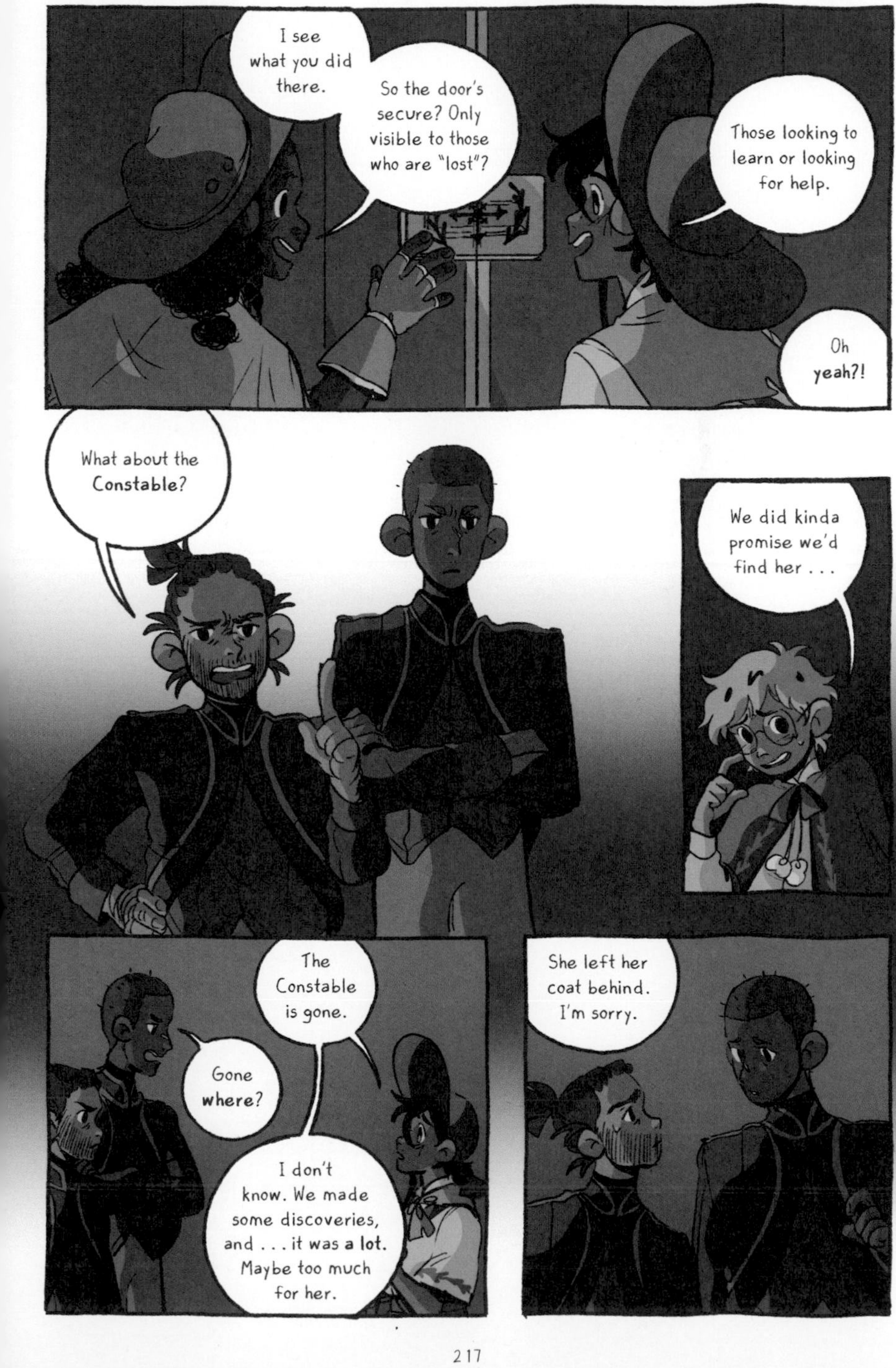
I see what you did there.
So the door's secure? Only visible to those who are "lost"?
Those looking to learn or looking for help.
Oh **yeah?!**
What about the **Constable?**
We did kinda promise we'd find her . . .
The Constable is gone.
Gone **where?**
I don't know. We made some discoveries, and . . . it was **a lot.** Maybe too much for her.
She left her coat behind. I'm sorry.

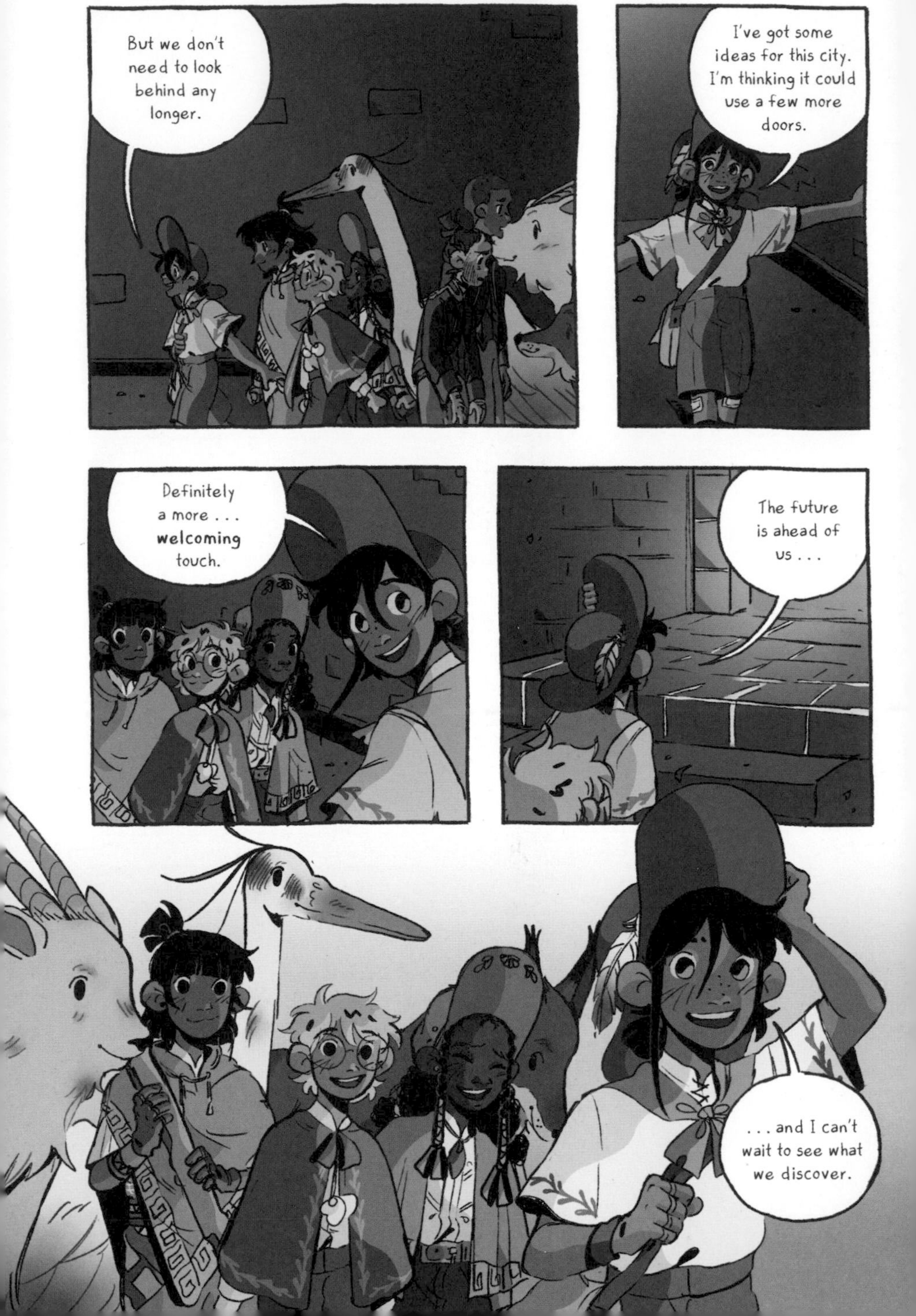
But we don't need to look behind any longer.
I've got some ideas for this city. I'm thinking it could use a few more doors.
Definitely a more . . . **welcoming** touch.
The future is ahead of us . . .
. . . and I can't wait to see what we discover.

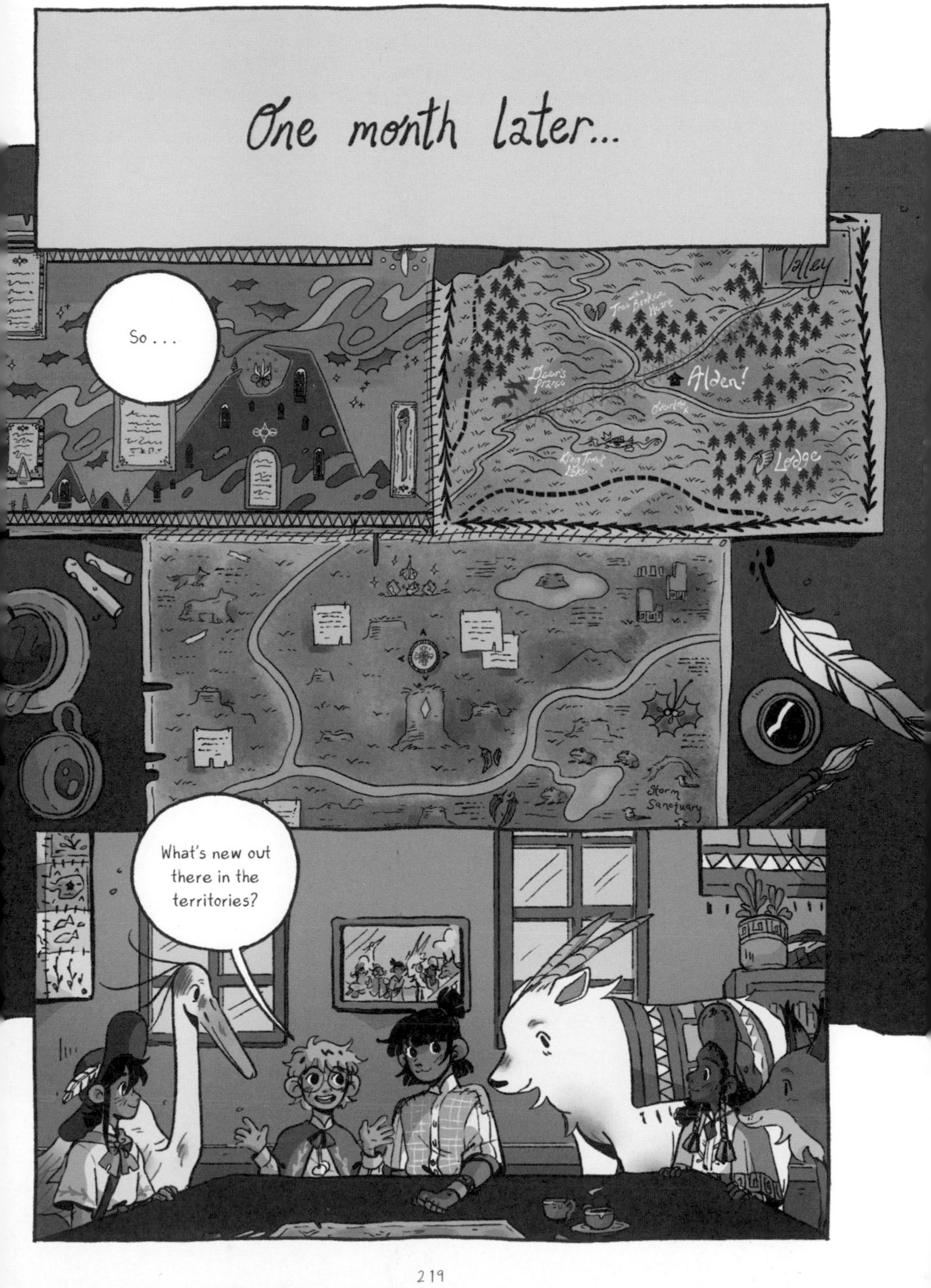
One month later...
So . . .
Valley
Alden!
Lodge
King Trout Lake
Storm Sanctuary
What's new out there in the territories?

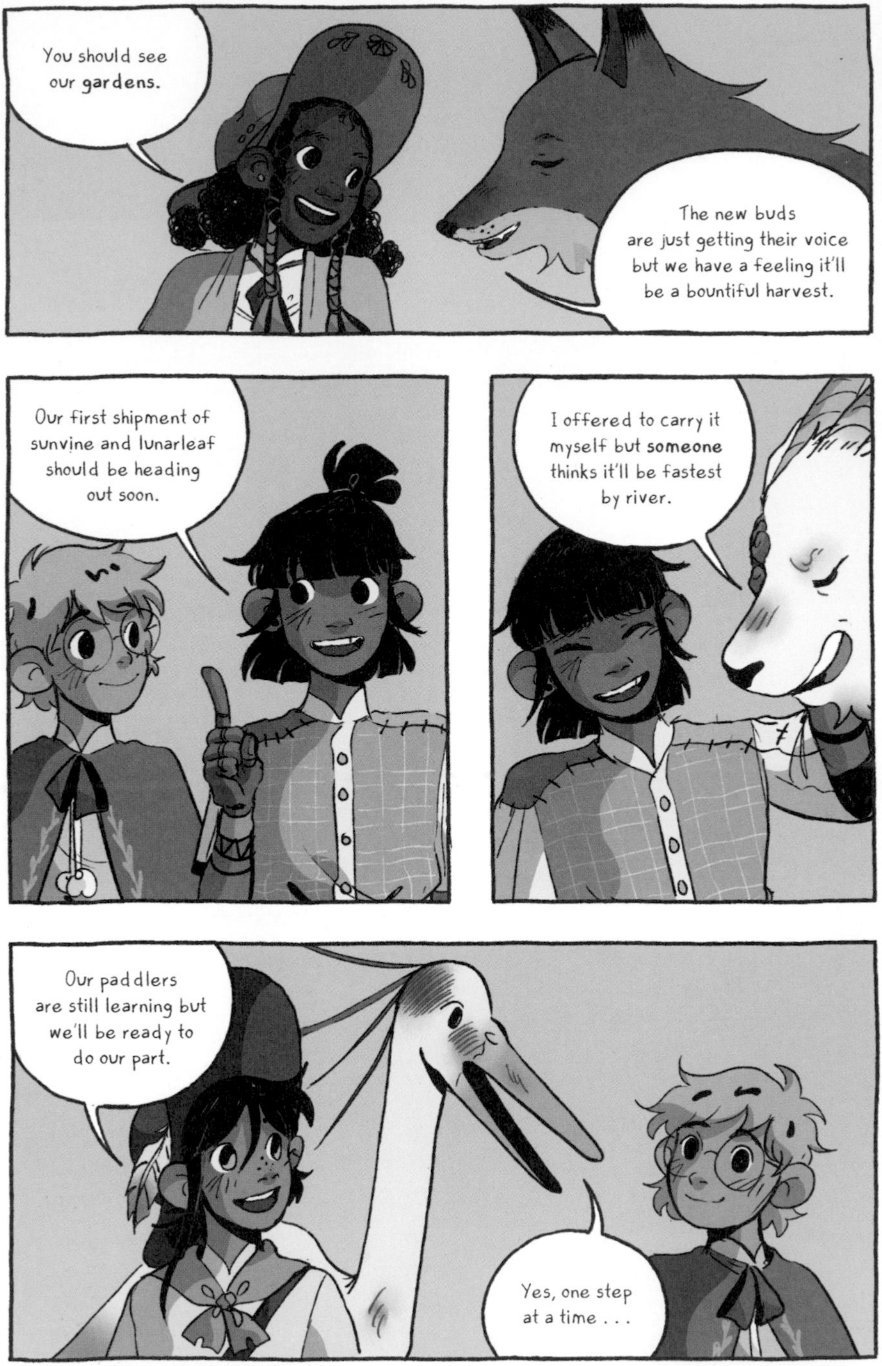
You should see our gardens.
The new buds are just getting their voice but we have a feeling it'll be a bountiful harvest.
Our first shipment of sunvine and lunarleaf should be heading out soon.
I offered to carry it myself but someone thinks it'll be fastest by river.
Our paddlers are still learning but we'll be ready to do our part.
Yes, one step at a time . . .

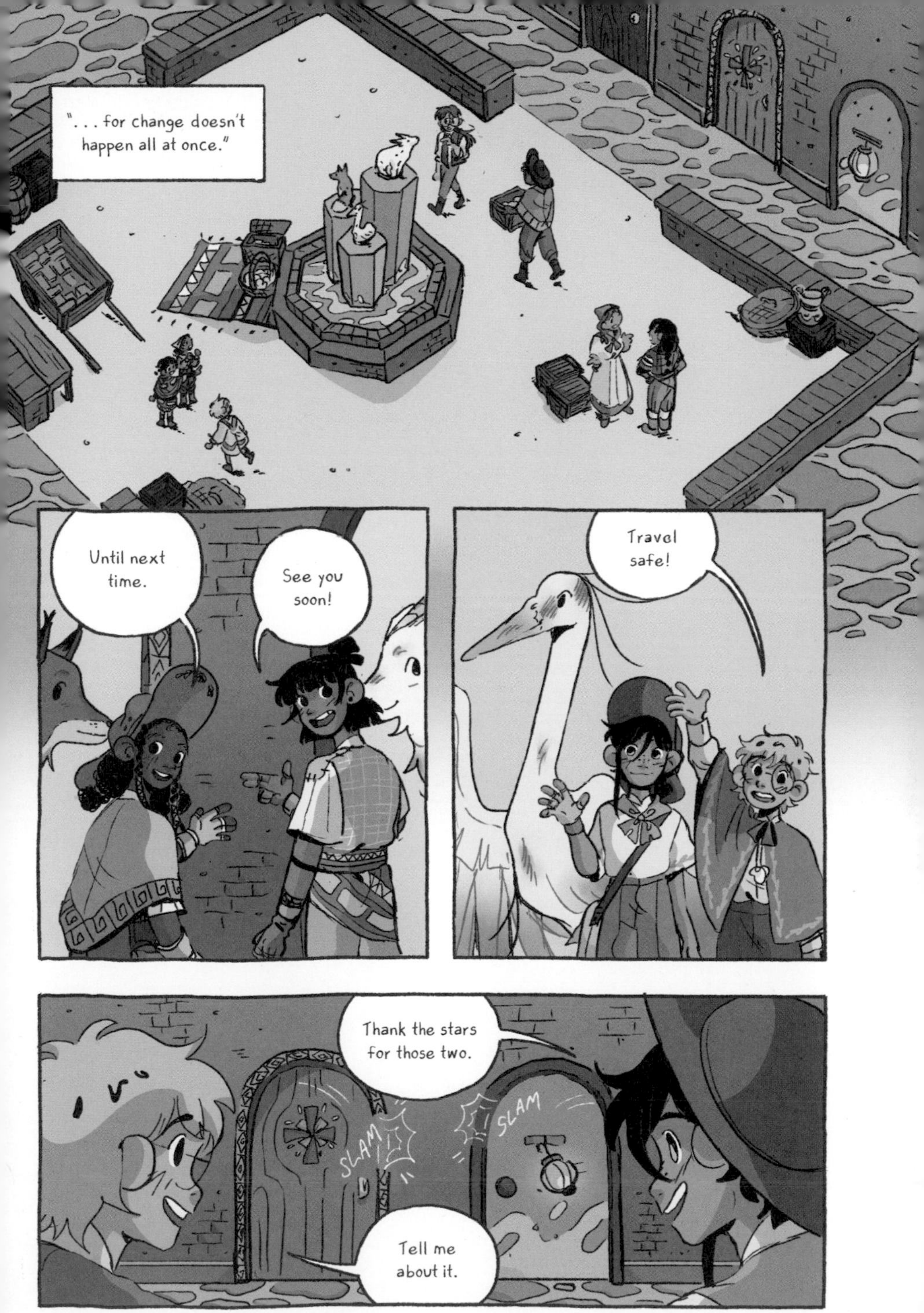
". . . for change doesn't happen all at once."
Until next time.
See you soon!
Travel safe!
Thank the stars for those two.
SLAM
SLAM
Tell me about it.

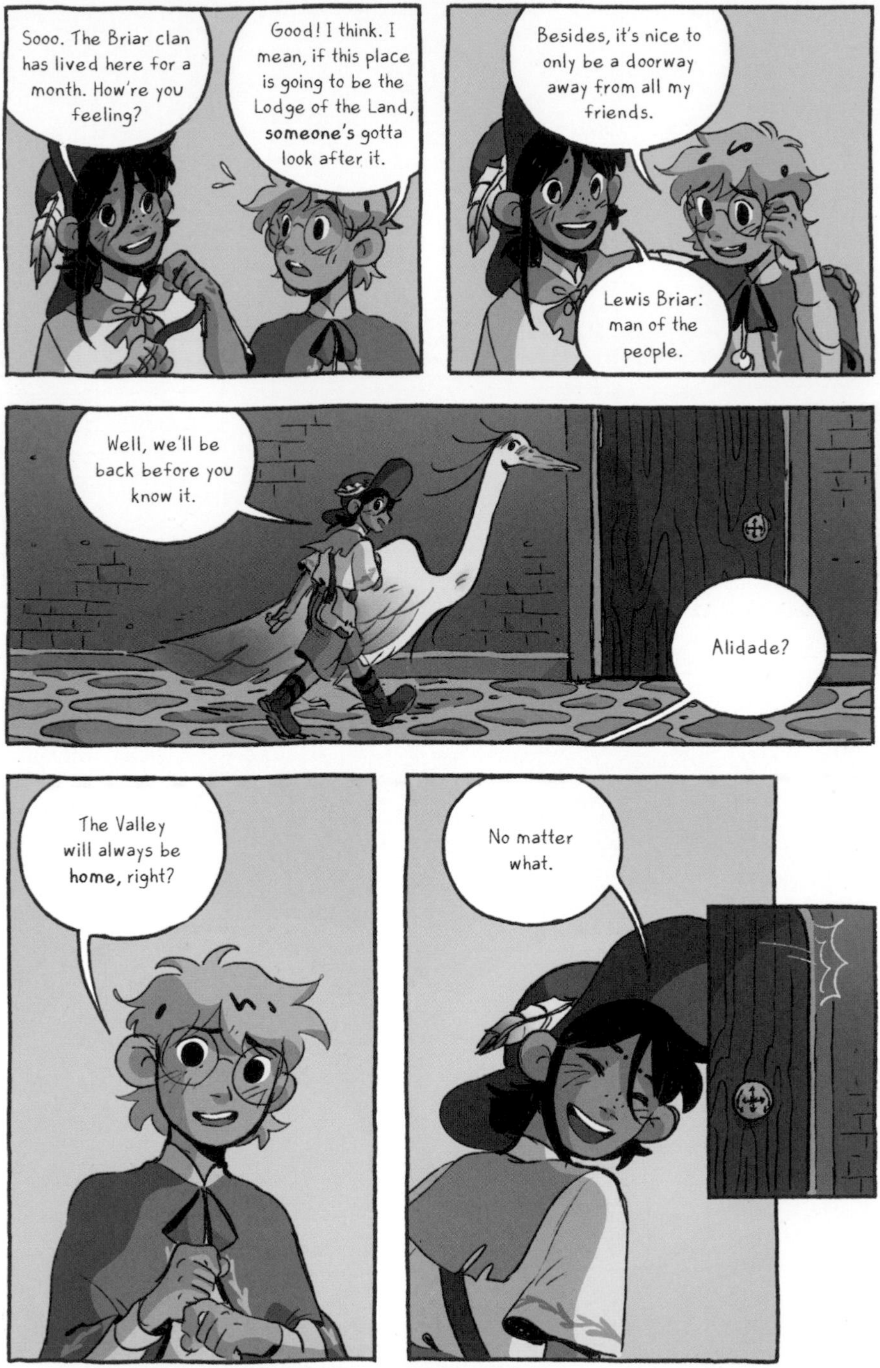
Sooo. The Briar clan has lived here for a month. How're you feeling?
Good! I think. I mean, if this place is going to be the Lodge of the Land, **someone's** gotta look after it.
Besides, it's nice to only be a doorway away from all my friends.
Lewis Briar: man of the people.
Well, we'll be back before you know it.
Alidade?
The Valley will always be **home**, right?
No matter what.

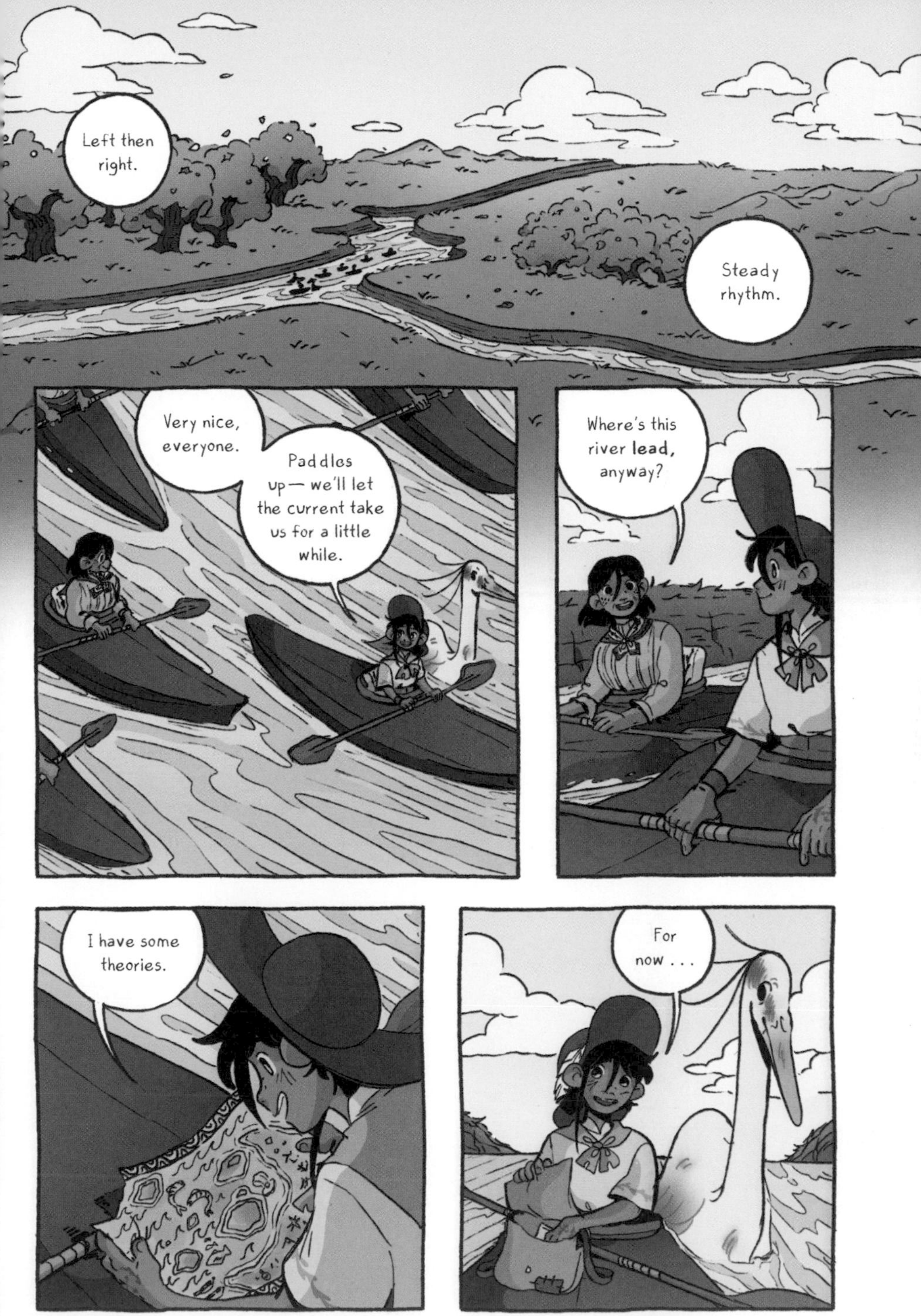
Left then right.
Steady rhythm.
Very nice, everyone.
Paddles up— we'll let the current take us for a little while.
Where's this river **lead,** anyway?
I have some theories.
For now . . .

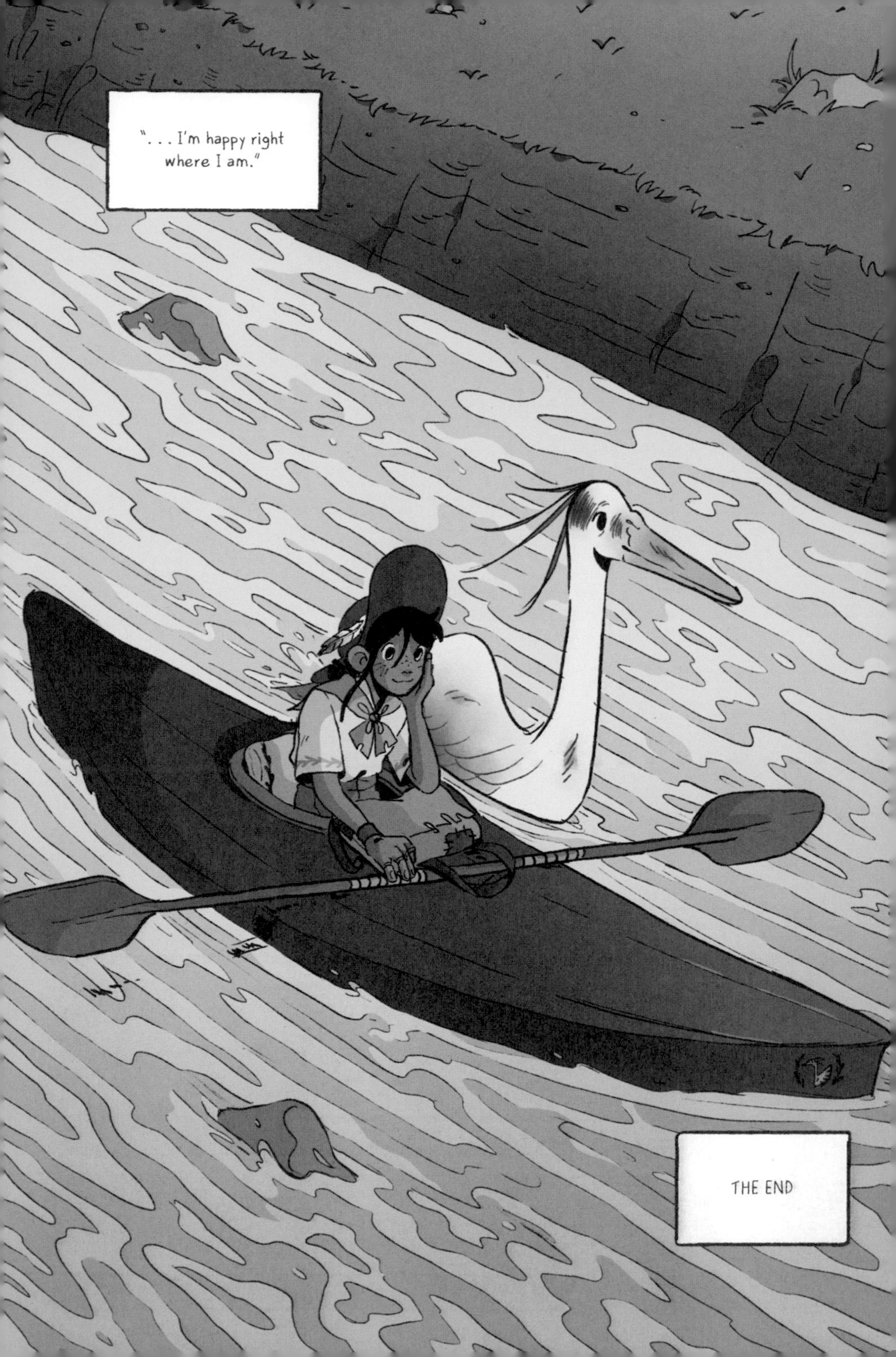
". . . I'm happy right where I am."
THE END

the whole plains were orange!

Tallgrass Poppies

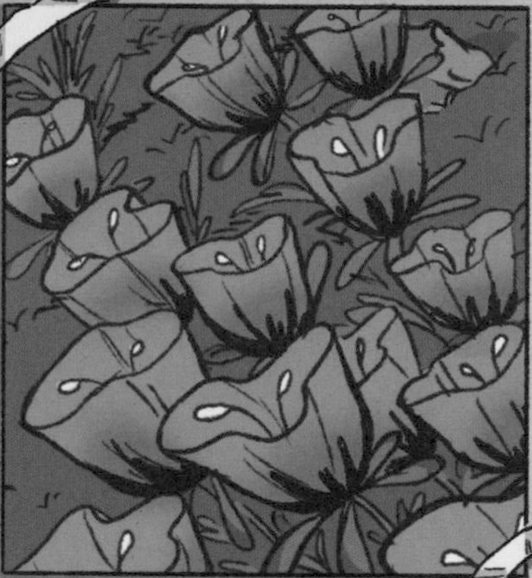

one of the Brightest I've seen!

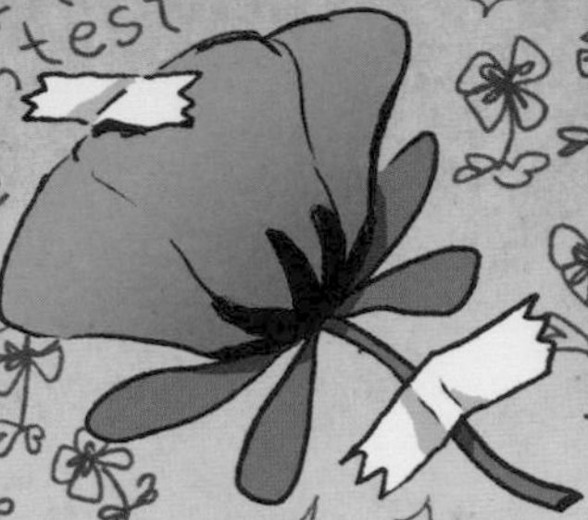

grows in HUUUGE numbers!!

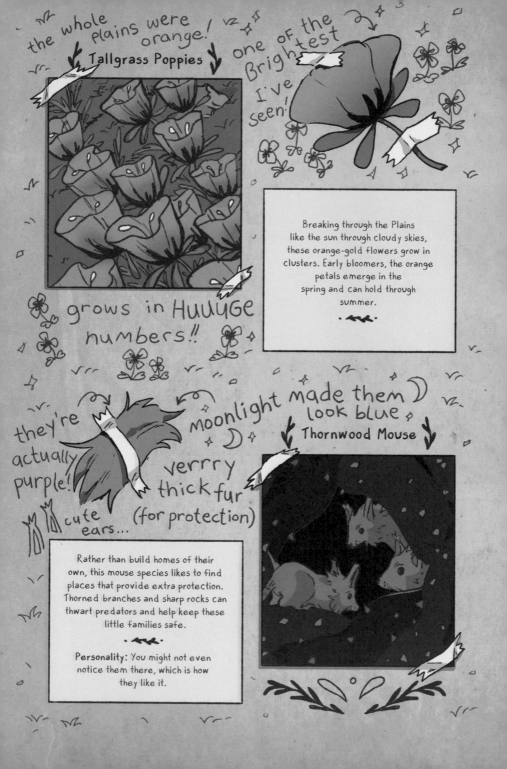

Breaking through the Plains like the sun through cloudy skies, these orange-gold flowers grow in clusters. Early bloomers, the orange petals emerge in the spring and can hold through summer.

they're actually purple!

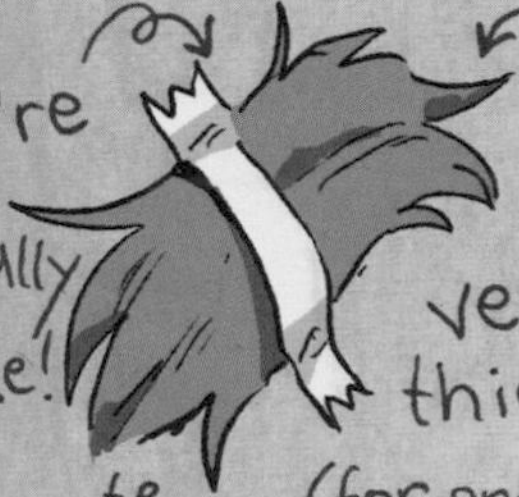

moonlight made them look blue

verrry thick fur (for protection)

cute ears...

Thornwood Mouse

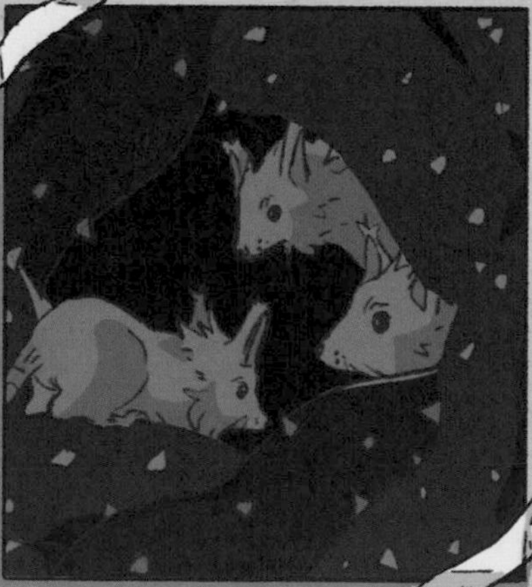

Rather than build homes of their own, this mouse species likes to find places that provide extra protection. Thorned branches and sharp rocks can thwart predators and help keep these little families safe.

Personality: You might not even notice them there, which is how they like it.

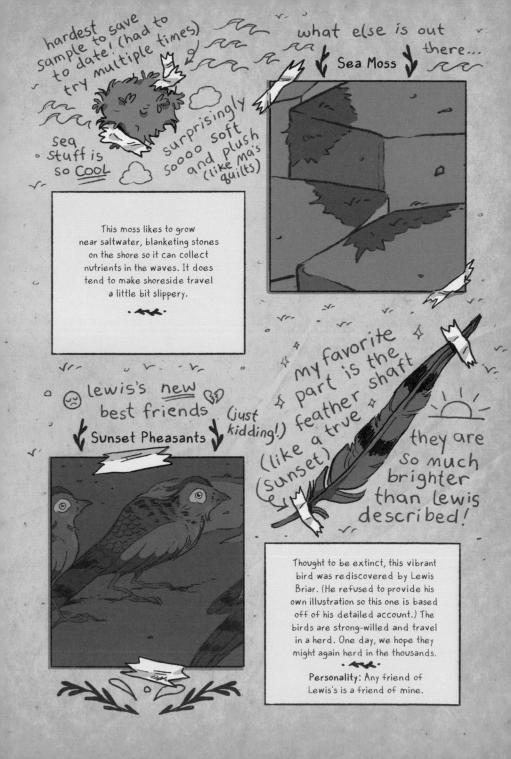

hardest to save sample to date! (had to try multiple times)

what else is out there...

Sea Moss

sea stuff is so COOL

surprisingly soooo soft and plush (like ma's quilts)

This moss likes to grow near saltwater, blanketing stones on the shore so it can collect nutrients in the waves. It does tend to make shoreside travel a little bit slippery.

lewis's new best friends (just kidding!)

Sunset Pheasants

my favorite part is the feather shaft (like a true sunset)

they are so much brighter than lewis described!

Thought to be extinct, this vibrant bird was rediscovered by Lewis Briar. (He refused to provide his own illustration so this one is based off of his detailed account.) The birds are strong-willed and travel in a herd. One day, we hope they might again herd in the thousands.

Personality: Any friend of Lewis's is a friend of mine.

Drawing the Memri of the Plains

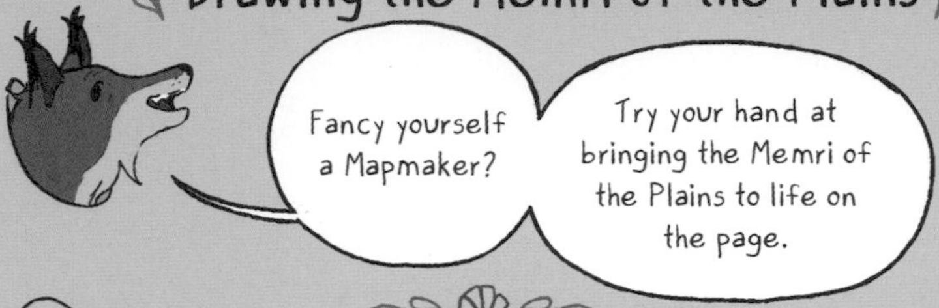

Fancy yourself a Mapmaker?
Try your hand at bringing the Memri of the Plains to life on the page.

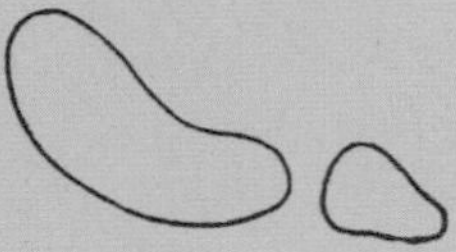

(1) We start with a sleek and agile frame. "Graceful," one might say.

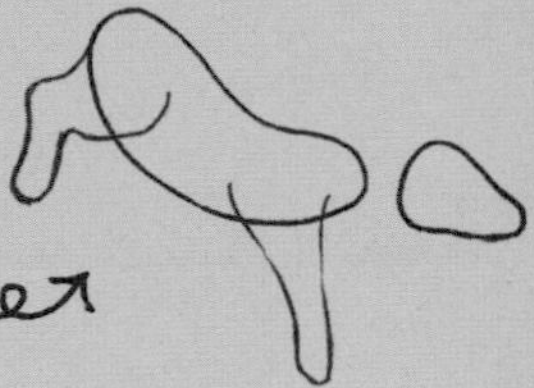

(2) You then of course need quick feet. I'd hate to be drawn standing still.

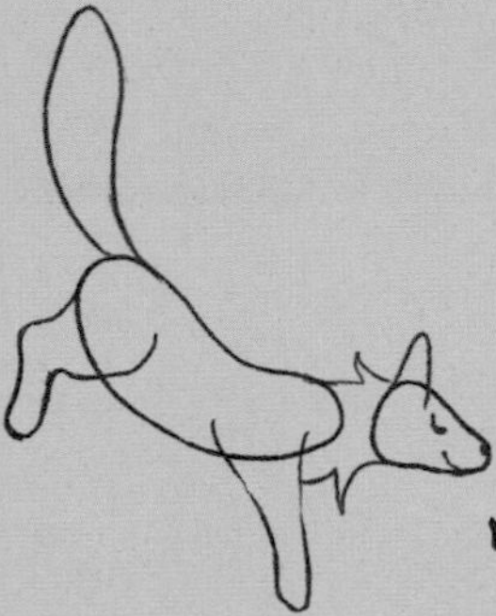

(3) Don't forget a little personality. Maybe a smile or a wink.

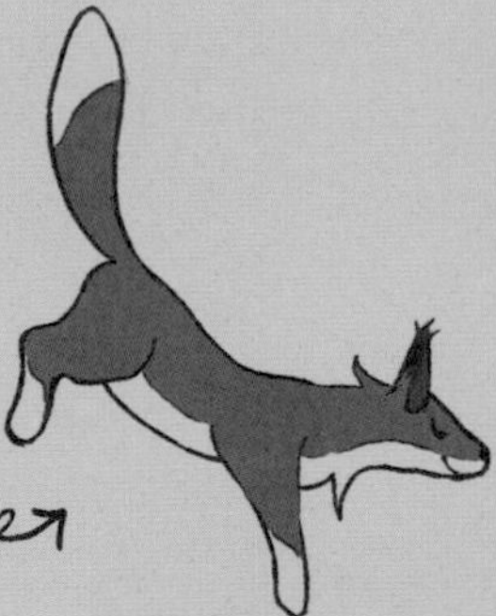

(4) Lastly, erase the guidelines and add details of your own. Just don't forget a few speed lines to capture my movement.

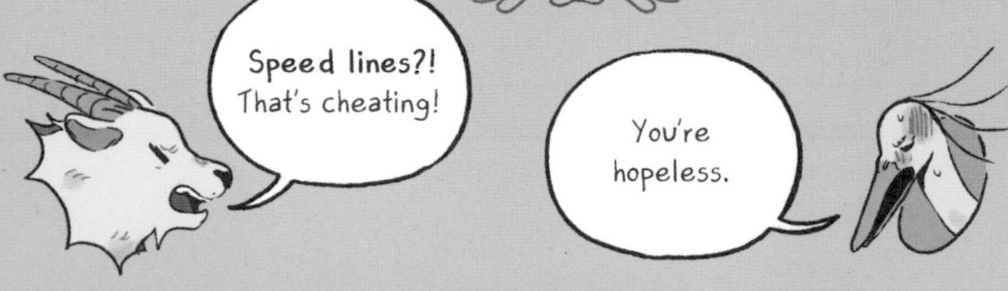

Speed lines?! That's cheating!
You're hopeless.

Character Concept Art

Ripley Range

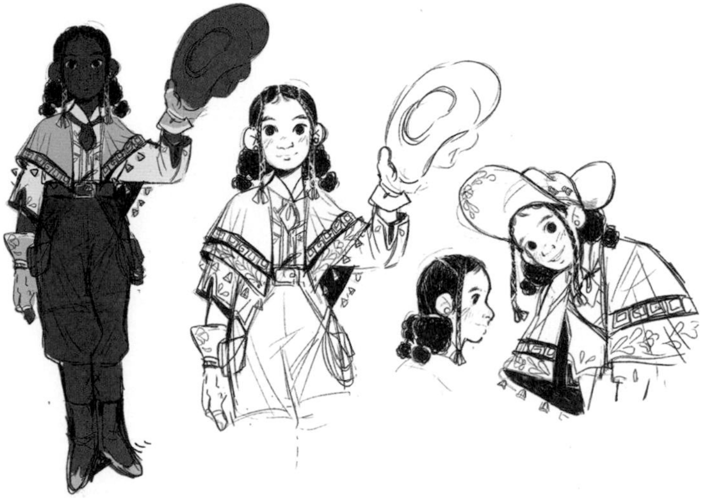

Ripley loves the expansive outdoors and the work of being a Mapmaker. She loves interacting with people in her territory, hearing their perspectives, and including those personal insights on the map. She's big and bold, with clothes fit for the terrain. She's got a look where you see her and can't help but think she's cool.

The Range Family

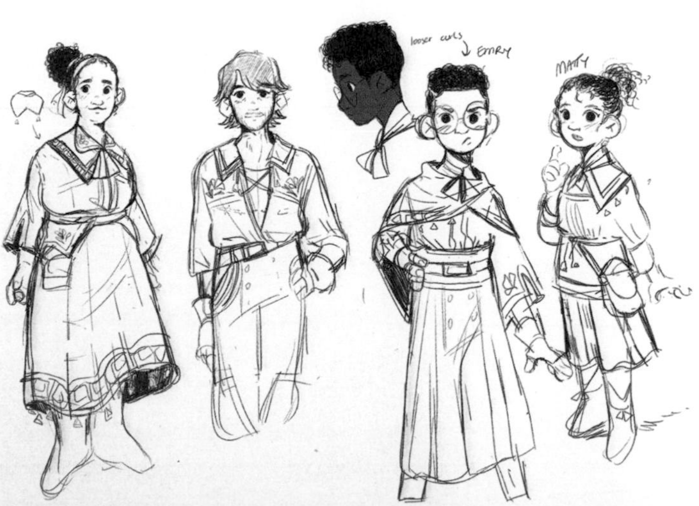
looser curls
EMRY
MATTY

World Concept Art

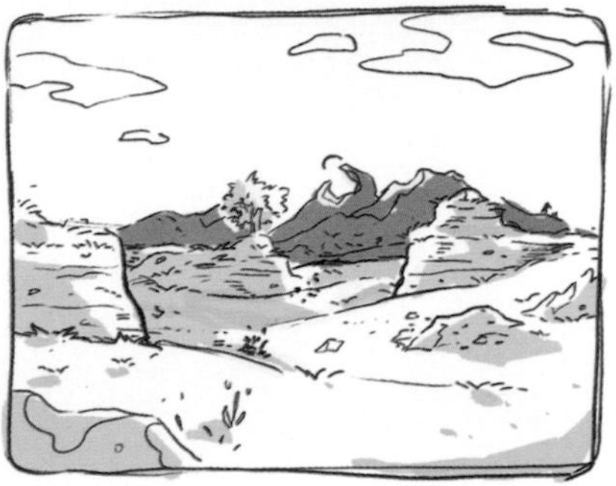

Unlike the Valley and Mountain, which had their people congregated in one location, the Plains have towns and communities scattered about. Most of these are farming or agricultural communities. Rather than big farms, every house or building has a space on the roof or balcony where gardens are grown.

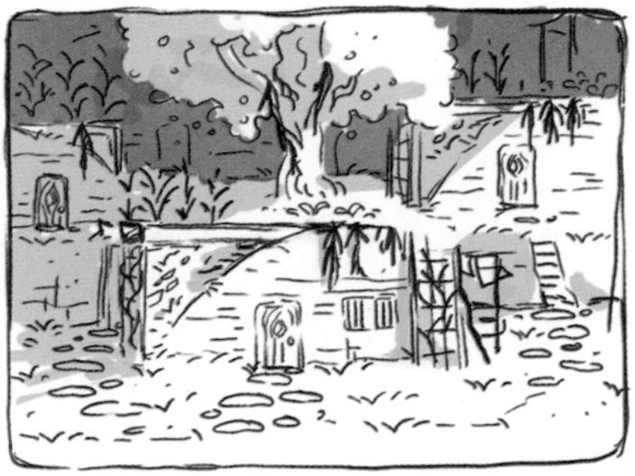

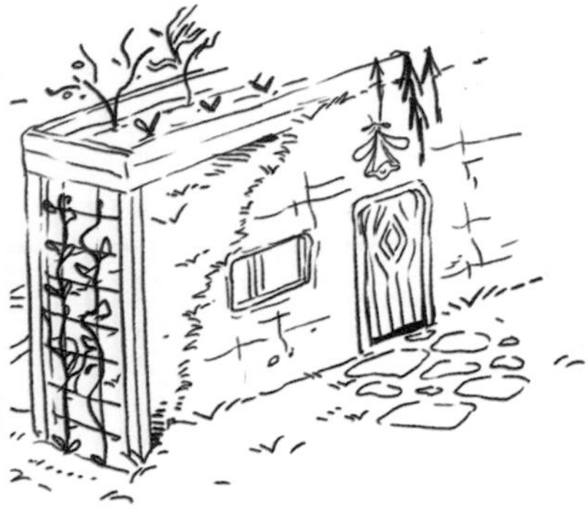

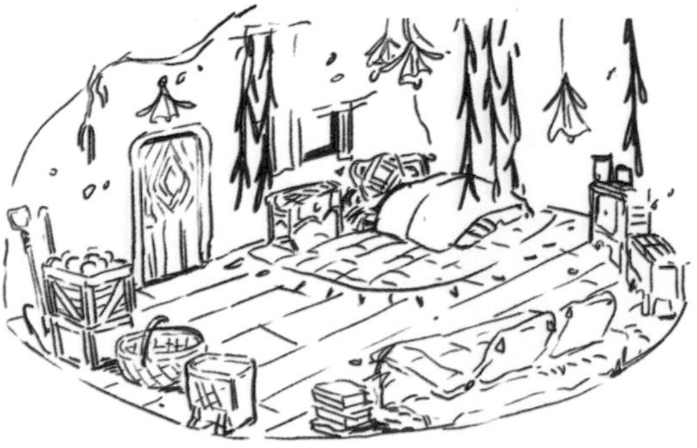

The Barrenlands
and Pheasants

The pheasants that Lewis befriends were initially
designed to be much larger, so Lewis could ride on their
backs. But, ultimately, the herd of smaller birds fits
better narratively. Lewis riding a large running bird,
though, is still a great concept.

Note from the Writer

Not a single page of the Mapmakers trilogy could have been written without the encouragement and sacrifice of my entire family. I can never thank them enough. (But I'll keep trying!)

From start to finish, Amanda and I have been surrounded by an incredible team of collaborators: Sara Calhoun, Patrick Crotty, Danny Diaz, Cynthia Lliguichuzhca, Walter Parenton, Bob Bianchini, and our fearless leader Whitney Leopard. We could not have asked for more talented stewards to guide us through this process.

We've been so fortunate to have the support of countless booksellers and librarians who've helped this series reach readers. I'd like to specially thank Paul, Casey, and everyone at my local shop, the Silver Unicorn Bookstore, for being such champions of the series and kids' graphic novels.

Lastly, I'd like to thank our readers. These characters will always hold a special place in my heart, in no small part because of all of you who joined us on their journey.

—Cameron

CAMERON CHITTOCK is a writer of comics and graphic novels, including the *Mapmakers* trilogy and *Teenage Mutant Ninja Turtles x Stranger Things*. When he's not scribbling down ideas, he can be found exploring New England with his family.

cameronwtchittock.com

Note from the Artist

This whole series wouldn't have been able to become what it's drawn out to be without the support of all my loved ones. I'll be eternally grateful for you being there beside me over the course of this long journey.

Echoing Cam, this series wouldn't have been what it is without our amazing (and constantly growing!) team, who shared the same willingness to collaborate that only made this series feel more alive.

Many, many thanks always to Cam, who gave me a chance to tell this story alongside him. Thank you for letting me walk and grow alongside you over the past few years, becoming a collaboration partner an artist always dreams of.

And to the readers who joined us all on this journey. The shapes of our world and our characters were drawn from the love I hold in my heart for them, and it brings me so much joy to be able to share them with you! The art for this book was created on the unceded lands of the Chochenyo-speaking Ohlone people.

—Amanda

AMANDA CASTILLO is a comic artist, illustrator, and storyteller who loves to tell warm and heartfelt stories, whether it be through drawings, words, or both. When not creating comics, Amanda enjoys making warm meals for loved ones, tending to plants, and just simply sitting outside.

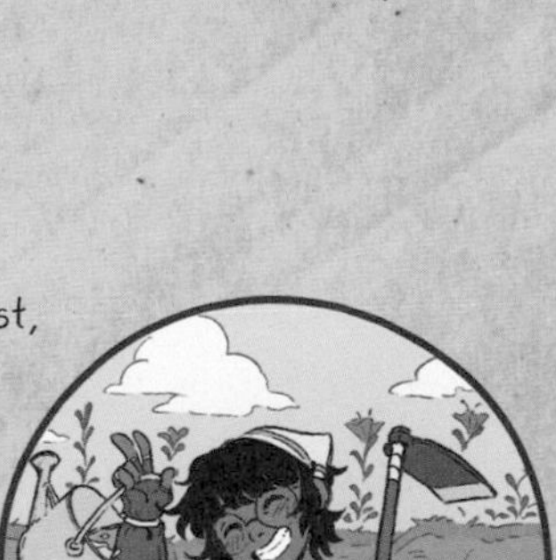

amanda-castillo.com

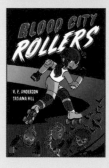